The
Surrogate

- n.   1. a surrogate mother.
- adj. 1. taking the place of, as in sexual surrogate

Medical Fiction

by

Dimitri Markov
n.d.p. of DH Marks

1996
Revised 2018

The Dangerous Doctors Series
by **Dimitri Markov**
n.d.p. for DH Marks

- **BloodBird** - When the organ isn't the only thing transplanted

- **The Surrogate** - A young woman trapped in the greed and power of the IVF industry

- **Her Charm Was Contagious** – A dangerous doctor and a patient who just loved everyone to death

- **Vera Mortina** - When the patient is not the sick one

- **Transit States** - collected poetry of DH Marks

Available as paperback on <u>Amazon</u> and on <u>Kindle</u>

About the author

Dimitri Markov is the writer's name for Donald H. Marks, a physician and writer of intense medical fiction on the theme of **Dangerous Doctors**. Markov gets his too-near-to-real-live material by observing others in the greater healthcare field for their actions, beliefs, hopes, fears and fantasies. Markov employs his lifetime of medical experience to explore the ill-defined boundary between medical fact and medical fiction. His **Dangerous Doctors** series of medical fiction includes: Vera Mortina, Her Charm Was Contagious, BloodBird, and The Surrogate. These works tell the (fictional) stories of good doctors, nurses and various health care providers, and doctors who are dangerous because of their faults : anger, jealousy, insecurity, greed, and mental illness. Dangerous to patients, dangerous to themselves, and certainly dangerous to those doctors and nurses they work with every day. Themes include *in vitro* fertilization, paranoia and insecurity of aging, commercialization of medical care, and the transplantation of consciousness. If you enjoy true-to-life medical fiction by Robin Cook, Michael Palmer, Patricia Cornwell, Carol Cassella, Kathy Reichs, and Arnaldur Indridason, and the writing style of Scott Turow, then you should be reading Dimitri Markov's **Dangerous Doctors** series. In that sense, it will probably be dangerous for you to relate to your own health care providers the same way again. The author welcomes your comments : DimitriMarkov52@gmail.com

Personal blog site for the author:

https://dhmarks.blogspot.com/

Acknowledgment

I would very much like to thank all my initial readers for their valuable assistance in comments, punctuation, plot issues, and encouraging feedback. Comments and correspondence to DimitriMarkov52@gmail.com

Preface

All the characters and events in this book are of course just totally, totally fictitious. How could it be otherwise? The author certainly would be very surprised nevertheless if readers do not relate to some circumstances in a more or less personal way or recognize certain character traits in their own acquaintances, particularly those in the health care fields.

Prologue:

The fertilization of an egg by a sperm is one of the greatest wonders of nature, an event in which magnificently small fragments of animal life are driven by cosmic forces toward their appointed end, the growth of a human being. As a spectacle it can be compared only with an eclipse of the sun or the eruption of a volcano . . . It is, in fact, the most common and the nearest to us of nature's cataclysms, and yet it is very seldom observed because it occurs in a realm most people never see, the region of microscopic things.

- George W. Corner, Director Emeritus,
  Department of Embryology
  Carnegie Institution of Washington

Chapter 1

Haven County, New Jersey Fairgrounds

On the opening day of the annual Haven Arts Festival, Marina Bonnaserra, a trim and pretty 32-year old nurse with a serious demeanor, stood patiently by her display of carefully selected oil paintings. From her vantage point in the exhibitor area, Marina, an amateur artist, could easily watch the occasional visitor who stopped by her exhibit or others nearby to look briefly, and then pass on. This art show was the first of the fall season and a favorite of Marina's. It gave her the chance to luxuriate in the fresh October air for hours, something she rarely could do. It also afforded her opportunity to network with other amateur artists and was a means to meet new people. Those were skills she never had been particularly adept at, but one that she desperately wanted to develop.

Marina liked to think of herself as uncomplicated, but she had one passion and one obsession that she admitted to. She jokingly referred to painting with oils as her passion, the outgrowth of favorable talent and years of training, which had been her hobby since her mid-teens. Painting's solitary nature and non-competitiveness suited Marina very well. Her one obsession, on the other hand, was rarely discussed, and even more rarely acknowledged, as it lay sequestered within the most painfully private area of her mind, from where it could do her no harm.

Marina had occupied her particular stall at the art fair in this medium-sized town in central New Jersey for several years. The tall wooden display frames in the community center parking lot stood like stands of a newly growing forest, and her own display frame tended by contrast to make her diminutive five feet two height even more petite than she already perceived it to be. The ten small paintings on display, impressionist oils of the local countryside she had carefully chosen, seemed to go appropriately with her bright, flowery dress and the simple brown ribbon she wore in her sandy-colored hair. Her soft, soothing artistic style complemented her quiet, reflective personality in a very natural way, and the synchronicity centered her sense of place.

Marina smiled at the curious and the mildly interested as they milled around the collection of her works. A few were local artists, and others she recognized from the community. There were rare questions, a few compliments and occasional nods of approval, and their murmurings blended indistinguishably in the background along with the rustling of leaves in the wind and the rumbling of cars on the gravel parking lot. Her works

hardly were big sellers, but that had never been the issue
for her. Her "profession" of nursing provided her with a
good livelihood, especially for a single woman without
children. Charlie Kincade, her long-term friend and
sometimes companion, jokingly referred to her status, and
to his, as "SINK," standing for Single Income No Kids,
and it described them both too perfectly. Yet, although
Marina had little hesitation using the descriptor SINK in
reference to Charlie and a few others, she found it
annoying when used to describe herself -- she resented its
yuppie and other connotations.

Later in the afternoon, after most of the crowd had
looked, made their purchases and passed on, a thin
redhead in her early thirties came over to Marina's
plywood stand, towing like excess baggage an obviously
disinterested little girl behind her. Marina watched
unenthusiastically as the woman tried to look at the oils
despite the child's distracting, constant bickering.
Fortunately, at least there was no one else around who
would be disturbed by the complaining child.
   "You paint these?" the woman asked, nodding her
head at some oils. She took a cigarette out of the pack
stuffed in her western-style leather purse, then lit it with
the burning end of the one she currently was smoking.
She coughed clouds of smoke several times -- some
coughs were prolonged, wet affairs of a seemingly painful
nature -- not always covering her mouth as she did. After

dropping the spent cigarette onto the grass, she crushed it out with the toe of her sequined black cowgirl boot.

"Yes, I did paint them. Do you like them?" Marina asked, trying not to seem too proud. The woman didn't appear to Marina the type to like paintings or collect them, although Marina had long ago found such generalizations useless. At least she showed some interest and had taken the time to comment to Marina. Up to this point in the day, Marina's works had not been generating a lot of conversation.

"Oh, yes, I do like them. They're very pretty. I guess I like soft art." The woman tried to say more, but the little girl with her began pulling on her clothes, and she started to back off, apologetically. She opened an outer flap on her shoulder bag, took out a pack of cigarettes and lit up all in one quick movement. Then she took a long drag, exhaled the smoke out through her nostrils, dragon-like, and coughed again. The smoke swirled in the crisp afternoon air, and then vanished. "Sorry about her," she said, glaring at the little girl with her. "Kids want to run around at a park, not look at art. I guess it's just natural." The girl smiled up upon hearing that her needs were finally understood, then jumped playfully.

"No, really, it's all right," Marina tried to reassure her, glad to have the opportunity of conversation. "If you like, I could take your daughter for a short walk while you look at the other exhibits," Marina offered, smiling at the child. "I need to walk around a bit myself."

"Thanks very much. Actually, she's not my daughter, she's my niece. Say hello, Vanessa." The little girl smiled briefly, and then hid behind her aunt's dress.

Looking again at the girl, Marina could now recognize they weren't a mother-daughter pair, and looking closely at the woman, she asked, "Don't I know you from somewhere?"

"Well, yes, you do look kind of familiar."

"I got it. You work for Dr. Vernor, don't you?" Marina thought she had seen this woman there. She used Dr. Ryder Vernor for her occasional physical exams and her rare illnesses. His office seemed to have a comfortable, unrushed atmosphere that set it apart from other medical offices she had been to. She liked that.

"Yep, that's me," she replied. "I'm his secretary and receptionist. Look, I'm real bad with names, so I'm sorry but . . ."

"I'm Marina Bonnaserra," she said, extending her hand and smiling.

"Right, I knew it, but I just couldn't think of it, with my niece tugging on me and all. Hi, my name is Vena Kleinman," she smiled nervously, and extended her hand in return. She took another drag on her cigarette, and exhaled out of a corner of her mouth, away from Marina.

"Yes, I remember you now," Marina said. The personnel had changed several times over recent years at Dr. Vernor's office, including the receptionist. "You know, I used to go to school with Dr. Vernor's wife, Lissa." Although never close to Lissa, Marina had first chosen to use Dr. Vernor for that very reason. After her first visit, Marina knew she liked Dr. Vernor as a person, a competent and caring physician, and thought him to be rather good looking too. She wondered why such a nice man chose someone as pushy and pretentious as Lissa for a wife. Oh well, she shrugged, to each his own.

"No, I didn't know that. What a coincidence," Vena replied coldly, without smiling.

"Look, about your niece. I can take her for a while if you'd like to look at some art. I need a break anyway."

"You got kids of your own?" Vena asked as she tried to size up Marina's suitability for the task. Her niece had already started moving toward Marina, looking her over and eagerly waiting for a chance to run away from the strict control of her aunt.

Marina returned Vena's smile and said, a sense of regret in her voice, "No, I'm not married." She suddenly began to stutter, and then blushed. She never quite knew how to respond to that question, particularly when she was asked off guard.

"Well, you should be, I mean, the way you seem to like kids and all. Anyway, my sister isn't married either, and she got her," Vena said pointedly, nodding impatiently at Vanessa.

Marina chose not to reply, and instead smiled back uncomfortably at Vena and Vanessa. Vena's comments made her think about a pamphlet she had recently seen at the hospital, advertising for their large infertility clinic. So many women wanting desperately to have children, pretty, young, married women, in all the perfect circumstances, and yet apparently totally barren. How tragic, how ironic, she almost shuddered. Actually, Marina had to admit that she had not just 'found' the fertility brochure, but had been well-aware of the clinic for some time, might be interested in some of their services, and had arranged to pass conveniently near their offices so that she could just happen across one of their brochures without having to go through the embarrassment of requesting one.

"What I mean is you don't need to get married if you like kids. I know a lot of women who got kids without being married. Let's you stay free. You know?" Vena explained, and then coughed again.

I should be so lucky to be that free, Marina thought, as she smiled at the darling little Vanessa, hovering about like a precious angel. "Are you all right?" Marina asked, concerned that Vena might have a case of bronchitis or, worse yet, pneumonia.

"Yeah, it's just a damn smoker's cough, that's all. I sure as hell don't have a cold, and I don't need none neither." Looking at her cigarette, Vena shook her head sadly and said, "One of these days I've got to give them up, you know?"

Marina smiled but said nothing, sure this conversation would only make her stutter worse. She hated her stutter, a burden that had been with her since her mid-teens, but, try as she might, she just couldn't govern it. Trying to consciously control her speech often ended up making her stutter worse. It was a vicious circle.

"You seem to do well around them, children I mean," Vena said, gesturing toward her niece. "I guess you must have a lot of patience anyway, you being the artist type."

"Yes, I guess so," Marina said, taking Vanessa by the hand to go on a short walk. "I guess so," she repeated, more to herself, then asked, "Do you mind if I buy Vanessa some ice cream?"

"Nope, not at all. Thanks. Vanessa, now you be a good girl, okay?" Vena barely heard Marina say she would be back in a few minutes, as she hungrily took her first free moment today to do anything besides argue with Vanessa, and began by looking more closely at Marina's paintings.

Chapter 2

Marina's walk with Vanessa proved relaxing and enjoyable, and they definitely shared a common interest - ice cream. Like the walk, the art show itself was over before anyone realized it, and Vena and her niece were soon gone. After the art show ended for the day, Marina's friend Charlie Kincade, who had spent the day in his office reviewing legal briefs, helped her load all the paintings and the display stands into her minivan. Each of her oils was carefully wrapped in heavy cloth and laid on a special rug in the back. After that, she drove her van - Charlie followed in his Audi - to her house, where they unloaded the paintings into her art studio.

In his early forties, Charlie Kincade was a full partner of the small and not-too-thriving law firm of Cornwall, Kincade and Santos. The firm took in general legal work and lived off business contracts, real estate transactions and whatever else came its way. Its offices were on Main Street, Haven, in an older brick building stuffed between an exercise gym and a medical office.

Kincade felt held back by his partners, whom he perceived to be not overly assertive. They never seemed to pursue the "juicy" clients other firms attracted. He believed that, as a lawyer, he should be making more money, but never quite got there. This left him feeling trapped in his firm, although not entrapped enough to develop sufficient interest or the courage to leave. He was a pragmatist, and he realized that, with today's lawyer glut, any attorney would kill to be even an associate, let alone a partner, in an established group practice like his. So Charlie stayed put and waited for the perfect opportunity to magically appear.

Marina and he had dated on and off for over five years. Most of the time it was casual, occasionally it was hot. Lately, she reflected sadly, it was not. Marina often found herself having a hard time warming up to Charlie, and he to her, although she knew they both wanted to. They were both shy and reclusive by nature, and had a difficult time expressing their affection physically. Although Marina thought Charlie cute, he was only moderately good in bed, not that she was any expert or authority on the matter. They had their problems together, but she liked Charlie a lot and still hoped that their relationship someday would go somewhere. She was fairly certain he felt at least approximately the same way.

Occasionally, Charlie glanced Marina's way and smiled at her as they carefully unwrapped each painting from its cloth cover, and set them on end against the wall. Today she had sold only two, both to a local car dealer and self-described art expert - Dona Dorland.

"By the way, before I forget, thanks for the referral," Charlie told her, after an uncomfortable stretch of silence. Neither had ever been a great conversationalist. He laid the last of the paintings against the wall, then walked over to the small couch where Marina had been sitting, drinking a glass of wine, peacefully watching him work.

"Oh," Marina said, "so you called Dr. Vernor after all." She had only vaguely remembered telling Charlie about a conversation she had overheard recently while at her physician's office. Marina had thought it a good opportunity to try and help Charlie's modest legal practice and hoped that the information would generate the goodwill needed to sustain their relationship.

"Yeah, and you were right. Dr. Vernor was planning to change his lease and he did need some legal advice. Thanks again. I owe you one," Charlie said. He clumsily attempted to put his arm around Marina's shoulder, but withdrew when he seemed to encounter surprise. "So, who was the little girl I saw you walking around with earlier today?"

"Oh, she was the niece of a woman who just wanted a few minutes alone to look at my paintings in peace. You might know her." Charlie seemed to know a lot of different women, in her opinion.

Charlie paused for a moment. "No, I don't believe so." He got up and poured himself a glass of wine, then returned to his place next to Marina.

"Well, she's the secretary and receptionist for Dr. Vernor." She saw Charlie didn't remember, and so she dropped it. For a lawyer, he never seemed too adept at recalling people's names or faces, unless, of course, it suited him. "Vena Kleinman?" When he still showed no recognition, Marina said, "Well anyway, I offered to watch her niece for a while so she could spend some quiet time looking at the exhibits. That's all," Marina smiled nervously. She could see from the frown on Charlie's face that the subject of kids already was making him jumpy.

"I'm surprised, Marina. That's not something I would ever do, you can be sure of that. Taking around a bunch of screaming kids certainly isn't my idea of having a fun time," he chuckled. "And just think of the potential liability."

"I was not suggesting you ever do that, Charlie," Marina calmly told him, took a sip of wine and sat back on the couch. "Anyway, there was just one kid, not several kids, and she was very well-behaved. You don't always need to exaggerate so."

Charlie's emotions were prototypically inscrutable as he smiled uncomfortably at Marina. He shifted on the couch, avoiding looking at Marina, and quickly finished his wine. Then, he seemed to more or less pop up and poured some more.

"But, since you brought the matter up, I do think you have a lot to offer a child, Charlie. You might even surprise yourself and like one of your own if you would just give yourself a chance." Marina felt herself getting nervous in response to the subject of children, and started to feel all tight inside. She forced herself to just shut up before she dug herself into a hole. It seemed lately that her five-year relationship with Charlie was getting more strained and was heading nowhere, just like this line of conversation. Was she wasting her time dating him, should she look for another man in her life? The fact was, Charlie never seemed protective or possessive, and she thought he probably wouldn't even object if he knew she was dating other men, although she was not, never having found that easy to do. That really bothered her. God knew, Charlie was almost certainly dating other women, probably sleeping with them too. Right now, she wanted to avoid a fight with Charlie more than anything. She didn't want to screw up their evening again.

"What's the matter, Marina? You look real sad all of a sudden," Charlie said as he put his wine glass down on the table, and reached out for her hand.

Marina smiled tightly, squeezed his hand, but felt all choked up and could say absolutely nothing.

"Hey, you can tell me," Charlie joked and half-reassured her. "You know, Marina, I know a lot of secrets, other people's secrets, and I never tell anyone." He held up his crossed fingers like a boy scout. "Attorney-Client..."

Marina looked at him, took hold of his other hand, but avoided talking. She found most people became anxious around a stutterer. She also knew from experience that people who brag about knowing other people's secrets can never really be trusted to keep them. Charlie definitely was one of those people she could trust only so far.

"Look Marina, I know what you're thinking," he nodded seriously. Rather than proving that assertion by revealing exactly what that was, he instead offered, "I think this is going too fast, too far." Charlie readjusted his weight on the couch, subtly moving a few inches away from Marina in the process.

"No, no, I wasn't thinking that at all, Charlie. What specifically are you talking about?" She stuttered a little more noticeably now, at least to her own ear, the negative feedback acting like a catalyst for a disastrous and irreversible reaction.

"Us, Marina, us." He gulped down the rest of his wine, then got up, walked over to the kitchen and poured another glass from the bottle. He finished that glass off even before he had returned to the couch.

"I don't want to argue about this again, Charlie. How come lately whenever we talk, we fight?" Marina felt herself tighten up as the stress of the conversation brought her stuttering more out into the open.

"I, I ah never agreed to have children," Charlie firmly told her.

"Children? Oh, for God's sake, Charlie." she exclaimed. "Okay, look, let's not get into that again." Marina felt the need to pull out each word she spoke; she agonized at the strange way the words must have sounded, but forced herself not to feel embarrassed, and to continue. "I didn't even bring children up this time. It's not even an issue right now, is it? For God's sake, Charlie, we're not even married, yet." Marina let the "yet" fall helplessly off the end of the sentence, silently, like the last hopeless breath of life or the last melting flake of snow on a window. "Why don't we just go out for a peaceful dinner, Charlie, like we had planned to?" She had nothing in her own place he would be interested in eating. When she was home alone, which was most of the time, she rarely cooked and infrequently ate anything substantial, and it was a wonder that she actually had to watch her intake at all - she had a propensity to easily gain weight. Cooking for only one person was a pain, a chore, and something she avoided.

"Hey, I mean I don't think I even want the little rats running around my house," Charlie persisted. "I kind of like things the way they are. And I like our relationship the way it is. Nothing more. You understand, don't you?" he tried to say soothingly, then reached for his wine glass and frowned when he noticed that it was empty.

"Nothing more, meaning, you don't want to get married, right?" It was the truth, Marina knew it, and it hurt her very essence and her deepest sense of self-worth to say it. But if marriage and having a family were her goals, and it had been so for a long time, then she had to finally admit that Charlie Kincade was never going to be the means to that idyllic end. Maybe no one would want to marry her, she wondered. Looking at her distorted image reflected in the wine glass, she wondered if there something innately wrong or undesirable or fundamentally not attractive about her? She could feel a strong wave of depression washing over her, pulling her down, drowning her in self-doubt and self-pity, making her feel like a complete failure. She just wanted to cry.

"Look, I never said that, Marina. I just don't think that now is a good time to think about all those things, that's all," he told her, his face getting very serious. "My legal practice is just now starting to take off."

"You've been saying that about your practice for years, Charlie." Marina tried to laugh, but it ended up sounding like a scoff. "Nothing has changed. And about us, why, all you want is the benefits of a marriage, like companionship, sex, . . . "

"Don't you? Look," Charlie said, turning toward Marina and taking her shoulders in his hands. "You of all people like the freedom of being single too. You tell me that you enjoy my company, and I know you enjoy the sex, at least I think you do." A smirk crossed his lips, an idea formed in his eyes.

"Why are you bringing this up right now, Charlie?" she pleaded. "You're going to ruin a perfectly good evening, you know." Marina wished she could start the entire evening's conversation all over again, like running a DVD backward, editing out the rough parts, the uncomfortable issues to be avoided once again, then replaying it, but she knew that life was just not like that. What was done was done.

"Hey, I saw how you took after those kids at the exhibit this afternoon. You got that goofy look in your eyes again. You even drive a minivan. See, you can't wait to have kids."

"There was one girl, Charlie, just one. And I got the minivan to transport paintings. It's a practical choice, that's all. It's got no implied statement." God, he's making a federal case out of this, she thought.

"And the way you looked at me. Hey, I know what you're thinking--Mating Season. Look, babe, I really don't want kids, believe me. I don't want to be dipped in honey and strapped on the anthill of marriage again either, babe. Not me, no way." He backed away a little further on the couch from Marina. Taking a small cardboard box of rum-soaked cigarillos from his shirt pocket, he asked her, "Do you mind?" gesturing at the cigarillos.

Marina waved her hand to suggest to Charlie that the smelly cigars, although not pleasing to her, were also not a major issue right now. She really did hate the persistent odor they left in her clothes, her hair, her furniture, and also worried about her asthma kicking in. It wasn't real asthma, as Dr. Vernor had explained it to her, just something called hyperactive airway disease. When she had first heard that description, she had laughed, for it was the first time anyone had used the adjective hyperactive to describe anything about her. The breathing problem, though, was not a laughing matter, and the suffocating sensation of air-hunger, triggered by irritants in the air like cigarette smoke, were a terrifying experience. Now, though, was not a good time to make a point about her distaste for tobacco smoke, and she wearily forced herself to be conciliatory, once again. Yet, after a few seconds, it was all starting to come together in her mind. Marina looked back at Charlie, crossed her arms and said, with a mixture of resignation and determination, "Sure, I understand." She paused, and then added, "Maybe you're right."

"What do you mean?" Charlie lit the cigarillo and

took a big drag, slowly exhaling the smoke up and away from Marina as he puffed his cheeks up like a big fish.

"Well, whenever we've been talking lately, we argue. This isn't at all what I want in a relationship, Charlie. Maybe we just should stop seeing each other the way we have. Okay?" In her heart, she knew that wasn't what she really wanted to do, and intended just to give Charlie a slight push into saying something reassuring to her like, "Oh, no, I don't want that, Marina." She really liked Charlie, and he was actually a nice enough man, once she had taken the time to know him. Long-term commitments definitely scared him off, though, and she had strenuously avoided pressing the point. Yet after several years, whatever fears he had of a more permanent relationship with her should by now have been allayed. She was ready for more from him and was sure he was too. He may not have realized that just yet, but nevertheless she was absolutely certain it was in his best interests.

"Why, is that what you want?" he asked, but it came out sounding more like a statement, and his face was certainly not at all covered with disappointment.

Marina fought to maintain her composure. "Charlie, this relationship isn't at all what I want," she said defiantly. She paused a moment to look at some colors reflecting off the window, giving herself the time to regain her composure, and not cry, especially not in front of him. "Charlie, I'm going to be thirty next year," she lied a bit, still not mentally prepared to have left her twenties. "There are things I want to do before I get too old."

Smiling sardonically, he shot back, "I'll bet I know just what those things are, too. Okay, Marina, I agree. Can't we just be friends? I think that maybe your goals here are just too different from mine."

Marina watched with disbelief as her only significant relationship with a male slid into the dumpster, her only tie with normality washed away after years of effort, and the futility of saving it made her begin to cry. She looked back at Charlie, who appeared as perplexed as she, both wanting desperately for the evening to not end on so disastrous a note. She reached out and gently took his hand in hers.

Charlie moved to take up the few inches between them, and carefully placed both their wine glasses and his cigarillo in a little decorative cork holder on the coffee table. He put his arms around Marina, gently drawing her closer to him, caressing her, hugging her, and when she seemed to respond, he began kissing her, softly at first to test her reaction, then with greater passion when she didn't resist.

Marina sighed softly, and moved closer into Charlie's embrace in response. She could feel the regret at their arguments slowly being replaced with relief, then arousal, and then quickly transforming into a hopeful sense of longing for the reassurance of his physical touch. Although she in no way deceived herself into denying that her longer-term need was for a more meaningful companionship than simply something physical, she certainly could welcome the reassurance of his sweet embrace. It was a means of bonding that she knew worked well for him, and she employed it as often as she could.

Charlie's kisses, tentative at first, grew in passion, and she soon found herself hungrily sucking his probing tongue deep into her mouth, suggestively playing her tongue against his, and she felt more at ease as the warm, wet feelings excited her even more. His mouth tasted tart from tobacco, but she ignored the bitterness, just as she had learned to overlook so much that was imperfect or undesirable in her own life. Sex was infrequent and something she really didn't spend a lot of time thinking about, but when the opportunity presented itself, her intimate feminine nature readily responded. She wanted Charlie's caress now, more than in a simply sexual way, for it was a way for her to be assured that all was not lost in their relationship, and also just to reaffirm that Charlie continued to value and desire her as a woman. She needed that too.

Slowly, Charlie's warm hands ran up and down the sheer fabric covering her back, stroking her and soothing her in ways that only human touch could. The more Charlie touched her in a caring way, a sorely missed way, the more Marina felt on fire, felt the tension, the sexual urgency bursting out, and she felt smothered, suffocated, gasping for air, panting, and yet blocking her next breaths by pressing her mouth tighter against his. Without explanation, she gently guided his hands, and Charlie eagerly followed her suggestions as more than mere acquiescence, but as consent, participation, and encouragement.

Charlie leaned over, pulled Marina down and rolled on top of her, deep onto the couch, way down into the love nest they were creating together. She didn't resist, wouldn't have even if she were capable of doing so, her sexual feelings now so aroused past the point of no return, hoping beyond hope that his feelings for her were more than superficial lust, unable to believe otherwise. The excitement made Marina's breaths come in short, sharp bursts, pants, more like gasps, warm breaths, moist rushes of sweltering air filled with soft moans and the suggestive rustling of clothes. She felt intoxicated, highly vulnerable, her head swirled, and she could smell her own strong scent of arousal flushing the air all around them like a chemical attractant for two animals at the height of mating season.

Charlie adjusted his weight, and then moved to center himself over Marina's tensed body. Gently pulling her blouse up, he moved her bra over the top of her breasts but paused to stare for a moment at a faint scar near her nipple.

Less than a quarter inch long, the old surgical incision had involved the edge of her nipple, and had left a subtle darker coloration to it. Marina was certain that Charlie had noticed that minuscule, trivial, inconsequential and yet hated scar before. How could he not have, she wondered, although he had never before inquired to her as to its origin. Why are men always so breast-conscious, she wondered. Maybe it was because they were at heart all such big babies, or maybe because they viewed potential mates as continuations of their mothers. At any rate, if Charlie wasn't going to ask her for any details, Marina knew that she certainly wasn't going to go into any prolonged explanation and volunteer the origin of that scar, especially now, at this very private and intimate moment. The very memory of the months of reconstructive plastic surgery she had had to endure so many years ago still pained her.

Charlie's interest in the scar seemed quickly to wane, and within seconds he was back at his main task, driven by a basic human need to achieve a summation, a climax, a culmination to the drive, a drive which Marina was now completely in sync with. He didn't seem to her at that moment to require any foreplay to get sufficiently excited, and in fact appeared to be on the verge of climax already. Charlie never had, unlike her, required any foreplay, romantic, playful, preparatory or otherwise, Marina reflected with some degree of disappointment. Yet, so much the better. The tension she was feeling at that moment was really becoming overwhelming, as was her anxiety. She absolutely had to have him, right now. The thought of imminent intercourse in itself was so intense that it almost suffocated her, although her basic needs, motives, drives she was certain were quite dissimilar to those of Charlie.

The Surrogate

Charlie, she reflected, seemed to approach each activity in his life, including eating and sex, as a task, and, being an attorney, appeared to think in terms of 15 minute intervals, like his billing increments Even at passionate moments like this, Marina could never be completely certain whether Charlie was acting more like a raging bull or an analytical lawyer. He set about with a singular concentration to seek relief in the only way he knew how, and they moved together toward that common pleasurable destination in an imaginary land neither could cohabit for longer than a half hour every few weeks.

Relieved that his concentration had returned back to the rest of her and away from her breasts, Marina's excitement was free again to grow. With Charlie's every action, she countered in unison, as if they were dancing, dancing in coordinated, single-minded counter actions of increasing intensity. Her head swam from the warmth and the excitement, as she fought to maintain even a semblance of control for one last second, almost unable to breathe as Charlie's mouth and hers were locked in a never-ending kiss. She knew it had been way too long since she had last made love, and longed for his body to be next to hers, a part of hers, together, and she prayed for it to last for hours, although she knew from experience that would never be, at least not with Charlie.

No longer in control of his mind or his body, Charlie held both of Marina's hands tightly in his, fingers intermixed, stretching their arms out over their heads. But then, by having her arms pulled over her head, in some strange, obtuse way Charlie had somehow triggered the wrong button on some cerebral DVD player. And suddenly the wrong disk began to play, and tragically, there would also be no way to stop the derailing their love journey would now take.

. . . Faint scratching sounds disturbed Marina, dragging her out of her lust-binge, pulling her from below a level of conscious awareness and down into some dark, distorted corner of reality. Marina opened her eyes for a moment and felt horribly disoriented as she looked around to see what was disturbing her. All the familiar surroundings of her house seemed to be rapidly dissolving and she felt wildly confused and she felt terribly threatened. Now, instead of her living room, she appeared at first transported to a strange alley, and then lying alone in a dark, dirty parking lot. There was a smell of asphalt and dirt and garbage, and she was being held down on the ground, and her hands were bound tightly together and pulled above her head. The feelings of fear and threat and anger suffocated her, making her gasp wildly for breath. She felt a terrible painful biting and gnawing at her nipples and knew her life was in danger.

Marina panicked and struggled to get up. Some primal instinct told her to run away from there as fast as she could, to escape right now. Terrified, she discovered she couldn't. Someone was holding her hands firmly, pinning her down, thrusting his hips against hers. Marina tried to scream, fighting back with all her strength, but she was too weak and her mouth was covered with a hand. She thrashed her head back and forth and fought to escape, but couldn't move. Looking up, she saw that wisp of a Latin man with a thin mustache, the tormentor of her nightmares, a detached grimace of indifference marking his cruel, gaunt face …

Marina screamed, then reached up in a frenzied terror between reality and memory and dug her fingernails deeply into her attacker's chest, drawing blood. The man screamed and jumped off her, and she knew that she was finally safe. But now when she looked up, the driveway was gone, as was her tormentor, and instead, she was at home and was dismayed to see Charlie running into the bathroom looking for bandages. She rolled over and groaned in embarrassment and regret and failure.

Minutes later, they were both terribly agitated and confused - Charlie for his feelings of having offended her, although he could not imagine what he had done or said wrong. Marina, in turn, was upset for aborting their mutual orgasm. Yet, they both knew that there was little else that could be said, and after some quick apologies and a few clumsy attempts at explanation, Charlie was gone into the night.

Marina rearranged her clothes to cover herself up, and as she heard the door close with a slam, and his car start and speed away, she lay down and cried on the couch for a long time. The horrible experience left her feeling humiliated and depressed and a failure and not in control of her senses at all. She wondered if truly she were insane or on the verge of insanity. When would she cross that abyss again, she wondered? The last time had also been during sex, when her hands were pulled up over her head in the same way. Did this mean she would have such terror-filled nightmares each time during sex, destroying the mood, the intimacy, the very act? Would she never be rid of the memory of her rapist from so long ago? Fear of this terrifying nightmare reoccurring was a terrible, strong inhibition to intimacy. Depressed, she went into the bathroom, disrobed, and showered for over half an hour. When she had finished, she still felt unclean, as she often did, even after showering.

An hour after an agitated and horribly confused Charlie had left so abruptly, Marina put on her coat and went for a walk. She had had this nightmare, or flashback, if that was what it was, in Charlie's presence before. It was embarrassing for her and frightening for them both. Each time they had managed to get past it and to come together again after a while, and she was sure it would be that way this time, too. She could only hope so.

The night air was chilly, the ground was lit only by a quarter moon partially obscured by clouds, and the earth seemed utterly indifferent to her solitary walking and her seeming insoluble plight and the anguish of her inner thoughts. She appreciated how Charlie seemed to understand the painful depths that Marina had come from, and charitably thus far had never made a point of her embarrassing flashbacks. Certainly, though, Marina knew it must have had a strongly inhibiting effect on him and on his desire to have sex with her. At one point, Charlie had suggested counseling for Marina, mentioning that it had helped clients of his who have had problems dealing with violent crimes. She had followed up on the idea, although being basically distrustful of counselors and psychologists - she had never known one who was completely normal. She had actually been in and out of counseling for the last sixteen years, with variable effects, and now she considered resuming therapy, before it was too late.

The cold night air made her hip hurt as she walked. It was a chronic injury -- the slight limp aggravated the pain and brought back long-suppressed memories of a cold March evening in Haven some sixteen long years ago. Back on that day, life had inexplicably created a new set of harsh realities. Long-repressed vital forces had struck out boldly in self-defense against death. Half-frozen tips of the outermost branches of aging maple trees on the walkway in front of her house, long barren during winter, had brazenly developed proud sprouts of tiny green buds that flouted logic. Broken branches, scattered like the bones of so many long-dead birds, had littered those streets of her past, serving as reminders of the previous night's fitful wind storm.

Marina remembered that day as vividly now as if she were still there. Further down her street, patches of frost and piles of icy snow had blanketed the sloping, expansive front yard of the Bonnaserra residence in Haven. Inside, separate and shielded from the elements, a younger Marina Bonnaserra had waited.

At sixteen, Marina had been fair of spirit and appearance, trusting to the extreme point of dangerous naiveté, and virginal. Although strenuously attempting to appear calm and uninterested, her stare that night down the empty street in front of her house was as incessant as it was high tension. Her feelings transcended in sputtering spurts from boredom to concern to a worried annoyance. Finally, to pass time, she had alternated between lying coiled spring-like in a corner of her living room couch and pacing back and forth in front of the picture window. Every few minutes, Marina had checked the flashing clock display on the VCR or glanced into the empty kitchen, but immediately returned her stare to the nearly vacant street outside, wondering again if something was wrong. Even today, whenever she saw a VCR flashing, she had this memory of her placid life at 16 so violently interrupted.

Back then, Marina was five-foot-one, a little on the thin side, with deep brown expressive eyes, and hardly thought herself to be particularly pretty or special. Her face had begun to feel the ravages of a running battle with acne, aided by a near addiction to chocolate. She was an only daughter, and although not spoiled, perceived her parents to be overprotective and terribly out of touch with what life was really about. It had taken Marina months of painstaking persuasion and persistent argument before her parents had finally agreed to Marina's first un-chaperoned date. After that fateful decision, Marina thought she would faint in an emotional, dizzying surge of happiness, unable to see the evening through. She felt a surge of contradictory emotions - flushed and hot and dizzy and more than a little scared, all at the same time - as that night, her night finally approached. This was something she wanted terribly, and yearned for - because now she would finally be treated as an adult.

At that moment, despite her contradictory excitement and confusion and apprehension, she couldn't wait for her new reality to unfold, just as she had fantasized it would so many times before. Yet, the evening didn't at all start off as planned, for Pascal, her date, hadn't arrived on time. Instead, Marina was left to worry as she wondered if he had an accident, forgot, or worse yet, changed his mind without even the courtesy of informing her. With Pascal, Marina had to admit, any of these explanations was possible, although she still had no doubt he would eventually arrive.

Only moderately popular at school, Marina was active in the biology, art and Honor Society clubs - all characteristically sedentary activities. She tended to complete all her homework, handed assignments in on time, got better than average grades, and was sensitive to being teased with names like "good girl." Cautious and innocently trusting by nature, she had always played by the rules - other people's rules - and expected her acquaintances to also play the same predictable game and in the same way.

An agonizingly long forty minutes passed before a black BMW careened down the quiet street and bounced into Marina's driveway, nearly knocking over the mailbox in the process. The bottom of the car had made an audible abrasive scraping noise - even today she could still hear it - as it rubbed over the curb, prompting Marina to nervously peer over her shoulders. Fortunately, her parents didn't appear to have seen or heard the near-collision, and she felt relieved. She didn't want to provide them with yet another reason to be nervous about her date, make a scene, or worse, change their minds and withdraw permission.

Pascal was someone Marina had looked up to. She admired Pascal for his good looks, his athletic abilities, and even his success in the classes they took together. He dressed simply and in the current style of all his friends, not distinguishing himself by taste in clothes. Pascal was also someone her own mother and father had seemed to have faith and confidence in. Marina didn't bother making her parents aware of certain - how could she put it - inconsistencies in his personality. Pascal did at times have a reckless impulsiveness and a bizarre lack of concern for personal safety, but these were also characteristics which excited and attracted Marina to him. This young man had been, after all, the son of her mother's friend at the PTA. That night, so many years ago, Pascal was simply to drive

Marina to the movies and deliver her safely back home. It was a limited assignment, and one agreed to well in advance by all parties concerned and after much discussion and negotiation.

Moments after parking his parent's car, Pascal had hurriedly walked into the large foyer, smiled sheepishly at Marina and held her hand. She in return held his hand tightly and smiled. Marina's parents soon joined them, making the room seem quite a bit smaller. Although he appeared somewhat uncomfortable, Pascal greeted Marina's parents, shaking Mrs. Bonnaserra's hand, perhaps a little too strenuously. Even before Pascal could advance into the house one foot further, Mr. Bonnaserra had pulled him into a small area off the foyer for an unexpected conversation. The hurriedly whispered words all passed in one direction, and judging from the look on Mr. Bonnaserra's face, were said in utter and complete seriousness.

Marina had resented her father's intrusion into her affairs - after all, she was now sixteen - and she bridled at her exclusion from the man-to-teenage boy conversation. She and her parents had already agreed that any further interference or conversation was unwarranted, and she had flashed a stern look in her father's direction reminding him of their agreement not to embarrass her. Mr. Bonnaserra smiled uncomfortably and reluctantly stepped back, leaving Marina free to drive off in Pascal's parent's car.

Marina's best friends had sensed something terribly wrong with Pascal for years, and, in truth, their observations had not totally escaped her. Yet, up to now, she had preferred to see only those parts of Pascal which were good, and which reinforced her own favorable impressions of him. That night, though, Marina couldn't avoid becoming aware of problems soon after leaving home. Pascal was much more aggressive than Marina expected or preferred, particularly since she was more inclined to remain in charge of herself. It was a trait her mother possessed in dealing with men, and one which she had had felt compelled to emulate. Although close to her mother in some ways, she still occasionally found herself fighting, even into the present, to be her own woman.

At the theater, Pascal's hand had snaked its way around Marina's bare shoulder within minutes of their being seated, leaving her surprised and uncertain. She flashed a neutral glance - not one of disapproval, but with a 'go slow' message attached. Still, when she didn't signal her displeasure by withdrawing away from him, Pascal's open hand next found its way onto the front of her blouse, momentarily caressing her breast. She almost cried out, but was too frightened and embarrassed to even turn her head and look at him. Instead, Marina attempted a weak look of displeasure, and held her breath. Marina remembering her mother's parting urge that night for her to be, or at least seem to be in control. Yet, she almost felt too terrified to move, and she still remembered how it took all her inner resolve to gently but firmly grasp Pascal's hand and remove it back to his lap. Still, at that point, Marina wouldn't have characterized the evening as having turned in the wrong direction.

Pascal had behaved himself for the next few hours, but at the drive-in after the movie, Pascal's knee had unexpectedly touched Marina's under the table. Not sure if it was intentional or an accident from the close seating, Marina blushed, but didn't withdraw her knee, and the contact lingered. Even today, she could still feel that unwanted touch, not because it was so momentous in itself, for her knee had been touched on occasion since then in much the same way and for the same reasons. At the time, though, strange and powerful feelings were beginning to confuse her thoughts, taking charge and controlling her every action in mysterious and totally unfamiliar ways. That night, she had felt more a woman than ever before, and had desired to finally be treated as one by her date and especially by her mother and father.

To Marina's relief, Pascal's touching and groping her, welcome and unwelcome as they simultaneously were, progressed no further, and it appeared to her that Pascal would finally act like a gentleman. Her opinion of him had changed, though, and looking over at Pascal, Marina clearly saw more an acne-pocked teen than a mature and trustworthy young man who could be gentle and respectful with her. Still, Marina remembered how she somehow felt guilty that she had disappointed Pascal or felt sorry for him or worried that she wouldn't see him again. Those contradictory emotions persisted still, although now they were mixed with guilt and a desire to please and were directed toward Charlie Kincade.

Marina had reached out, as she had seen her mother

do on so many occasions after arguing with her father, and held Pascal's hand to reassure them both that the evening was not a loss. He had returned her smile and grasped her hand tight. His grip was firm, perhaps too firm, full of intent although not painful, and his palm had felt sweaty.

Later, they had driven toward Marina's home, carrying on a light conversation about music and dancing. Marina felt relieved, and glad that her evening wouldn't be a total horror story. She still wanted to have good things, exciting things to report about her date with Pascal when she met her friends at school. Doubtless, they would have expected no less.

After driving quietly for a few minutes, Pascal had unexpectedly slowed in a strange part of town. Then, without explanation, he turned sharply and parked in a grassy field. Marina's apprehension level shot to astronomic proportions as she wondered what Pascal had in mind and whether he was receiving her messages at all. Up to that point, she thought he had, but she was no longer certain. Marina inhaled deeply and tried to relax.

There was barely enough moonlight inside the car for Marina to see Pascal's face, and as she gazed at his endearing smile, hidden partially by shadows, she felt a warm flush. Surely this was still the same person she had known for years, and nothing had changed between them, she had tried to reassure herself. Momentarily not in control of her emotions, she slowly inched closer to him, then tilted her chin up to receive his kiss. She had wanted this ending to their date for months, and wouldn't have been able to finish the evening without it.

In the ensuing moments, her inexperience almost put her at a crucial disadvantage. Marina's head swirled and she felt nearly out of control of her own emotions. Breathless, she had panicked as Pascal's powerful hands moved out, touching her and groping her in ways she had never been touched before, embarrassing and electric ways. Fighting against her most strange and powerful urges, she almost agreed to do the one thing she probably comprehended the least.

She remembered being no match for Pascal's athletic body, and soon had found herself totally unable to control his increasingly insistent physical advances. Marina firmly pushed his hands away, pleaded with him to leave her alone but fearing he wouldn't, when unexpectedly, he stopped. Instead, Pascal straightened his clothes, sat upright and stared forward out of the front car window. For several minutes he breathed deeply, seemingly stunned, as he regained his composure before talking again. She remembered the tense atmosphere waiting to see what he would do, and the peppermint on his breath in the enclosed space of the car. Obviously more angry than disappointed, Pascal instead attempted to laugh and make light of the situation rather than pursue it any further.

In a few moments, the conflict had seemed to be over and they had again driven off toward Marina's home in silence. Marina remembered feeling glad she had insisted on not doing things she was uncomfortable with, and pleased and grateful that Pascal had actually had the maturity to listen to her and respect her choices. She had seen the unfortunate results of dates gone too far in too many girls she knew of - pretty Christine Lincoln had come to mind - and she had decided long ago not to end her school years, her opportunity for college, in so tragic a way. Gradually, Marina began to feel in control again, yet, when she looked over at Pascal, she realized just how easily he could have overpowered her. It was a chilling observation, one she carried with her the rest of her life.

Just a few minutes later, Pascal had again unexpectedly jerked the car off the road and parked in another empty lot. That time, he had smiled mischievously, then resumed his unwelcome touching, pressuring, and scaring of Marina. In a panic, Marina had grabbed the car door's handle and quickly yanked it open. Not thinking clearly, she desperately pushed herself out and ran away, quickly disappearing down the unfamiliar street. Although Pascal's voice echoed out to her from the shadowy background, she would not see him again that night.

The instant Marina Bonnaserra had fled from the car, she felt safe and back in control, but those feelings were fragile, deceptive, and they soon passed. Only moments later, out on the silent, midnight-deserted streets, her justified fear of Pascal was superseded by an even more serious threat. Even today, Marina still ran over and over in her mind how her evening had turned into a series of tragic, stupid mistakes, and she blamed herself. It was a mistake going out with that immature boy that night; going along with Pascal, parking in a strange place and letting him grab her body had also been an error. Her walking alone, there, she realized most of all, was probably an even more dangerous error. Those thoughts had filled her head with a dark feeling of terror and foreboding as she had moved quickly down the empty streets, seeking safety, partially wishing she were still in the car, relatively safe with Pascal.

Although there was no apparent reason to be alarmed, Marina had been painfully conscious of her aloneness, and of her vulnerability. She tried to minimize the echoes of her foot steps on the deserted concrete by walking on her toes. Yet, doing so only made her seem more obvious, and she desperately wanted to avoid calling attention to herself, as if anything more than her mere presence had been required to do just that.

Several times, Marina had thought she heard a sound - the scuff of a shoe, the rub of sneakers, a cough, a metallic click - or saw someone watching her, following her. But, each time she could see nothing when she turned. She hurriedly moved along, looking in desperation for an open store, a police car, anything to give her safety. Then, miraculously, she spotted a cab parked with its lights on about a block away, near an all night diner. Her hopes rose as she dashed across the street toward it.

From out of nowhere, she remembered two powerful hands darting out and grabbing her from behind, holding her strongly and suddenly as she had tried to run past an open but darkened alleyway. The hands seized her much as a small crab grabs at feeder fishes, holding them in a grip of death with one claw, hungrily tearing their flesh apart with the other.

Marina remembered struggling at first, but with one of her assailant's hands firmly covered her mouth, she had difficulty breathing. Screaming out for help seemed impossible, even if there had been someone around to hear her desperate cries or to care. Her efforts to fight free were futile, and the more she struggled, the harder he held her. His other hand around her neck, the assailant roughly threw Marina against a wall, slamming her head against the bricks. The sky filled with stars, she moaned, then quickly went limp, the cruel blow having knocked her nearly unconscious, and she could no longer resist him. As she was being dragged along by her feet, Marina had momentarily wakened long enough to see a thin, wiry young man with unusually tiny, close set eyes and a closely cropped goatee mustache. His cruel face was marked by oddly characteristic facial features, impassive and passionless, almost imp-like, with a pear-shaped face, gaunt, high cheek bones and fine eye brows, and Marina fought to remember his disturbed and violent face. Marina's head throbbed, her hips felt as if they had been pried apart and dislocated, and a sharp pain seared into her pelvis, and, finally overcome, Marina had lapsed back into merciful unconsciousness.

The Surrogate

By the end of that fateful day so long ago, Marina Bonnaserra had survived, but in the process had forever lost her innocence. Physically, she suffered from a vicious assault that left her injured and disfigured, in both physical and emotional ways. Psychologically, when she awoke and realized what had happened, she felt betrayed, attacked, violated, and filthy in ways totally beyond cleaning. In addition, she had experienced a profound anger and regret at having been so utterly stupid, a stupidity that had left her open, vulnerable, and she had sworn to herself that she would never allow herself to again be so stupid as long as she lived. She had lost much, she had learned more, and she had since not forgotten that attack nor the pain to this day.

Chapter 3

Marina finally ended her walk and returned to her house more than an hour after Charlie Kincade left. The evening had rapidly chilled down after sunset, and a strong breeze blew damp air in from the west. The house seemed eerily empty, almost unwelcome to her. Staring at the empty couch where so much passionate hope ended so prematurely, and instead went terribly wrong, she cried a bit, then, feeling better, sat up and made a cup of tea. She brought the tea to her bedroom, dressed for bed, and then tried reading, hoping to fall asleep. Instead, she read for hours, unable to sleep. She always had insomnia when depressed, and arguing with Charlie and then clawing him during sex, involuntary as it was, definitely depressed her. She started to think of the fun she had taking Vanessa for a walk, and how she had bought them both ice cream. Other women no less deserving than she had such pleasures in their lives, and why not she? It was then that Marina knew exactly what she needed to do to give her life meaning and direction. Not made impulsively, the decision had actually been forming for months, perhaps years, and Vanessa had been simply a catalyst to bring it to the fore.

    Born and raised in Haven, Marina was recently graduated with a Master of Science in Nursing Administration. She had been employed at Haven General Hospital for less than two years, first as a ward nurse, and then, when that proved both intellectually boring and physically too stressful, for a short but unsatisfying stint in the admitting office, and most recently as the Quality Assurance nurse. An administrative position, her QA job required her to maintain an eternal vigilance on the procedures and occurrences at Haven General. It was an assignment Marina tried to complete with the enthusiasm of a zealot, as she had approached most of her life's important activities. This attitude, not shared by most at Haven General, had unfortunately made her few friends.

    The position of QA nurse paid adequately and left her free time truly free, unlike that of the staff nurses. Her duties required no patient contact, something Marina had never been particularly good at and which pleased her to no extent, although at times she had to admit that she found the job somewhat boring too.

    Marina helped the hospital maintain its quality, but more importantly, she assured that Haven General could meet its yearly re-certification inspections. She took her responsibility as seriously as any administration-bound nurse. Marina suffered, however, under the irony of having responsibility for assuring the quality of medical and nursing practices in which she herself lacked up-to-date experience. Such deficits were an all-too-common paradox for those who no longer practiced the professions they were entrusted to supervise.

Marina's next day at work was as uneventful as it was quick, and after arriving home the next evening, Marina wearily sat at her table and opened the newspaper. She first looked at the local news, then the "Current Living" section, scanning a few movie reviews. Nothing interesting was playing, and she abhorred the more popular films, centered on violence and sex. The next section contained the local crime stats, and concerned the local robberies, arrests for DWI, divorce settlements, and lastly, the rape statistics. Sometimes, fortunately, days would pass without one, but at least twice each week in Haven, a seemingly average medium-sized city, there would be several sexual assaults. She had no idea why they occurred with such frequency, or what, realistically, could be done about it, only that they were truly crimes against the very fabric of society.

She wondered once again whatever became of the bastard who had raped her years ago, and why the police had never found him. Hopefully he was dead and rotting in hell. She realized over the years the police seemed to have just given up on her case, and too soon, too easily, in her opinion. Long ago she had resigned herself that the local police would never solve her own rape. They had forgotten, and with her parents now both dead, part of her wanted to forget too, but she couldn't. The rest of her, the limp from her still-painful hip, the stutter, the disfigured nipple, and worse - the agonizing memory, the terrifying dreams, those wouldn't let go. She supposed that forgetting, letting go would have a therapeutic effect, might be a catharsis, but she couldn't forget, nor could she forgive, not until justice was done.

Today again, there were no rape trials reported in the newspaper. That was, at least, certainly good news for others.

Chapter 4

Haven, New Jersey

"Enough is enough," Marina thought as she wearily put down the oil palate she had been using for the last several hours. She had been home for the weekend, alone, and as usual had hours to do with as she wished. Friends of hers who knew of her available free time were often quite envious, their own weekends booked solid with kids and dinners and movies, and yet Marina was just as often envious of the reasons they had for not having free time on weekends - those very spouses and children. Why them but not also her?

Her position in the administrative side of nursing left her much time to herself. It was a conscious choice, and one well-suited to her solo personality. Perhaps the lack of patient contact held the greatest attraction for her, allowing her to avoid 'messy' things like human fluids and strong emotions, and dealings with strangers.

For years, Marina had adapted to spending a good part of her free time painting. It was relaxing, creative, and best when performed alone. Morning had always been the best time for her to paint, although not too early.

The Surrogate

She liked to organize her life a bit first, then put her phone on answer, and settle down for some serious painting, assuming that the mood struck her. Sometimes it didn't, in which case she would wait until the right frame of mind arrived. Creativity couldn't be forced, and until she was ready, she well knew from experience, any creative efforts on her part would be a total waste of her time.

The painting studio was a large, open area off the living room. It had once been a sewing and meeting room for the original inhabitants, who, according to lore, were Amish farmers. Marina had extended and expanded the windows, adding an entire wall of sloping garden windows on a side not facing into the sun. Marina hated direct sunlight, and found it impossible to paint in.

The eighteenth century restored farmhouse in which she lived had been in her family since she could remember. Her father had purchased it as an anniversary surprise for her mother when Marina was just three-years-old. They had nurtured and repaired and restored the old farmhouse and the surrounding land, at great expense and time, until it was more than a symbolic representation of what it once was. It had become a reflection of life, first of her parents, and now of hers, a living metaphor. Unfortunately, at those times when she felt most alone and isolated, it also seemed like a prison.

Most available wall space was covered with paintings, all oils, and almost all hers. Some dated back to her first efforts in high school. Even then, she had shown unusual promise as an artist. She far exceeded her teachers' abilities early on, and delighted her mother often with her paintings as gifts. Her father wasn't much of an art lover, or, according to her mother, a lover of any other form of art or music, and he showed little interest in Marina's artistic talents. Everyone expected Marina to continue on to art school, and all were shocked when she chose the profession of nursing. Even today, she had to admit to herself she had no logical reason for this choice, no inner burning desire to emulate Clara Barton, no specific love of biology or of the healing arts. Perhaps it was simply a rejection of her past, pre-college, education and life, so centered on the humanities.

About half of her paintings were landscapes and seascapes, the other half were studies of men's faces. The style varied from impressionist to portrait; Marina only tried surreal and other more severe forms on a few occasions and quickly found the style not to suit her. She had also tried sculpture and music, but quickly gave them up after determining that she could never achieve excellence there.

The portrait of one man in particular stood out; he was young, Anglo to Nordic, with tiny, mocking eyes, low cut ears and in several paintings wore a sharply angled goatee. A cruel sneer covered his thin lips. Ten or twenty variations on this one man at various ages, and in different hair styles and colors covered several walls. Marina looked at one of the oils and felt years of tension, repeated daily, surge into her neck, twisting the muscles, and she turned away quickly, not wanting her day spoiled so early. His image made her feel sick to her stomach, and she once again swore out loud to kill that bastard some day.

Marina dropped her brush in an old ceramic turpentine cup, splashing a few drops onto the newspaper covering the old wooden work table as she did. She swished the brush around a bit to wash off the outer layer of paint, allowing her to reuse the brush again, and tried to clear her head and regain her composure. After setting her easel a little straighter, she slowly got up from her padded artist's stool and looked about.

Marina felt stiff from having sat at her easel for several hours and took a well-needed stretch. She pulled her legs out, then her back, then her arms overhead, then finally rolled her neck and smiled, although her smile seemed a little forced. The aches and pains in her shoulders and back she was certain were caused by lack of exercise were still there. Once again, like a recalcitrant alcoholic avoiding AA meetings, she vowed to go back to the exercise club she still paid membership dues to but rarely visited. Marina found the other women and particularly the men she met at Haven Racquet Club vapid, and dull people always were a turnoff for her. 'They,' in turn, referred to Marina, although always behind her back, as an elitist, or uptight and standoffish, which only showed they didn't understand her at all. She was much too complex to be dismissed that easily.

Looking at her watch, Marina was surprised when she realized she had only an hour to get changed and drive over to Haven General Hospital. Marina had been putting off going to an introductory *In Vitro* Fertilization seminar at Haven General for a long time now, but had resolved this time she would do it. Although she had inquired once before by phone, and had tentatively made plans to attend, at the last minute she developed a case of severe anxiety made worse by embarrassment at being seen there in public, and backed out. Then, a few days ago, she received a copy of the Conceptions Foundation brochure in the mail, sent with a note of encouragement from Denny Cruite, the Foundation's director. "You can do it too; you're strong." Cruite's note said, making reference to a chance conversation they had previously had on the subject in the hallway at Haven General. Cruite's comments made Marina scoff in a self-deprecating way.

Marina had come to realize she would never have children if she waited for someone as indecisive and evasive as Charlie Kincade. She liked him a lot, and still hoped very much for their relationship to go somewhere someday. Yet, as Vena Kleinman had so recently explained to her, why should she wait to have children? She was young, healthy, attractive or at least attractive enough, and fertile as far as she knew, although her biological clock was inexorably ticking away. This was despite the painful episodes of pelvic inflammatory disease she occasionally developed, leftovers from an infection she suffered after her abortion at age sixteen.

The Surrogate

The memory once again pained her, distracted her, made her angry and resentful, and she shook her head and fought to dismiss her unwanted remembrances. Staring intensely into her reflection in the glass, she asked, "Are you doing this because you really want to, or because you think it's what other people expect will make you more complete? You better make up your mind now." Then, deciding this was no time for another bout of indecision, she pulled herself together and marched out the door.

Marina knew deep inside she was able to, willing to, take on the responsibilities of parenthood, single or not. She also very well knew the answer to her loneliness was never going to be Charlie Kincade or someone as equally indecisive and unwilling to just make a simple commitment as him. After the debacle at her house the other night, she wondered if she would ever even see him again. He had not returned her phone calls to try and patch things up, although that wasn't all that unusual. No, the answer to the emptiness she felt was a child, a Vanessa of her own.

Marina pulled her oil-stained painting blouse over her head, then chose a colorful sweater to match with a new flower print blouse, one that would complement her skirt. Then, looking in the mirror, she quickly fluffed up her hair. Marina checked her makeup one more time, which she hated to use in excess and was thankful she didn't need much of, anyway. Her mother never permitted her to use a great deal of makeup as a teen, telling her she was naturally beautiful. Yet, Marina's mother was both biased in her opinion, and naturally contradictory, saying on other occasions she thought Marina to be plain, with a crooked smile. Thus, Marina grew up with one more reason to be self-conscious of her physical appearance.

There was one part of her body she did think rather beautiful - her eyes. They were round, of an excellent proportion, attentive appearing, and topped by long and fine eyelashes. Marina's eyelids were of a soft lavender color, often described by her mother as heliotrope. Her eyelids were a frequent source of compliment - that is, when compliments were paid - and Marina often took the opportunity to apply just the lightest shade of shadow to accentuate their purplish blush.

Looking back at her image, Marina sighed, "that's good enough for government work." It was a phrase she had carried since studying art in a state-sponsored program years ago.

As she stared at her image in the mirror, she could see her apprehension of attending the seminar was obvious, very obvious. Her motives seemed simplistic and superficial, almost transparent, and feeling that way troubled her. Having other people read her so easily angered her, made her feel too open, vulnerable.

A half hour later, Marina pulled her minivan into the newly enlarged employee's parking area by the front of the hospital. Haven General Hospital was undergoing one of its seemingly continuous expansions, and the construction had all but choked off traffic flows. The vast parking lot stretched to the right and far beyond the orange silk wind sock which flapped smartly in the breeze by the heliport. The heliport itself was a mere roped-off area of parking lot with some lights arranged around the circumference. The presence of a heliport was more a matter of corporate prestige for Haven General Hospital than of community service.

Marina quickly walked the short distance from the parking lot to the main entrance, dodging the traffic as she went. Security guards nearby busily hollered directions to everyone passing by.

About the same time she received the Conceptions Foundation brochure from Denny Cruite, Marina had also noticed a series of medical information advertisements in the local newspaper. The articles discussed women's issues such as weight control, breast self-exam, and fertility. An offshoot of articles ran on advances in pregnancy, including screening for birth defects, and alternate birth techniques.

One article discussed the potential to achieve pregnancy for those not normally able to conceive; it discussed common reasons for infertility and newer treatments. Near the end of the article, Dr. Baatard, the author, mentioned that sometimes single women choose artificial insemination techniques -- *in vitro* fertilization -- for childbearing. There, it had caught her eye. Implicitly, IVF was presented as an option for women not requiring the heavy constraints of marriage. In concept, at least, it had appealed to her. More curious than ever that Baatard could be right, Marina arranged to attend an informational seminar mentioned at the end of each article. That led to her coming here today.

Marina entered the remodeled lobby of Haven General and looked around for directions to the conference. Large red banners draped all the walls of the spacious, newly refinished hospital lobby. Oversized red paperboard posters were prominently displayed on easel stands positioned in the corners and to both sides of the entrance way. These placards directed visitors wishing to attend the fertility conference to follow the arrows and proceed to the auditorium. It was all so organized, so efficient, planned to be easy, just like IVF itself, she supposed. She stood straighter, adjusted her purse strap over her shoulder, inhaled deeply, and proceeded on.

Just inside the auditorium, several groups of young women with fresh, determined faces milled around, speaking quietly among their small groups. They each wore a uniform red dress suit, matching red shoes, and had their hands full of glossy red brochures to distribute as they busily directed guests into the auditorium.

And I worried about finding the conference, Marina thought, shaking her head. Upon entering the large down-sloping auditorium, one of the ladies at the reception desk smiled profusely at Marina. "Hello and welcome to the Conceptions Foundation seminar," the receptionist nearly sang out. "I'm Heather. What's your name?"

Marina stared blandly at the receptionist. Heather, how typical, she thought. Not wanting to start the evening with a dose of her sometimes caustic sarcasm, Marina

politely gave her name, and she waited, nervously
drumming her fingers on the desk top. After noticing that
Heather couldn't find her name on the computer printout
list, Marina tried to allay Heather's puzzlement. "I only
made the reservation at the last minute, by phone, last
week, and . . . my name may not have been entered." She
felt her stutter return with the last few words and began to
blush.

"That's really okay, it's no problem," Heather smiled
calmly. "I can register you here right now, and there
should be plenty of room for you to attend today."
Heather made a few notations on a clipboard, then looked
up at Marina. "Here are your Conceptions Foundation
brochure, your parking pass, and a financial screening
form." Several major credit card insignia displayed over
the tables and also were imprinted on the financial
screening forms.

After Marina took the papers and started looking
through them, Heather asked, "Did you remember to
bring your insurance papers with you?" Heather flashed a
perfect full-mouth smile at Marina and waited like an
excited puppy for Marina's reply.

As Marina looked at the huge diamond ring on
Heather's perfectly manicured hand, something about it
annoyed her, perhaps its abject banality, its unabashed
ostentatious air, its stuffy, comfortable smugness. Typical,
she thought, well-aware that it was her jealousy speaking.

"I don't understand," Marina replied. "I thought this
was an introductory presentation, not an actual clinic
visit."

"Yes, that's true, of course it is. I was -- we were --

just thinking ahead, that's all. What I mean is, most health plans cover *in vitro* fertilization," Heather smiled, as if her response was actually God's promised answer to the world's suffering. "I was just wondering if you brought your health policy card. That way you would have the numbers handy to write down on the financial screening form, should you decide to go ahead," she nervously added.

How convenient, Marina thought. "Yes, of course. I'm a nurse, and I'm employed right here at Haven General." She opened her purse, took out her wallet and handed over her employee's insurance card to Heather.

"Thanks. The total procedure can be a tad expensive, that's all," she added, as if she weren't stating the obvious. "Is your husband employed here also?"

Marina paused, then said, "No, I'm single," as she glanced at the papers she was handed. She apprehensively waited for the inevitable question about her partner, but fortunately none came.

Heather's mouth was gaping as she pondered realities outside of her young, newlywed, giggly world. "That's fine, really. There's no pressure here," she tried to smile, although her face appeared more uncomfortable than relaxed.

Sure, Marina thought. There's no subtlety here, either.

"Please help yourself to some vegetables, fruit, drinks, and our other goodies," Heather continued, gesturing over to a nearby table. "We should be starting soon."

Marina took a sampling of the fruit and some sparkling mineral water, and then sat near the front of the auditorium, on the far right. She always chose the center right, at church, the movies, and conferences, and Charlie joked how it was a subconscious expression of her political beliefs. Marina knew that to be nonsense -- her seating preferences were simply born out of habit, and to the speaker on the podium she was seated to the left. It was all relative.

Marina tried not to look self-conscious, and was comforted to notice that many of the other women were also here without a male partner. She could see that, just as Baatard had only recently reinforced, her own decision to have a child despite not having a man around, was not at all unique. She remembered how, before her mother's untimely death in a freak car accident a few years ago, she would say to Marina, "you're such a smart girl, don't you want to get married?" The remarks at one point got so annoying, Marina avoided calling or going over to her mother's farmhouse at all. Her mother's solutions were not necessarily going to be hers, and she was not automatically going to become another Mrs. Antonio Bonnaserra. No, not her. She was her own woman now. She came and went as she liked, and apologized to no one for her actions. Marina liked living her life that way, and wasn't interested in changing it. But why then, she wondered, was she even here today at this conference? Wasn't she contemplating making the biggest change possible in her life, bigger than marriage and certainly more permanent?

The lights in the auditorium gradually dimmed, and a very thin, diminutive woman with an ice-like no-nonsense grimace and the look of distaste continually on her lips addressed the audience. Marina figured her to be probably in her early forties, but her dress, her walk, her makeup made her appear much older. She too was wearing a red blouse and red skirt with matching red shoes, and a little on the excessive side of gold necklaces and gold bracelets. The woman's outfit and body habitus made her appear somewhat severe, as she assertively portrayed the part of the business woman. Pendulous pearl earrings "adorned" her ear lobes.

"Hello, my name is Denny Cruite," the woman in the red business suit announced, her voice thin, high, and tense, then, after a short pause added for emphasis, continued, "and, along with my husband Nevin," Cruite paused again and smiled thinly at an older man seated on the other side of the podium, alone, "we founded the Conceptions Foundation."

Marina had half-expected the woman to introduce herself as Nancy Reagan. 'Just say no.'

Nevin Cruite, the bag of bones Denny so casually referred to, was a worn, sickly appearing man. His gray suit draped over his skeleton of a body, much like a sheet covered old and abandon furniture in a deserted house. Looking at Nevin made Marina feel uncomfortable, and she directed her attention back to Denny Cruite, herself not that pleasant a sight either.

Denny's paper-white face was prematurely wrinkled, probably from cigarette smoke, Marina thought, and it made her look harsh. Characteristic crow's feet splayed her eye corners. Marina wondered if Denny Cruite was not well, or on some chronic medications, for she possessed an unfortunate combination of thin hips, thin lips and thinning hair which only accentuated her feeble appearance.

Denny made Marina feel uncomfortable and reminded her of her grade school principal, a strict disciplinarian, and Marina unconsciously sat straighter in her seat. God, Marina thought, someone ought to tell this woman that Sherwin Williams isn't a cosmetics line.

Marina thought that as Denny was looking into the audience, she seemed to be frequently staring over at her, but could never be certain of this. The sensation, the perception, though, was somewhat unpleasant in itself.

After waiting while, like a trained puppy dog, Nevin smiled to the audience, Cruite continued. "I want to welcome you all to our Conceptions Foundation seminar." Cruite paused long enough to look over the audience and size up the group a little better, sort of get the feel, the pulse of the crowd, and then continued with the force and zeal of a Sunday morning preacher. "Now, how many of you are interested in becoming pregnant?" Denny almost sang the question out, smiling expectantly and bubbling over with enthusiasm. She anxiously scanned the audience, staring each person directly in the eye, almost begging for positive responses.

Marina looked around, and although she wasn't usually inclined to reply in public, hesitantly raised her hand along with most of the women sitting around her. She reminded herself that she was acting under peer pressure, and cautioned herself not to get 'suckered' into doing something.

"And how many of you are just sick." For a moment, the speaker crackled, and then only static came through, causing Denny to stare anxiously at the audience. Usually, someone from the hospital's audio visual department was present to assist with the slides and handle emergency situations like this, but at this moment, none was to be found. Then, one of the men on the stage got up and walked over to the back of the podium, bent down, did something to the wires, and the speaker came back on. The man was in his early to mid forties, powerfully built with muscular upper arms the size of bowling pins crammed tightly in a worn blue sport jacket.

"Thank you," a flustered Denny gratefully told him, and greatly relieved, she continued.

"As I was saying, how many of you are just sick and tired of unsuccessfully trying and waiting, trying and waiting, while your biological clocks keep ticking away? Huh?" Denny's voice had a slight pseudo-Texas accent, mixed with an annoying singsong rhythm, and her foot literally tapped back and forth to the cadence of her presentation as she repeated "trying and waiting." Denny's face projected the image of an impatient, driving, determined woman fettered with the trappings of marriage and held back her whole life by men, but Marina was certain that, in reality, Denny was restrained by no one; Marina admired that in a woman.

Again, Marina saw the hands fly up, and thought a 'Yes,' although she didn't raise her hand this time. She watched out of the corner of her eye as an overweight woman in a wheel chair raised her hand, and wondered briefly about this person's difficult circumstances. Yet, she reasoned there would be no reason why someone restricted to a wheel chair couldn't conceive a child, and certainly would be no less capable of loving a child, although the idea of her giving birth, thinking about the actual mechanism, the mechanics of the act, well . . .

"Good," Denny said, surveying all the positive responses. "Well, I didn't want to wait either, and 'thayat' is why Nevin and I started Conceptions Foundation over eight years ago. Yes we did, didn't we Nevin?" Denny smiled over at Nevin and paused before continuing. "We got pregnant, yup, and we had our child, despite horrendous odds," she told the audience, her voice quivering as she said the word horrendous, "and you can too." Denny shook her head from side to side, and closed her eyes, then struggled to continue. The audience presumed the fight was against painful memories. Denny thrust her outstretched hands to the group assembled and fixated on her as she smiled widely and said, "And WE want to bring what WE discovered to other women in need."

The audience was abuzz with excited background

discussion which lasted until Denny signaled for silence by repeatedly making a T sign with her two hands.

"Now, first, may I introduce to you our Conceptions Foundation staff. From right to left are our clinical nurse specialist, our clinical psychologist, and, of course, our founding obstetrician, Dr. Damon Baatard." Denny began to enthusiastically clap as she faced the staff on the stage and forced a wide smile out of her thin, painted chicken lips.

Marina sensed a slight exaggeration in Denny's applause, and probably in her general presentation. She could see a great deal more histrionics than scientifics here, which disappointed her. Nevertheless, she had invested enough time and courage in coming today and she wasn't about to trust her gut feelings and to just walk out before the inevitable sales come-on.

Marina thought she saw Nevin briefly glance her way, then quickly turn away. Unconsciously, she uncrossed her legs and adjusted her skirt down over her knees.

Looking at Dr. Baatard, Marina thought he appeared distantly familiar, and she wondered if perhaps she had once seen Baatard around Haven General, or noticed his picture in a newspaper article. Baatard seemed to be the prototype of all physicians she had known: calm, confident, focused, self-centered, sitting stiffly straight and properly stylish and professional in a tailor-made suit.

Coincidentally, Marina looked for but didn't notice a wedding ring on Baatard's hand. Although she wasn't sure why she looked for the ring, it was something she frequently did - often unconsciously - when noticing others for the first time.

After some polite applause as each Conception Foundation staff was introduced, Denny continued. "And now, Dr. Baatard will present an introduction to the concept of assisted fertilization. After this, we'll have presentations by the nurse coordinator on Conceptions Foundation from a patient's perspective. Then, the clinical psychologist will discuss the psychosocial aspects of assisted fertilization. After all 'thayat,' Heather will brief you on all the different convenient financial arrangements you can make with The Foundation."

A soft murmur permeated through the audience, until Denny said, "And finally, I'll try to summarize the evening. And following this," Denny smiled and sighed, as if she had already worked herself to the bone, "we have a special guest. Ms. Jody Ebbegest, a successful Conceptions Foundation mother, will give you her experiences from a patient's perspective." Denny smiled to herself as she held her hands up and led the audience in applause, ever so politely. She nervously straightened her skirt, pulled her knobby little knees together tightly and nodded a go-ahead to Dr. Baatard.

Baatard lectured for about a half-hour, covering basic concepts in conception, the most frequent causes of infertility, and the different techniques of IVF. He kept the technical level of his presentation down to a common level, simple enough for the high school graduate, yet tantalizingly interesting to the more sophisticated. He spoke confidently from his graphically perfect slides and his crisp color overhead projections, each professionally prepared, and never used notes or paused and risk breaking the concentration, and he literally exuded confidence and yet still managed to maintain a certain endearing feel - the appeal of the common man, a strong but understanding father figure, a supportive brother/husband. Baatard seemed to those hopelessly barren to be exactly the approachable, sympathetic but omnipotent male physician they needed if they ever were to become successful breeders.

Baatard began his presentation by reviewing the female reproductive tract. He then covered the female reproductive cycle, a topic he hoped those in the audience had at least gone over once before while still in high school. In preparation for the details of IVF itself, Baatard gave a brief discussion of hormones. He explained how hormones are complicated organic molecules which influence basic cellular activities, and how the proteins which direct their intricate synthesis are formed by linking hundreds of amino acids together in highly specific chains that conveyed information. The directions for assembling the amino acids are contained in genes, themselves linear linkages of highly complex inherited information. Proteins provide structure to body cells and act as organic catalysts, which regulate chemical reactions within the body. Hormones, Baatard explained, are secreted by specialized cells in the body called endocrine tissues, which form collections termed endocrine glands.

* * *

On a strictly subconscious level, Marina's hormonal cycles were functioning on auto pilot. The monthly torrential flood of hormones prepared Marina's sexual organs for the task of reproduction. Up to this point in Marina's life they had prepared her well, leading to a comely appearance, supple albeit somewhat small breasts, shapely hips, and about sixteen years ago, acne, some effects of which still lingered. The hormones also directly and unpredictably affected Marina's central nervous system, the seat of both her self-awareness and her turbulent and often contradictory emotions. That second effect Marina was on occasion wholly unprepared to understand or control.

* * *

After pausing to allow some of what he had said to sink in, and for note-takers to catch up, Baatard continued his presentation. He noted that among each person's hormonal tissues was a small collection of disparate and essential secretory glandular tissue - the pituitary gland. This complex gland was located only one inch directly behind the bridge of the nose, encased in a bony recess deep within the skull, a scooped out area of bone shaped like a Turkish saddle and anatomically described as the sella turcica. Descartes, the French philosopher, once referred to this essential gland as the seat of the soul. This was centuries before an understanding of neuroanatomy, endocrinology and biochemistry revolutionized medicine. More sophisticated societies subsequently determined the pituitary not to be the seat of the soul, although they still didn't manage to locate where exactly the soul did reside. Nowadays, the intelligentsia doubted its existence altogether, and dropped the search.

Baatard droned on about how the pituitary gland consists of multiple intermingled collections of cells whose specialties were to secrete different hormones - chemical messengers - into the blood. From its lair in the sella turcica, the "Master Gland" controlled an enormous group of basic bodily functions. It also regulated all other hormone-secreting tissues, including the ovaries in women and the testes in men, the thyroid and other endocrine glands.

Marina took notes and tried to follow along as best as she could in the brochure, and watched intently the rush of overhead color slides. She did better than usual, she thought, understanding the medical jargon associated with *in vitro* fertilization - her training as a nurse undoubtedly helped. Nevertheless, she found it difficult to take notes in the subdued light in the auditorium, especially given the speed of information presented.

When Baatard's presentation was completed, he

paused to ask the audience if there were any questions.

After looking around to notice if anyone else had raised their hand first, Marina raised her hand.

"Yes, miss," Dr. Baatard said, clearing his throat. "And what is your question?"

"How much input does the mother have in what type of child she gives birth to?"

Baatard seemed perplexed at the question, and glanced around, seemingly for support. "Could you be a little more specific?" Baatard asked.

"Yes, I was wondering if, for example, it's possible to choose the sex of the child?"

"That's a very good question, actually, and one that's asked a lot. Yes, we can pre-select passively or actively," Baatard continued. "That is to say, we can exploit some techniques which select for the survival of male sperm before fertilization. In addition, for *in vitro* fertilization, as opposed to artificial insemination, we can try to select ova based on sex before the actual implantation. We can even selectively abort after implantation too, if the sex of the fetus isn't the desired one. Does that answer your question?" His response caused a fair amount of discussion in the audience, some of it neither subdued nor calm.

"Partly." Marina paused for a moment, collecting her thoughts, then asked, "For the mother in her thirties, there's a special risk. Could you describe your ability to screen for birth defects."

"Yes, well, Miss . . . " Baatard paused.

"Bonnaserra."

Baatard stopped for a moment, as if he were trying to

remember something, then continued, "Yes, Miss Bonnaserra, we can screen for physical defects too. As I was pointing out in my presentation, we can look for a variety of physical and mental deformities. We can't detect all, mind you, but quite a lot. If we detect problems at any stage, pre- or post-fertilization, after implantation, or up to four to six months of pregnancy, we can, in some circumstances, terminate the pregnancy. In other words, abort."

Everyone on the podium, and most of the audience, turned toward the direction of a loud gasp, almost a shriek, coming from the back. A woman was being helped to her feet and escorted to the exit by a small group of women, all angrily complaining about what they had just heard. A hospital security agent, a woman specifically chosen for her gentle but firm handling of confrontations, followed them out, to assure there was no disruption of the presentation. Baatard waited until they had left before continuing to answer questions.

Marina raised her hand again, this time to ask about an article she had read in the paper discussing in utero selecting for intelligence. The article had mentioned Dr. Baatard's name, as a prominent infertility specialist familiar with that area, and also his association with The Conceptions Foundation. Although Baatard was able to answer several other people's questions, he never got back to Marina before ending the question and answer session to move on with the next speaker.

As Marina listened to the various presentations, she began to see how IVF really could be the answer, her answer. Having gone this far, she felt there was little reason to turn back now. All the relevant clocks were ticking, including her biological one, and with much more indecision, she would effectively close out her opportunity to have her own family, short of some unexpected Prince Charming showing up in the Quality Assurance office tomorrow. She placed no reliance in fairy tales.

Chapter 5

Haven Fertility Associates, PC.
Haven, NJ

Toward the end of a long clinic day at Haven Fertility Associates, Garza, Baatard's longtime nurse practitioner, rumbled her noisy cart down the corridor past Baatard's office. The reverberations of the cart's metal wheels against the worn linoleum floor made an annoying din, accentuated by the crash and rumble the cart generated by bumping into each door it passed. The cart's wheels were loosened from years of use, and, coupled with the narrowness of the corridors and the technician's advanced age, made the navigation even more difficult.

"Hey, you ignoramus." Baatard yelled out at Garza from inside his office. A short, serious woman, a little on the chunky side, with matching brown skin, eyes and hair, Garza had once been an independently operating midwife herself in another life and in another country. "Don't bang my door with your stupid cart every time you wheel the stupid thing past." In the distance, the steady, intimidating chant of abortion protesters disrupted the usually placid neighborhood. Baatard had already angrily called the police twice this morning alone, but it was little use. The protesters had their rights to annoy him, so he was informed - the right to intimidate his patients, and the right to act like barbarians and disrupt his medical practice. As he listened to their constant annoying chants and shrieking, Baatard felt his stomach react with its characteristic flush of acid. One additional annoyance in an already annoying day, he thought.

Baatard reached into his coat pocket, took out a couple of antacid tablets that he always kept close by, and promptly popped several into his mouth like candy. He tried to ignore the dry, chalky taste and the unpleasant burning effervescent feel before swallowing them in one mouthful. He then washed the antacids down his gullet with a gulp of decaffeinated espresso he had brewed up in a small unit in his office, the bitter taste of the espresso only accentuating the acid further. He put the cup down on his desk, next to some billing justifications he needed to complete, and returned to reviewing some medical charts.

Garza ignored Baatard's outburst, having heard it many times before, and instead, hurriedly guided the electrically propelled shopping cart-like device out of the hallway and into the waiting room, unavoidably bumping some more walls and doors as it went along. The cart was filled to nearly overflowing with black medium-sized plastic trash bags, each neatly sealed closed with plastic tape. On the side of the bags were red and black symbols, with a matching symbol on the breast pocket of Garza's frayed green cloth jacket and also on the side of the cart.

From her position seated in Baatard's waiting room, waiting for her initial infertility evaluation to begin, Marina could hear Baatard yelling out something. It was too garbled for her to understand, but she deduced from the tone of Baatard's voice and the embarrassed and angry look on the office help's face that it must have been an obscenity. She already was apprehensive about coming to the clinic, and learning that the doctor she was about to request assistance with the most private and intimate of matters behaved like a Neanderthal only made her feel even more insecure. Experience had taught her to expect such rude behavior by physicians, infected as a group with a God complex.

Garza passed through the waiting room with her cart and literally fled into the hallway, and was gone in less than fifteen seconds, leaving a trail of unusual food scents behind. Marina tried but couldn't make out what the small print on the bag's labels said as the cart wheeled passed her, but had the uncomfortable impression she had seen the symbol before.

Baatard's waiting room was a simple area, and more an extension of the receptionist's section. Five small Naugahyde chairs crowded along the walls, each chair facing its empty counterpart. A low lying square wood table, jammed into the center of the room, was covered with outdated magazines, aged dried coffee stains, assorted plastic credit card emblems, and brochures for various illnesses and for a few local banks. With the ability to see only one to two consults an hour, there was little need for greater seating capacity, and this left both the patients who waited and the receptionist who sat behind a sliding glass window with little room to move around.

Marina picked up a brochure entitled "Newer Ideas for *In Vitro* Fertilization" from the table and glanced at the articles, to keep her thoughts occupied on anything other than her immediate agenda. Although resolved to go ahead with the assisted fertilization, Marina still had many internal conflicts and doubts, too many loose ends that needed closing. The brochures Marina casually examined had obviously been prepared by some slick PR department especially for the obstetric office environment. The opposing purposes of sales and education were none too subtle, and Marina immediately began to filter what she read.

Marina's eyes nervously darted around the room as her thoughts momentarily drifted to another obstetrician's office some sixteen years past. Her consciousness became flooded with a powerful mixture of anger and guilt which she fought to immediately shut out in an act of sheer self-preservation. The brochure bent in half in her tight grasp.

"Ms. Bonnaserra," the casually dressed receptionist, whose name tag said "Sharlene," called out. She opened the door which led from the reception area to the examining rooms for Marina, and as Marina approached, Sharlene looked at her strangely, and then said, "You know, for a moment I almost called you Ms. Vernor."

"Why was that?" Marina asked, knowing only one female named Vernor - and that was Lissa.

"She's the wife of Dr. Ryder Vernor, and you look more than a little like her." Sharlene appeared slightly uncomfortable, as if she regretted opening her big mouth.

"Oh, I know Lissa Vernor," Marina replied, "but I think you're mistaken. I don't really look like her at all." Marina remembered Lissa as being a little on the wild side, a cheerleader with a perfect figure and an aggressive but complying personality, a girl who seemed to be able to date anyone she wanted, and whom she remembered as being far prettier than she. Lissa had once told Marina that she would only marry a doctor or a lawyer, because only they could give her the life style and respectability she deserved, and Marina wasn't surprised when she married Ryder Vernor. Not being a close friend or a member of the in-crowd, she had not been invited to the wedding, and had seen little of Lissa since.

"I also know Dr. Vernor," Marina said. "I've been his patient in the past for different things." Marina speculated why Lissa Vernor would be coming to this office, but didn't ask, her own situation foremost in her mind.

The Surrogate

Sharlene ushered Marina into the back clinic area to an examining room, past a plaque on the wall which displayed:

Doctor: Baatard
Patient: MB

Sharlene placed Marina's chart in a plastic holder outside the door, then motioned Marina to be seated inside. "Dr. will be right with you."

Marina found the way the receptionist dropped the article 'the' as she said "Dr. will be right with you," rather than, "The doctor will be right with you" annoying and a little ostentatious, and it was one more annoyance that raised her anxiety level. As Sharlene closed the door, Marina saw a young woman dressed only in a paper disposable examining gown shuffle by. The gown was held loosely together by paper tabs on the back, her head was hung low, and she was sobbing quietly into a handful of tissues. Marina quickly looked away.

Marina glanced around the sparse but clean room, then took a seat. The chair was of an arty, modern design, heated to a comfortable temperature and emitted a soft, relaxing purr and seemed a little expensive for a medical examining room. The room's subdued light and the few reproductions of impressionist art displayed on the walls at least tended to make Marina's wait comfortable, and she was most thankful for the absence of "waiting music."

After a few minutes, Garza came in the room and pounced onto a swivel stool in front of Marina. The chair, in response, registered a complaint in the form of continued squeaks.

"Good afternoon, Mrs. Bonnaserra," Garza said, "and welcome to Haven Fertility Associates." Garza held a clipboard in one hand and extended her other hand to Marina.

Marina nodded Garza's way, briefly shook her hand, but said nothing. Garza glanced at Marina, and then quickly looked away, and yet Marina perceived a hint of recognition in Garza's eyes. She started to ask Garza about this when she was interrupted.

"Before doctor sees you, he would like you to answer a few questions about your medical history. Shall we begin?"

"Fine," Marina replied, already taken aback by Garza's gruff, almost inappropriate manner, particularly for such an up-scale operation as The Conceptions Foundation.

"Age?"

"Thirty-two, just a few months ago."

Garza looked askance at Marina, then said, "Okay, and I presume your genetic sex is female?"

"Yes, female, of course." Marina began to feel uncomfortable. Didn't she look female, for Christ's sake?

Seeing the puzzled look Marina was giving her, Garza said, "We take nothing for granted here, Marina."

"I guess in an infertility clinic you do see all kinds." Marina was certain that a nurse, let alone a non-medical professional, should have experienced no trouble recognizing her as authentically female, unless there was something less than feminine about herself she had not been aware of. That last possibility made Marina became even more uneasy and a little self-conscious.

"You got that right. Now, what is your sexual orientation?"

"I beg your pardon," Marina said. She had never been asked this rather inappropriate question before, felt offended, and considered telling this gruff Garza so, too.

"These are different times we live in, Mrs. Bonnaserra, and a brief sexual history always plays a part in our evaluation. I don't see why that question is unclear. I mean, if you don't . . . "

"Fine, fine. I prefer men, if that's what you mean," Marina nervously smiled, trying to maintain her composure. Garza's body odor was beginning to bother Marina and she almost had to get up and open the door a little. Having so unpolished a staff member seemed totally incongruous with the slick, professional image of this IVF clinic, and she strongly considered mentioning that to Dr. Baatard.

"Are you currently using any form of contraception?"

"No, I'm not." The occasions of need were, fortunately or unfortunately, infrequent, and she preferred time-of-use methods like a rubber prophylactic, uncomfortable and unnatural as they were, to the pill, whose dangerous side-effects had scared her off. She also was attracted to the rubber's ability to cut down on the transmission of infectious diseases like herpes and HIV. Those she surely didn't need. She had once imagined that using a rubber prophylactic or contraceptive foam might also decrease spontaneity, as opposed to the pill, which required no planning and preparation, but that had never actually been a real problem in her experience.

Garza seemed to smirk again, which annoyed Marina, her sexual habits and her level of activity being none of Garza's personal business. And yet, here she was, disclosing intimate details to this downright inappropriate stranger. Under ordinary circumstances, Marina supposed that a single woman of her age would be using some form of contraception if she was sexually active. Not to use any form of contraception implied the opposite - that she was either sexually inactive - for whatever reason, was foolishly carefree or that she was stupid, unless she WAS trying to become pregnant. Yes, of course. That explanation was consistent with her being in this IVF clinic after all, and made her feel a little less strange.

A seemingly routine series of questions on her past medical history followed, and Marina tried to answer each as carefully as she could, although some clearly seemed irrelevant. She was asked about any past medical illnesses, past surgeries, any history of sexually transmitted diseases - syphilis, gonorrhea or Chlamydia. Marina's life was of such a level of simplicity and lack of 'complications' these last sixteen years she had little trouble answering.

"Are you infected with hepatitis, herpes or HIV?"

"Not that I know of, although I never have been tested," Marina said, shaking her head. She had never seriously considered being tested before, but now wondered. Charlie Kincade was the only man she had been with in a long time, although she would never admit that to him. Although she had no reason to think he slept around, she wouldn't be at all surprised either. Maybe she shouldn't be so trusting.

"Well, you probably would know by now if you had any of those things," Garza nodded, knowingly. "And how many years of unprotected intercourse have you had?"

"Approximately twelve," Marina said, preferring lying to embarrassment.

* * *

Operating deep within Marina's subconscious, hormonal surges caused several developing ova - human eggs - to burst forth from their follicles. The unrestrained rupture on the surface of Marina's ovary had been building for hours, yet lasted for merely a millisecond, and in the process, enormous amounts of vital, unrestrained energy spewed forth.

The explosive release of the ovarian follicles was nearly painless to Marina. Although her body temperature did increase a degree or two, Marina was aware only of a slight warmth and of a flushed feeling which she innocently attributed to the summer heat.

Moments later, the stimulated and developing ova were free in Marina's pelvic cavity, where gentle fluids washed Marina's egg the short distance into the waiting opening of the Fallopian tube, there to be entrapped by waving arms of thin tissue.

The ovarian follicle whose home the egg had left behind on the ovary's surface was now free to develop on its own. Still more estrogen and progesterone poured from the follicle and pumped into the general blood circulation, the powerful primordial sexual hormones traveling throughout Marina's body, and to Marina's uterus, thickening and enriching and preparing the blood nest to accept a fertilized ovum, should one arrive. Up to this point in Marina's young life, none had.

* * *

"Have you ever been pregnant?" Garza asked, a trace of sadness covering her face as she spoke.

Marina paused, wondering if the subject of pregnancy, or some particular knowledge, expressed or implied, about Marina had caused the change in Garza's expression. "Once," she admitted.

"What was that? Could you speak up a bit?"

"Once, I was pregnant, once." A long string of unpleasant memories flooded back, and she felt pressured, confined, accused.

"Oh," Garza replied, her tone implying she was not completely surprised. "Well, did you deliver?" Garza literally stared into Marina's eyes as she spoke, as if there was some special recognition taking place, and Garza nodded her head affirmatively without saying a word, as if realizing some unspoken truth.

"No," Marina replied, almost in a whisper, turning her face toward the wall, feeling helplessly exposed. She stared at her broken and distorted reflection in the metal paper towel holder, her face pained and pale white and suddenly aged. What had happened to her so long ago still made her feel like a criminal - both a criminal and the victim, and she still suffered under the guilt.

"Then, I guess that means you had an abortion?"

"Yes, that's right. I had an abortion," Marina almost whispered, staring into her folded hands on her lap. She rarely uttered those words, and as she did so now, felt her composure slipping away. Strange, she thought, how she still felt in some ways like a terrible, shameless murderer. Her child would be sixteen now, if it had been born.

"Oh, I'm sorry, really I am. Well, I guess that makes you G1 P0 Ab1," Garza said to herself as she busily wrote notes in Marina's chart.

"Excuse me, what does that mean?" Marina hated eclectic abbreviations, from the military to medical. She felt they put her at a disadvantage, and there was just too much at stake here, and too much she didn't understand to allow that to occur. She had to know everything that involved her, unlike that last time. Although as a nurse she might have been expected to know what these abbreviations stood for, she just didn't. Maybe it was just the unusual, pressured circumstances. It was at times like this she realized how being administrative actually hindered her, distanced her from her own profession.

"Oh, it's just GYN shorthand," Garza reassured

Marina. "The G1 stands for gravida-1, meaning you carried a child once, the P0 means parturition zero, that you gave birth no times, and the Ab1 means you had one abortion."

"Oh, I see," Marina said, feeling extremely flustered.

"That is correct, isn't it? I mean, that IS what you told me?" Garza repeated.

"Yes," Marina replied tersely, trying not to make eye contact. "That is what I said. I assume that's all you want to know." Garza made her feel very uncomfortable, and she had a burning need to get this dreadfully stressful interview over with.

"Yes, of course it is. There's really NO need to get touchy now."

"I'm not getting touchy," Marina angrily shot back. She felt flushed and hot and was afraid her annoying stutter would return. Damn, the embarrassment. "It's just that it was a most unpleasant and awkward time, that's all," Marina tried to explain.

"It often is," Garza nodded understandingly. "When did your abortion occur?"

"Almost sixteen years ago," Marina replied softly, looking at the floor. She wanted to ask Garza why she needed so much detail on this one question, but held her curiosity, assuming it had something to do with her IVF evaluation.

The Surrogate

Sixteen years ago, Garza had been working in an abortion mill, and at the end of one particularly long day in that distant clinic, Garza had been slowly walking into the cramped break room in the back of the clinic, next to the shared rest room. There, she had poured herself some coffee, lit a cigarette and had tried to relax.

She had no other plans for that evening, a fact she had been glad of, particularly at that time; being alone for so many years had made her accustomed to being on her own schedule. In other circumstances, she felt she certainly would have been more sought after as a woman. Back home in her native Guatemala she would be considered pretty, young, intelligent. She was a college graduate, and fluent in two languages. Now, in the US, she was lumped together with all the other Spanish-speaking women. Short and squat, thick-lipped, dark of hair and eyes and skin, and too serious. Few men looked twice at her, even those from her own country, preferring the superficial Anglo suburban girls who ended up so tragically in their clinic. This too made her resentful and reclusive.

Garza took a particularly deep drag from her cigarette, and felt the warmth expand her lungs. Exhaling too had its own hot sensations, and she sipped some coffee; it was 'last of the day' coffee: bitter and strong and the way she liked it. After that, Garza stared into the remaining dark liquid for some time before moving again, deep thoughts rummaging around like rats in the basement of her mind.

As Garza anxiously thought about her work at the clinic, uneasiness quickly degenerated into depression.

She had feared for some time that her routine at the abortion clinic was becoming too 'routine,' and she wondered if she were becoming a little like the callous doctors in her clinic. The very thought revolted her: "I would rather die than be like him," she scoffed.

Later, much later, Garza collected the plastic bags of nonmedical waste from around the various clinic offices and stacked them in a pile by the back door. Before taking the bags down the back ramp to the trash bin, Garza needed to deactivate the security alarm, and this she did the same way she had hundreds of times before. The code she had chosen was the numeric equivalent of "FETUS," a fact only she knew, and was her little 'inside joke.'

The community in which the clinic had been located for perhaps six years was beginning to show the signs of urban blight and neglect, accompanied by an annoying increase in petty crime. Break-ins had occurred at the clinic, usually kids looking for drugs, and for equipment to sell. Pain pills could be sold too, particularly the strong "prescription" samples left by the drug detailers - the professional representatives who earned their name by emphasizing to physicians selectively favorable details on the overpriced products they left behind. Searching any further in that clinic for drugs was a waste of time for the local petty thieves - the clinic stocked no narcotics, and only a limited amount of samples of non-narcotic pain medications were kept around at any one time. Maybe looking for pain medications hadn't been their motivation, for the break-ins still happened. But what else, Garza thought? She had laughed at the impasse, and concluded: Kids are slow learners.

Garza pushed open the heavy metal back door, and walked the trash bags down the then-darkened ramp leading to the rear of the clinic. After tossing the bags - one by one - into a trash bin in a corner of the parking lot, Garza hurriedly turned to go back inside. She had never felt safe outside, alone, unlike her years in Guatemala, even with all the political violence. Then, before she could start back, something had made her pause.

Garza thought she saw a flower pattern of cloth mixed between all the assorted bags and pieces of garbage in the trash bin: it was something clearly out of place. Turning back, and looking a little more closely in the dim light, Garza thought she could make out the color of flesh. As she leaned forward and partially into the trash bin, balancing her chest on its hard metallic edge, anxiously pushing aside mounds of rubbish, she suddenly touched something soft. Garza looked closely: it was a human hand, and the unexpected sight made Garza gasp out loud.

The hand lay open as if reaching out for help, quite empty and motionless. Looking even closer, Garza could make out the brown-red stain of old blood on some nearby pieces of newspaper. Her heart suddenly raced as her adrenaline glands reflexively squeezed a shot of epinephrine into her blood stream. She felt deeply sick and frightened - her brain was frantically screaming warnings to her to run.

Garza rushed back in the clinic and pulled the door

secure behind her, then called the police and hurriedly told them what she had just seen. After hanging up, she turned on all the outside lights to the parking area. One of the beams shone slightly to the right of the trash bin, its top flipped back like a gigantic coffin. That done, she forced herself to get a grip on her composure, then ran back outside. She wondered if she had stumbled across another drug-related murder, or an overdose, or perhaps, she feared, it was someone from her clinic - patient or staff. One of the girls did look particularly depressed today before leaving, and Garza thought she might have worn a similar flowery pattern of clothes.

Somehow, Garza had managed to lift her non-athletic frame up over the metal side of the trash bin and climb inside. She remembered worrying, as she climbed over the trash bin's rough edge, about the discarded needles of local junkies that might have been tossed inside, and cut medical glass from her clinic, also contaminated with blood. Infections like hepatitis could kill worse than any bullet. The dark contents had a foul smell of rotting food and animal excreta, and she couldn't even see where or on what she stood.

As Garza anxiously shoved mounds of rubbish aside, she thought she heard the faint rustling of rats among the lower reaches of the trash can. Fighting an urge to get out and run, Garza pushed concerns of personal safety to the back of her consciousness as she crawled toward where she had seen the cloth and the hand.

Garza was sitting alone on a pile of refuse in the center of the darkened trash bin when the first of several police cars had arrived minutes later. The head of a partially clothed and unconscious female, possibly in her teens, lay like a dead weight on Garza's lap. "She's alive," Garza had told the police, and those words had made her feel angry, ashamed, and dirty. She still felt that way even today, sixteen long years later, whenever she recalled that painful day, with almost as much detail as if it had just happened to her. "It looks like she's been sexually attacked; we better get an ambulance," were the last words she remembered having had said that terrible night.

Chapter 6

Garza hurriedly scribbled some additional notes in Marina's chart, but only asked a few more questions. Shortly after all Garza's questions had been answered, the door opened and Dr. Damon Baatard entered, as if on cue. A symbolic stethoscope protruded, unused, from the right pocket of his light blue sport coat. Marina immediately recognized him from the Conceptions Foundation seminar, and had the same vague feeling of familiarity. Dr. Baatard seemed a little shorter and older to her now than he did at the seminar, and his mannerisms were definitely gruff and impersonal, as opposed to the polished image he presented to the audience. The same sense of confidence and control she had noticed from him at the seminar was still present, and it was professionally comforting. Baatard's presence immediately changed Garza's attitude, the way she sat in her chair, even the way she held her notebook, now seeming more professional, organized and proper. Marina too felt a change in the way she related to Garza, and now to Baatard. It was definitely more patient-physician. Marina had noticed such subtle transformations occur before, and wondered what interpersonal mechanics actually caused them to happen.

Dr. Baatard was forty-five years old, of Belgian background, and a native of New Jersey. Baatard had practiced in the specialty of gynecology and obstetrics for nearly a third of his life. The son of a surgeon, he had known since grade school he would become a physician. With his parent's support, he had carefully tailored his classes in high school and college toward just that end. Being an above-average student, he had managed admission to several medical schools of his choosing without too much trouble at all. Once enrolled, he had mastered the difficult medical curriculum reasonably well.

Not a star, not an outstanding student, but not interested in being one either, Baatard looked upon medical school as a milestone to his career. Once he was graduated, he had no trouble gaining admission to the obstetrics and gynecology residency of his father's choice, which he completed before he was twenty-eight. During the residency, he had occasionally moonlighted in various abortion mills, and covered for local practitioners, as did his fellow residents. After several years in a group practice as junior associate, he tried a few years of solo practice in Manhattan before meeting up with Denny Cruite.

Baatard stared at Marina as if he knew her, but didn't say anything. He observed Marina's absence of a wedding band almost immediately, for that was something he found helpful to look for.

Baatard took the chart from Garza, who then left the

room. He took several minutes to glance through it, assimilating all the information Garza had already extracted. "Hi, Marina. How are you?" Baatard smiled, taking a seat on the swivel stool, his words annoyingly lengthened, his gaze straight into the chart.

"I'm just . . . ," Marina started, but was cut off when Baatard spoke into a hand-held dictation unit.

"Initial Workup, Marina Bonnaserra, . . . " Baatard paused. He held the pause button, then asked, "What can we do for you today, Ms. Bonnaserra?"

"I would like to have a child, Dr. Baatard." Although that was why she was here, and she had thought by now she had come to terms with her unusual goal, contradictory emotions still ruled her mind.

Marina noticed that Baatard's finger nails were bitten down almost to the skin, an oddity she had occasionally seen in a man, and which she attributed to stress. This contrasted with the careful, tailored look of his clothes and his tasteful, but not excessive, use of jewelry, undoubtedly the mark of a woman's influence -- his wife's or Denny Cruite's.

"I see. Well, I trust you have been trying but have been unsuccessful?" Baatard asked, matter-of-factly.

"Yes, I guess that's true," she replied in a flat and low voice, looking away from Baatard and into her lap. She feigned a smile. Just being here, and answering all these personal questions was embarrassing. Getting past the noisy and intimidating Right-To-Life pickets outside the building was a chore and an embarrassment. Marina got a glimpse of Christine Lincoln, whom she had casually known in high school, but hadn't seen since, prominent in the picket line.

Marina wondered if perhaps she should have tried to locate a fertility specialist who was female, someone in another hospital, perhaps one in another city. That might have allowed her to be more comfortable. Although Dr. Baatard had an excellent reputation around the hospital, he now seemed too close.

"I see." Addressing the recorder again, Baatard continued. "Initial Infertility Evaluation, Marina Bonnaserra." He looked more carefully at the full color Medical Chart, with Marina's name and address at the top, followed by her social security number and blood Type. Also present was a Credit worthiness code, used internally and useful for the billing department. Fertility works were not covered by all health insurance plans and were expensive. Baatard saw that Marina's chart had a green sticker, meaning she was employed and quite able to handle any co-pay.

Underneath all this was a standard medical history and physical form. Marina seemed a straight-forward initial workup. Those were always so cookbook, he could probably do one in his sleep. By the time he got the case, the initial evaluation for all practical purposes was completed anyway. Baatard simply ran down the progressively restricted possibilities on a diagnostic algorithm; the answers were all too often the same. At this point, Baatard simply evaluated the suitability of the patient for *in vitro* fertilization techniques, and gave her a final, gentle push into acceptance, if needed. Women who made it this far had for the most part almost all already made up their minds, and any further encouragement was more to assuage guilt than settle uncertainty. Baatard's fees more than made his participation worthwhile.

Leafing through Marina's chart, Baatard said, without looking up, "I see you have attended the Conceptions Foundation seminar. Very good."

Marina nodded.

"Let's see, . . . you were evaluated for infertility once before, and the workup showed, . . . ah, it showed, . . . ah, yes, mild uterine fibrosis."

Marina remembered her past workup, a step actually taken more out of curiosity than a desire to become pregnant. She had accidentally had unprotected intercourse with Charlie, an incident brought out by the heat of passion, if passion and Charlie could be considered in the same sentence. Marina worried for weeks she would become pregnant, but she didn't. "Accidental" sex began to happen more frequently, as Marina gained confidence that she would likely not conceive. Eventually, she saw a gynecologist, but no cause was ever identified. The working hypothesis seemed to be possible infertility caused by residual scarring from her pelvic inflammatory disease.

"Okay, okay, we can deal with uterine fibrosis. The

main thing is that you can make eggs." Baatard smiled reassuringly at Marina for a few milliseconds, then directed his attention back to the relevant areas of Marina's medical chart. His facial expressions changed remarkably fast. He immediately noticed several interesting things. Marina was unmarried, she was a nurse employed at Haven General -- which raised warning flags -- and she was an amateur artist, and that she belonged to an organization called MENSA. "Could you tell me what is MENSA?"

"It's a national society." Almost as soon as Baatard had brought up MENSA, Marina had regretted filling out the history section of the intake form with such compulsive accuracy. Her compunction to detail had created difficulties for her in the past, and it seemed to her that she just never seemed to learn. She was also a little surprised that a physician would not have been aware of MENSA.

"For what, artists?"

"No, not really. MENSA membership is made up of persons who have unusually high IQs." She blushed as she explained the meaning, and turned away, as if admitting she had some embarrassing disease.

Baatard looked at Marina askance, his head tilted at an angle.

"Actually, I think it's a little silly, really, and pretentious," Marina said, defensively. She usually found derision when she mentioned MENSA, as if she were being an elitist. It wasn't that way at all, but she rarely discussed her membership, and if she felt hassled, never bothered defending her actions.

"Then why do you belong?"

"I belong because, I guess, the people at meetings are often interesting," she partially lied, "and it's a chance to network." In truth, she rarely went to meetings, and when she did, found them boring. Marina tried to force a smile, shifting in her chair and pulling her clothes a little straighter. She heard the first trace of her stutter showing up.

Baatard smiled and said, "Like being a Unitarian, huh?"

Marina returned a look of disapproval without comment. His remark made her wonder if Baatard could ever understand her motivation at all.

"And your chart indicates you're a nurse at Haven General. I haven't seen you on the obstetrics or gynecology wards."

"No, I work strictly in nursing administration." Marina noted the look of surprise and perhaps wariness on Baatard's face, a typical reaction by doctors. They seemed to be universally suspicious of nurses in administration, as if she were involved in policing their actions, questioning their billings, disputing their judgments, and adding needless aggravation to their already pressured lives.

Baatard nodded his head, then took a few minutes to outline for Marina the evaluation route he would take. He ended by saying, "I suspect, as you already appear to have also, *in vitro* fertilization may help you to achieve a pregnancy." He smiled reassuringly and confidently over at her from above the medical chart on the clipboard, then continued. "Assuming we can successfully obtain ova from you, do you have a sperm donor selected?"

Not expecting him to be so blunt, Marina blushed, and then replied, "Do we have to decide this now?" She nearly choked on the words "sperm donor." A sperm donor? Why the hell didn't I consciously deal with this before Baatard asked me, she wondered? I must look like a moron to him.

"Perhaps not," Baatard hesitated. "Remember, we have no secrets here, and as adults there's nothing we can't say or discuss with each other. Okay? As your doctor, you can tell me anything, anything at all, and it will remain right here," Baatard said, pointing to the office around them. He continued to write notes in her chart.

The thought of Charlie Kincade telling her the same line came to mind, and she didn't believe him either. "Yes, of course," Marina said. "Your honesty and privacy are appreciated. Because, Dr. Baatard, I don't plan to be pressured into sleeping with or even marrying someone just to become pregnant." Crossing her arms tightly in front of her chest, she looked straight at Baatard and said, "Do you have any doubt, Dr. Baatard, I could make a competent, caring parent?"

"No, not at all. Why, of course you could be a good parent," he smiled reassuringly.

"Good, because I have no doubt, none at all." Her worst fears of bringing up a child - maybe even children, who knows, mistakes happen - flooded her mind, belying the outward confidence she attempted to portray.

Baatard nodded agreement, and dropped the line of conversation. Instead, he busied himself filling out a series of lab request slips, then pushed the intercom button to bring in Garza again. "We can get your pelvic ultrasound and hormonal evaluations completed right here," Baatard told Marina. "In forty-eight hours we could be on our way. I think this can proceed pretty fast, that is if you would like to."

"Yes, I guess I would." Marina now contemplated how she would fill in the missing pieces. She felt pressured, uncertain, and even a little dirty as she considered putting a perfect stranger's sperm in her vagina. The whole idea made her shiver.

"Well then, let's get started. Here, please put this on," Baatard said as he handed Marina a disposable examining gown. "Just push the intercom button to let us know when you're ready." Baatard and Garza left the room while Marina changed.

Marina disrobed quickly and put on the simple yellow paper gown, and secured the back with paper ties. "I'm ready now," she spoke into the intercom. As she waited for Baatard to return, she realized how silly she still felt about trying to have a child, and using IVF. She also dreaded the inevitable "who is the partner" question being brought up again, although she knew that it was inevitable. 'Even when I don't want to be dependent upon a man,' she thought, 'I still am. I've got Baatard to contend with, and I've got to come up with sperm.' She speculated briefly on the possibility of fertilizing an ovum without sperm, having heard some reptiles could do this, and then laughed at the idea. That would make her Marina of the Immaculate Conception. Or the mother of a lizard. Yeah, right, she mocked.

While Marina waited for Baatard to return, she looked around the room. A stack of empty black bags lay on the counter top, folded flat. Each bore the red and black label she had seen on the full bags in the shopping cart being pushed through the waiting room earlier. Looking closer, she saw the lettering "Human Waste" in fine print. Feeling momentarily breathless, Marina quickly looked away, as if trying to hide an awful secret.

For some reason, Marina was reminded of the evidence bag the police had given her, containing her personal belongings, mostly torn and soiled clothes found on her and near the rape scene. They had given everything back to her after the investigation into her own assault and rape was closed. Apparently they had decided it no longer contained useful evidence, and was taking up valuable space in their evidence lockers. She had kept the clothing bag, not so much because she ever could extract more information, but so she would not forget. And remember she did.

Knowing that the animal who raped her was still free to attack other women or even herself angered Marina and made her fearful. She knew she could never feel truly at ease and safe until he was caught. Others - Charlie Kincade for instance - thought she was obsessed and should "just let it go." She tried to, if only for her own sanity, but she could not. Whether it was anger, an overriding desire for revenge - not a usual part of her personality - or the need to finish things, set them right again, she just didn't know. Marina did know, though, every time she looked at the small scar on her right nipple, that she could never undo the past. It was her scar, but also served as her badge and her reminder.

After a few minutes, Baatard returned to the exam room, again accompanied by Garza. "Marina, Ms. Garza is a nurse practitioner and she will be performing some of your initial evaluation today."

Garza nodded matter-of-factly to Marina, then looked toward Baatard.

Baatard continued. "Based on the medical history we have already taken, we have arrived at a list of most likely diagnoses." He glanced at the clipboard and checked off the tasks yet to be performed. "These exams are designed to strengthen and confirm our diagnosis and help us develop a treatment plan specifically tailored to meeting your individual needs."

It seemed all too neat and organized to Marina, as if she were merely another pre-formed pie on an assembly line waiting for the appropriate filling to be added or the top crust to be laid on. She resented medicine as it was now practiced, and wondered if there weren't a better, more personal way. Yet, by her own chosen profession, she too was a part of the system, and she too contributed to its problems. After all, she consciously chose administration over patient care, giving up the chance to make a one-on-one difference. One-on-one, she reflected, that always seems to be my weak area. For a moment, she thought about the few people she associated with, the gang at the billing office, administrators at work, local artists, and she saw the same failure pattern. Were they reinforcing her, reaffirming her attitudes, or simply similar enough to her own reclusive personality to be comfortable with?

Marina was directed by Baatard to sit up and then to slide back onto the examining table. Anticipating what was expected of her next, she let her knees fall to the sides, and then closed her eyes. Marina hated these pelvic exams, although it was a woman - Garza - and not Dr. Baatard whose examining fingers would soon slide into her vagina. Marina felt a little uncomfortable about having Baatard present and obviously viewing it all, despite his being the physician she had sought out, the 'grand fertility expert.' It was probably his maleness that bothered her the most, and she tried hard to dismiss the thought and keep to business. Even though she realized Baatard and Garza were both medical professionals, she still felt embarrassed and vulnerable. She was certain her own body held no particular interest to either of them apart from the many others they saw each day, yet, having her body exposed always made her uncomfortable, even with Charlie. Although she thought the whole pelvic exam experience a bit degrading, she kept her opinions to herself and bore it.

Before the pelvic exam began, Baatard took a moment to listen to Marina's heart and lungs with a stethoscope. Garza took Marina's blood pressure and pulse rate. That finished, Garza performed a brief manual pelvic exam with her right gloved hand, her other hand applying counter-pressure to Marina's abdomen. Then, Garza reached for a speculum and tried to insert it into Marina's vagina.

Marina felt some sharp pullings and a painful pinch. "Ouch," she protested, pulling her knees together and squirming around on the examining table.

"Sorry about that," Garza apologized, looking both concerned and perturbed.

Marina found Garza's apology too quick, too cool to be sincere. She had had specula exams before, and they had never hurt like this had.

Garza carefully looked through the opening the speculum made, and around inside Marina's vaginal canal for a few minutes. Then, in a monotone voice, Garza spoke to Baatard: "Normal vagina. Normal cervix. Normal adnexa."

Marina, eyes closed, again momentarily flashed back sixteen years to the abortion clinic in Haven. The sounds, the odors were all too uncomfortably familiar. She sensed a sour taste in her mouth, and felt faint. Marina struggled to suppress a scream, then opened her eyes and looked over her side and on the floor for a waste bucket with human tissues in it. That horror fortunately was far in her past, and instead, Marina now saw Baatard's face near hers, lamely smiling reassuringly. Baatard must have sensed a problem, for he took Marina's hand in his and held it.

Garza performed a Pap smear on Marina's cervix before finishing with the perfunctory and always disgusting rectal exam. "Rectal Normal," Garza called out, looking directly at Marina but showing no emotion. She rubbed her examining finger from the rectal exam onto some chemically impregnated paper lying near the sink, then waited for the chemicals to react with the trace of stool she had left. After a few seconds, no blue color appeared on the chemically impregnated paper, indicating the absence of blood. "Guaiac negative." Garza patted Marina's buttock, then said, "Okay, all done," as she gave Marina's hand an encouraging squeeze.

Marina made a point of giving Garza her most glacial of stares. There was something about Garza that made her nervous, or maybe anxious, something odd she sensed.

Garza and Baatard were relieved at the normal findings but not totally surprised. "According to the infertility algorithm we have developed, the diagnostic possibilities center on a problem with your ovaries or with your uterus," Baatard commented as he watched Marina's facial expressions in response to the exam.

Marina observed Baatard closely. She knew he probably was wondering if her infertility was really due to something physiological like uterine fibrosis, or, more likely, was her dearth of children simply due to a lack of intercourse. She was pained at having given him the opportunity to question and judge her in that way. Yet, either way, she realized, *in vitro* fertilization probably could help her become pregnant. And either way, Baatard would get reimbursed. She thought Baatard so superficial; she was certain she understood him and his motivations. In many ways he seemed to her like Charlie Kincade, and could probably be approached, managed in the same direct way.

The physical exam completed, Baatard called on the intercom for someone to join them. A few moments later, a thin, wiry man with dark complexion wearing a turquoise smock entered the room. His name tag identified him as "Muhammad, Ultrasound Technician," and he wheeled a large piece of complicated equipment toward the side of the examining table.

"We'll get an Ultrasound image of your ovaries next," Baatard said to Marina. "I need to be sure they are both there, and without any obvious deformities. Sometimes they're missing, or have cysts, although I'm certain you should have known this by now, particularly since you're a nurse."

Marina indicated she wasn't aware of having these problems.

"Polycystic ovaries can lead to infertility, although your absence of corroborating signs and symptoms makes this unlikely too."

Marina was familiar with the term, and nodded that

she understood.

Motioning for Marina to stay laying flat on her back, Baatard watched Muhammad take the ultrasound probe from the receptacle. Garza squeezed some clear gel from a tube onto the black plastic and metal probe tip for Muhammad. The transducer gel made a disgusting sound as it left the tube; the guttural noise made Garza giggle.

"This is going to be painless," Baatard reassured Marina. "Just don't move." He motioned a parting with his hands, and Garza reached over and opened the front of Marina's hospital gown, exposing her lower abdomen.

Muhammad methodically slid the ultrasound transducer probe's cold metal tip back and forth over Marina's glistening, oiled abdomen. Marina's abdominal muscles reflexively rippled and retracted under the probe's movement, and although tense, she consciously tried to stay still.

Thousands of ultrasound bursts emanated each second from the probe tip and penetrated through Marina's abdominal wall and deep into her tissues. Some waves were reflected back to the probe tip, and were detected, amplified and interpreted by the instrument's electronic circuitry. Within minutes of the scan's completion, an image of what Marina presumed to be the contents of her pelvis, highlighting both her ovaries, printed out from the machine.

Baatard, pointing matter-of-factly to the images, said, "Your ovaries look okay, but there may be some residual fibrosis around the fallopian tubes, bilaterally. Perhaps it's residual from the PID you said you had a few years back."

"And what is the significance of that?" she asked, already knowing basically what he would tell her.

"You may not be able to pass ova from your ovaries to your uterus. Since fertilization actually takes place in the tubes, if they're not open and passable, then no pregnancy can take place. In fact, you may even be at a higher risk of an ectopic pregnancy, which, as you know, can be very dangerous."

Marina nodded glumly. "What do you want to do now?"

"We could go forward with the workup, concentrating on your tubes. There are a number of tests we could perform to try and determine the patency, but they are, as you may know, painful, not totally inaccurate, and rather expensive."

With all this bad news, Marina barely noticed Muhammad pack up his equipment and wheel the cart out of the room. Right now, she was too busy absorbing the significance of what Baatard was telling her. The bottom line seemed, to her, that her ovaries were normal, which didn't really surprise her, but that her tubes may be blocked. And if her tubes were blocked, then simply injecting donor sperm into her uterus during the time of her ovulation wouldn't work. She would have to undergo IVF. "I know what tests you're referring to, and frankly, I don't want to go through all that."

Long ago, she had decided that her reproductive

system functioned normally, although that assumption may have been in error. She always suspected the diagnosis of uterine fibrosis given to her by her last gynecologist was inaccurate, and apparently it may have been, or perhaps it was a kind diversion from truth perceived. Perhaps her tubes were blocked -- another slap in her face from her past, that bastard who raped her once again interfering with her life and her ability to become pregnant. But it was harder for her ego to accept what probably was even more the truth - that what she was really looking for some form of artificial insemination rather than simply assistance with an actual physical fertility impairment. Again she wondered if she would spend her whole life avoiding intimate contact with men. Would she continue to let an attack that occurred so long ago ruin her entire life? Running these thoughts through her mind only made her feel more like a failure than ever. "So, what's next?" Marina asked Baatard, shrugging her shoulders.

"If we assume for the moment that your tubes aren't open and can't transport the eggs, your ova, from your ovary to your uterus, then just that may explain your difficulty becoming pregnant. That severely limits your options, and I'm afraid that IVF may probably be the only practical way for you to achieve a pregnancy."

In actuality, she suspected that what Baatard was trying to do was justify the IVF procedures, the technology, the injections, and all the expense. She wondered if she was really deceiving Baatard, if Baatard was mistaken or just fooling himself, or even trying to fool her. She didn't care. Marina was using Baatard, using him just as much as she probably could easily have used Charlie to become pregnant. The details, the means, didn't concern her, just the end. Besides, she thought with a certain regret, both Baatard and Charlie used her, each for their own purpose. Baatard wanted her money, and Charlie, well, it was obvious what Charlie wanted, and what he didn't. And she didn't want to be used or even to feel she was being used. Her distrust of men, born sixteen years ago, remained as strong as ever. She suspected that was really why she avoided sleeping with Charlie, or with anyone else.

"Okay, then what's next," she asked glumly.

"If you're ready, and you want to avoid an expensive, risky workup that might not even yield a definitive answer, then I would suggest that you give the go-ahead to start IVF. It can be a long process," he nodded knowingly, "and the sooner we start, the sooner we can know how it may turn out."

Realizing that her choices seemed very limited, Marina nodded her acquiescence, and Baatard wrapped a small plastic tourniquet around Marina's arm and watched as Garza prepared to draw a blood sample. "Hold still," he warned Marina, "We're going to take a little sample of your blood."

There was a momentary pricking sensation, and Marina looked over and watched blood flow out of her arm and into a glass tube with a red rubber stopper. Her head started to swim, a salty taste formed in her mouth, and she quickly looked away. It was at times like this she realized why she chose administrative nursing.

After a few minutes, Baatard said, "We'll be checking the hormone levels in your blood, just in case, although I suspect they will be normal. Assuming that your hormone levels are within expected limits when the results come back from the lab, are you ready to go on?"

"I guess so," Marina smiled nervously. "What do you have in mind?" She watched as Garza cleaned off the venipuncture site and applied a bandage.

"Well," Baatard said, crossing his arms on his chest, "that really depends on what you want."

"I want a child. A normal, healthy son," Marina repeated.

Garza stood up to leave, but looked surprised when Baatard abruptly reached out, placed his hand on her lower hip and held her back.

"Where are you going?" Baatard asked her.

"Well, I, I assumed you would want to be left alone with Marina when you discuss treatment options."

"Please, stay close by," Baatard asked Garza. "The patient is still only in an examining gown." Looking into Marina's deep brown expressive eyes, Baatard continued, "Yes, you want a child. That's why every woman goes to the Conceptions Foundation seminar. But I think you want more than this."

"How so?" Marina smiled warily at Baatard. Were they communicating on the same wavelength, finally?

"You want a physically normal child."

"Of course I do. That isn't unusual, is it?"

"No," Baatard replied, "of course it isn't. Very little any of us do is unique. But you came to me, not to more - shall we say 'conventional' - fertility specialists. What I mean to say is, you want a child who is similar to you - intelligent, gifted in many ways." He scribbled some notes on a pad as he spoke, then played with a pen, at times rubbing the tip between the cracks in his teeth.

"Yes, that's true," Marina said, watching Baatard closely. She found his habits at times more than a little strange, and distracting. As a physician, and as a man, he was less than appealing to her. Certainly, she could have taken her insurance and gone anywhere, seen anyone, yet, there were definite reasons she chose Baatard. "I've read there are ways to enhance the selection process," Marina said, ready to begin more detailed negotiations.

Baatard nodded and smiled. "Of course there are ways to select. A great deal depends on what you want to select for. And remember, selecting for something also means selecting against other things. It's the other side of the coin, a side not everyone acknowledges." He picked up a plastic model of a fetus, about 30 weeks gestation, and slowly rotated it in his hands, much like a God toying with a mortal.

"I know what I want, and I'm willing to be a little choosy." She looked up at the ceiling, took a deep breath, and said, "I want a baby free of defects, without problems."

"Yes, of course you do, Marina. We all do. And as part of our services, all ova are screened for the presence of genetic defects. We check biochemically and with chromosomal analysis for neural tube problems, Myasthenia gravis, sickle cell, and hundreds of other genetic diseases. If any are found, the fetus is aborted, with your permission, of course. We try to leave as little as possible to chance."

"I'm relieved to hear that, Dr. Baatard. I remember your going over this at the seminar you gave. But I was also thinking of something else. I want all those tests done, but there's something else that I want to test for."

"Such as?" Baatard leaned forward in his chair, not having this conversation very often with a client. "If you're referring to sex," Baatard said, "we can also not implant certain ova if the fetus' sex doesn't please you. You did mention that you preferred a male child."

"Yes I do, but it's not exactly sex that interests me the most." Marina thought she saw Baatard suppress a smirk, but ignored him, this time. All men were such pigs. "Although I do strongly prefer having a son to a daughter, it's intelligence I'm primarily interested in," continued Marina. "I read recently about the Intelligence Genetic Complex. Supposedly it's highly correlated with innate intelligence."

"There's some evidence for that," Baatard replied. "There's a lot of research being done on this subject, and there appears a good correlation between the presence of the genetic markers in the intelligence genetic complex, the IGC, and innate intelligence. My own reading on the subject shows a probable relationship between the presence of the IGC and high IQ scores. But I think there's a lot more to do with intelligence than simply genes, you know." Baatard looked directly at Marina and kept his gaze.

"Good. I'm sure that is so," Marina said. "Now on the Nature versus Nurture argument, I'm strongly in the Nature camp. I've read in nursing journals that people are doing research in this area, but can you really screen for intelligence?"

"There are some articles on the subject of prenatal screening for intelligence, but the ideas are highly controversial. I imagine it's difficult to obtain adequate research funding."

"That's probably true," Marina continued. "I specifically came here because of your research interests, and your association with Conceptions Foundation."

Baatard nodded some more, but didn't say anything.

"So, you screen for certain chromosomes, this intelligence genetic complex, for instance." Marina remembered how some genetic diseases were associated with certain chromosome deformities that could be seen under the microscope.

"Yes we can. But, as I just said, selecting for also means selecting against. We don't talk about this side of the coin often."

"Why?" Her question was more rhetoric, curious to see what he might say. The probable answers were all too obvious.

"It makes people uncomfortable, and . . . "

"And what?" Marina replied as she sat up and crossed her legs over the side of the examining table. She had given this much thought and was mentally ready to accept what he was implying.

"And selecting for and selecting against isn't for everyone. That's what I meant. In other words, I'm saying that you may need to have an abortion, possibly several . . . at a very early stage, of course. You've had one before, and I'm certain it had its effect on you. It always does in women like you. Do you have any problems with this now?"

"None," she lied, looking directly into Baatard's eyes. She knew Baatard was both referring to discarding fertilized but unsuitable ova, her ova, and possibly aborting a viable fetus. A preterm abortion, for whatever reason, aborting one embryo growing, living in her own womb, that was entirely a different question, and one she hoped she would never have to face. She had problems with having an abortion under any circumstances -that was clear given the terrible rape and unwanted pregnancy she suffered through as a teen. Discarding ova before they were implanted was clearly different in her mind. There were still significant moral issues, and differences between this and a preterm abortion. Also, the IVF procedure and what selection techniques were allowed was still strange to her. She wanted to ask for as much information as she could, and she needed to be as assertive as possible.

"I want a child, exactly as we agreed," Marina said.

"Oh God, I know this sounds so weird. I must be the only person who has asked you for something like this." She felt embarrassed now, even having brought it up. After all, was intelligence the most important attribute of a child, or was it health, good looks, artistic or athletic abilities, cooperative personality, compassion, or any of a thousand other characteristics valued by parents and by society?

Baatard nodded at her, smiled reassuringly and waved his hand as if to dismiss her worries. "No, actually a lot of intelligent young adults are trying to take the initiative against nature's errors. They know the technology is there and they want, they demand the right to select out the features they would find unacceptable. No, Marina, you definitely aren't alone. You represent the future."

"I'm glad to hear that," Marina said. She felt guilty enough just being here, and also felt strange for conceiving in such a vicarious manner.

"But, to answer your question as best as I can, I think we can in some way screen for intelligence. Yes, I think that it can be done, although the technique is, if you'll pardon the pun, still in its infancy."

Marina let out a groan at the pun and sternly looked at Baatard as she slowly shook her head in disapproval.

"Sorry about that. Comedy isn't my specialty." Baatard shrugged his shoulders and smiled affably.

"Certainly anything you could do to help select for ova that will develop into a healthy and intelligent child will be appreciated." She thought for a moment, before asking, "You spoke at the IVF seminar about hormone manipulation." Baatard nodded. "I was wondering if using hormones to stimulate my ova is all based on the supposition I have some type of implantation problem"

"Not completely, Marina. Hormone stimulation also aids in our obtaining ova from physiologically normal donors as well."

Marina thought she understood the implications of what he was telling her, and smiled slightly to herself.

"So, even if you don't have an actual implantation problem, or uterine fibrosis, or even if you don't have anything at all wrong with you, physiologically, the hormone manipulation might still be useful."

"Good, Dr. Baatard." So, she was right, and the treatments weren't just a sham if there wasn't anything physiologically wrong with her. They could be of practical use in any case.

"This would be our initial treatment option in your specific case anyway. So, if I understand what you're getting at, hormone manipulation will work even if there's absolutely nothing wrong with your ability to ovulate. Now, does that answer your question?"

"Yes, perfectly," Marina smiled, still uncomfortable, but now better aware. She was right - they were communicating on the same wavelength and she was relieved.

"Of course, there are no guarantees."

"Understood." She wasn't looking for guarantees at

this point, just a chance.

"Good. Then, I can definitely recommend a trial of *in vitro* fertilization. We can harvest ova from your ovaries and select those which are free of genetic abnormalities. Then we can fertilize them and select further for males."

"Great. When can we start?" Marina wanted the pain of indecision and the embarrassment of artificial insemination and unwed pregnancy behind her as soon as possible.

"Well, I'm afraid there are still a few details we need to clear up first. Can I ask again, who do you plan to be the sperm donor, the biological father?"

"Can't we worry about that later?" Marina could hear her stutter becoming more pronounced, at least to her hyper-attuned ears, and began to close up.

"I'm afraid not, Marina. We could freeze your ova for long periods, but it's better to fertilize them and implant them fresh. You do have a sperm donor in mind, don't you?"

* * *

Each day for the past twenty years, unknown to Marina, her hypothalamus - a primitive pleasure center at the base of the brain - would release surges of gonadotropin-releasing hormone - GnRH. A tiny ring of microscopic arteries encircled the hypothalamus and bathed it much like a moat surrounded, protected and isolated a castle in ancient times. From the hypothalamus, the GnRH traveled far throughout Marina's body via her vast circulatory system. Although all the cells of Marina's body were exposed to the GnRH, some cells were exposed more than others, and some were definitely able to respond to the stimulating effects of the GnRH more than others. The GnRH was released in rising surges, each pulse ever more powerful and ever more frequent with the passage of months and years as Marina developed from an adolescent into a young woman.

Last week, toward the end of Marina's menstrual period, pulses of GnRH were released every four to five hours. Today, with the beginning of Marina's new menstrual cycle, the surges of GnRH were becoming stronger, flooding into her blood stream every hour, effecting her sexual organs and saturating her sensations.

Chief among the body's areas responsive to GnRH were a set of cells in Marina's pituitary gland. These individual units of life responded in kind to the hormonal stimulation by releasing hormones of their own. Luteinizing hormone - LH - and follicle stimulating hormone - FSH - were liberated from the pituitary into the blood stream. These in turn traveled to and stimulated Marina's ovaries. The ovaries then responded to the hormone stimulation of LH and FSH by releasing increasing amounts of hormones of their own - estrogen and progesterone - essential and primitive female hormones of immense power. The estrogen and progesterone went on to bind to receptors on Marina's hypothalamus, thus completing a feedback loop.

Itself also a pleasure center, the hypothalamus could

bind opiates, or mistake estrogen and progesterone for opiates, for sexual hormones were also nature's addicting pleasure drugs.

***

As the levels of estrogen and progesterone in Marina's blood rose to new heights, they increasingly bound back onto the hypothalamus. This attachment supplied the negative feedback needed to dampen the dangerous heat-generating nuclear reaction that built up monthly deep within Marina's pelvis. Lacking sperm, her procreative fires would once again be cooled.

* * *

Chapter 7

Haven Fertility Associates, PC.
Haven, NJ

As Marina's follow-up appointment time with Baatard drew nearer, her concern lay not so much on becoming pregnant but with receiving her first injection of hormone. Marina had always hated needles, ever since she could remember – Charlie called her a wimpy nurse, and just the thought of enduring multiple injections over several weeks made her skin crawl.

Even with many pressing, confusing questions clouding her thoughts, Marina still managed to arrive at Baatard's office almost thirty minutes before her scheduled appointment, a fortuitous combination of easy traffic and her mother's compulsive character traits. Sharlene greeted Marina, who reluctantly signed in to begin the series of injections that ultimately would lead to her becoming impregnated. In her heart of hearts, Marina knew that she needed to start as soon as possible, before she had a chance to change her mind and back out. It had taken her a long time to decide to try and become pregnant, and she still had to admit she wasn't entirely certain assisted pregnancy, especially using an anonymous sperm donor, was the correct thing to do.

Baatard's office waiting room was empty, and while waiting for her name to be called, Marina leafed through an outdated magazine addressing the needs of expectant mothers. The magazine articles seemed designed around supporting the advertisements, and she found them totally boring and mindless. The photos were of beautiful, smiling, young women blissfully immersed in the happiness of pregnancy and early motherhood. Marina had a difficult time identifying with women like that - 'breeders' as Charlie derogatorily referred to them. She quickly lay the magazine back down, lest she develop new doubts about whether motherhood really was consistent with her self-concept.

Marina had her thoughts preoccupied most of the last few days with visions of a pregnancy, her own pregnancy. Somehow, she just couldn't envision herself carrying a child - rounded out, bloated, swollen, nauseous much of the time. She almost found the idea somewhat amusing at first, but, when she tried to laugh, instead only became more uncomfortable, as she worried how this pregnancy, and later a child, would affect her life. In fact, when she reflected on it, she realized she really had not given a great deal of thought at all to the disruptive effect a child would have on her own lifestyle, and on her precious freedom to come and go. Marina loved her independence, and carefully guarded her quiet times at home, reading and painting, but she had tried to mentally prepare herself for the upcoming changes, certain that the benefits well outweighed the costs.

She had to admit she knew precious little of child care. Would she, for example, nurse her infant? She thought that she would do so, as she believed it would be healthier for the child, but was prepared to use a bottle just as well. Although Marina hadn't changed a diaper since baby sitting as a teenager, it didn't seem like rocket science either. Practical issues, all.

Nor had she dwelled, and intentionally so, on the difficult social situation that being an unwed mother would create. It was then she began to wonder, to fantasize really, what her baby would look like. Would it, would he, more resemble her or the sperm donor? If the baby didn't resemble her at all, what then would she tell him when he was older? What would she, could she, tell him at all about his father, his biological father? Would the biological father, the anonymous sperm donor, ever want to see his son, to know him, or even to know her? These questions puzzled Marina, and more than a little, they frightened her. There were no easy answers.

Within a few minutes of her arrival, Marina was brought back from the reception area, but this time was not taken to an examination room. Instead, she was placed in a special treatment room in back of the office complex. This room was quite different from the examining room she had been in on her last visit. Suction and gas outlets jutted from flush mounts high on the walls, electrical receptacles protruded by a light switch, swivel lights dangled down from the ceiling on long spider-jointed arms, and shiny tile covered the floor. The room had a sterile, dehumanized sense to it, and noise loudly reflected off the walls and floors. Marina noted the sharp chemical smell of what she presumed to be disinfectant. The odor brought back uncomfortable memories of another clinic some sixteen years ago, that clinic also concerning pregnancy. She felt her eyes moisten and her throat tighten up and she thought she might cry. At times like this, she wondered what really was the matter with her, and what was it she really wanted out of her life after all. Was she crazy, or going crazy, attempting something as foolish as IVF?

Baatard entered after the usual delay, but this time without uttering a perfunctory greeting, nearly slamming the door closed behind him. Marina quickly rubbed her sleeve across her face, grabbed control of her own composure, and attempted a smile. She took one look at Baatard's face, flush red and constricted, and asked him, "What happened to you? Did someone die or something?" She wondered if it was an abortion gone bad, and her throat constricted.

"No, thank God. It's just hard to be pleasant after spending a few minutes with slime balls." He roughly put down some papers on a counter top, then repeatedly clicked a pen open and closed.

"I guess you must mean lawyers?" Marina laughed cynically, remembering something Charlie had once told her.

"Well, yes. How did you know?" Baatard asked, a puzzled look on his face.

"It was just a lucky guess," Marina said, shrugging her shoulders and giving a faint smile. "You know, when a doctor gets angry after speaking with someone, and you describe them as slime balls, well, there aren't too many things you could be referring to."

"I guess so," Baatard nervously chuckled. "I didn't realize I was being so transparent. Anyway, I can't talk about the case, of course. Except to say it's frivolous." He adjusted the collar on his shirt, and stretched his neck out, turtle-like.

"Of course." Marina watched as Baatard's hands clenched around his stethoscope, twisting the plastic tubes into contorted angles. Baatard's face also became flushed, which tended to accentuate his chubby cheeks.

"So," Marina sighed. "What do you have in store for me today?" The thought of needles being jabbed into her skin already was making her edgy, and she imagined feeling hundreds of tiny fake pin pricks, and involuntarily shuddered.

"I mean, you can't always have things go as expected," Baatard continued, his mind apparently caught in a rut and not ready yet to concentrate on Marina. "Medicine is a very unpredictable thing, you know. It's an art that's practiced, not a predictable, repeatable science."

From her job as Quality Assurance nurse at Haven General, Marina had seen her share of accusations of malpractice against doctors. Most were unfounded, some ill-defined, and some patently false and vicious.

Occasionally there was a major mistake, not just an unfortunate outcome. The error could be one of omission - not doing something that should have been done, or one of commission - doing something that shouldn't have been done. More often than not errors were simply that - human mistakes, and not malicious or intentional – that they rarely were.

"We try to take precautions, to foresee every eventuality, to handle problems when they occur," Baatard persisted, whether to convince Marina or himself, it was not clear. "It takes years of education and constant learning to become a competent physician. I mean, it's not like we just don't care about our patients. They have no appreciation for what we go through, none at all, none."

"Of course," Marina replied, reassuringly, wondering how much longer he would carry on about his personal problems before returning to hers.

"Anyway, we're here to talk about you and your infertility therapy, aren't we?" Baatard forced a crooked smile, which vanished moments after its premature creation. He buttoned his coat, brushed his fingers nervously through his hair, sat down and crossed his legs, then uncrossed them and re-crossed them the other way. He flashed another tight smile at her, this one lasting only a microsecond.

Marina watched as Baatard looked down and noticed his shoe laces were undone; he did nothing about it.

Baatard reminded her in many ways of Charlie Kincade, an uncomfortable thought in itself. She remembered that Charlie had called again and left another short message in a pleading tone on her answer machine. He sounded like a wounded puppy dog, but she realized that was his intention and she studiously avoided the trap. She was undecided and actually anguished - but only to a small extent -about returning his call. Almost certainly, it would lead to another uncomfortable dinner date, and another clumsy attempt at sex. Unwilling as she was to admit it, her conscience was her best guide here: she was wasting her time on Charlie Kincade. Facts were facts. Her thoughts suddenly were jerked back as Baatard resumed speaking. One problem at a time, she thought, I can handle just one problem at a time.

"As I hope you have read in the brochures you received, . . . " he droned on, his dry manner of speech reminding Marina of a boring college professor she had endured years ago. She shifted around in her chair, then returned to listening to Baatard.

" . . . we are going to try and use hormone injections to stimulate your ovaries to produce egg follicles. Then, we are going to recruit these follicles with what we call a stimulated down-regulation cycle." Baatard started to draw some pictures on a pad using brightly colored marking pens that emitted a strong fruity fragrance. He added for illustration some color overlay diagrams he had made just for this purpose.

"Excuse me," Marina interrupted, feeling somewhat confused. "Can you slow down and explain about down-regulating again?" She knew how important it was for her to understand exactly what Baatard was proposing to do with her body; she had to understand, in order to reduce her anxiety to a manageable level, and protect her own best interests.

"Sorry. Okay, well, to begin with, today we're on approximately day seven of our menstrual period." He looked at her, then at his watch, smiled and made an affirmative humming sound, then continued. "This is the best time to begin, since we would normally be producing an egg at this time anyway."

Marina wondered why some male physicians she knew insisted on used the first person plural "we" when referring to their female patients doing female things. "We" weren't ovulating, "I am," she thought.

"We will try to mature several eggs," he continued. "That should make the odds of retrieving one better."

"That makes sense. The Conceptions Foundation pamphlet went into this, but maybe you better . . . "

"Sure, no problem, no problem at all," Baatard said as he nervously looked at his watch again, then forcefully lay a clipboard down on the desk with a thud. "Sure, no problem at all," he repeated. "Okay, look, Marina. We'll be giving you an injection of synthetic gonadotropin releasing hormone, which we call GnRH, to induce ovulation in our ovaries."

"What adverse events might be expected from being injected with that hormone?" Marina questioned.

The Surrogate

"There's no problem here, Marina. You normally produce this hormone, and so the injection is simply more of what you already have, but sooner, and more. I'm surprised you don't know that, as a nurse."

"I could use the review, that's all," she explained. Marina felt Baatard had a hell of a lot of nerve questioning her knowledge base. After all, she was sure his neuroanatomy and his dermatology, areas outside his specialty, weren't too great. Medicine and nursing were very complex, and it was only normal for people to be very familiar only with their own limited area of area expertise. She was sure it was also that way for lawyers – Charlie had once admitted so – and for accountants and car sales persons too.

"There's no problem with doing it, trust me. How could there be a problem injecting you with a hormone that you already make on your own?" Baatard opened his palms and smiled nervously at Marina, as if the answer were self-evident.

"I guess not," she replied. At that instant she thought Baatard reminded her more of an oriental rug sales person than of an infertility specialist, making her wonder if she had chosen the correct doctor.

"Rigggghhht. It's really perfectly safe; I give this injection all the time," Baatard said. "Trust me, okay?" He waved his hand in front of him, as if sweeping away any objections or doubts. For a moment, he looked down at his shoes, frowned, and then started to tie them. Bending over turned out to be too much trouble and he had to cross his leg first.

"It sounds reasonable, I guess," Marina replied

tentatively, her voice, though, revealing that she wasn't totally convinced. "But, can I expect any side effects? I mean, should I be watching out for anything in particular?" Visions of her lying stroked out and alone in her house for days panicked her.

"Well, yes there are some rare side effects reported," Baatard reassured Marina, "but only a few. They're also outlined in this pamphlet." Baatard handed Marina another small booklet, a flashy, colorful one designed so it could conveniently fit into a purse. The booklet, prepared by the same pharmaceutical company that produced the hormone, covered in more detail the hormonal treatment she was about to undertake. "The kinds of things that are most likely to happen are hot flashes and sweats. Rarely you could get depression and emotional lability."

"Thanks for telling me," she added ironically. "I feel more at ease if I know what to expect. You realize, I'm still a little nervous about this." She bristled at the thought of having to endure hot flashes or sweats, let alone depression and emotional lability. Her mother suffered from those symptoms, and they had made her life miserable. All these injections and her uncertainty over the procedure made her jumpy enough. She thought she remembered once reading about a woman committing suicide after starting hormone treatment.

"Yes, I can see that you're still just a little anxious,"

Baatard observed. "That's perfectly normal, I can assure you. I haven't mentioned a few other side effects, though. You might as well know a little more, since you're the inquiring type, and a health professional," he added a little gratuitously.

Marina now had to wonder if this hormone injection procedure really was as safe as she was being led to believe. She also sensed being talked down to, and that grated on her.

"More rarely, the hormone injections could give you headache, vaginitis, and possibly even some nausea and vomiting."

"Oh, that's not so good. I tend to get really bad headaches as it is." Another legacy of her rape, she reminded herself.

Baatard quickly glanced in Marina's patient chart. "But you didn't mention that before. Are you taking any medications?"

"Yes, but only when the headaches get really severe. I've been seeing Dr. Vernor about them from time to time. By the way, shouldn't you be speaking to Dr. Vernor about the procedure and the possible side-effects, as he is my primary care doctor, so that we can all be prepared?"

Baatard's face changed subtly, and he seemed surprised when the name 'Dr. Vernor' was mentioned. "I will, if you like. But you can also call our office if any of these happen and become a problem. One of the staff nurses, physician's assistants, or myself is available at all times to help you."

"What about Dr. Vernor? Can't I call him if I need a doctor? He's the person I routinely see for medical problems." All except gynecologic, she reminded herself, since she preferred to use a female physician for her routine gynecologic exams.

"Sure you can use Dr. Vernor, I guess, but I prefer you call here first and let us try to handle the problem, since we'll be the ones giving the medication. Okay?"

"Fine. Then what?" Marina asked, not wanting to make a point of this. She would probably call Dr. Vernor first, anyway. She certainly didn't need Baatard's permission.

"Okay, okay. I'm getting to that," Baatard nervously chuckled. He looked at his wrist watch, then at the wall clock, then over toward his door. "The GnRH is administered daily . . . "

"Sorry. The what?" Marina interrupted, confused at the abbreviation.

"The GnRH, the GnRH. You know, the synthetic gonadotropin releasing hormone I was just talking about. It's the hormone that you'll be getting next, I mean first, and it's to be injected beginning in the mid-luteal phase of your next menstrual cycle. These injections are then continued at a lower dose as we stimulate the ovary with additional hormones."

"Oh, more hormones? Like what?" Marina asked as she shifted uneasily around in her chair, crossed her legs, straightened her skirt, and smiled, briefly. All this was making her very uncomfortable, and she envisioned herself getting cancer or a heart attack from all the medications. She wondered if she could become pregnant from the hormones, and then have a serious medical problem from all the treatments while pregnant. What would happen to her child then?

"Look, don't take this wrong, but all this information was covered in detail in the brochures you were already given to read," Baatard reminded Marina. He looking at his wrist watch several more times in succession, as if he couldn't believe the time, then frowned. "It's in the brochure, it's in the brochure, read the brochure."

"Dr. Baatard, I may be a nurse, but embryology and fertility are not my strong points," Marina sternly replied. She objected to the implication she was negligent in not reading the brochures, or worse still, that she had not absorbed and understood all they had to say. She could see Baatard was either getting angry or impatient, but didn't know which and at this point really didn't care. "You may think that I ask too many questions, but I'm sure your other patients must ask just as many, if not more. I just need a little reinforcement here, that's all," she firmly told him, wondering if he treated all his patients this condescendingly?

"Okay, sure. Here," Baatard said, repeatedly jabbing at an illustration in an open pamphlet he held in front of her. "I guess I can spare a little time; I can go over it again for you, if I have to," Baatard said, emphasizing the word 'again.' "And I don't think you're stupid, trust me."

"Thanks a lot," Marina said, only half-heartedly. She never believed carpet sales persons, especially ones that told her to 'trust them.'

"Okay, next we'll use another hormone. This one is called human menotropic gonadotropin, we abbreviate it hMG, and we give it daily to stimulate our follicle development. Like all the other hormones, hMG can have side effects, and they're similar to those seen for GnRH. If we experience any abdominal pain, or a rash, we would want to come in right away."

"Why, would we be in danger?" Marina asked, trying to goad him into referring to her, not 'we.'

"Well, I wouldn't say WE. I meant you could be in some danger. Abdominal pain could indicate you're developing a rare but very serious syndrome."

"A serious side effect? But I thought . . . "

"I said RARE, Marina. It's called OHSS, and we would need to check for it. That's all."

"Oh, I see. What exactly does OHSS stand for?"

"Ovarian hyper-stimulation syndrome."

More rug sales person talk, she thought. He's trying to confuse and impress the customer. "Have you ever had this OHSS happen to one of your patients?" The thought of backing out occurred to her again.

"No, can't say that I have. But, I certainly know what to look for and I know how to treat OHSS if it occurs."

"I see," Marina said, only partially reassured.

"We'll be monitoring serum estradiol levels and vaginal ultrasound weekly."

'More needles.' she thought.

"Assuming you, meaning your menstrual cycle, progress normally, that is to say, as expected, egg follicles will develop. When at least three good sized follicles, ones with a diameter of, oh, sixteen millimeters, are noted on vaginal ultrasound, then we'll get our next hormone treatment."

"What? Another hormone? Is this different from the other two?"

"Well, yes. It's a different one altogether. I mean, it wouldn't make any sense, would it, to repeat giving you something I was already giving you?"

Marina shook her head "no," and fought against feeling intimidated.

"This hormone is called hCG, and it will trigger oocyte maturation. The hCG also was clearly and extensively covered in the booklet and the film, you know."

Marina shook her head, "I don't understand. I thought I just got injected with that one hormone, hM . . . whatever."

"No, the last one was hMG. Please pay attention to what I say. This is hCG, it's totally different. It's a totally different hormone, and it acts completely differently on your body."

"I'm sorry. It just sounds confusing," Marina smiled nervously and shook her head slowly. She could see Baatard was getting more frustrated by the minute, but decided he was amusing this way, and tried to push him a little more. Occasionally she played with Charlie Kincade this way, too. She had no other pets.

"Maybe, but just leave it to me," Baatard smiled

thinly. "Okay, okay, oocyte is a mature infertile egg, and hCG, well that stands for human chorionic gonadotropin. Look, Marina, I know this all sounds complicated, but all these damn hormones have these really long names, and that's exactly why we abbreviate them. But don't worry, just trust me and let me keep track of the abbreviations." He reassured Marina, waving his hands in front of him. Baatard smiled broadly, then said, "I do this all the time. Anyway, it . . . "

"Do what all the time?" Marina interrupted him, knowing innately that it would only fluster Baatard even more. After all, she thought, if he could intimidate her, she would at least extract some passive-aggressive revenge.

"Give all these injections, of course," Baatard tried to explain. "As I said, it makes your egg mature inside the follicle on your ovary's surface. So," Baatard said, abruptly standing up, "are you ready to begin with your treatments?" Without waiting for an affirmative response, Baatard quickly pressed the intercom button and asked for Garza to come in.

"Sure. I guess," Marina said, almost to herself. Sensing what Baatard wanted as he reached for a needle infusion unit and a tourniquet, Marina rolled up her blouse sleeve.

Garza drew the hormone injection from a tiny glass vial she had brought in with her into a syringe. As this was going on, Baatard cynically asked Marina, "Any word on the other issues that are still unresolved?"

"No, not yet, I'm afraid." She had not been able to force herself to give this much thought at all, actually. After all, she couldn't just ask someone for 'it,' like Charlie Kincade, or stopping some stranger randomly in the street. Hey, mister, she imagined herself asking, got any sperm?

"Oh. It's just that I remain moderately concerned we'll soon have harvested perfectly good oocytes, but we'll have no sperm donor. I'd hate to be put in that position if I were you."

"Yeah, I can see why," Marina admitted. She felt trapped and unprepared and foolish for being in several complicated and uncomfortable situations at the same time. She also felt angry at Baatard and angry with herself for having allowed all these stresses to be piled upon her shoulders.

"So, just for your information," he smiled, "I do have several backup plans."

Marina was relieved and listened intently. "A backup plan?"

"Yes," he smiled again, like a prepared Boy Scout. "For example, we could always freeze your oocytes and use them later. Although there are some problems with doing things this way, I must admit," he cautioned.

"I can guess what the other alternative is, and I have no problem with that, as long as you use a disease-free, intelligent, emotionally strong donor," she reminded him. Baatard nodded agreement, then she added, "And I want my child to be a boy. It has to be a boy."

"You indicated before to me that you prefer a male, and many women do, although most prefer to have daughters, but is there any particular reason why the child has to be a boy? I mean, that's totally up to you, of course, and it can be arranged. I just wondered, that's all."

Marina had known for a long time that she didn't want the responsibility of having a daughter. She dreaded the possibility of seeing someone who would grow up and repeat the same stupid mistakes she had made. She would feel accountable, and she already had enough guilt to deal with. No, she definitely didn't want a girl, and so Marina insistently and simply told Baatard, "The reasons are personal. Why? I thought it wasn't a problem for your clinic."

"Problem? No indeed. I'm asked to do this occasionally; it's not a problem, not for me." He looked at his watch again, then at the door.

Marina blushed and looked away. "That's good. Look, Dr. Baatard, I really don't care where you get . . . it . . . , you know what I mean. I mean, I, I just don't care to know . . . who. And I don't need to know, as long as it's healthy and disease-free and compatible. Do I?"

Marina could feel her jaw tighten up and almost freeze as she nervously tried to envision "The unknown sperm donor." How unromantic. She imagined a mysterious male figure lurking around in the shadows somewhere, ready to anonymously fertilize her without touching her. The very thought made her skin crawl. She wondered if she were becoming afraid of men, if she really disliked men, or simply hadn't met the right one yet, or ever would. Marina had asked herself these very questions many times before, but it was obvious to her that before she could answer them, she had to find the bastard who raped her. He was still around, she could feel that, and she had to get the low-life bastard before all else in her life would ever be normal again. He had disfigured her body, he had made her pregnant and made her suffer through an abortion; he gave her nightmares every time she tried to be intimate with men. She could feel herself cycling up in anger, breathless, her heart racing, losing control. Once again, she fought back to regain her emotions, calm herself.

"No, of course you don't need to know the identity of the sperm donor," Baatard reassured Marina, pulling her from her fears back to reality, although reality didn't seem any more appealing to her, either. "In fact, you won't know. Anonymous donors are, well, anonymous. Speaking of which, you're just in luck," Baatard said. "I thought this eventuality might happen. Actually, this isn't the first time this particular 'situation' has transpired, so there's no need to be self-conscious about it."

"I'm not self-conscious about anything, Dr. Baatard." Marina objected, reacting to his patronizing attitude. "I know what I'm doing and how I want to do it, thank you. It's my body and it's my life, after all."

"Of course it is. Good. We, that is to say The Conceptions Foundation, belong to a sperm bank association. Currently we have several suitable sperm donors that should fit your particular criteria quite nicely," he told her, displaying a list for her to see. There were no names, only alphanumeric codes, and no useful information could be gleamed by reading it, but only a vague reassurance that the list at least existed.

"Dr. Baatard, despite what you may think of me, I'm not self-conscious about using a sperm donor," Marina insisted unconvincingly, looking away and blushing. "Of course, I don't need to use a donor, I can easily get my own, you know, thank you. I'm a young, attractive, woman, aren't I? But I'm sure you can understand why it's difficult for me to discuss this."

"Yes, I do, and I make no judgments here at all" Baatard smiled reassuringly. "And of course, after fertilization of your ova with donor sperm, we'll screen the ova for genetic defects, select the desired sex, and even look into this issue of intelligence you're interested in so much. Of course, this type of screening and selection is just in its infancy, no pun intended." Baatard smiled childishly.

Marina groaned as she recalled Baatard used the same stupid pun on her before. She had not thought it was clever back then either, and considered reminding him of this as she stared at him askance. Charlie, too, had the same awkward problem of forgetfully repeating inane puns.

"We can't promise a particular intelligence level, just

as we can't guarantee really anything. We just try, but we aren't God."

As Baatard spoke, Garza, who had patiently stood by listening to the discussion, now applied a rubber restriction band to Marina's upper arm and cleaned off the skin with an alcohol wipe. Marina's veins popped full immediately, and Garza painlessly slipped a needle into Marina's skin. Marina flinched as the thin metal shaft of the needle slid into an arm vein without a problem. As soon as blood flowed into the plastic line, Garza attached a large plastic syringe full of a clear liquid. She first secured the intravenous line in place with white cloth adhesive tape, then injected 2 milliliters of Marina's first hormone injection. In seconds, the IVF treatment had begun.

* * *

The genetically engineered recombinant GnRH hormone surged out of the syringe tip, into Marina's bloodstream, and raced around Marina's body, frantically searching for the right biochemical receptors located on the surface of ovarian tissue cells. Once the receptors were found and bound the GnRH, genes on Marina's chromosomes were activated. This would first lead to protein synthesis, then the proper stimulation of the life-generating processes would begin, much as they had, quite unassisted, for millions of years.

Coincidentally, only hours earlier, a similar surge of Marina's own GnRH had already flooded her senses. The hormonal pulses were occurring every ninety minutes during this phase of Marina's monthly cycle, repeatedly pounding Marina's subconscious. The surge in GnRH hormone jarred each of Marina's ova like the endless pounding of waves against a breakwall, the unfertilized ova protectively embedded into the surface of her ovaries.

Nature had exquisitely designed the body so that only one ovum at a time typically would respond. Now the pace was accelerating too quickly for nature's intended plans; the artificial GnRH repeatedly surged forth against Marina's hypothalamic gland, the process mercilessly shocking her senses into an electric state of hyper-awareness. An unnatural deluge of blood-borne estrogen boosted the effect of GnRH. Together, the hormonal surges synergistically triggered several of Marina's thirty to forty thousand ova from their quiescent state into one of rapid development, beginning their own life cycle.

    * * *

After a few minutes, having decided that no adverse effects were experienced as a result of the injections, Marina left Baatard's office for the day. As a relieved Marina passed the reception desk, Sharlene put the phone on hold, and reminded her that a copy of her medical records had not yet arrived from Dr. Vernor's office. Marina promised to look into this, then left.

Chapter 8

Operating Suite
Haven General Hospital
Haven, New Jersey

Three weeks later

Lissa Vernor, the young wife of a local doctor, lay on the operating room table, her bloody abdomen sliced wide open like a freshly caught tuna. She had only a barely detectable systolic blood pressure and evidence of bleeding into her abdomen when she was hurriedly admitted in critical condition through the Emergency Room minutes before. Now, operating room personnel frantically circled Lissa's unconscious body, desperately trying to stem the deadly flow of vital fluid, each sensing a disaster was imminent.

Wide flat metal clamps pinned back the sides of a gaping midline incision line in Lissa's abdomen. The surgeons had used that wide an opening to effectively give them the increased exposure required to search, probe, and explore her bleeding belly. Inside, blood seemed to ooze continuously from everywhere and paradoxically from nowhere identifiable. A torrent of frothy red blood fought a running battle with an army of suction catheters, whose sickening choking and gurgling sounds filled the background.

"I need more goddamn suction in here," Dr. Baatard, the chief surgeon on the case, frantically called out. Although he was primarily an obstetrician/ gynecologist specializing in infertility, he was also well trained in general surgery, occasionally practiced gynecologic surgery, and of primary importance, knew the patient. Baatard desperately struggled to figure out where all the usual anatomic landmarks – liver, spleen, colon -- were, now hidden under the pool of blood swirling up in his patient's abdomen. Staying in control was of utmost importance to surgeons, and the high level of frustration Baatard felt at not being in control was evident in his cracking voice.

Instinct and years of experience told Baatard there was a "bleeder" somewhere, and it must have been at least a moderate sized one, perhaps a small artery. But where the hell was it, he thought. And why would THIS patient be bleeding? He considered on more than one occasion requesting an emergency vascular or gastrointestinal surgery consult, but each time he backed off. Baatard felt certain that he could resolve the problem himself if only he tried a little harder, explored a little longer.

The instrument nurse on the case, Deanna Baptiste, had the front of her green paper operating gown splashed with hundreds of tiny droplets of fresh liquid blood. Baatard's was the same. The individual blood droplets beaded up but took a long time to dry, and gave the paper material a glittery, sequined appearance under the fluorescent lights.

Deanna continually thrust the suction catheter tip deeper into the open operating area in the patient's lower abdomen, trying to remove as much of the blood as possible. She frequently had to move the tip around a bit to clear away any debris blocking its opening before pulling it back. Deanna needed to repeat the procedure every few minutes to keep the surgical field clear enough of blood for Baatard to effectively work in.

Blood surged into the vortex at the tip of the suction catheter, flowed through the clear plastic line, and was pulled with a low gurgling sound into the vacuum reservoir mounted on the wall. With this extent of bleeding, the vacuum reservoir trap reached its 500-milliliter capacity every fifteen minutes, half with blood, and half with frothy red foam and saline rinse solution. This continually filling reservoir contributed to the frenzied, hectic pace of the emergency surgery, and also added to the confusion, being one more thing to keep track of.

"The reservoir is almost full again," Deanna called out, trying to warn Baatard. "There won't be any more suction for a few minutes until we can change it." Deanna turned to the circulating nurse, Josh, about to ask him to change the bottle.

"No can do, buckaroo," Josh laughed nervously and quickly shook his head. "Look, I'm gowned and gloved," Josh smiled as he held up his hands and rotated them back and forth at the wrist, as both proof and defense. "Hey, you better ask the gas man to do it," Josh suggested as he looked over his shoulder and smiled harmlessly at Dwight, the anesthesia nurse, whose hands were not considered sterile.

Baatard noticed Rudy Salvatore, the surgical resident on the case, uncharacteristically kept his head down and did not say a word. He was usually up front in any surgical procedure he assisted on, eager for the experience, but now a surgical mask covered Rudy's mouth like a bandit, hiding his facial expression from view.

"No way, Bubba," Dwight protested to Josh. "I'm too busy. Who's going to watch the patient's blood pressure if I start messing around with this other stuff?"

"One of you better move, now, goddamn it, before the goddamn blood overflows into the suction line and contaminates the whole goddamn hospital," Baatard barked. He was well aware that, ever since the advent of the AIDS crisis, no operating room personnel volunteered to change bottles of unidentified body fluids. It only contributed risk to an already risky profession.

Dwight and Josh looked at Baatard, unsure how to best respond. His temper was well known, and no one wanted to risk having a scalpel thrown at them.

"Look, I can't find out where the goddamn blood keeps coming from," Baatard exclaimed, in helpless frustration, seemingly to himself. "I just know I didn't nick anything going in. SHIT." He noticed with relief that Dwight, in an apparent effort to appease him and avoid confrontation, had quickly changed the suction reservoir. Baatard felt he could always count on Dwight.

Why the hell had Lissa Vernor started to bleed like this, Baatard again wondered. She didn't have any bleeding disorders, at least as far as he could remember. He did check, he thought. Baatard ran through all the likely sources of bleeding he could think of. "Dwight," Baatard yelled out, "read me the admitting symptoms again. There must be something that can help."

"Sure," Dwight said, picking up the admitting room log. "Okay, the admitting doctor, Keith Tamborer, says she is a thirty-two-year-old female, complains of acute onset pelvic pain, nausea and vomiting. She collapsed at home and was brought to the ER by her husband, Dr. Ryder Vernor, the GP. Anyway, admitting vitals were: BP 40/0, heart rate 160 and faint, temperature 89.6. Physical exam says the ER nurse was unable to arouse her, and the lower abdomen was slightly distended and purplish. Dr. Tamborer put a needle into the patient's distended lower abdominal area and got back blood. There was a hint of bleeding from the vagina, and that must be when they called you for a gynecologic surgery consult."

Baatard nodded that it was. He looked down at Lissa. Even with her skin as pale as a Ping-Pong ball, and an endotracheal tube protruding from her mouth, she still looked good.

"Admitting labs were significant for, hum, let's see, . . . , look, the hematocrit is fifty-five. Man, she must have been real dehydrated." Dwight shook his head and rolled his eyes.

"That's no real help at all," Baatard said, disappointedly. His frustration level was rising in concert with the mounting pressure this complication was causing on his time. Lissa Vernor's unexpected surgery was forcing him to bump so many other things he had already scheduled that it made his head swim.

"Keep the suction on, goddamn it," Baatard cried out. He well knew from experience the prognosis for a successful closure in a case like this didn't look good. He delved deeper into Lissa's pelvic area, frantically pushing organs aside with his open, gloved hand, trying to locate the ovaries. Perhaps Lissa has an ovarian torsion, he thought. Twisted ovaries could bleed like this. But why would her ovaries twist? Could Lissa possibly have had pelvic inflammatory disease?

"Was she your patient?" Josh asked Baatard.

"What?" Baatard asked, trying to ignore Josh, who was always too perceptive for his own good.

"Dr. Baatard, was Lissa Vernor your patient?" he repeated.

"Why? What made you ask that?" Baatard mumbled, avoiding looking in Josh's direction.

"Well, you kind of looked like you knew her, that's all. I didn't mean to pry, you know," Josh replied, backing off a bit.

Two more long hours passed, with over thirty empty bottles of blood and plasma now stacked up in a corner pyramid like offerings at the Temple to the God of Hopeless cases. Mentally exhausted, Baatard finally threw his hands up in the air, his gloves caked with layers of dried and drying blood. "Look, people," Baatard addressed the O.R. personnel, "I just can't seem to be getting anywhere here, okay? I don't see any bleeding source, okay? Maybe she really isn't bleeding all that badly."

Deanna stared coldly at Baatard, and from underneath her surgical mask, muttered, "I don't think this is a very good idea. You remember what happened last . . ."

"Hey, that's really none of your goddamn business," Baatard quickly cut Deanna off. "What are you, anyway, a goddamn surgeon?" he yelled back at Deanna across the table, making everyone uneasy. Trying to avoid an obvious conflict, and realizing from the look on Deanna's face he had greatly offended her, Baatard toned down his voice. "Look," he said, "we'll tank Vernor up really well with saline and monitor her closely." He tried to look positive, laughed nervously and joked, "All bleeding stops, okay? Anyway, she doesn't have any clotting problems. She should achieve hemostasis on her own, really soon, just you watch." Baatard liked the way the word 'hemostasis' - which referred to the control of bleeding - sounded , professional, important, authoritative, and decided to try to use the word more often. Baatard looked again at the O.R. clock, knew he already was late for his fourth case - a routine tubal ligation - and hurried out after a quick closure.

"Hey," Baatard smiled over to Deanna as he walked past, and asked, "Are you okay?" as if nothing had happened at all.

"What the hell do you think, you bastard? I'm surprised you even asked. Don't you ever talk to me that way again in front of other people, understand?" Deanna turned back to her work, vowing never to have another conversation with Baatard again. Then she suddenly turned back and drove the point in more deeply as she poked and jabbed her index finger into his chest. "Don't you ever talk to me like that again, EVER."

"Hey, easy now. No offense intended," Baatard explained, falling back as he feigned shielding himself from the sword-like digit.

"You have no right to embarrass me like that. Who the hell do you think you are, mister?" Deanna demanded as she angrily stomped off toward the postoperative recovery area.

Chapter 9

Procedure Room
Office of Dr. Baatard

Over the next few weeks, Marina faithfully continued going to Baatard's office for her almost daily hormone injections -- the very act of doing so imparting a sense of involvement and action. With each hormone injection she received, Marina felt her hopes of finally having a child increasing. She often fantasized what her child would be like, and how much joy it would be to have him around her house and in her life. Just as studiously, she avoided considering the down sides, and there were several: lack of a stable partner, an unknown father, not to mention the end of her SINK life, her single, childless woman ways. She had finally taken the plunge, and truly expected to get drenched, and felt aglow at the very thought. If everything went as planned, she would suddenly be transformed into a mother, and soon. When she thought of all that she needed to do: buy clothes, baby furniture, a name, and all those thoughts almost made her dizzy.

Early the next morning, Denny Cruite opened the door to the Quality Assurance office at Haven General, and went inside. "Marina, how are you?" she said, flashing a charming smile and extending her hand.

"Denny, I didn't expect you," Marina said, a little

flustered as she looked up from a case record she was reviewing.

"Well, I was in the area and just thought I'd drop by and see how you're doing. Oh, let me introduce someone to you," Denny said as she turned toward a rather well-dressed Latino woman who had slowly followed her in, from a distance. "Lydia Ramirez, this is Marina Bonnaserra."

Marina nodded, and extended her hand toward Lydia, who seemed rather uncomfortable and out of place. Lydia's hand felt cold and hard to Marina.

"Lydia is a judge, and was here for a," she started to say something, but precipitously dropped the direction of her sentence when Lydia flashed her a particularly cold look. "I was helping her locate the medical ward. She's visiting a friend," Denny finished.

"Pleased to meet you, Lydia," Marina said. "Is there anyone I can help you locate?" The visit by a judge was rare, although attorneys occasionally came by looking for information. She routinely referred them to the hospital legal office, and shooed them away empty handed. Lydia didn't appear to be here on business, although Denny's mannerisms seemed odd enough to warrant Marina mentioning this to the nursing supervisor, who could pass the info on to the hospital legal office.

"Oh no, no, we're fine. Well, we must be going now," Denny said. Lydia smiled a thin attorney grin, and the two left almost as suddenly as they had arrived. Once outside Marina's office, Denny turned to Lydia and asked, "Well, do you approve?"

Lydia nodded back, "Yes, I am sure she will do just fine. Perfect donor, should have plenty of perfect eggs," she confirmed to Denny in a subdued voice. An image of dollar signs colored both their fattened cheeks.

With Denny and her lawyer friend out of sight, Marina tried to return to her chart review, but after only another minute of work, closed the file cover. Her follow-up appointment with Baatard was scheduled in half an hour, and she had to start over to his offices. Marina had taken particular care to follow Baatard's instructions exactly, not wanting to contribute to any failure of the IVF process. Other than some small black and blue areas in her upper arms from the frequent needle sticks, she had noticed few problems up to now. She quickly learned to keep her needle bruises well hidden by wearing long sleeve blouses, and laughed as she thought her arm looked like it belonged to a junkie, hoping the police never stopped her.

After her first procedure visit, Marina found she didn't actually get to see Baatard every time she received an injection of hormone; rather, they were usually given by Garza. On increasingly rare office visits, Baatard actually saw Marina, as opposed to the office nurses simply giving the injections and inquiring about problems or questions. At those times, he reassured Marina that the hormone injections eventually would further develop her ova. Baatard kept a positive and upbeat demeanor, and repeated the same therapeutic plan he had provided to Marina before she began her hormone stimulation treatments. As soon as Marina developed at least three good-sized ovarian follicles, she would start receiving a series of hCG injections. Before that point, any action to bring about ovulation was premature and bound to fail, and a demoralizing, not to mention expensive, failure was to be avoided at all cost.

As mean and unpleasant as Marina had observed Baatard with the personnel who worked under him – she had seen it only once, but sensed its omnipresence -- he was just as oppositely polite to his patients. Marina sensed this facade at some deep level, but was not consciously aware of this, or at least suppressed the awareness. Denial was as basic a defense mechanism as flight in the face of danger.

It was a beautiful autumn day outside, with a light wind rustling multicolored leaves in thinning trees, and Marina enjoyed walking the short few blocks to the Conceptions Foundation offices. Today was an ultrasound day, not an injection day for her, which should have made her less apprehensive, although her concern for a successful outcome actually made it somewhat worse. She had no need to be reminded that today was the third week of the stimulated down-regulation cycle.

Marina signed in at the reception desk, and was immediately whisked back to the procedure room.

Sharlene gave her a paper gown, and directed her to the attached changing room. By now, Marina knew the routine almost as well as if she had worked there. After changing, she re-entered the exam room and took a seat. In a few moments, Garza entered, along with Muhammad the ultrasound technician. Marina lay on the leather-cushioned table, opened a small area on the front of her gown, and Muhammad applied the transducer jelly and began his exam.

After taking an extra few minutes scanning Marina's lower abdomen, Muhammad made some measurements directly on the ultrasound film. Uttering some "uh huh" sounds to himself, he printed a copy of the scan appearing on the monitor. Marina sensed that, unlike previous ultrasound exams of her pelvis, this time Muhammad saw something different. When Marina asked Muhammad about this, he explained that for the first time he could clearly see her ovarian follicles. He then hurried out of the exam room. Marina could hear Muhammad excitedly reporting these findings to Baatard in the hallway outside the room. There was some technical conversation between them, followed quickly by several orders from Baatard. A few minutes later, Baatard entered.

"I think this is it, Marina," Baatard proudly announced as he sat on a stool by the side of the ultrasound procedure scanning table. He held the ultrasound printout steady in front of him as if it were some manifest document of truth and kept proudly looking at it as he asked, "Are you ready?"

"I don't know. Ready for what?" Marina asked apprehensively. She knew what Baatard was getting at --

inducing ovulation -- but at this point, she wasn't sure she was ready, especially without being given any time to mentally prepare. Marina was also bothered by what she sensed as a certain air of indifference, detachment on Baatard's part. Oh well, she thought, I guess in the final analysis I'm just one more patient. Nothing more.

"We've seen some good ova in your peritoneal cavity, and they're ready for harvesting right now. We just need to give the final hormone injection, then go in there and get the ova." Baatard gestured over to the waiting surgical equipment.

"I guess it's too late to back out now," Marina reflected, as she glanced nervously at the assemblage of devices arrayed like weapons menacingly around her. Soon, she sighed, she would be pregnant, and later, a mother at last. But a single mother, alone, without a support system. And then what, she wondered?

Garza smiled at Marina, then busied herself taking Marina's blood pressure and pulse. Garza left the blood pressure cuff lightly inflated, keeping pressure on Marina's veins, and cleaned the skin over a large vein with an alcohol wipe.

"Yes, it really is too late to turn back, especially after all the effort we've put out to get to this point." Baatard nodded to Garza, who injected a preloaded syringe labeled 'hCG' into a vein in Marina's arm. "Well, good then," Baatard told her. "Of course, what I mean is, are you ready today? Right now? And, do you have someone available to drive you home after the procedure?"

"Yes, I'm ready now, I guess. You caught me a little off guard, you know." She thought again about calling Charlie Kincade. As ridiculous as it now seemed, he was really the person closest to her, and the only one with whom she had a long-term relationship. Yet, under the circumstances, she felt embarrassed about calling him. It was all too awkward -- becoming pregnant without his involvement. It would put her at the disadvantage for certain. Ah, if only things had worked out differently between them, and Charlie had been family-, marriage- and children-oriented. But he wasn't, she would have none of trying to force him into her mold, and she would have to make do herself. "I don't think I have someone who can drive me home," she finally explained, feeling terribly disappointed. It was an admission of devastating significance, for now she realized just how alone her life really was. Soon, with a child, that would end. "I wasn't told to make those kinds of arrangements. Why will that be necessary?"

"The anesthetic we'll be giving you makes you very drowsy, and I'm afraid it won't be safe for you to drive yourself," Baatard explained.

"Well, I guess maybe I'm not ready, then." She was in a way relieved at having so easily postponed the procedure.

"But we already injected you, Baatard exclaimed, flustered. "Okay, okay, don't worry. We can put you up overnight in the outpatient surgery section of Haven General."

"But, Dr. Baatard, I didn't bring anything with me for an overnight stay." Seeing that events were developing an impetus of their own, she felt pressured, panicky, and reached out for one more bargaining ploy. "Just give me a few minutes to pack an overnight bag, and I'll be right back," Marina said, then headed for a quick trip home.

Chapter 10

Upon her return from her short trip home, Marina checked into Haven General's admissions office. She expected the paperwork to take some time, and was prepared for a long wait. Marina was pleasantly surprised when she was simply handed a packet of forms and directed up to the outpatient surgery area. Evidently, Baatard's office had already called in the admitting information on her -- besides, as a hospital employee, her billing and personal information was already in the hospital computer.

Baatard was waiting for Marina at the outpatient surgery nurse's station. "For starters," Baatard explained, "you'll need to get undressed and put on a hospital gown. You know the routine, I'm sure. Then, we'll start an IV line in your arm. Once we're ready, the nurse will anesthetize you."

Marina winced at the thought of another "needle" and gave a concerned look to Baatard as he described the procedure. It all sounded easy when she explained about injections and even did venipuncture on others, but was squeamish when she herself was the patient.

"After you're unconscious, we'll then insert an ultrasound-guided probe into your vagina." Marina frowned, and opened her mouth to raise an objection, and Baatard said, "Look, Marina, it's really quite simple and uncomplicated." Watching how nervous Marina appeared, he added, "It's exactly as was outlined in the brochures and the little video you saw at the Conceptions Foundation seminar that you attended. You do remember?"

"I guess so," Marina replied, a little hesitantly. She hated needles; she hated even more the thought of being unconscious, helpless and not in control of her body. It made her think of her only other time in a hospital, some sixteen years ago, and experience she would never allow herself to forget.

"Then we'll poke a hole through your rear uterine wall," Baatard added, almost gratuitously.

Marina winced again, her mind reeled with images of excruciating pain as she was slowly impaled on a stainless steel probe.

Baatard tried to minimize the procedure's risk by putting his finger in his mouth and pulling it against his cheek, producing a popping sound. Smiling lamely, he told her, "That's all there is to it - just a little pop."

Marina glared at Baatard, exclaiming, "Really, Dr. Baatard, this is NOT a joke." Again, Baatard's inane behavior reminded her of Charlie Kincade, and she felt terribly alone and wished Charlie would be here, right now, and even momentarily reconsidered calling him. She wondered if he cared enough for her to actually leave work to be with her, and give her the support she needed, then decided against making the call. She was a big girl, an independent woman, she admonished herself. Besides, what a terribly uncomfortable position for her to place Charlie in.

"I know, Marina. I'm just trying to ease your apprehension," Baatard tried to explain. "Believe me, I take this very seriously."

"You can do a lot to ease my apprehension by not treating me like a child or some bubble-headed baby machine," she scolded him. She wondered again about switching to another fertility specialist, although it was all obviously much too late. Marina hated herself when she was so confused and indecisive, traits she had fought against her entire life, traits she had learned from her mother, and traits she hoped her son would not have.

"Right," Baatard said, then paused and looked closely at Marina. "I hope you don't think those are my opinions of you."

Marina put her hands on her hips and stared sternly at Baatard, telling him, "I certainly hope not," but realized there was no way he could be anything but just one more chauvinist physician.

"Okay, as I was saying, after the puncture of the very back wall of your vagina, we'll advance the probe within your pelvic cavity. Then we'll slowly and carefully move the probe tip toward the mature follicles on your ovaries, guided again by ultrasound," Baatard added with a sigh. He held up a color photo of the female pelvis with follicles on the ovaries to help illustrate the probe's course. "And then we'll harvest the eggs. Now, before we start, I have to ask you to sign this surgical consent form," Baatard said, handing a pen and a printed form to Marina.

"What do you mean, surgery? I thought I was only getting some ova harvested? No one ever said anything about being admitted to the hospital to have surgery done." She knew she was letting her anxiety run away with her senses. Everyone who worked here knew a consent form was necessary, and that, for medical-legal reasons, even outpatient surgical procedures required that a consent form be completed.

"Yes, exactly. You're not having 'real' surgery done, but this is still considered a surgical procedure because it involved anesthesia and cutting, so we have to provide you with what's called 'Informed Consent'.' All we're doing here is explaining to you exactly what we're going to do. That is, what the procedure consists of, what are the benefits, the risks, and alternate procedures. It's a legal formality, that's all," Baatard shrugged.

"Oh," Marina said, a little intimidated and embarrassed at her confusion. As a Quality Assurance nurse, she certainly should have expected to receive a formal informed consent briefing. She realized that she was probably not being misled or taken advantage of, but still felt that way.

Marina and Baatard were both startled when the door to the procedure room opened, and Denny Cruite walked in. She looked around, smiled at Marina and walked over to the examining table.

"Denny, what are you doing here?" Baatard

exclaimed.

"I was in the corridor visiting a friend who's hospitalized when I happened to hear the nurses say that one of our patients was in the procedure room for an ova harvesting procedure." Smiling slightly at Marina, Denny said, "I'm just so happy that you decided to go through with IVF," Denny smiled squeezed another rushed smiled as she took Marina's hand in hers and patted it lightly.

Denny Cruite, as founder and Director, was heavily involved in the daily management of The Foundation. Although with The Foundation from its conception, she rarely got involved in the procedural side of things. She had no training in the health sciences and actually abhorred the sight of blood.

Denny's hand felt cold and clammy, and reminded Marina of the grip of the elderly and infirmed. Gently but firmly, Marina pulled her own hand free. Marina always felt uncomfortable in some vague way when around Denny, ever since first seeing her at the presentation at Haven General, and was even more so now. She didn't dislike Denny, though, and in a way also admired her for her sense of direction and inner confidence. Marina could see that Denny was wearing her standard coordinated red business outfit, and wondered if Denny had just given another presentation.

"Oh, Marina, you are such a pretty woman," Denny smiled. "I'm sure your husband must be very proud of all the extra effort you're putting yourself through to give him a child."

Marina stared back, almost too taken off guard to adequately reply, Denny's insensitive comments making her feel uncomfortable. "Yes, I hope it's all worth it," was all she could say. She could sense a level of insincerity in Denny's voice, but had absolutely no idea what was motivating her. She suspected that Denny's behavior toward her might be different than toward other Foundation clients, but could only wonder why.

After a few seconds, Denny smiled, commented to them both that everything seemed to be going well, and left.

Baatard took a few moments to regain his composure, obviously thrown off by Denny's unexpected visit, then said, "Sorry about that. Now, back to the informed consent for the procedure I just finished describing for you."

Marina nodded acknowledgment that she had heard this.

"There are some risks too. These include the possibility of infection."

"Infection." Marina exclaimed.

"Well, it is, after all, a minor surgical procedure, and you could always get infected, I guess."

"You guess?" Marina interrupted. She didn't want a doctor who guessed.

"In theory, yes. But in fact," Baatard corrected himself, "we take such care these days with aseptic technique it's really very unlikely. The probe does pass through the vagina on its way, and the vagina is NOT a sterile environment." Baatard wrinkled up his nose, then continued. "That's certainly one potential source of contamination."

"Oh."

"There could also be some other problems, with bleeding, for example. After all, this is technically a surgical procedure. But, bleeding too is a rare complication. And there could be problems with the anesthesia, and some other, minor or unlikely problems. So, do you have any questions?"

Not wanting to sound like a complete idiot by asking more questions - after all, she was a nurse. - Marina quickly signed the consent form and handed it back to Baatard. She wanted to avoid being reminded the answers to any questions she might have were simply to be found in some brochure she should have read.

"Good. Now, please excuse me for a few minutes while you get set for the procedure," Baatard said as he left the room.

Garza directed Marina to change into an examination gown, remove her panties, and lay down on the procedure table. Marina did so and hopped up on the hard examining table, and winced at a slight tinge of pain as her hip twisted a little. The cold plastic covering chilled her bare bottom and caused goose bumps to form on her skin.

Marina still had some misgivings and a good deal of apprehension about these procedures, but was as determined as ever to see the IVF through, and always tried to keep the end in sight.

While lying on the table, waiting for Baatard to return, her mind began to drift and she wondered why

Charlie still occasionally called and left messages on her recorder. Maybe he's changed, maybe he really wants to make a commitment. Then reality set in, and she thought it more likely he was lonely and simply wanted someone to sleep with. Despite that, Marina had never completely lost interest in Charlie and briefly debated the best timing to return his calls, if ever. She still cared for him, and even remotely hoped their relationship would still develop someday. Marina wondered again what Charlie would think about her doing this today, and what she would tell him if she ever got pregnant. She knew that eventually she would be finding out the answer to that question.

Garza applied a tourniquet, then inserted a small needle into a vein in Marina's arm. She covered the entry point with a pad of surgical gauze, then secured the plastic needle hub down with a line of white adhesive tape. Baatard, who had just reentered the room, then injected a short-acting anesthetic and another unit of hCG hormone into the clear plastic line leading into Marina's arm. Garza and Baatard had to wait only a few minutes for Marina to fall into a light sleep, then continued with the preparations for the procedure.

Marina's unconscious mind drifted inside the procedure room, then up and through the ceiling and down to another clinic, also in Haven, but this one existed only in the past, in a bad dream some sixteen years ago. She had been there with her mother, and she had already been several weeks pregnant. The clinic had occupied half the first floor of the brick warehouse-looking structure. The other half of the first floor consisted of a flower shop to the left front and a hoagie sandwich shop to the right front. A single plastic vase of flowers in the window of the flower shop looked wilted and carelessly arranged. The floor and counter of the hoagie shop appeared dirty. The smell of salami and onions filled the air, even into the clinic.

Inside the glass entry doors, Marina and her mother, Carmela, had stepped into an old unpainted hallway that smelled of mildew. After walking up a short flight of stairs, they saw a small clinic reception desk to the left. Several small offices were behind the reception desk and also to the left of the entrance hallway.

Marina slowly walked up to the reception area, her mother at her side. Somehow, coming to this clinic reminded her of a visit to the principal's office at school. A large, older woman dressed in a muumuu dotted with food stains was busily talking on a phone, looking through a stack of charts, eating a buttered breakfast roll and drinking coffee. Her name tag said, "Flo," and had a yellow happy face sticker attached below it. Without directly looking at Marina or acknowledging her existence, Flo gruffly asked Marina what she wanted.

"I called yesterday afternoon," Carmela replied, preferring to speak for her daughter. After not hearing a reply, Carmela whispered, "It was about an abortion." Abortion clinics in New Jersey were difficult to locate, and this one had been recommended to her, in strictest confidence, by a good friend. Looking at the shabby, and perhaps not even clean surroundings, Carmela had seemed to wonder if coming to this particular clinic was all that good an idea. After all, her daughter's safety was her primary concern. If, God forbid, something bad should happen to Marina as the result of a botched abortion, would Carmela even be able to live with herself? She felt guilty and more than a little cheap subjecting her precious, innocent daughter to these depressing surroundings. Hadn't she already been put through enough?

Flo flashed Marina the uninterested blank stare of someone who had heard this too often before. "I assumed as much. That's why everyone else is here today," she told Carmela, gesturing over to the others already in the waiting room. Her face held a look halfway between disgust and indifference. "So, you're prepared to pay?" Flo's rough voice made Marina feel uncomfortable.

"I beg your pardon?"

"We need to take care of the financial arrangements first," Flo stated in a disinterested voice. "How are you going to pay for the service? Health plan, check, credit card?" Flo looked closely at Marina, who said nothing, and then gave Carmela a perturbed look. "You did get briefed on the phone before coming here, didn't you? You're here for an abortion, aren't you?"

"Yes," Marina told Flo.

"Right. Well, there's a fee. That was explained to you

on the phone, I'm sure. This isn't a charity clinic, you know."

"Yes, I can see as much. But, don't worry, we have some money. I brought it here, just as you told me on the phone," Carmela said, patting her purse.

Flo took the cash for the fee from Carmela Bonnaserra and counted it carefully, several times. Then, Flo said to Marina, "Have a seat, little one. I'll put your name on the list. First come, first served. You can use the time to complete the patient information form," Flo instructed, shoving toward Marina a clipboard with several faded and photocopied forms on it. "The anticipated wait is three hours. Oh, and by the way, so you don't have to keep asking me questions, . . . "

"Really, I don't want to be a bother," Marina interjected. The coarse and unfriendly atmosphere already was making her feel even more uncomfortable than when she had first driven down.

"Please, don't interrupt, honey," Flo scolded Marina. "Now, as I was going to say, the bathrooms are through the doors to the right, snack machines are to the left. I advise you not to eat anything, just in case the anesthesia makes you nauseous. If you have any questions or you want something else, you can come back here and ask me."

Marina watched Flo drop an insincere smile, but the look on Flo's face was unmistakably, "Do not disturb." Marina was certain there would be little which could motivate her to ask Flo for anything.

"And remember, we don't give change for machines," Flo sternly told them both. She quickly slipped the glass

partition closed without waiting for a response from
Marina or Carmela, and directed her eyes away from them
and back to her work and her food.

Marina had made this journey reluctantly, not
knowing what to expect, and what she was seeing and
hearing was totally new and frightening to her, and much
worse than she had even imagined. She had at one point
thought about asking some of her friends about their
experiences, but wasn't certain who had ever been
pregnant, let alone had an abortion, except perhaps for
Christine Lincoln, the cheerleader. It just wasn't
something you talked about at her school.

Marina couldn't have imagined the clinic would look
so different - so unfriendly, and so dirty - from how her
mother had described it to her yesterday. There were no
windows, no pictures, and no background music. Marina
quietly sat next to her mother in the cramped and poorly
lit waiting room, and worked on completing the crudely
copied forms she had been given. About ten other teenage
girls, each apparently middle class, many also clearly
upset and frightened, also packed the room. None of the
other young women, each her approximate age, white,
well dressed and pregnant, spoke. The girls were for the
most part unaccompanied by parents or male friends.
Several other girls were smoking, making Marina cough
and causing her to worry about kicking in an episode of
her asthma. Marina noticed a torn No Smoking sign on a

wall, covered with graffiti, but instinctively knew better than to ask Flo to enforce it.

A side arm on the waiting room chair rose diagonally and reminded Marina's of her desk at school. Marina looked at all the forms on the clipboard just handed her, which was now her current assignment, and tried to respond as well as she could. Her mother helped her answer questions, but only when asked to. The form did have many inquiries about Marina's past health but seemed to have more to do with insurance forms and financial responsibility and persons to notify in case of . .
.

Marina finally finished answering the last question on the pre-visit questionnaire almost an hour after she started. She found the questions boring, more than a little repetitive, and some of them slightly embarrassing. Several uneventful hours then slowly passed. Each time Flo the receptionist opened the glass divider to call out the name of the next patient, Marina leaned forward expectantly, but only to be continually disappointed.

The gradually changing group of pregnant girls packed together rarely spoke to each other. Occasionally they exchanged fleeting glances and feeble smiles. Marina quietly sat in her seat and spoke to no one. From time to time, she lifted her eyes from the floor to briefly look around the room, having quickly learned that, in this group, more than momentary eye contact was to be avoided. Several of the other girls acted tough and gave the impression they knew the clinic's routine.

The long wait, on top of her pregnancy and the cigarette smoke and the crowdedness, was beginning to make Marina nauseous again, her stomach churned and she developed a headache. She tried simultaneously to forget and remember and not think about what she imagined was soon going to happen to her. Marina thought she might die, and half-hoped she would.

The long periods of silence were broken from time to time by a girl entering the waiting room, or one leaving. Occasionally Marina heard someone cry, sometimes in the waiting room, and once from another, unseen room. Other than that, it was boredom, pure and simple.

After a while, a young Latino woman wearing a light green nurse's uniform opened the door to the waiting area. "Marina Bonnaserra," she called out.

Marina was surprised, and jerked around in her seat to stare blankly at the nurse who stood in the open door. Instead of her usual turning and going back in to the examining area, the nurse, whose name tag said Tina, stared back at Marina for the longest time.

"Oh, no," Marina exclaimed out loud, nearly jumping out of her chair. She had realized it finally was her time, her turn to have her pregnancy terminated. Also evident was that, for some reason, this nurse was staring at her in the oddest way. A few of the other girls looked disapprovingly at Marina but said nothing. "You look at me like you want to say something," Marina said to Tina when she had gotten up close.

"You just looked familiar, that's all," Tina said, and

gave her a strange smile.

"I've never been here before," Marina stuttered out, absolutely certain she had never seen the nurse before in her life.

"Then, I must be mistaken." Tina said as she took Marina's hand and led her and Carmela out of the waiting area to the back. They walked down a short corridor with aging fake wood panel walls and worn floor tile. Coming up to a door labeled "Procedure Room," Tina pushed a metal door open with her foot and gestured for Marina and Carmela to enter.

Tina had taken a seat in an old wooden arm chair situated to one side of an aging examining table. Marina sat on the opposite side in a swivel stool with a horrible squeak, and almost hit her head on the metal ankle stirrups as she sat. The metal table in front of her reminded her of an instrument of torture she had once seen in a horror movie, a mental image that really was not helpful at the moment. Carmela stood back against the wall. Marina thought her mother looked uncomfortable.

"It smells like disinfectant," Marina commented to the nurse, making a face and trying unsuccessfully to create light conversation. Tina grunted a sort of affirmative response. No one else spoke. Rebuffed, Marina looked down into her lap. Her slightly widened midsection held the less than 2-month old fetus no one wanted. It was the child she was going to have killed, killed for her convenience. The horrible implications of that act were almost too strong and vivid for her teenage mind to contemplate or for her to handle emotionally. For a moment Pascal came to mind, then her horrible ordeal, and that evil man's cruel face. Right now, she could barely keep from crying; again she considered running away. Unfortunately, she knew doing that wouldn't solve her immediate problems, and would only make matters worse.

After a few minutes, the clinic doctor entered the room. He seemed to Marina to be about thirty, maybe a little less, and wore faded jeans and a sweater under a soiled white smock, and sneakers. Wire frame aviator's glasses, tinted blue, covered his eyes. A closely cropped beard decorated most of his chin and cheeks and had a slight reddish tint to its brown color. Marina noticed he had no rings on his fingers, bit his nails extensively, almost to the extent of self-mutilation, and wore an impressive gold braid watch. He took the clipboard from Tina without looking at her and quickly glanced through it.

"Hi, 'howareya'. I'm one of the clinic doctors," he blithely restated the obvious, without specifically identifying himself. His voice was thick and sounded as if he had a cup of gravel in his throat. "And you're Marina Bonnaserra?" he nodded at Marina, who timidly glanced back. "And you must be the mother, Mrs. Bonnaserra." He stood up briefly and shook Carmela's hand too.

Moonlighting from his regular practice with a large gynecologic and obstetric group downtown, the doctor had performed perhaps five abortions today already, and had many more to go. The first few each day meant something to him, but after a while, well . . . Having seen so many pregnant teenagers and their mothers, he had actually lost track months ago of their names, a fact which at first had puzzled him. Gradually and without a clear intention to do so, he had eventually stopped routinely asking; he suspected they often didn't want to tell him.

"Look, Marina, let's get down to basics here as I haven't got a lot of time to waste," he said unenthusiastically. He glanced at his watch, then at the chart, then back to his watch again. "Are you here of your own accord?" he asked, glancing over at Carmela Bonnaserra. "What I mean is, . . . "

"Yes," Marina insisted sorrowfully, "I want to be here." She felt her face blush and could have kicked herself. "No, I don't mean that I want to be here, really. What I mean is that I know why I'm here. I need an . . . "

"Please, don't interrupt when the doctor is speaking," Tina quickly corrected Marina.

Clearing his throat, he firmly told Tina, "I think you can let the girl speak for herself. Marina, could you tell me in your own words why you're here?"

"I'm not a girl, DOCTOR." She couldn't remember having been given his name, and examined his coat for a name tag. He had none, and she tried to remember to ask. "I'm sixteen, and I got pregnant because I was raped, not because I'm some silly, sleep-around teenager. Anyway, I guess now I need an abortion."

"Sure, I understand. I see this kind of thing all the time, and I'm not judgmental. Trust me on that one," he winked. After flipping through her chart again, he commented, skeptically, "I don't remember seeing a mention of rape on your medical record."

Marina blushed, was too embarrassed to elaborate, and simply shrugged.

"And how can I help you, Marina?"

"As I said, I guess I want to get an abortion," Marina repeated, looking down in her lap. She could hear the beginnings of her stutter poking its ugly head out, and her throat reflexively tightened up. Again, she fought the almost irresistible urge to get up and run. She didn't want to be here, she didn't want to be pregnant, and she regretted the embarrassment she had caused her mother. Up to this point, she thought she wasn't afraid, but felt that was rapidly changing. "It's my right, isn't it?"

Not commenting on that, the clinic doctor asked, "When was your last period?"

Marina felt flushed and hot and confused, then looked at the clinic doctor as if he were crazy. No one other than her mother had ever asked her that before, not even her family doctor. She was, however, painfully aware of the answer, almost down to the hour. "It was about twelve weeks ago, I guess, doctor . . ." She was still a little uncomfortable that the clinic doctor had never even given her his name. She found the experience depersonalizing enough without even knowing the name of the abortion doctor.

"Well then, I guess that places you at about eight to

ten weeks pregnant, doesn't it?" he said, matter-of-factly. "That's pushing the limits, but I think we can do it. Now, Marina, here are your options. Quite simply, you can have an abortion, you can have the child and give it up for adoption, or you can keep the child. It is, after all, your child," he said, looking over at Tina, who sternly looked back at him.

"Look, doctor. I don't want options. I want an abortion," Marina blurted out. "I'm only sixteen years old; I don't want a baby. Not now. I've got my whole life ahead of me. Maybe later, but not now. Please," she said, gesturing pensively at her enlarging abdomen.

"So, I take it you definitely want to have an abortion," the abortion doctor more stated than asked, the disinterest, distraction evident in his every manner, and he took little care to disguise it.

"Yes, an abortion," Marina insisted, her voice quivering with uncertainty and fear. She sternly looked over at the doctor, who didn't have any reason to raise an objection. Looking at her mother was another matter. What would have been her mother's attitude if her pregnancy had resulted from an ill-prepared sexual escapade rather than a rape? Would things be so detached, civil, or rather more harsh, accusatory and angry, she wondered?

Interrupting Marina before she could finish her thoughts, the abortion doctor proceeded to spend a short five minutes discussing, or rather lecturing, on the subject of therapeutic abortion with Marina and Carmela. "There are basically two ways we do abortions here," he had informed them, with the air and interest of a civil servant performing the same dull and disinteresting task tens of times each day. "We can chemically induce one by giving you this pill," he said, frowning as he held up a large orange and yellow, lozenge-shaped pill.

"I heard about that in school, and I really don't want to do the abortion that way. I'm afraid," Marina said, not looking directly at the doctor.

"Oh, I see. You're very intelligent and well-informed for a sixteen-year-old, Marina." The doctor and Carmela both looked surprised. "Anyway, I couldn't agree with you more. This pill is really messy and loaded with problems. I don't think you would want that," he said, searching their faces for agreement. "Well, alternatively, we can surgically bring about an abortion."

That was what Marina expected the doctor to say, and to do, although she still wasn't sure she could go through with it. Thinking about the results of her not having an abortion were, though, even more confusing to her young mind. Could she, who still thought of herself as both an adult and an adolescent, bear a child, handle the responsibilities, the demands on her time and patience? Maybe she had been too hasty in dismissing the possibility.

"Is that safe?" Marina asked. "I mean, surgery . . . " Her head reeled with visions of operating rooms, surgeons, anesthesia, knives and blood. A chill ran up her spine and she shivered involuntarily.

"Oh, yes. It's quite safe. We perform well over twenty to thirty abortions on an average week here," the doctor understated the facts. "It's not really surgery, anyway, at your stage," he reassured her. "It's only called that. We really just use suction."

Marina flinched, looked into her lap and said nothing. Terrible visions of how suction could bring on an abortion filled her head with terror. She envisioned her abdomen being cut wide open and a large bathroom plunger being forced inside her and a crying baby pulled back out. If she survived, would she be so irreparably damaged as to be unable to ever bear children again? Would she ever want to?

After talking some more and answering a few questions from Marina and Carmela, the doctor handed a consent form to Marina.

Marina took it, signed it quickly without reading it, and handed it over to her mother before the paper soiled her hands. Carmela read the document more closely, also signed the consent form without comment, and returned it to the Doctor.

The Doctor took the form, looked it over carefully, signed it and handed it to Tina. "Here, witness it," he told her. After Tina signed in the signature witness box, The Doctor told her to get Marina ready. "I have at least three others waiting," he said to them, taking a bite out of a burrito he had stuffed in his pocket as he hurried out of the room.

"Mrs. Bonnaserra, you better go with him too, Okay?" Tina said. She motioned with her head out the door, and Carmela exchanged furtive glances as she left.

After Marina had changed into an examining gown, The Doctor and Tina returned. Marina was already seated on the end of the examining table. Tina directed her to lie back and place her heels in the metal stirrups. The Doctor took a seat on the stool by Marina's feet and then matter-of-factly asked her to move her knees apart.

Marina had only done that with a man once before, when she was raped. Although she remembered nothing of that degrading moment, the experience left an indelible mark in her subconscious. She felt embarrassed and in a way debased again, and wasn't sure she would ever let a man 'move her knees apart.' Instead, she stared uncomprehendingly at The Doctor and Tina.

When Marina didn't move fast enough, an impatient The Doctor placed his hands on her knees and tried to pry them apart, and Marina angrily reacted by strongly pushing her knees together. "Hey, what are you doing?" she yelled out. She pulled the examining gown down tightly over her knees, glaring back at The Doctor.

"Hey, easy, Marina. It's only part of the exam," Tina had tried to explain. "Look, you're only taking up precious time here we could use elsewhere. Please, try to remain calm and cooperate, will you?"

"Now Marina," The Doctor explained, "I hope someone already would have taken the time to explain to you what's going to happen next." The Doctor glanced menacingly at Tina, who only looked away without replying.

"No, no one said anything to me about what was going to happen here. This all scares me very much," she said, her voice cracking, on the verge of crying. Her mind was occupied with visions of gigantic vacuum hoses being shoved painfully into her private parts, and these vague ideas terrified her.

"Okay, look, I don't have a lot of time to tell you everything, but I think this should go relatively quick." The Doctor got up, walked over to the sink, washed his hands briefly with the remains of a discolored hand soap bar. He then used some paper towels that were stacked loosely to the side of the sink to dry his hands.

Marina noticed that The Doctor's hands were still wet, and wondered just how clean they really were, and where they had already been today. "I want my mother back in here, please," she pleaded. She wondered if this seemingly careless doctor even had the knowledge and experience to be doing an abortion, and if he had the requisite cleanliness. Marina also wondered if any women had died under his care. She searched his eyes, but saw only indifference and annoyance at the delay.

"I'm afraid that having your mother in here during the procedure would not be a good idea, Marina, trust me. Now, I think that the fastest and easiest way to do this is what we call a suction abortion," The Doctor explained.

Marina felt her heart race and a salty taste develop in her mouth, her head was swimming, and she considered running away, or screaming out for her mother. But she was no longer an innocent teen, and instead, out of fear simply lay there passively and did nothing. She had been the victim once before, and now she felt like the victim all over again. For someone who was so innocent, why was she being made to suffer so?

"Marina, have you ever had a speculum exam?" The Doctor asked.

Marina fearfully shook her head "no," as a cold chill ran through her pelvic area. "Oh, my God," Marina said, realizing what The Doctor was referring to. She felt Tina hold onto her hand and give it a squeeze, and tightly squeezed back for support.

"Okay, well this is something that every woman gets at least once a year for most of her adult life. You might as well learn about it and get used to it right now." The Doctor walked over to a cabinet and held up a speculum wrapped in clear plastic for Marina to see. "This is a disposable speculum. Did you ever see one of these?"

Marina nodded yes. She had learned about the speculum exam in her sexuality course in school, but had never actually seen one, least of all had it inserted in her vagina. "Look, doctor. I don't think I really want to go through with this," she stuttered out.

"Marina, this won't hurt at all. Trust me," The Doctor smiled. "I'll only be inserting this so I can get an adequate look and to make room for the rest of the equipment I'll need to place in there. That's all."

"The rest of the equipment?" Marina nearly shrieked. She nervously glanced around the room to see what other equipment he was referring to. "I want my mother."

"Relax, it's just the suction equipment we already spoke of," The Doctor tried to reassure her. "Please cooperate with me, Marina. We really don't have a lot of time. I've got a whole bunch of other girls waiting to get this same thing done, and none of them are giving me such trouble. Okay?" he nervously smiled. "First, before we get going, we're going to give you a little sedative to help you tolerate the pain and the nausea."

"You're going to put me out?" The thought of losing control, and opening herself to anything happening without her knowledge and consent frightened her. She again wanted her mother in the room, even though she well knew her mother would never be able to stay for the procedure. Blood and needles were not her mother's strong point.

"No, no, no, you will not be unconscious," The Doctor told her. "This is only to cut down any pain you might experience, and make the total procedure a bit more tolerable. Now, to begin with, we're going to insert an IV into a vein in your arm, then we're going to inject a little medicine in your blood. This won't hurt a bit. Now, please, lie still." Tina reached for a rubber tourniquet and wrapped Marina's right arm above the elbow, then inserted a small plastic catheter into the vein which popped up full of blood. The catheter was taped into place on Marina's arm, with the plastic tube residing in the vein, and the other end connected by means of a plastic tube to a bag of fluid. Tina injected two different syringe contents into the line, and soon Marina began to painlessly float in the air, awake but totally separated from her body and anything that was happening to it.

A drugged Marina slowly moved her knees together, and turned her face away from The Doctor. She uttered a low groan of protest, closed her eyes tightly, and balled her hands up into tight little fists. This was not at all what she had envisioned. She wanted out, and she wanted to have her mother in the room with her right now.

Tina tried to hold Marina's hand again but this time Marina withdrew it. She wanted to be separated as much as possible from what was happening to her. She wanted to pretend that she wasn't even here, in this room, lying on this table, allowing this strange man to violate her.

The Doctor took a pack of sterile gloves from a box in the cabinet and put them on. Marina heard the snapping sound of plastic and smelled the talc powder, and another shiver shot through her body.

"Now, once the speculum is in, I'll simply place a suction catheter into your vagina, through your cervix and into your uterus. Then the unit will suck out the products of conception. Do you understand what I'm saying?"

Marina nodded yes, then shook her head no. "What are products of conception?" She suspected what he was referring to, and hoped she was wrong. But she had to ask.

"By that I'm referring to the fetus," The Doctor said indifferently. He sat back on the stool, reached over toward Tina and snapped his fingers impatiently. Tina opened the clear plastic sterility wrapper on a speculum and handed it to The Doctor, and he took the speculum and said, "Now, look Marina. I need to insert this speculum into your vagina. Okay?"

Marina muttered, "Oh, my God," to herself, covered her face and looked away from The Doctor and Tina. Her knees trembled, and she started to sob quietly.

The Doctor tried several times to insert the speculum, but found the entry difficult, and he then tried inserting a well-lubricated finger into Marina's vagina first, gently plying the vulva apart, before trying the speculum again.

Marina let out a loud squeal of protest, causing The Doctor to slow his efforts down, although he seemed not convinced he was hurting her. Despite some anxious pushing and twisting, entry proved too difficult and, frustrated, The Doctor had to withdraw the speculum once again.

Marina cried out in pain as the speculum was withdrawn. She felt degraded and humiliated and hated this doctor and all other men who hurt her so. Her private parts felt raw and bruised, like someone was trying to force a tree stump up her pelvis.

The Doctor asked Tina for some additional lubricant jelly, which she liberally squirted onto his examining glove. The gel made a disgusting, rectal sound as it exited the tube, which under different circumstances might have been considered amusing. The Doctor again lubed up Marina's vulva with the gel, then liberally rubbed some additional jelly onto the outside of the speculum before inserting it, this time successfully.

"Ouch, that hurts," Marina protested, withdrawing

her buttocks. She began to cry but it came out instead a soft whimper.

"Please, don't move," The Doctor told her. Tina put her hands on Marina's shoulders to try and keep her restrained.

Marina cried out in pain several more times as the speculum was forced deeper into her vagina. She imagined her inner body organs being torn along the way and was certain she was being mutilated and was bleeding internally by now. An almost uncontrollable, primal survival urge to get up and run out of the clinic swept over her body. This time, she realized without looking around, doing so was clearly impossible.

All her doubts about the choice she had made now came rushing out into her open consciousness. Marina swore never to allow herself to be put in this position again. She hated Pascal, and if he represented men, then she hated them all. They had done this to her, they had caused this embarrassment and pain, they had taken advantage of her. But, never again.

Once the speculum was firmly and securely in place, The Doctor put a fiber optic light source in Marina's vagina, quickly identified her cervix, and noted the opening - the cervical os. "The os is closed," he commented to Tina. This was to be expected, as Marina had never delivered a child. An additional few minutes of dilation were required before an opening large enough to pass the suction catheter through the os could be created.

Tina picked up another sterile plastic-wrapped package, a long thin one, and opened it. She dropped the contents, a red rubber rod the diameter of a pencil, with a tapered end, into The Doctor's gloved hand.

"Okay, Marina. This won't hurt. Just lie still," The Doctor said, trying superficially to reassure her.

"Hey, wait a minute. What are you going to do with that?" Marina asked, reaching up apprehensively toward The Doctor's hand with hers. She had no intention of letting him hurt her with that 'thing.'

"I'm just going to widen the opening to your cervix, that's all. Please, don't touch anything, and keep your hand at your side. All this equipment is sterile," The Doctor scolded, making no effort to disguise the look of impatience covering his face.

Marina nodded she would try not to touch any of the sterile equipment, and lay her hands back down at her sides.

"This really won't hurt at all," The Doctor tried to reassure as he inserted the dilating probe into Marina's cervical os to enlarge the opening. A few streaks of blood had already formed on the cervix from the trauma. This was not unexpected, and he calmly blotted the blood with a cotton tip applicator. "There, that didn't hurt, did it?" The Doctor didn't wait for Marina's reply before continuing with his procedure.

At The Doctor's nod, Tina flipped the switch on a large mechanical device. The room was instantaneously flooded with a dry odor of rubber, oil and something else - Marina couldn't be sure exactly what. She thought it may have been the smell of cooked meat. The examining table shook from the harmonic vibrations of the motor. Marina flinched nervously, then asked, "What's that sound?"

"Oh, it's just the suction pump, that's all," Tina told her.

"Oh," Marina said, nervous tears forming in her sad eyes. She already had quite vivid visions of a suction pump, and of what it would be suctioning from deep within her. A chill ran up her back.

Tina attached the thin clear plastic catheter to the suction line with a twist and handed it to The Doctor, but as The Doctor grabbed for the tubing, the pump unexpectedly went quiet.

"What the hell happened? Why did you turn it off?"

Tina looked at the switch, certain she hadn't touched it. It was still in the ON position, but the power light was off.

The Doctor noticed the power light off too, and yelled, "Check the goddamn plug, will you?' he asked, although he could already see for himself that the electric cord was plugged into the wall.

Tina moved the ON-OFF switch back and forth, and pulled the plug out and reinserted it, but to no avail. She looked up at an increasingly annoyed The Doctor, and helplessly shrugged her shoulders.

"It must be a blown fuse. I hope we've got spares,"

The Doctor growled as he got up, walked over to the unit, pulled open the fuse box cover of the antiquated machine, and found the fuse. He pulled it out of its holder and held it up to the light, easily seeing the broken filament and the charred glass, indicative of a blown fuse. A replacement was next to the holder, and he slipped it in, closed the cover, and nodded to Tina, who flicked the switch, and the pump came back on. "Electronics is my hobby, at least it used to be," he explained.

The Doctor washed his hands again, then redirected his attention to his patient. Noticing the tears in Marina's eyes he asked, "Does this hurt you? We haven't even done anything yet."

Marina could detect little authentic concern in his voice, and sobbed, "YES," then asked, "I'm going to die, aren't I?" She wondered whether she was referring to her fetus or herself. Her ability to think clearly was flooded by a torrid mixture of guilt, anger, fear and doubt, and clouded by all the drugs she had been given. At that moment, she had felt totally incapable and unprepared to take control of her fate. That she hated the most.

"No, of course you're not going to die," Tina jeered.

"We wouldn't let that happen," The Doctor added, unconvincingly. "I do this all the time and nothing bad like that ever happens, believe me." The Doctor gave a confident smile to Marina, then said, "Now, stay completely still; this won't hurt a bit." He quickly slipped the suction catheter into the opening he had just made in Marina's cervical os. Fresh drops of blood lined the os, the result of small areas of trauma he had created. Once the catheter passed through the os and into the uterus, it began to make several crescendo gurgling sounds.

The flood of different smells, each disgusting, and the horrible sounds mixed with the pain made Marina want to vomit. Marina briefly shifted around the table top, more from anxiety than discomfort or pain. "What's happening now?" She could only guess, and felt her panic level rising.

"We're just suctioning out the fetal tissue, that's all. Now, be a good girl and don't move" The Doctor said.

Marina hated the way the clinic doctor sounded. It was almost the same condescending way Pascal had tried to control her the last night he had tried to "make it," as he put it. At least this wasn't in the back seat of a car, she thought. She couldn't object then, and she couldn't now, and she vowed not to allow herself to be trapped this way again.

There was another loud gurgling and sucking sound, then silence. "There, it's over," The Doctor announced.

Marina was surprised at the suddenness and quickness of The Doctor's announcement. She had expected a lot more, but wasn't going to argue with him. There was almost no pain, and she felt relieved, almost glad, at least at first, until the horrible significance of what had just happened began to sink in.

The Doctor cavalierly tossed something into the waste pail next to the table; his action happened too quickly for Marina to see what it was. There was, however, something odd and disconcerting in The Doctor's face as he saw Marina's glance at his actions that had made her suspicious.

The Doctor superficially exchanged some quick, encouraging words, looked at his watch several times in a row, and then patted Marina on her buttock. "Good girl. Just stay here for an hour until we're sure everything is okay, and then you can leave. Look, I've got to run. I got a ton of your friends left to do today. See you," The Doctor said over his shoulder as he rushed out of the room. Tina again checked Marina's blood pressure and pulse, then followed The Doctor out, leaving Marina alone.

After The Doctor and Tina left, Marina had adjusted her uncomfortable position by rolling over onto her side. She remembered what the doctor just said to her and thought, no, you definitely won't be seeing me again. I'll never let myself be put in this position again, never. She buried her face in the pillow, and cried deeply and for a long time. She had never felt so alone and ashamed in her life.

Another half hour passed with agonizing slowness as Marina lay alone, interrupted only by Tina occasionally coming in, taking Marina's blood pressure and pulse, checking for bleeding, then just as quickly leaving. Marina had dozed off without much effort, but was soon pulled awake when she heard the shriek of a young girl's voice from another room. Although there was only one loud cry, Marina could hear some continued light sobbing, followed by footsteps and the closing of a door. Vague images of abortions gone badly flooded her mind and filled her imagination, and her thoughts wandered back to her own just-completed abortion. She remembered how she had wanted to ask the doctor about her baby. Even thinking the words 'her baby' sounded almost unreal, and so much in the distant past. Yet, it was only less than an hour ago that her baby was still alive, and she was still a mother. She felt choked up and began to sob into her pillow again. She knew the terrible, painful truth was that now she no longer had a baby, and perhaps never would again. After what had happened to her body, would any man even want her? Would she ever be able to have a child again, physically or mentally? She had desperately wanted to ask the doctor about its sex, to know even one fact about the nameless life that was no more, but at the time had been too intimidated and afraid to even speak. They probably couldn't tell this early, she thought.

As her eyes wandered about the room, Marina noticed a yellow plastic pail in the sink. She could see in there the medical instruments The Doctor had just used on her abortion. A small squeeze bottle of dish soap stood next to the pail. The water the instruments were submerged in had a faint red tint.

Shortly, Carmela Bonnaserra was allowed back in with her daughter. She held Marina's hand, asked how the procedure went, then began to cry herself. Marina could see that the stress had been heavy on her mother, too.

It was another thirty minutes before the short-acting

The Surrogate

analgesic began to wear off. Soon, the pain in Marina's pelvis became excruciating, and the nausea almost overpowering. Marina spit some thin, clear foul-tasting liquid into the sleeve of her examining gown. She wanted to faint, and she wanted to vomit, perhaps she wanted to die. She didn't know which one or all of these were true.

Marina remembered the waste basket next to the table, and reached down into it. She saw the small plastic trash bag the clinic doctor had thrown in earlier. It was loosely tied. Marina pried open the bag using her fingers on one hand, then looked inside.

The bag contained a small shimmering lump of soft material lying atop some bloodstained tissues. It looked moist and pink and was about the size of a small goldfish. Marina rolled over onto her side some more, wincing with the pain, then lifted up the basket a bit closer to her face so that she could see better. She was shocked when she clearly saw a tiny eye looking right back at her. Marina shook the basket a bit. She thought she saw a tiny arm on the goldfish or whatever it was. Curious, she moved her head down closer. Then suddenly, she thought it moved. Marina cried out in the realization of what she was viewing, dropped the basket onto the floor with a loud bang, and then fainted.

Several hours later, Marina had awoken on a cot in a room labeled "Recovery." It was only slightly larger than her own bedroom, with one light hanging from the ceiling, a dull fading green paint on the walls, and no privacy separating the five other cots which were jammed in the same room. Carmela Bonnaserra was seated next to the head of Marina's cot, quietly reading a book. On each of the other cots lay a girl who also had just finished with an abortion. Most of the sheets were soiled with red and brown stains - the lingering remains of still other girls who had once been in similar circumstances. The sharp scent of vomit mixed with the sweet, warm smell of blood.

Marina stayed in the 'recovery room' for several more hours, until she felt well enough to dress. Lying in that hellish, depressing ward certainly was motivation enough to leave. Carmela and Tina held onto Marina, supporting her while walking to Carmela's car, but Marina was far weaker than they had anticipated, and they soon found themselves nearly dragging her along. It didn't take long for them to resort to a wheel chair.

Their horrible clinic experience at last behind them, Carmela drove Marina home. Each time the car shook, Marina's head pounded and a knife-like pain cut deep into her pelvic area. Several times, they had to stop the car by the roadside and allow the pain to subside before proceeding. When the uncomfortable return trip was finally over, Marina was actually relieved to find her father not at home. At that difficult time, both she and her mother wanted only to avoid sharp questions and explosive arguments. On the surface, Antonio Bonnaserra's absence didn't seem unusual, given the early evening hour.

The Surrogate

Marina went upstairs, showered with some effort, changed into clean clothes, and collapsed into bed. Exhausted and still experiencing some persistent abdominal discomfort - which the nurse had reassured her was really not atypical and should resolve on its own - she nonetheless seemed to herself to have survived as well as could be expected. She was glad this horrible experience was over, finally, and vowed never to let this happen again. Marina had also decided not to speak to Pascal again. She was incensed at the disrespectful way he had treated her that night - that was, after all, the reason she had been forced to flee into the nightmarish darkness all alone. Pascal had been the cause of her having had to suffer through the violent physical assault, the grotesque physical deformity, an unwanted pregnancy, and a horrible abortion. In her mind, Pascal had hurt her just as deeply as if he had raped her himself.

Chapter 11

Inside the pleasantly outfitted *in vitro* fertilization suite, Baatard noticed that Muhammad had returned and was busy making adjustments on the ultrasound unit. Its operation was essential to the ova harvest procedure. Garza took Marina's blood pressure and pulse, and noted them and Marina's respiratory rate on a log chart.

Baatard, already covered in operating room garb and face mask, slipped on a pair of sterile gloves. Seated atop a stool mounted on four large wheels, he maneuvered his arms to a comfortable position between Marina's legs; Marina's feet were already resting in metal stirrups.

Baatard next took a disposable plastic speculum, one with a fiber optic lighting system built in, and inserted it into Marina's vagina. He noticed that Marina's outer vaginal lips were still slightly moist, but that the moisture appeared to be thin and more damp than wet. Baatard surmised that Marina had quickly showered when she went home for her overnight bag, and was grateful that Marina, at least, never grossed him out with an overpowering, fishy pelvic odor like some of his fat, older patients.

While carefully watching the ultrasound picture on

The Surrogate

the large viewing screen, Baatard gently slipped the specially designed ova harvesting probe deep into Marina's vagina. The unit was about ten feet long, although only less than a foot actually entered the patient, and was about one inch in diameter. It was similar to the flexible proctosigmoidoscope used by gastroenterologists on another, nearby body orifice.

Using the ultrasound imaging equipment to constantly visualize the flexible probe's location, Baatard guided the shaft up the back wall of Marina's vaginal wall. Marina involuntarily shifted on the table and emitted a soft groan as he moved his instrument forward.

"I think that she might need a bit more anesthetic," Baatard told Garza. He took a syringe Garza handed him, filled it from a vial on the medication cart, and then injected it into Marina's arm. Baatard then filled another syringe from a different bottle, and injected it too. Moments later, Marina lay still and made no further sounds.

"What was in the second syringe, more anesthetic?" Garza asked, trying to keep a record on the medication log sheet in the procedure book.

"No," Baatard said. "It was more analgesic. I think she might have had a little discomfort." He gave a concerned glance down at Marina, and then told Garza, "We better put a call in to the nursing station and request for an anesthesiologist to come by, just in case we might need some additional help here."

Garza made the request on the intercom as Baatard checked the vital signs monitor to be certain Marina's heart rate and blood pressure were adequate. Then he nodded to both Muhammad and Garza his intention to proceed. Gently but firmly, Baatard pierced the rear vaginal muscle layer with the probe's tip. Now free in the space of Marina's pelvic cavity, the probe was guided under ultrasound visualization toward the ovarian follicles, which waited ripe on the ovary.

Baatard, Muhammad and Garza each carefully visualized the whole procedure with the ultrasound unit, whose technology realistically made this all possible. "It looks like there are three good sacs on the right ovary," Baatard said to Muhammad. "Let's try them first."

Muhammad leaned over his equipment, stared intently into the display scope, and then changed some settings on the control panel. "I'm okay here," he said.

"How's her breathing?" Baatard called out.

"It's shallow and eight per minute," Garza replied. "I just listened to Marina's breath sounds. They're adequate, and her blood pressure and heart rate are also within normal limits." Garza's interest alternated between the vital sign monitor, the ultrasound camera, and the video signal from the tip of the fiber optic probe. She held onto the receptacle end of the probe, waiting to get a tissue return.

Watching the probe tip appear on the ultrasound screen as it approached the first sac, Baatard said, "I'll be ready for Mr. Thirsty, soon."

"What are you talking about?" Garza asked, giving

him a quizzical look.

"You know, the suction line for the puncture tip?" He looked at the serious glare Garza was giving him, and said, "Look, I'm only joking, Garza. Lighten up, okay?"

Garza leaned over and spoke into Baatard's ear, so Muhammad couldn't hear. "Look, Damon, we've been working together for a long time, right? I just think it's not really appropriate to joke during a procedure. Especially if someone else," she motioned at Muhammad, "might overhear. And think what might happen if the patient was a little awake and heard that."

Unimpressed, Baatard repeated, "Lighten up, Garza. And, don't call me Damon when others are around. Okay? It gives the wrong impression."

"Okey, dokey," Garza replied caustically and coolly smiled.

"As I was saying, it might be a good time for the suction line," Baatard said, not looking up. He looked in the fiber optic viewing port of the probe and could actually see the egg sacs waiting, appearing like tiny little ripe cherries on a stalk as they bobbed around in front of his eyes. He gingerly held the control lever of the puncture tip, and slowly but firmly advanced the probe.

In his imagination, Baatard could almost hear the microscopic pop of the follicle sac as it was ruptured by the probe tip. He asked Garza for more suction, but continued to look only between the ultrasound picture and the probe's viewing port. He kept the probe stationary where it entered Marina's vagina, one hand firmly gripped on its shaft.

"We got something coming out the suction port, and

it looks like a small amount of bloody fluid," Garza told Baatard. The presence of streaks of blood was not unusual or abnormal for this procedure, and did not signify that a bleeding problem had developed. Garza carefully directed the returning fluid into special tissue culture dishes. "I hope there are eggs here," she added, as she watched the yield from the suction line.

"We all do," Baatard told Garza. An unsuccessful ova harvest would mean that whole procedure would need to be repeated, an annoyance at best, and an additional risk and expense to the patient. "Say, where the hell is Frank?" An embryology technician was always present at ova harvesting, and the protocol dictated that Frank Lieu, the senior embryology technician for The Conceptions Foundation, should have arrived long before the procedure began. Baatard shook his head angrily as his opinions of Frank Lieu were once again confirmed.

"I don't know. He should have been here by now. I'll call him," Garza said.

Baatard repeated the puncture/harvest procedure two more times, draining each ovarian follicle sac on the right ovary completely. "Are you sure there are only three sacs on the right?" Baatard asked Muhammad. He often was able to find four, sometimes more, when they tried looking more carefully. The more eggs harvested, the better, especially with such a selective patient as Marina, Baatard thought.

The Surrogate

"Yes, there are only three sacs large enough to identify. Do you want to try the left side?" Muhammad suggested, as he leaned forward and made some adjustments to the control panel of the ultrasound unit.

"Okay, I think we might as well, seeing as we're already here anyway. The more eggs we can find, the better our chances are of the *in vitro* fertilization being successful. He looked at the O.R. clock on the wall. It showed an elapsed time of thirty minutes. "We better get a move on. I've still got three more cases this morning alone," Baatard said to Garza as she came back in the room. "Maybe you should call out and have the next case put in a room and prepped."

"That's already been done," Garza reported, absorbed in her work. "And I had Sharlene notify the embryologist to get his butt on over to this room, too."

Garza was dependable and careful, and Baatard liked those characteristics in her. He recognized early on in his career that he needed someone with him who could complement his weak areas and help him succeed. That was why he had asked her to move with him when he left the Central Haven Obstetrics and Gynecology clinic so long ago. Now, in his position seated next to Garza, Baatard could feel her gently but noticeably press her thigh against his. He decided to ignore it, and also her strange glances, as usual. This time, though, he didn't withdraw his thigh from her. Instead, he looked over at Garza briefly, returned her smile, and then tried to concentrate on the case. As a woman, there were characteristics of Garza he found somewhat attractive. They had occasional lunches together, a few dinners, and had even slept together on several occasions while on a trip to IVF seminars. Although their relationship had never taken off, it definitely wasn't dead either.

The ultrasound unit revealed four more egg sacs on Marina's left ovary, and Baatard was slowly able to move the probe, still under ultrasound guidance, over toward the first two ovarian sacs without difficulty. Suddenly, he felt a great deal of resistance to moving the probe further. Damn, he thought, the probe seems to be caught on something, perhaps a piece of adhesed tissue.

Baatard looked up, irritated at the delay, and yelled out, "Can't you goddamn people see there's something holding me up? You KNOW I'm in a goddamn hurry and for some strange reason TOTALLY UNCLEAR TO ME I just can't seem to get your help." Frustrated, Baatard tried gently twisting the probe a little, first to the left, then to the right, and finally rotating it. Occasionally that helped in situations like this. When the probe didn't free up, Baatard became impatient and his technique became coarser and more abrupt. He realized this, and his self-awareness made him even more anxious and impatient.

"How can we help you, Dr. Baatard?" Garza asked, her voice sounding worried. "Please, you know that when you get annoyed during a procedure you might rush and make a mistake. Please, Dr. Baatard, that wouldn't help things at all."

"Okay, okay," he griped. Baatard knew Garza

understood him better than anyone else, although he
wouldn't admit it to her or anyone, and although he
wouldn't let her know it, he was thankful she was here.
She had saved his ass more than a few times from making
a serious mistake, and even once from being discovered
after having made one. He owed her for this.

"Let's try rolling Marina slightly onto her right side.
Maybe that will free things up a bit," Baatard suggested.
"Maybe the probe got caught on some damn ligament or
something." He looked over at Muhammad for some
bright ideas, but got no help, which did not surprise him.
Muhammad, strictly a technician, shrugged his shoulders,
smiled uncomfortably, then returned to his instruments.

Garza and Muhammad rolled Marina onto her right
side. Unexpectedly, her anesthetic began to wear off a
little as they did so, and Marina groaned slightly and tried,
in her stupor, to straighten out her left leg. This caught
everyone by surprise, especially Baatard.

"Watch out," Garza yelled, reaching desperately to
restrain the slowly shifting leg. "She's trying to move."

"Quick, she's waking up," Baatard yelled out to
Muhammad. "Give her more goddamn diazepam."
Baatard watched helplessly as Muhammad instead
ineffectively tried to hold Marina's leg steady with his
hand.

"But I'm not licensed to give drugs, Dr. Baatard,"
Muhammad objected. He seemed surprised and confused
that Baatard would even ask him to inject drugs into a
patient, something clearly out of his training.

"I don't care what the hell you're licensed to give,
goddamnit, just give the goddamn meds," Baatard yelled

back. A small ball of spittle formed on Baatard's lower lip, and his eyes were wide open in shocked apprehension. He could see a disaster in the making, and tried at all costs to avoid it. When Mohammed hadn't yet moved, Baatard screamed back at him, "Give the diazepam to her NOW or you won't have a fucking license or a fucking job this time tomorrow, you idiot."

Events were moving too fast and Baatard feared that he was losing control. Visions of the recent Lissa Vernor debacle floated in the back of his mind, and he hoped and prayed that another disaster wouldn't be in the making. The fact that this patient was also a quality assurance nurse at the hospital only made him more anxious and upset.

"Look, easy there. I'll give her some more anesthetic," Garza called out. "You know Muhammad isn't licensed to do that, Damon." But before Garza could move, she gasped and watched in horror as Marina's leg stretched out even more and pressed against a loop of the probe's fiber optic cable, causing the probe to jerk back sharply about an inch out of Marina's vagina. Just as that happened, bright red blood began to return from the probe's suction port.

"Oh no. We've got a bleeder here," Garza called out. The agitation in her quivering voice belied the calm she still tried to project. The probe's sudden movement out had apparently cut a blood vessel somewhere deep within

Marina's pelvic cavity. Not being able to actually visualize what had just happened, only time could tell how serious this would be.

The confused yelling, the inflammatory word 'bleeder' nervously called out, and the pain caused by movement of the probe deep within her pelvic cavity all pulled Marina from her lightly anesthetized state. She looked down toward her groin, and when she noticed a rivulet of her own blood trailing from her vagina, she let out a fearful moan. Baatard, Garza and Mohammed all stopped what they were doing and stared at Marina for the briefest second of realization, then continued trying to salvage and stabilize the situation.

The additional dose of anesthetic Garza had just injected into Marina's intravenous line rapidly took effect at about this time, and Garza was finally able to roll Marina, now a limp slab of meat, onto her back and straighten out her limp legs. Garza watched Muhammad shake his head as he looked at his ultrasound scanner, and asked him, "Do you see anything?" Blood continued to flow out of the suction catheter at a respectable rate.

"If you mean: do I see the source of bleeding, the answer is no," Muhammad said, obviously offended at the way he had just been publicly humiliated. "But this ultrasound unit is really not good for finding bleeders. The visual port on the probe is far better for that." Muhammad looked expectantly over at Baatard.

"The fluid is still coming out sero-sanguinous, about 100 milliliters total." Garza's voice was beginning to crack.

"Okay, let's take out the catheter, and," Baatard

instructed Muhammad, "you better put in a call to the Department of General Surgery office. Ask for a surgical consult ASAP." Baatard could see small rivulets of blood now trickling from Marina's vagina, and ineffectively stuffed some gauze bandages in the opening. "And where the hell are the anesthesiologist and Frank?" he yelled at Garza and Muhammad, who could only return anxious shrugs. Garza flashed Baatard a look of surprise and disapproval at his crude hemostasis technique. It seemed more show than serious effort.

"How's her blood pressure?" Baatard snapped, ignoring Garza.

"Okay," Garza reported, making some adjustments to the intravenous line. "Her heart rate and breathing are still within normal limits, too." She looked up as the anesthesiologist, a young black woman shrouded in green OR garb, entered the room.

Baatard nodded, but there was no way he could have disguised the worry in his face. He was glad the anesthesiologist he had asked for earlier had finally arrived, and quickly briefed her on the problems they were having. After confirming that the necessary arrangements to cover his ass by calling in the surgeons had been made, Baatard documented in Marina's surgical chart that she had an adequate blood pressure and was breathing. The surgeons arrived just then, and Baatard went over the briefing again, before being reassured that all was under control and he could now leave.

Relieved, Baatard headed out of the procedure suite to prepare for his next case, then turned back to Garza, and told her, "Be sure to get her goddamn eggs out to the lab before the surgeons contaminate everything. Things will get kind of messy and confusing, you know." Looking around, Baatard angrily asked, "And where the hell is Frank?"

Just as the words left Baatard's mouth, Frank Lieu entered the room, bumping into Baatard in the process.

"Where the hell were you?" Baatard snapped, as he kept walking in the opposite direction.

Before Frank could reply, Baatard was already half way out of the room. As he hurried down the corridor, Baatard wondered for a moment why he had not heard any more about the outcome of his postoperative patient, Lissa Vernor. He decided that no news was probably good news. This only reinforced his belief that Lissa's bleeding had stopped on its own, just as he had predicted it would. At least he wouldn't have to deal with a bad outcome on another physician's wife. That was always one of his worst nightmares, and so time-consuming.

A half-hour after returning to his office in the late afternoon, Baatard heard a knock at the door. His nerves were shot, he was dead tired, and all he wanted was to be left alone for a few minutes. He rolled his eyes helplessly and groaned. Sharlene pushed the door open, came in and quietly pushed it closed with a swift bump from her buttocks. "Hi, Damon" she said softly.

"Oh, hi," Baatard replied tersely, trying to

concentrate on a handful of papers in front of him. He wondered what the hell she was doing here just now. She could be so inappropriate at times.

"I just wanted to tell you that Garza called, and everything looks okay on the Bonnaserra case." Not getting a response, Sharlene pouted her lips playfully and said, "I hope I'm not bothering you."

"No, no, not at all. I just have a lot of work that I need to get done, that's all." Sharlene was acting strange, even for her. "I, ah, I felt you pressing against me in the elevator earlier today. Did you need more space?"

"No, I had plenty of room," Sharlene smiled. "I just like to feel you close to me, that's all."

"Close to you, or close in you?" Baatard smiled. Nervous from the near crisis in the Bonnaserra case, he decided he could very well use some relaxation just now, something he wasn't at all getting a lot of lately. He had enjoyed a few quick moments with Sharlene before over the years, just as he had with Garza, and although never memorable, they were convenient.

He deftly placed the phone on answer, then got up from his desk. Moving in front of Sharlene, he turned down the room lights, and locked his office door. A recent trip to the front had shown that almost everyone else had left for the day, except for a receptionist who was busy answering the phone and stuffing envelopes, and he felt his privacy was reasonably safe and assured.

The Surrogate

Baatard smiled down at Sharlene. He considered her still pretty for her age, in a simple kind of way. Now, she looked particularly appealing in a rather revealing, casual blouse and skirt. She wore it cut short, about an inch above her knees when she was standing. There were many times when he had noticed it ride up higher as she sat.

"Yes," Sharlene replied, as she put her hands around Baatard's hips and pulled him close. She tilted her head up and received his full mouth kiss, sucking his tongue deep into her mouth, licking and stroking his tongue with hers, mixing their juices together. "Oh, baby," she moaned hungrily.

Baatard was getting uncontrollably excited, and once again, he ignored the strong smell and taste of nicotine on Sharlene's breath and in her mouth. It revolted him, but he could endure it for the moment. He could smell her thick, strong feminine scent and became even more aroused. Reaching down, he roughly pulled her loose skirt up to her hips. To his surprise, he touched only skin. She was wearing absolutely nothing underneath. Unbelievable, he thought.

Eight minutes passed - fast, for that many minutes. Baatard tried to manage Sharlene's weight as he surreptitiously stole a look at his watch, trying not to attract her attention.

He heard her say, "Oh, Baby. Not bad, Damon." She moved off him and pulled her skirt back down over her waist. "Next time, try to slow down a bit, and let us both get something out of it. Okay?" The look on her face was more exhaustion than pleasure.

"Yeah, sure Sharlene. That was very good," Baatard only partially lied. "I really wanted you, Sharlene," he exaggerated, more for her benefit. He looked at his watch again, then added, "But, I . . . "

"I know, I know. You're late for another procedure. No problem. See you after work?"

"Sure, I guess, I think so. Let me call you, okay?" He quickly cleaned up a bit at the small sink in the corner of his office, then hurried out. Passing his front desk, he stopped to leave word with the receptionist where he would be. The receptionist glanced a knowing smile at him, making him think she might have been aware of the little love tryst which had just transpired. Tough, he thought, if she doesn't like it or bad-mouths me, I'll fire her tight ass.

"Funny about that woman," Sharlene said to him as they walked down the corridor together a few minutes later.

"Who? What woman?" He wondered if Sharlene was referring to Garza or to one of his patients. "What do you mean?" he repeated.

"Miss Bonnaserra, that's who. She looks an awful lot like another of your patients, Lissa Vernor, don't you think?"

"Yes, I guess so," Baatard shrugged. Now that he thought about it, that was the second time Sharlene had said that about Marina, and he was beginning to see the resemblance himself.

Baatard left his office building and headed over to the hospital via the connecting indoor ramp. His head was one large bundle of confusion, filled with the 'quickie' ecstasy of Sharlene, the near disaster of Marina Bonnaserra and the difficult Lissa Vernor case. And looming in front of all that was an endlessly long list of procedures that he still needed to complete before the long day ended.

Chapter 12

Haven General Hospital

Deanna Baptiste, mentally exhausted from the long, detailed surgery on Lissa Vernor, was relieved when she could finally drag herself off the ward. She was embarrassed and seething with anger over the public harassment she again had received from Baatard. It had happened before, Deanna sighed, and she had let past episodes slide by without complaining. This time, she thought, he's gone too far.

Years of hospital stress were having a draining effect on her body, and Baatard only seemed to accelerate the decay. Now, when she was handed a phone call from her nursing supervisor assigning her mandated call, she was, to put it mildly, not overjoyed.

Mandated call meant that a nurse was required to work a shift, whether she wanted to or not. Mandated call - almost a form of involuntary servitude - was usually applied only in extenuating circumstances. Most frequently, the nursing administration used mandated call to cover a ward's staffing needs when the assigned nurse called in sick and there was no other backup available. Extenuating circumstances were becoming rather frequent, though, and Deanna was growing a bit tired and annoyed with all the extra work. This was the second time in one week Deanna was asked by her supervisor to stay on in the recovery room, and at Haven General, being asked was equivalent to being ordered to work. Deanna found it more than annoying, although she had to admit she could always use the added money.

This time the mandated call was to watch Lissa Vernor after her surgery; Deanna was to substitute for a no-show nurse. Deanna had suspected the mandated call would be coming, given the nursing shortage and the high rate of absenteeism lately from a virus circulating in the community. Her already being familiar with this particular patient did make her the most likely choice - that, she had to admit.

Lissa Vernor required intensive, one-on-one nursing for several reasons. Lissa was in critical condition after emergency surgery. The blood loss had been massive, and no one really knew if all the bleeding had even stopped. There was also a need to keep the surgical adverse outcomes lower and one-on-one nursing might help here too. Most important, this patient was the wife of a physician affiliated with Haven General Hospital - Dr. Ryder Vernor. Doctor's wives were treated like royalty, if only by the hospital and its employees.

Another reason for the especially careful treatment Lissa received was related to the yearly hospital recertification. Hospitals with unacceptably high rates of serious complications and deaths after surgery - 'high risk units' - were marked by the state's hospital accreditation committee. High risk units were then required to undergo frequent inspections and audits of their protocols and staff credentials. Even if successful, these time-consuming proceedings could take months. Worse, they might affect the hospital's ability to perform surgeries during the investigation. This hurt the bottom line - for surgeries were moneymaking, billable events.

An hour later, Deanna sat by the nursing station monitor console, a high-tech collection of electronic equipment constantly beeping and flashing. Electronic devices with their digital readouts and high-pitched monotone beeps were everywhere. They made Deanna feel like she was on a space station and not at all in a hospital.

Deanna nervously watched Lissa Vernor's blood pressure monitor every few minutes. She knew from experience that having suffered as much blood loss during surgery as Lissa had, her postoperative course would be rocky. Lissa's low pressure continued to show, at best, a systolic of 55 mm of mercury, which in Deanna's book was severe hypotension.

Blood delivered oxygen and nutrients to all the tissues and organs of the body. In addition, blood removed carbon dioxide and waste products, and there was an imminent danger of Lissa's blood pressure becoming too low to adequately perfuse her critical tissues: the brain, kidneys and heart. Once these organs shut down, the inadequate blood circulation would quickly lead to death, Lissa's death.

Every thirty minutes, Deanna checked the plastic urine bag which hung down from the side of Lissa Vernor's bed. Urine flow out of the bladder catheter would have meant adequate blood perfusion of Lissa's kidneys; disappointingly, none came, and only a small amount of dark yellow urine pooled in the bottom of the bag.

Concerned that her patient was in trouble, Deanna keyed Baatard's cell number into the automatic paging system. Thinking about Baatard always made Deanna confused, and the insulting way he openly treated her in the O.R. only made her angrier. She messed up on entering the third number into the paging system, tried again, and correctly entered the recovery room phone number. After hitting the pound sign to end her entry and send the message, she hung up and waited.

Deanna sat alone at the nursing station, drumming her fingers on the desk and watching the electronic monitors for five long minutes before the phone finally rang. She anxiously picked up the phone on the first ring.

The voice was gruff, and clearly annoyed. "This is Doctor Baatard. Who's this?"

"It's Deanna, Damon. I'm calling about . . . "

"Deanna? Look, Deanna. Don't you know I'm in the middle of surgery, goddamn it? Okay, okay, what's the problem?"

"Now how would I know you're in surgery again? I'm not clairvoyant," Deanna angrily shot back, but then forced herself to get the conversation back on track, to keep control, not to let Baatard's rudeness divert her.

Looking down at her nursing notes, Deanna told Baatard, "Your post-op's abdomen has continued to distend. Her blood pressure is still low and she's had no urine output. Maybe she's still bleeding."

"What are you now, a goddamn doctor, for Christ's sake?" Baatard chuckled derisively. "And what do you want me to do about it, anyway? I looked for a bleeding source, didn't I?"

"Yes, but . . . "

"And you were there, weren't you?"

"Yes, but . . . "

"Then don't call me again unless it's a real emergency, for Christ's sake, and quit playing doctor. Look, Deanna, why don't you try one of the OB-GYN residents first? Yeah, call the gynecology residents over to look at her. They need the experience. And don't call me Damon in public. It's unprofessional."

After Deanna heard the phone loudly hang up, she felt like a fool for having called Baatard in the first place, even though it was his protocol. "You're unprofessional, and you're fucking with the wrong person, Baatard," she muttered to herself. Deanna picked up Lissa Vernor's hospital chart and as calmly as possible documented the low blood pressure, the call to Baatard, and a toned-down version of their conversation, while a plan formed in her subconscious.

The next hour passed too slowly. Deanna noticed Lissa's abdomen was not only more swollen, but now it was actually getting tense. The overlying skin developed a disconcerting purplish discoloration, probably from old blood underneath. Worse yet, the patient never woke up, something Deanna was not accustomed to having happen this long after surgery. Not wanting to wait any longer, Deanna decided to follow Baatard's suggestion. The gynecology resident would have to evaluate Lissa's deteriorating condition.

Deanna looked up the gynecology resident's pager number from a list of this month's on-call residents taped nearby onto the wall. She quickly keyed in the cell phone, entered the recovery room phone number into the text message box, hit the pound sign, hung up, and waited. This time it took ten full minutes for a reply; she again picked up the phone on the first ring.

"This is Dr. Salvatore," a groggy voice said. "Ah, did someone page the gynecology resident?"

"Yes, Rudy. This is Deanna. I'm covering the Recovery Room tonight," she said, relieved to hear his voice. Rudy Salvatore was the most reasonable and caring of the residents, and Deanna felt she could trust his judgment and could depend on him to help.

"What can I do for you Deanna? And, could you please make it quick," he told her in a hushed voice.

"I'm sorry to call you, but I have a problem. Can you come over to the Recovery area?" She realized that her page must have woken him. Residents slept odd hours and grabbed naps when and where they could. It was a dog's life, especially for the first year. Initially, she thought that explained why residents treated the nurses and medical students so bad. Then, as she got to know more medical students and doctors personally, she realized that they were all really compulsive-obsessive sociopaths to begin with.

"Yeah. Maybe. I don't know. First tell me what the problem is," Salvatore replied, his voice tainted with sarcasm. "Does one of your post-partum patients have constipation again?"

Deanna heard Salvatore yawn, and resented the condescending nature of his voice. "No, it's the post-op bleeder case - Lissa Vernor," Deanna tried to explain. She waited through several seconds of silence, then asked, "Hello, are you there, Dr. Salvatore?" She listened carefully and thought she heard him mumble something softly. Another voice, faint, perhaps female, whispered in the background, and this both irritated and offended Deanna.

"Oh, it's Vernor, huh?" After another long pause, Salvatore seemed to have woken enough to collect his thoughts. "Yes, Vernor, sure I know about the case. Why?" Salvatore pulled out a stack of index cards wrapped with a rubber band from his pocket. He cleared his throat and tried to recall the rapid fire information and directions given when Dr. Baatard signed all of his patients out to him.

"She's still hypotensive, she has no urine output, and

I think her bleeding is continuing into her abdomen."
Deanna looked over at Deanna's monitors: the blood
pressure was a menacingly low 50/40. She noted this in
the vital signs chart, along with the fact she was relaying
this to a physician. Deanna felt jumpy, nervous, as if she
imminently expected something bad to happen, which she
did.

"I can understand that," Salvatore said under his
breath.

"I'm sorry, I didn't catch that," Deanna replied,
wondering if Salvatore was trying to imply anything
without directly challenging his superior - Dr. Baatard.

"Nothing, it was nothing. But why are you calling
me about this now? Did something new happen?" He
yawned into the telephone receiver again.

"Vernor's abdomen is distended, purplish, and tense.
On top of that, she's running a low grade fever." Deanna
waited for a few seconds of silence, then said, "Hello, Dr.
Salvatore?"

"Yeah, I'm still here, Deanna. I'm thinking. Did you
call Dr. Baatard?"

"Yes, and he said to call the resident."

"That figures," Salvatore muttered.

"Can you please come down and examine your
patient?" Deanna sensed a problem getting Salvatore to
come on to the ward; perhaps Salvatore too knew there
was a screw-up when Lissa was closed without
identifying the bleeding source. Deanna meticulously
documented her conversation with Salvatore in the
Nurse's Notes section of the patient's hospital record
while she was talking. It was simply a case of Cover Your

Ass - CYA as people so often said.

"Uh, is the patient complaining of any pain?"

Deanna again heard Salvatore yawn on the phone. "She hasn't woken up yet." Like you, she thought. "I'm telling you, there's a problem here. I can feel that something bad is going to happen, and soon."

"Sure, sure. Okay, I'll be right there." Salvatore, exhausted from his third 36-hour shift in a row, hung up the phone, rolled over in the on-call cot and promptly fell asleep again.

Salvatore was shocked awake, torn from a deep sleep in the dark on-call cubicle within five minutes of hanging up Deanna's phone call. His beeper, painted bright red and restricted to Cardiac and Respiratory Arrest CODEs, gave off a constant high-pitched scream. He shot up straight in the single cot, confused and completely disoriented for a few seconds.

"Code Blue. Recovery Room," the 'CODE' beeper blared out, echoing against the tiny room's bare walls.

Salvatore jumped out of bed, pulled the sash tight to keep his scrub pants held up, then slipped on his sneakers. He dashed like a lunatic out into the darkened hallway, following closely on the heels of the rest of the emergency response team.

As Salvatore ran into the Recovery Room, the monitor above Lissa Vernor's head showed she had a dangerously low systolic blood pressure of only thirty to forty, and no detectable diastolic pressure. "Shit," Salvatore cursed. He knew that blood pressure would be too low to adequately perfuse the coronary vessels and would lead to a myocardial infarction - heart attack.

Medical people crowded everywhere, most of them yelling questions and orders at each other. Salvatore had to elbow his way through all the confusion over to the bedside. Once there, Salvatore grabbed Lissa Vernor's limp, doughy wrist; he detected no pulse over her radial artery. Shit, she's already dead, Salvatore thought. Now what the hell am I going to do, and how am I going to explain this to that bastard Baatard? Tiny bits of his recent conversation and warning from Deanna flashed in his mind. Now he regretted not seeing this patient immediately, knew he should have, but couldn't get enough peace of mind to make up an adequate excuse just now. Too much was happening at this moment, but he made a mental note to do that later.

Marina Bonnaserra, lying in bed in a distant cubicle, awoke for a moment. She heard all the racket and saw the frantic efforts to revive Lissa, but had no idea what was happening, and lay awake watching what little she could observe.

Salvatore shoved two fingers into the crevice along the front of Lissa Vernor's neck, but he couldn't detect a carotid pulse. "Shit," Salvatore muttered, "she really is dead."

"What did you say?" Deanna asked Salvatore. She had heard him completely, but couldn't believe he had already given up hope. There was absolutely no reason to give up just yet, and Deanna wouldn't allow that.

"Nothing, nothing," Salvatore muttered. He looked around him at the confusion, feeling totally helpless and alone, for he realized he was in command but had no commands to issue. Events had taken on a life of their own.

Deanna noticed tears forming in Salvatore's eyes, something she had not seen from him before. Sensing Salvatore wasn't fully in control of the CODE or of himself, she assumed direction of Lissa's care, and of her life. Deanna didn't know if Rudy Salvatore was too tired, or too inexperienced, or simply too indecisive. Details didn't matter; she had seen other house staff collapse in the face of a medical crisis before, only to be saved by a nurse. "She's not dead yet," Deanna firmly told Salvatore. Her face, her manner displayed the clear thinking and direction and confidence Salvatore lacked, and Deanna could already see him accede by default to her authority. "This is still a CODE. No one is going to stop before we even start, not while I'm here. I'll begin chest compressions."

"Okay, okay, run the IV wide open, people," Salvatore anxiously called out. Taking the cue from Deanna, his approach seemed to change and he said as confidently as he could under the circumstances, "Let's try to get her pressure up." Trying to re-assume control of the CODE, Salvatore directed one of the other nurses to perform chest compressions. He wanted, he needed

Deanna free to think and help him avoid having another of his assigned patients turn into shit.

Deanna, an unmistakable look of disgust and contempt covering her face, thrust a strip of tracer paper fresh from the electrocardiogram - EKG - monitor over to Salvatore. "She's got sinus tachycardia, Rudy." Lissa's abnormally fast heart rate - sinus tachycardia - was most likely caused by her depleted blood status. The actions that needed to immediately be taken were clear in Deanna's own mind, starting with infusing more fluids, which was vital. As long as Salvatore acted appropriately, Deanna would 'let' him give the orders. Even if she was really in control, and the most capable, she was still only a nurse, and with the patient's physician in the room, no one would follow her orders. One thing for certain, Deanna's confidence in Salvatore, and in all physicians, was diminished even further.

Seeing Salvatore's tears more clearly, Deanna leaned over and asked him, "Hey Rudy, are you all right?" Residents had lost their emotions before in her presence, something that hampered their performance immeasurably. She had to know if that was what was happening here. It would help her help Lissa, and help Salvatore too.

"Yes, of course I'm all right. No problem." Salvatore straightened up, wiped his face with his coat sleeve, took the EKG tracer strip and examined it. His hands trembled, and a confused, lost look covered his face. The fact was, he had never been good at reading EKG's even under the best of circumstances, and that was only one of the many reasons he decided not to choose internal medicine as his specialty. This EKG strip showed a rhythmic and uniform jagged line, cutting sharply first in one direction, then changing to rip in the other direction about 130 times a minute. He didn't recognize the pattern at all, but eagerly accepted Deanna's interpretation of sinus tachycardia. "She's probably really low on fluid volume," Salvatore said. His mind raced to explain what was happening and quickly find a way out, fast, before Baatard could yell at him again. And before Lissa Vernor died.

Salvatore looked carefully at Lissa's hopelessly bloated body, then told Deanna, "Her abdomen is more distended. Maybe Baatard didn't catch the last bleeder before closing, after all." It was obvious to everyone that continued fluid loss could explain the EKG tracing.

"No shit, Sherlock" Deanna whispered to Salvatore, her feeling of revulsion growing by the minute. She was way ahead of him once again. "The patient needs blood fast, oh wise one of medicine and surgery."

"Right, right. I, I can see that. Okay, call the blood bank. Get four units of packed red cells up here in a hurry, and run them in rapidly. And you better use a blood warmer, too."

"Sorry," said Deanna, shaking her head. "We already tried that. The Blood Bank says they're completely out of her blood type again. Lissa already exhausted their supply from all the bleeding she did during surgery. And they don't know when more will be available." Deanna shrugged her shoulders, then bent over to take Lissa's blood pressure again.

Turning to Deanna, Salvatore was momentarily distracted by the loose fit of her green surgical shirt. He was allowed a particularly good view of Deanna's pendulous breasts as she bent over the patient toward him every few minutes. Salvatore had noticed before that Deanna often wore rather loose-fitting bras, and instinctively knew what to look for. Shaking his head to regain his thoughts, he called out to the ward clerk, who was circling in the background. "Please, call Dr. Baatard."

"I already tried that, but he's in another surgery, and can't be disturbed," Deanna interjected. "You know how angry Baatard gets, so I wouldn't call him either if I were you." She subconsciously stood a little straighter, allowing her blouse top to fall against her chest.

"Shit," Salvatore said to himself. "Okay, why don't you call the Chief Gynecology resident."

"I already have," Deanna said, "and he's on his way in from home."

"Good," said Salvatore. He turned his back to the group and quickly wiped his face with his scrub shirt, smearing a mixture of fresh perspiration and old tears against his cheeks.

Deanna thought Salvatore looked terribly frightened and confused, and she heard him say, almost to himself, "If I can only keep her going until more blood arrives, she should be okay."

Looking at Deanna, Salvatore asked, "The chart notes a slight fever. Why does she have THAT, do you think? Has she been coughing?"

"I don't know why she's got a fever. Her urine looks clear and no, she isn't coughing."

Not having enough time to work up the fever, Salvatore told Deanna, "Okay, okay, maybe it's some mild lung consolidation from the surgery. We better culture her up, though. You know, blood, urine, the usual. And get a portable chest X-ray." Thinking it over some more, he added, "And I think we better put a culture swab into her vagina also, just in case she's got toxic shock syndrome or something."

"Better get her through the CODE first," she reminded him.

Two more liters of saline solution ran into Lissa's arm through an intravenous setup over the next half hour. Salvatore had taken hold of Lissa's hand and stood at her bedside during much of that time. Fortunately for the patient and for Dr. Salvatore, Lissa's blood pressure slowly came back up toward a range compatible with life. Deanna noted on the monitor, however, that Lissa's heart rate was still 130+. "She probably still isn't getting enough oxygen to her tissues," Deanna told Salvatore. "You need to get hold of some real blood, fast, if we're going to pull this one off." Crises that ended badly usually cascaded downhill just like this. Deanna was prepared for the worst, but still hoped for a positive outcome.

"How about an emergency request for donation?" Salvatore asked one of the lab technicians who had responded to the code and had stayed in the room.

"That's already been done," replied the lab tech, shaking his head, "but you know, these emergency calls have been happening so frequently lately, the response is just not too great. Doc, her surgery just busted the blood bank."

Just then, Deanna and the lab tech heard someone yelling and barking orders on the other side of the room and looked over to see who it was.

Salvatore also looked up to try and see where all the yelling and screaming was coming from. It was his worst nightmare: Dr. Baatard, dressed in surgical garb, was marching up to the post-op's bed, his face puffed up and red, and obviously in a very foul mood. Salvatore desperately looked around but could find no place to hide.

"All right, goddamn it. What's the goddamn problem?" Baatard grumbled, seeming both annoyed and surprisingly disinterested.

"Please, Dr. Baatard, watch your language around the patient," Deanna scolded him.

"The patient is in a goddamn coma," Baatard tersely reminded Deanna. "She can't hear anything. Now, Salvatore, what the hell's going on here?" Baatard crossed his hands in front of his chest, and rocked back and forth on his heels in an intimidating manner.

"Hypotension, secondary to hypovolemia, probably secondary to continued intra-abdominal bleed, sir." Salvatore quickly let go of Lissa's hand. "We did get her pressure up."

Deanna, again getting none of the credit she deserved, simply rolled her eyes toward the ceiling.

"Thank you, Dr. Salvatore. I really needed your assistance on this one." At first glaring at Salvatore, Baatard tried to look calm, shoving his hands into his pockets, and in a quiet tone asked, "Okay, Dr. Salvatore, can you tell me just what course of action you recommend for this patient?"

Salvatore watched carefully as another one of the nurses bent over his patient, also opening her scrub top to his view inside. A beautiful set of breasts bobbed and swayed only inches from his face, causing him to again lose his chain of thought momentarily. He began to turn away when the nurse unexpectedly looked up at him, but stopped when she returned a very subtle smile. What's the matter with me, he wondered? Am I some kind of sex addict, or a deviant? I'm only inches from a seriously ill patient, and I've got to keep my mind on her and nothing else, he thought as he struggled to get a hold of himself.

Salvatore nervously suggested, "Should we consider a surgical re-exploration?"

"Wrong, asshole," Baatard sneered, shaking his head in disbelief. His attention was redirected to the bedside.

"Dr. Baatard, your language is really inappropriate." Deanna protested. She sensed a ruse on Baatard's part to deflect the blame onto Salvatore, and realized Salvatore was too naive to be aware of this or to adequately defend himself.

Baatard ignored Deanna and continued digging. "You

open up that abdomen, Dr. Salvatore, and all you'll find in there is blood and loose tissue and more blood. You can go back in, but I can guarantee you won't find the bleeding, if there still is any bleeding this long after surgery. I didn't find it, and you definitely won't find it either," he half-sneered. "Besides, right now it's a mess in her abdomen; you can't find anything. No, Dr. Salvatore, surgical re-exploration is definitely not the answer, goddamn it."

Baatard grabbed the vital sign clipboard out of Salvatore's hands and yelled a flood of orders out at Deanna. "Check all her clotting factors, get her an emergency transfusion of six units fresh whole blood, infuse lactated Ringer's solution at one hundred fifty cc's per hour until her pressure is adequate, and measure the hourly urine output."

Baatard turned to Salvatore, pointed right at his forehead and added, "I want YOU to stay right here. You let me know when the blood finishes going in, and what the clotting studies show. And Salvatore, . . . "

"Yes?"

"I want you to find out, if it's not too much trouble, why the hell your patient has a fever. You don't need my help for a simple fever workup, do you?"

"No, Dr. Baatard, I don't need your help on the fever workup. I've already started one, as a matter of fact."

"I'm glad to hear that," Baatard replied caustically.

"But, about the transfusion, we've checked and there isn't any blood available," protested Salvatore. Deanna and the lab tech nodded agreement before moving away.

"Oh? Well, I'll see about that," smiled Baatard,

watching Deanna out of the corner of his eye as she paced back and forth in front of the nurse's station, then disappeared into the medication room for a few minutes. When she came back out, Baatard noticed the sleeves of her surgical scrub top, pulled up before, were now down. He tried to smile at her, but failed to get her attention. Baatard briefly watched Deanna as she then sat by herself at the Nurse's work desk and play with the chart rack, nervously nibbling at her nails. After finishing scribbling a few notes in Lissa Vernor's chart, Baatard left the ward.

Baatard first stopped in the patient family waiting room to speak with Lissa Vernor's husband. Dr. Ryder Vernor happened to be a family practitioner from whom Baatard occasionally received patient referrals. Understandably, Dr. Vernor was quite upset about his wife's unexpected illness. Baatard knew that the terror that Dr. Vernor was feeling would be doubled by his own first-hand understanding only too well what already had happened to Lissa. Intimate knowledge of events that occurred coupled with an understanding of what was likely to follow enabled doctors.

Chapter 13

The conversation with Dr. Vernor took less time than Baatard had expected - only ten minutes. It also turned out to be less uncomfortable than Baatard had anticipated it would be, considering all the unfortunate circumstances. Ryder Vernor was, of course, depressed with the disastrous outcome, but apparently accepting of what had occurred. Perhaps, Baatard felt, he could at least comprehend, if not fully accept. Perhaps acceptance would be asking too much.

As a physician himself, Ryder Vernor certainly knew the score as well as Baatard. To Baatard's relief, there had been no angry outbursts, no emotional crying, and no threats of legal action on Vernor's part. There certainly could have been, and some would even consider such behavior part of the normal grieving response. Yet, Baatard was left with the clear impression that Vernor seemed truly appreciative of Baatard's efforts and in agreement with the course of care his wife was receiving. Yet, Vernor also seemed perhaps just a little too accepting, a lingering observation which puzzled Baatard.

Although Baatard routinely avoided trying to put himself in his patient's or their family's position, he found himself doing so in this case. Perhaps it was because both Ryder and he were physicians, but for whatever the reason, he hoped that he would try to display as much patience and understanding as did Ryder if he were ever under similar circumstances.

After speaking with Dr. Vernor, Baatard stopped by the office of the Director of Laboratory Services, his friend George Zimmer, to inquire about the availability of additional blood for Lissa Vernor. As expected, his direct intervention helped. From Zimmer's office, Baatard returned to his own office in the attached medical complex.

Baatard knew he had a full load of patients waiting to be seen back at his office. The delay caused by Lissa Vernor, though unavoidable and not his fault, would make for some unhappy campers. Tough shit, he thought, then laughed to himself.

Baatard decided that it would be prudent to stay in the immediate area of the hospital and medical complex, for he not only had Lissa Vernor's case to contend with, he also needed to remain accessible until he knew for certain that Marina Bonnaserra's bleeding had stabilized. And if complications were to occur, he needed to be available for Marina also.

Although not intentionally Baatard's fault, the Bonnaserra bleeding did occur during an invasive procedure he was performing, and was at least technically his responsibility. Baatard doubted Marina would be the type interested in a lawsuit, although he never could know for certain when it came to those things. Once hemostasis was achieved, Baatard planned to immediately transfer Marina's care to another service, probably to General Surgery.

Now, with Lissa Vernor also so critically ill, Baatard wanted to be available for any sudden changes in her condition. Baatard had already developed a particularly uncomfortable, negative view of Lissa's probable outcome, one he preferred not to dwell on right now. Baatard reflected that he had not had so many seriously ill persons under his care at any one time for months, maybe years. Although seriously ill patients generally meant big billings, he could feel the pressure beginning to get to him. He would rather have his patients free of complications than be able to bill in cases like that. Besides, billing for infertility workups had given him the best reimbursements he had ever had, and were more than enough to justify de-emphasizing his other activities.

Baatard had just gotten inside the door to his office when Sharlene pulled him aside. She cleared her throat, then moved Baatard directly into the reception office, where she told him, "Denny Cruite is on the phone. Do you want to take it?" although he would have preferred having a few minutes to clear his desk of some must-do paperwork first, something he saw in Sharlene's face indicated that he needed to speak with Denny.

"Why, is there something wrong?" Damon asked, then coughed nervously.

"Not that I know of, but she sounds a little annoyed."

"Denny always sounds a little annoyed," he quipped. "Okay, I'll take it in my office." He walked quickly down the hall, went in his office, shut the door partway, for privacy and to cut down on outside noise, and picked up the phone. "Hello, Denny?"

"Hello, Damon. How are you?"

He could tell from the animated edge in her voice that something was up, and so he told her, "The usual, and a million things going on. What brings your call?"

Denny thought quietly to herself for a moment before saying, "Damon, can I tell you something in confidence, in strictest confidence?"

"Of course, Denny. Is something the matter?"

"No, not at all. As a matter of fact, when you hear what I have to say, I think you'll agree that things may be looking pretty good for us. Did you ever hear the term 'chump change'?"

Although she apparently didn't intend for her question to sound that way, a certain bitterness laced her voice, warning Damon. He had learned over their years of professional association that Denny had her own agenda, and didn't always share it with his. "No, I can't say I have," he said.

"Neither did I, until recently, but it means, loosely translated, an inappropriately small amount of money."

Damon suspected that her call had something to do with money, and now wondered if there was a billing or a reimbursement problem, or another patient complaint?

"That's what the Conceptions Foundation means for you, Damon. You're capable of so much more, and yet at the rate you're going you're destined to perform the same procedures until you retire, and with diminishing reimbursements, I might add."

"I don't see what you're getting at, Denny." Apparently this was not a billing problem, and her tone was such that he could now sense there was no problem. That made him doubly suspicious.

"You know, Damon, I had a very interesting conversation with some very prominent ladies at a Conceptions Foundation presentation at our home last night."

Confused, he asked, "Last night? I wasn't aware there was a Conceptions Foundation seminar last night. Why wasn't I informed." Speaking at the Foundation seminars was very important to Baatard, as it was an excellent opportunity to network, to recruit new patients for the lucrative procedures, and he almost never missed the opportunity. Speaking there, introduced as he was by Denny, almost as a personal endorsement, meant direct dollars, big dollars in his pocket, so big that he often took pains to eliminate other competing speakers wherever he had the chance. Denny also hosted private briefings at her house, for very special potential clients, women who chose to maintain their privacy and their separation from the masses of common humanity who attended the public seminars. They were catered events, designed to meet the approval of Haven's elite. Baatard had remembered Denny casually mentioning such private meetings, as opposed to their popular public seminars, but it seemed long ago, and he had assumed, not having heard further, that such meetings, while seemingly a great PR idea, never had actually gotten off the ground again. Now, apparently he was wrong.

"Mrs. Doreen Johnston, the Chief Financial Officer of Haven General, attended the most recent one, along with Lydia Ramirez, the family court judge," she smiled with the well-fed satisfaction of a house cat after dinner.

He had heard Denny mention Lydia's name before. "Isn't she the wife of the president of Generic Pharmaceuticals?" Baatard was impressed at the list of wealthy and powerful people, some of whom he recognized.

"Yes, that's her, all right. It was just Nevin and me, and the two guests, and Nevin wasn't feeling too well, again. We started with our standard presentation, but things quickly changed to a discussion of your research."

"It's not really research, especially in the way Generic Pharma means research. It's more of a special interest, and a specialty area of knowledge." He hoped that Denny didn't create any misunderstanding or mistaken expectations of his abilities.

"That's very modest of you, Damon, but anything special you have going for you could give you a marketable edge, as far as I'm concerned. Anyway, they were very impressed with The Foundation's capabilities."

"Then I assume, from the tone of your voice, that they are interested in IVF, and you want me to see them, probably in a very private setting." Baatard had a real problem taking care of the spoiled, pampered, castrating women Denny occasionally referred to him, but the money was excellent. Some in his community were more than willing to pay exorbitant amounts for special service, sort of like a private health spa for fertility.

"Look, Damon, I'm well aware that you don't particularly enjoy seeing some of the people I've sent to you over the years, but you have to admit that you and I and The Foundation all have benefited immensely."

"Okay, sounds like just more of the same this time, right?"

"Not exactly. Let me put it to you this way, Damon. Let's say there is a particular woman with approximately ten times your net worth, with a high-visibility job, but also a lot of family pressure to bear a child. Perhaps it's the woman's parents or her husband's parents, or maybe it's simply internal doubt of her capabilities as a total woman, or maybe she's always wanted a child, but, well, you know how these motherly things can get shoved aside on the competitive road to success." Denny chuckled a little, then continued, "Now you're thirty-five, you've got the money, but you still don't have the time or the physical stamina or you don't think that your career can handle the strains of carrying along an extra twenty pounds for several months. Or you're like Lydia Ramirez, and you want to run for State Senate, and you think that being childless makes you look harsh and unfeminine. What are you gonna do?"

"Undergo IVF?" Baatard offered, certain that was where Denny was going.

"Wrong. These women don't really want a kid, any

more than they really want a lover ten years younger, any more than they want a penis, a new ruby ring, a Porsche or a hole in the head. But, if they could have a kid without all the muss and the fuss, then they might go along with it," Denny smiled, then coughed loudly, another wet, painful cough.

"Maybe you ought to see a doctor," Baatard suggested. "You sound awful."

"Probably, I guess," she shrugged. "I think that I got it from Nevin."

"Okay, now let me guess, you're planning to branch into the private adoption business?" Baatard asked, skeptically.

"No, not exactly. Look, Damon, these women don't want to adopt for the simple reason that they can't deal with the uncertainty of what they are getting. You know just as well as they do that there are several undesirable traits that you can't really check potential adoptees for. Things like propensity to alcohol or drug abuse, or intelligence." She said that last word with an intensity entirely different from all her other points today.

Baatard could see her point. Lydia Ramirez as family court judge could become very embarrassed if some snoopy reporter discovered that the mother of her adopted child was in prison, sentenced by Lydia herself on a prostitution charge.

"Why, if you could supply some of these women with

a newborn with guaranteed intelligence and no known disease, and of a specified sex, it would be worth an absolute fortune. You could almost literally name your price," she exclaimed gleefully.

"We charge a lot now, Denny," he commented, caustically. "How much more could we reasonably get?"

"Think of it this way, Damon. We charge twenty to fifty thousand now to the general public for our standard services, right? Well, for most of the people we see, that's between twenty and eighty percent of their yearly income. But, and here's the beauty of what I'm proposing, the two people I was speaking with last night have combined yearly incomes in the five to twenty million dollar range, five to twenty million, Damon," she repeated for emphasis. "Strictly on a percentile basis, that comes up to about ..."

"You've got to be kidding, Denny." The numbers were adding faster in Baatard's head than comprehension would permit. "Nobody would pay a million dollars for a surrogate adoption." There were other ways to adopt, outside of the slow and cumbersome public system. Alternatives already existed, for the right amount of money, and certainly didn't cost half a million or more.

"Sure that's a lot of cash, now I'm not talking any surrogate adoption here, Damon, but something very different. Look what we could be offering here, Damon. Sex selection, guaranteed health, good gene line, and most of all intelligence. I'd say that's worth at least a million plus to the likes of Mrs. Judge Lydia Ramirez."

Baatard's thoughts finally began to take in the barest significance of what Denny was proposing when they were interrupted by some noise heard on the phone, apparently in the background, and he asked, "Is everything all right, Denny?"

"No, it is not. Those Goddamn abortion protesters are back again. Can you believe it?"

Baatard heard a knock, and someone yelling something to Denny, who hurriedly said, "Damon, I've got to hang up, there's some kind of a disturbance outside."

"Who are they this time?"

"The usual - that pest Christine Lincoln and her crowd of religious whackos. Didn't you say you knew her?" When Baatard didn't reply right away, Denny said, "Good bye, Damon, and good luck with Mrs. Ramirez."

"Mrs. Ramirez? What do you mean?"

"You sounded interested in the possibilities as I presented them, as I expected you to be, so I took the liberty of arranging an introductory meeting for her."

"When?" Baatard exclaimed, as he grabbed for his appointment list.

"Don't look on your appointment list, Damon, because you won't see her there. I took the liberty of calling Sharlene and arranging for it myself." After more loud noise on the phone, Denny said, "Look, I've got to go now. Good luck, and call me to let me know how it went, okay? And be good, be your best, because this is important to me, to us. Good luck."

The Surrogate

Baatard instantly felt unsure of whatever Denny was proposing, and the fact that he actually knew almost nothing of what it was that she was proposing, nor did he have even the barest inkling of what Denny had told or promised or obligated to Judge Lydia Ramirez. His hands shook as he put the phone down, and he felt trapped, nervous, threatened, compromised, abandoned, as if all that he had accomplished and all he had worked for and looked forward to his entire life was somehow being threatened. Still reeling from Denny's call, Sharlene knocked at his door, and said, in a skeptical voice, "I guess you know about your unscheduled case."

"Yes, surprise, surprise," he grumbled as he got up from his desk and walked over to her.

"I know what you mean, but what could I do when Denny called? Besides, you do have sort of an open time slot. Someone canceled." Seeing that Baatard was offering no resistance, she said, "Well, at least she's private pay. Anyway, Mrs. Ramirez is here. Do you want me to sign her in, and take the basic info?" she asked in a low voice.

"I guess," he said, unenthusiastically.

Sharlene opened the door and moved forward to take up the few inches left between the front of her sheer, cream colored linen blouse and his arm. Baatard was quickly overwhelmed by the cigarette odor which constantly surrounded Sharlene like a cloud of air pollution. He had not been able to break her of the habit, and now had to move back a few inches from her to breathe. Several times in the past he had found her minimally interesting and even somewhat attractive, at least enough for a momentary fling now and then. She was, though, simply a diversion from the other women he was currently dating. He never thought of such divergence as disloyalty, but rather harmless recreation which actually reinforced his appreciation of his steadies. Despite that, it was difficult replying to Sharlene's constant flirting, since "making it" with her was akin to kissing an ashtray, and often was just as exciting.

Sharlene nodded her head toward the waiting room, occupied only with a well-dressed woman sitting alone, but said nothing.

Baatard thought about the 'add-on' briefly, then told Sharlene, "Sure, take care of the preliminaries, and I'll see her then." From a distance, Ramirez looked more like a drug company representative or an insurance agent than a family court judge, and his stomach made a growling sound.

Sharlene left, but returned only a few minutes later, and Baatard took the new patient record Sharlene had handed him, and started paging through. "But, the new patient chart is totally empty," Baatard complained, handing it back to Sharlene. "It looks like no pre-visit screening interview was done."

"Nope, none. I gave Mrs. Ramirez the introductory packet, but she just handed it back and said she didn't fill in questionnaires. I wasn't going to insist she do anything," Sharlene told Baatard, shaking her head. "The way she spoke to me, the way she looked at me, it made me real anxious."

Baatard nodded understandingly, having been well-acquainted with exactly that feeling around attorneys.

"Anyway, she 'informed' me that she's not accustomed to being kept waiting, that she's a very busy lady, and she's expecting to be brought back immediately," Sharlene said mockingly.

"Yeah," Baatard said, caught up in some thoughts. "I'll bet she's got a wad of crisp one hundred dollar bills stuffed in her purse right now. You can't trace those," he quipped. "Look, I'll be in my office finishing up my charts from the last few patients. Just bring Mrs. Ramirez in when you're ready. And let me know what the surgeons say after they look at Ms. Bonnaserra."

"By the way," Sharlene reported, "Deanna called over and said to tell you Bonnaserra still has a good blood pressure, and she's starting to wake up."

"That's good," Baatard said, relieved. He was confident that he couldn't have caused more than a minor nick to a small blood vessel during the ova harvesting, and was confident Marina would recover. This same complication had happened a few times before, and was not uncommon for him or for his colleagues in the community. Besides, it was really Marina's fault that she bled, Baatard rationalized.

Walking out for a moment to the lab area, Baatard poured some coffee from the old stained plastic brewer, then liberally sprinkled on some powdered creamer. Some of the powder fell on the table top, and Baatard brushed it off onto the floor. Rather than sinking down into the coffee and dissolving, the powdered creamer in his cup formed a layer of floating white scum on top, and, disgusted, Baatard put a finger in the coffee and confirmed his suspicion. "Sharlene, the goddamn coffee is colder than a witch's tit in winter." He angrily poured the unappetizing cold liquid suspension down the drain, being careful not to spill any more coffee on his white coat.

Sharlene stuck her head out of the reception area into the hallway, a look of embarrassment on her face. "Dr. Baatard. Watch your language, please."

Baatard smiled innocently at her, then walked back down the hall to his office, to meet Ramirez.

A few minutes later, there was one light knock at Baatard's office door. Sharlene pushed the partially open door inward, handed a new patient chart to Baatard, and motioned for Mrs. Ramirez to enter.

Baatard figured Ramirez looked to be a youthful thirty-five, with stylishly trimmed black hair, and decorated like a Christmas tree in a lavish amount of expensive-appearing jewelry. Her pleasingly athletic body was probably more muscular than fat, and appeared somewhat disproportionately top heavy. Her face was heavily made up, in an attempt to disguise years of stress which led to premature aging.

Ramirez extended her well-manicured hand as she slowly strolled into Baatard's office, and Baatard offered her a seat in the swivel leather chair in front and to the right of his desk. The pervasive scent of expensive perfume followed her in.

"Hello, how are you," Baatard asked, extending his hand. "I'm Dr. Damon Baatard."

Ramirez smiled coolly, and said, "Yes, I know." She coughed lightly into her hand, and said, "Thanks for seeing me without an advance appointment." Her chest had a soft rumbling sound to it as she spoke, as if fighting a case of pneumonia. Her eyes fixated cat-like upon Baatard's, cutting like a laser through Baatard's facade right to the soul, as if sizing him up for doing a special favor.

"Not at all. Not everything in life can be scheduled in advance." Baatard was sure that Ramirez did in fact schedule everything in advance, and wondered why, or if, her visit here today might be different. Pregnancy usually didn't need to be rushed. "Now, how may I help you?" he asked, after sitting back down.

"Well, recently I had the, uh, pleasure of, uh, attending a private forum on *in vitro* fertilization. I want so much to have children," she paused, "under the right circumstances, of course. You know?"

Baatard concentrated on Ramirez's speech, her particular accent, which so contrasted her appearance that, although comparatively subtle, actually seemed to get in the way. He also instinctively knew immediately that he didn't trust anything Ramirez said to him. Everyone who entered his office wanted something from him; usually he knew what it was. This time though, Baatard wasn't sure at all, and that bothered him, made him suspicious.

"You were, I believe, described as a founding

physician at The Foundation, and Denny was kind enough to arrange for a private meeting with you," Ramirez calmly explained.

"Yes, that's correct." He noticed Ramirez methodically look at each of his medical certificates on the walls and at the photos on his table. Ramirez stared curiously at the plastic anatomical models of the female genitalia and the fetus at various developmental stages, each arranged neatly on top of the book case, and Baatard felt uneasy at being so openly examined. Ramirez gave him the feeling that he was being sized up as a person in addition to being certified as a physician, and that important facts about his personal life were being compiled for some obscure purpose.

"You got a lot of degrees, Dr. Baatard. That must have taken a lot of years in school."

"Yes, it does take a lot of time to acquire all this training, but it's necessary. But let's get back to your visit today." Baatard sat up straight in his chair and tried to look as serious and professional as possible. Looking at the blank chart Sharlene had handed him, Baatard asked, "My receptionist tells me you haven't yet filled out the patient information questionnaire. We need that done before we can proceed." Ramirez looked slightly annoyed. "It gives us a lot of information we need to understand your problems," Baatard smiled, trying to sound helpful. "The usual procedure is to fill out the information form, and . . . "

"Yes, well I, uh, do understand how it was supposed to work, Dr. Baatard, you know?" Ramirez leaned back in the chair, causing it to squeak. "But, I'm afraid the usual way may not at all do here," she replied coyly.

Baatard shrugged his shoulders, then asked, "Oh, how is it that the usual way for patients to enter my obstetrical practice isn't suitable to you?" Baatard leaned forward slightly, flicking on the silent "record" button by his desk side.

"No recorders, please, Dr. Baatard. I'm much too shy," Ramirez smiled again. She leaned forward, rested her palms on Baatard's desk top, and grinned menacingly.

"Of course. One can never be too careful," Baatard stammered, taken completely aback. He was truly astounded; almost no one knew of the recorder.

"Too careful of what? I'm afraid that I don't understand."

"Uh, no, no. It's nothing, nothing at all, really," Baatard said, struggling not to sound nervous, although he already knew he had failed miserably at that. "So, I assume that you have been trying to have children and have been unsuccessful." Baatard briskly waved his hands in the air as he said "trying," and studiously watched Ramirez's face. He saw only annoyance.

"Yeah, we been trying all right," she stated, sounding more like an admittance, an unpleasant look appearing on her face as she sat back from the desk. When she crossed one leg over the other, her dress rode up, revealing much of one thigh, enclosed in black nylon, and she made no effort to readjust.

"Well, have you seen another physician about this fertility problem before?"

"Yes," Ramirez replied, "you could say that."

Baatard always found an affirmative response to this last question a bad prognostic indicator. "And have you and your husband already had the usual, extensive workups?"

"That is correct." Ramirez lazily stretched her arms straight out in front of her, re-crossed her legs, and yawned. "Dr. Baatard, will this take much longer? I have an appointment with my personal trainer soon, and a big case to hear later today."

"The initial visit does take about an hour, I'm afraid." Baatard had never been put in such a strange, uncomfortable situation before, and swore that he wouldn't allow this to happen again. Ramirez possessed one of those uniquely grating personalities which immediately turned him off.

"As you wish," Ramirez replied as she stared directly at Baatard's forehead -- Baatard could almost feel its penetrating intensity, "although I think your efforts will be a waste of your time and my time. I've already been completely and extensively evaluated, to no end, I'm afraid."

"And what was found?"

"I have what are called poly, uh, poly . . . "

"Polycystic ovaries?" Baatard interjected, helpfully.

It was starting to come together now.

"Yeah, that's it. I've got them - polycystic ovaries. At least I had."

"So they got better, or the cysts were surgically removed?"

"Hell no," Ramirez said, slamming her palm onto the desktop. "They removed my ovaries. Both of them."

"Oh, I'm so sorry. That operation must have been very stressful for you," Baatard replied, seeing more clearly the extent of her problem.

"You bet it was," Ramirez said. "I got it done before I was married, and, like the marriage, I still have the scars from the surgery."

He simply nodded, then asked, "Did they remove your uterus also?"

Ramirez hesitated for a moment before answering, "I don't think so. My last doctor said that she saw it on an exam with that pricey ultrasound machine all you doctors like so much. And I know I've definitely got a vagina," she smiled.

"That's good. Without a uterus, you realize, a pregnancy would be difficult, but not impossible. We can use hormone injections to create an artificial hormone cycle and support a fertilized ova's implantation and development, but we can't simulate a uterus. At least not yet, with current technology."

"Now, I'm on all these hormone replacements. Can you believe it? A young, good-looking woman like me, on hormone treatments." she exclaimed.

Baatard tried to nod understandingly. All he wanted right now was for this most unusual woman to leave his office and go back to whatever court and whatever gym she wanted to spend her time in.

"Still, I suppose that it was worth all the frustration and medical bills."

"I guess so." Baatard, minimally fascinated by the conversation, tried to at least seem agreeable, "but, I can see that there are going to be several major impediments to achieving a successful pregnancy here, particularly now that you've told me that you have no ovaries, and that your hormone cycle is artificially generated."

Baatard made some additional notes in Ramirez's chart. From Ramirez's last response, Baatard knew that she must have already seen at least one other fertility physician and had an adequate workup, which raised the question of why Ramirez was here today. "I assume that you'll be willing to transfer your medical records from your previous gynecologist?"

"Yeah, sure, sure," Ramirez said, waving her hand in front of her. "Whatever you need, I'll do. Whatever it costs, I'll pay, you know."

Baatard was relieved. That, at least, was a good sign in many respects.

"Well, can you get me pregnant?"

"Possibly. If you want to. But, could you tell me, why you want to become pregnant? I mean, it's really none of . . ."

"Exactly," she cut him off. "Stick to the issues, Dr.

Baatard. Can you or can't you?"

"Possibly," was all he was willing to answer, having learned long ago to not make promises he might not be able to keep. "But, it will be extremely difficult and there can be absolutely NO guarantees. What I'm saying, Mr. Ramirez, is . . . "

"I know what you're getting at, Dr. Baatard. You don't want to be blamed for trying and failing. Hey, I can understand that. If I were you, I'd be a little afraid too, you know?" Ramirez started to laugh again, but it ended up in another wet cough. She almost choked for a minute, then heaved one gigantic retching gag before spitting up something big and wet and yellow into a handkerchief. Finally, Ramirez was able to continue.

Disgusted, Baatard's stomach churned, and he felt a little nauseous.

"But you really don't need to be afraid, you know."

Baatard swallowed hard, and he heard his voice crack as he said, "Thanks for the reassurances. You have been told quite a lot, and you seem to remember technical things quite well."

"I make my living remembering things, Dr. Baatard. I'm a quick study." Ramirez smiled confidently, straightening up a bit in her chair.

"That's good, Mrs. Ramirez," sighed Baatard. "As for your apparent problem, there may be a way we can help with this." Looking a little puzzled, Baatard asked, "Tell me, were you dissatisfied with your previous physician?"

"No, not exactly dissatisfied," she explained, then looked right into Baatard's eyes as she said, "Let's just say, Dr. Baatard, she was not able to give me what I needed, and I'm accustomed to getting exactly what I need, exactly what I want, and exactly when I want it. So, with Denny's enthusiastic recommendation, I changed to you. But there was no legal action, if that's what you mean."

"Good," Baatard smiled. He briefly considered whether Mrs. Ramirez's previous doctor was even alive.

"I knew when I listened to the seminar at Denny's home that YOU would be able to give me what I need," Ramirez flashed a mean jack 'o' lantern grin as she anxiously leaned toward Baatard.

"Well, I'll certainly try. I hope that I can help." He began to wonder what exactly it was that the previous doctor had been unable to do for Ramirez/Infertility workups were so cookbook, the available options so limited, and his own approach might not be terribly different. In this case, did that mean he also wouldn't be able to give Ramirez 'what she wanted' either?

"I, we want a child very much, but not just any child, Dr. Baatard. If we are going to go through all this hell again, not to mention expense, we want to get a smart kid. I want a boy, and he better be healthy," Ramirez replied, menacingly. "You know what I mean?"

"Of course, Mrs. Ramirez, of course, everyone wants those things in every child. And, with good genes and careful in uteri screening, we can help assure quite a lot these days." At least she isn't asking me to do anything illegal or unethical, Baatard thought. Yet.

"I know, Dr. Baatard, I know." Turning toward the window, Ramirez said, "Your usual and customary efforts and assurances are, of course, appreciated."

Baatard smiled. "Good, at least we have an understanding before going into this."

"But that just isn't good enough," Ramirez added. "We want a special child, and I don't want any mistakes."

"Then I'm afraid I still don't quite understand." Baatard felt suddenly hot and closed in. He wished he had left his office door open a bit, and he vowed to immediately get a panic button installed in his desk to call Sharlene or the police or building security.

"Okay, let me spell it out a little more for you," Ramirez said, her voice dripping with annoyance. Ramirez turned back to Baatard, stood up and began to slowly walk behind Baatard's high-back chair.

Baatard nervously looked over his shoulder as Ramirez walked in back of him. The collar on his shirt began to feel unusually tight, and he wondered if Ramirez was going to grab him by the neck and choke him into submission, and he wanted to get the hell out of there now.

"I'm a busy person, a very busy person, you know. And although I suppose on one level I want a child, or, maybe I should say, my husband, who is also my campaign manager – did I mention that I am running for appellate court?" she paused, then continued what seemed more like an internal dialogue than a conversation, "- thinks I should have a child, I really don't have the time or the interest to go through nine months of physical hell, potentially disfiguring my body that I work real hard to maintain in the process."

"I could, if you like, arrange for an adoption," Baatard offered, waving some papers in front of him to clear the air a bit. At least for the moment, Ramirez didn't appear to be planning to grab him, as he sometimes felt that she somehow would. She generated an uneasy feeling in him, he didn't know just why, exactly, but she did.

"I really prefer not to have an adoption, Dr. Baatard," Ramirez snapped. "I want this to be truly my own child, not adopted. It's has to be my child, Baatard. Got it?"

"But, without ovaries, you realize, don't you, that's impossible." He was suddenly fearful that no matter how hard he tried, he could never satisfy Ramirez. He wasn't God and he couldn't just create ovaries after they were surgically removed.

"Yeah, I know that."

"That is, unless you happen to have some of your ova stored before your ovaries were removed."

"Hey, nice try, but I don't think so."

Baatard's heart sank.

"But, there's another part of the story I didn't tell you about yet. And don't you dare tell anyone about this," Ramirez warned him, "or," Ramirez started to say, then stopped, instead giving Baatard a blood-curdling stare.

Baatard's face visibly paled. He had heard rumors about town of the vicious Ramirez family, their political connections, the implied ties to drug money, and he considered making a dash for the door. It was only Ramirez's strong hand holding his shoulder down kept him in the chair.

"Hey, it was just a figure of speech," she smiled. "Don't get nervous. Okay?"

Baatard now knew he should have listened to Sharlene and not taken the case. Once you start, it's much harder to stop, especially with something like this. This vicious woman, a criminal who judged criminals, scared the shit out of him.

"When I was younger, before I was married, I got a bad case of Chlamydia, and I ended up with scars on my tubes, and so now I can't have kids. All because of some idiot kid."

"I thought you had polycystic ovaries," Baatard asked, trying not to cringe in his seat. He knew there was nowhere to hide, and only wanted the interview over with as soon as possible.

"Yeah," she wearily admitted, "I've got that too, I'm afraid. I got problems with both my ovaries and my tubes; I'm afraid I'm falling apart, right?"

Baatard started to say some things to reassure her, but Ramirez coughed up another clot of yellow phlegm into a handkerchief, and followed that up with a long, noisy, disgusting wet blow of her nose before he could continue. "Doctors are trained to ask questions, Mrs. Ramirez, that's all." Baatard wondered if the less he knew, the better off he would be. For a moment, he actually fantasized that he might simply stick someone else's fertilized ova into Mrs. Ramirez and be done with it. Who would know, anyway?

Yet, he would know, and he knew that to do so was immoral, illegal and highly unlikely to pull off, anyway, and the thought was quickly banished from his consciousness. He had never successfully gotten away with anything illegal in his life, and the few times he had tried had turned out to be complete disasters that he remembered and regretted to this day.

"Well, in my line of business, asking too many questions can be bad for your health," she laughed, a nervous, quiet chuckle.

Baatard tried to laugh too, but couldn't.

"I see what you mean, but without an ovary or stored ova, I just don't see how I can help you."

Ramirez was unprepared for Baatard's verdict, and leaning toward him, she calmly said, "I want a child, I want a child, I want a child. I don't know any other way to tell you what I want, and I don't understand what it is you don't seem to understand. Denny Cruite seemed to think that you could do this service for me, or I certainly wouldn't have bothered to come here, but make no mistake about it, I WANT A CHILD AND I WILL GET A CHILD, NO MATTER WHAT. Now, you can do this service for me, or someone else can, and I suggest that you give a great deal of thought to what your failure to perform will mean for the both of us."

"But, but, but . . ."

"And on paper the child's got to be from me and my

husband. You know what I mean, Dr. Baatard?"

"But, like I said, unless you have ova harvested and frozen before your ovaries were removed . . . "

Now, since I apparently haven't any ova, I suggest that you find some, you fertilize it with sperm from my husband, and you either implant it into me, or into someone else. Got it? But understand this; even if it's another woman's body that's held the kid, on paper it's got to be from me and my husband." Ramirez grasped Baatard's hands, then dropped them and took hold of Baatard's shoulders, smiled in a threatening way and winked, "Money is no object here, know what I mean, Dr. Baatard?"

Baatard tried to move away from Ramirez's strong grasp, but was nearly shoved back down into his chair. "Well, the child certainly can be from your husband, assuming he can supply sperm. About locating an oval donor, well . . ."

"Denny Cruite specifically told me that would be no problem, so if you think it is, then perhaps you better talk to her," Ramirez told him, dryly.

Baatard cursed Denny for committing him to anything without speaking to him first.

"Look, Dr. Baatard, this is going to cost a bundle of money, right? I know that, I'm not stupid. That doesn't worry me, okay? I mean, money's no problem here. I don't care how you get it done, just do it and don't tell me about it. Okay?"

From that point on, there was little more that needed to be said. Baatard and Mrs. Ramirez did talk a little longer, trying to come to a complete understanding on all the details. Baatard mentioned that he would need to perform a pre-implantation history and physical on her, and asked her to arrange for that, and Mrs. Ramirez made some vague promises to that effect, although she seemed not at all enthusiastic about undergoing implantation.

A half hour later, Baatard escorted a visibly upset Mrs. Ramirez from his office. Turning to shake hands, Baatard smiled weakly and said, "This was an interesting and most unusual meeting, Mrs. Ramirez. Let's both think about it a little, and I'll get back to you. Okay?"

Ramirez started to say something, then huffed, turned and walked out.

Baatard asked Sharlene to have Mrs. Ramirez sign a release to transfer her medical records from her previous gynecologist.

After Ramirez walked out the door, Baatard shook nervously, "What a goddamn weirdo." He had managed to get through perhaps the toughest interview of his professional career, and still managed not to promise to do anything illegal or unethical. He was angry and disappointed at Denny, though, for committing him to perform any fertility service. Still, as he thought about what Ramirez and Denny were proposing, he realized his consent was never really required, only his actions.

Chapter 14

"There's a woman here to see you, Ms. Cruite," Denny
Cruite's secretary buzzed on the intercom, then whispered,
"And she's not very happy.".

"Shit, can't I be left alone for one goddamn minute to
get anything done," Denny muttered to herself. Her
secretary's voice sounded preoccupied and distant, and
the difference caught her attention. Looking over at her
appointment calendar, she said, "I'm not scheduled to see
anyone. Who is it?"

"A Mrs. Ramirez."

Denny choked, then nearly spilled her cup of coffee
as she put it down. "Tell me it isn't the same lady that was
just in here, please."

"I'm afraid it's the very one."

Denny vividly recalled speaking with Ramirez less
than two hours ago, and had really thought that their
conversation had gone well.

"She knows she hasn't made an appointment, but
wonders if you could . . . Hey, what are you . . . "

A woman's voice came on the intercom. "Hello,
Denny. I hope you got time to see a paying customer."

Ramirez elbowed herself into Denny's office, and
took a chair in front of her desk. Denny's secretary
popped her embarrassed face into the door, apologized,
then quickly left.

"Hey, Denny, you don't look too happy to see me. How come?" Ramirez asked, with no attempt to hide her insincerity.

"I'm just surprised to see you, that's all," Denny stammered. "What can I do for you?" She anxiously looked over at her office door, which her secretary had closed when she left. That was the custom, but now Denny wished it had been left open, even a little open.

"I just came from Dr. Baatard's office," she frowned.

"Yes, and did you find the visit helpful?"

"Not really. He seemed to be totally unaware of our conversation. Didn't you call him while I was on my way over, as you had promised?"

"Yes, no, but . . ."

"Well, that explains why he seemed so surprised. I would be too under similar circumstances," she glared at Denny, "especially when people don't keep their promise to me. I don't like that."

"You are interested in assisted pregnancy, and we will provide it, Mrs. Ramirez," Denny insisted confidently. She tried to return the conversation to establishing his purpose for her initially being here, unwelcome and forced as it was. I'm quite sure there won't be a problem with you receiving medical care through The Foundation and one of its participating physicians. Let me speak with Dr. Baatard. Maybe I can help allay your fears."

Ramirez said, "Good. That's what I thought you might say. I show my thanks in many ways, and my wrath too."

Denny quickly got up to escort Mrs. Ramirez from her office door, again almost knocking over the cup of coffee sitting on her desk in the process. "Let me speak with Dr. Baatard. I'm sure there was just a simple misunderstanding and there's really no problem. You'll be hearing from me," she nervously smiled. Once Ramirez left, Denny sat staring at her closed office door for several minutes, trying to cool down, wondering just what had gone wrong between Ramirez and Baatard and what she was going to do now.

Chapter 15

Haven Fertility Associates, P.C.
Haven, New Jersey

Within a half-hour after Lydia Ramirez left his office,
Sharlene's grating smoker's voice sounded on the
intercom. "Dr. Baatard? Ms. Cruite is on the phone."

Baatard looked at the phone for a moment before
answering it. Denny Cruite almost never called him at the
office, even though their business practices had become
so intimately linked. She never called, that was, unless
there was a problem, and somehow he already knew it
would be Ramirez.

"Hello, Denny. I must say this is a surprise." Baatard
almost said that her call was a pleasant surprise, but
couldn't bring himself to lie so early in the day. He, like
many others at The Foundation, referred to Denny as The
Dragon Lady, and limited their contact with her to
business only.

"Why?" Denny asked, coughing deeply.

"Well, it's just that I didn't expect to hear from you
today. Business meetings with The Foundation usually are

reserved for Thursdays, and you rarely call me at the clinic otherwise," he nervously chuckled.

"Damon, I want to get right to the point. I just had a visit from Mrs. Ramirez."

Baatard couldn't believe what he was hearing. Wasn't Ramirez just in his office? Hadn't they just discussed her particular needs at length, and even come to some sort of preliminary agreement? His mind flooded with explanations - none of them good. Had he offended Ramirez? Had he not been clear on the limited confidence he had in the restricted options he could offer that bizarre, self-centered woman?

"What a coincidence." Baatard told Denny, trying to sound surprised but not perturbed. "You know, I just had a visit with her also. Isn't she a weird bird?" The beginnings of another chuckle died before leaving his lips and a feeling of impending doom shrouded the conversation - a dark, foreboding and deadly sensation.

"She's a vulture, Damon, and vultures eat dead meat, if you know what I mean, but I'm afraid that that's entirely beside the point."

Baatard started to reply, then held back. He had nothing to say. He tried to swallow hard, but his mouth was too dry.

"And she's somehow disappointed with a meeting she just had with you, and that's just not good. Damon, what happened between you two?"

For the first time, empathy and concern were detectable in her voice, and Baatard wondered if it was it transference from her own worries, or his?

"Nothing, really. You say she's disappointed? But I

thought the meeting went well, considering. Look, let me say for the record before we start here: I'm a professional."

"Of course you are, Damon."

"I won't let some pushy woman attorney dictate medical procedures to me, and neither should you. Got it?" Baatard felt truly intimidated for the first time in years, even though he had yet to be formally threatened, and he didn't like the feeling at all.

"You must be out of your goddamn mind, Damon. You don't know who you're crossing here, believe me. I think you better tell me everything that happened at this little meeting between the two of you."

"I'd be happy to. Mrs. Ramirez discussed the cause of her infertility problem, and her desire to have a child. She said she had polycystic ovaries, and that they were surgically removed, both of them. Then she told me she was evaluated by some other infertility doctor, unnamed, and that person couldn't give her 'what she wanted'."

"And just what was it that she wanted from you, Damon, that was so unusual or difficult? The woman apparently had no ovaries, so your options were fairly limited, I'd say."

"That's just it, Denny. Although Ramirez never actually said what she wanted me to do, I think she wants to use her husband's sperm on some donor ova and use these to impregnate either her or a surrogate. Look,

Denny, I'm a doctor, not a psychic, and I can't read that
woman's mind." Baatard waited for several seconds for
Denny to say something, anything, but all he heard was an
amazingly calm, agreeing, 'Uh huh.' Baatard was
appalled, now realizing that Denny and Ramirez
apparently were coming from the same place. He had very
little room to move. If Denny was in agreement, Baatard
reasoned, then perhaps she could at least be relied on for
another kind of help. Perhaps Denny was already
anticipating what Baatard could ask next, or was waiting
to volunteer it, and he quickly tried to turn the
conversation around. "Can you believe it? Where the hell
does Ramirez want me to get donor ova?" Baatard already
knew.

"Sounds good to me. What she's asking for isn't so
strange, Damon. We have ova available for donation,"
Denny calmly told him, too controlled and calm.

That was, after all, correct, Baatard thought. Despite
the specter of working with such an abrasive character, all
Baatard was being asked to do at least seemed legal and
ethical. She was, after all, not just a lawyer, but a judge.
He still was uncomfortable, but began to feel less tense,
particularly with the Foundation's Director seeming to go
along with it. Legal IVF assistance was something he
could do for Ramirez, and he wasn't being asked to do
anything else. At least not yet. Baatard knew that he
would have to maintain his vigilance, to protect himself
from unsuspecting requests. Not everyone was as honest
or ethical as he perceived himself to be.

"It's been done before," Denny continued, her voice
an annoying monotone whine. "You know that. All you

have to do is find a woman who has frozen ova stored with The Foundation, ova she has no intention of using. Then you make her an offer. It's a simple donation deal. What's the problem this time, Damon?"

"Nothing, I guess," he said reflectively, thinking how uncomfortable he had felt when Ramirez walked behind his chair and held onto his shoulders. "It's just that I don't like the woman. She gives me the creeps, and I'm surprised you don't dislike Ramirez either. I simply don't trust the woman, and I really think there's something else here up her sleeve." Denny was right, though. The Foundation had performed such ova donations before, albeit in reverse. It was in many ways akin to sperm donation, and yet, it wasn't. The ethics were much more complicated, and the legal issues of parentage were not well-developed at all, and therefore Baatard tended to stay away from such messy issues.

"I really don't think you can know my opinion of Judge Ramirez. Whether I like or dislike her isn't your concern, nor is it relevant to the infertility business at hand," she coolly stated. "Look, Damon. We've got ova, plenty of ova. And I want to go ahead on this; there's really no reason not to treat her as we would any other client. I think it's best for both of us, and for The Foundation, don't you agree?"

"Denny, are you letting this pushy judge to dictate medical procedures to you? You need to be very careful

with anything you agree to with this person, believe me."
He could only begin to imagine the public relations and
legal repercussions if this ever got out.

"No, not at all, Damon," Denny laughed. "And don't
characterize Judge Ramirez as a pushy broad, please."

"First of all, I didn't, but why not? Isn't that what she
is?" Denny seemed so stupid and naive at times, and at
others, so goddamn crooked herself.

"I've got no way of knowing that, Damon. As far as
I'm concerned, Mrs. Ramirez, I mean Judge Ramirez is a
client who's going to be referred to as a patient, hopefully
your patient. It's worth a lot to both of us."

"Exactly how much could this be worth, Denny?"

"Try fifty thousand for you, complete, no billing, no
deductible," she said, running her palms against each
other. She smiled to herself when she considered her own
cut, which was much more substantial. But then again,
she did most of the work. Baatard could never have
attracted this type of client on his own. He was a
competent doc, but this took a different skill class
altogether.

Baatard gasped. "Fifty thousand? You sure?"

"Absolutely. And let me put it to you another way. If
you won't agree to participate, I've got other infertility
specialists who will, and that person will get the hundred
thousand. That will take care of my problem . . . "

"Your problem?" Baatard interrupted. Now he
definitely didn't like the tone of her voice, and what she
was implying.

"Yeah, my problem. I KNOW that I have to satisfy
Ramirez, and I want to. I want the money, and you should

too. It's not illegal, it's not drug money, so what's the problem? You too damn rich?"

"No, but . . ."

"But nothing, Damon. Do you have any idea exactly how much we can bill for services like this? Do you? And the fame, and the referrals. There are a lot of Lydia Ramirez out there, and I know some of them already have been making inquiries. God, just thinking about it makes me excited." She smiled, and uttered a deep, sexual groan.

"Money, money, money. That's all you ever think about."

"You've certainly never complained about the money before, Damon. Maybe you haven't realized that yet, but your problem will be if I have another of the Conceptions Foundation physicians take care of Lydia without you." Denny Cruite listened for a complaint from Baatard, but he was tellingly silent.

"Now, Damon, if I were you, I'd get hold of some suitable ova really fast. This isn't rocket science here. I'd fertilize those goddamn ova with some good sperm, implant them into Mrs. Ramirez or whomever the hell else Ramirez wants to use, and get it over with. You can piss her off on your own time, but don't involve me. I got enough problems of my own."

Baatard was momentarily dumbfounded, and unable to reply. He had a gut feeling that something bad was going to happen, both in the procedure he was being asked to perform, and to him. Once again, he wished he had never seen Ramirez. Why him, he asked, looking forlornly up at the ceiling?

"By the way, how did Marina Bonnaserra's procedure work out?" Denny asked.

"There were some minor complications, but I think she'll be okay. Why?" He had noticed before that Denny seemed unusually interested in Marina Bonnaserra, although so very little distinguished Marina from any of the hundreds of other IVF clients. Baatard wondered if perhaps any of their clients, current or potential, had expressed concern to Denny about Marina's bleeding. After all, it wasn't that atypical an occurrence and it did resolve without leaving any permanent injury.

"Minor complications?" Denny almost laughed, before wheezing loudly. "Hey, that's not what I heard. Look, Damon, I want you to keep me informed on her progress. Understand?"

"Yes, although discussing a patient's progress is confidential information. Why the sudden interest in this one particular patient, Denny. You've never inquired about the outcomes of complications before."

"It's just good management practice to keep your ear close to the ground, so to speak. She's a pretty woman, Damon, and talented too. I'm sure her husband must be very proud."

"She's not married, Denny," Baatard explained.

After a short pause, Denny started to ask, "Oh. Then, how did she, how did you . . .?"

"She's using our sperm bank."

"Oh, now isn't that interesting." Denny paused in

thought for a moment before continuing. "Anyway, I want you to keep me informed of her progress, okay? And Damon, I wanted to tell you that I really enjoyed your presentation on the Intelligence Genetic complex that you gave at the hospital a few days ago. Your research is fascinating." Baatard nodded acknowledgment at the comment. "How do you even have the time to think about something that complex and theoretical, let alone actually do any research?"

He remembered how surprised he felt when Denny showed up at the combined Obstetrics-Gynecology, Internal Medicine and Human Genetics conference. She had never expressed anything more than a passing interest in this subject before, and usually directed all her energies to money-making activities. "Thanks for your compliment. Yes, human genetics is complex, but most often of little practical, immediate use. In the case of the IGC, though, things may end up being quite different. I wouldn't term this finding theoretical at all. In fact, I'm rather convinced that the IGC both exists and can be selected for."

"Really, selected for. That's truly remarkable, Damon. Selecting people for intelligence, why, that's almost like Brave New World, or the Nazis."

"The ethics of science is neutral, Denny. It's how you use it that makes all the difference. Take atomic energy, for example. When put to good use it can supply electrica¹ energy to an entire city, or harnessed to destroy a cancer, but when used as a weapon, its destruction knows almost no bounds." Although he still publicly proclaimed that science was inherently neither good nor bad, privately, he was no longer convinced. Certain concepts and objects of nature were by their very nature dangerous and best left alone.

The second phone line rang, and he put Denny on hold while he answered. Sharlene would have gotten it, and by ringing him meant that he should pick it up. "Dr. Quinnan's on the line," Sharlene called back. "Can you take it?"

Events were simply occurring too fast for him to absorb and deal with. "Yes, sure. I can speak with him now." I hope so, Baatard thought. He switched back to Denny, assured her that he was only interested in cooperating, and promised to call her right back. Then, after the appropriate clickings of call transfers, Quinnan got connected. Damon Baatard suspected what Quinnan wanted; he rarely called for other than patient-related reasons.

"Heh, heh, heh. I saved your ass again, Baatard," Quinnan growled into the phone. "The bleeding has stopped on the Bonnaserra case, at least for now."

"Thanks for calling me, Quinnan. That's good news." With all the problems concerning Ramirez, Baatard had not placed as much effort in following this patient who developed a complication as he usually would. He was glad that the surgical consultation had been completed. "I was worried about her," Baatard lied, as he saw his reflection of relief in the office window. "What did you find when you explored Bonnaserra's peritoneal area?"

"I didn't need to. Pay attention, Baatard. The bleeding stopped on its own. There was no need to operate, heh, heh, heh."

Baatard, finding Quinnan particularly obnoxious today, replied, "Well then, don't claim any credit for doing nothing. I could have done that. Okay?" Baatard tried to imitate Quinnan's irritating voice, but knew he wasn't giving it justice.

"What's that? Do nothing? Yeah, you could have done that, all right. Your patient would have been far better off, too."

"Very funny, Quinnan. You know that's not what I meant." He hated it when other physicians - let alone 'lower' health care personnel - were critical of him.

"Do you really think you could have handled the bleed, Baatard? I don't, heh, heh, heh. Look, Baatard, here's a piece of advice. Don't do something you can't undo. Okay? I don't deliver pizzas, and Luigi's across the street doesn't do general surgery. Get my point, Baatard?"

"Yeah, I get the message." It was a stupid analogy that was well overused and overdone.

"Baatard, do you want me to discharge this Ms. Bonnaserra, or do you want to?"

"Actually, I might as well keep her there. Later today I can do the embryo transfer we've been planning, and she can then be discharged tomorrow. Besides, I think she lives alone; the extra day of rest will be good for her."

"That's fine with me, Baatard," Quinnan said with a coarse laugh. "It means less work for the old Quinnan, you know. I have just one request, though. Don't perform any more invasive procedures on this patient for several weeks, Baatard, eh. We wouldn't want any more bleeding, now, would we? And Baatard," Quinnan asked.

"Yeah?"

"Thanks for this interesting consult. And, have a nice day. Heh, heh, heh," he jabbed.

Baatard could almost feel the sarcasm as he heard another gruff laugh on Quinnan's end. He slammed the receiver down on the desk, and thought, That's the last time I use that critical SOB for a consult.

Almost as soon as the phone was down, it rang again, intruding once again on any attempt Baatard might have made to do anything else besides having painful conversations. Shit, Baatard thought, now what?

"The Radiology Department at Haven General wants to talk to you. Can you take it?" Sharlene asked.

"Yeah, put them through." Calls from Radiology were always business only, almost always important, and had to be taken.

"Dr. Baatard, this is Dr. Fillipo-Mendez," the caller said. "I'm calling you about that pelvic ultrasound on Lissa Vernor."

"Okay, sure. What did you find?" Baatard tried to focus his thoughts back on Lissa Vernor, her unexpected bleeding, the unsuccessful surgery, and the reasons for his ordering a post-operative ultrasound exam of her abdomen.

"There's a lot of fluid buildup in her pelvic area, probably from all the bleeding and interstitial fluid shifts. Also, there's a moderate amount of intestinal swelling."

"Right, okay," Baatard commented. That was not unexpected. The intestinal swelling might indicate dysmotility, or worse yet, ischemia. "Did you see the ovaries?"

"Yes we did. They're both there, and of normal size," Dr. Fillipo-Mendez said.

"Were there any ovarian follicles or tubular swelling?" Baatard asked, interested in any signs of a pregnancy.

"No, didn't see any evidence of that either," Dr. Fillipo-Mendez said. "And, I know you were interested in the uterus. We got a good shot of that too. Everything looked okay to me. I saw no abnormalities, and also no gestation sack."

"Nice job. Thanks, Dr. Fillipo-Mendez," Baatard said, then quickly hung up. He was upset that Lissa Vernor's surgery had not gone as expected, but, bad outcomes happened; he had some and his colleagues certainly did too. It was part of being an obstetrician and a gynecologist. He also had a hard time taking the blame for the outcome of a disaster that may have begun before he was even involved with Lissa's care. How true that was in her case, he thought.

His mind, however, was preoccupied with the

troubling Ramirez case and the advice Denny Cruite had just given to him. The question was what he should do? After several long minutes, Baatard asked Sharlene to get Frank Lieu on the line. Once connected, Baatard directed Frank to compile a list of ova that were potentially available for donation, and bring it over to his office ASAP.

Chapter 16

Later that afternoon, Frank knocked on Baatard's door. "I got the list you wanted, Dr. B. We got six sets of ova I know for a fact we aren't going to use." Frank handed the computer printout to Baatard, who carefully read through the names on the database list. Baatard had already asked Frank to obtain a sperm sample from Mr. Ramirez, which he would designate HR-39.

Two of the women with available ova were, coincidentally, also wives of prominent businessmen in the community. Almost certainly they wouldn't be willing to donate their ova to another woman. Those spoiled, socially conscious women just didn't do that type of thing, Baatard considered. Several of the remainder were professionals, some single, some not, and he doubted they would donate either, although he never knew for sure until he asked. But asking could be touchy and he preferred not to. He also suspected that once he disclosed the name of the potential parents, his requests would be refused, no matter how much money Ramirez would put up as an inducement. Anyway, Denny did much better at asking potential female ova donors than he ever could.

Toward the bottom of the list he noticed Lissa Vernor's name. The way things were going for her, it certainly didn't look like she would ever have a need for fertilized ova.

Baatard put the available ova list down on his desktop and turned his chair toward the window. The sky was overcast and gray; probably it would rain later. Maybe it would clear by the time he left much later in the evening, he hoped. Baatard kept thinking about Ramirez, and about his conversation with Denny, and found it hard to concentrate. Well, he thought, the decision here is both simple and obvious.

"Okay, Frank, here's what I want you to do," Baatard finally said after he had finished collecting his thoughts. "When you obtain sperm specimen HR-39, I want you to screen it for potency and viral sterility and genetic stability as you usually do, okay, and then I want you to use HR-39 to fertilize all the LV-1 ova." Frank nodded that he understood, but seemed surprised at the request. "Call me and let me know how it works out. Okay?" Baatard finished.

"HR-39? LV-1? You sure? You got permission?" Frank asked incredulously, still apparently not realizing the details of what was going on.

"Frank, Frank, I appreciate your concern," Baatard said, controlling his anger at his orders being questioned by an underling. "I have all the necessary documents, or at least I will have them by the time you're done. Don't worry, just do what I ask you to do, please. And, for the record, Denny Cruite also knows about this."

As Frank left his office, looking at the list and

mumbling to himself, Baatard had for the first time serious concerns about how much of The Conception Foundation's private affairs Frank was really aware of, and exactly how trustworthy and loyal an employee he might be. They were important concerns, and he was certain that if Denny were even half as cunning as he thought she was, she would be wondering the same, and somehow he knew, Denny would take "appropriate action."

Shortly after the clinic doctors departed the clinic each evening, the nurses finished their charting and other paper work and then left too. The billing clerks usually stayed until 6 p.m., entering their charges and their cash receipts into the office's computerized billing system. Garza, the hired staff's supervisor by seniority, was usually the last to leave each day. After saying goodnight to the billing clerks, Garza, certain she was now alone, began her evening duties before herself finally going home.

Garza first checked that all the electronic equipment was turned off, the doors locked, and the security system turned on. Then she performed a nightly ritual entrusted by the clinic doctors just to her.

Going into each procedure room, Garza methodically collected the biohazard/human waste bags from the medical waste receptacles for disposal. The bags were carefully labeled with biohazard emblems, and contained bloody bandages, disposable scalpels, empty suture packs, and the mangled and discarded 'products of conception.' State and federal rules dictated special handling, and common sense only reinforced that. The young and the poor - frequent clientele for an abortion - were often positive for hepatitis or HIV virus. Then, after a few minutes, Garza took her small collection of waste bags to the back of the clinic. Far against the rear wall of the laboratory area stood an aging floor model freezer unit. Too old for repairs, it would run until it too died, and then would be thrown out with the unwanted trash just like its own contents routinely were. Somewhere toward the back of that freezer, Garza located a white plastic tub. The tub had once been used to hold laundry soap in the utility room of the old wood frame house that Garza shared with several other families. It had a loose-fitting round plastic disk for a cap and a heavy plain wire handle attached firmly into the sides. A red and black biohazard label covered over the soap manufacturer's brand name. Below that was another label, this one indicating the container held human bio-waste. Garza faithfully lined the plastic bucket each night with a fresh, black, plastic tie bag.

The existence of the white plastic bucket and the viewing of its contents were carefully restricted, entrusted by the clinic's directors to Garza alone. Dr. Baatard thought that seeing the culmination of only one day's work, the enormity of what they had done, collected all in one place and at one time, could cause "trouble." More of that both he and the clinic didn't need. Abortion clinics, never popular with society in general and religious groups in particular, were often the site of violent protests by committed people, both pro and con. Just working in one was stressful, and for the staff, could also be dangerous.

Soon, there was a familiar, faint knock on the back emergency exit leading down to the street. Garza didn't need to look at her watch to know who it was. The timing was enough. She took the collection of fetuses, tied the bag and placed it inside a second one, and then opened the back entrance.

Christine Lincoln stood there staring down at the floor, cheeks puffy and eyes swollen from recent crying. "I'm here for my babies," was all she said. Once her routine had become established, it was all she even seemed to say. Garza had tried to speak with her about her actions, woman to woman, on a few occasions but without success. Christine's bizarre stare was enough to squelch all attempt at conversation. Slowly, she reached out and took the bag Garza handed her, just as she had done several times a week for almost five years, and then left just as quietly.

Garza watched Christine leave, then shook her head in pity before closing the door and securing it. Back inside, Garza thought briefly on how many woman she knew who, like Christine Lincoln, had been driven over the edge in one way or another by the abortion experience. There was no resolution, and she herself at times approached that very abyss. Although she had never experienced the abortion of a fetus of her own, her work as a nurse in an abortion clinic left her with a surrogate experience, constantly reinforced. She shook her head sullenly, quickly finished up, then left for home.

Miles away, Christine Lincoln entered her small apartment and locked the door. She put her small plastic bag on the coffee table and turned on a few lights here and there, looking around briefly to be certain she was alone. Light made the emptiness go away. All women had to be cautious these days.

With only three rooms, her apartment was cramped, but neat. The living room had a half sofa, a coffee table and a TV, rarely used. A few books, mostly of a religious nature, lay sideways on a corner unit. The kitchenette had a small refrigerator unit, an electric stove, and assorted appliances. She noticed the answer phone message light was on, but knew there would be plenty of time later for that.

Taking her small plastic bag, Christine went into her bedroom. She saw documentaries of how abortion doctors unceremoniously tossed each wasted fetus into a trash bucket on removal from its mother, and she had seen it herself. The thought made her angry and sad. Each dead baby laying neatly lined up on her small coffee table was the result of one of the clinical abortions performed at the hated Haven abortion mill. At times like this, she had to struggle to not consider the enormity of their, and also her own, unfortunate, tragic actions. Christine thought angrily how Dr. Baatard in particular disgusted her. His uncaring attitude toward his patients, his staff, and toward the very lives he took many times each day was sickening. What Baatard, Garza and the others did for money violated her principles, and made her feel perverted, unclean. They were as dishonest to their chosen profession as she had once been to her own principles.

Garza seemed to understand her, and long ago in their shared empathy decided to give these babies, if not a decent life, than at least a decent burial. If only Garza didn't need the money, she would do something else with her life, Christine rationalized. Perhaps together they could change the fate of all these unborn children, convince the mothers to let their children live, and allow them to be born. Maybe she could even take care of them herself, and be the mother she once could have been, and should be. Her thoughts returned to the orphanage near Haven where she spent her first eight years of life, and she felt faint.

Christine felt the acid returning to her stomach and the tension to her neck as she thought about what tragic fate almost became of this "medical waste." She knew that, were it not for the intervention of her and Garza, in only a few hours a bio-waste dealer would have claimed the day's collection of discarded human tissue. Oh, yes, they would be disposed of 'properly,' she was assured. "Of course they would be," she would reply. Christine suspected this translated into incineration, or maybe something even less respectful to human life. The pain in her head throbbed and pounded incessantly and with increasing fervor, making her wince.

But for now, Christine had something else in mind for the fetuses, something unknown to Baatard, something she felt the clinic's directors would surely disapprove of. But it was an action she needed, for her own sanity, to perform as often as she could. For this was a solemn obligation, a bond, a fulfillment of her obligation to herself and to them. It was also her way of keeping functional and sane.

Christine carefully spread some clean plastic sheets over the top of a wooden table, then whispered, "Come out, little children," as she removed the collection of fetuses from the plastic trash bags taken by Garza from each of the procedure rooms. Today Christine counted seventeen human fetuses total, an average number for the clinic, and a number which probably left none unaccounted. Their gestational ages ranged from four to sixteen weeks, she estimated. They were also of various stages of development and of each sex. Christine usually could tell these facts from a visual examination of the remains. Sometimes that was not possible.

Lighting the stub of a large red candle she had used many times before, Christine placed the candle's base on top of a silver dish. The side of Christine's face glowed eerily in the yellow flicker of candle light as she methodically laid all the fetal remains in a neat row along the center of the table top. Drops of old brown blood stained her hands in several places. The raw scent of uncooked meat filled the air. She caught her strange, almost ghastly reflection in some glass, and turned away.

Each fetus faced Christine on the table top, as best as she could determine. Sometimes she had difficulty when the location of the head was uncertain, but she had developed a system and a ritual for even that unfortunate eventuality. Order was vital.

Finally, all was arranged to her satisfaction. Christine turned to the fetuses, each lying silently in a row. Then, she began to chant a prayer for the dead,
and for the unwanted,
and for the unknown,
and for the forgotten. But not forgotten by her.

Christine closed her eyes and forced herself to shut out her anger at Dr. Baatard and all the foolish, spoiled, uncaring girls who used the clinic today and who so carelessly left a small part of themselves behind. She struggled to fill her heart with love, if only for a little while, and if just for the sake of these unborn innocents now arrayed so peacefully in front of her. Now, those souls were beyond her help, and all she could do was honor their existence. The very idea of treating these babies as trash made Christine choke and she wanted to cry and strike out against the injustice she felt. But Christine contained her rage for now, as she had on countless occasions before. Soon the bucket would be emptied to make room for tomorrow's medical waste. Too soon, the trash man would arrive.

The Surrogate

Chapter 17

Embryology Laboratory

Conceptions Foundation

Haven, New Jersey

Frank Lieu, senior embryology technician at The Conceptions Foundation, still had at least half-a-day's work left to complete before he could even think about leaving. Twenty-nine years old, short and scruffy, Frank had been with The Foundation for the last two and a half years, almost since his arrival in the States. For the last nine hours straight, Frank had been overwhelmed with work in The Foundation's embryology laboratory, working straight through lunch without a break. Just now, the pressure made him feel anxious and nervous and also more than a little annoyed. Frank looked up at the time rushing past on the wall clock, then glanced angrily over at the ten vials of sperm still sitting on the lab bench, waiting to be processed. What the hell did that crazy Dr. Baatard want from him anyway, he kept asking himself?

Frank Lieu had emigrated to the United States three years ago. Six months before that he was graduated from a program in obstetrics and gynecology at Kowloon Hospital. An honors graduate of the Taipei Free University School of Medicine, Frank was conversant in Chinese, English and Japanese, though his knowledge of Japanese he admitted to no one. He had emigrated here with the hope of entering a residency program in Obstetrics and Gynecology in Newark, and then establishing a medical practice somewhere in the US.

Although Frank was a graduate of a respected foreign medical school, he now faced the daunting task of completing an approved three-year residency program in the US. This residency requirement was general policy in the US, and was designed to assure a basic competency of foreign medical graduates who practiced medicine here. Frank also was required to take a two-day long, complicated medical exam called the FLEX - the foreign-trained physician licensing exam - after his three-year residency program was complete and before he could finally practice medicine. Although he resented what he interpreted to be obstructionist, restrictive and racially biased requirements, he realized he had no choice but comply.

Frank's hopes to quickly obtain a medical license were, however, shattered soon after his arrival in America. Somehow he got caught up in a paperwork nightmare worse than his immigration had ever been. Now, he was kept busy just establishing legal residency and completing his work permits. In what spare time he had remaining, he still tried to prepare for the FLEX exam. Unfortunately, each day without direct patient contact left him further away from clinical competency, a reality which bothered him greatly.

The FLEX was not the final barrier - gaining entry into a residency program was -but FLEX was a formidable one regardless. Frank resented taking the exam; he was certain that its only purpose was to keep nonwhites out of the Anglo-dominated medical system. That made him scornful of people like the careless, greedy Dr. Baatard. Frank knew five times, no, ten times more about the intricacies of OB-GYN, and infinitely more about caring for neonates than the disrespectful Baatard. Yet, it was Baatard who now seemed to hold the key to his very future in this country, for Baatard had promised to assist Frank in obtaining one of the highly sought-after, exclusive OB-GYN residencies at Haven General Hospital. It was that promise that kept Frank slaving away in the embryology lab.

Frank shook his head angrily as he strained to keep his mind on the day's work. Grabbing one plastic incubator dish after another, like hamburgers at a fast-food restaurant, Frank rushed through the ova thawing step. Too fast, he was moving way too fast for safety, he worried. This pressured pace made him nervous. Yet, it was the only way, it seemed, for him to keep up with the demands placed on the small IVF lab, which was required to move the innumerable individual fertilizations along as if they were only cars on an assembly line.

All this rushing put Frank in a worse mood than usual, and he was both angry and resentful. Having to hurry always made him that way, and Baatard clearly was at fault. It just seemed to Frank that, no matter how fast he went, there was always more to do. He knew why, too. It was all the advertisements for IVF - they were in the newspapers, on the TV. Frank even got the 'pleasure' of hearing them on the radio as he drove the one and a half hours to work and back to the cramped apartment he shared with his parents and cousins. Each time he heard the advertisements exhorting women to try the benefits of IVF, he could envision the waves of hopeful mothers-to-be, like lost puppy dogs, closing in on the lab where he worked. He imagined them to be like ducks waddling expectantly toward a pond where little children stood with bread crumbs to feed. In anger, Frank slammed closed the sterility door to the incubator, shaking the vials inside.

Late in the afternoon, several administrative employees at Conceptions Foundation had already begun to arrange their affairs for the end of the day. The corridors had that -it's going to be over soon - look, exhibiting more activity from 4:15 to 4:30 than during the rest of the day combined.

Frank had already made certain he was working alone; he disliked having others around when he had to concentrate, and today was definitely one of those high-concentration days. Having others around slowed him down, having to slow under all the work that needed to be done made him nervous, nervousness bred errors, and errors led to embarrassment and recriminations. Besides, he thought, he couldn't stand another screw-up like last week's. Although he was certain the death of an entire week's worth of fertilized ova really wasn't his fault, he was definitely on guard and much more cautious. The work involved in covering the mistake up almost wasn't worth it. Besides, if his supervisors had only been reasonable on how much could be done at any one time, the error certainly wouldn't have happened. Clearly, he thought, the fault wasn't his, but ultimately Baatard's.

Frank verified one more time that the heavy metal door to the lab with its biological sealants lining the sides was secure. Then he started the overhead vent fan on the sterile hood. The hood's electric motors kicked in with a complaining whine, dutifully sucking the lab's air through innumerable microporous filters before being released into the outside atmosphere. The hood, the floor, even the chairs seemed to vibrate from the clean air circulation motors mounted on the roof in separate red metal boxes. These air filter hooded areas allowed the experimental embryology unit to fulfill stringent EPA government requirements. The rules were designed to protect the local populace against pathogens, but Frank couldn't understand what danger fertilized human ova posed; it just wasn't here. What a waste of money, he thought, and money that he should be getting for all this work, and the extra work too.

Satisfied the air circulation systems were active,
Frank switched on the ultraviolet light air sterilizing unit
and activated the chamber interlock. Only a barely visible
deep blue light shown. A low level hum from the
ultraviolet lights now competed in the background with
the sound of the suction motors. The ultraviolet lights
would allow him to move sperm from the storage
chamber over to the ova's tissue culture trays without
danger of contamination. He could then begin the IVF
process for another one of Conceptions Foundation's
innumerable pampered clients.

Frank took hold of an ova donor culture dish with the
initials 'LV-1' on the vial cap. He thought LV probably
represented the ova donor's initials, although he never was
told; he just assumed. Like the sperm donors, an ova
donor's confidentiality was a carefully kept secret. No one
Frank knew of seemed to understand the codes, although
he assumed Baatard did, and he was certain that the
Foundation's miserly director, Denny Cruite, did too.

Frank was already even more upset and in a foul
mood for being rejected again for a date with Sharlene,
the receptionist at Dr. Baatard's office. This made him

have a little more trouble concentrating today than usual. Sharlene had seemed too sensitive yesterday, even for her, and had simply overreacted, in Frank's opinion. She had told Frank he was bothering her and that she "might have to report him." Shit, she was two inches taller than his five foot seven and weighed only about twenty pounds less. What the hell was she so uptight about?

Frank angrily slammed the freezer's heavy metal door closed, imagining it had been Sharlene's tiny head, and then waited for the vapor that formed out of the condensed moisture to clear. "Report me, Shit." Frank muttered in Chinese against all the background noise. Sharlene was Korean, and he should have known better than to ask one of them out. Surely, he thought, she rejected him because Koreans hate the Chinese, probably almost as much as Koreans despise and loath the Japanese. He felt that to be a well-known fact in his community and decided Sharlene was no great loss, for his family believed Koreans to clearly be inferior to Chinese.

After a few minutes, Frank was more in composure. He calmly put on a pair of heavily insulated gloves in preparation for retrieving a sperm sample. Reaching deep inside the ultra freezer, he firmly took hold of the top specimen rack by its metal cross arm and carefully lifted it out. The rack was filled with five-milliliter glass specimen containers, each holding approximately two to three milliliters of human sperm. Animal sperm for Baatard's private research experiments was kept in a separate ultra freezer, clearly labeled as such. Frank didn't know all the details of Baatard's experiments, for Baatard liked to personally perform much of his own work, but apparently they concerned Baatard's pursuit of the Intelligence Genetic complex - the IGC. Frank had read of Baatard's interesting and highly controversial work, some of which bordered on eugenics, and found it fascinating. Although Frank had even volunteered to assist Baatard, for free, Baatard, with a secretive air, declined.

Frank knew one of the tiny glass vials of donor sperm archived in the deep freezer was his. Yet, without the code sheet, if there really was one, he had no idea which one it was. Frank also knew some other donors, including Dr. Baatard himself, although that information was strictly off the record.

Frank struggled not to tip over the hundreds of tiny glass vials which lay precariously on their ends. Spilling the vials twice in two weeks would have been too much for him, and certainly, he realized all too well, for his supervisor, his 'direct'. Even once was too much, for that matter, he reflected. It had taken at least an hour last week to pick up all the damned little vials and return them to their places on the rack. Frank found this to be both boring and a complete waste of his time. He was much more capable, and destined for greater activities.

After a few minutes of looking, Frank found the correctly numbered glass vial containing the donor sperm Baatard instructed him to use. He left the vial out of the rack to allow it to slowly thaw at room temperature.

That done, Frank walked over to the CO_2 incubator and carefully slid out a tray of small plastic Petri dishes, each containing unfertilized ova. Each set of dishes represented the yield from one of Conceptions Foundation clients, harvested within the last two days. The flow of eggs from Foundation clients into his lab had increased incredibly over the last few months and was becoming nearly overwhelming. Frank had no idea how much the demand would increase in the future, and he suspected his employers didn't either. It seemed to Frank the volume of patients was increasing so fast that he would need to hire another assistant soon.

Frank used a computer printout to identify the correct batch of ova that had been harvested recently from a patient of Dr. Baatard's. Returning to the sterile air flow hood, Frank placed the tray of tissue culture dishes labeled "LV-1" inside, taking care not to slosh or spill the small amount of sterile tissue culture fluid inside each clear, delicate container. If the precious ova were exposed to air for even a few seconds without having an adequate growth media covering them, they could die.

Frank next looked over at the semen specimen in the vial still sitting on the table top. It appeared liquid, although it was usually too viscous and thick to judge its physical state just by looks. The vial's outside had a soft, frosty layer on it, suggesting there had been some heat transfer through the glass, probably enough to thaw the contents. This would explain the condensation he saw form on the outside around the label "HR-39."

Frank noticed the overhead micro cameras inside the hood flash on. They automatically monitored the transfer of sperm into the dishes, allowing Frank to observe much better than with the other, older, recently renovated hood unit.

Frank knew from the increasing traffic outside the lab's window that closing time was fast approaching and he would need to hurry and move things along. Yet, he did have to finish the "MB-1" ova before leaving for the day, even if he finished nothing else.

As he tried to reach over to the sterile glass pipette jar, Frank felt his arm being held back. Shit, he cursed to himself. His white lab coat had snagged on a rough metal corner of the liquid nitrogen deep freeze. Frank only briefly considered taking the time to free his coat. This would have required his stopping, putting down the vial of sperm, and freeing his sleeve. Angry and annoyed at his sleeve's insolence at slowing him, inconveniencing him, Frank tried the quicker way. Frank forcibly pulled on his arm, giving it a quick yank. This caused a slight rip in the coat; yet, incredibly, his coat remained stuck, defying him further. Looking around him in disbelief, he wondered how his life could have taken such a downward turn after such a promising beginning.

"Shit," Frank yelled out, his angry voice echoing off the walls for a few seconds; this was followed by a ripping sound, quite alone in the room. More than the fabric of his coat was thus ruined.

As Frank pulled his arm back, he accidentally knocked over the vial of donor sperm which had been defrosting on the desktop. Frank watched in helpless disbelief and horror as the vial rolled on its side, then along the counter top. Quickly leaning forward, Frank desperately tried to grab the vial of sperm, tipping over other equipment in the process. Unfortunately, he only succeeded in knocking the one vial he needed further along the counter top. His coat was still entrapped and this prevented him from going after the vial.

Just then, the phone rang, breaking his concentration. Frank jumped at the unexpected interruption, then he reached over, trying to hold the phone and simultaneously get hold of the precious vial of human semen.

"Frank, this is Dr. Baatard," the voice barked. "How's the LV fertilization going?"

Frank took a second to gain his composure. How the hell did Baatard know what he was doing, Frank wondered? "Fine, Dr. Baatard. No problem at all," Frank stammered as he helplessly watched in wide-eyed desperation while the glass vial finally rolled off the desktop and onto the floor, shattering in a thousand wet splinters.

"What the hell was that, Frank?" Baatard asked. "It sounded like glass breaking."

The Surrogate

"No, nothing's breaking around here. Everything's under control, Dr. B. But, I got a lot to do, so . . . "

"Well, I guess that twice in two weeks would indicate a depth of incompetence pretty hard to believe, even for you, Frank." Sarcasm dripped from Baatard's voice.

Frank stared at the little puddle of broken glass and semen on the floor, then rolled his eyes skyward. He couldn't believe his bad luck. Now, what would he do? He wasn't stupid, and resented having someone as unintelligent and uncultured as Baatard remind him to do simple things. "I, ah, I know you need me in a few minutes for harvesting, but, don't worry, I'll make it," Frank said, not looking up as he continued to work. "Sure, sure Dr. Baatard." Frank heard the click of the phone, then wondered just how he could handle this problem and still avoid discovery. The sperm sample that was just destroyed had HR-39 listed on the top. Assuming the vials were logically coded - and Frank had no idea who made up the codes for the anonymous sperm donors, then any other vial labeled with "HR" should be, or at least could be from the same donor. His rationalization made sense to him and gave him more confidence.

Frank pulled out the top rack of sperm samples and frantically searched through the almost hundred or so tiny glass vials for the initials "HR-39." To his amazement, there were none. Anxiously, he pulled out the next rack and looked through it too. Torrents of acid flooded into his stomach, eroding the lining and making him nauseous.

Just as Frank finished searching all ten racks and not finding another vial labeled "HR-39," he heard several people outside the airlock door. He looked around and was startled to see Dr. Baatard, accompanied by the Dragon Lady, Denny Cruite.

Frank reached into the sperm donor freezer, grabbed a vial at random, and carefully placed it on the bench-top to thaw out. Considering that the vial of sperm should be farther along in thawing by now, Frank placed the frozen vial in his hand to warm it faster. He then closed the liquid nitrogen freezer back up. The freezing cold glass vial stung his hand and adhered to the skin.

Baatard and Cruite looked inquisitively through the window into the embryology lab. Frank signaled all was okay, and Baatard flashed a stern half-smile before continuing down the hall with Cruite. Before leaving, Cruite sneered at Frank, much like a viper opens its jaw and flashes its forked tongue before biting its prey. Relieved that they had left, Frank went back to work.

The Surrogate

In all the confusion and rushing, Frank for some reason forgot to note the number on the glass vial of sperm he finally ended up using. Almost mechanically, he wrote down "HR-39" in his log book without really considering what he had done. As he slid the ova culture vials into the incubator, he was so nervous he was also no longer even sure what ova he had fertilized, or perhaps even fertilized again. At any rate, he reasoned, his being rushed into making mistakes wasn't his fault. It was 'theirs' and he hoped they got sued big time if anything really did go wrong. He laughed as he considered some rather humorous possible mismatches of sperm and ova he knew were available. After replacing the now-fertilized HR-39/LV-1 ova - they were, weren't they? - into the CO_2 incubator, Frank cleaned up. He then hurried over to assist in harvesting ova in the procedure room, where Dr. Baatard and another patient were waiting.

Frank knew the stairs could save him some time, at least, since he remembered having left his equipment cart near the procedure room. He ran up the stairway to the third floor procedure room, arriving exhausted and completely out of breath. Frank was startled as Baatard rushed out of the procedure room just as he was about to enter. Baatard's face bore a scowl and his eyes darted about, anxiously, defensively. Denny Cruite, face mask on, followed Baatard out.

"What are you doing here?" Baatard demanded, almost hitting Frank with the door as it flew open.

"I'm here for the ova harvesting," Frank tried to explain, gesturing at the tissue culture equipment he had wheeled along in front of him, like a lunch cart. "You did want me here, didn't you?"

"Yes, yes, of course I did. Well, I'm sorry to say that won't be necessary any longer," Baatard barked out. He and Cruite turned their backs to Frank, and whispered among themselves. The mood was glum.

"I don't understand," Frank said. His eyes darted back to the procedure room. A patient could be seen lying on the bed, and nurses and technicians were rushing into and out of the room.

"Look, Frank, there was an unfortunate outcome," Baatard said, his voice cracking and unsure. "The patient had an air embolism about fifteen minutes ago. She has to be taken to critical care." Seeing Frank's look of dismay, Baatard shrugged and said, "Hey, shit happens." Baatard's outwardly cavalier attitude did little though to hide his disappointment.

Cruite looked away, and said nothing. Frank could see from her facial expression she too was visibly shaken.

Despite his apparent nervousness and apprehension only seconds ago, Baatard's face quickly changed and was now nearly completely lacking emotion as he said, "Now Frank, I've got a ton of things to do besides explain this to you, so if you'll excuse me, . . . " He hurried off, not saying anything else to Cruite or looking back.

Cruite said nothing further to either Baatard or Frank, preferring to speak with a woman whom Frank recognized to be a Miss Yee, who had just joined them. Frank had heard that Yee handled legal matters for The Conceptions Foundation. The Chinese made excellent lawyers too, Frank thought. After discussing privately between themselves for a moment, Yee and Cruite both left, also in a hurry. Frank was left behind, unnoticed, holding onto his unused procedure cart.

Chapter 18

Haven Fertility Associates, P.C.
Haven, New Jersey

The next day

The private office phone line rang just as Baatard was rushing out of his office to start his third abortion of the afternoon. He usually was able to squeeze at least four to six abortions out of a good afternoon - afternoons he reserved only for that one procedure. On other days he would restrict himself to clinical evaluations, or only perform non-fertility workups. He had found it best not to mix too many things up, for that was confusing to him and to the staff. In addition, women not coming in for abortions tended to get upset if they caught wind of objectionable things occurring in their pristine midst.

The continual interruptions to an organized office day seemed to get worse each year instead of better, exactly the opposite of what Denny Cruite had promised Baatard when she lured him into joining The Conceptions Foundation. Frustrated once again, he slammed down the patient's chart he was fighting to read, and muttered, "Goddamn it."

"Can you take a call from Frank Lieu?" Sharlene asked.

"Do I have to?" Baatard joked, his eyes rolling toward the ceiling, searching for some divine explanation to the continual disorder in his midst. "I'm trying to get out of here for a scheduled procedure." He formed a clear image of that geek embryologist from Conceptions Foundation and laughed nervously as he wondered what new crisis or screw-up Frank had caused now.

"Unfortunately, you may well have to take his call. Frank insists it's very important, and that you know all about it," Sharlene told him.

"Sure. But tell him to make it quick. I got a million things to do besides talking to that goof ball. I can't understand what the hell he's saying half the time, anyway," Baatard muttered.

"What's that?" Sharlene asked.

"Nothing," Baatard gruffly told her. He wondered if Frank's call meant there were going to be some unexpected problems with the ova fertilization on the Bonnaserra case. Worse yet would be difficulty with the new assignment Baatard had just given Frank. Baatard hated unexpected problems. Frank seemed to be a walking set of difficulties and unexpected and unexplainable complications.

After a few minutes pause, Sharlene called back. "Frank said it would be better if he could come to your office. Okay?"

"Hell no," Baatard objected belatedly. "I'm trying to

get out of here, Sharlene. I've got another 'AB' waiting, you know that. Tell Frank it's got to be a call and not a visit."

"I'm sorry, Dr. Baatard," Sharlene called back. "It's too late; I'm afraid Frank is already on his way over here. I'll call over to the procedure room and tell them you'll be a few minutes late."

Baatard could feel the tension in his neck come back; knowing people, procedures, whatever were waiting for him, waiting behind each completed task to put another time demand on him, made him tense, more tense. Sometimes, he felt so pressured he wanted to scream. That, Baatard rationalized, was why he was so tense and terse - some said critical and rude - to those he worked with, and perhaps even with his family. They just couldn't understand the pressure he was under, and so they had no pity.

While Baatard waited for Frank Lieu to arrive, he looked over his sperm bank directory one more time. "Intelligent, disease-free, male; that's what Bonnaserra said she wanted," he recited to himself. Several sperm samples on the donor list would more than meet these characteristics.

Frank barged into Baatard's office after knocking loudly but not waiting for a reply, as if his knock was more of a warning than an announcement. "Hi, Dr. B. How you 'dooooin?'"

Baatard looked at Frank incredulously, and then suppressed a laugh as he imagined how Frank's protruding front teeth probably could function well as a can opener. He fantasized about taking a tin can and jamming the lid into Frank's teeth, then turning the can around until the top opened. "What's up, Frank?" You goofy loner, Baatard added to himself. "Are you here about the Bonnaserra ova?"

"Yes. I'm happy to say you got eleven ova during the harvesting procedure. Ten of them look at first guess to be viable. What's the plan, Dr. B? Freeze now and pay later?" Frank giggled as he shifted back and forth on his feet.

"Can you please stop calling me Dr. B.? It's annoying." Baatard strained to understand every word Frank mumbled, finding the accent almost incomprehensible.

"Okey dokey, sir."

Baatard winced. "No, I think we'll fertilize now, and transfer a few selected ova later. The rest can then be frozen." That seemed the prudent thing to do, and Baatard almost always chose to act from what he had learned worked best. Experience was his teacher, both professionally and in his relationship with others, and he thought himself to be a good student.

"And who will be the lucky sperm donor? I hear Ms. Bonnaserra is wanting," Frank smiled and chuckled, clumsily rotating his hips back and forth.

"Easy, boy. Calm down. No, I don't think you two are compatible," Baatard frowned. Then, fighting to keep a straight face, he played his own little practical joke, and instructed Frank, "I want you to use the sperm bank frozen specimen RS-39 on the MB-1 ova."

Frank looked confused, pulled out a stack of index cards and a black notebook from his overstuffed shirt pocket, and rummaged through. "Hey, I thought I heard that number before. Wasn't that sperm donor the one you said to use on the LV-1 ova?"

"No, that was HR-39, you moron," Baatard screamed, cutting Frank short. He could already envision a mistake being made. "You did use HR-39 sperm on the LV-1 ova like I told you to, didn't you?"

Frank's face turned pale white, and he nervously looked away. "Yes, of course not. I'm certain I used HR-39. Yes, HR-39, that was what you said to use on the LV-1 ova, and so that's what I did."

"Good. I'm relieved to hear that." Baatard said, not totally convinced. He had harbored continuing doubts about Frank's competence, and, he thought it was more than simply a language problem. "So, how exactly is that IVF going on the LV-1 ova?" He made a mental note to personally check on this by visiting the IVF lab, perhaps tomorrow morning before hospital rounds, no matter what Frank told him.

"Uh, well, it didn't work out," Frank mumbled, staring at his shoes. After a few tense moments of silence, Frank picked up his papers and looked like he was headed for the door.

The Surrogate

"Oh, shit. What do you mean?" Baatard yelled out, grasping the sides of his face with his hands. He couldn't believe what he had just heard, and couldn't understand why he hadn't at least been told until now. "Come back here and sit down, Frank, when I'm talking to you, damnit. We're not done yet. I think you better tell me everything that you know."

Frank slinked back to his chair. "Well look, that wasn't my fault, not all of it," Frank explained. "The tissue culture fluid was contaminated and started growing mushrooms. The ova were ruined and I had to throw them out."

Baatard, taken even more aback, had to think for a moment about what he had just heard. "Did you say mushrooms? What do you mean, mushrooms?" Baatard asked, almost unable to believe what had happened. "You're kidding me, right?"

Frank shook his head no. "Mushrooms, fungus," he repeated, shaking his head.

"For Christ sake, Frank, are you running a Chinese restaurant or an IVF laboratory?"

"Look, Dr. B, I'm sorry. There was a fungus growing in the tissue culture fluid. Mushrooms. It wasn't my fault." Frank looked around the room anxiously, and unsuccessfully attempted a smile. "It happens," he shrugged sheepishly.

"Who's fault do you think it was? Mine?" he said, his body shaking with anxiety.

Frank shook his head, and looked at the door like he was going to dash right through.

His hands trembling, he told Frank, "Okay, look, we

better remain calm. Exactly how many LV-1 ova were ruined, Frank?" Baatard yelled, "and were there any frozen ova left that you could use?"

"All of the LV-1 ova were used, and I guess they were all contaminated. Mushrooms," Frank shrugged, looking ashamedly away from Baatard. "All gone. Nada."

Baatard's spun his chair around and stared at Frank. "Now what the hell am I going to do?" Looking at Frank, he realized how much damage he could cause, and sternly told him, "Frank, no one must know. No one, understand?"

"Don't worry, Dr. B, no one knows about the mushrooms," Frank told him, shaking his head insistently, his face deathly serious.

Frank shook his head that it wasn't so, but Baatard could see that it was otherwise. "I'm ruined, Frank, I'm fucking ruined," Baatard cried to himself. Images clouded his mind of state police and hospital security coming up to his clinic and arresting him. He could hear them now accusing him of medical fraud, malpractice, and theft of ova. Baatard felt terribly betrayed and vulnerable and totally on his own. His only ally, or accomplice, unwitting as he was, was Frank Lieu, and that was certainly no solace. "Frank, I want you to listen very carefully. I want you to tell me exactly what 'people' know about this."

"No one else suspects, really. Look, Dr. B, I, I won't tell anyone, I promise." His face looked more worried now than it had ever been.

Unconvinced about Frank's reliability to keep such sensitive information confidential, Baatard firmly told Frank, "You're not to discuss this with anyone, understand?"

"No, Dr. B, no. But what if . . . "

"No buts, Frank." Baatard tried to gather his composure and quickly figure out just what he could still do to 'give Ramirez what she wanted.' "Now, this unfortunate mistake on your part, Frank, will necessitate a slight change in plans."

Frank's face turned ghastly pale, his body began to shake uncontrollably, and he swallowed hard and tried to leave again but Baatard held on to him. Baatard thought fast, trying to come up with a plan that would fix the damage, or at least control it. "Frank, I like you and I'm going to do my best to save you. But you have to work with me on this, Frank. Help me think of a plan." Baatard's mind raced alone, desperately examining every alternative he had used under similar situations in the past.

Frank listened attentively and took out his note pad. He offered no suggestions, now being almost too afraid to speak at all.

Unexpectedly, an idea came to Baatard, one that would solve his problems, one that he had probably subconsciously been considering all along. It was undoubtedly unethical, perhaps illegal, but he knew he had to do it. His own life probably was at stake. It was crazy, risky, foolish, unlikely to succeed, and brilliant. If he were wrong about others having found out about the contamination, and he had another chance, he would indeed be okay.

"Do you think there is any more of sperm HR-39 remaining?"

Frank meekly nodded yes, but his face belied the fact he had already looked and knew otherwise.

"Good. I certainly hope so, for your sake, Frank. Now, instead of using sperm RS-39 on ova MB-1 as we had planned, I want you to use sperm HR-39." He would get hold of some ova fertilized with Ramirez's goddamn sperm no matter what.

Frank nodded YES, then violently shook his head NO and looked extremely confused. "Sperm HR-39 on ova MB-1. Right, Dr. B. But does . . . "

"Don't ask, Frank, do what I say but just don't ask. We're talking basic survival here, our survival. Frank, I looked up Ramirez over at the library. Her name has been all over the newspapers for the vicious way she treats both lawyers who appear before her and the defendants whose trial she is supposed to assure is fair. She'll make both our lives miserable if she gets a whiff of this little mistake of yours. You don't want that to happen to us, do you?" Baatard jerked his body violently, feigning painful spasms as if he had been sitting on a high voltage wire.

Frank had stopped smiling long ago, and looked deathly serious for the first time Baatard could remember. "Anyway," Baatard continued, "when Bonnaserra's fertilized eggs get to the sixteen-cell stage, screen for the usual, you know, neural tube defects, chromosomal abnormalities, genetic diseases. Discard the bad eggs. Separate out the males at that point, freeze the females, and then look for the intelligence genetic complex. Call me with the results. Got it?"

Frank mumbled "HR-39" to himself, hastily scribbled some notes in his pad, then silently nodded.

Baatard watched Frank's scrawny butt move out the office door, then called back, "Frank, can't you remember to close the goddamn door?" Frank was already halfway down the hall, and Baatard had to get up to close his office door himself. He called after Frank and yelled out, "Plan for tomorrow."

"Right, got you, tomorrow, right-on, Dr. B. Oops, sorry," Frank mumbled as he frumped down the hall, his sneakers making a squeaking sound.

Within minutes of Frank leaving, the phone rang again. Baatard nearly jumped at the sound, the tension getting to be way too much for him. "It's Denny Cruite," Sharlene said. "She wants to see you in her office right away. Can you go over there now?"

"I guess so. Is there another problem?" he asked, almost rhetorically. His mind was preoccupied with the disastrous information Frank had given him, and the terribly risky response he had needed to make. What Denny could want from him just now surely would pale in comparison, but was also an unnecessary diversion. He had more than enough to do and to carefully consider.

"She didn't say." Sharlene almost hung up the phone, before she heard Baatard still talking to her.

"Before I forget, Sharlene, we still need to get Mrs. Ramirez in here pronto for a pre-implantation physical and ultrasound. Have you been able to make the arrangements yet?" Things were going to move very fast, he felt, and he had to get everything ready. There could be no loose ends.

"I'm still trying, but every time I call Mrs. Ramirez, she's either hearing a case, or unavailable, or ill. But I'll keep at it."

Baatard shook his head, wondering why arranging a simple fertilized ova donation for Ramirez seemed to be taking so unusually long.

Chapter 19

Conceptions Foundation
Haven, New Jersey

Baatard quickly arranged for one of his colleagues to perform several scheduled abortions for him, and then walked over to the Conceptions Foundation corporate offices. Denny Cruite didn't often call, although that seemed to be changing lately, and Sharlene had said Denny sounded rather anxious and urgent. Denny didn't even tell Sharlene on the phone what it was she wanted to talk about, which was also out of character for her. Already on edge, pressured, over-committed, Baatard was now anxious and suspicious.

Baatard looked with apprehension for abortion protesters as he approached the front of the Conceptions Foundation building. He preferred not to confront them or be seen by them when entering that building. Although he certainly wasn't afraid of the protesters, and in fact had said on many an occasion he wasn't going to allow those kooks to intimidate him, the string of murders of abortion doctors in recent years was definitely having a chilling effect on those few doctors who still performed abortions. Fortunately, no protesters were around just then.

Minutes later, Baatard was brought directly into

Denny's office, a plush, wide-open area on the top floor of
the Conceptions Foundation building in downtown
Haven. Perhaps the most stunning aspect was a large
picture window overlooking downtown Haven and the
North Bergen River. His office had no window, was a
quarter the size, and much more Spartan. Up till now, he
had been completely satisfied and hadn't noticed. Baatard
took a seat facing Denny while she finished a phone call.

Denny saw Baatard's reflection in the picture window
and curtly nodded to him as he sat. She took a long drag
on her cigarette, and blew consecutive smoke rings at his
image, obscuring his reflection. The cigarette was one of
the newer, colored designer types - the ones attractively
designed for women, yet something about the way Denny
blew smoke rings struck Baatard as decidedly unfeminine.

After hanging up, Denny slowly turned her chair
around to face Baatard. "Thanks for coming over so
quickly," she said, her face hardened with a haggard
expression.

Denny laid her palms down flat on the desk top with
an exaggerated calmness and forced a wide smile, and for
a moment, she appeared to Baatard to be a leaner,
feminine version of Ramirez. He didn't exactly know
what to make of that observation, and simply tried to
collect his thoughts before speaking. "Not at all. Until just
lately, you only called me infrequently, so I figured it
must be important." Baatard also thought Denny looked

particularly weary today, but opted not to mention it. He noted that her face appeared drawn and worn and tired. Her hair, usually spindly as it was, today looked almost frail and brittle, as if it had been bleached once too often. Even her chin, usually soft and white, looked a little red and studded with a few hair follicles. Her eyes were gray and had bags, her skin was shallow and blue gray, almost cadaveric. It was not an effect of the office lighting, of this Baatard was most certain.

"Yeah," she exhaled with the interest of a snake observing its prey, "it is important." Denny flicked some ashes from the tip of her cigarette into a porcelain ashtray, noticed Baatard's look of disapproval at her smoking and said, "I'm trying to quit, but I got too much going on right now to give it much attention. But I'm sure you know how that goes. Anyway, I didn't ask you here to talk about my trivial habits."

"It's really worth the effort to quit smoking, Denny. I could help you if you ever want me to. But, knowing you as I do, I'd say something else is bothering you. Do you care to tell me?" He had thought, with the Dragon lady, subtlety was a waste of time, and the direct approach worked best.

"Well, for one thing, my, ah, husband Nevin has pneumonia." She took another deep drag from her cigarette and held the hot gas in her lungs a long time before exhaling tiny wisps of smoke which lingered like a toxic fog around her upper lip. Her thin fingers which delicately held the cigarette betrayed a slight tremor.

"Oh, how terrible." Baatard said, aware that Nevin Cruite had not been feeling well. "What kind of pneumonia does he have?"

Denny shrugged. "They've got him in Haven General now, and he's getting IV antibiotics." She looked away, and fidgeted with a half-empty pack of cigarettes. Denny's face grew several years older and a shade more pale as she continued talking. "The doctors think he may not make it this time." She looked away and out the window.

"Oh, Denny, I had no idea. I'm so sorry. Is there anything I can do?" Baatard asked. It must be one hell of a pneumonia, he thought. He made a note to check around the hospital to see what bugs were circulating in the community right now.

"Thanks for the offer, Damon. I'll let you know."

"Well, I hope for your sake it's not contagious."

Denny's mouth opened, but she said not a word. For a moment, it looked as if she was going to cry, then she seemed to pull herself together before saying, "But, let's talk about a habit we both share, shall we?" She smiled a tiny, crooked, smirk of a smile, looking like a lizard about to zap a fly with a lash of its tongue.

"Like what?" Baatard asked.

"Like breathing, that's what," she said as she straightened and squirmed in her chair.

"I don't understand."

"Oh yes you do, you certainly do," she laughed ironically. "And I'm sure you'll be interested to know I just had another visit by Mrs. Ramirez." Denny took another deep drag on her cigarette, then coughed heavily, followed by a wheeze. "Sorry," she said, nervously covering her mouth.

"Oh. Well, what did she want?" Baatard asked, loosening the knot in his tie, and looking around anxiously.

"She wants you to give her what she asked for, that's all."

Baatard felt suddenly anxious and sweaty. He again regretted the day he agreed to take care of Ramirez's, and was terribly afraid that the whole affair would lead not just to his losing his medical license but to his losing his life. "Look Denny, I already agreed to perform IVF for her. That's exactly what she wanted from me, isn't it?" He opened his hands wide, looking as if he would do anything, refuse nothing, and cooperate completely.

"Yes, it is. You did the wise thing there, Damon."

Baatard tried to smile and appear relaxed and confident but simply couldn't. Who would he be fooling, anyway, he wondered? Talking about Ramirez made him uncomfortable. "If that's so, then why did you call me in here? What did Ramirez see YOU about this time?"

"Simple. She seems to think you can't give her what she wants. She thinks there's a problem somewhere. Is that true, Damon?" she asked, a sense of desperation in her voice.

"No, no. There's no problem at all. Really, I don't know what she could be talking about. Trust me." Baatard suddenly realized Frank's screw up was going to get him killed. Ramirez was widely reputed to have no tolerance for error.

"Look, Damon, let me put it to your straight. Ramirez said she's already used one fertility doctor before you, and she doesn't have time to try a third. If you don't produce, she threatened to, well, I'd rather not say what, Damon." Her voice was monotone, factual and broken.

"That's impossible, Denny." Baatard said, although he knew quite well it wasn't impossible at all. He thought about the threat to his life for a few seconds, then seemed to have an idea. "Denny, you're a witness to a threat against my life. We can go to the police, we can make a complaint against Ramirez, and get protection."

Denny laughed ironically, and then coughed. "You're so simplistic, Damon. Do you want my advice?" she said, more a statement than an offer.

"Yes. But if it's giving Ramirez what she wants, believe me, I'm already trying to do just that," Baatard said.

"Good. That's all I want to hear you say. Ramirez thinks I have influence on getting you to do things. I guess I do. I hope I do," she said, shaking her head. "I just hope Ramirez doesn't think you need any more motivation than you already have." She turned in her chair, and asked, "Damon, are you leveling with me?"

"Well, yes, no, not completely that is." He wondered nervously what exactly Ramirez meant by 'motivation.' "Look, Denny, there was a small problem. But it was only a minor setback, a mere delay, that's all."

Denny gasped, nodded to herself, and stared angrily at the ceiling.

It was obvious to Baatard that somehow Ramirez knew about the lab contamination, and Denny also knew. He wondered who knew first and told the other. Baatard considered for the first time Denny could be feeding information to Ramirez.

"I think you better tell me the full extent of this supposedly 'minor problem,' don't you?"

"Sure, Denny, sure. Look, it's really quite simple," Baatard said, faking a nervous chuckle. "Unfortunately, a small, totally unexpected problem has developed. The tissue culture for the ova I had Frank fertilize for use in Mrs. Ramirez became contaminated."

"What ova, what contamination?" Denny angrily asked. "No one said anything to me about this, and it's my goddamn lab that it happened in. Oh, shit. I'm going to kill that goddamn fucking Frank."

"Please, calm down, Denny. Yes, those were the ova destined for Ms. Ramirez, and it's unfortunate, but we both know those things happen. It's nobody's fault."

"Oh, God. So it's true. Ramirez said something to me about mushrooms and I thought she was crazy. But, she was right. "

"But how the hell could Ramirez have found out about that?" Baatard asked, remembering how Frank had used the word mushrooms.

Denny leaned forward in her seat and tapped another cigarette out of its box. "Mind if I light up another?"

Baatard knew that was not a question for him to answer. Denny looked thoroughly depressed. "I'd appreciate it if you didn't," Baatard frowned.

"You're naive, Damon, and I'm afraid your naiveté is going to get us both in a lot of trouble." Denny tapped another cigarette out of the carton, then slowly placed the nearly empty carton on the table in front of her. Using the still-lit butt of her current cigarette, she lit the replacement, switched it into the holder, and disposed of the old one. "Don't you know who you're trying to please here? Don't you know how serious this is?" she pleaded. Denny took another deep drag, then started to cough a wet hack almost before taking her next drag. Her thin frame shook and rattled like a paper bag full of dry beans.

Baatard also coughed, the poorly ventilated room reeked and choked so with cigarette fumes. He could almost feel the pain of her cough. "Look, Denny, I do think I know who we're dealing with here. And, just as for all my other patients, I'm going to try really hard to have a satisfactory outcome. We've already begun searching for and preparing fertilized ova to replace those lost by contamination. I just had a really hard time locating some ova I could use here, but it will get done."

Denny didn't look impressed with the problems Baatard was having, nor sympathetic.

"You know there's been a run on ova for just this reason. But, well, we are trying again."

"You are? Good, Damon, good, but tell me specifics, not generalities."

"Okay, my plan is simple, really. Marina Bonnaserra never specified whose sperm to use on her ova; she left that decision entirely up to me. Although I originally intended to fertilize Bonnaserra's ova with a banked sperm specimen, I decided to use Ramirez's sperm instead. I plan to instruct Frank to implant some of the male MB-1 ova in Mrs. Ramirez." Denny nodded agreement and smiled her approval. "There should still be plenty of male ova left to implant in Marina Bonnaserra herself," Baatard continued. "Bonnaserra will never know, and being so satisfied, will be none the worse."

As he suspected she would, Denny indicated only approval for what she was hearing, rather than approbation. "That's wonderful, Damon. I'm proud of your anticipating the problem and taking the decision to switch and use Ramirez's sperm with Bonnaserra's ova. That was simply brilliant. Yes, go ahead and do it, by all means."

"Look, I know it's practical, under these circumstances, but it's making me real nervous."

"I don't see why, Damon," Denny said, apparently not at all understanding what she was hearing.

"Because, Denny, I've already done something wrong by fertilizing the other, now-contaminated ova with Ramirez's sperm without first getting the ova donor's permission."

"Whose ova, Damon?"

"Lissa Vernor," he admitted, afraid the truth would get out eventually.

"But the woman is in a goddamn coma, Damon. Don't you see, no one knows, and so there's no need to worry here."

"Yes, but I think it's still unethical. And Frank knows all the details. I could lose my medical license, and maybe even go to jail. Now that the LV-1 ova became contaminated, it looks like I had to use whatever ova I could, if I didn't want to upset this Ramirez. Worse, I used the MB-1 ova, at least some of them, without permission too."

"In my opinion, neither action is criminal, as far as I can determine, as long as both actions can be explained away as errors," Denny said slyly, and nodded her approval.

Baatard nervously shrugged, and looked around the room. "Maybe so, but I don't see the need to discuss our progress and problems with Ramirez. It will just make her nervous," Baatard said, adjusting his shirt collar. "And I hope you won't either. Okay?"

"Sure, Damon. But, well, you know, these things have a way of getting out. Ramirez is already nervous, she's upset, and you know already what she told me." Denny appeared as if the death threat was directed against her too, which it probably was.

Baatard stared blankly at her, unable to think about anything but Ramirez's threats. He felt sick to his stomach as he faced the ruination of his whole life, his career, the place in society he had worked so hard for so many years to achieve. And for what? He had not solicited Ramirez, none of this was his fault. He was innocent, he was the goddamn victim here.

"Yeah," was all Baatard could say. It was evident to Baatard that Denny was scared too, and they were both fighting for their lives.

"I certainly hope so, because if Ramirez's not happy with you, it's not just your problem." Denny smiled sweetly at Baatard, then showed him to her door.

Baatard remembered that he had yet examine Mrs. Ramirez, and made a mental note to finally do so within the next day or two. As she had no ovaries, and apparently no frozen eggs, her involvement at this point would be only peripheral. He had already gotten some healthy eggs, and instructed Frank to fertilize them with Ramirez's sperm. The fertilized eggs would be screened to separate out the healthy males, and then he would simply implant them into Mrs. Ramirez's uterus. He could easily supply the necessary hormonal injections to support implantation and growth for nine months; it was routine. Once the baby is born, it will appear to be hers, and for all practical purposes will be just that, effectively giving Ramirez what she needs. Yet the thought that he had a workable plan in progress was of only incomplete consolation to Baatard.

Chapter 20

Frank Lieu opened the liquid nitrogen freezer in the back of the embryology laboratory and stood back a few feet. A smoky haze instantly formed from all moisture which condensed out of the atmosphere around the door. Frank moved to the front of the ultra-freezer unit once the chill and the vapor had dissipated. He put on a special pair of thick insulated gloves, then reached into the freezer and carefully took out a metal rack filled with small glass tubes.

Baatard did say CK-29, didn't he, or was it HR-39, Frank tried to remember. He checked on the order sheet one more time, saw he had written down HR-29, and pulled out the glass vial with CK-29 written in red wax on its black screw cap. There were some other notes scribbled down near "CK-29," but they were nearly illegible. Frank's notations were in his own confusing version of mixed Cantonese and English, and sometimes it was difficult to read, even for him. After replacing the rack back in the freezer, Frank placed the glass vial on the desk top to allow it to gently thaw for a few minutes.

An hour later, Frank could see as he swirled around

the bottle that the sperm specimen had become a semi-liquid. A light layer of frost lingered on the outside of the still cold vial. Frank attached a small black bulb with air control buttons onto a glass pipette tube from the pipette rack. After inserting the thin glass tip of the pipette into glass vial CK-29, he suctioned the seminal fluid into the pipette, and then transferred the sperm onto a small plastic Petri dish. It's definitely not a lot of fun this way, Frank frowned.

The tissue culture dish - only three centimeters in diameter - contained several milliliters of special nutrient broth with a red dye acidity indicator. As long as the culture remained free of contamination and of an adequate acidity, it retained its red hue. If a yellow coloration developed, this meant contamination, or something equally bad.

Microscopic ova belonging to Marina Bonnaserra, identified by the code MB-1, were incubating in the dish, attached by special proteins to the bottom plastic surface. Frank smiled to himself as he remembered the ova donor, then said in his own unique version of broken English, "I sure hope you like the children these sperm give you."

Frank fixed a scanning optical dissecting microscope over the dish, then he transferred the video signal to a television monitor. There, he could see the millions of sperm, their tadpole-like bodies swarming over the eleven individual MB-1 ova, each sperm cell fighting to fertilize an ova and become a human. The selection process was poorly understood but produced what amounted to a unique creation tens of thousands of times each day in places all over the planet.

After watching for a few minutes, Frank carefully covered the Petri dish and placed it into an incubator overnight. He checked the atmospheric controls to be sure the inside was 5% CO_2, then closed the hermetically sealed doors.

The next day, Frank was pleased to note seven of the MB-1 ova had fertilized with what he thought was HR-39 sperm. They were now at the four-cell stage. Frank carefully suctioned off the spent tissue culture fluid, rinsed the ova off with fresh nutrient medium, and then transferred each fertilized egg to a separate dish. Excited, Frank called Baatard to tell him the good news.

"Good job, Frank," Baatard praised him. "But now the hard work begins. Let me know how they look at the fifth doubling stage. Then we can be more confident." Baatard heaved a sigh of relief, knowing he could at least please Ramirez, and most certainly Marina Bonnaserra too, although pleasing Marina was no longer his main concern at all.

Later that day, a jubilant Frank called Baatard back. "The Bonnaserra ova still look pretty good, Dr. B. There are no indications of any genetic abnormalities, and no chromosomal aberrations. Five of the seven ova which fertilized are males, and listen to this: four have the intelligence genetic complex. These must have been some parents. I mean, can you imagine the odds of . . . "

"Thanks very much, Frank," Baatard interrupted, suddenly feeling extremely relieved. "Look, here is what I want you to do. Freeze all the females, the one male without the intelligence genetic complex and one of the males with that chromosome. Prepare the other three males for implantation right away, okay? I'll see you at Marina Bonnaserra's room at Haven General in one hour."

After he hung up on Frank, Baatard immediately called Sharlene on the intercom. "Phone over to Haven General, get hold of the head nurse for the floor Marina Bonnaserra is on, and arrange for a tentative embryo transfer later today. We can do the procedure right there in her hospital room. If the utilization review people hassle you, tell them the patient is private pay and we can bill her for this, and still discharge her the next day."

"Right," Sharlene said as she tried to keep up by taking notes.

"And remind Frank Lieu over at Conceptions Foundation's embryology lab. Tell him we're going to use the fertilized male MB-1 ova immediately and to get them ready. He should already be busy doing this, but with Frank, who knows? Okay?"

"Sure, I'll take care of it. And Damon, there's something I think you'll want to know."

"And that is? Make it fast, I'm in a big hurry." He busily pulled together papers and equipment as he spoke.

"Do you remember when you asked Mrs. Ramirez to sign a release for transfer of her past infertility workup to our office?"

Dimitri Markov

"Yes. Don't tell me you forgot to ask her to do it?"
Baatard under normal circumstances would have been
furious, but now he had to admit that not having the
records at this far point would be only an annoyance.
"Of course I asked her. I'm not stupid, you know."
Baatard wasn't at all certain of that, but rather than
voicing his sarcasm, simply said, "Let me guess. Ramirez
said she doesn't fill out forms." That certainly seemed to
be her style. Baatard wondered if the ice lady could even
write.
"No, that's not it at all. Will you let me finish, please?
She did sign a release form, and I tried to get the records,
but I'm afraid that won't be possible."
"Why is that, Sharlene?" As he waited for an answer,
he suddenly almost didn't want to know.
"I called over to the infertility group where Mrs.
Ramirez's last infertility doctor worked."
"Good job, Sharlene, but get to the point already. I've
got a million . . ."
"She's in jail, Damon." Sharlene interrupted him.
"Apparently she got convicted of insurance fraud and
medical malpractice, and got three to five in Trenton."
Baatard dropped the phone on the floor. He stood
there for several long minutes, unable to move as he
looked at the receiver bobbing up and down on the
tangled wire line, like a head, his head, in a hangman's
noose. He envisioned his torso similarly swinging in the

331

wind, and the implication was clear -- he was going to share the same fate as Ramirez's previous infertility doctor, unless, that is, he delivered. It took Baatard a while before he recovered sufficiently to pick up the phone and silently hang it on its cradle.

Baatard spent the rest of the afternoon glumly thinking about what he was going to do next. He saw visions of himself hopelessly trying to defend himself against a trumped up malpractice charge. He envisioned his own contorted face, muscles spasmed into an infinitely painful death grimace, high voltage electricity coursing through his body and burning his skin. But NO, he resolved, that would NOT be HIS fate. As he considered the four Bonnaserra ova, each possessing the intelligence genetic complex, each capable of evolving into a healthy, and probably brilliant male child, he could see not the egg, but the nucleus of his salvation.

He had a plan that would give Ramirez all she wanted. But there was one possible refinement to the plan, one additional CYA he had to attempt. Picking up the phone, he called Denny.

"Damon? Is there another problem?" Denny asked.

"No, oh no, no, there's no problem. Everything is proceeding according to plan. But, Denny, maybe we could make this ova donation a little more legal."

"Legal? What do you mean, Damon?"

"Well, Bonnaserra never specified what sperm to use, and since she left that choice completely up to me, I don't see any legal problem here."

"I agree, but I'm not sure Bonnaserra will be happy if

she ever finds out you used Ramirez's sperm, and that Ramirez is the father of her child. I certainly wouldn't," she nervously chuckled.

Baatard thought that was obvious, and said, "Bonnaserra doesn't even need to know I was initially planning to use another sperm donor. And I have no plans to ever tell her whose sperm I used. She already knows and has agreed to that part being entirely my choice and completely confidential," Baatard explained. "She doesn't want to know," he added.

"Good," Denny said, indicating by the tone of her voice that there were no moral, ethical or legal questions in her mind at all.

"As for the ova donation, I could simply ask Ms. Bonnaserra to donate a fertilized ova, or even to sell one. That way we wouldn't have to just take them." He knew he wasn't "just taking them," he was stealing another woman's ova, her child in effect. That bothered him, for he had never done that before. Yet, he suspected, no, he absolutely knew what tremendous potential these male ova with the IGC possessed. They would be intellectually superior, and probably would be worth an absolute fortune.

"No, I wouldn't do that, Damon. Marina Bonnaserra doesn't strike me as the type to sell ova," Denny told him. "I think that suggestion would turn her off, and it might make her suspicious and doubtful of The Conceptions

Foundation. I mean, what if she wants to know to whom her ova would be donated?"

He could see Denny's point, but persisted, "Maybe if you ask Marina yourself, make it a plea from The Foundation or something, she might agree?" He could feel the desperation in his own voice, and his heart racing.

"Okay, Damon, I'll try that approach, although I'm not at all sure it's a good idea. I'll let you know what happens."

"By the way, Denny, Marina's at . . . "

"I already know where she is now, Damon. But, thanks for the information."

Almost as soon as Baatard had put the phone down, it rang again, startling him. This time it was Garza. "Do you want to use a single implantation catheter for all three ova? Frank just called back to ask about it." After a long pause, Garza asked, "Hello, Dr. Baatard, are you still there?"

Baatard's mind, pulled from deep thought by Garza's questions, desperately raced for several seconds, trying to formulate a detailed plan from the opportunity he had. Finally, he said, "No, no, let's not do it that way. Garza, I want you to have Frank load three separate transfer catheters, each with one fertilized embryo. And make sure that Sharlene called over to Haven General to have the ward nurses make the necessary preparations for an embryo transfer. We can do it right there in Bonnaserra's room."

Baatard, for the first time in days, had a relaxed, incompletely relaxed, that is, and partially satisfied look on his face. Finally, he sighed, he had fertilized ova for

Lydia Ramirez. He had wanted to satisfy Ramirez and get her off his back in the worst way, and of course he wanted the hundred thousand, which would end up being the easiest grand he ever had made, and now, thank God, he finally could. He would take one catheter and use it on Bonnaserra. The other catheters he would use on Mrs. Ramirez. That should satisfy everyone.

Then, just as quickly as he had felt safe, his mood changed to one of extreme anxiety. Mrs. Ramirez, Mrs. Ramirez. He had somehow neglected in all the rush and confusion to examine her. By now, she should have had a pre-IVF workup, signed a consent form, and been in a procedure room prepared for ova implantation. How could he have been so stupid to overlook that? By his own incompetence, he may have just signed his own death warrant. Practically speaking, it was too late now to accomplish all that was necessary. Now what was he to do? He had ova and no place to put them. Damn, what have I done? he thought.

"Fine," Garza said, bringing Baatard back to reality. "I can probably have Frank bring the fertilized MB-1 ova over in fifteen minutes, if the hospital can have everything ready."

Baatard paused for a moment before answering Garza. He went over the situation again and again in his mind, searching desperately for a solution, any solution. "Yes, sure, have Frank do that. That would be great. And

Garza, I don't want to screw around waiting for the nurses to get things set up on their own sweet time. Okay? I got a lot to do today, a lot to do, so could you go over and check things out yourself? See you soon. And, only call me if there's a problem, okay?" Immediately, his mind was redirected to the problem at hand: where to put the fertilized ova that were to have been used on Mrs. Ramirez.

"I know," Garza said disappointedly, "you have a lot of things to do before the procedure, and time is money."

"Oh, if you only knew," Baatard ruefully said, "if you only knew."

Chapter 21

After her breakfast, Marina used her bedside intercom to call the ward nurse and inquire when she would be discharged. Marina was startled when the nurse abruptly told Marina she would be staying for her embryo transfer first before her discharge. Marina was apprehensive about the implantation procedure as it was, and surprises like this didn't help either. She was certain that Baatard had not mentioned to her that the ova transfer would take place today, so soon after her ova harvesting and subsequent bleeding complications. If today was to be the day, though, she had little choice but to stay.

Several times, the thought crossed her mind to get up from her hospital bed and leave before being impregnated, but each time she tried to calm her anxieties, and managed to talk herself into staying. The final moment for IVF seemed at hand, but paradoxically she felt she was less committed to carrying it out now than ever.

A short while later, the ward secretary brought in a beautiful basket of assorted cut flowers, bright red roses and pink carnations and baby breaths. Marina was surprised at receiving such a beautiful bouquet, and couldn't imagine who had sent it. At first, she assumed the flowers must have been from Charlie Kincade. Then she realized it couldn't have been him, since he didn't know about her hospitalization. She had never been able to bring herself to tell Charlie she was attempting to become pregnant, and that she intended to have a child without him. How could she even begin to explain all that to Charlie?

The scent of the flowers was as beautiful as their appearance, but despite their beauty, the thought of being unnoticed and so alone at an important time like this depressed Marina. She wondered how anyone would know or care if something happened to her while at Haven General. If, in attempting to create another life, she instead were to die of some tragic obstetrical accident, who would mourn her death, who would claim her body, or even arrange for her funeral? Would Charlie do it, would anyone? The thought was suddenly and devastatingly depressing.

She reached over to examine the tiny blue card stuck on a plastic fork among the flowers. "Hope your procedure goes well. Love, Denny." That's so considerate, she thought. Somehow, though, she also felt a little uncomfortable, and suspicious of Denny's motives. It was probably simply good public relations, and a courtesy done for all IVF patients of The Conceptions Foundation, Marina decided.

Marina stared at the card and the tight, stark writing style for a long time, then placed the card in with the flowers. The writing seemed masculine, she thought, and wasn't actually the first non-feminine characteristic she had ever noticed about Denny Cruite. The observation found a secure place in Marina's subconscious.

Marina thanked the ward clerk, then gave some excuses about allergies. She was about to give the flowers back to be placed at the nursing station, when there was a knock at the door. It was pushed open, and Marina was surprised to see Denny standing there, dressed in her standard red suit, perhaps on her way to another presentation.

"Hi, Marina, I stopped in to see how you're doing. I just learned that you're going to have your implantation procedure in only a few minutes, so I won't be staying too long."

"Thank you for coming," Marina stammered. "That's very thoughtful of you. And thank you for the lovely flowers," Marina said, gesturing at the bouquet. For some strange reason, Marina sensed there was another reason for Denny's being here. The Conceptions Foundation probably had hundreds of female clients in the IVF program, and there wasn't anything unique about her own situation, at least as far as she could understand. She almost found herself hoping for Denny to simply wave and then just go away.

"Marina, let me get to the point, if I may, since the nurses say you'll be needing to leave soon. There is a favor of you I'd like to ask. It's a special favor, one only you can say yes to."

Marina was right - there was an ulterior motive for Denny's being here. The way the conversation was going, Marina knew it would not be something easy or conventional. "What kind of favor, Denny?"

"Marina, our fertility laboratory informs me that you had seven successfully fertilized ova. Of course, some of these are going to be used in your implantation, but they don't all need to be." Denny looked away from Marina, and attempted unsuccessfully to appear nonchalant. "Assuming that everything is successful, and you become pregnant, we would, I would like you to consider donating one of the remaining ova to another woman."

Marina was simply shocked at the suggestion, and almost at a loss for words. Such a request was totally inappropriate under the circumstances. "I'm afraid I don't understand," she said, although she did only too well.

"There are so many intelligent young women in our community who are desperate to have a child, Marina. Fertilized ova of high quality, like yours, are so rare and precious. Ova donation would be completely anonymous," she said, a certain desperation mixed with a stain of embarrassment in her voice, "just as was the sperm donated to fertilize your own ova. We could even compensate you - - if you wish."

Marina was taken aback, and also slightly offended. Denny's sense of timing was surprisingly inappropriate and insensitive. This was neither the time nor the place to discuss such a proposition. "Can't you let me think about this a while? Maybe in a few weeks or a month, then we can talk some more."

"Yes, I suppose that would do. But, we really would

like to know right away, if you could only tell us."

Marina knew when she was being pressured, and resented it, particularly now, when she was in such a vulnerable position. She could only assume there was an acute need for a fertilized ova, and that she was one of many women who were being similarly approached. Now she realized the ulterior motive for the flowers. "Okay, if you must know right now, then the answer is no."

"But, Marina . . . ," Denny protested, looking like she had been handed a diagnosis of a terminal disease.

"Please, I appreciate where you're coming from, Denny, but this is not a good time to talk. In just a few minutes, I'm going for my ova implantation. I really can't think reasonably about something as important as donating my own fertilized ova at a time like this. I'm sure you'll understand." She was glad she had stood her ground. Denny, however, was another matter. Denny changed from appearing reluctant to being very annoyed and flustered.

Denny made little effort to maintain her composure and disguise the anger she felt. She superficially thanked Marina, appeared at least overtly polite and grateful, and quickly left. As soon as Denny was at the nurse's station, she entered the staff office, shut the door and called Baatard.

Baatard was disappointed but not surprised when Denny informed him of Marina's response.

"Well, it's really too bad, Damon. You know, when I told Ramirez . . ."

"You told Ramirez about this?" he exclaimed. He could see everything he had so carefully arranged starting to unravel, and he was helpless, surrounded as he was by incompetents, to do anything to stop the unfolding disaster. "Why did you do that?"

"Relax, Damon. When I called for you earlier, Sharlene told me you were unavailable and in a big rush. I asked her if there were any problems, and she told me they had still not been able to schedule Mrs. Ramirez in for a pre-implantation exam, and time was running out. As a favor to you, I got in touch with Ramirez."

"We've been trying to do that too."

"Yes, well Ramirez liked your idea of using Marina's ova very much, but she suggested that it might be more convenient for all concerned if you use another woman to carry the child, her child, and then she would simply adopt it."

"Assuming we could arrange for this, who would we get to carry the child? These things take a lot of effort to arrange, and there are a lot of legal issues and problems, you know."

"Maybe so, but Ramirez likes the idea, and so do I. Call me when you have given it more thought." Denny hung up without saying anything further.

Baatard stood in his office for several minutes, wondering where he was going to locate a reliable, willing surrogate mother on short notice, and satisfy the dangerous Ramirez and the dysfunctional and conniving Denny Cruite.

Chapter 22

Lancaster, Pennsylvania

Oliver Wade, long-term sheriff of Lancaster County, Pennsylvania, drove the police department's sole cruiser out on back road patrol. A thick morning fog had cleared, the roads were still wet and slick from melting frost and a light morning rain, and the air was damp and chilly. Wade, as he liked to be called, lived in Lancaster County his entire life. He owned a piece of land his family had held for generations and rarely traveled outside the county. With an impressive stature of six foot, two inches and two hundred ten pounds, a roughly trimmed reddish mustache, and a hulking gate, people seemed to know his line of business even when he was out of uniform.

Already alerted by a local Amish farmer who had seen two cars racing, Wade had seen the smoke rising from the car wreck while still several miles away. He was the first official on the accident scene. Wade slowed his late model Chevy patrol car as it came around the slick, rain-soaked curve, taking caution to avoid driving over the fresh skid marks in the road near where the 'victim's vehicle' went over a steep rocky embankment. In the background he could hear the high-pitched siren of the ambulance he had requested.

Wade saw the late model light blue Ford sedan laying on its side like a wrecked ship listing on a sandbar several hundred feet down from the road's edge, still smoking. The Ford's New Jersey plates contained "MD" in the sequence, suggesting it was owned and principally driven by a practicing physician.

The destroyed car's hood was wrapped tightly around a power pole, whose thick wood shaft snapped in two as if it had only been a pencil. A large gray power transformer lay on the Ford's hood, also still smoking. Wade could tell from this, and the occasional sparks coming from the car's hood, that it was best to stay back and not touch anything just yet.

Wade got back into the patrol car and radioed in for an electric utility crew to come out and secure the power line. This was standard procedure before he and the ambulance technicians attempted a rescue in cases like this. Using his binoculars, Wade could observe two women in the front seat of the car. Both occupants were strapped in with seat belts, both were motionless and one was without apparent chest movement. Wade shook his head after seeing what he could expect when he finally got into the destroyed car.

Fifteen minutes later, Wade and the paramedics finally got a clearance from the electrical utility crew, and quickly made their way through the dry hillside brush down to the crash site. Wade choked a little from the putrid smell of fresh burning flesh merging with the sharp dry odor of overheated electrical equipment and hot oil mixed with dirt. Even more than a vision of the horrific wreck, he would retain the memory of that smell for days.

They pulled open one of the doors using large iron bars and checked for pulses; the young victim's face had a dusky blue appearance. The younger of the two accident victims, she had no apparent chest movement. On exam, the paramedic found that, as expected, she had no pulse.

Wade stayed at the scene to supervise the removal of the dead passenger, then completed his accident investigation and photographing. It was a dry task he had performed all too often for his liking, resembling in his mind vultures picking through leftover bones. Wade made sure the wreck was towed away but kept for further examination, then he left for his office.

Chapter 22

Garza met Marina in her hospital room to give a pre-procedure briefing and answer any questions Marina might still have, but she was the last person Marina wanted to see right now. Moving to the side of Marina's bedside table, Garza smiled and said, "Well, today's your big day." Marina only nodded at the obvious, and she continued, "Let me tell you a little about what's going to happen to you."

Marina lay back and listened as best she could, trying to absorb the stream of facts and still psychologically accept what was about to happen. Although, being a nurse, she had a reasonable understanding of what was to occur, she still felt anxious and more than a little scared.

After she was finished with the short briefing, Garza asked, "Got any questions?"

"Just two," Marina said. "Will it hurt, and how long will it take?" Those were her bottom line when it came to procedures involving her own body.

Garza looked disbelievingly at Marina, shook her head and frowned. "This really isn't a big deal. Didn't you take the introductory briefing and video course?"

"Of course I did." Garza knew that, and Marina resented the rhetorical questioning. This wasn't grade school. "What does that have to do with my questions? Why do you and Dr. Baatard keep asking me that? Look, you may not think I'm very smart, but sometimes I like to hear things more than once."

"Okay: no, and about fifteen minutes," Garza said, shaking her head. "It always seems that it's the health care provider who is the biggest baby about these things."

"Thanks a lot," Marina replied, half-jokingly.

"Okay, now that that's all done, we're going to take your blood pressure, heart rate and temperature. Then things will get moving." Garza quickly and efficiently took Marina's vital signs and recorded the readings onto Marina's chart. After that, Garza went over to a corner and sat in an aging plastic chair and waited, reading a copy of People magazine.

Baatard came in only a few minutes later, humming the "Hi Ho, Hi Ho" song from Snow White. He pushed what seemed a lunch cart loaded with medical supplies on top. Following close behind Baatard was a short thirty-ish Oriental man, carrying a black plastic lunch pail type of container.

"Hi Marina," Baatard said. He saw Marina's anxious and surprised stare in the direction of the other man, and explained, "Oh, this is Frank Lieu. He's the embryologist for Conceptions Foundation"

"Yes, I think I recognize him from the video tape," Marina replied, as she uncomfortably watched Frank gawk at her with a childish smile. She pulled her blanket up to completely cover her legs, then said, "Really, Dr. Baatard. I'm quite nervous about having this procedure.

Can we just go ahead and get it over?" Marina pulled her robe a little more closed in the front, and again adjusted the blanket to more completely cover her legs. Frank made her feel more uneasy than even Baatard did, which was saying a lot. "Look, Dr. Baatard, are you certain you screened the embryos exactly as we discussed?"

"Yes I did, I sure did. I think you will be most pleased." He looked at her anxious face, then added, "But, there are no guarantees."

"Of course. Good," Marina acknowledged. "So, what's next?"

"Well, it's really easy enough. All this procedure entails is insertion of this very thin catheter into your vagina." Baatard held the embryo transfer catheter up in the air for Marina to see. "We'll pass the catheter through your cervix and into your uterus, and deposit the fertilized ova there. This should take only a few minutes, and then you can be on your way." Baatard snapped his fingers to emphasize how fast he anticipated the procedure would take. "By the way, did you happen to see Mrs. Denny Cruite?"

"Yes I did. I guess you know what she was here about."

Baatard nodded that he did, and looked away.

"Well, I was taken aback, to say the least. And I told her I needed time to think about it before saying yes or no."

"But, . . ." Baatard started.

"The answer for now is definitely NO. I need time to consider this more, although I really don't think I'll be changing my mind." She sternly looked at Baatard, making him understand that she wasn't going to be bullied into a response. "And what about him?" Marina asked, looking in Frank's direction. "Why do strangers need to be in the room? This isn't a public showing, Dr. Baatard," Marina frowned disapprovingly.

"Mr. Lieu is the embryologist. He's a highly trained and skilled technician and his presence during the procedure is essential."

Marina shrugged in a way which indicated that, although she didn't approve, she was willing to acquiesce on a point she didn't think she could win.

"Now, just be a good girl and cooperate."

"Excuse me, but I'm not a girl." Marina firmly corrected Baatard. "I'm a woman and I'm your patient. I would appreciate it if you don't refer to me as a 'girl' again." Marina looked sternly at Baatard, then grudgingly began to move her knees apart, guided by gentle pressure from Baatard's hand.

"Well, I'm sorry, Marina, I mean, Ms. Bonnaserra," Baatard said.

Marina gave a glacial stare followed by a nod.

After Baatard and Garza put on sterile gloves, Baatard took a narrow-mouth disposable plastic speculum and inserted it into Marina's vagina.

The speculum was ice-cold, and Marina reacted by pulling her buttock away from Baatard. "Ouch." she complained.

The Surrogate

Baatard realized what was happening when Marina squirmed back, and muttered an insincere, "Sorry." He then sternly told Marina, "Please, don't move. Okay?" as he continued to push the speculum into her vagina. Baatard bent over at the waist and looked down Marina's vaginal canal, then commented, "Good, very good. I can see the cervical opening - the cervical os - very clearly. Hand me a catheter, Frank." Baatard held out his open hand stretched in back of him, but continued to peer down Marina's vagina, held open by the speculum. Baatard repeatedly opened and closed his hand and snapped his fingers to emphasize to Frank to get a move on it, but remained frustrated by Frank's typical slowness.

Marina's vaginal canal was lit by a small fiber optic cable built into the body of the speculum. Experience taught Baatard to judge by the size of the speculum and the fit, that is to say the amount of resistance the vaginal canal gave the speculum, that this speculum had been the only thing in there for some time. He smiled knowingly to himself.

Marina saw Baatard smirk, and asked, indignantly, "Is there something humorous you see there, Dr. Baatard?"

"No, not at all, Ms. Bonnaserra," Baatard carefully replied, not looking up.

Frank handed Baatard a slender plastic disposable catheter; it contained one living being, even if only at the sixty-four cell stage. Baatard placed the catheter tip into Marina's cervical os and fed it slowly up deep within the uterus until it would advance no further.

Marina squirmed around uncomfortably in the bed,

then moaned and protested, "Ouch."

"Does it hurt you?" Garza asked, without displaying much real interest.

"No, yes, I don't know. I'm all right, I guess," Marina finally said.

"Please, try to stay perfectly still, just for a few more minutes. Okay?" Baatard told Marina as he gently squeezed the handle grip on his end of the embryo transfer catheter one fourth of the way until he heard a click. This sound suggested to Baatard that an embryo had been released from the catheter and was now free to attach to Marina's uterine wall.

Baatard started to reach out for another ova transfer catheter, and then suddenly paused. An idea, more an inspiration, strange, twisted, bizarre, unethical, and one eminently practical again was raised in his consciousness. Looking at the second plastic catheter, Baatard visualized, realized once again how he could satisfy Ramirez, and still do so according to Ramirez's own bizarre specifications, and still satisfy Denny and perhaps most of all, for only a little effort on his part, he would be at least one hundred thousand dollars richer. At first dismissing the idea, Baatard quickly changed his mind again and realized he could very well go through with this, he needed to, and he would. It was his only real choice. He remembered a line from Macbeth: "Desperate diseases are by desperate measures cured, or not at all," and could clearly see its relevance here.

Looking up at Marina over the sheets and between her knees, Baatard smiled slightly and said, "That's all there is to it. Now that wasn't too bad, was it?"

Marina, her face shrouded in a completely serious look, didn't reply. She found the procedure degrading and threatening and it made her uncomfortable. The idea of becoming pregnant and of being a mother filled her with enough apprehension and anxiety, already. She could only imagine what Charlie Kincade would say about it.

"Anyway, I hope the embryo attaches and develops well. We should know fairly soon," Baatard reassured Marina. He saw Frank looking his way, about to say something, and then stopped.

Marina pulled her hospital gown down to cover her legs, then asked, "And now what?"

"What you'll be doing is coming back for daily blood tests. If we detect rising estrogen levels, this will suggest to us successful implantation of the embryo has taken place. Then, about a week after that we'll begin taking ultrasound exams of the uterus. Once a gestation sac is observed, we're on our way." Slapping Marina's thigh, Baatard said, "Good girl," without first carefully considering his words. Seeing the angry look develop on Marina's face, he immediately said, "Sorry."

Marina again nodded, but said nothing, realizing that Baatard was simply too uncouth an ox to appreciate why he offended her.

"Any questions?" Baatard asked, then, not waiting for an answer, Baatard got up, told Marina, "See you in a week," and walked out. On his way out of the hospital room, Baatard reached over to the cart covered with fertilization implantation equipment, deftly grabbed the remaining two embryo transport syringes off Frank's tray and kept walking.

Frank appeared totally confused, and took off into the hospital corridor after Baatard, catching up to him in the hallway, yelling, "Dr. Baatard. Dr. Baatard."

Baatard kept walking, ignoring Frank completely. He seemed to know what Frank wanted, and he wasn't interested.

"What are you going to do with the other ova?" Frank continued to ask. "I thought you were going to use them here?" Frank insisted. He was out of breath and very upset at this change in the expected, the planned course of events.

"Frank, Frank, Frank," Baatard said, smiling wryly and slowly shaking his head as he continued walking away. "You need to exercise more, boy. You're all out of breath."

"But what about the other fertilized ova, Dr. Baatard? I thought . . . "

"Well, I was going to use all the fertilized ova, yes. But I decided it wasn't a good idea to expose Marina to the risk of multiple simultaneous pregnancies. That's a medical decision only a physician can make, Frank," Baatard smiled condescendingly. He patted Frank on the shoulder. "You're not a licensed physician in this country, yet. Anyway, do you remember that woman we determined to be carrying triplets last week?" Baatard asked.

"You mean Mrs. . . . "

"Yeah, her. Be careful about using patient's full names in public," Baatard cautioned Frank. "Patient confidentiality, you know."

Frank nodded he understood.

"Well, we had to go in and 'waste' one of the fetuses at ten weeks, just because she couldn't 'emotionally deal' with triplets. And you remember what problems that led to, don't you?"

Frank nodded he remembered.

"Well, I don't want to risk those problems here, that's all, Frank," Baatard said.

"No, but what about the other syringes, the other fertilized ova?"

"Why, they simply are no longer needed, Frank," Baatard explained as he kept walking away.

"But, what are you going to do . . . " Frank stammered.

"Do? I'm going to dispose of them, of course. We can't very well freeze these embryos at this point, now can we?"

Frank, confused, shook his head. "No, I guess not."

"See. There's no need to worry," Baatard smiled at Frank. Patting Frank on the shoulder, Baatard told him, "You're doing a fine job here at Conceptions Foundation."

Frank Lieu stood with a paralyzing motionless in the hall, seeming to be more confused than he had ever felt. Baatard could sense Frank's doubts and concerns, and this in turn made Baatard more uncertain than ever of Frank's reliability.

"Everyone is so pleased with your work, and I appreciate your concern. Keep it up, Frank," Baatard said as he walked away from the only person who knew which sperm were used to fertilize the LV and MB ova, and the altered disposition of all the fertilized MB-1 ova. Now, Baatard realized, there were two major tasks he had to accomplish. First, he had to determine how he would adopt out any child which resulted from the implantation of Marina's fertilized ova into their only logical recipient -- Lissa Vernor. But her feckless husband Ryder would be the key here. and just as important, was the ultimate 'disposition' of Frank Lieu, the de facto historian. Frank's own actions would be the major determinant of both their futures.

Chapter 23

Intensive Care Unit

Haven General Hospital

Baatard took the elevator from the OB-GYN ward Marina was on down to the Intensive Care Unit. There were two other duties he had to perform, and he couldn't afford to avoid it much longer. First, he stopped at the Nurse's Station, and using the justification that Lissa may have had a recurrence of her bleeding, got a nurse to bring a pelvic exam setup into Lissa's room, then went down the hall to Lissa's room.

Lissa was the only patient in Room 714 West, a small room crammed with three beds and nightstands, and a small attached bathroom. The curtains were drawn around Lissa's bed, and only half the overhead lights were on. A TV set to the news channel played in one corner, probably as a hideout for the nurses on break. Baatard walked over to Lissa's bed, took her hand and said, softly, "Hi, Lissa. How are you?" He expected no reply and wasn't disappointed. There was not the slightest change in her flat facial expression, not the finest twitch of her fine eyebrows signifying sensation, nor movement of the lips which once laughed out loud.

The ward nurse entered the room and set some packaged medical equipment on a bed stand near Lissa. "Here it is. Do you want to examine her now?" she asked, still skeptical of the motive for a pelvic exam on a comatose woman.

"Yes, that will be fine. I'll do a quick manual exam, then a speculum exam, and then finish off with a pap smear. This should take only a few minutes." Wanting to get the transfer over with as soon as possible, before there would be any possibility of challenges to him, he helped the nurse move Lissa's hospital gown up over her knees.

He put on his gloves, squeezed some lubricating jelly out, and then inserted some fingers of his right hand into Lissa's vagina. There should be plenty of room for this, he thought. Then, taking the plastic speculum, Baatard inserted it into Lissa's vagina. Peering down, Baatard could clearly see her cervix. Good. Reaching over, he took the ova catheter and inserted it into the vagina and up to the cervical opening and through. A small dot of blood appeared, but quickly coagulated. Squeezing the syringe handle, Baatard released the egg into Lissa's uterus, then withdrew the catheter and placed it on the bedside, out of sight of the nurse. He quickly obtained a Pap smear, ran the scraper against a microscope slide, and then withdrew the speculum.

While the nurse was covering Lissa and cleaning up the bed area from the procedure, Baatard took the ova catheter, coiled it and stuffed it into one of the large pockets of his white coat, and left the room to the nurse's station. There he wrote a short procedure note, carefully omitting any reference to the ova transfer. He walked down the hall in the opposite direction.

As Baatard walked down the ward past the family waiting room, he quickly looked in, then just as quickly stepped to the side when he saw Dr. Ryder Vernor waiting inside there, alone. Baatard took a deep breath, tried to give the appearance of being relaxed but concerned, and went in.

Ryder stood against the window, looking out. His clothes were wrinkled and soiled and he hadn't shaved. Once an active young doctor in his early thirties, he now looked old, worn out, stooped, and distracted. Baatard knew that Ryder was hurting; he could certainly understand why. If it had been his wife who had stroked out, rather than Lissa Vernor, he would certainly be feeling the same way. What he was about to do next was without a doubt the one task Baatard hated the most.

Their talk together took almost thirty minutes. Baatard thought that Ryder must have given these same courtesy conferences himself. Ryder had that certain sense of familiarity with what Baatard was saying and going to say next, which, when combined with being on the receiving line, made for all around uncomfortable feelings. Baatard found Ryder to be, at least on the surface, as well-informed and understanding as when they spoke last - shortly after Lissa Vernor's surgery. Somehow, though, Baatard had to think that Vernor wasn't being completely candid with him. Ryder seemed almost too reasonable, too accepting, and too passive. The other side, aggression, was conspicuously missing. Baatard was well aware of the psychological stages one usually goes through in these circumstances: first denial, then bargaining, then anger, and finally resignation. Maybe Ryder had already managed to work his way to the last stage, a stage Baatard fortunately had never been in himself.

Once the "patient disposition task" was over, Baatard muttered some perfunctory apologies and empty words of encouragement to Ryder, then hurried out of Haven General and back to his office.

* * *

The first week of life was hectic for the fertilized ova, still slowly forming its life-giving attachments to Marina's uterine wall. The eight-cell zygote Frank had prepared and Baatard had injected had already divided after about thirty hours into a small sphere – a blastomere. Cell divisions came faster in the warm blood and nutrient-rich environment and within only three more days a small ball of cells - referred to in medical circles as a 'morula' - was formed. A net of nutrient-giving blood vessels attached the morula to the rich uterine wall. By the seventh day the morula divided into two layers separated by a fluid-filled cavity. The ever-increasing collection of cells - destined eventually to become human - was now known as a blastocyst.

   * * *

Chapter 24

Haven General Hospital

Several Weeks Later

Dr. Rudy Salvatore glumly sat alone at Lissa Vernor's bedside, unable to leave, for the third day in a row. Baatard only rarely came by any longer, there being little he or anyone could do at this point for Lissa. Salvatore also noticed that Lissa's husband, Ryder Vernor, also came by less frequently with every passing day. When Ryder did visit, it was only for a minute or two. He would look sadly at his wife, hold her hand, fleetingly kiss her on the cheek and then leave. Salvatore couldn't even imagine what the pain for Ryder must have been like.

Salvatore felt quite certain he at least could leave any time he wanted to, but he still stayed. As he stared into Lissa Vernor's unresponsive, expressionless face, he remembered the times just so recently she had laughed, told jokes, made dinner, spoke to friends, had plans, and he tried to hold back his tears, for he thought that crying openly was most unprofessional.

Salvatore would get up occasionally to eat, go to the bathroom, see his other patients, make some calls out, but he always returned to check Lissa's eyes. It always came down to that, he thought: checking her eyes. And for the second time this hour, Salvatore slowly got up, took the portable ophthalmoscope from his pocket, pulled open Lissa's eye lids, and shined the light in. "Lissa, please look at me."

The optic fundi were normal, her discs were flat, he thought, but the pupils were still dilated. There was no constriction of the pupils to the light source. This could only mean that Lissa's cerebral injury extended to her brain stem - that most basic, primitive and essential component of her entire central nervous system. Salvatore switched off the ophthalmoscope's light. "Lissa, are you there? Can you hear me? Can't you say something, anything to me?" he whispered. "Please."

Steve Tanabe, a neurosurgical resident, and Salvatore's close friend since medical school, came over to Lissa's bed. Baatard had called Steve only a few minutes ago, and asked him to look in on The Sim doc, as Salvatore's friends called him. "Hey, man, don't you think you shouldn't get so emotionally attached?" Tanabe asked, placing his hand on Salvatore's shoulder. "I mean, it's not going to help her any," Tanabe said, "or you."

Salvatore looked away from Tanabe, and then remarked, "Her pupils are still dilated and unresponsive. Hey, it doesn't get any worse than this, does it?"

Tanabe also performed a quick neurological exam on Lissa. The result was, unfortunately, the same. He shook his head after sadly confirming what Salvatore had already observed, then said, "Look, Rudy, it's not your fault. Bad surgical outcomes happen."

"Okay, it's not my fault. But I knew this woman, Steve. I knew her before her brain turned to squash." Salvatore looked disbelievingly at the side of Lissa's scalp where the intracranial pressure monitor screw went in. A small sensor pierced through Lissa's skull to monitor the pressure inside the brain case: too much pressure could lead to instant death. There were some short-term, temporizing medical treatments that could be taken to reduce the brain swelling that caused the pressure rise. Unfortunately, no therapy existed to reverse the underlying damage and restore Lissa's consciousness. Salvatore wondered if the pressure screw and the medications were really more for his and Dr. Vernor's benefit now.

"Lissa was such a good person. Shit, I can't deal with this anymore. I quit." Salvatore angrily threw his stethoscope onto Lissa's bed, took off his white coat and headed off the ward.

Tanabe tried to catch up with Salvatore, but gave up, shrugged his shoulders, and continued with his patient's rounds. Stopping back at Lissa's bed, Tanabe wrote a note in the Physician's Orders section of her chart: "Transfer to Chronic Care." Baatard had asked Tanabe to be sure this was done. Tanabe pulled out the blue order tab on the side of the thick notebook-like patient record; this flagged the ward clerk that an order had been entered. Wearily, he dropped Lissa's chart on the nurse's desk, and left the ward to finish his own work.

Chapter 25

The hospital pharmacist, Lynn Janislowski, also known affectionately as Jelly Roll to many people who worked the wards at Haven General, passed Salvatore on her way onto the ward. Salvatore almost pushed into Lynn in his haste to leave, but failed to respond to Lynn's greeting. Ignoring this, Lynn muttered, "I wonder what's wrong with him?" then continued pushing the large medication cart into the hospital ward's drug room. She picked up the drug dispensing sheet off the ward clerk's desk and ran through the day's unit-dose replacement needs, humming peacefully to herself.

After replenishing the non-prescription and prescription cabinets, Lynn turned to the narcotic shelf. She pulled the key chain from around her neck, unlocked the cabinet, and located the narcotic dispensing log. It was hardly touched; only a few codeine tablets, some Schedule III analgesic, and one ampule of morphine sulfate, scribbled down as "MS." Picking up the small cardboard box which normally contained three MS ampules, Lynn noted there were two amps missing. Surprised, she rechecked the log: this was a new box, which meant that there would still have been two ampules of MS inside if only one was used. In addition, there appeared to be a short count of five codeine tablets, each was 5 milligrams.

Deanna could hear Lynn's shrill, annoying voice calling over to her from across the nurse's station. "Oh, shit. What now?" She lay down the patient chart she was writing nursing notes in, and went over to see what the problem was.

"Deanna, why are there two amps of MS gone from the box, but only one signed out?" Lynn asked.

Deanna shrugged her shoulders, looked toward the sink and said in a flat voice, "I don't know, honestly. But I'm not the only nurse who has access to that room, you know."

"But, the log says you're the only one who entered the locked cabinet." Lynn held up the narcotic log book in her hands.

"Oh, yes. Well, I forgot to write it down, but there was just so much doing here this morning. A little earlier, when I went to draw up some MS, I noticed some succulent material in the ampule after I opened it. I figured the stuff was a contaminant and the ampule was useless, so I wasted it," Deanna said, matter-of-factly.

"You what?"

"I dumped the MS contents into the sink," Deanna said as she looked innocently over at the small sink in the medication room.

"Sure, I understand what you meant, Deanna, but I don't understand your method. Hospital procedure clearly states that . . . " Lynn started to remind Deanna.

"But I had to do something, Lynn. The patient was in a lot of pain, so I had to use some codeine tablets. You pharmacy people don't understand the stress of working on the medical surgical wards. There are thousands of patients, all screaming out in pain at the same time. The pressure is tremendous. Besides, I'm just a floater today. I don't normally work the wards," she pointedly reminded Lynn.

"Deanna, I think you're exaggerating a bit, don't you? But I do know how much we ALL have to do here. Everyone is short of staff. I just wanted to . . . "

"Look, I meant to confirm the change a little later with her ward physician, Dr. Salvatore. I know him and I'm sure he wouldn't object. Unfortunately, you know how things get around here and, well, I never got around to it," she said, avoiding looking Lynn in the eyes.

"What patient of Dr. Salvatore are we talking about here, Deanna? The ward records don't show anyone at all receiving MS?"

Deanna smiled, fidgeted with her keys to the medication cabinet, and then looked back to the nurse's station. "Look, I have to get back to work. There are new patients being transferred in and I have to finish the paper work. You understand, don't you?" Deanna backed away from Lynn, smiling politely. She was conscious of a tremor in her hands, and struggled unsuccessfully to control it.

"Sure, sure," Lynn said. "But, please, Deanna. Try to be better on keeping records. You never know when we could get audited. MS vial consumption must exactly match chart orders. It's hospital protocol," she said, slowly shaking her head, a puzzled look on her face.

After leaving the ward, Lynn went back to her office. It was a nondescript cubicle in a hallway off the main corridor by the inpatient pharmacy. Once inside, she switched on her pharmacy department computer, then logged into the medication audit program.

Lynn ran a program that compiled the numbers of medication accidents and accidental wastage and compared it to the total usage of narcotics and controlled medications. She also compared accidents and wastage of non-narcotic medications. Then Lynn compared the hospital-wide output to one restricted to shifts and floors Deanna worked on the last six months, including those shifts when Deanna was off. Realizing the search could take hours of computer time, Lynn logged off.

* * *

During the following weeks of life, the embryo alive inside Marina's uterus showed continued growth of its cell mass. The developing ball of cells was now well-situated on the enriched warm lining of Marina's uterus. Soon the blastocyst transformed into a two-layer disk, still without visibly identifying human characteristics but definitely alive. Pulsating blood vessels from the blastocyst proliferated at an astounding rate and automatically attached feeding conduits to Marina's uterus. A final home for a fetus and a nutritional supply strong enough to last nine months were being assembled.

* * *

Chapter 26

It took several hours for Deanna and the hospital's social worker to finish the transfer of Lissa Vernor to Haven Convalescent Hospital, and, when it was all done, the whole activity left Deanna feeling empty and in a way cheap and soiled. Deanna watched as Lissa was carried like excess baggage out of the room on a transfer gurney. No sooner was she out than a team of aides came in to disinfect her vacated bed. Obviously, another patient needed it. Deanna stood by the bedside, running her hand along the still-warm impression left by Lissa's body, shaking her head sadly, wishing secretly it were instead Baatard being transferred out on a stretcher.

When the transfer was over with, Deanna quickly walked past the hospital cafeteria, down the narrow corridor between lockers and linen carts and around the corner, a new force and purpose now in her stride. Once there, she entered a small phone booth built into the wall and carefully closed the door. Deanna looked outside the door again to be sure she was alone, then called a long time friend of hers - Vena Kleinman.

Deanna had once worked with Vena in Dr. Ryder Vernor's office, before she took a position in the operating room at Haven General. They still met from time to time, occasionally after work for drinks, and had shared their problems before. Vena was as close to Dr. Ryder Vernor as Deanna felt comfortable in getting right now.

Deanna had no doubt, from what she had been told
and what she had witnessed herself, about the cause of
Lissa Vernor's stroke. Even more than the damage caused
Lissa, she herself was hurt by Baatard's constant barrage
of insults. What about her own pain and suffering?
Deanna's thoughts never progressed to her own motives -
she just went ahead and made the call to Vena. She had
come to expect verbal abuse from surgeons, and had
learned to ignore it. Like a fool, she had thought her on-
again, off-again 'special' relationship with Baatard would
at least move him to treat her somewhat akin to the
physical closeness they occasionally experienced. What a
fool she was, she laughed ironically.

Deanna quickly told an astonished Vena what she
knew of the Lissa Vernor debacle, and what her
suspicions were. Someone needed to know the truth of
what had happened in the O.R., so Lissa's damage
wouldn't be forgotten and conveniently swept under the
professional rug.

Vena, of course, was aware of what had happened to
her boss's wife, but not how it had occurred. Ryder
Vernor didn't discuss his wife's tragedy very much around
the office: doing so made him more depressed than he
already was.

Deanna admitted to Vena that she was at a loss on
how to proceed, and was very fearful of taking any direct
steps herself. Deanna was certain that even were she to

talk to someone anonymously at Haven General Hospital, she would be turned in and fired. Physicians at Haven General were treated like gods, and their transgressions were assiduously kept closely guarded secrets.

Vena thanked Deanna for the information, assured her of confidentiality, and said that she knew just what to do. Vena, in reality, did not. After ending Deanna's call, Vena thought for a long time about how best to handle the information with which she had been entrusted. Her feelings about Lissa were ambivalent at best, particularly given the odd relationship they both shared with Ryder. Her loyalty to Ryder was firm, which was more than she could say for Lissa's.

Solely on inspiration, Vena called Marina. Marina seemed to be the most level-headed person Vena had met in a long time, even they didn't exactly associate socially. Marina had also known Lissa for years, although apparently not too well. And Deanna remembered that Marina worked at Haven General, although she didn't recall in which capacity.

"Marina, you know Lissa Vernor, Dr. Vernor's wife, don't you?" Vena asked.

"Yes, I've known Lissa Vernor since high school," Marina replied, still surprised at receiving a call from Vena. They had only met a few times, usually at Dr. Ryder Vernor's office, and once at an art showing.

"Well, you won't believe this, but Lissa's in a coma."

"Yes, I heard about it through the hospital grapevine. Isn't that terrible." Although Marina knew the general problem, she knew none of the details at this point. In her position with the Office of Quality Assurance at Haven

General, she naturally was informed of all adverse or unexpected outcomes of patients, and she expected that eventually she would be getting Lissa's chart too. As she approached her mid-thirties, Marina found that serious medical problems happening to people her own age disturbed her. Reviewing the medical records of others, she often found herself worrying about her own increasing vulnerability.

"About a month ago Lissa got really sick," Vena related. "Dr. Vernor said she seemed at first to have a stomach flu, but it just got worse. Lissa had to be taken to the emergency room. They did some tests and I guess they found bleeding and needed to operate on her. I don't know all the details, but from what I was told, Lissa had a lot of bleeding during surgery."

"I don't understand, Vena. You say she had bleeding from a stomach flu?"

"I only know what I heard," Vena explained, trying to control herself, before continuing. "She bled a lot during surgery, and afterwards she had a severe stroke. Lissa never woke up, and they had to send her to a convalescent hospital."

"I just can't believe it. How horrible. But Vena, why are you calling me about this?"

"Good question, Marina. Well, the oddest thing happened and I can't really tell you too many details without revealing who told them to me. But, someone involved in Lissa's care thinks Dr. Baatard made an error in her surgery which resulted in Lissa's coma."

"Oh, how terrible." Marina exclaimed, thinking about all the times Dr. Baatard had taken care of her, the surgical procedures, the fertilization, her own bleed during a procedure performed by Dr. Baatard. If Baatard had erred in the care of Lissa Vernor, he had plenty of opportunities to harm her also, and the very thought, even the possibility made her skin crawl. "But Vena, what do you want me to do with this information?" She vaguely knew what was coming.

"I don't know, really," Vena lied. "But, I don't think Ryder, Dr. Vernor knows any of this. I think he should, or at least the hospital should, don't you? I remembered you worked there, and I just thought you'd know the appropriate channels to take."

Marina was noncommittal and politely thanked Vena for the information before hanging up. She thought for a long time about what she had just learned. Assuming any of it was at all accurate and reliable, then Vena was right: someone at Haven General needed to know. And, in her position as QA nurse, she would be the one.

At first, the most logical approach Marina could think of was to call Haven General's legal office. They should be notified immediately. Yet, she thought this might compromise the confidentiality Vena had promised. Instead, Marina decided to first initiate a review herself. Since Lissa's adverse outcome occurred during surgery, and it was unexpected, the case would come to Marina anyway for review. Her earlier inquiries wouldn't attract too much attention, she reasoned.

Marina was certain Baatard, even more than most doctors, possessed a great deal of pull at Haven General and she didn't want to cross him. Marina also fully expected the hospital would side with Baatard if there was any doubt. Further, she began to feel uncomfortable with Baatard supplying her IVF care. The last thing she wanted, now that she was finally undergoing IVF, was a stupid or careless mistake.

* * *

The two-layer embryonic disk that Marina's egg had transformed into now again changed its character, operating under a will of its own. It converted in complexity into three layers, directed to do so by only poorly understood laws of nature. A primitive central nervous system, body cavities and a heart all formed. The body of the embryo was now divided up into ridges called somites and actually resembled a tiny sea horse. A human awaited.

* * *

Chapter 27

Marina occasionally took a morning off from work in order to attend pre-trial hearings for accused rapists. It was an odd routine, but one with a purpose. Today several men accused of raping a young woman were being arraigned. A few of the aspects of the case resembled the tragedy she was subjected to so long ago. More than listening, she hoped to get a good look at the faces of the accused. Although it was now nearly eighteen years later, Marina was almost religiously convinced she would still recognize her attacker if she saw him long enough and stared at him carefully. After all, she had painted his portrait tens of times, many from the perspective the passage of years might have taken. Although she had been disappointed up to now, she could not give up the way the police so easily did - she owed it to herself.

Marina was surprised in a pleasant way when she met Charlie Kincade as he stood in the hallway outside the pre-trial courtroom around 9 a.m. Charlie was talking to a group of anxious-looking people, whom Marina assumed were his clients. He nodded her way, excused himself and walked over to her.

"Hi, Marina," he smiled. "I've been wondering what happened to you. I've called your house more than a few times, but you've never returned my calls." He looked more concerned than annoyed or offended.

"You look good, Charlie," Marina said, placing her

hand gently on his arm. She paused for an uncomfortable few seconds, unsure of what to say next, or more precisely, how much to say. She found attempting pregnancy, especially the circuitous way she was going about it, most awkward. "Please, don't take my not returning your calls as a snub. Something very important has been going on in my life and I just haven't been ready or able to speak with you again just yet, that's all."

"Oh. It sounds pretty serious," he smiled, uncomfortably.

"If you mean, am I dating another man, the answer is no. But, I can't tell you what it's about, not now at least. If something comes of it, you'll be one of the first to know, okay?" She wanted to be vague, lest her ova's implantation didn't work out. It was embarrassing enough just talking about what she was attempting.

"Sure, thanks Marina," Charlie said, a puzzled look on his face.

"So," Marina said, straightening herself up a bit, "what brings you here this morning?" She looked over at the people Charlie was talking to. "Those clients of yours don't look the criminal type."

"Oh, them. Well, they're not criminals at all, Marina, although there really is no 'criminal type.' This case is real exciting. Didn't you read about the Manuel Rossa trial?"

Marina shook her head. She was pleasantly surprised to see Charlie so involved and interested in his work.

Hopefully that was a good sign that things were finally working out for him at his office.

"I'm surprised. Aren't you the one who reads the court section every day?"

His dig stung. Charlie had indicated in the past he thought that she was obsessed with finding her rapist and that after so many years she should just "give it up." But that was not going to happen. It might work for others, but not for her.

"Anyway, this case is fascinating. I defended Mr. Rossa six years ago on a rape charge, and he lost."

Typical, Marina thought. She still liked Charlie as a friend, although she sometimes wondered why. But, she doubted she would ever use him as a lawyer if she needed one. He didn't seem to project the confidence of a winner.

"There were no witnesses, no physical evidence, but Mr. Rossa had dated the victim earlier the week she was raped. They had argued, and Rossa couldn't provide a credible alibi for his location the evening of her violent rape. The prosecution came up with a local drug dealer who testified he thought he may have seen Mr. Rossa at the victim's apartment. I think the police got to the drug dealer first and altered his testimony. Anyway, Mr. Rossa got convicted."

Marina had a hard time feeling bad that anyone got convicted of anything, let alone for rape. Although she hated to admit it to herself, she seemed to feel that all men were guilty of rape until proven innocent. Her stomach began to knot up in a tense ball, and she suddenly wanted to terminate her conversation and get far away from the courthouse and the accused rapists.

"I've never believed Mr. Rossa did it. He's a very gentle, intelligent man. It's just not in his character."

"It sounds like a real injustice," she scoffed as she struggled to regain her composure. "Rapists are all such sweethearts, you know."

"For an artist and an educated person, you're a hard woman, Marina."

"That's certainly an insensitive thing for you to say, Charlie, especially since you know what hell I had to live through. Well, I guess that unjust convictions can happen and innocent people rarely can get sent to jail." She had no doubt wrongful convictions did occur, but the alternative of not sentencing every convicted felon because he persisted in claiming innocence was not too good either. Her rapist was still free, after all these years. The possibility that he was now dead had occurred to her, but she had dismissed it, as Charlie was fond of saying, for lack of evidence. There were times when she could almost feel the beast's evil presence, and was certain he was still alive, and possibly nearby. Did he remember her as well, or at all?

"Yes, the system's certainly not perfect. I'm the first person to agree with that. Anyway, in this case, Mr. Rossa's family was devastated. Although they never said it, I think they always have blamed me for his conviction, and I've been trying to right that wrong for six years. Then, last month I found a way to do it," Charlie beamed with pride.

"Let me guess. You found a witness to Rossa's being elsewhere, or you found the real rapist," Marina said.

"No, well sort of. It's even better than that," Charlie beamed. "There's a type of genetic evidence that's being used in criminal cases. It's called genetic identity testing."

Marina told Charlie she had heard of it. The science was interesting, but she wondered if it could also spring free a guilty person.

"What I did was a big gamble because if I were wrong, I could have provided additional evidence against my client which would have extended his sentence. But Mr. Rossa urged me to proceed, which only further convinced me of his innocence."

Marina wondered why Charlie wasn't so persistent and aggressive where their own relationship was concerned. She liked those qualities in a man.

"I remembered there were some clothes, including the victim's underwear, from the trial. I checked, and they were still in an evidence locker. I got the D.A. to agree to send certain stains on the pants and panties for genetic identity testing. Not surprising to me, the semen came back totally incompatible with that of my client."

"Very clever, Charlie," Marina said. "But Charlie, are you absolutely, completely convinced you're letting an innocent man go free?" Accidentally releasing a real criminal was, in her mind, a greater danger than unjust conviction could ever be.

"Look, Marina, I can understand where you're coming from, but in this case, the man is totally innocent."

Marina nodded angrily, her muscles in her neck tensed up and she could feel a flush of blood rushing into her face. "No offense, Charlie, but you can never understand where I'm coming from on this. Trust me." After she said this, she could see he was offended, and decided to back off. "So, I suppose you got the judge to admit Mr. Rossa was innocent and they let him go. That's a wonderful achievement," she told him, not trying in the least to hide her heartfelt sarcasm.

"Not exactly," Charlie told her, evenly. "Look, the judge reviewed the case, and threw out the original conviction. What it means is, even if they would want to retry Mr. Rossa, they don't have enough evidence for a conviction. Unfortunately, that's not the same as a statement of his innocence. But, it's enough to get him released," Charlie smiled but it was not a completely comfortable one.

Just then there was a loud cry of happiness and cheering and applause. The family rushed forward to embrace Mr. Rossa; after a few moments, Charlie left Marina to join them. Marina looked carefully at Mr. Rossa just in case, but could see instantly that he was not the animal she so doggedly searched for. The man was in his early to mid forties, powerfully built with muscular upper arms the size of bowling pins crammed tightly in a worn blue sport jacket. Marina was certain she had never seen him before.

Marina couldn't help but notice the man's greasy hair, gold earring, and several oversized rings on each hand. Pock marks, probably from some childhood illness, scared his face. His facial features somehow made a chilling impression on Marina, and without staring at him she tried to remember as much detail as she could. She thought that she might want to use some aspects for a portrait some day, perhaps another "special" portrait -- her training in art made it relatively easy for her to pick up physical characteristics like that.

Almost as if instinctively, Rossa turned around and noticed Marina staring at him. His eyes critically looked over at her, slowly inspecting her face, then moving down the front of her sweater, lingered over her breasts, then down to her hips, over her legs, and Marina felt as if he was actually touching her intimately with his eyes. Then Rossa cracked the most unfriendly of smirks before turning back to Charlie. His judgmental look made Marina feel uncomfortable, almost as if she had been flung open for inspection and violated. For an instant she thought she recognized something about him, and then just as quickly realized how ridiculous that was and dismissed the thought.

Marina left Charlie and the Rossa family to celebrate, and went inside the courtroom. There were other men accused of rape, and she wanted to have a good look at them.

While seated waiting for the defendants to be brought in, Marina wondered what she would do if by some miracle she finally confronted the man who raped her. That eventuality had actually never been faced, but she never gave up her hope that it would someday happen. She wasn't a particularly strong woman, nor was she partial to physical violence, but her anger persisted. Even if she thought she saw her attacker, she had to wonder if anyone would even believe the unprovable accusations of an obsessed female, especially after so many years had passed.

Marina's attention suddenly shifted to the conversation Charlie just had with her. She found it most interesting that stains found on a pair of panties could be used as evidence to identify a criminal years after a crime had been committed. An image of the evidence bag given her from the police came to mind. In the bag were the clothes she had worn that fateful night so long ago. As she remembered it, there were many different stains on her clothes. Some were obviously dirt and grease. Marina wondered if one of the stains was semen, and how she could go about determining this.

Chapter 28

Haven General Hospital

As the Quality Assurance - QA - nurse, Marina was
automatically notified whenever there was an unexpected
or untoward complication on any patient admitted to any
service. She had heard about the Lissa Vernor case almost
as soon as the surgery was complete, and had already
requested the operative and Surgical Intensive Care Unit
charts long before Vena had called her. Nevertheless,
Vena's call was a red flag indicating that this particular
case required more than her usually extensive review. It
could also easily end up a real political hot potato.

   The foreboding, voluminous Lissa Vernor inpatient
records arrived several days after Lissa's care at Haven
General was complete and Lissa had been
unceremoniously transferred to a convalescent facility for
custodial care. Before even touching the hefty stack,
Marina tried to clear her head of any preconceived
notions, a task she aspired to each day but somehow never
could completely achieve. Her patient-doctor relationship
with Dr. Baatard, and her personal knowledge of the
patient - Lissa Vernor - admittedly made an unbiased
view somewhat difficult. Marina opened to the first page
of Lissa Vernor's voluminous medical records and began

to read.

Within minutes, Marina had finished the Problem List: the front sheet of most inpatient charts. The Problem List summarized the major medical and surgical problems that the patient had, along with a list of current medications, allergies, and the name, address and phone number of the patient's immediate family.

Marina got into the Surgical Summary next, and then the Surgical Intensive Care Unit Summary. "This is going to be a wild one," she said to herself as she began to realize the complexity and enormity of the situation. Marina straightened herself up in the uncomfortable hardwood chair supplied by the hospital and surveyed the damage documented in front of her.

Marina had not been given specifics from Vena about what she thought, or rather had heard, had gone wrong with Lissa's surgery. This left Marina with the impression Vena and her source weren't sure themselves. But, Vena seemed to somehow know what actually happened during the surgery, implying to Marina that Vena's source must have actually been there. Someone who was there would have seen the flow, the complete story, and understood more, and Marina respected that. Inside information from nurses, Marina had found, usually was correct.

After another hour of carefully reading and rereading Lissa Vernor's inpatient chart, it was still not clear to Marina what, if anything, had gone wrong with Lissa

Vernor's surgery. Clearly there was bleeding. Troubling, no source was found, although there was more than ample documentation the surgeons had looked. Marina briefly considered trying to speak with Dr. Baatard, but dismissed this until first clearing it with her superiors and the hospital attorney.

Several hours later, Marina's attention still was fixated on what she read. Marina turned to Section Seven of the main set of hospital records: the Nursing Notes. She momentarily stopped, put her phone on answer, poured herself another cup of coffee, and resumed reading. It all seemed there: the nurses admitting assessment, the progress notes, the documentation by Deanna Baptiste that the surgeons were notified several times of an apparent bleeding problem post-operatively. Lissa Vernor certainly was not doing well in the recovery room, but the care she received seemed appropriate, at least it was as far as Marina could determine from her perspective as a nurse.

Marina turned next to the nurse's notes from the recovery room. While unable to stop her reading, Marina used her free hand to pick up the phone to the hospital legal office.

Lemar Jackson, the hospital attorney, took the call. "Hi, Marina. How are you doing?" he asked.

"Not bad. How are you doing?" Marina asked, smiling as she twirled a pencil in her fingers. Lemar was one of the few men she occasionally passed in the halls who paid attention to her. Several times, she had expected him to ask her out, but he never did. Marina wondered what the problem was, but never pressed the issue, especially now that she was undergoing IVF. "Lemar, have you heard anything about the Lissa Vernor case?" she asked, directing her attention back to the matter at hand.

"No, can't say I have. Should I?"

"I think you will." She thought they all would.

"Then we better talk. How about my office in half an hour?" Lemar asked.

"See you, Lemar," Marina said, and then walked over to the ladies room to freshen up a bit.

Marina was shown right into Lamar's office off to one corner of the Legal Affairs Department. It was small and crowded, not much larger than her own and crammed with books, hospital charts stacked ten high, sticker notes on the wall, and two phones. "Lemar, I received a routine notification about the unexpected and poor surgical outcome on the Lissa Vernor case. I've been doing some reading, as you can see," she said, pointing to the hefty volumes she brought with her.

"So, who's the nurse who reported this to you?" Lemar asked coolly.

Surprised, Marina said, "Why? Do you think I work only from informers? It's just a routine review, that's all. This isn't the KGB, Lemar."

"Sure," he smiled, not at all convinced.

She gave Lemar a serious smile, crossed her legs and adjusted her position in the soft leather chair. Perhaps her being "tipped off" was more obvious than she thought. "Anyway, if there was a source, I'd like to keep it to myself for now, if you don't mind. But, take it from me, she is in a very good position to know what happened to the patient."

"So, there was an informant, and it was a female. Probably a nurse. And what did this source of yours allege happened? Was there malpractice?" Jackson asked.

"Hey, I'm not a lawyer, Lemar. I'm only a nurse in QA, that's all. But, this chart would have eventually made it to me for sure anyway."

"Why?" Lemar asked.

"Because there was a bad surgical outcome, of course," Marina told Lemar. "To keep it short, a patient - the wife of a medical staff - was admitted through the ER with internal bleeding." Lemar shook his head and moaned up at the ceiling as she said 'wife of a medical staff.' "The patient was taken to surgery, no bleeding source could be found, and she was closed." Marina started to continue her summary of the case, but was interrupted by Lemar.

"Was there evidence the patient was still bleeding at the time her surgical exploration began?"

Marina nodded yes.

"And was there evidence she was still bleeding when the surgical exploration was complete?"

Again Marina nodded yes. "Apparently, Lissa continued to bleed and may have stroked out as a result of the continued and uncontrolled blood loss." Marina finished, smiled slightly at Lemar and folding her hands on her lap. She caught Lemar gazing at her legs, and readjusted her dress downward. Although she liked Lemar professionally and as a person, when she considered all that was going on in her life now, she wasn't sure she had room for more than one lawyer.

"Do you think there was a problem with the care Lissa Vernor received?" Lemar asked, taking more notes in a small steno book.

"No, I don't think so, except perhaps not finding the source of bleeding. And, maybe not giving Lissa enough fluids or blood soon enough."

"Maybe she wasn't bleeding," Lemar asked.

"What do you mean? Of course Lissa Vernor was bleeding. They saw evidence of continued bleeding during the surgery. This is clearly documented in her medical and surgical chart, and in the O.R. report, Lemar."

"Could she have been oozing from all over the place instead of bleeding in just one site? I think I heard of that kind of thing happening." Lemar Jackson looked at the clock on the wall, then at his watch. "Shit, I'm late. Look, I have to go now, I have an important appointment. Why don't you leave what you have with me so I can look it over? And, could you ask around about this 'oozing' thing. I'm sure I heard of it somewhere. See you after work?"

Marina smiled and shook her head no. "We better

keep our relationship on a strictly professional level for now, don't you agree?"

"Yes, sure, I guess to avoid the appearance of conflict of interest on our parts," he replied, not looking too offended or disappointed.

Chapter 29

Marina's House
Haven, New Jersey

* * *

By the seventh week after the IVF procedure, what began
as an embryonic disk had become miraculously
transformed into a cylinder-shaped embryo. A head and
tail were clearly visible. Inside the head, a rudimentary
brain formed, although consciousness was still months
away. Tiny limbs, eyes, ears and nose all rapidly
developed, changing the appearance of the embryo to
something undeniably human. The embryo had now
become a fetus. The strong pulse of life, initiated long
ago, had evolved far.

* * *

After her ova implantation procedure, Marina returned to
her daily activities almost without limitation. Baatard had
instructed her to go about her life as usual, and she gladly
had taken him literally. She even tried going back to the

exercise club, but went only a few times before confirming her impression that the people there, particularly the men, were all intolerably boring and vapid. Painting alone in her studio or reading were her only forms of relaxation.

A few days after returning home, Marina picked up the phone to call Dr. Vernor's office. She needed to find why there was such a delay in getting a copy of her records transferred to Baatard's office. It would also be a good opportunity to see how Lissa was doing. Once Lissa had been transferred out of Haven General Hospital, her direct sources of follow-up were severed. "Vena, this is Marina Bonnaserra. How is everything?" she began, attempting to not seem so obviously interested only in pumping Vena for information.

"There's no change, really," Vena sighed. "Lissa is still in a coma."

"Oh, how terrible. It must be very hard on Dr. Vernor," Marina said. Now that Marina suspected that Vena may be spending time with Ryder, other than at work, she had to be more cautious about what conversations she had with Vena, what information she gave, and what she agreed to do in Vena's behalf. She considered the possibility of her being used as a pawn in a malpractice move by Ryder against Baatard, with malicious seeds being planted by Vena, even though she found it hard to give that much credence.

"Absolutely. Dr. Vernor is just beside himself with worry." Vena lowered her voice to a whisper before adding, "This is having a very negative effect on his practice, too."

"Oh my, I'm sorry to hear that."

"Say," Vena whispered, "did you ever do anything with the information I told you?"

"I did what I could. We'll just have to wait and see," Marina said. In fact, the informal review had progressed quite far, and Lemar in legal was now having his turn.

"Oh, and Marina, I know about needing to make a copy of your medical records. I'll try to get to it as soon as possible. Okay? With all that's been happening here, I'm sure you can understand why I just haven't gotten to it."

"Yes, well, look, I'll let you go back to your work. Just take good care of Dr. Vernor, okay?"

"Sure, I'll try," replied Vena. She smiled, and said to herself, "You can bet on that honey," after hanging up the phone.

The next day, an hour after eating a light dinner, Marina put down her easel for a few minutes. She felt suddenly hungry, unusual for her this time of evening, and headed for her small, old-model refrigerator. Marina looked with an utter lack of surprise on the total barrenness of the cold cavern. "This looks like as good a time as any to take a break," she sighed.

Marina got her purse and took the car to the market. As she started from her parked car to the grocery store, Marina thought she recognized Dr. Vernor. She called out for him, and when he didn't respond, Marina tried to catch up to him, thinking that this would be a good opportunity to offer her condolences over Lissa's tragic illness. As she approached Vernor's car, she thought she noticed his office receptionist, Vena Kleinman, in the passenger seat waiting for him. Confused and surprised, Marina backed away, unsure how to handle what might easily become an awkward situation.

Marina had thought about the Manuel Rossa trial almost daily. In her opinion, Charlie Kincade had been particularly brilliant and persistent in his successful handling of the case, two qualities she wouldn't normally have ascribed to him. The freeing of an innocent man made her proud to know Charlie, and she even considered dating him again. She was sure that he would be agreeable to that, any time she showed an interest. How Charlie would react to her attempt at pregnancy was uncertain at best. Like most men she knew, Charlie probably would interpret her attempt at IVF as a rejection of his masculinity. Of course, her motives were much more complicated than that.

The new technique of genetic analysis, which Charlie had exploited so well in the Manuel Rossa case, fascinated her. She couldn't stop thinking about the clothes she had worn during her own rape, clothes now stuffed away in a paper bag in her room. They were old, soiled things, hidden away, far out of sight, but, like the memory of the rape itself, something she just could not discard. They were omnipresent nightmares, lurking just below her consciousness.

Marina took the paper evidence bag from her drawer

and turned it around in her hands. She had done this several times before, all those times becoming somber occasions. Scraps of torn and soiled clothing tumbled around inside. Her hands trembled as she reached inside the bag and took out her old panties. They were ripped along the seams and had a dirty feel to them, much as she still perceived herself, she sadly reflected. She held the cloth to her nose and inhaled; the stale, dirty odor made her choke. The memories generated by doing this brought tears to her eyes.

Later, she telephoned Charlie Kincade. He was, of course, surprised and happy to hear from her. Charlie immediately assumed Marina was calling regarding their relationship. He was wrong.

Chapter 30

Haven Hills Condominium

Baatard sat alone on the balcony of his town house looking west past downtown Haven. He had always found the view from his balcony breathtaking; often he could make out several business towers standing like giants above Manhattan, even from this distance. Baatard remembered well how his wife had fallen in love with this particular town house because of this very breathtaking view, had made an offer on the spot, and had his first dinner alone on this balcony. Now, severely depressed, he could care less about all his success, his position with The Conceptions Foundation, his research, the remembrances only a blur in the misty distance. It was gone, all gone. And what he had left was total aggravation: Marina Bonnaserra, Lissa Vernor, Denny Cruite, and that demanding Lydia Ramirez.

Baatard put his coffee cup down on the ledge, wiped his forehead with his shirt sleeve, and then went back inside. He sat alone for a long time in a small plastic chair in the empty kitchen, staring at the wall. His thoughts were preoccupied with another upsetting encounter with Ramirez at his office. The woman scared him and he could almost sense the violence swirling below the surface, and the uncomfortable fear he had in Ramirez's presence. Most of all he wanted Ramirez dead, for he was certain Ramirez was a threat to him and all he stood for and had worked so hard for. Several times, he nearly got up the nerve to accuse Ramirez to her face of threatening him, but he didn't, partially because he had no proof whatsoever, and partially because he was fearful she would pull out of her contract, and leave him several hundred thousand dollars poorer.

All these problems made Baatard feel severely depressed and threatened. He wanted to run away from it all, give it all up, change his name, and have no responsibilities at all.

Baatard's thoughts kept returning to Ramirez. Soon he forgot Haven, his obstetrical practice, and everything else for that matter. Ramirez was dangerous and unpredictable, and more than ever, Ramirez was a threat to his very life. He had to defend himself, but with the police and the courts seemingly unable to stop Ramirez, what alternatives did he really have?

Unexpectedly, his remembrances flashed to Lissa Vernor and her unfortunate and unexpected surgical outcome. He had bad results before; hell, everyone had that happen. It was part of the game, something unfortunate, but also something to be expected. This particular 'unfortunate outcome' though, was a bigger disappointment, a greater blow. He had already heard disturbing, ugly rumors of Quality Assurance hearings - probably more like a medieval inquisition - and Baatard was certain it was all because Lissa Vernor was the spouse of a staff physician. He had thought about this often before, and always he asked if his feelings of regret over Lissa Vernor's poor surgical outcome were related to his perception of guilt and helplessness over other pointless losses in his own life, and Baatard stared for a long time into the living room which now seemed so empty.

It took a long time for Baatard to regain his composure, and when he did, he thought about Ryder Vernor. Although Baatard had never actually liked Ryder, he felt sorry for him. Baatard now knew all too well how it felt to lose a loved one; he had experienced the same hurt himself. In a way, he wished he could help Ryder, he wished there were some way to bring back Lissa, but knew there wasn't.

Now, because of Ramirez, Baatard had another unpleasant task he needed to take care of. Several days ago, he had in desperation started a dangerous process, set an illicit play in motion. The second act began as Baatard called Ryder Vernor on the phone.

Ryder was surprised and puzzled, and from the tone of his voice, more than a little suspicious when he took the call from Baatard. Nevertheless, Baatard managed to arrange for a meeting later that morning between the two of them right there at Baatard's town house.

Ryder arrived on time, and first spoke to Baatard through the remote outside intercom. Baatard buzzed the electric door lock to allow Ryder into the secure condominium building, and greeted him warmly at the front door. He could see Ryder was wary, and tried his best to put Ryder at ease.

After some small talk, Baatard said, "Look, Ryder, you can't imagine how sorry I am about Lissa's tragic illness and her terribly unfortunate outcome. Believe me, if there was anything I could have done differently, you know I would have. I'll never forget her, and I certainly can't replace what you've lost."

Ryder nodded, then said, "I appreciate what you're saying. But, Damon, I don't think we have a lot to talk about. And I really don't understand why you asked me over today."

"Ryder, you don't think I was at fault, do you? I mean, haven't I explained to you all that happened?" He tried to seem as wronged and hurt and misunderstood as he was capable of appearing.

"Yes, but still, . . . it's all very hard to accept. Look, I don't blame you, at least from what I know. But, I understand all adverse outcomes like this go to a QA hearing. I want to hear what they say about it." Ryder Vernor looked into his hands for several moments, then sighed, stared out the window and said, "And I plan to review the hospital record myself, if for no other reason than for my own peace of mind."

Baatard hadn't expected this, and was taken aback.

"At this point, Ryder, you're a family member, and not the patient's treating physician," Baatard cautioned. "I'd be careful, if I were you, and submit your request to examine Lissa's medical records through the hospital attorney." He could see nothing good resulting from Ryder meddling, searching, and poking into his every action. Nothing anyone did was performed to perfection, and under the microscope almost everything could look imperfect. Medicine was indeed an art and not a science, rather than the other way around as popularly believed.

Ryder looked surprised and annoyed, but nodded he understood. "Maybe so, but I still want to review the records, Baatard."

"Yes, yes, I understand, and I feel quite confident when you review Lissa's hospital chart you'll see I wasn't at fault. Really, I assure you. I tried, we all tried." He had lost much of his regret, and now felt annoyance at his being inspected, reviewed, challenged. Damn Ryder, and damn his wife.

"Maybe so. So, what did you bring me here for, anyway? You weren't worried about a law suit, were you?"

"A law suit? No, not that." Baatard tried to laugh, but knew it didn't come off convincing. "But there's something you need to know about that you won't find in Lissa's hospital record."

"What's that?" Ryder asked.

"You didn't know, Ryder," Baatard said, looking at his hands folded on his lap, "that your Lissa had been seeing me for several months before her illness." Remembrances of Lissa when she was well flooded his mind, warm images of a vibrant soul trapped in a dull marriage. Perhaps Baatard related to Lissa so well because he felt she in some ways suffered as he once did.

"No, I didn't know that." Ryder turned around in his chair suddenly, his eyes wide open. "She was seeing you for what reason?"

"It was for professional services, of course." Baatard knew of other people Lissa was seeing, too, and not for professional reasons there, but he didn't carry tales.

"Of course," Ryder said, visibly relieved. "But, frankly, I'm quite surprised. How could she? I never even saw any bills."

"Lissa asked that we not mail statements to her, and she always paid by money order."

"This is incredible." Ryder angrily exclaimed. He got up and paced back and forth. "Was she ill? Was this related to her bleeding? I just don't see how this was possible."

"Well, I don't know about how she kept the medical expenses from you, but women have a way about doing those things. Believe me, I'm an authority on that one." Baatard briefly smiled, and then grew solemn. "But, Lissa asked me to keep this a secret from you and anyone you knew. As my patient, I had to respect her request for patient confidentiality." Her request was not uncommon, in his specialty, Baatard reflected.

"She was successful, then. I'm really quite surprised,

and I must admit that I'm more than a little annoyed at you for not telling me. So, why was Lissa seeing you?" Ryder sat back down and stared angrily at Baatard.

Baatard thought from the look on Ryder's face that he knew the answer to his own question. "First, let me assure you Lissa was not ill at all. No, not at all. And, let me also say the reason I was seeing her had nothing to do with my getting her as a patient through the ER on that fateful day. That was strictly coincidental. I was up for the next GYN admission, she came in with blood in her abdominal cavity and possibly some vaginal bleeding, and I was called. I'm trained in general surgery, too, you remember."

"I see. No, I didn't know that."

"Yes, it's training that comes in handy. Many gynecologic surgeons are also trained in some general surgery. Naturally, since I was already seeing Lissa as a patient, and familiar with her, I think she got better surgical care than if she had gotten assigned someone unfamiliar with her surgical and gynecological history." It was unintended, but true.

"Maybe so, Damon, but I still think you should have told me about her seeing you then."

"At that time, Ryder? Well, then I couldn't have imagined her having such a disastrous outcome, and I still was under confidentiality instructions from her. I really am terribly sorry." Baatard took another drink from his can of cola, and then played with the tab top, eventually breaking it off with a hollow, metallic click.

Ryder shifted uncomfortably in his chair, looked directly at Baatard, and then asked, "So, why was she seeing you?"

"She was being evaluated for infertility, Ryder."

Ryder nearly choked. "Infertility? You're kidding me, Baatard. She never discussed this with me." Ryder's face had turned beet red, he nervously laughed, then abruptly stood up and walked over to the window and looked out.

"Lissa told me she wanted to have a child." Baatard looked in Vernor's direction, but got no response. "I assume you were not entirely in favor?" Lissa had told him that once.

"Why? What did she tell you? What other personal information of ours did she share with you? GODDAMN IT." Ryder yelled, slamming his fist onto the window ledge.

"Not a lot else," Baatard said. "It isn't true then you didn't want a child?"

"Well, I did know that she wanted a child, but we never really settled on doing it. I mean, we never agreed to do it. I don't know if it even would have worked out," he said, shaking his head in confused disbelief.

"How's that?" Baatard asked.

"Well, you see, we were having some, ah problems," Ryder said.

"You mean with her not being able to conceive?" Baatard asked.

"That too, I guess. No, I was referring to problems with our marriage" Ryder murmured. "So, I really don't understand why she would want a child with things going the way they were."

"It's quite common, Ryder. You should know that, being a physician yourself, especially in family practice. Women often try to bring a child into the picture to sort of, you know, cement things together." Baatard remembered how that had once been true in his circumstance also.

Baatard could hear his automatic answering machine intercept several calls with a recorded message and beeping in the background, but ignored it. He waved his hands into the air - an act of dismissal to the answering machine and to all the intercepted interruptions. Then, he reached over to take a drink from the can of soda he had put down on the coffee table. "Would you like one?" he offered Ryder.

"No, thanks. So, what did you discover?"

"Apparently Lissa had some form of tubular dysfunction. I planned to stimulate her production of ova, harvest the ova, and fertilize them." It sounded simple back then; and it usually is.

"Fertilize her ova using what, may I ask, for sperm?" Ryder's voice was becoming increasingly irritated.

"Since it would have tipped you off to ask you for a sperm specimen, Lissa asked me to use the sperm bank. I planned to use a compatible donor so it might not be too obvious, someone perhaps who physically resembled you and had a compatible blood type." He had used that ruse several times before with great success, rarely generating suspicion or angry surprise. The potential legal issues of parentage were horrendous, but as yet not addressed,

Ryder shifted around uncomfortably.

"You can't imagine how pleased we both were, and surprised, to find you listed as a donor."

"Yeah, how convenient," Ryder commented, sarcasm evident in his voice. "I didn't mention that to Lissa. Yes," he said reflectively, "It was something I did a long time ago, in my college days."

Baatard recalled that the date on the sperm donation from Ryder was only a few years ago. The time sequence he gave didn't quite fit, but that didn't matter now. "Yes, it would definitely have been convenient," Baatard agreed. "Using your sperm would accomplish a pregnancy for Lissa and it would use her ova. You would still be the father, and all would be well."

"I see. It would have been as if she got pregnant naturally. She could sleep with me and not have to expend any effort in the process. That's my Lissa, all right." Ryder said, a bitter and sarcastic tone to his voice.

"That's a strange way of looking at it, don't you think?" He could sense a great deal of resentment here; surely their marriage must have been troubled. Dysfunctional sex was often the first symptom.

"That's your opinion, Damon. But, you're an outsider, and believe me, you wouldn't know what it was like to live with Lissa Vernor."

"What do you mean?" He knew what it was like to live with someone you learned to hate, and had heard stories about Lissa's bizarre antics. Perhaps he did know some of what Ryder was referring to.

"It looked a lot better than it really was, that's all. Anyway, the way you were to work it, I would be the genetic father and Lissa would be the genetic mother. How convenient," Ryder commented sarcastically. "I suppose she could always blame the pregnancy on a failure of birth control."

"Yes, I guess these things happen," Baatard agreed.

"Yeah," Ryder said. "It's all so neat and perfect, like Lissa." He puckered and twisted his lips and made an expression not unlike having bitten into something both bitter and sour.

"Yes, the explanation, at least as far as the pregnancy was concerned, would have fit. About the marriage, your marriage, I can't speak," Baatard said.

Baatard looked over at Ryder, who sat silent, absorbed in thought. Ryder gave no acknowledgment of what he, Baatard, was saying. "So, it's unfortunate Lissa couldn't have gone through with her wishes. She loved you a great deal," Baatard said, trying his best to look sad. He wasn't so sure that was the truth, but felt it an appropriate although somewhat gratuitous comment. "Don't you see, Ryder, Lissa's trying to have a baby was for you and for your marriage more than for her? She loved you, Ryder, above anything else. In a sense, she would die for you." Although neither man truly believed this, Ryder seemed deeply moved yet troubled by the comment, as if both men did believe it after all.

Ryder looked at his hands, then at the floor. He started to leave, then said, "Frankly, I'm overwhelmed,

Baatard. I feel numb, and I don't know what to think about all this. It's such a shock."

"These are hard times for you, Ryder, and I appreciate that. Why, I can't even begin to imagine how such a tragedy would affect your life."

Ryder shook his head, then said, "I've got to get going."

"Thanks for coming, and call me if you need anything, okay?"

"Yeah, sure. You know, it's unfortunate Lissa didn't get what she wanted, isn't it. But then again, Baatard, none of us do," he laughed ironically. "Do we, Baatard?"

Baatard wondered, as he escorted Ryder to the front door, just what he meant by that last remark. Did Ryder know intimate details of his own less-than-ideal past marital life too?

Baatard extended his hand, then said, "Please, if there's ever anything I can do, let me know. I'm very sorry this has happened."

Ryder looked deeply into Baatard's eyes, then left without saying anything further. The stare was not something Baatard could easily read, nor forget.

Chapter 31

Haven General Hospital

Two hours had passed since the official closing time of the administrative offices at Haven General Hospital. Dr. Ryder Vernor rapidly walked down the near empty halls of the executive wing, stopped near the usually open door of the Medical Records Department, now closed, and quickly went inside. Ryder quietly closed the metal frame door behind him.

The typical flurry of activity had ended for the day, and most of the medical records clerks had already left for home. Ryder entered the outside area, with its shelves of records piled in several disorganized attempts at organization, and individual booths for dictation of reports. The one medical records clerk still there saw Ryder enter and asked if he needed help.

"No, thanks, I just want to catch up on some chart work and dictation. I'll be all right." Ryder waited until the clerk returned to the back area, then he went over to the master files, which were arranged alphabetically. Lissa's chart was not there.

Ryder tried the master chart catalog and again looked up his wife's name. An old dog-eared pink index card was inserted at an angle under the name Vernor; the card showed Lissa's chart was already checked out. He expected as much.

From the tracking system of crossed out names, Ryder learned that Lissa's chart had previously been to several departments for review. Lissa's records were now in the surgical department offices, signed out to Dr. Rubin.

Ryder went to the surgical floor, then down the near empty corridor to the Surgery Department offices. He tried to open the door, but it was locked. If he was to review Lissa's chart, he needed to get inside.

Ryder fumbled to open the door to the Surgery Department offices with his hospital master key. This key had been given to all the hospital staff, mainly for entry to the main outer doors after hours, and to allow him entry into the house staff lounge. He had never used his master key to enter the Surgical Department offices, or for that matter any departmental offices at night, but it seemed like the easiest, the first thing for him to try at this point. Ryder put the master key in the door lock and was relieved when it opened the door with a magnetic clicking sound.

Dr. Meyer Rubin's outer office was a mess of papers, charts, and message notes scribbled on pink pads. Group photos of surgical residents were encased in uniformly inexpensive frames and hung irregularly on all the walls. Ryder looked around quickly for his wife's hospital records, moving from desk to desk, checking all the shelves. He worried that at any minute someone would come in and challenge him. To his dismay, none of the many charts he found belonged to Lissa.

Going into Rubin's inner office, Ryder couldn't find any patient charts at all. He then went into the adjacent department conference room through a connecting door and quickly looked around there too.

A long mahogany table with a green felt cover occupied most of the center of the room. The felt cover was heavily stained and worn through in several points. A wide assortment of chairs was unevenly pushed under the table and more were jammed against the walls, giving the room a crowded, heavily used look. More group photos of surgery staff and residents from past years adorned all available wall space. On several book shelves were medical records and assorted folders stuffed with papers. There was a slight musty odor in the air, and coffee stains dotted the fabric of the chairs and the carpet.

Ryder found Lissa's charts in one messy pile on a top shelf. Her name was scribbled on a torn half sheet of ruled paper and attached with a rubber band to the top of the stack. Excited, Ryder stood up on a chair to get a better look. Then he heard the outer door open.

The night janitor, whistling to himself, emptied the trash by Dr. Rubin's secretary's desk, and noisily shoved the wooden chairs back into order. He shook his head at the mess left for him every day. "I wonder how they can get their work done," he complained to himself. "I sure hope they don't treat their patients so sloppily." As he opened the conference room, the janitor was surprised to find Ryder seated at the table, reading from a book and taking notes. "Hello, Dr. Vernor. I didn't expect to see you here."

"Oh, hi," Ryder replied, trying not to look out of place, but only slightly surprised. "I needed to look up something, and the medical library showed the book I was looking for was checked out to Dr. Rubin. I used my pass key to get in; I didn't want to bother you."

"It's no problem, doc. If you need anything, just call," the janitor smiled as he left to work on the offices down the hall.

Ryder put down the book he had hurriedly opened and went back to retrieve Lissa's charts from the book case. His wife's made up most of the ponderous records on that shelf, and committee proceedings made up the rest. Ryder anxiously picked up the stack and, seated at the table, started reading through them as fast as he could. Most of what he read in the reviews he already knew from talking to Baatard and others who were present during and after Lissa's emergency surgery.

Ryder came across the section which described the fever Lissa developed toward the end of her hospital stay. He had heard about this too, but as Lissa's temperature had resolved in only one day, he had almost forgotten about it. Ryder took his mini tape recorder out of his pocket and quickly dictated notes for details he knew he couldn't remember or have enough time to write about.

One of the committee reports Ryder read was from the Internal Medicine department. It discussed the finding of abnormally high hormone levels in Lissa's blood. Ryder wondered if they were related to Lissa's effort to become pregnant. Funny, how she was trying so hard, against impossibility, he thought. He wished she had discussed this with him first. Maybe then all this wouldn't have happened. Ryder tried to suppress a surge of guilt so he could concentrate on the chart review; he knew time was limited.

Still not finding an explanation to the surgical disaster that ended in Lissa's stroke, Ryder started leafing through the laboratory reports in the back of the chart. There were innumerable blood count slips, each attesting to his wife's critical anemia. The clotting labs didn't show any abnormality; this didn't surprise him. He also saw a few x-ray reports, again none of which was abnormal.

Toward the back of one chart, under the urine analysis slips, Ryder found a group of microbiology lab reports. They were probably from the evaluation of Lissa's fever, he reasoned. The blood and urine cultures were all listed as 'no growth', which made sense, as Lissa's fever had resolved on its own, without antibiotics.

The last report was taken from a vaginal swab, which was unusual, Ryder thought. He guessed the residents were just trying to be thorough in their evaluation of the fever. Perhaps they had considered toxic shock syndrome, although there was no report of Lissa having the characteristic rash. There was no growth of pathogens reported from the vaginal sample, and no indication of the toxin that caused toxic shock syndrome.

Baatard was definitely being thorough, Ryder thought. Then Ryder found a report of some cells present on the vaginal swab tip: a few epithelial cells, a few Gram-negative bacteria, and rare sperm cells. Sperm cells. Shocked at what he had just read, Ryder put down his paper and the recorder and stopped taking notes.

Chapter 32

Marina walked into the high-tech lobby of Northeast Forensic Laboratory, Inc., known by its acronym NEFL. Charlie Kincade had finally recommended NEFL to Marina, but only after several memory proddings on her part. He was as opposed to her pursuing her rapist as ever, and almost begged her to finally let go after all these years. He just could not understand how deeply she was committed to finding and bringing to punishment the animal that violated and nearly killed her so long ago. Charlie's inability to understand her dedication had always stood in her subconscious as perhaps the major impediment to their relationship finally taking off.

Marina knew she could not depend on Charlie or on the police to help her. And, she could in a way rationalize their having given up and even somewhat accept it. But, she did at least expect support from Charlie.

When the NEFL receptionist called her name, Marina walked into the consultation office carrying a paper bag. This aging evidence bag contained clothes soiled and not washed clean in over sixteen years, and mirrored her memory and even her life. She stopped short of the office, unable to choke back the tears, and went into the ladies room first for the few moments needed for her to regain her composure before returning to the necessary task at hand.

Chapter 33

Haven Fertility Associates

Baatard sat at the custom-made wooden consultation desk in his office, alternatively playing with a plastic model of a uterus and drawing doodles on his list of patients to be seen. Being in his office on a no surgery day always bored him so. He looked at his watch, then at the clock on the wall, then again at his patient log for the day. Shit, he groaned, seven more complaining Bozos to go before lunch.

He recognized the names of several of his "repeats" on the list and winced his eyes in mock pain. Baatard moaned out loud at the name of one, whom he remembered as a middle-aged, rather fat chronic complainer. He could never provide adequate relief for her multiple pelvic complaints nor enough answers for an infinity of annoyingly meaningless, trivial questions. He vividly recalled her particularly strong ever-present body odor, and nearly gagged. Baatard prayed that she wouldn't require a pelvic exam today; he hadn't eaten yet and he was certain if he had to go 'in there' he wouldn't be able to even look at, let alone smell, food for a month.

Baatard shuffled through his in-box while waiting for the next patient to be brought to his office. He lifted out his medical journals and set them off to the side in a separate stack, perhaps to be read at a 'later date', unspecified. Baatard opened a few flashy, colored medical equipment advertisements, quickly glancing through them and discarding them into the 'circular file' on the floor by his desk.

Getting toward the bottom of the in-box, he noticed an envelope from Haven General Hospital. It was labeled CONFIDENTIAL in big bold red print. Baatard stared at the letter, not believing what he was seeing, as if he was not actually the person to whom the letter was addressed. After a few seconds, he got up to shut his door before opening the envelope. Inside, Baatard found a short letter from the hospital Quality Assurance nurse, his patient Marina Bonnaserra, her name conjuring up several negative images in his mind.

The letter was a request to 'informally' meet with him to review a case, unnamed. "Shit," Baatard said out loud, slamming his hand onto the desk top, forcing his coffee cup to jump sideways. The thought of being grilled and questioned and challenged by one of his own patients, a nurse no less, placing him at a less than superior footing, irked him to no end.

Baatard knew damn well which case Marina was referring to. Although he was confident there would be no problem, as he was absolutely certain he had done nothing inappropriate, he fumed as he thought how this was one more example of interference with the autonomy of his practice. Baatard briefly considered the possibility that a colleague, or more realistically a competitor, had put the hospital up to this. He speculated on who it might be for a few minutes before finally dismissing the idea as baseless.

Baatard quickly slid the QA letter into his top drawer, then picked up the phone and called his malpractice carrier. Their legal department would need to be aware, just in case there really was a problem.

Chapter 34

Dr. Rubin, a concerned look on his face, opened the door
to his inner office and personally escorted Marina
Bonnaserra in, offering her a chair. Rubin had seen
Marina at some previous QA hearings, but had very little
interaction with her. Rubin noted with curiosity she was
the first woman in his office in months who wore
perfume.

"Thanks for seeing me on such short notice," Marina
smiled politely as she sat. She avoided using the title
"Doctor" whenever possible when addressing physicians,
whom she generally had little respect for. Although she
really didn't know Dr. Rubin, and had to admit she had no
basis for judgment, she would reserve using the title
"Doctor" for a later date, if it was warranted and the
occasion called for it.

Although Marina had been the QA nurse at Haven
General for almost two years, this was her first time in the
Office of the Chief of Surgery. Rubin seemed outwardly
pleasant but more formal than she would have expected,
and wore an expression of benign disinterest, which
troubled her. Looking around, she was impressed with the
spaciousness, the quality of the furniture, the rugs and the
drapes, particularly when she contrasted it with her
cramped, noisy cubicle in the nursing staff offices outside
of the medical records area. The desk and shelves were
very messy, which she thought was typical for a man, but

which also reflected badly on Rubin's secretary. "I'm glad you want to look into the Lissa Vernor case so soon after the fact," she told Rubin. "I think you can agree with me this is heading right into . . . "

"Let's not speculate on where the review might be heading, okay, Miss Bonnaserra? There's no real way for us to know that," Rubin angrily said, cutting Marina off in mid-sentence. Rubin had a deep frown on his face and the troubled furrows on his forehead were now accentuated. He shifted his considerable weight around in his chair a little in an attempt to get comfortable. Then, he sternly told Marina, "I just don't want to have my conclusions biased by your preconceived notions, no matter how well founded you may think they are. Look, Marina, Miss Bonnaserra, Nurse Bonnaserra," Rubin stumbled, searching for a common ground to speak from, "Dr. Baatard is one of our finest and most gifted gynecologic surgeons. I have every confidence in his judgment and actions, and I really am surprised you're insisting on a formal review hearing. Hemorrhage is a known complication of surgery, I'm sure you realize."

"Oh, yes. I'm quite aware of this," Marina said, nervously smiling. "But, all adverse events undergo a QA evaluation of some degree, even if not a full hearing, Dr. Rubin. I don't understand why you find it so unusual in this case?"

"There are various levels of QA hearings, beginning

with a simple chart review and stopping there, or going all the way, as you're insisting in this case, to a formal peer review hearing. Unless there's obvious gross negligence, which I see no evidence of, a chart review should be satisfactory. I would have thought that would apply to the Lissa Vernor case. The bottom line is this, Miss Bonnaserra, I'm concerned that any excessive attention to this particular adverse outcome might bring the attention of the hospital certification auditors. It also might delay our on-going preparations for re-certification. And that could cost big bucks." He tried to chuckle, and feign concern, but ended by choking on the phony sound.

"Yes, that's true. However, in this case, even your own hospital legal counsel thinks . . . "

"What do you mean, my hospital legal counsel? I wasn't aware that our legal counsel was involved in this case." Rubin snorted. Rubin grabbed his intercom switch and yelled out, "Ask the hospital counsel familiar with the Lissa Vernor case to come to my office right away, please."

"But, . . . " Marina tried to call out, then stopped when she noticed that Rubin wasn't currently paying attention to her.

Rubin's secretary called back in a few minutes and informed him the attorney in question, Lemar Jackson, was out of the office until tomorrow.

"That's what I was just trying to tell you," Marina said. She could see Rubin was more than annoyed, he was fearful and pressured. Someone had already been speaking with him, perhaps Dr. Baatard himself.

Ignoring Marina, Rubin told his secretary, "Okay,

then have them send up anyone else who is available."
Rubin was only further annoyed when his secretary called
back to inform him no one from legal was available to see
him for several hours at least. Apparently they were all
giving depositions at a major case against Haven
General's E.R.

"Did you have a chance to review the records I sent
up?" Marina asked Rubin.

"Yes, of course I did," Rubin replied, defensively.
"They're right over there," he added, pointing through the
connecting door. He could see a large stack of bound
patient records on a cluttered shelf in the Surgery
Department library. He momentarily considered that he
remembered having placed the stack of charts for Lissa
Vernor a little more close to the center of the bookshelf,
and arranged a little less neatly. He dismissed this as
trivial, and continued his conversation.

"Then you know the patient was admitted with a
hemorrhage, and bleeding which preexisted the surgery,"
Marina confidently told Rubin. "Lissa Vernor, you will
recall, was admitted with hypotension and blood found in
the peritoneal cavity."

"Yes, exactly," beamed Rubin. "So you do agree,
then, that Dr. Baatard was not the cause of her adverse
outcome post-op." He seemed both surprised and gratified
and suddenly relieved, as if he had just discovered both
his and Baatard's fears were utterly groundless and

baseless.

"The problem, it seems, centers around the possibility Lissa Vernor's exploratory surgery was closed without first identifying or controlling the bleeding," Marina explained.

"But Dr. Baatard did look, didn't he? Sometimes a closure such as you describe is necessary. Why, I've done this myself. I hope you aren't planning to investigate me too now that you know this," Rubin laughed.

"Of course not, but, but . . . "

"Dr. Baatard looked for that bleeder for over six hours, as I understand it?" Rubin nodded his head in Marina's direction, waiting for her to respond in the affirmative. "He and his assistants, that is. There were others there too, I believe. Those guys were pretty persistent, if you ask me." Rubin took off his glasses as he looked at Marina as if she were needlessly annoying him, then scribbled some notes on a pad.

"Yes, I think so," Marina replied.

"Marina, look, I know you're an experienced QA person, so I also know I'm not telling you anything new when I ask you to keep an open mind and not jump to conclusions. Okay?" he smiled.

Marina realized what Rubin was telling her was very true. In her experience, and in what she read in professional QA journals, over 95 percent of malpractice cases were strictly bullshit. The vast majority of QA inquiries were based on misunderstandings or human errors, rather than intentional, or careless mistakes. Having someone of Rubin's stature express confidence in Baatard made her feel good, also. After all, she was still nominally under Baatard's treatment for infertility.

The desktop intercom went off with a loud, irritating grating sound. "Yes," Rubin snapped in a tone of voice which made no effort to disguise his annoyance. "I thought I asked not to be interrupted?"

"I understand that," his secretary said in a whisper. "But there's a Mr. Charles Kincade here. He's very insistent on seeing you." Rubin puzzled at the look Marina developed of surprise and joy when she heard Charlie's name.

"Let's both take our speaker phones off, okay?" Rubin snapped, "and please, can you speak a little less loud?" Rubin heard the change in sounds, then continued. "That's better. I think privacy is better for things like this. Now, I don't know this person. Who is he? What does he want?" Rubin muttered some apology in Marina's direction for the interruption, then continued talking.

Marina was quite surprised to hear Charlie's name, and wondered what he was up to.

"Mr. Kincade's a lawyer," the secretary explained, her voice cracking slightly. "Mr. Kincade has a court order releasing copies of all of the Vernor patient's medical and surgical records to him." Not hearing a reply, Rubin's secretary continued, "Hello, Dr. Rubin, are you there?"

Marina wondered if Dr. Ryder Vernor, already using Charlie Kincade for a business transaction, had discussed his wife's case in the context of a potential malpractice suit. She was fairly certain Charlie didn't have any experience with medical malpractice. This was a highly specialized legal field, not something to be undertaken lightly. She would have thought, if Ryder were considering a malpractice claim, Charlie would have referred him to a specialist.

"Yes, of course I'm here. I was just thinking," Rubin said.

"Well, what do you want me to do?" his secretary asked.

"What do I want you to do? I'll tell you what to do. I'm not a lawyer. That's what we pay lawyers for. I hate talking to lawyers. Call up the legal department, get hold of a lawyer, and refer Kincade whatever, . . . "

"Charles Kincade," his secretary offered.

"Thanks," Rubin jumped back. "Refer Mr. Charles Kincade over to the legal office. There's nothing I can do here about this." Rubin shrugged his shoulders, smiled weakly at Marina, then hung up the phone.

"Some lawyer's here with an order for Lissa Vernor's records," Rubin said. "I can't deal with that. I shouldn't have to; I'm a physician, not a records clerk. Ha." he laughed sarcastically, although his face progressively showed him to be worried. "So I sent him to the legal department. There's no lawyer available in legal right now, so that should slow this Kincade up, whatever he wants," Rubin said.

Marina thought it best to give no indication that she knew Charlie Kincade. If that came out later, she might have to address it, as her personal involvement with Charlie might put her in yet another potential conflict of interest with the Lissa Vernor case, considering her employment with Haven General Hospital.

Further, she was still a patient of Baatard's. Could she objectively evaluate his care of another patient while she was also actually his patient at the same time? The more she considered her complex, intertwining involvements, the more she wanted to pass off this QA assignment to someone else. The problem was, there was no one else. Haven General had only one QA nurse.

Marina had tried to discuss her concerns with Lemar Jackson, suggesting to him that Haven General contract the review of the Lissa Vernor case to an outside consulting group. Not surprisingly, Lemar assured her that would be unnecessary. Whether Lemar was giving her a vote of confidence or simply trying to save Haven General some money was problematic. Yet, Marina was still uncomfortable with potential conflicts of issues. The use of outside contract reviewers had been an option taken before, when the workload became too great, although the hospital usually complained about the additional cost. She filed the problem away and intended to raise it again using outside reviewers only if an actual conflict-of-interest developed.

After spending the next hour again reviewing Lissa Vernor's records with Marina, the meeting broke up. Once Marina left, Dr. Rubin, his face a dark scowl, asked his secretary to find out who in legal had finally spoken with Kincade. A few minutes later, he was connected to the hospital legal secretary. It was she who had actually spoken with Charlie Kincade. The hospital legal office secretary told Rubin that she had simply taken Kincade's request and told him she would give it to the appropriate persons. Kincade seemed to her to be satisfied when he left, the secretary reported. Rubin asked the secretary to arrange a meeting between himself, Marina Bonnaserra and Lemar Jackson as soon as Jackson returned. He knew problems like this never went away, they only got bigger.

Lemar Jackson returned to his offices at Haven General later that afternoon. He was surprised and totally unprepared to find Dr. Rubin and Marina Bonnaserra expecting to meet with him immediately. Presuming this would have to do with the Lissa Vernor case, he quickly scooped up a note pad, some internal documents, a hand recorder, and took off to Marina Bonnaserra's office in the QA area.

The tense meeting between those three lasted only thirty minutes, but covered the Lissa Vernor case, the liability issues, and the standard of care practiced by Baatard. Marina mentioned the possibility of conflict of interest on her part, but both men dismissed it as a non-issue and urged her to remain as the QA nurse on the case. Uncomfortable, and also upset that he was devoting too much time to what he perceived as an unfortunate but not totally unexpected surgical mishap, Rubin abruptly left after complaining he had too many other pressing matters to attend.

In reality, Dr. Rubin had heard enough. According to Jackson, there might not have been medical malpractice on Dr. Baatard's part, but there certainly was enough doubt and probable cause to allow QA to insist on a formal hearing. Rubin knew he couldn't stop the hearing from taking place; he couldn't even try to.

What angered Rubin most was Jackson's reminding him that Haven General was required to report the QA hearing, regardless of its outcome, to the state hospital re-certification agency. Rubin wanted to avoid a painful, lengthy and costly hearing concerning what he felt to be an unexpected but entirely explainable bad surgical outcome. Such an extensive investigation would hurt Baatard and it would also hurt Haven General. No one would benefit.

Back in his office, Dr. Rubin picked up a hand-held dictation unit and started a short memo. He knew that his hand was forced and he no longer had a choice. Rubin recognized trouble when he saw it, and was sure the best way to keep it limited was to cover his ass by convening a committee to affix and distribute blame.

Rubin requested that a full surgery department committee be assembled. In addition, Rubin requested that the Chief of the Hematology and Oncology Department also review the hospital chart in question. Rubin wanted emphasis placed on the unexpected bleeding Lissa Vernor had. Although Rubin still saw absolutely nothing wrong with the care Baatard gave to Lissa Vernor, the presence of Kincade on the case so soon after it went to QA review made him anxious.

The next day, Marina decided it was finally time to visit Lissa Vernor. She had been planning to do so since Lissa's surgery, but with her fertilization attempt and the complications, she had not managed to get around to it. First, she called Dr. Vernor to ask for permission.

Dr. Ryder Vernor was both surprised, gruff and not too encouraging after receiving Marina's call. After a few minutes of explanation, Marina did manage to extract a less-than-enthusiastic approval.

The visit to Lissa Vernor was perhaps the most memorable Marina had ever had in a hospital. Although unexpectedly clean, the convalescent hospital, located just outside of Haven, was at the same time sterile in its emotional environment. The nurses seemed uncaring, and the patients clean but unattended, as if Marina's visit had been expected and prepared for.

Lissa lay in a large open ward of four women, each unconscious, each body neatly dressed in a clean flowery nightgown, each body covered with sheets and a blanket tucked in at the same position under their chins. The head of each bed was tilted to exactly fifteen degrees, and there was an identical portable night stand with plastic flowers and an air freshener parked by each bedside.

Marina walked over to Lissa's bedside, pulled up a chair, and took Lissa's hand to hold from under the sheets. There was a deathly stillness in the air, a thick suffocating sterility that gave her the feeling of being in a graveyard and made her want to get up and leave. Lissa's hand was cold and clammy, without any sign of life other than a faint twitching. Lissa's eyes were closed, and her breathing shallow but with an odd, cavernous echoing quality to it. Marina found the whole experience was more than unnerving.

Feeling guilty for not having gotten to know her better, Marina carried on a one-way conversation with Lissa for a while. She didn't see the logic in doing so, but thought that if there were any chance Lissa could hear, it might help. Maybe this was the first time Lissa had heard a human voice directed to her in all these months.

After about thirty minutes, Marina tucked Lissa's hand back under the sheets and left. Shaken by the experience, she would not return. Seeing Lissa lying like a vegetable, she couldn't help but feel that Baatard was responsible, even if only in a small way. Could she be subjecting herself to the same risks of injury at Baatard's hand? The possibility left her shaken and cold.

Once Marina left the convalescent hospital, a nurse's aide went into Lissa Vernor's room to straighten up. She pulled the blanket down tight, then lined up the night stand parallel to the bedside. After quickly looking around at the other patients and noting the volume reading on one of the urine bags, the aide left the room, quietly closing the door behind her. The aide never noticed the small tears that had just developed in Lissa Vernor's eyes.

Chapter 35

Marina's House
Haven, New Jersey

After her ova implantation procedure, Marina developed a new sense of confidence, self inspiration, a surge of creativity which had been lacking for so long. Its origin was unexplained, its presence unexpected, its effect welcome, and it was as if the new life that had been implanted deep within her had in another sense given her new life, life renewed, life reborn. Each weekend, Marina now was able to sit untroubled for several hours at her easel on the open patio, her mind amazingly, refreshingly receptive and creative.

It was late afternoon, and Marina had just returned home from the office an hour ago. The phone rang almost as soon as she began working on a new idea for a painting. She usually put the phone on answer before beginning any activities which required creativity or concentration, but had unfortunately forgotten today.

"Ms. Bonnaserra?" the voice asked.

"Yes, this is she." Marina didn't recognize the person speaking, but reacted cautiously to its dry, unfriendly quality. She wasn't expecting any calls, and rarely got any while at home, except from Charlie Kincade.

"Ms. Bonnaserra, this is Garza from Dr. Baatard's office."

Marina's heart began to pound and she associated voice to name to face. "Yes, what can I do for you?" A thousand thoughts raced through her mind, all centered around the IVF procedure. This could be the call she had been anxiously waiting for, finally telling her she was successfully implanted, that is to say: pregnant, a mother-to-be. Or, Garza could be calling to inform her the implantation didn't 'take'. Unfortunately, Marina couldn't get a good read either way from Garza's terse voice, devoid as it was of any tonal qualities.

"Ms. Bonnaserra, Dr. Baatard asked me to call you. He wanted to be the one, but he just got called into emergency surgery and thought you wouldn't have wanted to wait."

"Yes, what is it?" Her heart was racing as if she had just completed a marathon. She prepared herself for the worst, for the big disappointment, but prayed for the best.

"Congratulations. Your pregnancy test this week is positive," Garza sang out. "The implantation was successful."

Marina broke out in a wide smile and sighed. "Finally," she said to herself. She flopped back down into a chair, exhausted. Her first instincts were to yell out and run around her house and clear into town and tell everyone she met. She wanted to laugh and cry and thanked Garza profusely a thousand times before hanging up, despite Garza being about the last person she would have wanted informing her of such joyous, welcome news. Marina looked around, happier than she had been in years, but paradoxically found no one near with whom to share her joy. Soon, she would be alone no more. Marina reached for the phone, thinking she might call Charlie, then changed her mind and placed the receiver back down. What would he think, her becoming pregnant while having dated him? Even though the circumstances were explainable, they were awkward at best, she had to admit.

Lost in concentration, Marina almost didn't hear the ring of her portable phone a few minutes later. The unexpected sound made her jump. She was fearful of answering it, afraid it might be Dr. Baatard's office telling her they had made an unfortunate mistake and she wasn't really pregnant, that it had all been a dream. Marina decided that she was being ridiculous and answered the phone.

"Hello, is this Marina?" asked the caller.

"Yes, who is this?" Marina cautiously asked. At first, she didn't recognize the caller's voice. Marina slipped her shoes off and rested her feet on a chair on the other side of the table.

"Why, Marina. This is Vena. How are you doing?"

"Vena? Just fine, thank you. As a matter of fact, I'm more than fine."

"Oh?" Vena asked.

"Yes, I'm pregnant." Vena wouldn't have been her first choice of persons to share her joy with, but fate had it that way. As Marina told Vena, thoughts rushed up from her subconscious reminding her of the last time she was pregnant. Feeling momentarily sick, Marina had to fight to repress the memories. She became angry and resentful when she realized another unfortunate comparison: just like last time, the father of her child was conspicuously absent, and unknown. Vena's whiny voice jerked her back from the verge of crying.

"Congratulations. So, who is the lucky man?"

Ignoring the question, Marina asked, "How is Lissa doing?" She figured that, since Vena didn't mention anything, Lissa had not shown any sign of improvement. That still didn't explain, let alone justify, Vena's driving around in public with Dr. Ryder Vernor, a married man of importance to his community.

"I'm sorry to say there's been no change," Vena told her coolly. "She's still in a coma."

"How terrible," Marina said, only somewhat surprised. Although realistically, Marina didn't hold out much hope for Lissa ever regaining consciousness, that was always possible, and it was wrong to so easily give up hope. She was left with an empty feeling as she wondered if she should visit Lissa again in the convalescent hospital. "Please tell Dr. Vernor how sorry I am to hear that."

As she listened to Vena's chatter, Marina was reminded that her outpatient records from Dr. Vernor's office still hadn't made it to Dr. Baatard's office for review, yet. She had requested them some time ago, and although they were probably irrelevant at this point, as she had already achieved her pregnancy, Marina liked her loose ends all tied up.

Vena said she would relay Marina's condolences, then started some small talk around Marina's pregnancy.

"It was very nice of you to call to inquire about my health, Vena, but is there any other, perhaps more specific reason for your call?" Marina quipped. Her annoyance level rising, Marina wanted to cut to the underlying motive and subject she was sure existed, but at the same time avoid sounding too nasty. She hated both deception and pointless conversation. Her feelings toward Vena were hostile, probably related to Vena's moving in on Lissa's territory while Lissa was so helpless. Although, Marina had heard that Lissa had done the same thing to other women countless times before. Facts were facts. Still, she really had no excuse for not being civil toward Vena. Her negative feelings were her own problem, and not Vena's.

"Actually, I did call you for another reason, Marina. I had the most coincidental thing happen to me the other night."

"Oh, why don't you tell me about it?" Marina's curiosity was almost at a new high, as was her guard. She put her paint brush in a cup of thinner and walked with her portable phone into the kitchen. Marina could see that Vena's interruption would last a while, and although she resented the invasion of her privacy, at least just for this one time she would talk civilly to Vena. Marina still felt too full of joy from her own good news to return to her somewhat reclusive and secretive nature.

Marina opened her refrigerator and poured herself a cup of iced cappuccino into a champagne glass. Sitting near the window, she again put her feet up on a nearby chair and stared out into the meadow off to the side of her house.

"Well, I was trying to help Dr. Vernor do some household type chores, his wife being ill, you know, . . . "

"Yes, I guess so," Marina interjected.

" . . . and I want to help Ryder, Dr. Vernor out as much as I can. We've developed such a good relationship working together the way we do."

"Yes, I'm sure you have," Marina said. She wondered if Charlie ever had anything going with one of his secretaries, but decided that he would be too prudish for that.

"And I thought for a moment I saw you in the parking lot near our, near his car that night. And, well I just wanted to know if it was you. That's all." Not hearing an immediate reply, Vena continued, "Was it?"

Avoiding a direct answer, Marina said, "How is Dr. Vernor dealing with his wife's illness? It must be devastating." Marina could almost feel the strong sense of anxiety Vena projected.

"He is devastated. As a matter of fact, Ryder, that is Dr. Vernor, is considering suing Dr. Baatard."

"Oh, I see. Well, I'm not surprised," she said,

wondering if she would need to notify the hospital legal office of this information. Haven General could be named as a third party, or another deep pocket.

After a pause, Vena repeated, "So. Was it you I saw?"

"Oh, for God sakes, Vena. What's the matter with you, anyway? I can't say, really if I may have seen you in some parking lot somewhere. Why do you need to know so badly?"

"I don't NEED to know, Marina. I was just curious, that's all. Look, Ryder, Dr. Vernor asked me for help getting a reception together. It's for people we know from the exercise club. You know, the one you never can get over to."

Marina harbored little guilt at not exercising. The club was more a social gathering place for business types, a dating zoo, and the people working there were not knowledgeable at all about the equipment, much of which was out-dated and ill-maintained. "It's difficult to always do everything one wants to," Marina said defensively, "or to do what one should," she added.

"Yes, I guess it is. Anyway, Dr. Vernor is shy and wouldn't want my being with him outside of work getting around."

"I can understand why," Marina said cryptically, nodding her head. She wondered why any successful man would want to be seen associating with Vena Kleinman. Then she wondered if a successful man would want to be around her, either, as few ever had been. But this was no time for being hard on herself.

"After all, I guess he still is technically married,"

Vena said, nervously.

"Yes, that's certainly true. He is married. But, don't worry. I don't carry tales," Marina said, then started to laugh. So that was the reason Vena had called. It seemed Vena was more interested in protecting and preserving her awkward relationship with Ryder than in protecting his or her integrity.

"I really don't understand what's so funny about this."

"Oh, nothing. You're correct, it isn't a very amusing situation, it's not funny at all. It's just that the name Vena Vernor is so silly sounding, so . . . so inappropriate, like the names just don't go together," she giggled.

"Okay, Marina, you've had your laugh. This situation isn't easy to work out at all."

"No, I guess it isn't. I agree with you there, Vena. Good-bye," Marina said, taking the opportunity to end the conversation before Vena could ask about her own marriage-less pregnancy. That was one discussion she did not want to get into, and regretted bringing it up. She tried hard to suppress the laughter in her voice, and taking care to switch on the answer phone before returning to her studio.

About an hour later, the phone rang again. Marina was surprised when the voice leaving a message belonged to Baatard. Anxious that the call would be related to her new pregnancy, she switched off the recorder, and greeted

Baatard.

"Marina, first let me congratulate you on your pregnancy. I'm very happy for you, and I do hope that you end up with just the son you've dreamed of."

Taken aback by Baatard's uncharacteristic gentleness, Marina thanked him.

"You're probably wondering why else I called. Well, it's nothing to do with your pregnancy." He paused a moment, then said, "Actually, it's got everything to do with your pregnancy. I know from the letter I received that you're the QA nurse assigned to review the Lissa Vernor case."

Marina confirmed that she was, and could see where this conversation was going. She immediately suspected that either Rubin or Jackson had spoken to Baatard about her, and probably their concerns about the potential appearance of conflict of interest. Would Baatard already be trying to exert pressure and influence her?

"I guess this puts you in an uncomfortable situation," Baatard chuckled nervously. "I mean, if you think there is any possibility that Lissa's bad outcome was due to an error on my part, I could well understand your not wanting to continue having me supply your IVF services. You might even be worried that your very actions in the performance of your duties might adversely affect the quality of care I give you. Let me assure you in no uncertain terms that nothing could be farther from the truth."

"That's very kind of you to call me about this, Dr. Baatard. Actually, it has been on my mind quite a lot. There's another side to this, too. Since I work for Haven

General, and I'm also your patient, I thought there might be a conflict of interest."

Baatard made a grunting sound to indicate he could see her point, then she continued, "But, I've spoken to Dr. Rubin, and to the hospital legal counsel, Lemar Jackson, and they both don't see a problem. Therefore, along with the reassurances you just gave me, I am continuing on as the QA nurse for the review of the Lissa Vernor case. After all, I make no final judgment, and in many ways I function simply as a coordinator for the formal QA committee."

"I can certainly go along with that, Marina. But what about . . ."

"Well, so far the IVF has been going along very well. Dr. Rubin has expressed a lot of confidence in you, and so far I've seen nothing in the hospital records that convinces me you're at fault. And your care of me seems to be just fine, so, at least for the moment, I'm not going to change doctors." She remembered once again Vena's call about there possibly being a problem with the care Lissa Vernor received. Actually, this had not been the first case by a long shot of alleged malpractice by an inside tip. Rarely had she known such inside information to pan out. Now, Marina was impressed by Baatard's insight, and his sensitivity to the issues, and to her feelings. No, at least for now, she would keep her new pregnancy under his care.

Chapter 36

Marina called up Ryder Vernor the next morning. She had wanted to ask him if he knew any detailed information on his wife's surgical care that might explain her underlying problem, or what happened to her as a result of the care she had received. Marina had not had a need to see Dr. Vernor as a patient for months now, and had last spoken only briefly when she asked permission to visit Lissa. After explaining to Vena that she wanted to ask a medical question, she was put through to Ryder. Apparently he wasn't exceptionally busy.

"Yes," the gruff voice said, "what can I do for you."

"This is Marina Bonnaserra, Dr. Vernor. How are you doing?"

"Me? Why should I have a problem? It's my wife who's the one with a problem, you know. Didn't your visit to her scare you off?"

"No, not really. Why should it have? We used to be acquaintances, and I was just trying to find out . . . "

"Look, Ms. Bonnaserra," Ryder said, abruptly cutting her off, "I appreciate your concern, but really, there's been no change, and there's really nothing you, or I, or anyone can do. So, if you have nothing else to discuss, I'm a busy man, a very busy man." Ryder hung up the phone without waiting for a reply. He glanced out again into the adjacent waiting room. It was still empty. He slowly got up, closed his door, laid his head on the desktop and cried.

"Hello, this is Nurse Ivory Peoples, from the Haven Convalescent hospital. Is Dr. Baatard there?" Peoples asked in her thick Jamaican accent.

It was late after clinic and Sharlene had already left, leaving Baatard to answer the 'personal' line. "Yes, this is Dr. Baatard. What can I do for you, Ms. Peoples?" He ran over in his mind what trolls he had warehoused over at Haven Convalescent, that dump, and who might be giving him problems today. It was probably something to do with bowels, either incontinence or constipation.

"Dr. Baatard, there's something happening to one of your patients. I just thought you'd want to know about it right away." Her voice was high-pitched and anxious.

"Well, what is it?" He knew from the tension in People's voice this was not a call about a simple medication error or constipation. "What patient is it? Did someone fall out of bed again?" He put down the day's stock quotes, picked up a pencil and slid a blank note pad in front of him.

"Well, it's not exactly a problem. I don't know how to say this. Something like this has never happened before, and it's quite unusual, you know."

"You said all that already. Get to the point, Peoples."

There were a few long moments of silence, then Peoples said, "I think one of your patients is pregnant."

441

She spoke very rapidly, as if trying to avoid staining her mouth with the words. After another uncomfortably long silence, Peoples continued. "Hello? Dr. Baatard, are you still there?"

"Um, exactly which of my patients is it?" Baatard slowly asked Peoples.

"It's your stroke patient. What do you want us to do? I mean, under the circumstances . . . "

"A stroke patient? Which stroke patient?" Baatard waited a few long seconds before asking, "You don't mean Lissa Vernor, do you?"

"Yes, she's the one."

"You have got to be kidding." he nearly screamed. "There's just no way she could be pregnant," Baatard insisted, as he tried to contain himself, then asked, "Are you sure? I hope you have the correct patient. This is NO joke, Peoples."

"I agree, this is no joke, Dr. Baatard," Peoples replied in her most serious voice. "I know my patients, and I even checked the wrist name tag to be double sure."

"Okay, okay, it's no joke. I can see that. But, how do you know she's pregnant, Peoples?"

"Believe me, Dr. Baatard, I know. Either she's pregnant or she's got one hell of a weight problem."

"But, how could it happen? She's in a goddamn coma."

"Please, Dr. Baatard. DO you need to swear?"

Ignoring her rhetorical question, Baatard suggested, "Maybe one of your staff was responsible. Maybe one of those low-life sickos you employ to save a few dollars did this on the night shift."

"Dr. Baatard, I think it more likely the patient was pregnant before her admission here. Don't you agree? I can assure you that . . . "

"You can assure what? You can't assure shit, Peoples."

"Really, Dr. Baatard." Peoples exclaimed.

"Look at what has happened, will you. What am I to tell the husband, Dr. Vernor? What kind of situation does this leave him in, huh? Did you think about that, huh? Okay, okay, I'll be right over."

"Good. Thank you, Dr. Baatard."

"And Peoples, . . . "

"Yes, Dr. Baatard?"

". . . order a portable abdominal ultrasound to be performed now so we can see what exactly is inside there before I arrive. I want to be absolutely, positively, definitely certain. I want to actually see the goddamn kid by ultrasound before I say anything about this to her husband. Understand?"

"Yes, Dr. Baatard."

Baatard started to put down the receiver, then picked it up again and said, "Hey, Peoples. Lissa Vernor WAS my patient. But I transferred her chronic care to Dr. Hernandez several weeks ago. You should be calling him, don't you think?" He remembered transferring Lissa's care at Dr. Vernor's request, and after hearing through some friends of his that Ryder Vernor was threatening legal action.

Peoples too heard about the transfer of patient care responsibilities, and also attributed it to the rumors of an impending law suit. "I tried to, but Dr. Hernandez left for the week to attend a medical meeting. He supposedly signed all his patients out to you," Peoples replied. "That would include Lissa Vernor, I presume."

Shit, that's right, thought Baatard. "Okay, okay. I'll be right there. And, Peoples, keep this quiet, will you? And get me a urine sample from her too, okay? Send it for a pregnancy test."

Ivory Peoples heard the click of the receiver, and immediately began the preparations for a visitor. Picking up the microphone lying on the nursing desk, Peoples screeched an announcement on the overhead speaker. "People, we going to get a visitor. Dr. Baatard." Peoples heard the groans come from different directions down the hall. "You know what we going to do, so let's get to dooooin' it. Okay?"

Next, Nurse Peoples called up the radiology department at Haven General Hospital and requested a portable ultrasound exam of Lissa's abdomen. When Mohammed called her back to ask about the details, she repeated that Baatard wanted to be "absolutely, positively, definitely sure Lissa was pregnant."

"That sounds like Baatard, all right," Mohammed the ultrasound technician said. "I'll be right over."

Calling her aides together, Peoples ordered them to clear all the wheelchair patients from the halls, mop up any urine puddles on the floor, and change any soiled bed clothes. As this was being done, Peoples walked up and down the hallways, her large bottom swaying in counter-pulsation to her steps, widely spraying disinfectant and deodorant mists into the air from cans she clutched like castanets in both hands.

Baatard arrived in a huff at Haven Convalescent within the hour. Rushing in from the parking lot, he pushed the swinging wooden side door open with such force it banged loudly against the wall, startling everyone at the nurse's station and making them look up.

Bypassing the nurse's station, Baatard marched straight to Lissa Vernor's room. There he found his patient - his former patient, he corrected himself - unconscious as before, lying in bed, eyes closed. But there seemed to be a subtle difference in the texture of her skin, and some puffiness of her face. "I've seen that look before," Baatard commented to Nurse Peoples, who was standing attentively by Lissa's bedside. Mohammed was also in the patient's room with a portable ultrasound unit, and nodded his head in agreement.

Baatard took the urine sample from Peoples and tested it with a spot pregnancy assay kit he had brought with him from his office. It tested positive for HCG, confirming that Lissa was very pregnant. Yet, he really didn't need a pregnancy test to reach that conclusion.

Lissa's sheets were pulled back for the ultrasound exam, and her robe drawn up, exposing her slightly rounded belly. Her abdomen looked a little distended, her cheeks a little more full.

Trying to ignore the sickening ubiquitous background odor of feces and urine from all the other patients, Baatard told Peoples, "She definitely looks pregnant. I don't need any damn ultrasound to tell me that. Any fool can figure this out."

Mohammed rode the metal ultrasonic transducer probe on a film of mineral oil which coated Vernor's abdomen like holy oil on an offering. The transducer probe slid slowly back and forth, and every once in a while Mohammed reached over and changed a switch setting on the control panel or make a note in his log book. Film recordings of the most interesting images were made, and all the data were stored on magnetic tape.

Mohammed looked up from his screen and spoke to Baatard as soon as he finished the scan. "Got it," he proudly announced. "Just a minute for the hard copy." Not very long after that, Mohammed handed an imaging film to Baatard. "See, right here," Mohammed excitedly said, repeatedly jabbing at an interesting area on the photo, causing it to flip back and forth in his hand.

Baatard spotted a tiny spine and a miniature skull on the film. "I agree, it does look like a fetus to me too. Lissa definitely is pregnant. I wonder how the hell THAT happened." Baatard asked, staring accusingly at Peoples.

Baatard did some quick calculating, measured the fetus' skull dimensions from the photo, and pronounced, "This fetus has got to be about six months old, assuming Lissa got pregnant just before her unfortunate illness." Looking at Peoples, Baatard frowned as he said, "We better get the father on the phone so I can talk to him. I can only imagine that this will be very difficult for him to handle."

Chapter 37

"Pregnant? You have got to be kidding," Ryder Vernor yelled at Baatard as they stood in the hall outside Lissa's room. Ryder had raced over to Haven Convalescent almost as soon as Peoples had called him. The very thought that his unconscious wife Lissa was six months pregnant was as ludicrous and impossible as it was insulting. "There must be some kind of mistake," Ryder said as he paced nervously back and forth, then told Baatard and Peoples, "This is impossible, absolutely impossible. I had a, . . . , " Ryder paused, then stopped talking.

Baatard caught the interruption, and was left very curious just what Ryder was about to tell him. "Impossible? I don't see how it's impossible. Lissa is definitely pregnant," Baatard replied, trying to remain as calm as he could. The hallway was no place to carry on a medical conversation, let alone an explosive argument, and he said, "Tragic it is, impossible it isn't. I examined her myself." Baatard looked closely at Ryder and said, "I'm sorry. What were you going to say about it being impossible?"

Ryder ignored Baatard's question, and asked, "Hey, how come you're here, anyway, Baatard? Where's Dr. Hernandez?"

"Oh, he's gone for a week, and I'm covering all his patients for him. Look, Ryder, let's try to be logical about this. Okay, okay, I know how upsetting this must be for you, but . . . "

Vernor looked at Baatard, his face turning beet red, before he exploded, "Like hell you do. I don't see how I can go through with this with my wife in a coma and no mother to care for an infant."

"I've had my own personal experiences with tragedy, too, Dr. Vernor," Baatard said, then asked, "Do you mind if I ask you a few questions?" Baatard glanced over at Peoples as he was talking.

Peoples turned her head away, but looked back to watch Baatard every once in a while as she busily made notes in Vernor's chart.

"No, I don't mind, as long as I can ask some of you too," Ryder replied.

"Okay, that's fair enough. Let's start by logically trying to date this pregnancy. When was the last time you had intercourse with your wife?" Baatard waited for the usual objection by Peoples to any conversation mentioning sex, and was surprised when none came. She seemed totally fascinated with this unusual incident, and wasn't going to say anything to slow down the conversation. Here right in front of her, the daily TV soaps were being played out in real life.

"I think that we had sex last maybe the day before her admittance to the hospital. I mean, it was a long time ago, you understand."

It must have been a really memorable occasion,
Baatard commented to himself. "That puts her pregnancy
at about six months, and goes along with the ultrasound
measurements, and with my exam. Doesn't that seem
reasonable to you?" Baatard asked. "I mean, after all, she
was TRYING to get pregnant, you know."

"Well, I guess so, but you told me . . . "

"Well, there you are. The hormone stimulation
sometimes works in unexpected ways. Apparently her
tubes weren't completely incapable of conducting eggs
after all. That must explain how she got pregnant."
Baatard looked carefully at Ryder's reaction, which
consisted solely of exasperated speechlessness. "Under
other, more happy, circumstances I would have been, as
her fertility doctor, pleased with this outcome. Her
pregnancy was achieved with my help, but unfortunately
now she's in a coma. Oh, such tragic circumstances. I'm
truly sorry, Ryder. Really, I am," Baatard said, shaking
his head in feigned sorrow.

"Baatard, this is impossible. You don't understand."

"Hey, I know this will put you in a very difficult
situation. You're almost a single father, but at the same
time you aren't. You're married, so getting a mate to help
with the child will be nearly impossible. Man, I really
wish there was something I could do to help," Baatard
said, shaking his head.

Ryder stood motionless and silent, his face
prominently displaying his confusion, his internal turmoil
for all to witness.

After waiting through a few moments of stillness,
Baatard continued. "From what I have known of

circumstances such as these, a C-section is the only appropriate delivery technique. Don't you agree?"

"Yes, well I guess so," Ryder replied. "But why hasn't anyone noticed this before now? Damn it, doesn't Hernandez examine his patients, Baatard?"

"I don't know how Hernandez could have missed this either," Baatard agreed with Ryder. Baatard disliked Hernandez anyway. He shook his head slowly and put his arm around Ryder's shoulder. "I guess it could be a combination of your Lissa being covered by sheets all day, and Hernandez not expecting this. Anyway, one thing is for sure - Lissa is going to deliver a baby, your baby, in about another three months."

Baatard waited for Ryder to reply, but all Ryder could seem to do was stare depressingly at the floor.

That is," Baatard carefully suggested, "unless you want to, ah, terminate the pregnancy." Baatard made the allusion softly, all the time looking down at Lissa's bed. Out of the corner of his eye, Baatard watched Peoples angrily blush and turn away. "I must admit that, at six months, an abortion will be dangerous and hard to justify to the ethics committee. But, I think that, under your wife's particular circumstances, well . . . "

"Terminate the pregnancy?" Ryder replied, his voice rising. "Hell, of course not. Baatard, we have got to talk. Anyway, you can't abort her at six months."

"Abort him, Ryder. It's a male child," Baatard

corrected Ryder.

"Oh." Ryder replied, looking away.

"But there is another way I could think of that might help you here. Let me call you in a few days, after you've had a chance to assimilate all this, and we'll talk some more, okay?" Baatard flashed a supportive smile, gave Ryder an encouraging pat on the back, and then left.

Ramirez, sitting at her desk at work reading some legal briefs, received a call from a guard at the Haven Municipal courts.

"I got something you may find interesting here," the guard said. "You know of a broad named Marina Bonnaserra?"

"The name's not familiar. Why?" Ramirez lied.

"She's been coming to a lot of rape trials lately. I tried to get a conversation going with her, and I found out she's looking for someone. Who, I don't know, but I kind of get the impression she was raped once and she's still looking for the guy who did it. Know what I mean?"

"Yeah. Obsessive shit, huh? Do you think she was raped recently?" Ramirez asked.

"Nope. Can't say I ever remember hearing of her case coming up. Maybe it's still under investigation," the guard speculated, "or before my time here."

"Okay, look into it for me, will you?" Ramirez asked the guard, who, in a simple and ongoing exchange of favors, had provided his share of useful information to her over time.

Chapter 38

Marina's House
Haven, New Jersey

The next several months were the busiest and most exciting times for Marina. At work, activity at the QA office had dropped to a welcome lull. Even activity in the Vernor case slowed down, as committees and outside experts busily prepared their reports.

At her home, the pregnancy just about totally disrupted every aspect of what had been up to now a single and organized life. Initially, Marina was careful with what and how much she ate and, as a consequence, put on only a few pounds. As time progressed, though, she began to swell up like a watermelon. By the end of her third trimester Marina had gained nearly thirty-five pounds. Realistically she had to admit that most of the added weight was not from her baby. She was trim before her pregnancy, and expected to return to her former shape after delivering, although it might require more dedication to exercise on her part.

At first, Marina tried to maintain the limited exercise she cared to do under normal circumstances. walks in the park and leisurely strolls around the mall. Soon, her feet began to swell and her legs hurt and she detested any form of exercise at all. Baatard warned her against too much inactivity, and although she listened attentively and appreciated the importance of what he was telling her, she was at heart a creature of habit and resisted changing her sedentary ways to any great degree.

A nagging low back pain became an unwelcome and frequent companion. Despite this, she still managed to 'force' herself to get out and walk for 15 minutes most evenings. Baatard was as reluctant to supply Marina with medication for the pain as she was to take it. The package insert which accompanied the medication noted that it could cause birth defects; the warnings had been enough to frighten her.

Several times, as the QA process concerning Lissa Vernor slowly developed, Marina had again considered changing doctors. She wondering how smart it really was to continue seeing someone she was also investigating for QA reasons.

There were the obvious conflict of interest questions, although Lemar Jackson had assured her it would not become a problem, at least not yet. Also, there was the confidence factor. Yet, Haven wasn't that big a community, and she suspected that most of the other OBs would not be that interested in a change of doctors in the third trimester her choices in alternate obstetricians were not that great. At least she knew Baatard and was used to his office and his mannerisms. In addition, the more she read about what had happened to Lissa Vernor, the less she could find Baatard at fault. He seemed to have committed no act of commission or omission that would have led to the adverse event. She began to conclude that perhaps Baatard's, and for that matter Lissa's, luck had just run out. Worse yet, she hated her own indecisiveness.

Curiously, Marina found that the pregnancy had the opposite effect on her relationship with Charlie Kincade than she ever would have predicted. At first she avoided seeing Charlie, afraid of how he would react to this news. Eventually, she decided to accept one of his infrequent invitations out for dinner.

They arrived at the restaurant, a local Italian place of passable cuisine, separately but at the same time. Charlie noticed her enlarged midsection almost immediately, and although he tried to avoid staring, it was all too obvious. Marina was quite along in her pregnancy and had developed a slight puffiness of her cheeks and the skin of her upper arms, in addition to the rather enlarged abdomen. Yet, instead of reminding Marina of how bloated and heavy she looked, Charlie instead complimented her by saying, "You look unusually radiant tonight." He also pulled out the chair to her dinner table in an uncharacteristically gentlemanly gesture.

Marina was surprised at Charlie's unusual flattery. She was also amused as she watched Charlie incessantly stared at her midsection. The waiter came by and she ordered a diet cola, and Charlie got a gin and tonic. Being in the mood to be a little bit of a tease, she waited to discuss her altered appearance for a long time, deciding to first let Charlie bring up the topic.

Charlie stammered at first, and looked a bit uncomfortable as he asked, "I know this sounds ridiculous, but you look a little bit, you know, pregnant." He chuckled nervously, then looked away. The drinks arrived, and Charlie downed his in one gulp, then signaled the waiter for another.

"Well, I'm definitely not becoming obese, Charlie. I look this way because I am pregnant." Marina smiled sheepishly, reached across the table top and held his hand. She had never seen Charlie appear to be so uncomfortable in all their years together.

"Oh, for god's sake, be serious." Charlie nearly choked, as he gawked at her full lower abdomen.

"Well, yes, I am serious," she tried to smile. "I was hoping you'd at least offer your congratulations."

"Fine. Congratulations. Now, do you care to tell me who the father is? I, I never even knew you got married." He stared uncomfortably at her ringless hand still loosely holding onto his.

"I never told you about a wedding because I never got married. Actually, you're one of the few persons I've told about my pregnancy, and I was hoping you'd be at least a little more supportive."

"Supportive?" he nearly yelled. "You want me to be a little more supportive? Why don't you ask whoever you're living with for support? Or perhaps I should put it another way, whoever you're sleeping with? No, I don't want to know." Charlie dropped Marina's hand as if it could transmit leprosy, and covered up his ears with his hands. "Excuse me, Marina, I didn't mean to say that. It's, it's none of my business, really." The waiter came by again, and it was both an unwanted intrusion and welcome just the same, in the way placing their orders served to break up the tension. They both glanced at the menu, Marina ordered pasta and Charlie ordered a steak.

"Charlie," Marina protested, her face flushed, "I don't like your tone of voice at all."

"I'm sorry, Marina. It's the questioning lawyer part of me again." He abruptly moved his chair back, as if getting ready to walk away.

Marina could see that Charlie was getting angry and confused, and searched for a way to ease his anger and confusion. Under similar circumstances, she had to admit she might react that way too. "I'm not living with anyone either, Charlie. And I didn't sleep around and get pregnant."

"Then, I don't understand what you're saying, Marina. I don't believe in Immaculate Conception, you know."

"Well, I'm no Virgin Mary. That much you know for certain," she winked at him. "Charlie, it's like this. My biological clock is ticking. I want to have a child before I get too old. That's normal, isn't it?"

Charlie shrugged, as if conceding that, although he knew she wanted one, he didn't.

The Surrogate

"I can't wait forever, Charlie. I know how you feel about children, so I never asked you to - you know - to participate." She waved her hands in the air, as if to demonstrate what she had a difficult time putting into words. "And I never really thought you wanted to get married. I didn't want you to feel I pressured you into doing something you weren't ready to do."

"Thanks, Marina," he said ironically, "but I don't understand. How did you . . . you know?"

"If you're worried about my having been with another man, well you can forget that. I used *in vitro* fertilization. I used my own ova and they were fertilized from a . . . a, a sperm bank."

Charlie took a quick gulp of water from his glass, then choked and coughed up the water on the front of his shirt as she said 'sperm bank.' "A sperm bank? You used a sperm bank?" he stammered. Charlie apologized profusely, then wiped up the mess with a paper napkin. People at surrounding tables were looking at them strangely. Their entrees arrived, and they both paused to consider their thoughts. Marina took little bites from her pasta, and Charlie cut some steak and started to chew.

"Please, could you lower your voice?" Marina blushed and turned away. Charlie nodded condescendingly. "I just decided to go it alone and not wait around any longer. I didn't like the idea of being a dependent little puppy dog hoping for some prince in shining armor to rescue me some day from the curse of maidenhood. That's just not me, Charlie."

"But, but you don't even know who inseminated you, for God's sake," he stammered. "I mean, he could be a goddamn drug dealer or a criminal for all you know."

"Those are people in your world, Charlie. The vast majority of people are perfectly normal, at least I think so."

"It's not just you I was thinking about, Marina. What if your child wants to know who his father is? Did you ever think of that?"

"I thought of a lot of things, Charlie. The sperm bank said they would provide me with a profile of the donor, if I ever want one." The Conceptions Foundation was a leader in donor and recipient education and information, at least in this regard. Marina could well imagine a time when she might want to know more about the father of her child, even though he was a father only in the genetic sense. Yet, Charlie seemed unimpressed.

"Believe me, this was a very big decision, and it's also very complicated, very complicated," she repeated. She looked down at the table and stared into her empty plate for a moment, then, searching for a way to end the line of conversation, said, "Look, there's the dessert cart. Care to join me?"

From that point on, Marina's relationship with Charlie surprisingly improved. They dated more frequently and became almost the best of friends. Marina wondered at first if he stayed so close to her out of guilt or a desire to be a father in some vicarious way. However,

The Surrogate

as Marina's pregnancy neared the seventh month,
Charlie's visits to her house again became less frequent.
Although Charlie explained it away by complaining of a
crushing workload and the demands of his law practice,
Marina attributed the distancing to his feeling
uncomfortable around a pregnant woman, particularly one
he had once been intimate with but not impregnated.

Chapter 39

Haven Convalescent Hospital

Nearly two months later

Shortly before seven in the evening, a private ambulance quietly pulled into the loading area of the ER of Quayle Medical Center, in Trenton, New Jersey. Its lights off, the ambulance driver parked, then she and the attendant quickly got out and opened the back door. They pulled out a collapsible gurney, popped open the wheels, and slid a body out the back and onto the bed. The patient's head was uncovered, and the patient was apparently alive, although there were no signs in the dim evening light of animation whatsoever.

The attendants wheeled the patient in through the ER doors, then immediately out the back of the ER and onto the patient transport elevator, stopping on the third floor. Apparently the cart was expected, for instead of going into a room, it was taken directly into a small operating room suite. A nurse helped the attendants transfer the patient to the operating room table, and waited for them to leave before beginning the preparation of the patient for a surgical procedure. Once the initial prep was complete, the nurse left to make some notifying phone calls.

A few minutes later the anesthesiologist arrived, and administered some intravenous drugs to the patient designed to relax muscles and prevent pain. Shortly after this, Dr. Damon Baatard entered the surgical suite, and began an elective cesarean section. Within minutes, a healthy baby boy was delivered, who was quickly transferred to the nursery. The mother's surgical wounds were closed, and she was immediately transferred out of the hospital and back to Haven Convalescent Hospital in a manner similar to her almost unnoticed arrival.

Lissa Vernor was in and out of the hospital in less than three hours, and little notice was placed on her having ever been there, except for the unaccompanied baby she had never seen, and had left behind.

"Goddamn annoying thing," Baatard cursed as he angrily punched off his beeper's continuous alarm. He had hated wearing a CODE beeper ever since his days as a medical resident: he hated the intrusion, he hated allowing people the freedom to bother him whenever and wherever he and they were. Unfortunately, he also found a beeper increasingly essential. Modern medicine and the pressures of his practice required his constant and instant availability. Others might have felt honored at being so sought after; Baatard was not, remembering a quote from the French General DeGaulle; "The cemeteries are filled with indispensable people."

Baatard was on his bimonthly morning rounds for the few elderly patients and consults for the last hour at Haven Convalescent when he was paged. He looked down at the flashing number on the top of the text message and recognized that it belonged to the birthing center at Haven General Hospital. Unsure just which of his 'term' patients it would be, he quickly walked over to the nurse's station and told the ward clerk, "Hand me the phone, will you."

"I'm sorry. Did you ask for something?" the clerk absentmindedly asked Baatard. She was seated next to the drip coffee brewer, and within eye shot of the TV monitor and her favorite programs. Baatard could see that, unless it was urgent, she intended to stay right there, ensconced in her chair.

"No, nothing. I can get it faster myself." Baatard reached around and grabbed the phone from the clerk, dialed the Labor and Delivery number displaying on his text message, and said, "Baatard here. What's the problem?"

"Dr. Baatard," one of the delivery nurses started, "your patient Marina Bonnaserra is here."

"And?" Baatard asked, trying to suppress his annoyance at being interrupted on his rounds. God knew, he hated to be at the dreary convalescent facility at all, and every delay keeping him there even a minute longer than absolutely necessary was a major pain. The gynecological needs of patients in convalescent facilities was rarely challenging, and even more rarely financially worth his while. On top of that, the stench at Haven Convalescent this morning was particularly overpowering. Still, his need to maintain regular contact with this particular facility was even greater.

"And she is having contractions every six minutes," the nurse continued. "What do . . . "

Baatard cut her off, as he wondered how long it would take for her to get to the bottom line. "Is Marina's cervix dilated?" Baatard growled, looking at his watch. "That's all I need to know. Just tell me if her cervix is dilated." Baatard anxiously calculated how long it would take him to finish his business at the convalescent hospital, how much longer to make the drive over to Haven General Hospital this time of day, and which route would be best.

"We don't know yet. The obstetrical resident is checking her now. Ms. Bonnaserra said her water broke about an hour ago."

Baatard listened as the nurse droned on, barely paying attention, preferring instead to watch a cute new nurse's aide bending over a short ways down the hall. He tried not to stare too obviously as her skirt rode up her thighs. Then, he almost turned away as she noticed him gawking when, instead of a scowl, she calmly returned his glance and smiled.

Baatard was jogged back from fantasy to reality by the dry, formal voice of the labor and delivery nurse who was still on the phone. In many ways, it reminded him of the uncomfortable tone of conversations he had had too many times with his second wife. "We have initiated the standard protocol. Unless you want a resident to deliver your private patient, I think you'd better hurry in."

Baatard knew what the nurse was getting at when she empathized 'private patient'. He didn't know for sure who the nurse was, but was certain from her twangy accent that she was Philippine and that she was eating while speaking with him.

"I'm on my way. Okay, okay. See you soon. Try to use breathing exercises to slow things down a bit, will you?" Can't they even leave me alone for five goddamn minutes, Baatard cursed as he rushed to fill in the Progress Notes on his patients? That was all that was left between him and the door. Jokingly, he had referred to the documentation of his monthly visit as 'Lack of Progress Notes' once to Nurse Peoples. As he remembered it, she didn't think he was funny. She never did.

Baatard rushed out the double back door into the small parking lot, sucking in the fresh air. The smell of urine and feces inside the building was so strong, it would still take another five minutes before all background stench left his mouth, and he would probably smell it on his clothes for the rest of the day. Baatard rapidly made the short drive to Haven General Hospital and within five minutes found himself in the Labor and Delivery Suite.

Gina Lareno, one of the newer Nurse Practitioners,

met Baatard as he entered the birthing room. "Here," Gina said as she without warning handed Baatard a small bundle wrapped in a blue blanket. "It's a boy. Isn't he beautiful?" Gina looked over at Marina and said, "The mother's doing well too, aren't you mom?"

Baatard looked down at the child, and tried to exhibit surprise at its being a male. "Wonderful," he said. He speculated how he was still going to bill for a delivery performed by a resident, although he was certain his billing office could handle it. Baatard briefly considered that the nurse practitioner and not the resident may actually have delivered the 'little bundle of joy.' He didn't know which actually had, and didn't plan to ask.

"Well that certainly was a quick delivery, wasn't it," Baatard said to Marina with a nervous laugh.

"Yes, and it was a lot easier than I expected," Marina replied. "But, the stretching and the tearing hurt a lot. I felt like I was delivering a watermelon."

"There's always some pain, sometimes a lot more. From what I've heard, you're pretty lucky." Baatard performed a cursory exam of the newborn, then said, "He appears to be a perfect baby. Let's check you out, too." Baatard whispered some instructions to Gina, handed the infant to her, then he left for the nursing station to complete some paperwork.

Gina took the signal from Baatard and moved the newborn to the nursery. When Gina returned, she helped Marina get ready for a bedside exam. She instructed Marina to empty her bladder first, then removed the large absorbent pad covering her groin and helped Marina lay down in the bed.

Baatard and Gina performed a brief exam of Marina's perineal area, noting some minor lacerations of the external vulva, but none which were extensive enough to require suturing. The tissue around the anus was also not torn, and there were no open cuts in the vaginal wall. Marina had indeed had a mild delivery. "And the placenta?" Baatard asked Gina.

"All the products of conception are accounted for and intact," Gina reported. This meant that the thin, delicate placenta was not torn as it passed out of Marina's vagina during delivery of her child, and that parts of the placenta were not left behind in Marina's uterus. Remnants of placentas could have caused bleeding or clotting problems later, or worse yet, infection, and checking that an intact placenta was delivered along with the child was standard procedure throughout the world.

Marina looked at Gina, and then at Baatard and said, "I want you both to know that I appreciate all that you have done for me. Thank you so much, Gina, and Dr. Baatard." She was genuinely pleased with the way her IVF had gone, and especially with the outcome, and now more than ever was glad she had chosen not to change physicians during her pregnancy. Baatard had worked out just fine, and with little to no action lately at Haven General on the Lissa Vernor QA review, she had almost forgotten about any concerns she had once had. Looking appreciatively at them both, Marina said, "He IS everything that I wanted. I plan to name him Austin. What do you think?"

"Fine name, fine name. Nice name," Baatard told Marina, his concentration momentarily directed to Austin's paperwork and then at his watch. Gina nodded her approval too. "Why Austin?" Baatard asked.

"Because it's masculine. Austin is a strong sounding surname. That's all," Marina said, smiling and shrugging her shoulders. "Besides, it's not common."

"I guess so. Anyway, you and your child will be able to stay in the birthing room for at least one day, and maybe longer," Baatard told Marina. "That is, if you want to and the room isn't needed. And, Marina, congratulations again."

"Thanks for your help, and I think I'll take you up on your offer. I feel real tired, and Austin and I want to get some rest before going home."

Never one to sleep well outside her own home, Marina had a difficult time resting in the hospital. She continued to wake up every half hour, feeling slightly disoriented and with a mild headache. Her pelvis felt bruised and stretched beyond its limits, constraining her ability to move around at all for the first day. Hospital sounds and smells crept into her subconscious and seemed both unknown and unwelcome. Gina noticed Marina's problem and offered her a sedative. Unfortunately, this didn't help at all.

Later that evening, Marina experienced a strange, new, terrifying nightmare. It was different from the recurring nightmare of her rape which had plagued her for years. That one she had almost managed to live with, buoyed by the hope of the eventual apprehension of her rapist and finally extracting her fullest revenge. In this new nightmare, she dreamed of seeing four boys in an orphanage, children she didn't remember having met but who still seemed familiar to her. The orphanage was burning and the children were crying out to Marina for help. Tragically, she was unable to save them. Marina tried desperately to run to the orphans but seemed to be stuck in molasses. She just couldn't move quickly enough despite the frantic effort she struggled to make.

Marina awoke with a start, sitting straight up in bed, looking around for the burning building, her heart racing and her face sweating. Her perineal area was still quite sore and raw from childbirth. Her eyes darted wildly around in the subdued light, looking for the children in the burning building. Then, recognizing she was in no orphanage, Marina grabbed for the call light. Within a minute a nurse's aide came in.

"Can I help you, Ms. Bonnaserra?"

"Yes, where is my child?" Marina asked, searching anxiously around her room.

"When you fell asleep, we placed her in the warmer, right here, next to your bed."

"Him," Marina corrected the aide. "My child is a boy, Austin Bonnaserra," she said definitively, wondering why the aide could have been confused. Austin was, after all, swathed in a blue blanket.

"I apologize, Ms. Bonnaserra."

Marina looked in the warmer at her bed side, and was reassured to see her Austin, all pink and comfortable. Marina leaned over and examined him more closely, looking for chest movement - the telltale sign of breathing. She was relieved to see Austin's chest flutter, his inspirations more like a quiver. His face held a peaceful, intelligent look, almost a glow to it. Turning to the aide, Marina said, "But I thought I heard Austin cry. Now he looks so quiet."

"None of the babies on the ward are crying now, Ms. Bonnaserra. It must have been a bad dream. Try to go back to sleep." The aide turned the lights down low and began to close the door. Just as Marina began to fall asleep again, the aide asked her, "Do you need another sedative?"

"No, thanks," Marina wearily told her, struggling to remain polite. Within minutes, Marina was again dreaming.

Chapter 40

Haven General Hospital
Post-Partum Ward

The next morning Marina woke around six, pulled from a deep but restless sleep by rattling sounds. Teams of nurses were going into each patient's room and noisily taking temperatures and blood pressures, without consideration of waking their sick patients from needed sleep. Even though she too was a nurse, she found it hard to relate to the activities of ward nurses. She preferred her cushy administrative position to the messy and physically strenuous ward, with its patient contact.

As was her habit before breakfast, Marina turned on the morning TV news on her bedside unit. She rarely got out of bed while at her own home until she listened to the TV for at least a few minutes. Unlike the hours worked by ward nurses, hers didn't require her to be in her office until at least 8:30, which suited her just fine, as she hated to be rushed in the morning. This turned out to be additionally convenient, in that leaving home at a reasonable hour should make any future arrangements for

Austin's child care less difficult.

The cafeteria staff brought in Marina's food tray right after the TV came on. Marina gingerly lifted back the plastic food cover and peered underneath. Yuck, she thought as she surveyed the moderately warm scrambled eggs and cold bacon. The food was arranged, make that thrown, in a most unappetizing way on her green plastic partition plate.

As Marina reached for the all-important coffee, she noticed the TV news anchor saying something about a "Miracle" baby. Marina reached over and turned up the sound volume with her remote.

"At seven thirty last night," the announcer started, "a miraculous birth took place at Quayle Medical Center, here in Trenton. A 6 pound, four ounce boy was born to Lissa Vernor. Tragically, the mother has been in a coma for the entire pregnancy, having suffered a stroke nine months ago while in surgery. Her husband, Dr. Ryder Vernor, a family practitioner from Haven, New Jersey was unavailable for . . . "

Oh, that poor woman, Marina thought. She wondered what Vena must have thought about this, being sort of a caretaker and surrogate spouse for Ryder Vernor. Marina was frankly surprised that Vena had neglected to mention Lissa's pregnancy. Surely Vena would have known. Maybe Lissa Vernor is beyond feeling now, but this has got to be rough for her husband, Marina thought. What a mixed blessing for them both.

"Well, Marina, how are you doing?" The loud, rough voice startled her, and she almost spilled her coffee as she jarred her table. Marina looked up and found a visibly angry Dr. Baatard standing by her bedside, apparently visiting on his morning rounds.

"Oh, you surprised me." She took a few moments to regain her composure before saying, "I'm doing just fine, thank you."

"Good. The staff pediatrician tells me your child is just fine, also. I saw Austin earlier, and he certainly is a handsome boy," he said, overtly struggling to sound pleasant.

Marina was surprised that a pediatrician had already been by to examine Austin without her being aware of it. "Yes, Austin is just what I wanted. You know, I still can't believe I'm a mother. Thank you very much for all your help."

"You're welcome. Now, let's check your perineum to see if there's bleeding, or any tearing." Baatard made certain there was a nurse in the room, then closed the door and pulled the drape around Marina's bed. He put on a plastic glove, and then carefully examined Marina's vulva, vagina, and anal area; it all looked appropriate for twenty-four hours after delivery. The vulva was a little raw, but without infection or bloody oozing, he observed.

"Hopefully I can go home today," Marina told Baatard. She longed for the privacy, the quiet, and a chance to be alone with her new child, her wonderful new son Austin.

Baatard checked Marina's vital sign clipboard. Her

temperature, blood pressure and heart rate were all well within normal limits. "I don't see why not," he told Marina. "Let me write the discharge orders when I go past the nursing station. You'll need to take iron supplements daily, a stool softener, and I want you to call my office in two weeks for a follow-up appointment. You can arrange for your own pediatrician to see after Austin. If you don't already have one selected, I can recommend some local ones to you."

"Right," Marina said. "Actually, I was planning to take Austin to a family practitioner I've seen in the past, Dr. Vernor. But, I heard he's having some more family problems, and . . . " Marina noticed a certain subtle darkness come over Baatard's face as she mentioned the name 'Dr. Vernor'. It was similar to the distasteful facial expression he had a long time ago after meeting with "slime balls."

"Oh, yes, well, I see what you mean," replied Baatard, having difficulty in hiding his displeasure in hearing Ryder's name.

Marina wanted to ask Baatard if he knew anything about the birth of the Vernor child, but before she could, Baatard started toward the door.

Marina remembered that Baatard hadn't mentioned any restrictions on activity, and asked him about that.

"I don't want you to perform any strenuous sports, particularly ones involving stretching of your groin, for at least two weeks. You can shower as soon as you want to. And no intercourse for at least that long."

Marina noticed Baatard's face become unusually serious and rigid, as if he were exerting a great amount of stress in trying to control its expression. She could only speculate on what was going through his mind, and didn't like it.

"At any rate, call me if I can be of assistance. I'll see you again in two weeks."

"Bye," Marina called out after Baatard, seeing he was already halfway out the door. Right after Baatard left, Austin was brought in from the nursery for his morning feeding. She had intended to breast feed Austin, and would have preferred to, believing the gift of food from her body to Austin's to be the essence of continuing her donation of life. Unfortunately, with only one functional nipple, she needed to supplement the breast feedings with formula. Although one nipple was probably adequate for a newborn's nutritional needs, she didn't want to take any chances.

Marina carefully took Austin from the nurse, and snugly held him close to her. She gently pulled back Austin's blanket and looked carefully into his face. Not having a great deal of experience with babies this age, she wasn't sure if he could yet recognize her features. Children had never been a strong point for her anyway. But to hold Austin, well it was exactly as she had imagined it would be, and more. Austin was hers, of her own flesh and blood, at least half of him was, and she loved him dearly. She held his hands and kissed his perfect, tiny fingers, then his angelic face. She thought she could recognize her features in his face, but saw some rough facial characteristics there also. Perhaps they're from the sperm donor, she reminded herself. Marina briefly considered who it might have been, then dismissed the speculation as something never to be answered. It seemed in that way almost like an anonymous adoption. She imagined that, at this point, it really didn't matter. She knew who the mother was.

Marina talked to Austin while feeding him, trying to tell him how glad she was that he was there, and how much she hoped for the future. She was amazed at how easily he responded to her.

Shortly, Marina got dressed and an aide from hospital transport took her by wheel chair to the Nursing Station. She was relieved that she could finally check Austin and herself out of the hospital, completing the end of a long ordeal and the beginning of a new life for her and for Austin. On her way off the ward, Marina's wheel chair nearly collided with Denny Cruite. Marina was startled from the near collision and was very apologetic.

Denny seemed to Marina to be a little thinner and maybe a little more sickly than the last time they had met. Her clothes, still the standard red business dress, seemed to hang a little more loose. Had Denny been losing weight, and why?

"Congratulations, Marina," Denny said, her voice noticeably a touch deeper and coarser than usual. "Oh, and this must be the new baby," she cooed, staring down at Austin. "May I hold him?"

Although not at all comfortable with the idea, Marina couldn't readily formulate an objection. Carefully, she handed Austin over to Denny.

Denny seemed to know how to hold babies, which didn't surprise Marina very much. She made some inane baby sounds, then smiled strangely and handed him back to Marina. "You're one lucky lady, Marina. I'm so proud The Conceptions Foundation could help in some small way in bringing this beautiful child into the world and into your life. Seeing him just makes me want to have a child of my own all over again," she winked.

"Yes, it's wonderful, isn't it," Marina said. They talked for a few minutes about mothering subjects, then Denny invited Marina to meet for lunch after she settled into a routine back at home. As she left the ward, Marina had a strong suspicion that Denny had another agenda here, but couldn't imagine what it might be. She decided, however, not to call Denny back.

Austin had a ravenous appetite, and fed just as often as he slept. The sensation of warmth, close physical contact, of feeding another's need, all were new and welcome to Marina. But later on Austin's first day of life, the site of Austin pulling on her one normal nipple during feeding triggered, for some totally unrelated reason, long-suppressed memories.

Marina was forced back to that horrible night some sixteen years ago when her body was defiled and deformed by the beast. She still remembered the terribly intense pain in her right chest, her inner thigh and in-between her legs, and the sticky feel of oozing blood. And she also remembered how, in a brief moment of regained consciousness, she had vaguely seen a woman staring at her face in the shadows and the trash, perhaps trying unsuccessfully to recognize her.

Back then, the woman who had rescued Marina tried to shield the facial lacerations from further injury and contamination, giving the best comfort she could until the ambulance arrived, extricated her from the trash and rushed her to the emergency room.

Once the ambulance had brought Marina to the hospital, a group of ER staff swarmed over her helpless body, starting a perfunctory intravenous line for fluid support and as a route for drug administration. As a nurse, she now knew most of their efforts had been aimed at supporting basic life functions and identifying the extent of injury, but back then, all she knew in her near-stupor was terror. An extensive skeletal and neurologic exam had been performed, and anything that might be broken was x-rayed. Sex-related crimes were more often a matter of aggression and hatred than of lust.

The Emergency Room doctor who directed the care given Marina was a thin, dark older man with serious, sad eyes, whose name tag said Dr. Daliwhal "Hank" Chandrachankar. He had long since retired. Better and more simply known as Daliwhal, and also as Hank, he had been in charge of the Bonnaserra case from her first arrival through the ER doors.

An increase in local crime had made Daliwhal an expert at treating sexual assault and the particular accompanying police demands, and he seemed to fancy himself almost an attorney, the way he was getting used to terms like 'evidentiary', 'intended victim,' and 'perpetrator'.

As per routine, several specimens of fluid and swabs were collected from Marina's vagina. Blood samples were sent for drug and alcohol screen, and for a baseline AIDS test. Marina's status at that moment, before any virus could replicate and change her blood test pattern, needed to be documented.

Daliwhal had busily worked toward identifying a source of bleeding on Marina's chest, when he suddenly stopped his actions, unable to believe what he was finally staring at. It took him a few moments to regain his composure and resume his work. He always was amazed when a new horror could shock him - he thought he had just about seen it all. Stepping outside the room, he asked one of the ER technicians to call the surgeons down right away. Then, Daliwhal began cleaning out a most unusual chest wound, in preparation for the surgeons who would undoubtedly further explore its extent. The tissue was obviously contaminated, and would require a drain rather than a complete closure, in order to avoid a closed infection - one that might lead to sepsis and perhaps death. Shortly, one of the requested surgeons entered the room, accompanied by two detectives. Daliwhal turned to them, his hands shaking, almost unable to speak.

The Surrogate

A one inch square area of skin was savagely torn from Marina's left breast, and roughly encompassed the top of the nipple and surrounding skin. The edges were raw and rough, as if some wild animal had been hungrily feeding there, before being forced to leave. The surrounding flesh was discolored blue and purple, the result of bruising and bleeding into the subcutaneous tissue.

Certain from the size and the spacing of the bite marks that these unfortunately were human bites, Daliwhal continued to probe the cut tissues. He liberally injected an anesthetic along the wound edges as he methodically worked his way along the edge. It was further evidence that they all were, after all, animals, Daliwhal thought. Fortunately, the number of people that were sick enough to inflict such heinous damage were limited, and whoever it had been, was deranged, evil.

The probably human origin of the bite made the wound management even more difficult. Human bites were much more an infection problem than animal bites were. At least rabies had been less of a consideration. In that time so long ago, Hank had tried to keep his mind from roaming too soon into developing a picture of the monster that could have done this.

Chapter 41

Marina's life with Austin soon settled into an easy routine of feedings, diaper changings, walks and naps. Although tedious and simplistic, she found motherhood to be not at all disappointing, and never regretted her choices in the least. And maternity leave was also a welcome respite from her job at Haven General.

Later that first week, while food shopping with Austin, Marina spotted Vena Kleinman from a distance. "Marina, how are you?" Vena nearly choked in surprise. "What a coincidence." Looking into Marina's backpack, Vena said, "Oh, your baby is so cute. She even looks a little like you, too."

"It's a boy, not a girl," Marina corrected. "His name is Austin, Austin Bonnaserra." Marina tried to smile and forced herself to be polite. She did make an effort to like Vena, but always ended up finding Vena lacking in certain social graces.

"I'm sure the father and you are very proud," Vena crooned as she twisted her dagger in Marina's flesh.

Offended, Marina instead ignored Vena's implied dig and countered by saying, "And how is your relationship? With your new friend, I mean."

"Oh, so far, so good," Vena signed. "Look, I'm pretty

hungry. Do you have time for lunch?"

Marina could see Vena hadn't a clue how she felt about her. Without a ready excuse, Marina was caught aback, and, besides, Marina wanted to learn more about Lissa and her new child, so she hesitatingly accepted.

Marina, with Austin nestled comfortably in her backpack, walked down the street with Vena to a natural food restaurant and store. The restaurant was Vena's choice, but was one Marina had avoided after finding it too trendy and superficial. The owners had no idea what the term "natural food" really meant. Marina and Vena took one of the few tables, near a shelf of vitamin supplements.

"To answer your question," Vena said, "Ryder is very lonely and unhappy. His medical practice has suffered, and he's barely making enough to pay his bills. I'm sure that, under the circumstances, you could understand this."

"Of course," Marina nodded, empathetically. "I heard on the television news about Mrs. Vernor giving birth, and I assume that is what you're referring to?"

Vena nodded her head.

"How tragic. No wonder Ryder is upset, with his 'significant other' so ill," Marina replied. Marina realized she left herself vulnerable for a caustic retort from Vena, but let it go, hoping Vena was not clever enough to pick it up. Besides, they were both adults, and she realized she had no reason to be so judgmental about Vena.

Marina looked over the 'natural foods' menu, and had to study it carefully before she could locate even one item that sounded the least bit appetizing. She was glad she wasn't too hungry, because she could see that otherwise she would starve.

"In fact, Dr. Vernor, Ryder, was seriously considering suing Dr. Baatard. Ryder thinks Baatard just totally screwed up as far as the handling of his wife's case was concerned."

As the QA nurse, Marina of course knew more about that then she was at liberty to tell Vena. From what she knew, though, she was beginning to doubt whether Baatard was really at fault. At least from the IVF procedures Baatard had performed on her, she had no reason to doubt his clinical expertise, although his personality certainly could use a little polish. Certainly, she would be willing to recommend Baatard as a physician to other women needing fertility assistance.

Occupied so completely with her pregnancy and her delivery, Marina really hadn't had a lot of time lately to inquire further into the Lissa Vernor records. She suspected that when she returned to work this would be one of the cases waiting a more detailed Quality Assessment review. Something Vena had just said didn't make a lot of sense, and Marina asked, "You said he was planning on suing, but not anymore?"

"Yes," Vena continued, "Ryder was getting ready to sue Dr. Baatard, but then all of a sudden, he changed his mind. Don't ask me why, either, because I don't know. Anyway, I'm surprised that you didn't find out about any of this, considering . . .," Vena said.

"Considering what?" Marina assumed Vena knew she worked QA at Haven General, and was referring to that. Marina wondered why Vena always was so quick to make little, annoying innuendoes. There were times when she really didn't want to be around Vena, and certainly wouldn't associate with her otherwise. They were such different people.

"Just that a friend, a close friend of yours was going to handle the case, that's all I meant."

"You mean Charlie Kincade?" Marina asked. Now she realized what the mousy little tramp was trying to imply, in all its petty ugliness. Marina wondered how Vena knew about Charlie Kincade, and that he was acquainted with her at all?

"Yes, that's who. Apparently you had something to do with him getting Dr. Vernor as a client," Vena said.

"Well, I guess that's true," Marina acknowledged. For some reason, she felt very defensive about this, even though she knew she really had no reason to. "I did refer Charlie to Dr. Vernor on another matter. I guess he naturally got to handle this other problem too."

Marina wondered if this had anything to do with Charlie calling her so much again lately. She did feel a little guilty at not having returned his calls. Marina had just assumed that he wanted to go out again, and she didn't know if that's what she wanted to do, although she was getting to miss him more than usual. Especially now. Although, she thought, it might be interesting to see how Charlie would act around Austin. Maybe he had changed, maybe he would actually be comfortable around an infant if it was hers. She wondered again if there was a conflict of interest in discussing Lissa's case with Charlie, since she was still nominally a patient of Baatard's, and also worked in the QA department at Haven General handling the Lissa Vernor review.

"Speaking about screwing up, Vena," Marina smiled, "messing with a married man can be a big mistake. I hope you're taking precautions."

"You mean Ryder?" Vena asked, surprised and blushing. "Oh, for God's sake, Marina, get real. His wife's a goddamn vegetable."

Marina nodded, and felt that she really shouldn't have even said that. Vena would have had every right to tell her to mind her own business. Besides, she could really see Vena's view - at what point was someone married, and when was he then widowed? Yet, she wondered from Vena's reaction to the question and the way she answered it if there were other men in Vena's life too. Charlie Kincade, perhaps? Marina wouldn't have been at all surprised.

"It's a difficult situation all around, Marina. Cut me some slack, will you. We are, I am, using birth control, if that's what you mean. We got some foam," Vena chuckled nervously, making a disgusting look with her face and sticking out her tongue. "It's strawberry flavored."

Vena's comments made Marina's skin crawl and her stomach churn, and she lost all appetite for food. Marina's opinion of Dr. Ryder Vernor also instantly changed, and she had to chide herself for being such a prude. "That was one thing I meant by precautions," Marina said, nodding her head with a knowing smile.

"Hey, give me a break, Marina. It's not like he's screwing around on some normal wife somewhere, is it?"

"I don't know. Is it? I guess the situation is unique," Marina agreed. "But I don't think that foam will keep you from getting a sexually transmitted disease." At times like this, Vena seemed so simple-minded.

"Oh," Vena replied, obviously not having considered that eventuality at all. "I guess not. But at least I can't get pregnant."

"Perhaps. By the way, who is caring for his child?"

"We are, I am," she blushed. "Ryder's not too good around children, and this IS his first, you know. He's also having a hard time warming up to the baby. You see, I've had to sort of move in."

"Vena, . . . " Marina said, disapprovingly. She suspected Vena would say this, placing her de facto next in line to be Mrs. Vernor when Lissa passed from the scene.

"That is, I've almost moved in, I meant to say. Not completely, just some clothes and makeup. You know. But not everything." Vena began playing nervously with her key chain, looked away from Marina and said, "And I'm telling the truth when I say I'm helping with things around the house. That explains my being there a lot." After that conversation, neither Vena nor Marina seemed very talkative, and both, feeling uncomfortable, hurried to finish lunch and leave.

Marina was left wondering why Ryder Vernor had

changed his mind about suing Dr. Baatard. Perhaps
Charlie would know the answer to that, although she
would have to clear any questions with Lemar Jackson
before she asked this of Charlie. She also wondered why
Ryder was having a difficult time warming up to his first
son. Was it his wife's hopeless condition, which Marina
would have expected to have drawn Ryder even closer to
his son, or was there something else that was making
Ryder keep his distance?

Chapter 42

Haven General Hospital
Department of General Surgery

Marina enjoyed her time at home with Austin, but after a few weeks also began to find it in some respects a little boring. At first she tried to spend time reading, then devoted more and more hours to her art, when she wasn't interrupted for childcare needs. Yet it surprised her how frequently she found her mind drifting back to her work at Haven General. She would never have guessed that what she had placed so little emphasis on actually had occupied so much importance in her life. Perhaps it was her modest career which gave her a sense of purpose and direction in the morning, and she certainly did miss the adult interactions. Certainly, Austin didn't provide any intellectual stimulation, at least not yet.

Soon, Marina arranged to place Austin in the on-site child care program her hospital provided, and started back to work at her office. The change in atmosphere was invigorating, and the interaction with adults welcome. Top on her list of tasks to resume was the Lissa Vernor case. She had been hearing so much about it from Vena, that her curiosity had grown. One of her first actions would be to interview Deanna Baptiste, the recovery room nurse.

Deanna had been nervously waiting in the nursing staff lounge when Marina called her in. Marina watched Deanna as she reluctantly came in to her office. Deanna wore a crumpled scrub suit, soft white work shoes which had apparently not been polished in quite some time, and a cheap good luck bracelet and bright red plastic earrings. Marina had noticed Deanna on several other occasions and had harbored her own set of opinions and suspicions about her.

After some perfunctory greetings, Marina said, "Thanks for coming today."

Deanna nodded politely in Marina's general direction, sat stiffly in a wooden chair to the right of Marina's desk and crossed her legs. She covered her mouth and emitted a wet cough.

"I realize your being here and talking with me puts a lot of stress on you." Marina thought a conciliatory approach would be best; she wanted to coax as much information from Deanna as she could. Deanna didn't have to help her at all.

Deanna occasionally nibbled on her nails as she replied, "Yes, it does make me nervous. What's this all about, anyway?" Her eyes darted around the room, shifting from Marina's face to the wall clock to the door and back. She impulsively took a pack of cigarettes from her purse and asked, "Do you mind if I smoke?"

"Yes, I do mind," Marina indignantly replied. "There's no smoking anywhere inside the hospital. You should know that. Anyway," Marina sighed, "I asked you here about the Lissa Vernor case. I understand you know quite a lot about it." Word around Haven General had it that Deanna, who was present at Lissa's surgery, was pissed at Baatard and therefore was most likely the informer that Vena had cryptically referred to in her phone call earlier.

"I was there, if that's what you mean," Deanna said with a feigned air of indifference, as she studied her tacky wrist bracelet.

"I think you were more than simply there," Marina nervously scoffed. "Tell me, Deanna, what do you think really happened?" At this point, she wasn't sure herself, and she sensed the nasty presence of lawyers, Charlie Kincade included, floating around the periphery.

"I don't know what you're getting at, Marina. Am I being accused of doing something wrong?"

"No, of course not. I'm only looking for information, that's all. It's part of my job in Quality Assurance." That was putting it mildly, she tried to smile in a reassuring manner.

"Okay. So why me? Why don't you ask Dr. Baatard or the anesthesia nurse or someone else?"

"I'm planning on doing just that. First of all, let me say no one mentioned your name to me," Marina partially lied, and suspected Deanna knew that. Somehow, she didn't think that would hurt her credibility with Deanna too much, as she was certain Deanna lied all the time.

"Sure, I believe that one all right," Deanna laughed nervously. She reached inside her scrub over-jacket, took out a cigarette lighter and played with it. "And pigs fly, too."

"If that's what you suspect, forget about it. You were there, I saw your name in the nursing notes, and I want to talk to everyone involved. That's all."

"Maybe I need to get a lawyer before I answer any of your questions." Deanna shifted around in her chair, carefully buttoned the sleeves on her over-jacket and glanced back and forth between the clock and the door. When Marina's phone rang, Deanna nearly jumped out of her chair, then nervously watched Marina as she spoke a few words, postponing her caller until later.

"Who was that?" Deanna asked.

"Just someone from the legal office." Marina could see Deanna get all uptight from her reply, and could have kicked herself for being so careless. "It's not concerning you, Deanna. This isn't a legal proceeding at all. And besides, no one thinks you did anything wrong. It's just simply a routine internal investigation of a poor surgical outcome."

Deanna looked down at her hands. "Oh, routine, huh."

"Yes, routine. All surgical deaths and most poor outcomes come to some form of quality assurance review or another. You're familiar with quality assurance reviews, aren't you?"

"Yes, I guess so," Deanna replied, adding defensively, "although I've never actually been part of one, you understand."

"Well, it's simply a fact-finding exercise, that's all. We can learn from it, that's its purpose. As a matter of fact, I plan to ask similar questions of Dr. Baatard."

"What," Deanna cried out, looking around quickly, her eyes wide open. "Is he here now?"

"No, of course not," Marina tried to reassure Deanna. "Please, Deanna, calm down."

"Does Dr. Baatard know I'm here, talking to you, in your office? Does he know you're asking me about the Lissa Vernor case?" Deanna got up from her chair and paced back and forth around the room, ending up at the window in back of Marina's chair.

"No, no way Deanna. This is strictly confidential. Your being here and everything you tell me is strictly off the record. Promise," Marina said, trying to smile confidently and reassure Deanna that all was all right.

"Sure," Deanna said. "Okay, I guess that sounds reasonable to me. Now, what exactly is it you want to know?" She cocked her head to one side like a little bird.

"I understand you were present for the entire surgery." Marina picked up some surgical records from her desk top and started leafing through.

"Yes," Deanna said as she bent over Marina's shoulder to look at the documents.

"And these notes indicate you were also there to work the recovery room on the same patient."

"Yes," Deanna told Marina. "The other nurse was a

no-show, and somebody had to cover." She smiled nervously at Marina.

"Good. Now tell me what happened, in your own words." Marina took her pad of paper and pen to take notes. "Please, it's all right with you if I take notes, isn't it?"

"I guess so. I'll try to tell you whatever I can. Sure, no problem. You ask whatever you need to, Marina."

Deanna emerged from Marina's office after an intensely long hour, nervously shook Marina's hand, attempted a weak smile, then walked alone down the hallway toward the hospital entrance.

Marina sat alone in her office for a long time, collecting her thoughts. Interviewing Deanna was difficult, but doing so revealed a great deal of circumstantial evidence which implicated Baatard, at least to some degree, with the adverse outcome of Lissa Vernor. This made her reassess her opinion of Baatard, and the confidence she had in him as a physician. Marina went out for a bathroom break, then poured herself some coffee before coming back in.

Almost an hour after Deanna left, Marina had finally managed to record all her thoughts and note as many facts as she could from her conversation with Deanna. Now, she could think about speaking with someone else.

Marina called for Dr. Rudy Salvatore to be brought in

from the Haven Hospital Volunteer's Office, where he had been waiting. Salvatore had also been present at the ill-fated surgery of Lissa Vernor, and had participated in her post-operative care, before mysteriously disappearing from his hospital duties.

While waiting for Dr. Salvatore, Marina picked up a drug audit report concerning Deanna and re-read it. The drug audit had been prepared by Lynn Janislowski from the hospital pharmacy. Apparently there was some problem with a narcotic drug count discrepancy.

The implications of the audit were quite serious, and Marina had to agree with Lynn - further action might be required. Now that she had the opportunity to question Deanna first, Marina took the drug audit file, placed it in a sealed hospital envelope marked "CONFIDENTIAL" and sent it to Dr. Rubin for his action.

Dr. Salvatore had taken an extended leave of absence from his residency after he had suddenly and without explanation left Lissa Vernor on the ward that dark day about ten months ago. The medical-legal term for his irresponsible action might actually have been patient abandonment. Marina had a difficult time locating Salvatore, and an even more difficult time convincing him to come in for an interview. Yet, no less than for Deanna, his input was essential to developing a complete QA report.

Rudy Salvatore was much less cooperative than Deanna. He only answered a few directed, pointed questions, and gave very terse replies. Rudy denied any knowledge of Lissa's problem, referring all questions to Dr. Baatard. After only fifteen minutes, Salvatore demanded to leave and Marina had no choice but to let him.

As Salvatore reached the door of Marina's office, Marina leaned far back in her swivel chair, crossed her legs, sternly looked at Salvatore and called out to him, "Oh, Rudy."

He stopped, turned back to Marina and said, "I really have nothing else to say to you."

Undaunted, Marina persisted, "One of my nursing friends saw you the night that Lissa Vernor was admitted to the hospital." It was a piece of information given to her in strictest confidence, and Marina was holding it in reserve, hoping up to now not to have to use it.

Salvatore's face almost dropped off and he stopped moving out of the office. He returned, and quietly closed the door in back of him. "So?"

"Well, is that true?" Somehow, in her woman's heart Marina knew it was. She suspected that the sort of activity she was alluding to was much more common than anyone suspected.

"I'm sure a lot of people saw me at the hospital. That's where I spent most of my time, you know." He slowly sat back down in the chair, the look on his face changing from concern and annoyance to one of guilt.

After several tense seconds of silence, Marina asked

Salvatore, "I don't suppose you would want to know where my friend saw you?"

"Where what?" Salvatore replied, shifting back in his chair, avoided looking in Marina's direction. He absentmindedly played with his electronic watch, making the high-pitched beep go on and off, on and off, while making every effort to appear calm and disinterested.

"Where my friend saw you," Marina repeated.

"I don't know what you're getting at, Marina. I thought this wasn't going to be a police investigation."

"It isn't." She knew well from experience when a man was lying, or not telling all he knew, and that was happening here.

"It certainly sounds that way to me. You're interrogating me, and I think that before I answer any of your libelous, slimy insinuations I should have my attorney present. I wonder how you would like to be on the receiving end of a slander lawsuit, Nurse Marina, Ms. QA."

"Now, Rudy, calm down. I didn't say anything negative about you, did I? I'm only trying to get at the truth," Marina said, backing off a bit.

Salvatore made some skeptical mutterings and looked away.

"My friend said she saw you by the on-call room in back of the emergency area," Marina pronounced with a flat tone and a sense of finality. She might as well have said she saw him with his pants down.

"So?"

"So, you weren't alone," Marina said. "Come on, Rudy. She saw you with Lissa Vernor, that's who. What do you have to say about that?"

"Well, I was with the ER crew that brought Lissa up to surgery, so of course I was seen with Lissa Vernor in the ER That's where Lissa was admitted."

"I'm not getting through to you, am I? I'm talking about BEFORE Lissa was admitted. This person saw you two together before Lissa was admitted, before she got sick." Marina wondered if Ryder was aware of a possible affair between his wife Lissa and Rudy Salvatore. Perhaps, she considered, Ryder isn't the genetic father of Lissa's child, after all. That could at least explain Vena's observation that Ryder was having difficulty feeling close to his son.

Rudy coughed. "Oh, yes, now I remember," he said, preferring to direct his attention to examining the ceiling lights. "I found Ms. Vernor looking for her husband, and I stopped to talk to her." Rudy smiled and folded his hands.

Marina scratched her head, breathed deeply, then asked Rudy, "So, what was going on between Mrs. Vernor and you?"

"Going on? I don't understand?"

"Come on, Rudy. Don't try to baloney me." Marina wondered for a shocked instant if she herself could believe what scandal appeared to be developing, what infidelity was being implied.

"Nothing was going on," Salvatore protested. "Mrs. Vernor, Lissa, was the wife of my attending physician. I only knew her through Dr. Vernor. I happened to see her at the hospital. That's all."

"That's all?" Marina knew Salvatore was fabricating the story, and suspected why.

"Yes, that's all. There certainly was nothing wrong with that, for Christ sake. I guess Lissa, Mrs. Vernor, was looking for her husband."

"You guess? Did she say that to you?" Marina asked, trying not to raise her voice.

"Yeah," Salvatore said, not looking at Marina. "I guess she did. I, I don't remember that long ago."

"The ER admitting note says Lissa was brought in from home," Marina reminded him.

"Well, I guess she didn't find Dr. Vernor at the hospital and then went home to look for him. She must have gotten sick later and then was admitted."

"Did anything happen to her at the hospital which could have caused the abdominal bleeding?" She could envision several intimate physical activities that might fit into this category, and strongly suspected Rudy Salvatore could also.

"No. Not that I'm aware of," Rudy added in a low voice, unconvincingly. "Look, I'm not a suspect in a criminal proceeding, am I? Otherwise I'll bring a lawyer with before the next time I talk to you."

"No, this isn't a criminal investigation, Rudy. I'm only trying to figure out what happened to Ms. Vernor, that's all. And I'm trying to get your career back on track again. That too."

"My career." he laughed. "I don't see you trying to help my medical career at all."

"Well, how can I help you unless you let me, Rudy? You never even told me, told anyone why you left your patient's bedside that day."

"That's very personal. I'll tell you this, though. I couldn't see the sense in what I was doing any longer, and I needed time to think. Is there anything wrong with that?"

Marina shook her head in pity. She knew Salvatore was trying to deceive her, maybe he was trying to deceive himself also. Marina could see neither attempt was successful.

"I don't have to sit here and take these accusations," Rudy said as he got up and stormed out of the office.

Marina yelled out at Salvatore's back, "I'm not making any accusations, Rudy. Please, let's talk a little more." Salvatore, however, kept on walking.

Disappointed, Marina had to let him go. She had no solid reason to hold him, and certainly no authority, although her intuition told her otherwise. And, she didn't want to burn a bridge between them. Marina was certain she would be having future meetings with Dr. Rudy Salvatore.

Chapter 43

Haven Community Hospital
Department of Surgery

Meyer Rubin held the final reports on the Vernor case in his hands for a long time before finally deciding what action he would, could take. The document, loosely attached in a Haven General booklet cover, had arrived moments ago from the Quality Assurance office, and included a cover letter with summary from the QA nurse, Marina Bonnaserra. The conclusions, though at first glance ambiguous, were carefully couched, and they could just as easily have been construed as devastating. Rubin thought the report was written almost as if Marina had started out with one opinion, and then had changed her mind. Changed her mind after finding out what, Rubin wondered?

As soon as Rubin had finished reading the initial QA report, he had a long meeting with the hospital attorney, Lemar Jackson. As a result of that meeting, Rubin requested a second, but informal, review by representatives of relevant hospital departments. It took several weeks for those departments to find appropriate specialists who had the time and the interest, and another several weeks for the actual documents pertaining to Lissa

Vernor's adverse outcome to be read and reports formed. Now, Rubin had in his hands those reports from the Surgery, Hematology, and Obstetrics departments, and soon would have to act on their uncomfortable and inconclusive findings. Rubin again calculated how many days he had left to serve in this administrative capacity as Chair, Department of Surgery, before being allowed to return once again to the more comfortable surroundings of the surgery suite.

Rubin had to admit to himself his thoughts were more on legal issues than on quality of care as he placed a call to Baatard. Baatard -- the name could just as easily be Rubin, he reflected. Or Bastard. He tried to laugh, but couldn't.

Baatard's receptionist answered a call placed by Rubin's secretary, and the call was transferred back.

"Damon, this is Meyer Rubin." After several moments of silence, Rubin said, " . . . Damon, . . . are you there?"

"Yes, Meyer. It's just that I'm surprised to hear your voice. What brings your call?" Baatard fell under the Department of Obstetrics and Gynecology, although he did have limited general surgical privileges.

Rubin began with the least direct lead-in he could devise, and asked, "I was wondering how you are doing."

"I'm surviving, I guess," Baatard replied glumly, his voice dry and terse.

"That's great, Damon, real great. Look, I was wondering if I could speak with you for a few minutes." Rubin could sense the tension on the phone.

"Perhaps. I've got a full clinic here right now. Speak about what?"

"It's about QA issues, Damon. That's all." Rubin could easily perceive Baatard's suspicion, and it made him wonder if, or rather what, Baatard was hiding. Rubin had always read Baatard as slightly less than forthright once he had started dealing with the likes of Denny Cruite, the Dragon Lady. The upper management and the department chiefs at Haven General all were upset with Denny Cruite; her pressure sales tactics cut into their bottom line at a very difficult time in health care economics. Funds that could be supporting the less-than-occupied obstetric and gynecological wards of Haven General were freely flowing into The Conceptions Foundation outpatient procedure rooms. It was also well known that The Conceptions Foundation planned its own outpatient clinics, its own laboratory, and radiological services. The Foundation was becoming the fast food of obstetrics, and marketed on the mass media more like a new car than as a highly professional service. Denny's grating, aggressive personality didn't help things either.

"QA issues? Meaning what?" Baatard asked innocently as he switched on the phone recorder switch, and moved his pen and paper nearby to take notes.

"Well, I want to talk to you about the Lissa Vernor case."

Baatard hesitated before replying. "Oh. I really don't think there's much to talk about, do you?"

"We'll see, Damon, we'll see." Rubin knew from experience he would need to set a lot of things straight before any public meetings took place and any facts which could prove potentially embarrassing to Haven General came out. Other local hospitals were beginning IVF programs and would jump at the chance to publicly humiliate Baatard, and by association The Foundation and their affiliated medical center - Haven General Hospital. He could just envision all the battling attorneys crawling over the garbage dump of embarrassing documents right now.

"Don't you think I should have my lawyer present while I discuss this with you?" Baatard coughed, then chuckled nervously. The brief laugh died halfway out of his open mouth, and became, instead, a gasp.

"I can't really say; it's totally up to you. Of course, at this stage, everything is very informal. I just want to talk, that's all. Okay?" Rubin hoped he was coming across more honest than he felt at the moment. He was never good at deception and was glad he didn't choose to become a lawyer. Even the thought of spending his life defending issues he didn't believe in, or worse, knew were false, made him sick.

"Like I said, I don't really think there's much to talk about, but if you insist, then I guess that you can go ahead." Baatard had anticipated this call for a week, at least, and had already cleared it with his attorney, Ellen

Yee.

"As you know, whenever there's a bad outcome in one of our surgeries, the case goes for an automatic QA review. It's automatic, mandatory, and part of the quality assessment program at every hospital. The review is for learning purposes only. This applies equally to all the staff, and isn't punitive. Okay?"

"Sure. I know all that, Meyer. So, what's the point?"

"So, Damon, after an informal review by the hospital QA nurse, the Lissa Vernor case was referred to the Surgery Department for additional review," Rubin said, as he played with his pen, nervously clicking it open and closed, open and closed, hating every minute of these messy administrative issues. He picked up one of the Lissa Vernor files -- a large, heavy bundle tied loosely with a red cloth sash around it - and moved it from a pile on the corner of the desk to dead center.

"I don't understand. Did the QA nurse find something wrong with the care I gave?" Baatard asked.

"No, of course not. But, because of its serious and totally unexpected outcome, we were forced by our own hospital bylaws to get some additional opinions. Now these were informal opinions, not officially part of any committee, and mostly were to assist me in evaluating the situation. The results of the Surgery, Obstetrical and Hematology Department reviews were pretty consistent and equally inconclusive." Rubin knew he wasn't interested in having a QA review, for any of several reasons. He wanted to drop the whole ridiculous case, and felt in many ways like a medieval accuser at an inquisition, but he had the hospital's best interests to consider foremost.

"My God. You got all those people involved rendering opinions in a simple adverse outcome? Don't you realize what effect this could have on my good reputation, my referral base?" 'My income.' he thought.

"Yes, I tried to consider all those things. I have to look after many different interests as Chair of the Surgery Department, you know." It was a thankless and pressured job, and he wouldn't wish it on a friend, nor ever volunteer for it again.

"Look, Meyer, I'm not the first surgeon to close up a bleeder. You and I know that. Maybe what we have here is a little creative elimination of a competitor, huh?"

"No, way. Now, don't start to get paranoid on me, Damon. You know these people. They're your peers, your colleagues. They haven't been able to find fault with your handling of the case. And I couldn't agree more. After all, I've closed up many a case myself despite the possibility of continued mild bleeding, and never had a problem like this."

"Good. Is that the end of it then?"

"I'm afraid it isn't that simple, Damon. Even though I surmise that your luck and that of Ms. Vernor had just run out that time, we're trying to be as thorough as possible."

"I don't understand. You just said that . . . "

"Yes, I did say it appears that you aren't at fault. We all agree that you had every right to anticipate that, in the absence of a bleeding disorder, bleeding should have stopped on its own. Unfortunately, it didn't, at least until the stroke, which may have itself been caused by the continued bleeding."

"Okay, then your investigation is concluded. Right?" Baatard asked.

"Almost. Look, Damon, the hematology consultant's report is most interesting. A drug screen performed on Lissa's blood taken at the time of her admission to the emergency room found an unusually high level of gonadotropin. There apparently were only two possibilities for this: either Lissa had an ovarian tumor, or she was being given the drug as a medication."

"Well, I didn't see an ovarian tumor during her surgery, although I wasn't really looking for one," Baatard added, defensively.

"Right," continued Rubin. He could almost feel Baatard being evasive. Rubin hated to press further, hated treating Baatard like a cornered rat, but had to persist in his questioning. "There was no evidence for a tumor, and anyway she was rather young for that, don't you think?

"Yes, of course she was. There's also no mention of hormone treatments on the emergency room list of medications the patient was on," Baatard stated with conclusiveness in his voice, as if trying to bolster his arguments.

"Yes, I recall that, too," Rubin agreed. "Yes, but do you think that was accurate?" Rubin asked, trying to take notes on the conversation with his free hand.

"What exactly do you mean?" Baatard angrily shot back.

"Come on, Damon. You know exactly what I mean. Lissa Vernor probably was on some form of hormone therapy. You're in the hormone administration business, aren't you? Do you know anything about that?" Christ. He wished Baatard would quit screwing around with him and just tell him what he needed to know already.

"Well, you seem to think I do."

"Never mind what I seem to think. Can you please give me a straight answer?" Rubin demanded.

"As long as the patient is alive, I'm bound by my professional agreement with her regarding patient confidentiality."

"You mean this is a patient confidentiality issue?"

"I didn't say that."

"But you just told me . . . "

"Look, all I said was that she told things to me in confidence, she strictly directed me to keep this information to myself, and she hasn't instructed me otherwise," Baatard explained.

"How can she change her directions if she's in a goddamn coma? Come on Damon, be reasonable."

"No, you be reasonable, Meyer. What if I discussed her private matters with you after her specifically instructing me otherwise. Then, if in a few months a miracle occurred and she decided to wake up and found out and objected, I could get slapped with one hell of a big law suit. Are you going to indemnify me against that?"

"Well . . . that's very hypothetical. Anyway, she's no longer your patient," Rubin pointed out.

"That's a technical point, and it's an action that Lissa Vernor didn't take. Her screwy husband changed treating doctors." Baatard paused a moment before continuing. Clearly, being evasive served no purpose now at all, he decided. "But, yes, she was seeing me for infertility," Baatard finally admitted, certain it would eventually come out anyway.

Rubin paused a moment before continuing, using the time to gather his thoughts. He had already suspected what Baatard just revealed to him, but also realized that Baatard's office chart of Lissa Vernor could soon be public knowledge anyway.

"Lissa was seeing you for infertility?" Rubin asked.

"Lissa wanted me to keep it most confidential, even to keep it from her husband," Baatard told Rubin. "She wanted to get pregnant and was unable to despite several years of unprotected intercourse. I found absolutely no reason whatsoever for her fertility problems. Everything worked perfectly. But, you know how that goes."

"Yeah," Rubin agreed. It was widely held that as many as half of infertility workups had nothing discovered, yet went on to pregnancy, and probably would do so even without hormonal interventions. The reverse side, IVF, wasn't really that great either, with at best a 25 percent success rate. And for all that money.

"I began her on a trial of hormone manipulation. It was part of a standard, routine ovarian hormone down-cycle regulation in preparation for ovarian stimulation. But I can't see how this relates to her poor surgical outcome."

Typical, Rubin thought. "I'm surprised, then, Damon. Haven't you heard of OHSS?"

Baatard recognized the abbreviations for the rare ovarian hyper stimulation syndrome. "Yes, of course I do," he muttered as he began to see where the conversation was going.

"Good. Then I'm sure you must know that OHSS can cause unexplained generalized blood oozing from every serous membrane, and can lead to hypotension. Maybe you didn't find a discrete source of bleeding during her emergency surgery because there wasn't a discrete point. Did you ever think of that?" Rubin smiled to himself.

"You only do what you can do, that's all," Baatard sighed as he threw his free hand up into the air. "I'm no closer to perfection than you are, Meyer. You know that. I never claimed otherwise."

"I'm not looking for perfection here, Damon. I'm only trying to explain to the best of my ability what happened to Lissa so that the hospital certification people and the lawyers have nothing to complain about as far as Haven General is concerned."

"CYA, huh, Meyer?" Baatard said.

"It's strictly administrative, Damon, not personal. Look, I know you have had more than enough questioning for one day. Why don't we call it for now? If I have anything more to ask, I assume I can always get back in touch with you. Okay?"

"Sure, Meyer, Sure," Baatard said, hanging up the phone and turning off his phone recorder.

Chapter 44

Haven Convalescent Hospital

"Nursing station. Can I help you?" Ivory Peoples gulped as she hastily put down a sandwich she was eating so she could hold the phone. She had been seated there for the last hour, leisurely reading a copy of Bethel Baptist Church News while she "supervised" her team of nurse aids and LPNs.

"Yes, this is Dr. Ryder Vernor. Hi, Ivory. How are you?"

"Not bad, doc. Are you calling to find out about your wife?"

"Yes, I am," Ryder replied, glumly. He tried to check in every day at first, but as the months wore on, his calls concerning Lissa gradually became less frequent, as did his visits. He suspected that, in Ivory's eyes, it looked bad, but he couldn't continue to be consumed by guilt. There was really nothing he could do for Lissa now. He needed to move on.

"Same old, same old," Ivory told Ryder, shaking her head sadly.

The Surrogate

"I wish it were otherwise," Ryder said. In many ways, that certainly was true.

"Me too, doc."

"Actually, I was wondering if you could do me a favor. Would you draw for me a red top tube of blood on Lissa and send it over to Haven Reference labs? They'll have an order slip waiting when the blood arrives."

"No problem. See you, doc." Normally, Peoples would take an order only from a patient's treating physician. In this case, Ryder was both a physician - one of the few she respected - and the patient's family. She went into Lissa's room and drew the blood specimen, directing the lab results to Dr. Ryder's office. Peoples neglected to make a note in Lissa's medical record of the order to draw blood.

Before going to the office the next morning, Ryder picked up his medical bag and brought it into the nursery. Vena was already inside the small room, which had until recently been a home study and office area. Its low ceiling slanted down toward one side, making the windowless room appear smaller than it actually was. Ryder and Vena had chosen the cartoon character wallpaper and put it up themselves. The baby furniture had been provided by Lissa's parents, who rarely visited. A photo of Lissa hung over the side of the crib where Ephrim could easily see it, placed there by Ryder.

Ephrim was being changed by Vena and gotten ready for child care when Ryder asked, "Can you help me hold Ephrim a bit? I want to take a small blood sample from him."

"Sure, but why?" Vena asked. She held Ephrim while Ryder cleaned off his left heel with an alcohol swab. Not getting a response, she asked again, "Why are you doing this, Ryder? Is something wrong?"

"Wrong? No, this is just a routine test," he tried to reassure Vena. "We do it on all infants shortly after birth." He quickly jabbed a small sterile aluminum barb into the heel, causing Ephrim to let out a wail. Ryder let a few blood drops form on the small superficial stab wound, then guided the blood flow into several small capillary glass tubes. He then carefully sealed the ends of the capillary tubes using a stick of special red wax. The bleeding on Ephrim's heel stopped easily within a few minutes.

"There, that's all there is to it," Ryder reassured Vena. "Thanks for your help holding Ephrim still." Ryder hugged Ephrim, who had by now stopped crying, and kissed him on his forehead. Vena then took Ephrim over to the changing table, cleaned his foot and put on his socks before the morning trip to the nursery.

"There, there, Ephrim, that didn't hurt, did it?" Ryder crooned to try and soothe him. He kissed Ephrim again and felt his bond with his son finally growing stronger. The physical resemblance of Ephrim to him was there, he was sure of it now. Others saw it, except strangely for Vena. "Nobody is going to take you from me, nobody. You're all I have left now," Ryder told Ephrim, his voice choking up slightly.

Vena appeared upset at Ryder's last comment, but continued busily stuffing a yellow cotton baby bag, then slung it over her shoulder. She anxiously forced a tight smile as she asked, "I don't understand, Ryder. Who could take Ephrim away from us?"

Ryder looked at Vena, handed Ephrim to her, but didn't reply. He lifted his sleeve to his face and wiped away what appeared to be a tear, then went into his study, closed the door, and called Baatard on the phone. He had gotten out of more stupid messes than this before. Surely Baatard would understand and be reasonable.

Vena could hear Ryder yelling on the phone in the study even with the door closed. At one point she thought she could hear another man's voice, if it really could have been that loud from the phone's handset speaker. After a few moments more, there was silence. Then Vena heard Ryder make one more phone call, this time without yelling, before coming out of the study, his face furrowed and angry.

They drove to child care, then on to work with hardly a word of conversation spoken between them. The medical office complex where Ryder had his office was nearly deserted this time of day. They entered the underground parking garage through the side near a sign for "Hospital Staff Parking," and then to the special doctor's parking area. Before getting out, Ryder handed a business card to Vena, then told her, "Vena, listen very carefully. I want you to keep this card in a safe place." She nodded seriously. "You need to call this person right away if anything happens to me," he continued. His face belied the calm he was trying to project. He had the distinct impression he was going to die, and if that were so, he feared there was probably very little he could do about it. Running away with Ephrim would not help, for he was certain there was no place far enough, safe enough he could reach.

"For God's sake, what's going to happen to you?" Vena asked, her face unable to hide the concern and uncertainty she was feeling. "Ryder. Are you sick or something?" She noticed Ryder had scribbled the name and number of someone on the back of the card.

"No, I'm not sick. But, well, you never know." He knew what they were discussing, and so probably did she.

"Ryder, I know when you're not telling me everything. What's going on here?"

"Look, I can't go into the details, not now, at least. Actually, I don't want to even think about all the details. All I can say is that Baatard talked me into doing something wrong, something terribly wrong." How could he have been so stupid?

"So, then don't do it," Vena shrugged.

"Yeah," Ryder laughed. "I just wish it were that easy. The person I made a certain agreement with isn't, shall we say, willing to revoke a contract." He regretted ever seriously considering Baatard's proposal to give up his son for adoption. It was made at a moment of weakness, of self-pity, of irresponsibility. Fortunately, he had realized what a foolish mistake he had almost made, and at the last minute, had driven to Trenton and taken his son home. Baatard had raised hell, but Ryder knew in his heart that it was the right thing to have done. Baatard had hounded him several times each day, every day since then, pressing for Ryder to give up his son. Now, he had to completely void the contract and find a way out. Ryder even considered going to the police, but he knew that Baatard had carefully constructed things. Baatard had probably done nothing illegal or unethical at all. Adoptions under similar difficult circumstances were occasionally arranged. And Ryder had certainly benefited from the arrangement, too. He could still hardly understand how a baby was worth so much money to another couple.

"What contract, Ryder? What are you talking about? Please, Ryder, tell me," Vena pleaded. She looked at Ryder, then in a moment of self-realization, blurted out, "Oh, no. It's not about Ephrim, is it, Ryder? Please, Ryder, tell me it's not about Ephrim."

"No, Vena, it's not about Ephrim any longer, as far as I'm concerned. Just remember, it's always wise to plan for all eventualities." He said nothing else as they exited into the foul cold weather and on to the office. He felt foolish, and alone, and dishonest. And he felt totally incapable of protecting the one person he cared about the most - his son, whom he had betrayed.

During the morning at the clinic, Ryder's foreboding words were foremost on Vena's mind, making it very difficult for her to concentrate on her work. Ryder's cryptic comments left her frantic with worry.

Unfortunately, Ryder had, for some reason, chosen to close himself off from her when she tried to discuss the problem with him further. Yet, Vena clearly sensed a danger to Ephrim, with whom she had formed a strong mother-son relationship. Even though Vena realized full well she wasn't the natural mother, her concern and sense of protection were none the less deep.

As the day wore on, without her being able to learn just how Ephrim was endangered, Vena needed to share her own fears with someone, anyone. Her first thoughts went to Deanna, with whom she was probably the closest, outside of Ryder, or perhaps even including Ryder. Unfortunately, when Vena tried calling, Deanna wasn't at work, and she didn't answer at home either.

As Vena stared at the card, anxiously turning it over and over in her hands, another idea came to her. Vena left the office for a few minutes, and using a phone booth in the lobby of their building, called the name Ryder had written on the card.

When Charlie Kincade answered the phone, he could immediately sense from Vena's voice that something terrible was bothering her. Charlie and Vena had met before on a few occasions when Charlie had visited Ryder at his office, and were somewhat familiar. Charlie listened as Vena explained what little she knew concerning the vague but ominous statements of Ryder's. Strangely, Charlie seemed as much in the dark as Vena was.

Charlie offered to discuss Vena's concerns with Ryder, and if he were to learn anything, he promised to urge Ryder either to explain the nature of the problem to Vena or at least allow him to. Beyond that, Charlie was bound by client-attorney privilege to remain silent.

Chapter 45

Early the next morning, a conservatively dressed man in his early forties presented himself at the reception desk at Baatard's office. Sharlene greeted him, and from his professional appearance, she thought him probably a detail man for some pharmaceutical company.

"Hello, I'm Charlie Kincade," the man said, introducing himself. He held a small briefcase in one hand, and clutched some envelopes in the other, and he temporarily put the envelopes down on the counter as he handed a business card to Sharlene. As Sharlene looked down to search the appointment book, Charlie explained to her, "I'm an attorney and I represent Dr. Ryder Vernor."

A look of extreme displeasure clouded Sharlene's face, and she closed the appointment book, now remembering the appointment.

Kincade shook Sharlene's hand vigorously, then gave a wide smile, which faded almost as soon as it was formed. Glancing disapprovingly around the rather sparsely furnished office, he nodded in the general direction of several patients who were waiting in the reception area, but said nothing.

"Oh, why yes, Mr. Kincade," Sharlene said. "I'm surprised to see you so soon."

"I don't understand. I called for an appointment, didn't I?"

"Yes, but that was only thirty minutes ago."

"Well, is there something the matter?" Kincade asked, reacting to the glacial stare he received from Sharlene.

"No, not as far as I'm concerned." She paused for a moment, then added, "I just wonder if you understand how hard Dr. Baatard works, and how much he cares for his patients. You people must get a lot of pleasure persecuting doctors the way you do."

"Oh, you must mean prosecute. Well, I'm not with the DA's office, you know."

"No, I know the difference between prosecute and persecute, I'm not stupid, and I mean you people persecute doctors."

"You people?" He knew what she was getting at, having had it implied so many times before. Being a social pariah - an attorney - he had gotten used to derogatory statements and nasty innuendoes, or at least learned to ignore them long ago.

"That's right. And you know exactly what I mean too - lawyers. I think it's disgusting. Anyway, you don't care what I think, now, do you"

"Funny, I was just wondering that about you," Kincade replied, then curtly turned his face the other way. "So, if you're through criticizing me, let's get on with it."

"Certainly, Mr. Kincade," Sharlene said,

sarcastically. "Anyway, Dr. Baatard is expecting you. Come in."

As Sharlene tried to lead Kincade into the back area, he asked, "Do you mind if I use your phone first?"

"You'll have no waiting to see Dr. Baatard, at least at this moment, so you won't have the time to make a call. That is, unless it's an emergency. Is it an emergency?"

"Is what an emergency?" Kincade asked, beginning to become flustered and impatient at the implied challenges he received from the nosy receptionist.

"The call: is your call an emergency or would you like to see Dr. Baatard right away? He IS available now," Sharlene repeated. "He delayed seeing one of his patients just so he could squeeze you in this morning. If you go off to make a call, well I just can't guarantee that he will still be available to see you. Then you might have to wait, like those mere mortals in the waiting room."

"Oh, I get it. Sure, I'll go in first," Kincade said, glancing condescendingly at Sharlene. She annoyed him, and if she had been working for his office, she would have been canned long ago. Presentation to the public was so important for professionals. Marina had mentioned to Kincade the apparent contradiction that existed in Baatard's office before to him. The Conceptions Foundation was a high-profile, strictly elective service that served the well-insured and the well-to-do, whereas here, Sharlene wasn't nearly polished enough, and neither was another employee Marina referred to once, a nurse named Garza.

Once in Baatard's presence, Kincade exchanged light greetings, then sat in one of the soft leather "consultation" chairs in front of the desk.

Baatard had tried to contact his attorney Ellen Yee first before agreeing to see Kincade. Kincade's call was so abrupt, so unexpected, and only thirty minutes ago that it had caught Baatard completely off guard. Ellen Yee had been unavailable, and Baatard hadn't the presence of mind to ask Kincade to hold off. Attorneys made him nervous, he wanted to show he had nothing to hide, and was quite confident of his actions. Perhaps, he thought, if Kincade got that message, he would be less likely to press any suit against him. "So. What brings you here, Mr. Kincade?"

"Simply this, Dr. Baatard. Dr. Vernor is quite distressed at the outcome of his wife's surgery. He feels that somehow you're responsible for her stroke."

"That's just not so." Baatard yelled out.

"Please, let me finish. I'm not here to accuse you of anything or be your enemy. Believe me, in this matter, I'm your friend."

Baatard's face left little doubt he didn't believe anything Kincade was telling him, least of all that Kincade could be his friend.

"Anyway, Dr. Vernor thinks that your negligence entitles him to monetary awards sufficient to provide for Lissa's care long-term."

"What?" Baatard nearly yelled. His hands were shaking, and he felt his blood pressure rising. The nerve of that Dr. Vernor.

"That's all he's looking for, really. Dr. Vernor doesn't want a penny from you personally, and he doesn't want to accuse you of malpractice. This is only a vehicle, a means to an end."

"And what would that end be, Mr. Kincade? My professional destruction?"

Kincade shook his head No. He intuitively felt that Baatard was going to be rather easy to steer into his own direction. Baatard was obviously nervous, and Charlie Kincade could sense it, smell it, feed on it.

"It certainly doesn't sound that way to me," Baatard added, uncomfortably.

"Oh, but it is. Trust me. For example, Dr. Vernor also might demand punitive damages for grief, loss of marital benefits, et cetera. But, with cooperation on your part, all that is negotiable." That wasn't entirely true, but Kincade found saying so often worked wonders in cases like this.

Baatard shifted uncomfortably in his chair, and looked glumly into his hands.

"It's my understanding that Haven General's Quality Assurance team is already investigating Lissa Vernor's disastrous surgical outcome." He suspected this would force Baatard more into the defensive. He also thought that, with Marina being the QA nurse handling the review, he would have to distance himself from her for the time being. The Vernor case might actually be fortuitous in that regard by providing him an excuse, he thought. The issue of Marina's pregnancy and child had taken him completely by surprise, and left him at the time totally unsure of how to deal with it. The whole situation made him uncomfortable.

"You certainly seem to know quite a lot about supposedly confidential hospital proceedings," Baatard told him.

"I have my sources, Dr. Baatard. We all do, I'm sure you'll admit. What I propose to you is a way to avoid a nasty malpractice hearing, a hearing that could severely damage the image of Haven General, your image in the medical community and the success of your practice." It was the old carrot and stick approach, and it often worked.

Baatard squirmed around in his seat some more, and nervously drummed his fingers on his knee.

"And last, a costly malpractice award could be very damaging to your personal finances. Look, I want to help you, Dr. Baatard. Let me help you. Let me be your friend." Charlie Kincade restrained himself, lest he begin to sound disingenuous and lose the control he was clearly establishing over Baatard.

Kincade had barely been present in Baatard's office for five minutes, when Baatard had enough. His voice was breaking as he said, "I really don't want to discuss this further without having my malpractice carrier present. Okay?"

"That's fine with me, Dr. Baatard," Kincade smiled. "And that's certainly within your prerogative. But I do think that we, that is to say all parties here, should try and avoid the malpractice courts. No one is a winner there."

Baatard, visibly shaken, nodded his head in agreement.

"Say, before I go, do you mind if I use your phone? I almost used it before coming in to see you, but when I learned you were available, I came right in instead. I didn't want to make you wait."

"That's very considerate of you," Baatard smirked.

"There's no need to be sarcastic, Dr. Baatard. I meant it when I said I'm your friend, I want to be your friend, and you should want to be mine, for, right now, Dr. Baatard I could be a lot closer and helpful to you than your own mother, more useful than even your own attorney. Be that as it may, I need to firm up a luncheon date. Do you mind?" he smiled, adding, "It's only a local call."

Charlie Kincade was deriving untoward pleasure from Baatard's suffering. He resented Baatard for being in such a monetarily successful position, considering all the long hours he also put in seeing clients. On top of that, Charlie didn't find Baatard all that likable a person, and wondered why, with all she knew, Marina remained a patient of his. When Kincade was through, he was sure Baatard would regret agreeing to see him at all.

"You can go into my connecting office if you like, and close the door for privacy."

"Thanks." Kincade sensed from experience with similar clients that, like a puppy trying to please his

master, Baatard would do anything for him to seem
reasonable and cooperative. It was a typical reaction of
adversaries.

"I really am not worried." Baatard tried to get up a
smile, then added, "about the phone calls, I meant. That
is, I'm not worried about you making long distance calls,
that's all I meant."

Kincade smiled, "I know what you meant, Dr.
Baatard. There's no need to be worried about me, I won't
hurt you." Charlie smiled reassuringly at Baatard, then
went into Baatard's office, quietly closing the door behind
him.

After a few minutes, Kincade came back out.
"Thanks for the use of your phone. Say, I saw a certificate
on your wall which said you're a founding physician of
Conceptions Foundation. That's fascinating."

"Well, I suppose it is. That depends on what you like,
now doesn't it?"

"Yes, I certainly wouldn't enjoy medicine at all,
although I do find it very, well, very, . . . interesting.
That's it, interesting." Charlie Kincade had once applied
to medical school, a fact he rarely admitted to anyone. He
was roundly and quickly rejected from all twenty-one
schools he had applied to, creating the basis of a general
animosity toward physicians he held to this day, and
perhaps the only general dislike he shared with Marina
Bonnaserra. It was one of only a very few long-term
grudges. Charlie rebounded from the rejections by
applying to thirty law schools, and was accepted to three,
none of which were first rate, but, in the end, he got his
law degree and passed the bar; that was all that he or that

anyone, cared.

"But what about law? I mean, don't you find that keeps your interest too?" Baatard said, puzzled.

"Oh, sure I do, sure, sure. But, medicine, I think I'd like that even more, but," Kincade sighed heavily, "despite its being interesting, it's messy, dangerous, and legally too vulnerable."

"What?" Baatard retorted. "You mean law isn't? That's not what I've heard."

"Yeah, I guess it is too. Anyway, medicine's not for me. I prefer predictable things," he said as he again smiled and straightened his tie. "Have a good day, Dr. Baatard. Thank you for your time, and we'll be back in touch." He buttoned the front of his jacket and briskly and firmly shook Baatard's hand. "By the way, which way to the bathroom?"

"Turn right at the glass door."

"Thank you again. By the way, we should do lunch one day. Don't you think?"

"Perhaps. When this is all over." Baatard straightened his tie, and buttoned the front of his jacket.

"Oh, it never ends," Kincade laughed. "It never ends," he repeated, almost to himself as he walked out the door. Kincade came back through the door in only a minute, and told Baatard, "I was serious about lunch, okay?"

"Sure, sure, if you think dining with barracudas suits

your taste, Mr. Kincade," Baatard replied. He made a slightly annoying buzzing sound as he said "Kincade."

"Yes, I see."

Sure, Baatard thought. Sure.

Chapter 46

"Deanna," Denny told her at their meeting in Denny's bright red Mercedes 450SL, parked inconspicuously in the middle of the Haven Mall. "I got a very disturbing memo today from the hospital pharmacist, Lynn Janislowski."

"Oh, about what?" Deanna asked, not too coolly, sitting right and staring straight ahead.

"The essence is that she thinks you're on drugs, you take drugs at work, and that you're a danger to yourself and others." Denny calmly looked over at Deanna, who tellingly didn't return the glance. "What do you have to say for yourself?"

"What can I say? It's not true."

Denny chuckled bitterly, then pulled out a paper from her pocket. "Evidently, this isn't the first time you've had a problem with drugs. I took the liberty of checking a little more deeply than our incompetent personnel department, and guess what I found?"

Turning toward Denny, tears forming in her eyes, Deanna asked, her voice laden with resignation, "What do you want? Are you going to turn me in?"

"No, as a matter of fact, I'm not."

"I, I don't understand."

"Oh, I think you will. It's quite simple, really. Actually, it's a bargain. It's a win-win situation. I want something, and you want something."

"What do I want?" Deanna asked, suspiciously.

"Deanna, don't interrupt me when I'm talking, okay?" Denny scolded her. "What you want, my dear, is drugs, am I right?"

"No, actually, I want to get off drugs. I want treatment. Can you help me?"

Unprepared for that answer, Denny thought for a moment, then said, "You never asked what I want."

"Okay, what do you want?"

"It's really quite simple -- service in kind, you might

say." She handed Deanna a small paper surgical package, and then outlined exactly what she wanted Deanna to do with it. And although Deanna didn't comprehend the why, she understood the how, and she agreed to doing Denny's bidding, exactly as requested, no questions asked. She preferred anything to a return to jail.

Shortly after arriving at the clinic, Vena called into Ryder's office on the intercom. "The O.R. is on the line. Can you take it?"

"Sure, put them through." Ryder thought about it for a moment, then added, "But I can't understand what they would want me for. I don't think I'm standby backup assistant surgeon today." Ryder picked up the O.R. schedule and checked it again while waiting for the call transfer.

"Dr. Vernor, I hate to call you on short notice," the voice from the O.R. sounded muted and hesitant.

Ryder immediately recognized the caller's voice and wondered what was coming next. He put down his coffee and donut and moved a pad and pencil in front of him on the desk.

"This is Deanna in the O.R. I'm handling scheduling today, and I'm afraid you may be the only assistant surgeon available right now. You know what a small town we have here," she laughed uncomfortably, then paused while waiting for a response. None came. "You probably can't do a case today, can you?"

As Ryder listened to Deanna talk, he detected something uncomfortable and secretively strained about her voice. He couldn't identify what the difference was, but its presence was undeniable and made him cautious. "I can, I guess, although I have a pretty full schedule as it is," he lied, scanning the half-full appointment book. "I'll have to move things around a lot, but I think I can come. What and when?"

"Are you sure you don't have something else to do?" she asked.

"No, not really. If you want me, then I'm free."

"Oh. Well, then the case is a BTL, at 10 a.m.," Deanna said.

Ryder recognized the abbreviations for Bilateral Tubal Ligation, and replied, "Okay. But remember, I'm not the surgery type. That's why I went into family practice, you know."

"Then why do you get involved in doing surgery at all?" Deanna asked, her voice picking up.

"Sometimes I really wonder too. Probably because it's a change of pace." Besides that, Ryder was relieved that at least now he could do something which would provide a reasonable compensation for his time. Having assisted on one before, Ryder felt comfortable with what would be required of him. With Baatard, all he had to do was hold retractors, buzz a sporadic bleed, and occasionally suture. He looked at his sparse office schedule again, then at his watch. "Okay. I'll come by in an hour to scrub in."

Forty-five minutes later, Ryder Vernor stood alone at the scrub sink outside the O.R. He had already spent the last five minutes vigorously rubbing iodine dye soap into his skin, and then used a sterile plastic scrub brush to clean under his nails. According to the aged green plastic timer over the sink, he had another five minutes to go. Ryder had never believed in the least bit that performing this ritual would sterilize the skin, at least any more than temporarily. He resented taking ten minutes from his day, even with as much time open as today's was, to do it.

Just then, Baatard rounded the O.R. corner and stopped abruptly in front of the scrub sink. Forcing himself to remain civil, he nodded at Ryder, and said, "Deanna told me you agreed to help out. I appreciate that." He was still furious with Ryder for trying to back out of the surrogate adoption contract. The baby had been promised to Ramirez, and it was too late, and totally unacceptable, for Ryder to change his mind like this.

"I'm here to assist on a BTL," Ryder said, defensively. "I don't know how they ever talked me into assisting you on this case, Baatard. I don't really like surgery, and we don't have a particularly good relationship now either."

"I feel the same way."

"Look, I didn't ask who the surgeon was on the case, or I might have changed my mind and not agreed to do this." Ryder turned back to the sink and resumed scrubbing, this time more vigorously than before.

Lest his own animosity affect the case's outcome adversely, Baatard nevertheless tried to be a little conciliatory. He had more than enough of adverse outcomes lately. "Okay, I know you're being inconvenienced, and I appreciate your doing this, Ryder. But I guess you were the only one in town available," Baatard offered, a puzzled look on his face. "You know how everyone clears out on a holiday," Baatard nervously tried to chuckle. They stood shoulder to shoulder at the scrub sink for several long silent minutes before finishing hand sterilization. The tension was palpable. After they finished their scrubbing, they both lifted up their hands, arms rigidly bent at the elbows, and entered the O.R. through the open door.

The operating room was empty save for one surgery technician setting up the O.R. table. Baatard watched Deanna as she came in briefly through the other door, her face mask on. She handed a package of medical equipment wrapped in disposable paper to one of the O.R. technicians, gave some instructions, and then quickly left as the scrub nurse came in.

The scrub nurse handed Baatard and Ryder sterile towels to dry off with, then helped them in putting on sterile paper surgical gowns. The gowns were held open for them in front, with the arm holes pointing forward.

The Surrogate

Baatard and Vernor simply walked forward, hands outstretched like robots, until they were inside. The gowns were wrapped and secured from behind for them by the scrub nurse, who then helped Baatard and Vernor into sterile gloves. Masks, hats and paper booties were already on before they scrubbed.

Baatard's patient, a divorced accountant in her late thirties with three children, was brought in on a gurney and transferred to the O.R. table. BLTs were a common form of sterilization for those not desiring the use of oral contraceptives, foam, other devices, or abstinence. This was his second case of the morning, his last was one of his older, fat patients, whom he remembered by a slight fishy odor coming from her groin, and a stubble of thick gray hair growing just under her lower lip. Baatard took a sterile paper drape, and along with the scrub nurse, pulled the cover down the length of the patient.

"You douche, I'll clamp," Baatard tersely told the scrub nurse. He congratulated himself for so deftly avoiding that odious chore.

The scrub nurse carefully covered the patient's abdomen with iodine-based wash, painting in wide strokes with a sponge on a stick, then following with more vigorous scrubbing.

Dimitri Markov

Baatard asked for a towel, then patted the surgical field dry. "You buzz, I'll cut. Okay?" Baatard told Ryder.

"Fine," Ryder said, taking hold of the electro-cauterization probe. He turned around to make sure the electrical lines were connected, and that the unit's power was on. "I'm ready," Ryder signaled as he played a bit with the floor pedal, watching the indicator light flick on and off. He noticed a little water on the floor by his feet, and mentioned this to the circulating nurse.

Deanna, who floated in and out of the O.R., told Ryder she would take care of the water spill. She casually threw a few sterile cloth towels from a utility cart down toward the edge of the spill, then quickly returned to her work.

Baatard took a number ten scalpel from the instrument tray, an extremely sharp blade in the shape of a half moon, got a "GO" nod from the anesthesiologist, and commenced the surgery. Before making his first incision, Baatard was momentarily distracted when Deanna walked back into the operating room and stood at the back of the anesthesiology cart. So used to her loquacious persona, Baatard found her almost total silence today unnerving. He hoped no one else picked up on it.

Deanna looked around at the floor near where Ryder was standing, then walked over to the wall just in back of Baatard and stood still.

As Baatard took hold of the scalpel blade, he noticed as much of Deanna's eyes as he could see above her face mask. They were wide open, and slightly red, clearly showing she had been crying. He started to ask Deanna if she wanted to, needed to leave the operating room, but held back when he noticed her hands trembling.

Deanna, as if acknowledging the concern in Baatard's eyes, leaned over and, nodding in Ryder's direction, whispered, "I'm all right, don't worry about me."

Baatard returned his attention back to the patient and to the surgical procedure at hand. His intestines rumbled and he belched a little, leaving a sour taste in his mouth. His stomach was bothering him again, as it had been doing daily as of late, and he vowed once again to drink less coffee. For now, he decided that he needed to take some antacid, something which was hard to do given his situation in the O.R. and the fact that he had on sterile gloves. He instructed Deanna to get some antacid from the cabinet, put it in a plastic cup and bring it over for him to swallow.

Turning back to the patient on the table, Baatard first made a long, superficial midline incision from the umbilicus to just below the ribs. There was little resistance as the scalpel blade sliced through the superficial layers of fat. Some mild bleeding in the subcutaneous fatty tissues began almost immediately to ooze up through the cut skin. The instrument nurse took an absorbent cotton cloth and lay it along the incision edge to help absorb some of the excess blood before it flowed out of the incision line and onto the patient's abdomen. Ryder helped out by clamping several small bleeders with micro forceps.

Ryder leaned over and tried to "buzz" the bleeding at the source - the incision edge, by placing the electro-coagulation probe tip into the pool of blood next to the nearest big bleeder. Blood was beginning to fill the deep incision line already, despite the presence of the absorbent cloth and the suction catheter. A small red rivulet began to overflow and run onto the patient's abdomen.

The instrument nurse put another absorbent cotton cloth in the incision to help sop up the blood and keep the operative field clear. Part of the instrument nurse's duties were to count the number of absorbent cloth towels used during the surgery, and by their extent of soaking with blood, estimate the patient's blood loss. She also ran the tip of the suction catheter in the wound to draw up blood. The blood made a sickening, gurgling, choking sound as it was pulled into the suction line, and the air held the characteristic smell of freshly cut flesh.

A patient could bleed out two to three units of blood - each 450 milliliters - in only a few minutes of uncontrolled oozing from a fresh incision. If the blood loss exceeded a certain amount, it would have to be replaced. That meant subjecting the patient to the risks of blood transfusion, particularly hepatitis and AIDS, and was to be avoided at all costs.

Ryder stepped on the foot pedal to activate the buzzer unit but looked up in surprise when nothing happened. There was no electrical buzzing sound, no coagulating blood, no smoke trail, no odor of burnt meat. Instinctively, he started to say something to the anesthesiologist, then abruptly stopped as his words came out garbled.

Baatard and Deanna looked over at Ryder, then nervously at each other. "You better check the cable on the butt pad, Deanna," Baatard recommended. "The buzzer doesn't seem to be working." As the only person not scrubbed, Deanna was the only one free to do this.

Baatard looked over at Ryder as he tried in vain to get the buzzer working again. By now, Ryder looked a little disorientated, but didn't say anything. Failure of electrical equipment happened occasionally, and it didn't appear to the other O.R. personnel too unusual when Ryder had to play around with the connections.

Ryder slowly slid the buzzer probe down into the plastic holder so it wouldn't fall on the floor, then bent down to check the electrical connections. His actions seemed slow, uncertain, and poorly coordinated. Unexpectedly, Ryder emitted a low, sickly moan like a mortally wounded animal, and never came back up. Instead, he slumped over, hitting the tile floor with a noticeable thud. Ryder's arms and legs twitched a few times, his body flapped and the back of his head slammed repeatedly against the metal table legs, shaking the instruments above and alerting everyone to the problem. From that fateful point on, Dr. Ryder Vernor lay unconscious on the floor like a limp doll, his operating scrub suit soaking in a pool of saline solution next to a broken plastic IV bag.

"Hey, Ryder," Baatard anxiously called out. Getting no response, he quickly threw a sterile drape over the bleeding incision line of the patient to protect it, and ran over to Ryder's lifeless body.

After quickly checking Ryder, his suspicions were confirmed, and Baatard called out, "He's got no pulse. Let's get some help over here, goddamnit. Call a CODE in the O.R." Baatard looked around and quickly decided he couldn't properly run a cardiopulmonary resuscitation on the cramped O.R. floor.

Baatard felt himself panicking, his chest tighten and a frightened feeling crawl over his body as he tried to fight the sense of total loss of control that was taking over. His hands were trembling visibly and his voice cracked as he yelled, "There's not enough goddamn room to run a CODE in here. Let's pull Dr. Vernor into the hallway. Move, people, MOVE." All Baatard could think of was how suspicious and uncomfortable it would look to have Ryder die in his presence, especially after he had been the surgeon under whose care Lissa had suffered a stroke.

Baatard felt a shiver run through his body like a jolt of electricity. He could feel his hands, then his whole body begin to shake uncontrollably, and he could only hope it was not noticeable to the others.

The anesthesiologist and the circulating nurse helped Baatard pull Ryder's limp body by his feet out of the way, and into the hall. By that time, the CODE team had arrived and the anesthesiologist had already begun CPR. As Baatard looked up, he was surprised to see Deanna cowering against the corner wall, her hands to her mouth.

"What happened?" the young ER resident who was in charge of the emergency response team asked Baatard and Deanna.

"Dr. Vernor was assisting me in surgery one moment, then he suddenly slumped over. Maybe he had a heart attack?" Baatard speculated, shrugging his shoulders, his voice quivering noticeably. Baatard pulled his face mask down from over his mouth to fight a strong sense of suffocation. He noticed he was also beginning to feel a little nauseous.

Deanna, standing nearby, gave both Baatard and the resident a disgusted look, then turned and went back into the O.R.

"Do you know his age?" the medical resident asked.

The Surrogate

"Maybe thirty-five, I think," Baatard replied. Baatard looked down in Ryder's direction, watching several medical students ineffectively attempting CPR. "Maybe he's a little more than thirty-five, I really don't know. Look, I just opened up a person's abdomen, and I need to get back in the case. Okay?"

"Of course, Dr. Baatard. We have it under control," one of the residents said while continuing chest compressions.

The resident now performing CPR whispered to another resident, "Isn't this guy the one whose wife stroked out just last year." They both turned their head and stared at Baatard, and their looks were incriminating.

As Baatard returned to the O.R., he turned back and saw the residents switching cardiac compressions. Over toward the shoulders, another person was ineffectively intubating - placing a large plastic tube through the mouth into the trachea of -Ryder, and a third was attempting to start an IV line in Ryder's arm. Baatard had seen futile efforts like this before and grimly knew how it would probably turn out. He realized what everyone must have been thinking, and he felt like a trapped animal.

Fighting to refocus his thoughts, Baatard quickly scrubbed his hands again, changed into a new set of sterile gloves and gown, and reentered the O.R. Once back in, while the case was being reset with sterile gear, Baatard leaned over and whispered to Deanna, "Hey, look, I can imagine what you're thinking."

"Is that so?" she shot back, in disbelief. "I doubt it." Killing, even at the hand of another, was new for Deanna, and seeing the actual process and the awful result left her nervous and disturbed. Viewing death was not new, but she had always been on the life saving side before, and this was totally different, but absolutely necessary for her preservation.

"I, we had nothing to do with this, just remember that. It must have been a heart attack."

Deanna stared at his cold, heartless face with a look of pure hatred, then turned and walked away, crying to herself, without saying anything else.

Marina Bonnaserra heard the Cardiac Arrest call blare on the loud speaker near her office door. Normally not one to congregate around crises, nevertheless she felt compelled this one time to follow the flood of people.

Something inside told her she needed to go. She rounded the entrance to the operating room suites just as Ryder Vernor was being wheeled out on a gurney. Medical residents still stood about his lifeless body performing chest compressions. Staring at Ryder's dusky blue face and dilated eyes, Marina had to cover her mouth and back away, shocked and nauseous. It took her only a few minutes to ascertain from others what apparently had happened, and it would be only a few days more before the medical records found their way to her office for review.

Upset and unable to work, Marina left early for home, stopping at the hospital day care facility to pick up Austin. According to the caregivers, he had been active most of the morning, then had become rather subdued and remained quiet until she had picked him up. Marina asked about a fever, diarrhea or any other reason for his change in mood, but it was without explanation.

As Marina held Austin, he smiled contentedly at her, made some 'goo' sounds, and didn't appear to be ill. Yet, Marina thought she too could sense a change in his mood. She knew she would have to keep a close watch on him this night.

Chapter 47

Upon arriving home, Marina found that she had received a tightly wrapped manila envelope in the mail, marked North East Forensic Laboratory. She walked into the nursery area, placed Austin, who was sleeping, into his crib, and went back to the living room. As she picked up the envelope, she could see her hands still shaking from witnessing Ryder's resuscitation effort at Haven General. She took the envelope into her kitchen and opened it up. Inside, she found a series of reports outlining the chemical nature of various stains on the clothes she was wearing when raped some sixteen years ago.

The forensics report detailed listings of certain proteins, something about electrophoresis banding - Marina had no idea what that referred to - and some information on blood and tissue types. Although she now had more information about her attacker than she ever had, she had no idea how to use it. But that was just a matter of time, she thought. The next day, she would make copies of the documents and forward them to Charlie Kincade, and to the Haven Police bureau. Maybe now, some action would be taken, she hoped. For aggravated sexual assault, there was no Statute of Limitations.

Marina knew that she now had a key to finding the bastard who had raped her, but instead of feeling relieved, she was angry and more determined than ever, for she knew that she had to end for once and for all the rage that seethed deep within her body all these years for the crime that with the passage of years seemed so insignificant that everyone but her had long ago forgotten.

The tragedy she had just witnessed left her terrified and terribly threatened; first Lissa, she thought, and now Ryder. Was there a pattern? Was she herself in any danger, or Austin?

Shaking her head, Marina wondered if she was becoming paranoid. Despite her attempts to place those distant illnesses and deaths, so seemingly unrelated to her, in perspective, she nevertheless had a distinct feeling of uneasiness that just would not go away, and she found herself not being reassured at all. As she looked around her house, she realized all too well just how vulnerable she was. Her house was isolated from others -- it was at least a quarter mile to the nearest house, and they were never home. The doors and windows had locks, but those could easily be circumvented, as she had discovered on several occasions after locking herself out. In comparison to Charlie Kincade's security system for his condo, the only private home system with which she was familiar, Marina had virtually no central security system at all, and she vowed to correct that as soon as possible.

Later that day, Marina drove to a pawn shop outside

of Jersey City where a casual acquaintance she had met during one of her journeys to the courthouse worked. She came out in only a few minutes, this time carrying a small brown paper bag. Inside the bag was a .22-caliber handgun, twenty rounds of ammunition, and the name of some ranges where she could get instruction and practice.

Chapter 48

Haven Family Practice Clinic
Haven, New Jersey

Vena stood alone near the reception area at Ryder's office, impatiently watching the office door, waiting for it to open. The surgery Ryder had gone to assist in was scheduled to be completed over an hour ago, and for some unexplained reason, he still hadn't returned. The phone rang intermittently - the office staff had gone out for lunch and forgot to forward all calls to the answering service, leaving all the phone line lights lit up. Finally, Vena called over to the O.R., and it was then she learned the awful news of how Ryder had just collapsed during surgery.

Those words were almost too horrible to comprehend, but somehow she knew that it was true. Not Ryder, it couldn't be Ryder, Dear God, let it not be him, Vena prayed. A shock ran right through her, impaling her body on a rigid bolt of electrical tension, and Vena screamed from the pain, then broke down crying.

Vena took a few moments to recover enough to continue listening. When she did, she heard the nurse recount all the deadly details to Vena: the operation, the emergency CODE, the short hospitalization in Intensive

Care before his heart finally stopped. She realized how utterly hopeless the situation was, when she heard the nurse ask her, "What do you think will happen to Lissa and Ephrim?"

Vena slowly shook her head, looked at the floor and sadly replied, "I just don't know." Ryder had never discussed custody issues with her, and now she could see that she, as neither the mother nor the wife, really had no rights to Ephrim, none at all. She wondered if what had just occurred to Ryder was the problem, the unnamed danger Ryder was so concerned about a few days ago. As Vena grabbed her purse and ran over to the ICU, she had no doubt whose fault it was. By the time she had arrived, Ryder had passed away, and his body was being prepared for removal to the hospital morgue.

After Ryder Vernor's tragic collapse in the operating room, Baatard underwent several hours of questioning, first by the police, then by the hospital attorney, and finally by Dr. Rubin. Detective Bruce Mitchell, although suspicious and distrusting by nature, approached the investigation of Ryder's death from the beginning as a either work-related accidental death or natural causes, rather than a criminal homicide.

Baatard found it very difficult to think anything, to concentrate, to decide what to do next, and had to cancel the rest of his surgeries for the day, perhaps for the week, he thought. Lissa's unfortunate outcome while under his care could be explained, but now, with Lissa's husband having an apparent heart attack while working with him, it could seem to everyone to be more than just coincidental. Yet, Baatard knew it had appeared to be just that - coincidental, and he desperately needed to establish that fact with the police and with the officials at Haven General.

Later that day, Vena began the heart breaking task of notifying Ryder's family, whom she had met on only one occasion, and also Lissa's parents of his death. Ryder's father, although devastated, was able to maintain his presence of mind and committed to fly to Haven immediately from the Vernor home in Virginia. He told Vena that he would probably arrange for his son's body to be brought back home to Virginia for a local funeral. Her world rapidly collapsing around her, Vena left the office early, unable to think of a single reason to keep it open. She went over to their, to Ryder's, apartment to be alone, to think things through. The answering service was instructed to cancel appointments and refer all patients to Dr. Hernandez.

Suddenly, Vena remembered that Ephrim needed to be picked up from the day care center soon. Although Vena could bring Ephrim home, she soon realized she had no legal authority over Ephrim, no right to keep him, being neither mother nor guardian to him. Then, recalling what Ryder had instructed her to do in case of an emergency, Vena first walked over to Ryder's work desk and called Charlie Kincade. Ryder must have known something was going to happen, she thought, and this must have been the emergency he was referring to.

Kincade was almost speechless when Vena told him about Ryder's tragic and untimely death. It had been only a matter of days since Vena called him about Ryder's cryptic and foreboding remarks, and it seemed as if Ryder's prophecy had indeed come true. "Vena," he cautioned, his voice trembling, "listen very carefully. Here's what you must do. Don't talk to anyone. Even if the police call, refuse to talk to them without my being present. Make sure you stay with Ephrim, and do not, I repeat, do not entrust Ephrim's care to anyone. Is he there with you now?"

"No, he's in child care."

Vena didn't like the fearful tone of Charlie's voice, and wanted to ask him what exactly he was concerned about. At the same time, she wasn't sure she really wanted to know. "You must go to get him immediately, and keep him with you at all times, okay?" Charlie insisted.

"But what will you be doing, and where will you be?"

"I can't take the time to explain now, but I've got several important steps to take immediately concerning Ephrim. Look, I promise to call you later today with details."

Vena got the clear impression Charlie Kincade had worked all this out in advance, almost as if he were expecting something.

The Surrogate

After she spoke with Kincade, Vena noticed near the side of the bedroom desk some reports from a company called Genetic ID, Inc. She had not seen the envelope before, and wondered if Ryder was just recently looking at it. Inside the envelope, she found the genetic analysis of blood from Ryder, his son Ephrim, and his wife Lissa. Scribbled on the envelope were the words, "sperm" and "urine." Vena stuffed the papers in her purse, then went to pick up Ephrim.

Chapter 49

Charlie Kincade opened the thick manila packet from
North East Forensics Laboratory as soon as the copy
arrived from Marina. He read the rather short report, then
had his secretary call Marina Bonnaserra.

"I just got the copy of the forensic lab results on the
clothes you brought them. It was pretty much as I
suspected."

"Finally, we have something," Marina sighed,
confidently. She had gone sixteen years without so much
as a suspect, a clue, a lead. And that was despite the many
trials she had attended, all the pleading ads she had placed
in the newspapers, the fliers she had nailed to lamp posts
offering a reward for any information leading to the arrest
of the man who had assaulted her, even these efforts were
a failure. Until now. "Well, what did it show? Who was
the man?"

"The good news is we got a good genetic ID.
Someone else's tissue is on your clothes all right."

"I'm not at all surprised. Now we can go to the police,
right?" She envisioned an astonished and grateful
detective, a wide-scale but short investigation, and a rapid

arrest and severe punishment.

"Well, that's where the bad news comes in, I'm afraid."

"What do you mean, bad news, Charlie?" She could feel the indignation swelling within her, and couldn't believe that even with new evidence, the police still wouldn't help her.

"It's like this, Marina. We have the perpetrator's tissue type, but we have no one to match it. It could belong to anyone."

"But, you used this type of information to clear one of your own clients, didn't you? How could it be so useful back then but not now? It freed an innocent man, didn't it?" she cried, "so why can't it catch even one guilty one?"

"Sure it did. The genetic tissue type of the victim didn't match the man who had been convicted of the crime. Under the circumstances, the courts had no choice but to release him. Your case is different. We have some man's tissue samples on your clothes, but until you can supply me with something to match it against, I'm afraid it's just short of useless. The lab told me they tried to explain this to you. I did too, if you remember."

"Well, I guess they did," she admitted. Marina remembered NEFL's caution on the usefulness of the data they might, if they were lucky, be able to provide. She guessed that in her enthusiasm to get the bastard that raped her, she had minimized what they said, hoping they were really being cautious. "But, Charlie, I had to find out what I could. Maybe I don't have a person's tissue to match against now, but I swear I will someday. And when

I do, we can get that man, that low-life animal, and finally bring me some peace of mind."

"Look, Marina, a lot of people are victims of crimes, terrible crimes, and a few are fortunate enough to survive, like you were. Almost all learn to let their past be over, and to go on with their lives. Maybe you need to do the same."

"You've got a lot of nerve, Charlie," Marina scolded him, offended at how little support and understanding he really could provide to her. "You weren't assaulted, you don't have nightmares every night." Still, Charlie wasn't the first to tell her this. He and others had urged her to get some counseling, some therapy, which she had tried as far back as her teen years just after the rape. The sessions had always turned out to be a waste of her time and her parent's money.

"Okay, okay, but we aren't much better off with this new information than you think, that's all I'm trying to tell you."

"Believe me, Charlie, I'm better off with what I have than with nothing at all." Just having some tie, some information, on her attacker made her feel better, as if she had accomplished something finally. She had found out something the police and Charlie hadn't. And she refused to give up until she had the bastard who raped her behind bars.

After Marina hung up from her call to Charlie

Kincade, she called a police detective she had some contact with over the years concerning her case - Bruce Mitchell. Bruce seemed polite and tried to be helpful and encouraging, but Marina could tell from the tension in his voice and the constantly ringing phones in the background that he was overextended. She was sure he had seen many more cases of rape and assault than she could ever imagine, and to Charlie, apparently, disappointingly, her own case was just one more. Marina was disappointed but not too surprised when she got almost exactly the same story from Bruce that Charlie had just given her.

After hanging up, she was left wondering where she would get a tissue sample from her attacker with which to make a match. Thinking about it in this light, it seemed to her she was almost no better off than before, still needing to find the man before proving his identification.

Chapter 50

Bruce Mitchell met with the Haven hospital pathologist later in the afternoon two days after Ryder died. As the investigating detective of an unexpected but not suspicious death, Bruce had also just finished sitting through the postmortem. It was the most unpleasant of tasks he had to perform as part of his official duties. Even the most gung-ho of his associates avoided autopsy duty.

"He probably had a lethal arrhythmia. His postmortem exam was fairly unremarkable," the pathologist reported.

"He was kind of young for a heart attack, wouldn't you say?" Bruce asked.

"Ordinarily, yes. He was only thirty-two years old. But he occasionally smoked, and he had a high-pressure career. Anyway, I found nothing unexpected," the pathologist said.

"Shouldn't you see something, some kind of blockage, if it was a heart attack?"

"For a blocked artery leading to a heart attack, yes, ordinarily, but the coronary arteries were entirely open, so

I think a lethal arrhythmia is more likely."

"But don't you think that's kind of strange?" Bruce asked.

"Not at all in his age group, inspector. It could have been due to an arrhythmia - a bad heart rhythm - or a non-blocking spasm of the coronary arteries."

"What would cause an arrhythmia, particularly one in a young male?"

"Just about anything, I'm afraid. The list is long and includes insufficient oxygen supply to the heart, electrical conduction defects, electrolyte problems, and a million other things," the pathologist said, "but often it's without a causal explanation."

A thought came to Bruce, and he asked, "Electrocution? How about electrocution?"

"Well, yes, I guess so. The heart is controlled by bio-electrical activity. Any electrical disturbance could interrupt the natural heart rhythm. But there was no evidence of electrocution at the autopsy. Why do you ask?"

Not directly answering the question, Bruce asked, "What was Dr. Vernor doing just prior to his collapse?"

Reading the cardiac arrest team report again, the pathologist said, "Apparently Dr. Vernor was buzzing a bleed. Let me call over to the O.R. and see if one of the nurses who was present at that surgery is here today."

A few minutes later, one of the circulation nurses who had been on the case with Dr. Vernor came in. After some introductions, Bruce asked the nurse about Dr. Vernor's actions around the time of his collapse.

"He didn't complain of chest pain or shortness of

breath, if that's what you want to know" the nurse related. "He never seemed to have any problems, as long as I knew him. Then, at the O.R., he just keeled over, that's all."

"And what was he doing just before that?" Bruce asked.

"Buzzing a bleed."

"Which is . . . " Bruce asked? He remembered that the hospital pathologist had used that term earlier.

"That's when you touch an electro-cautery tip into the source of a bleed. It sears the vessels closed with heat caused by an electrical current."

"There was an electro-cautery tip?" Bruce thought out loud. "Could I see the tip used by Dr. Vernor?"

"You can't. You see, they're considered contaminated medical waste, and are disposable."

Bruce seemed surprised and very suspicious.

"All disposable equipment contaminated with blood is autoclaved after the case is closed. That's standard everywhere, to cut down on blood-borne infections. So, that particular tip is gone," the nurse apologized.

"Can the electro-cautery tip short out?"

"I never heard of that happening," the nurse said.

Bruce remembered some related facts on another case he had recently been handling. He felt very uncomfortable upon hearing about the electro-cautery probe, particularly its being unavailable. Bruce quickly finished his notes, then left to finish his report.

After speaking with Dr. Meyer Rubin about the
Ryder Vernor tragedy, Baatard changed out of his surgery
scrubs and hurriedly walked over to his office. As he
entered the reception area, he was both surprised and
annoyed to see Charlie Kincade waiting for him.
"Goddamnit," he said out loud. Finding it was too late to
go in the back way - he had already been seen - he
decided to try the direct approach.
"Oh, Mr. Kincade," Baatard barked, unable to
conceal his annoyance. "It's you again. What do you want
from me now? This is really a bad time."
"That's an understatement," Kincade nodded.
"I really don't feel like talking to you, and even if I
did, I would want my attorney present. I'm sure you
understand."
"Ah, if I only thought you really cared," Kincade said
sarcastically. "This isn't a social call, Dr. Baatard. I have
something for you." Kincade looked at Baatard coldly as
he handed Baatard a sealed envelope. The office symbol
of Kincade's law firm was embossed in raised red letters
on the front of the envelope. Before Baatard had a chance
to open it, Kincade said, "I'm sure I'll be seeing you again,
Dr. Baatard. In court," he added, then turned and left.
Baatard watched out of the corner of his eye as
Kincade left. That arrogant son-of-a-bitch, Baatard
thought, as he stood in the center of his empty waiting
room. Baatard looked at the envelope a long time before
opening it. Inside he found about ten pages of legal
documents, with a short cover letter. "Shit," he sneered as

he kicked the wall and moved back to his office.

Chapter 51

Baatard made an appointment for later that afternoon in the office of his personal attorney, Ellen Yee. Middle-aged, Baatard guessed about forty, single as far as Baatard knew, Yee was one of several junior partners in the firm of Rebromowitz, Schneiderman and Luftkin. Of the almost thirty lawyers associated with the office, only Yee took medical malpractice cases. It was her specialty, and an interest she had developed since her second round of rejections of medical schools almost twenty years ago. Unknown to all concerned, she, Charlie Kincade and Dr. Ryder Vernor shared a commonality.

Baatard knew other doctors who used Yee's services; she had a reputation of fighting tough and winning. Fortunately, he had had few dealings with her in the past, all of a minor nature.

Baatard handed Yee the papers he received from Vernor's attorney, Charlie Kincade. "Look at this, will you," Baatard complained. "This attorney Kincade is requesting copies of Lissa Vernor's office record. Can you believe it? I think having to endure the scrutiny of a formal hospital review should be enough. Don't you?"

"You should have looked more closely, Dr. Baatard," Yee admonished after skimming all the documents. "Attorney Kincade requests all records on the Lissa Vernor case, both clinic and hospital."

"How do you know that?" Baatard asked. "I just gave you the papers and you hardly even looked at them yet.

"Kincade already called me, Dr. Baatard. I'm your attorney of record, remember? He tried the Haven General Hospital legal office first, and they referred him to contact me. Procedurally, Attorney Kincade isn't supposed to visit you at all without contacting your attorney, as I understand he recently did, so if it happens again, please call me first. Anyway, requesting those documents is exactly what you would expect him to do, wouldn't you?"

"Yeah, I guess so. But what the hell is he looking for, goddamnit? I already got the whole goddamn hospital looking at the Vernor case."

"Exactly which Vernor case are you referring to?" Yee asked pointedly.

"Oh, yeah, I see what you mean. Lissa Vernor, of course. I'm under a microscope about that one already. I just don't see why I need to provide more goddamn documents to Kincade when the hospital QA investigation is still ongoing."

"Maybe I can get Kincade to wait until the hospital investigation is complete. I'll see what I can do," Yee said. "The problem is, Dr. Baatard, that Kincade is also asking about any internal investigation at the hospital, and requests copies of those proceedings too."

"What internal investigation? I'm not under any

internal investigation." Baatard started to scream, but realized that he was losing control, and forced himself to calm down and maintain his professional demeanor. He knew he had done nothing wrong, and would not be forced into acting like he had. That road led only to defeat. He straightened up his body, looked Yee in the eye, and, pronouncing each word slowly and calmly, told her, "I'm not accused of malpractice or professional misconduct or anything. This is simply a QA hearing, that's all."

"I think Kincade is referring to any special reports the Chief of Surgery requested in preparation for the QA hearing. You are right, the QA hearing is an internal investigation and is most probably what Kincade is referring to. But there may also be other internal investigations pertaining to you that you aren't aware of, yet."

Baatard didn't like the way she let 'yet' drop off the end of the sentence, foreboding, foretelling, forewarning. "How the hell would Kincade know about these things?"

"I don't know, but I'm not surprised, Baatard. Perhaps he has sources within Haven General. And by the way, Kincade has copied this request to the Haven General Hospital Administrator. He also copied the state Board of Medical Quality Assurance, the BMQA, Baatard."

"Why did Kincade do that? No one is accusing me of medical negligence."

Yee shook her head in a pitying manner. "He's fishing, Baatard. We all do it," she said, trying to reassure him. "Kincade is looking for any past complaints, any prior restrictions of hospital or license privileges, any

problems with drug or alcohol abuse, episodes of
psychiatric care, things like that. He's smart, Baatard. And
his actions suggest to me he's experienced, very
experienced."

"Great. I'm so happy for him." Baatard couldn't
believe how things were snow-balling out of control. He
looked up at the ceiling and wondered who in heaven he
had upset.

"I assume you're clean in those regards, Baatard,"
Yee said, looking over her thick lenses at him.

"Yes, of course I am." Generally speaking, that was
true. Another thing was beginning to bother him - he was
finding the way Yee referred to him as 'Baatard' rather
than Dr. Baatard, or even Damon, a little grating. Should
he make a point of this to the woman who possibly was
his best friend right now?

"You'll tell me everything I need to know, Baatard.
It's the best, the only way I can help you. I must know
everything, even if you don't think it will be of use, even
if you're ashamed. I have to know it all."

"I have told you all," Baatard angrily snapped.
Goddamnit, he wondered, what the hell was she getting
at? Did she think, or know, he knew something else? If
so, he would rather have her just say it, come right out,
rather than play these mind games.

More than ever, he could see himself being set up
here. But why? Was some clever competitor using the

Lissa Vernor case to hurt his practice, perhaps to hurt The Conceptions Foundation by implication? It was possible, he guessed.

"No need to get angry here, Dr. Baatard. Just don't hold back. Anything you tell me is covered under attorney-client privilege." Yee tried to smile reassuringly.

Baatard wasn't buying. "So, Kincade asks BMQA about me. Now I suppose they're suspicious. Does that mean I'm going to get investigated by BMQA?"

"By his inquiring? My, no. The hospital will notify BMQA anyway about the QA investigation. The BMQA knows everything. As long as the outcome is good, everything's okay. So, a lot depends on whether the hospital makes a clear determination of lack of negligence or not."

"Well, they can't find any negligence on my part," Baatard confidently stated, "because I'm not negligent." Unfortunate as the outcome was, intentional it wasn't.

"Good. I certainly hope not. And, by the way, there's something else that you may be interested in knowing," Yee said.

"What else could happen today?" Baatard asked, throwing his hands up exasperatedly.

"Charlie Kincade is now the legal guardian of Lissa Vernor, and Vena Kleinman is now the legal guardian of Ephrim Vernor."

"What," Baatard shouted, turning around. "How the hell did that happen? What's going on around here, anyway?" Baatard yelled as he slammed his fist into his other hand. "You have to reverse that order, or declare it invalid or do something, anything," he blurted out. All air seemed to squeeze out of his lungs as he considered losing the huge chunk of money he had been promised.

"I don't understand why you're so upset about this, Dr. Baatard. This Vernor child is nothing to you," Yee said as she backed away from Baatard another foot and pushed up her glasses with a finger. She motioned her displeasure with his impulsive, violent gestures, waited for Baatard to confirm her statement, then repeated, "The Vernor child IS nothing to you, is he, Baatard?"

"Yeah, of course. Ephrim is really nothing to me. Nothing at all. It's ridiculous to even think so," Baatard nervously chuckled.

"Dr. Ryder Vernor took that legal step only last week, it seems. Perhaps it was at the request or recommendation of his attorney. Perhaps he had a premonition."

"Premonition Shit," Baatard laughed coarsely. "Don't be ridiculous. There are no such things as premonitions."

"Don't be so quick to dismiss things like that, Baatard. Eastern philosophy teaches that people who are in touch with their inner selves can know great truths. That is one of the many great failings of Western philosophy. Anyway, I've already asked Kincade for clarification."

"Good. But I need more than clarification here, Yee. I need that Goddamn guardianship declared invalid, INVALID, do you understand me? I'll explain more later, but for now, GET IT VOIDED," he ordered her, he pleaded with her.

"Yes, well I'll see what I can do, okay?" Yee tried to calm him, obviously taken aback by the magnitude of his reaction to the court order.

"And, what has Kincade clarified?" He could only imagine, and none of it was good.

"Nothing yet. He doesn't have to respond," Yee said, shrugging her thin shoulders and trying to wrinkle her very delicate eyebrows. "Baatard," Yee asked, stretching out the word and tilting her head to one side in a way which reminded Baatard of a Siamese cat. "Level with me. What is Kincade looking for? What does he want? I can be much more effective if I know." Yee pushed her glasses back up her nose again, sat back down, folded her arms, and waited.

Baatard, feeling more alone than at any time in his life, looked pleadingly at Yee and said simply, "I think I'm being set up." He turned around to make sure the door to Yee's office was closed, then reminded Yee of her pledge of client lawyer confidentiality, which he reminded her was analogous to his oath of patient-physician confidentiality. Yee acknowledged, and with that understood, Baatard then began to tell Yee the incomplete truth about some exclusive and entirely legal fertility services he was providing for a very wealthy and powerful client.

Chapter 52

Charlie Kincade opened the large manila envelope, heavily sealed with wide bands of masking tape and marked CONFIDENTIAL, which had just arrived in his office via express courier. On the outside were the clear markings of BMQA Disclosure, Inc., a specialty investigatory company he occasionally used. The envelope contained a small dossier of papers, mostly photocopies, and a summary report. Charlie picked up the stack in one hand, a tuna croissant sandwich in the other, kicked off his shoes and started to read. It didn't take long for him to discover these were exactly the papers he had requested weeks ago, and gave him more ammunition than he had bargained for.

The first set of copies was from the Wisconsin Board of Medical Quality Assurance, that state's BMQA. It represented the governmental agency responsible for licensing and monitoring health professionals in Wisconsin - every state had one. Having learned the technique from a seminar he had attended, Charlie used to go state by state when fishing for trouble; it was a long and costly process. Now, with the creation of the national physician's database, he could get what he needed faster, cheaper and missed less through BMQA Disclosures.

Charlie read eagerly about Baatard's past problems with some not exactly sanctioned practices involving infertility evaluations, a questionable sperm bank, bad records and billing practices and other claims. How the hell could he have missed all this, Charlie wondered? And how had Haven General's Credentialing Committee missed these facts? Apparently the complaints against Baatard had gone all the way to the hearing stage before being dismissed for lack of evidence, leaving Baatard's license untouched. This was all several years ago, and Baatard seemed to have been without question in the ensuing years.

Interestingly, Baatard's Wisconsin license application showed that Baatard had a New Jersey license prior to his Wisconsin license. There was no mention of a BMQA problem in New Jersey, and no other difficulties. Charlie Kincade made some mental notes and decided to ask Baatard about these records, at a time and place of his own choosing, a time and place which hopefully would catch Baatard off guard, surprise him, get him to say something unintended.

Charlie forwarded a copy of all the records to the Physician's Credentialing Committee at Haven General Hospital, and also "unofficially" copied a set for Marina Bonnaserra at her home address.

At 9 a.m. the next morning, Ellen Yee, having made an appointment the previous afternoon, presented herself to the law offices of Cornwall, Kincade, and Santos, P.C.

Yee walked up to the narrow reception window cluttered with credit card emblems, introduced herself and waited. The reception area was much smaller and cramped than in her own offices, and the furniture looked older and worn.

Shortly, Kincade, rather than a secretary, came out and quickly escorted Yee back into his office without saying a word.

Kincade and Yee had known each other for some time. Although never confronting each other on the same case before, they had politely and casually spoken in the court house and at legal social gathering on several occasions. Kincade found Yee to be distant, uninteresting and cold. He never knew what Yee thought of him, nor did he care.

Yee got right down to business. Pushing her glasses up her nose with one finger, she announced, "I represent Dr. Damon Baatard. I understand you claim to be the legal guardian of Lissa Vernor?"

"That is correct," Kincade replied, sensing a problem in the making. "I not only claim to be, I AM," he confidently stated. "Dr. Vernor appointed me guardian only two weeks ago. The papers were appropriately certified and filed with the county clerk."

"And who is handling the affairs of the son, Ephrim Vernor?"

"I am taking care of that too," Kincade said. "Vernor awarded Vena Kleinman custody of Ephrim Vernor in case of his inability to care for him. Ms. Kleinman has appointed me attorney of record for both her own personal affairs and those legal matters relating to her custody of Ephrim Vernor."

"My condolences to the boy. Anyway, I'm afraid we cannot accept that appointment. Vena Kleinman has no relationship to Ephrim Vernor - genetic, familial or custodial. This makes no sense whatever and certainly is not in the child's best interests. I plan to file papers objecting to this later today."

"On what grounds?" Kincade asked. The last thing he expected was to have anyone object to his or Vena's appointment, especially Dr. Damon Baatard.

"Exactly as I just said, counselor. In addition, I will object on the grounds of conflict of interest. Your clients are also the parents." Yee explained.

"One of my clients, one of the parents, is dead. The other is in a goddamn coma."

"Exactly."

"But how are they supposed to care for the child?" Kincade asked.

"I'm surprised you don't find it unusual that your client, whose wife - also a client of yours - is comatose under suspicious circumstances, dies shortly after appointing his lover the legal guardian of his child. Surely, someone will find this suggestive." she scoffed. "Who, may I ask, was named beneficiary of the Vernor's estate? You too?"

"Now, wait a minute. I don't like your slimy tone of voice or your ugly implications. Just what is all this suggestive of? I think you had better be careful of what you imply."

"Yes, well anyway, as you will see, I represent Dr. Baatard for several interests. I also present you with this document," Yee announced as she leaned forward and handed Kincade a thick envelope, flashing him a triumphant smirk in the process.

"Why is the legal guardianship of Ephrim Vernor a concern of yours?" Kincade said as he started to read. Surely Baatard had enough problems on his hands without this. It just didn't make sense.

Yee glared into Kincade's eyes and barked back, "That will become evident with time, Mr. Kincade. I trust you're familiar with these documents."

Trying to quickly look over the paper, Kincade said, "I, ah, think so," he stuttered, putting down his cell phone that he had been playing with as he stared at the letter. "This is a surrogate parentage agreement."

"Well, are you familiar with this type of document or are you not?" she demanded.

"I think so," Kincade said, as he stared more closely at the documents, eyes wide open. What he was seeing was totally insane.

"Good. Then you understand this represents a binding, irreversible legal contract. Ephrim Vernor was born as part of a surrogate parentage agreement between the Vernors and a private client of Dr. Baatard."

"What the hell are you talking about? I know nothing

about this, and this doesn't make any sense whatever. Neither Dr. Vernor nor Vena Kleinman had ever mentioned anything to me about a surrogate parentage agreement for Ephrim."

"It is a binding legal contract, not a document that must make some particular sense to anyone, least of all you. The contract expresses the wishes of the Vernors. You and I must simply execute those expressed legal wishes. We aren't here to question them. Both the Vernors are your clients, are they not?"

"Yes, but . . . "

"Good. Then I trust you'll execute their directions. I would like to take care of this business transaction as soon as possible."

"But, but Ryder, Dr. Vernor, never mentioned anything like this to me. In fact, by his assigning custody of Ephrim to me in case of an emergency, Dr. Vernor implied quite the opposite. It would be most unusual that, under the circumstances, he would fail to tell me about something as important as a surrogate parentage agreement. This is most unusual," Kincade repeated, shaking his head. "But, but, . . . " For the first time in years, Kincade was totally surprised, and unable to reply.

Kincade turned momentarily to take a portable phone handed to him without a word by his secretary. "Excuse me for a minute," Kincade said to Yee. "Yes, at eight, yes, two, smoking, of course." Kincade handed the portable phone back to his secretary, then continued. "I'm afraid I can't honor these documents," he defiantly told Yee.

"I don't see why not. Surrogate contracts are . . . "

"You can stop right there, Ms. Yee. I said, I see no

reason to honor this ridiculous document. What part of 'NO' don't you understand? It's obviously not authentic. If you disagree, then you can call for a child custody hearing. But until that time, no goddamn way," he said, angrily shaking his head. Kincade was interrupted again by his secretary holding the portable phone. "Who is it this time? I really can't be interrupted with non-urgent calls just now, please."

"It's a call for Ms. Yee," the secretary said, a worried look on her face. "It's Mr. Ramirez," she added as she handed the phone to Yee.

Yee calmly took the phone from the secretary, listened for a few minutes, then said, "Yes. No. Yes, he's right here with me. No, he didn't say where the child is. Wait a minute and I'll ask." Yee looked sternly at Kincade, then asked him again, "Where is the child Ephrim Vernor now?"

"I don't see how that concerns you." The mention of Ramirez's involvement shocked Kincade, and made him wonder just who the prospective adoptive parents really were. He didn't know of too many Ramirez's, and wondered if it was judge Lydia Ramirez. Could Ramirez be involved, perhaps even be the adoptive parent? He quickly dismissed the thought as ridiculous.

Yee relayed to her caller Kincade's response, then said, "That is most unprofessional, Mr. Kincade," her own anger now beginning to show. "And also most unwise."

She said good-bye to her caller and handed the phone back to Kincade. Yee sat straight in her chair, displaying no emotion whatever while she waited for Kincade's next move.

"Oh, you think so? Well, I think this secret surrogate parentage arrangement for Ephrim is bizarre. Baatard will only get that child over my dead body," Kincade said with a mock in his voice. As he said it, those very words rang with a haunting hollowness to them. "Frankly, I'm surprised that you would have anything to do with arranged adoptions either. Good day, Ms. Yee," Kincade said as he quickly got up and showed Yee to the door. Worried now about being the next victim, Kincade called a friend of his in the police department who was interested in the Vernor case.

Moments later, Detective Bruce Mitchell took Kincade's call.

Chapter 53

Home of Marina Bonnaserra

Usually a sound sleeper, Marina awoke suddenly in the early morning hours, torn from a deep sleep, certain she had heard an unexpected sound. Lying there alone in the darkness, all appeared quiet, peaceful. The sun had not risen yet, occasional cricket chirps interrupted the quiet country darkness, and the curtains moved gently with a light breeze. She could hear the reassuring sound of Austin's soft breathing in the crib next to her bed, oblivious, in his innocence, to all of life's problems. She again vowed to not put off for another day getting a security system installed.

The dimmed red indicator on the bedside radio flashed 4 a.m., hours before her usual time to get up. Marina continued to lie motionless, listening, and heard only the occasional rustle of wind. Still feeling an ill-defined anxiety, she got up and walked around the house, checking the doors and closing all the windows, listening, listening. All seemed quiet now, and reassured, she returned to bed. Then, just as she drifted off to sleep, she heard it again: a high-pitched cry, like that of a small animal, a painful, sharp, a piercing cry, a cry hauntingly devoid of words, only sound, and then in an instant it was again gone.

Only half awake, Marina turned in the darkness to Austin's crib next to her bed in the now-cramped room they both shared. Marina kept Austin within sight almost all the time. She switched on a small yellow night light, then, relieved that he was there, picked him up.

Austin seemed not too wet, but was rather warm. Marina took Austin's temperature with a small electronic thermometer. It read 100.3 degrees - a mildly elevated temperature. Now quite awake, Marina immediately gave Austin some acetaminophen drops.

Austin seemed better at first, but when Marina lay him back down he rolled over in the crib and threw up the pink medicine she had just given him. Thoughts of ear infections and meningitis floated around in her head, memories and fears from her own childhood. She cleaned up his face, changed his diaper, and gave him some apple juice in a bottle to cool him down. Then Marina called Haven General's Emergency Room, hoping to speak with the on-call doctor. The nurse advised Marina it would be best to bring Austin in rather than ask anyone to attempt making a diagnosis over the phone.

Her mind went back to her son, lying crying next to her. She worried he might have something seriously wrong. Again, she tried giving Austin more acetaminophen; this time, fortunately, he kept the liquid pain reliever down.

Marina bundled up Austin, placed him securely in a

car seat, and drove over to Haven General Hospital. She signed him into the emergency room, the only clinic open that early in the morning. She would have preferred going in to meet Dr. Ryder Vernor instead of a complete stranger, but that was of course impossible. After waiting a short amount of time, Austin was examined by an older, disgruntled doctor named Dr. Victor Frank, who seemed to be in a hurry even though the waiting room was almost empty. "It's a virus," he mumbled to Marina, obviously in a bad mood. "It's nothing serious; use Tylenol every four hours and call me if there's a problem." Dr. Frank grudgingly reassured Marina, then mumbled good-bye as he walked out the ER door.

With a negative personality like that, Victor Frank has no right to see patients, Marina thought. She had similarly concluded, even without a medical degree, that Austin had a viral illness. Yet, she was happy to have been reassured, and gladly put Austin back in his car seat and drove home.

Her phone was already ringing when she arrived home shortly before 9 a.m. It was Vena Kleinman, and she sounded very upset. "Marina, I hate to bother you, but something terrible has happened and I had to talk to someone."

Marina thought Vena to be the last person to want to confide in her. They managed to get along, but she felt certain Vena wasn't all that fond of her. She thought it probably was because of her rather judgmental attitude, an attitude Marina realized she of all people really had no right to assume. Lately, Marina felt anything but morally superior.

"You probably won't believe this, but Charlie Kincade, Ryder's lawyer just called. Baatard is claiming he has legal custody of Ryder's son, Ephrim."

"I don't understand. How could Baatard claim that?" Marina asked. This came as a total surprise, and was most odd.

"Apparently Baatard says Lissa Vernor's pregnancy was part of a surrogate parentage agreement, and he has legal custody of Ephrim."

"Didn't Dr. Vernor tell you about this surrogate parentage agreement?" The whole idea sounded preposterous, bizarre.

"No, not at all," Vena told her.

"It doesn't make sense to me. I can't imagine Dr. Baatard would even want to adopt Ephrim. After all, I don't think he's married or has the time for children." A picture of her last visit to Lissa Vernor, lying comatose in a convalescent hospital, suddenly came to her mind, and she felt very uncomfortable.

She somehow couldn't picture Baatard with a newborn child. And if he wanted one, well, he could just as easily have arranged adoption through The Conceptions Foundation or some other more conventional method. Unless, there was something special about this child Ephrim Vernor. She wondered for a moment what that could be.

"I don't know anything about Dr. Baatard's personal

life, but Charlie thinks Dr. Baatard may simply be acting as an intermediary, and not as the actual adopting parent."

"Me neither. What does Mr. Kincade advise you to do?" Marina asked. Certainly, Charlie would never agree to anything as preposterous as this.

"Mr. Kincade is asking for a formal custody hearing. He thinks this whole thing makes no sense whatsoever."

"Good for him. I couldn't agree more. I'm sure Dr. Vernor would have discussed with you something as important as this, unless . . ." She had another idea, outrageous as it may have been.

"Unless what?" Vena asked.

"Unless he didn't know about it. I mean, maybe the agreement was between Mrs. Vernor and Dr. Baatard." Marina wondered for a moment if Baatard could really be the father, knowing how Lissa used to sleep around, then chided herself for having such a mean thought.

"How could this surrogate adoption agreement be valid unless Ryder knew and agreed to it also," Vena objected? "After all, Ryder was the father, wasn't he?"

Marina chose not to voice any doubts she had. Even Lissa's tastes must have had their limits.

"Ryder would have to agree with this too, wouldn't he? But why would he have done that? No, Marina, Ryder never made any such agreement, that much I can say for sure."

"And you say he didn't discuss this at all?" Marina

was more certain than ever that something very unusual surrounded the circumstances of Ephrim Vernor's birth, something that made him very, very special. From what little she had seen of Ephrim, though, she couldn't imagine what that might have been. He seemed simply a normal baby boy, much like her own Austin.

"No. Not at all. As a matter of fact, Ryder just recently suggested the exact opposite," Vena said.

"What exactly do you mean?" Marina asked.

"Ryder was very upset and yelled at someone on the phone the day before he died. At the time, I wondered if the argument was related to Ephrim."

"Oh, why was that?" Marina asked.

"Ryder mentioned a 'contract,' one he wanted out of."

Marina planned to mention this last bit of information to Charlie Kincade as soon as possible, just in case Vena had somehow forgotten to.

"Marina, I'm terrified. You know, I'm Ephrim's only remaining guardian. With Lissa in a coma, and Ryder dead, maybe I'm marked for death next."

"I doubt that anyone is marked for death, Vena. Please try to stay calm and not let your imagination run away with you. As far as we know, Lissa's stroke was the result of a surgical bleed, and Ryder's death was also accidental, possibly a heart attack." Marina was not at all sure of this herself, and knew Vena wasn't either. "I agree, though, that you do need to be as careful as possible for the foreseeable future, for your sake as well as for that of Ephrim. And I'm going to call Charlie Kincade about this right now."

Chapter 54

Haven General Hospital

At 11:00 in the morning, Dr. Damon Baatard, accompanied by his attorney Ellen Yee, filed into the Executive Conference room at Haven General Hospital. The meeting room was on the main floor, next to the auditorium where Baatard often sat in on Conceptions Foundation seminars. Baatard would have preferred the former reason for being there, or any other reason than a QA hearing for that matter. He seethed with anger that anyone would be so insolent as to accuse him of culpability in a bad surgical outcome.

Dr. Rubin was already present at the meeting, seated along with the chiefs of the Medical, Obstetrical, Nursing and other Departments, the hospital attorney Lemar Jackson, Charlie Kincade and Dr. Rubin's secretary. Marina Bonnaserra represented the QA Department. Dr. Quinnan in this case had to represent the Surgery Department, as the Chief of Surgery was also the Chair of this meeting. Baatard recognized them all, the self-appointed little gods each one, seated around the extended rectangular mahogany table like disciples at the last supper, and pointed them out to Yee. Apparently she already knew some of them, a fact which didn't escape Baatard. Baatard wasn't sure who represented Christ, but he was certain who was being proposed for crucifixion.

The chiefs of the other services all nodded curt and formal greetings to Baatard, but unlike other occasions none came forward to speak with him. Today, they preferred to sit in a glum, detached silence rather than be accused of harboring bias toward a 'colleague'. Baatard found it all too disgustingly proper and distant for his liking.

After everyone made their introductions, Lemar Jackson, the hospital attorney spoke. "Good morning, ladies and gentlemen. Dr. Rubin and the Board of Governors of Haven General Hospital welcome you. We appreciate your willingness to volunteer your time and expertise and thank you for attending this meeting. The hospital Office of Quality Assurance, under the direction of nurse Marina Bonnaserra, has convened this meeting. You, as peers of Dr. Damon Baatard, a trusted member of the hospital staff, are called here to review the unfortunate outcome of the Lissa Vernor case."

"Excuse me," Yee interrupted, raising her hand.

"Yes, Ms. Yee?" Jackson said, already feeling a touch of anticipatory exasperation. "You really haven't given me a chance to even finish my opening remarks."

"Did I understand you to mean that Ms. Bonnaserra decided on her own to convene this meeting?" Yee persisted, waiving her open hand around the room at all the participants. Then, her voice dripping with sarcasm, Yee noted, "I'm amazed she has such wisdom and power."

"No, of course not," Rubin anxiously replied, interrupting Jackson. "Ms. Bonnaserra, in her capacity as Quality Assurance nurse, reviewed the case. She was one of several whose opinions went into calling this meeting. I also was one of those persons, as was Mr. Jackson and several others. These days, calling a meeting like this is almost mandatory after a bad surgical outcome and shouldn't be construed as our judgment of guilt or innocence, negligence or lack thereof."

"I see," Yee said, not seeming at all surprised at Rubin's comments.

"And I object to your referring to Dr. Baatard as a member, a trusted member, of the hospital staff," Kincade interrupted.

"But he is." Rubin interjected, "And please don't interrupt like that, either you or Ms. Yee."

"That's your opinion and prejudices the opinions of those present," Kincade said.

"Ms. Yee, Mr. Kincade," Rubin said sternly, "let me remind you that you're both here as observers, and that this isn't a court of law. This is a fact-finding meeting only. And I really want to keep the proceedings on track so we can all get out of here in a timely manner."

"As for your question about Ms. Bonnaserra, no, she didn't make the decision to convene this meeting on her own," Jackson said, confirming Rubin's comments. "But I do intend to get to that part, if you'll just be patient and let me." Jackson turned back to address the Chiefs of the different hospital services. "All adverse occurrences are reviewed at this and every certified medical center. The Lissa Vernor case is being treated no differently than any other QA review."

"I certainly hope so," Baatard leaned over and grumbled to Yee. He was confident his care of Lissa Vernor would be vindicated and he would eventually be found not to have committed any acts of commission or omission that led to her unfortunate outcome. It was Ryder Vernor's death that worried him.

Baatard's thoughts were interrupted by Jackson. "This meeting is being held in accordance with the Haven General Hospital official rules and regulations, Section 4, Subsection 2. I believe you were all provided copies of the hospital regulations, the medical chart in question, and other pertinent material several weeks in advance for your reading." Jackson held up his voluminous package of papers as an example.

Everyone nodded yes, most holding or opening stacks of documents arrayed in front of them.

Dr. Rubin spoke next. "As we all are more than aware, this meeting is called to discuss the extensive investigation on the unfortunate outcome of the surgery of Mrs. Lissa Vernor. Mrs. Vernor is the wife of the recently deceased Dr. Ryder Vernor, former staff physician here at Haven General Hospital. She is, of course, unable to attend because of her disability. Ms. Vernor is being represented by attorney Charlie Kincade, who is also her legal guardian." Rubin nodded in Kincade's direction and forced a polite smile. Kincade nodded back and returned a thumbs-up sign.

"Dr. Rubin, Dr. Rubin," Yee called out.

"Yes, Ms. Yee?"

"I want to point out there's no relationship between the injury suffered by Mrs. Vernor to which you just referred and any actions taken by Dr. Baatard."

"Well, Ms. Yee, that's just what we are going to discuss here today. I can neither agree nor disagree with you just yet. Now, before I read the conclusions of the internal investigation, is there anything anyone would like to say?" asked Rubin, furtively looking around the room, trying to avoid obviously looking into eyes and thereby inciting a positive response.

Everyone looked nervously around at each other, shaking their heads to indicate 'no.'

Kincade took exception to this, raised his hand and told everyone, "I think these entire proceedings are suspect and any results that you may present today are irrelevant." He was surprised to notice Yee nodding agreement, which worried him.

"How can you possibly know that, Mr. Kincade? You haven't even heard what I'm going to say," Rubin exclaimed, obviously irritated.

"Perhaps counselor is clairvoyant?" Yee sneered.

"The case has gone way beyond Lissa Vernor," Kincade said. "One of my clients is in a coma because of the actions of Dr. Baatard." Yee yelled out "I object," but

Kincade insistently argued forward. He wanted to forcefully state his position before things progressed out of hand. This was, after all, Baatard's turf. "My client's husband has died unexpectedly, also in suspicious circumstances, and also involving Dr. Baatard. And now Dr. Baatard claims to own their child. What is this, the Mafia?" Charlie waved his hands in the air, and then sat back down.

"Dr. Rubin, I most strenuously object," Yee shouted out. "We find these remarks slanderous to my client's good name and reputation and most prejudicial to the outcome of these proceedings."

"Mr. Kincade and Ms. Yee, will you please sit down and quit interrupting these proceedings," Rubin said. "This is neither a court of law nor a police investigation. It is merely a fact-finding body, part of the quality assurance proceeding. It's designed to improve future care by identifying better ways of delivering medical services. It's simply that. We are here to learn from our mistakes."

"I object," Yee screamed, "to your insinuation my client could have delivered 'better' care or that he may have made a mistake." Rubin groaned, "Oh, for God's sake," but Yee persisted. "No one has established that the care given to Lissa Vernor was deficient or that different care would have affected the outcome of Ms. Vernor's treatment. No one has shown that a mistake, as you so unfortunately put it, occurred at all."

"Okay, okay, Miss Yee," Jackson said, "we get your point."

"Ms.," Yee corrected him.

"I think Dr. Rubin meant 'Different care'. Dr. Rubin?

. . ." Jackson asked, waiting for a confirmatory clarification.

"Yes, precisely," Rubin said, choking nervously while drinking some water. "I meant different care."

"Now, you have not established different care by Dr. Baatard and all the others caring for Lissa Vernor would have been more appropriate or would have resulted in a more favorable outcome," Yee explained. "At this point, this is merely idle speculation on your part and Ms. Bonnaserra's, and I find it most objectionable. We have no intention of letting any unjustified remarks or insinuations harm the good professional name or career of Dr. Damon Baatard."

Baatard, obviously impressed, flashed an appreciative smile at Yee.

"Okay, Ms. Yee," Jackson said. "Look, no implication was intended. And, let Dr. Rubin and me remind you, Dr. Baatard may be your client outside these doors, but in here, as far as we're concerned, you're just an observer. And that goes for you too, Mr. Kincade. These aren't legal proceedings, and you have no role here other than as an invited observer." Jackson sternly looked at Yee as if to say 'understand' but neither said anything.

Much open discussion broke out between the people at the hearing, and Dr. Rubin had to take several minutes to restore quiet and order.

Kincade stood up, put his hands on his hips, looked

piercingly at Baatard and continued, "I was simply pointing out that Dr. Baatard was the physician under whose care Lissa Vernor severely bled and had a devastating stroke." Kincade thrust out a pointed finger at Baatard, and said, "Dr. Baatard was also present when Lissa's husband, Dr. Ryder Vernor died. I may not be a forensic scholar, but the events look like they could be connected. Don't you agree, Dr. Rubin," Kincade asked, looking around at everyone in the room to further emphasize his point? Again, Rubin had to take several minutes to quiet down the heated discussion which followed these accusations.

"I also just learned my clients' newly borne child is involved in a custody battle with Dr. Baatard." Gasps arose throughout the room, followed by astonished stares at Baatard and nervous and subdued discussion. Kincade observed that this was not general knowledge. Kincade watched Rubin slouch down in his oversized lounge chair which he had moved into the room. Rubin looked uncomfortably at Baatard and Yee, apparently about to say something. "Did you know about that, Dr. Rubin?" Charlie pressed for an answer.

Rubin appeared confused and startled at Kincade's pressing the question. He once again looked over at Baatard and then to Jackson, as if seeking help. "No, no, I guess I didn't," Rubin admitted.

"Doesn't this all seem strange and suspect to you, Dr. Rubin?" Kincade asked, sweeping his hands over the entire room.

Rubin leaned over to his left to confer with the hospital attorney. After whispering between themselves for several minutes, and pointing back and forth to Kincade, Baatard and Yee, Rubin spoke. "I can only comment on the facts which have been presented to me on the Lissa Vernor case, Mr. Kincade. I have no legal interest in any extraneous matters, and I can only suggest that if you have questions, that you should direct them to the police. Now, to continue, I . . . "

"I've done just that," Kincade interrupted.

"Good. Now, to continue. After several weeks of investigation, and hundreds of hours of effort on the parts of many different doctors and nurses, we are prepared to review our conclusions. First, the Department of Surgery will speak."

Dr. Quinnan picked up some papers and began to address the group. "I'm the Assistant Chief of the Surgery Department." He droned on for almost half an hour, reviewing the care of Ms. Vernor, the complications, and outlined all the records reviewed and who made the reviews. Finally, he announced, "We have determined that Dr. Baatard's care of Lissa Vernor, from a surgical standpoint, although of an unfortunate outcome, was appropriate and without error."

Baatard flashed a satisfied smile at Yee, but avoided looking at anyone else.

"Thank you Dr. Quinnan," Dr. Rubin continued. "Dr. Baatard is a member of the Haven General Hospital Department of Obstetrics and Gynecology. To avoid the appearance of bias or conflict of interest, we asked an outside gynecological surgeon, one not affiliated with our medical center or with Dr. Baatard, to examine the records."

"Dr. Rubin, Dr. Rubin," Kincade interrupted.

"Yes, Mr. Kincade."

"Who selected this outside consultant?"

Rubin conferred again with the hospital attorney, Jackson, then replied, "The outside consultant was selected by mutual agreement between Attorney Yee, Dr. Baatard's malpractice carrier, and the state Medical Society." After waiting for any objections from Kincade, Rubin continued. "Unfortunately, that consultant couldn't be here today due to prior commitments, so I'll read her report." Rubin looked in Kincade's direction to see if there were any objections. Surprised to find Kincade silent, Rubin quickly opened the sealed report. He leafed through a few pages, then said, "Yes, here it is under the Conclusions section: The consultant's report is that Dr. Baatard acted in an appropriate manner, and she could find no fault in the gynecological care Lissa Vernor received."

"Of course she received good care," Baatard said, shifting nervously in his chair. He looked at Quinnan, who smiled and gave a thumbs up sign in return. With his peers beginning to line up in his corner again, Baatard began to feel better about the proceedings.

"Dr. Baatard, please hold your comments until the proceedings are complete," Rubin admonished.

Rubin recognized the irritating, grating speech, "Dr. Rubin, Dr. Rubin," coming from his left side and asked,

"Yes, Mr. Kincade?"

"I've not seen most of these documents. I need a copy of all these reports today."

"These are confidential hospital documents, and I'll need to take your request up with the hospital legal counsel, Mr. Kincade," Rubin said.

"But, the hospital legal counsel is right here," Kincade said, pointing to Jackson, "sitting right next to you. Let's get the opinion now, shall we?"

Jackson looked over at Rubin, then said, "Hey, wait a minute, not so fast. I need some time to consider the legal implications of this complex case, Mr. Kincade. This will take several weeks, yes, several weeks at least. I'm sure you'll appreciate . . . "

"Yeah, yeah," Kincade sighed. "I would have at least thought it appropriate for me to review these pertinent expert testimonies . . . "

"This isn't a court of law, and these are expert opinions, not testimony," Jackson corrected Kincade.

Rubin cleared his throat, stiffly straightened the papers held out in front of him with a snap, then continued. "The Department of Medicine has reviewed the records, particularly from the standpoint of the bleeding and the initial illness which brought Lissa into the hospital, and we'll hear from them next."

A thin young man of ruddy complexion, wearing a turban, introduced as a Dr. Chandar, spoke up. He first quietly looked around the room, surveying the faces, then in a low but confident voice spoke. "The Department of Internal Medicine was asked to review the Lissa Vernor case from the standpoint of the bleeding and the high hormone levels. We could find no evidence of tumor, bleeding disorder, or other definite medical condition which might explain all the findings. We have found no error in the preoperative evaluation or in the preoperative care, from a strictly medical standpoint, that the patient received. In addition, we can find no error in the postoperative care the patient received, again from a strictly medical standpoint."

"Why do you keep emphasizing 'from a strictly medical standpoint'?" Kincade asked.

"It is simple," Dr. Chandar replied. "Because we are not surgeons. Now, to continue. Our main thought here is that it was unfortunate more blood was not available for the patient."

"But I did request it, and I even personally intervened to get some," Baatard interrupted.

"Yes, we noted that. Thank you, Dr. Baatard," Chandar said. "Now, our conclusion is that although no definite etiology has been established, the case is most consistent with ovarian hyper-stimulation syndrome, OHSS."

There was a great deal of conversation generated by this last finding, prompting Rubin to speak. "This OHSS is a very rare syndrome. Until I read the report from the Department of Medicine I can't remember ever hearing of it." Rubin smiled and looked around him, leaning over the wide table stuffed into the small conference room.

Baatard stared in amazement at Rubin when he heard the word OHSS. He winced and shifted his position in the wooden chair, coming to rest at an angle, leaning against one of the chair's solid wooden arms. The chair squeaked as Baatard moved around and caused several people to stare at Baatard each time he moved.

"Apparently, your suspicion of OHSS is based upon an unusually high level of hormones in Lissa's blood. Is that correct?" Rubin continued.

Chandar replied, "Yes, it is, although OHSS also is consistent with the total symptom complex. Of course, we'll never know for sure, but this is our best assessment of what may have happened."

Rubin then put down his papers, rested his hands on the table top and said to the group, "In speaking with Dr. Baatard, I've learned the patient was taking hormone therapy."

Turning to Baatard, Kincade said, "This is very new to me." Kincade leaned down to look at some papers, then said, "Was Lissa Vernor being evaluated for infertility? Was she being treated by Dr. Baatard?"

Dr. Rubin interrupted, looked pleadingly at Kincade and told him, "Please, Mr. Kincade. This isn't a court of law, and the rules of evidence and examination aren't being followed here. We aren't here to cross-examine physicians who aren't on trial. You agreed beforehand your presence here would be only as an observer."

"I thought the expert reports may have pointed to the existence of a tumor or some genetic condition," Kincade offered.

"Mr. Kincade," Baatard replied, in a condescending manner, "as I said before, there was no evidence of a tumor at the surgery. This is a matter for physicians, not for attorneys, who typically know little of the intricacies of medicine. And since my patient, . . . "

"Lissa Vernor isn't, I believe, your patient, Dr. Baatard," Kincade interrupted. "I was told by a Ms. Vena Vernor, and independently by a Nurse Peoples at Haven Convalescent Hospital, that the care of Lissa Vernor was transferred." As soon as he said those words, he regretted it. He didn't want Baatard to know he had been speaking with Vena or Peoples. Now, Baatard would undoubtedly intervene and poison these sources from future use. "Dr. Vernor, when he was still alive, changed his wife's care to Dr. Hernandez."

"That's true. While she isn't currently my patient - not due to any choice of hers, I might add - I still think of her as such. Besides, I was referring to her when she was my patient. And just who the hell is Vena Vernor?" Baatard demanded.

Kincade looked embarrassed, glanced over at Dr. Rubin, then explained, "Sorry. I meant Vena Kleinman, Dr. Ryder Vernor's receptionist. She was given custody of the Ryder child by Dr. Vernor."

"I have custody of the Vernor child." Baatard interjected. "But, back to the reason we are here, I can't discuss so openly the care I was giving to my former patient without her consent," Baatard angrily finished.

"How the hell is she going to consent when she's in a coma," Kincade blurted out, exasperated. He considered whether now might be a good time to pressure Baatard, make him lose his confidence by bringing up his problems with BMQA, then decided instead to hold that card until he really needed it.

"Dr. Baatard, would you please explain to this group why Lissa Vernor was taking hormone treatments?" Rubin asked, trying to diffuse an argument. "I think that would be helpful and would not reveal any confidential medical information. And Mr. Kincade, will you please watch your language."

"Yes, I'll explain that," Baatard told Rubin, certain this would come out eventually. "Lissa wanted to become pregnant. She sought me, in my position with The Conceptions Foundation, to evaluate the difficulty she was experiencing conceiving."

"And what did you find out?" Rubin asked.

Baatard leaned over and conferred with Yee for several minutes. After some additional arguments between them, Baatard replied to Rubin's question. "I could find nothing physiologically wrong with Mrs. Vernor. Sometimes, a trial of hormone stimulation helps in some nonspecific way to increase fertility. That was what she was receiving. That accounts for the elevated hormone levels."

"Well, from the look of your face, Dr. Baatard, I

would think the term OHSS means something special to you," Kincade quipped.

"Yes, in retrospect, the unexplained hemorrhage could have been caused by OHSS. It's a very rare complication of hormone treatment, and can involve oozing of blood and body fluids into various body cavities. Nevertheless, my looking for a specific source of bleeding was appropriate. I couldn't assume that zebras were coming when I heard hoof beats."

"I'm sorry," Kincade spoke up. "What zebras? What are you talking about, Dr. Baatard?"

"It's an old medical expression. It means common problems are common. That is to say, in this instance, if you see blood, look for bleeding, not oozing or something else equally obscure."

"And several other experts have agreed with this action of my client," interjected Yee.

"I couldn't assume there was a generalized oozing. I had to look for a source," Baatard repeated. "And as for the care Lissa received, well, that too was most appropriate for hemorrhage in general, and OHSS in particular. We gave her volume support, and blood. When Mrs. Vernor exhausted our blood bank's supply, and more couldn't be obtained, I personally intervened with the director of the blood bank so more blood became available. And it was."

"There, you see, all the experts have agreed that Dr. Baatard's actions in behalf of Lissa Vernor were appropriate. I think perhaps the Haven General QA nurse had a bias against my client in bringing this unwarranted investigation," Yee said.

"Just what do you mean by that?" Jackson asked.

"Just this. Are you aware that the Haven General QA nurse is emotionally involved with the attorney for Lissa Vernor?"

"Wait a minute," Marina shouted at Yee. "That's just not true at all."

"I think otherwise, Ms. Bonnaserra." Turning to Dr. Rubin, Yee demanded to know, "Could Nurse Bonnaserra be passing confidential hospital documents to Attorney Kincade?"

"Oh, no, of course not," Rubin said as he shrugged his head innocently, and quickly looked away. The stare he made into Marina's eyes, searching for confirmation, belied his certainty.

"By this, I am referring to documents which were slanderous, confidential, privileged information, and in violation of hospital procedures," Yee said.

Kincade and Rubin both gave an embarrassed and confused glance at Marina.

Rubin and Marina had a discussion between them, then Rubin asked for a short break. He motioned for Jackson, Marina and Kincade to follow him out of the room. Several minutes later they returned, and without explaining what they had discussed, Rubin asked for the proceedings to continue.

"What did you discuss out there without me?" Yee asked Rubin.

"We talked about procedural issues only, Ms. Yee. We'll be sure to try and include you in on appropriate discussions in the future," Jackson said, then added, "circumstances allowing, of course. However, we have no reason to think that Ms. Bonnaserra's former relationship with Mr. Kincade influenced in any way the QA proceedings."

Kincade and Bonnaserra were both too embarrassed to say anything at this point.

Yee, too, seemed unwilling to press her point. "Dr. Rubin, I'm prepared to summarize my client's presentation," Yee said.

"Look, Ms. Yee," Rubin interrupted, "this isn't a court and your client isn't on trial. This is a formal hospital proceeding, and you're here only as a guest and advisor to Dr. Baatard. I'm afraid there's no place here for you to present any summation."

"I'm aware of that, Dr. Baatard," Yee angrily replied, "but . . . "

"As far as we're concerned, Dr. Baatard isn't your client. There's no provision in the hospital rules and regulations for you to present anything at such a proceeding as this, and, therefore, only Dr. Baatard will be allowed to speak."

"But, Dr. Rubin, . . . " Yee protested.

"No, Miss. Yee. No." Jackson sternly repeated. "Now, if you have something to say in summation, Dr. Baatard, please do so now." Jackson momentarily winced when he remembered Yee wanted to be called Ms. Yee, but said nothing when Yee seemed to ignore this.

"I just want to emphasize my care of Lissa Vernor

was appropriate," Baatard summarized. "I'm sorry she suffered so severe a complication, I really am, but I didn't cause the bleeding problem in the first place, I treated Lissa Vernor appropriately, both in surgery and after, and although her outcome was unfortunate, that wasn't due to any action or lack of action on my part." Baatard leaned back in his chair, having made his point.

Rubin nodded his head, then announced that the committee would have a short private meeting. Yee, Kincade and Baatard were asked to leave the room, and once out, Baatard and Yee moved off to the opposite side of the room from Kincade.

Kincade sat down on a wooden bench, and quietly looked at a stack of papers. Baatard nervously tried to extract Yee's opinion on how the proceedings were going, but she seemed distant as she excused herself and headed off to the Lady's Room. After they were out of the room for twenty minutes, Jackson asked them back in.

"The Quality Assurance Committee convened to evaluate the case of Lissa Vernor is now prepared to present its conclusions," Dr. Rubin said. "The committee finds that the actions taken by Dr. Damon Baatard were appropriate. There will be no further internal investigations on the Lissa Vernor case. There are no adverse effects on the hospital rights or privileges of Dr. Baatard."

When Rubin finished talking, a general discussion

broke out between everyone present. Baatard hugged Yee, then got up to shake the hands of all the consultants present, and the hands of Rubin and Jackson.

"Dr. Rubin, Dr. Rubin?" Kincade asked, waving his hand.

"Yes?" Rubin replied, annoyed with himself for not keeping the meeting organized and directed. He wanted to show that he was in control, and now, he reflected, he had not done that.

"Here you have it, Dr. Rubin," Kincade said. "Dr. Baatard is telling us Lissa Vernor wanted to get pregnant. Yet, he has provided no information that would lead us to understand why she would want to go through all this trouble, and then give up her baby for adoption. I think this is an inherent contradiction, and leaves a major gap in Dr. Baatard's testimony. This is not something a woman would do at all."

Although the meeting was officially over, Kincade's remarks had a certain compelling logic to them which could not just be dismissed. Taken aback, Rubin conferred with Jackson, then asked for a short recess, leaving the room with Jackson and Yee. They returned in a few minutes.

"Mr. Kincade," Jackson said, "let me repeat that this committee is restricting itself to the care Ms. Vernor received under the direction of Dr. Baatard while she was a patient in this hospital. We cannot consider other matters. It is BEYOND the mandate of this committee."

Kincade angrily shook his head, then interrupted again, "One other thing, Dr. Baatard. I'm not a medical type person, you know, so bear with me."

"Of course, Mr. Kincade," Baatard said. He impatiently looked at Rubin, wondering why, after ending the meeting, Rubin allowed it to continue.

"I take it since you said OHSS is rare, that few people get it."

"That's correct. I'm not sure I've ever seen a case," Baatard commented.

"Well then, Dr. Baatard," Kincade said, walking over to where Baatard was seated. "What could induce it, I mean, what could bring on something so rare?"

"Hum," Baatard said, thinking for a moment, before replying, "that's a good question." He looked momentarily in Yee's direction, saw her narrowed eyes unmistakably urging him not to speculate, then quickly added, "Although I can understand the Department of Medicine's opinion that OHSS was consistent with Mrs. Vernor's elevated hormone levels, a definitive etiology probably never will be known." Glancing in Yee's direction again, she appeared approving and relieved.

Rubin and Jackson turned to each other, Jackson nodded in a way which indicated that further questioning was unnecessary and unlikely to be helpful, then Rubin hurriedly spoke. "Yes, well I suppose that's so, Dr. Baatard. Well, I want to thank everyone for meeting here today. The official findings of the QA Committee stand. I officially adjourn this meeting."

Yee and Baatard both cast negative looks on Marina

as they passed close to her on their way out of the meeting room. Yee's was one of pity, but Baatard's was one of betrayal, and hatred, pure and simple.

Once at home after the hearings, Marina nearly collapsed into the couch. She was totally exhausted from all the arguments and only wanted to relax. This was the most detailed, pressured, involved QA case in which she had ever been involved, and she was glad it was finally over.

Austin evidently had a hard day in the nursery, and he too was very tired. After a small meal and a new dry diaper, he fell asleep early.

Marina poured herself a glass of iced cappuccino from a bottle she had chilling in her frig, went into the living room and opened the new issue of Art Today which had just arrived in the mail. The front cover featured a reproduction of the Mona Lisa, altered with a strange, knowing smile and a wink. Underneath was the caption "Mona Lisa exposed." Marina turned the page and read an article about an art historian who proposed Da Vinci was really a transsexual whose bizarre habits included cross-dressing. The woman Da Vinci painted, the author claimed, was Da Vinci himself dressed in drag.

Marina thought the article, although provocative, was also quite preposterous. Da Vinci may have based Mona Lisa's face upon his, and simply altered the facial characteristics slightly. It was a technique she knew artists to sometimes employ, but she knew a woman when she saw one painted, and Mona Lisa was definitely a woman, not an altered man's face. Marina put down the magazine and went back to her studio to do a little painting to soothe herself before going to bed.

Chapter 55

Office of Dr. Damon Baatard

It was half past three the next afternoon, and Charlie Kincade had been waiting impatiently for over a half hour in Baatard's small reception area. Acting on a hunch, Kincade wanted to talk to Baatard some more; there was something about the Lissa Vernor case that didn't seem quite right. Oh, he had heard the presentations at the QA hearing and the board's conclusion that Baatard's care of Lissa seemed without fault. He understood as much as any nonmedical professional could. With the QA committee's findings on record, a malpractice action would not likely be successful. But still, there was something about Lissa's infertility treatment that didn't add up.

Kincade had considered it quite possible Baatard would not agree to see him without Yee being present, especially after the QA hearing yesterday at Haven General. And he did, after all, represent as legal guardian Lissa Vernor, and was legal representative for Vena

Kleinman and her custody of Ephrim Vernor. Kincade had thought about calling Yee first to get permission to speak with her client, but instead decided to try this way. The employment of 'surprise' as an interrogative technique sometimes worked, and although visiting Baatard was technically inappropriate, it wasn't something over which he could lose his law license for. After all, Baatard wasn't accused of anything. Yet.

Kincade smiled impatiently at the one other person waiting with him in the reception room, a mother with a young infant. The woman appeared to be in her mid to late thirties, a little on the heavy side, wearing a plain-looking pantsuit. Kincade thought that her choice of clothes did nothing to show off the physical beauty he suspected lay underneath.

"Your child is miraculously quiet, Miss. . . ." Charlie said, trying to start a conversation.

"Yes, she is. She's sleeping, the little angel." The woman, who introduced herself to Kincade as Christine Milltown Lincoln, quietly explained she was also waiting to see Dr. Baatard.

Although fighting to appear serene on the outside, inside, Christine's mind reeled from the macabre ceremony she had again performed. Only a few years had passed since Garza had brought Christine into the clinic late after work, allowing Christine to view first-hand what devil-work Baatard and his colleagues performed, and it was shortly after that life-changing revelation that Christine began performing her sorrowful ceremony for the unborn dead. Christine had been shocked beyond words, far more than any evil she had ever seen or imagined could have existed.

Kincade was a little more anxious than usual, having missed a luncheon date with someone he had been trying to ask out for months. Yet, he had to admit that he really felt more sorry than interested in the woman he was meeting. She was an older woman, but one left with a pleasant figure and apparently eager to be compliant. He had nothing better going on now that Marina wasn't returning his calls.

Baatard rushed out into the reception area after about thirty minutes and apologized superficially for keeping Ms. Lincoln waiting. Kincade could tell from the look on Baatard's face that he was surprised and not at all pleased to find Kincade waiting in his office unannounced. Baatard nodded only briefly and superficially to Kincade, but said nothing to him at first. Instead, Kincade noticed a puzzled look develop on Baatard's face.

As Kincade got up to shake Baatard's hand, Christine Milltown Lincoln carefully put down her child carrier on the seat of the waiting room couch. Suddenly, she sprang up and lunged toward Baatard like a ravenous leopard, yelling "Murderer, baby killer. You killed my baby." Lincoln grabbed Baatard around the throat and pushed him against the wall, shaking loose some hanging paintings.

Baatard, momentarily startled, lifted his arms up close to his chest, trying unsuccessfully to break Lincoln's frenzied grasp around his neck. Reflexively, he tried to shield his face from Lincoln's hands. "Hey, what the hell's the matter, lady?" he cried out.

Baatard tried to move away from the attacker, but like a crazed maniac she held her grasp tightly on his neck. Red streaks formed on his skin where she had dug her nails deeply in. Baatard continued to struggle from her grasp, but when this failed, he managed to throw Christine Lincoln solidly back against the wall, breathless and exhausted.

Lincoln barely missed Kincade as she slammed hard against the opposite wall, hitting her head with a loud thud. "Murderer, baby killer." she continued to scream uncontrollably.

Building security, having been called by Baatard's receptionist, Sharlene, responded almost immediately. They grabbed Christine and started dragging her, kicking and screaming, from Baatard's office.

With Christine now under control, Baatard took a moment to try and regain his composure. Such insane disruption had never occurred before in his office, Baatard thought, as he anxiously scanned the waiting room. A very uncomfortable Kincade had picked up the baby carrier and backed out of the way and against the far wall. "For God sakes, Kincade, it's only an infant, not a rattle snake." Baatard chided him. "It won't bite you." Both men were surprised that the baby had not cried with all the noise and jostling that had just occurred.

Kincade gingerly moved the covers aside to look at the infant's face and see if it was all right. Baatard looked in over Kincade's shoulder. They were both astonished to find that the carrier contained only a baby doll.

One of the security guards yanked Christine's right hand behind her back. He used his knee to press her forward toward the hallway and ensure her compliance.

Lincoln yelled out a scream of pain and protest, shouting up at Baatard, "Go ahead, you bastard. Have me arrested. I want every woman to know what a murderer you are."

Baatard, considering all the damage adverse publicity could cause, hesitated, calling to the security guard, "No, wait, bring her back in here. I want to talk to her first before you take her in."

Surprised, the guard held back. Looking up at Baatard, the guard said, "Wait for what? We're getting her out of here before she causes any more problems."

"Listen lady," Baatard started, ignoring the guard's protest. "Are you out of your mind? What's the matter with you?"

Lincoln shook herself loose from the guard's grasp and stood up. "There's nothing wrong with me. It's you that is killing people. I demand that you stop murdering babies in your clinic."

"Look, I think that it would be a lot better if we both calmed down, particularly you. Why don't you go home and get yourself composed? Then you can come back here in a few days and we can talk things through."

Christine nervously shook her head "no."

"If you leave peacefully now, then I'll consider not pressing charges against you. Okay? What do you think about that?" He recognized that certain twisted, demented look on her face. She was crazy, all right, Baatard thought, crazy but dangerous.

Christine Lincoln looked disgustedly at Baatard, then glared at Kincade. "Are you a murderer like him?" she demanded of Kincade.

"Murderer? Me? No, no, not at all. I'm not even a doctor. I was just here to see him, and I know nothing about what you speak."

"But do you believe in abortions?" she pressed.

Kincade stared at Christine, then glanced back to Baatard, then looked back at Christine's angry face before saying, "Well, I, I believe in a woman's right to control her own body and I believe in reproductive freedom for all women," Kincade replied, almost too automatically. When the expression on Christine's face became even more disapproving and angry, he quickly added, "but I also believe in everyone's right to live."

"Humph. Then you're no better than him," a disappointed and apparently disgusted Christine told Kincade. "Just have him let me go."

"Okay," Baatard told the security guard. "But get her out of here. Take her completely outside the office building and let her go. I don't want to press charges. I only want her out of my office and out of the building. And take her name and address so you can prevent her from coming back in to cause a disturbance like this again." Turning to Lincoln, Baatard said, "I want you to go home and think over what you did here very carefully.

You have no right to assault me, and that's just what you did. You can't commit violence in the name of nonviolence. Go home now, before I call the police."

"You don't have the nerve to call the police, you murderer." Lincoln yelled back. "If I go to jail, then even more people will know about the monstrous things you're doing to women here. Just wait until I get out of here. I'm going to tell the state licensing board . . . "

"Wait," Baatard said to the guard, having finally been hit where it hurts. "I changed my mind. I think I will press charges."

"No, no," Lincoln pleaded. "Look, I wasn't serious about doing that. Let me go, just let me go, that's all I want. I made my point. Okay?"

"Screw you," Baatard sneered as he looked down at her. Turning to the guard, Baatard said, "Let the bitch go, but get her completely out of the building." Baatard leaned down to Lincoln's level and snarled into her face, "Look, I don't care who you are, but don't ever do this to me again. There's no telling what consequences this may bring, now, is there?" I'm going to kill this fucking bitch, Baatard fumed to himself.

Lincoln got up, quickly took her doll and infant seat from Kincade, and quietly left, to wait for other, better times to make her moral point. She could see that today's setback was only temporary and didn't discourage her in the least, her convictions were much too deep for that.

Still, as she walked out of the building, an agitated look covered her contorted face, and it was not one of shame or regret, but that inward disgust brought on by painful memories. Although Baatard apparently didn't remember, Christine went back to a time some seventeen years before, when she had been a patient at Central Haven Obstetrics and Gynecology.

Christine Lincoln was at that time only seventeen, but often was mistaken for being at least twenty. Christine, as she preferred to be called, rather than the boyish Chris, was one grade ahead of Marina in school, and the two were only remotely familiar with each other. Precocious experiences, the stress of too many yelling matches, the scar on one cheek from an angry slap never returned, all this had prematurely aged Christine Milltown Lincoln. Occasional insect bites on her arms and legs and abdomen attested to sleeping in unclean bed clothes. These also had scarred Christine Milltown Lincoln. As a finishing touch, the rotten scent and yellow discolor of tobacco stained her breath and teeth and permeated her skimpy clothing.

Paradoxically, Christine Milltown Lincoln at times also appeared barely twelve-years old. Particularly to an adult in the cold light of day, she had seemed more a child than a teenager. Christine's wide blue eyes held a certain amazement that an elective abortion could be happening to her at all, for a cause and effect had not been well established.

It was also Christine's second abortion in as many years. Abortions at over three months gestation were always complicated, and illegal, at least in those circumstances. Garza, an experienced nurse midwife in her mid-thirties back then, had known these facts well, as did the clinic's doctors. She had seen it all, and even considering Christine Milltown Lincoln, perhaps she had.

Lincoln's uncomplicated abortion had taken less than fifteen minutes, during which time she had been totally conscious and not sedated, decisions made on the basis of cost-containment and convenience. Neither was a choice she would have made, had she been asked, but she hadn't been. Fortunately, everything seemed to have gone well, except for a small amount of blood loss and some moderate pain, which had by now become a severe cramp. Bleeding from the uterus had been greater than expected, although not enough for the clinic's doctors to worry over.

Christine had stayed for over an hour in the 'recovery room,' a converted and expanded storage closet emptied and used by those not able or anxious enough to leave immediately. There, she had rested alone on a wire cot whose uncovered mattress bore innumerable dried blood, urine and saliva stains, and the imperceptibly faint marks of dried tears. And there, Christine thought seriously for the first time about what had just transpired. Now she would have time enough to consider it all - her unborn baby's death, her meaningless life, her terrible loneliness, all this, including suicide.

Several hours later, Christine felt strong enough to

have left the clinic, and was accompanied and supported by her older sister, Eunice, who also had been a client of the clinic before. As they neared the door, Eunice noticed fresh blood running in rivulets down Christine's inner thigh. Eunice began to call out to her sister, but Christine's body reacted faster to the chain of events. Drained of vital fluids, Christine had slumped over, unconscious, like a five-foot four rag doll, and folding over, she had hit her forehead sharply on the floor with a loud thump.

It had taken over a half hour for the ambulance to come for Christine and rush her to Haven General Hospital. The nurses and aides left behind at Central Haven Obstetrics and Gynecology had been very upset, and understandably so. Their carefully orchestrated routine - designed around the maximization of patient flow - was terribly interrupted. Finally, the ambulance had left, and the clinic could now be closed for the day. Christine Milltown Lincoln was once again someone else's problem.

Within minutes of the ambulance speeding away, the abortion doctors, Damon Baatard included, had fled for the day, rushing out to perform rounds on their private patients at private local hospitals. The next morning, their hospital visits would include Christine Milltown Lincoln.

Returning to the present, the elevator opened, ending Christine's painful dream, and an older and scared Christine was escorted out the front door by building security.

Chapter 56

After Christine Lincoln left his office, Baatard slowly straightened his jacket and tried to regain his composure before turning to Kincade. "I'm truly sorry for this, this . . . disturbance. It's never happened before, believe me. I guess I'll have to see you now." Baatard motioned Kincade into his office.

Once inside his office and seated, Kincade said to Baatard, "What was that all about? What was she saying about you being a murderer and reporting you to the State Board of Medical Examiners? What other kind of problems do you have, Baatard?" Kincade asked, glad to have to opportunity to bring it up.

"Look, it's not what you think." Baatard nervously played with a pen, clicking it open and closed, and turning it around in his hand. He adjusted his tie and sat up straighter in his chair before saying "You know, I perform, that is my associates and I occasionally perform abortions here, but not every day." The correct number was two to five, every day, but he chose not to say that. "Obviously, not everyone approves, but we just try to provide a service."

"I can see that. But what has that got to do with her?" Kincade had heard of abortion rights protesters disrupting doctor's offices, but had never been this close to an actual protest before. He could see how it could be very effective in intimidating other women, and also their doctors.

"I, I think I recognize her," Baatard continued. "She had, I think she had an abortion sometime in the past. I don't remember any complications occurring at the time, but obviously something terrible is really upsetting her."

Kincade nodded, but doubted Baatard was telling the whole story, or telling it accurately.

"You do understand, don't you, what pressures performing this procedure places on her, on us, on everyone." Baatard turned his twisted face to stare out the window. "This severe a guilt-ridden, violent reaction doesn't happen too often, but I can't help but think that maybe something else might have been bothering her."

"I'll say," Kincade replied, shaking his head.

"You can understand what a heavy emotional burden we all live with when making these decisions." Baatard forced a smile and tried to look reassuring to Kincade, who appeared to Baatard not impressed. "Anyway, I'm sure you didn't come all this way just to discuss another woman's abortion," he said, leaning over his desk top.

Kincade attempted to focus his thoughts, then said, "Well, yes, I did have something to ask you. Actually, I have just a few things to ask you. You certainly seem to know your field quite well, and I'm sure you've been doing this for some time."

"Almost twenty years, actually, counting

moonlighting time as a resident." When Kincade looked as if he didn't understand, Baatard said, "I did my obstetrics and gynecology residency right here at Haven General some twenty years ago. Every once in a while, most of the residents performed 'odd jobs' for local clinics. Much of that was humping in those tedious abortion mills. For a while, back then, I did a hell of a lot of abortions. I still do them, but the circumstances are much better, and the risks much less."

"Risks?"

"Yes, the clientele at Haven General, and particularly at The Conceptions Foundation, are of a much higher socioeconomic status, so their background medical care and their health and nutrition status are better. This significantly reduces the complication rate. Also, here in Haven, there are very few AIDS cases, and therefore I see very few women with HIV infection here for cesarean sections or abortions. All that infected AIDS blood makes it much more dangerous for me, and for my staff."

Kincade nodded appreciatively, obviously impressed. "Let me say I understand, as much as a layman can, how difficult your work must be. And I also can understand and accept how your colleagues have found your care of my client Lissa Vernor without error. Actually, my goal isn't necessarily to fix blame on any one person at all, if there even is blame, but simply to uncover the truth."

"Truth?" Baatard asked skeptically, straightening up

in his chair. "Are you really interested in the truth, or are you just here in preparation for bringing a malpractice lawsuit against me?"

"I want to understand Lissa Vernor's bleeding problem better, perhaps more for Ephrim Vernor's sake. My client Lissa Vernor isn't planning a malpractice action at this time."

"How can you know that?" Baatard laughed contemptuously. "She's been in a coma for months,"

"Well, my last directions from her husband were not specific in that regard. I haven't decided either. Having the QA hearing go in your favor certainly makes that even less likely."

"Come on now, Mr. Kincade. You seem to be calling all the shots and making all the decisions for Lissa Vernor. In effect you are her." He knew Kincade would decide about any malpractice action based on his own agenda. What that could be was a matter of conjecture to Baatard, but, since it involved lawyers, surely was centered around money.

"I'm simply instructed to act in Lissa's best interests," Kincade innocently shrugged.

"Well, that may be. It's all a matter of viewpoint, now, isn't it?"

"What do you mean?"

"Simply this. I thought I was acting in Lissa's best interests, too. Anyway, I really don't want to discuss Lissa now. As for Ephrim Vernor, he's part of a surrogate contract. I really don't think you need to be concerned about his health. That will be his new, his adopted parent's responsibility."

"His adoptive parents? So, you're not the actual adopting parent, then?"

"Of course I'm not. And a real parent is exactly what he needs now, don't you agree?"

"No, why?" Kincade's face told Baatard he knew what slur was coming.

"Hey, it's obvious," Baatard said, opening his hands up. "His mother is in a coma and his father is dead, that's why. He's got no one to care for him."

"Vena Kleinman has been taking care of Ephrim since birth. That's why Dr. Ryder Vernor gave her custody. I think she's the most mother he's ever had."

"As I said, Ephrim has no one caring for him right now," Baatard repeated, sarcastically.

"There's no reason to be nasty, Dr. Baatard. I guess you don't know how shaky your surrogate case is."

"Shaky?" Of course he knew it was shaky, and that his actions were neither legal nor ethical, and regretted having suggested such a stupid idea to Ramirez in the first place. Yet, all the facts were secure, and as long as they stayed that way, he was covered. Baatard knew, though, that it was because of Ramirez's and Denny's threatening pressure that he even would have agreed to this insane arrangement.

"Yes. After all, why would Dr. Vernor sign custody to Vena if he already intended to turn over the child to surrogate parents? I mean, you aren't implying Dr. Vernor forgot about the surrogate contract, are you?"

Baatard looked away from Kincade, out the window. He wanted as much to back out of the agreement as Kincade and Vena wanted it voided, if only he could.

"Who are the adoptive parents anyway?" Kincade persisted.

"That's part of a very confidential contractual arrangement. I'm sure you understand these things all too well," Baatard replied.

"Yes, I guess I do." Kincade thought for a moment, then said, "Say, while I'm here I wonder if you'd give me an opinion on a medical question I have. It's not involving any legal issue with you or The Conceptions Foundation."

"I can make no promises, but I can listen," Baatard said. In actuality, he rarely trusted anything a lawyer told him, even his own legal counsel.

"What is your opinion of genetic evidence?"

"Well, I don't know a lot of detail, and it is such a broad subject. I mean, the courts accept it, don't they?" Baatard looked straight at Kincade, wondering what he was up to with these questions.

"What I really want to know is this, Dr. Baatard. I know that genetic evidence is highly specific. I know it's powerful enough to free an innocent man. I've used it for that. But, I have a problem. What would you do if you had someone's tissue type, but you didn't know whose tissue it was?"

"That's a very difficult problem. There aren't any genetic versions of a phone book you can look up someone in going by their tissue type. Although, I suppose that someday there will be." Baatard knew that

The Foundation kept an extensive database of tissue types from all the sperm and ova donors seen. But, that information was highly confidential, and Baatard didn't want Kincade to even know of its existence. "Why, do you have someone you think is innocent that you think this information will help?"

"No, quite the contrary, Dr. Baatard. I have a long-standing case I'm trying to solve. It was a crime most violent and perverse, and I really want an identity. There is a small stain on the clothing of a victim of a rape which occurred some sixteen years ago. I just hope that that stain will contain enough tissue for a genetic ID, but that's all I have, unfortunately." Kincade searched Bastard's face for a reaction; there was none. "So, what would you do, if you were in my place?"

Baatard shrugged his shoulders and offered his sympathy. "Could you forward a copy of the genetic identity to me? I could at least try a few things for you." Baatard could see that Kincade was surprised at his unexpected offer of assistance. What the hell, Baatard thought, even if it's a long shot.

With nothing more to say, Baatard walked Kincade to the office door before saying good-bye.

Chapter 57

Christine Milltown Lincoln returned to her apartment, more infuriated then frightened. She had intended to create a scene at Baatard's office, and indeed she had. However, the confrontation was only witnessed by Baatard and the one other man, not by even one other woman. To successfully intimidate Baatard into stopping the atrocities that went on in his clinic, she needed more media exposure and more leverage. Lincoln knew she could never be free from her constant nightmares until she first stopped Baatard and all the affiliated doctors of The Foundation from killing all those precious, innocent children. No matter what it would take, she was prepared to make any sacrifice to atone for what she perceived as her sinful past.

Lincoln took a long time to straighten up her clothes and regain her composure, all the while frantically going over in her head the development of a new strategy. Then she picked up the phone.

"Conceptions Foundation," the receptionist answered.

"Mrs. Denny Cruite's office, please."

"That's Ms. Cruite. I'll see if she is in."

Christine paced back and forth, holding her portable phone, rehearsing exactly what she was going to say. In another minute she was connected.

"Hello, this is Denny Cruite," the dry, business-like voice said. "How can I help you?"

"Ms. Cruite, my name is Mrs. Christine Milltown Lincoln. I attended a Conceptions Foundation seminar at Haven General."

"Yes, thank you for your interest in our Foundation. Are you interested in *in vitro* fertilization?"

"Well, I was," Lincoln replied, a certain hesitation in her voice.

"Oh? You no longer want to have an assisted pregnancy?" Denny asked.

"Yes, I still do. But there is a problem. You see, after the seminar, I made an appointment to see Dr. Baatard."

"That's wonderful. Dr. Baatard is a brilliant, gifted infertility specialist and one of the founders of The Conceptions Foundation," Denny replied, trying to appear as positive and enthusiastic as possible. Still, she could sense something strange, upsetting, edgy, almost abnormally detached in Milltown's voice. Warning flags waved all around her. "I trust your visit with Dr. Baatard was satisfactory in every way."

"No, it most definitely was not. While I was waiting in Dr. Baatard's office, I found out that he performs abortions. He kills babies right there. Well, I had no idea that he is engaged in killing babies. I want so much to have a baby."

"Look, Mrs. Lincoln, let me clarify things for you. Dr. Baatard only performs abortions during the first 3 months of pregnancy. You're not implying that this constitutes killing of babies, are you?" Denny countered.

"That's just not true. It's murder. It violates God's will. Only God can create a precious baby's life and only God can take it away. There are thousands of women all over this country that would die to have a child, Mrs. Cruite. And your Dr. Baatard is busy killing them."

"He is not MY Dr. Baatard," Denny said, defensively.

"But he IS affiliated with Conceptions Foundation, isn't he?" Lincoln demanded.

"Yes, but . . . "

"And you introduced Dr. Baatard as a founding member, didn't you?"

"Yes, but . . . " Denny struggled to get a word in.

"And your own brochure lists him as a member of the Board of Directors of Conceptions Foundation, doesn't it? Isn't all that true, Mrs. Cruite?" Christine Milltown Lincoln was now livid and nearly screaming into the mouthpiece of her phone. "I want to make myself perfectly clear, Mrs. Cruite. My group will do everything we can to stop Dr. Baatard from performing abortions."

"Well, I don't want to be confrontational, Miss. Lincoln, but let me also make myself clear. The Conceptions Foundation is operating within the law and within generally accepted medical practice guidelines. We intend to continue to provide a full range of obstetrical, gynecological, and fertility services to all women who want them. I might also add that I don't respond well to threats and intimidation. I look a lot more friendly than I am."

"The same goes for me too. Our beliefs are more important than our freedom. We demand, Mrs. Cruite, that Conceptions Foundation immediately dissociate itself from Dr. Baatard and from all doctors who perform abortions. We insist that Conceptions Foundation abstain from supporting or performing any activity associated with abortions."

"Listen here, Miss. Lincoln," Denny sneered into the phone, "I think you better get one thing straight right off. The Conceptions Foundation operates within the limits of and under the protection of the law. I'm sorry that you feel the way you do, but that's really not my problem, it's yours. We have no intention to succumb to your pressure tactics."

"I think you'll change your mind about that, Mrs. Cruite. You'll see what bountiful and glorious plans God has for all His children, unborn and born. Until that day, we plan to resume picketing Haven General Hospital, Dr. Baatard's offices, and The Conceptions Foundation offices."

"But what you're objecting to is only a small part of our services. We're also helping women to their right to create another life. We help women to become pregnant. We're not primarily an abortion clinic," Denny responded, exasperated. Visions of those annoying pickets coming back again nearly drove her crazy.

"Then we'll need to make other women understand the full range of what you're doing, including the nasty, evil deaths you cause."

The Surrogate

"I think you'll find picketing again most counterproductive." In other words, don't fuck with me, bitch, Denny thought. She wanted to reach right through the phone line and strangle that annoying religious crackpot. This was the same crazed fanatic who had picketed The Foundation Offices earlier this year, and had suddenly stopped.

"I don't think so. We're not a passive group and we're serious about obtaining our goals. If you don't concede to our demands, this time we'll begin disrupting your activities, both at your offices and particularly at your public seminars. We intend to let all women understand that you're engaged in murdering children, and not helping to bring about births."

Denny tried to reply, but the line suddenly went dead. Dumbfounded, it took several minutes for her to regain her composure. Visions of disruptive pickets in front of her clean, new building, of women turning away from her offices, of empty exam rooms filled with expensive medical equipment on lease, news of The Foundations stock valuation plummeting, all these things made her head swirl. She picked up a pen holder and threw it against the wall, and clenched her fists as she withheld screaming out loud. Then, getting hold of her emotions, she called up Dr. Baatard.

After the call was transferred into his office, Baatard was told Denny Cruite was on the line. "How can I help you, Denny?" he asked, guessing that she was calling about that annoying Christine Lincoln.

"Damon, what the hell is going on over there?" She wondered if Lincoln was as threatening to him, and how he handled her.

"What do you mean?"

"Do you know a Mrs. Christine Milltown Lincoln?" Denny asked.

"I'll say. She was just in here creating a real commotion. The woman's a pro-life nutcake. Why do you ask?"

"She just called me over here and complained about our association with you."

"Why? Because I perform abortions?" he commented, the high pitch to his voice letting on that he was hurt by this. "Was that what she was complaining about to you today?"

"Precisely. I want to know everything that went on there today, Damon. Every little detail."

Baatard related the entire uncomfortable incident with Lincoln, then told her about Charlie Kincade's visit. Denny screamed into the phone when Baatard related how Kincade had seen the entire confrontation with Lincoln.

"Kincade saw all that? What the hell was he doing in your office, Damon?"

"He said he just wanted to talk."

"Sure, I'll just bet he did. Why did Yee allow him to speak to you at all, especially without her being present?"

"I don't think Kincade asked Yee's permission."

"Then why the hell did you even talk to him? Look, Damon, please don't talk to anyone, especially the likes of

Kincade, without legal representation present. I sense big
potential problems here, Damon, trust me. Okay?"

Baatard promised to do that.

"And about the Lincoln woman, I think she's serious
and intends to disrupt our informational public
presentations at Haven General. That could have very
damaging consequences to The Foundation. I'm having
security stepped up, and I'll resort to court protection, if
necessary."

"Maybe we could stop performing elective abortions
for a while," Baatard suggested.

"What? No way. Get serious, Damon. We can't let
one fanatic disrupt the obstetric and fertility services we
provide to the public. Not every woman wants to be
intimidated by a crackpot like her. Besides, doing that
could cost us millions. No, you continue with exactly
what you normally do. Let me take care of this Ms.
Lincoln and her misplaced fanatic beliefs."

"Denny, before I forget, Kincade did ask one other
thing. He said it wasn't related to me at all, and was just a
point of curiosity. But, well, I think you might want to
know about it anyway."

"You bet I do. Okay, tell me what else he had to say.
Damon, I want you to think very carefully and be sure to
tell me every little detail. Leave out nothing, got it?"

"Yes, of course. He asked me my opinion about
genetic testing. That's all."

Denny nearly choked. "Genetic testing? Are you
sure? Did he say what he wanted to test?"

"Yes, he did. He said he's looking into the use of
sixteen-year old genetic evidence on a rape case. Beyond

that, he gave no details." There was a long silence.
"Denny, are you still there?" Baatard asked.

"Yes, of course," she nearly gasped.

"Is everything all right? You sound ill."

"Yes, of course everything is fine, just fine. It's nothing, really. Damon, did Kincade say why he was interested in this aged evidence or what he was testing or who was raped?"

"No, not at all. As I said, he gave no details."

"And what did you say to him, Damon?"

"I simply tried to explain to the gentleman that I don't know a lot about the subject. That's all."

"Good. The less you say to any lawyer about anything, the better we're all going to be. Okay?"

"Sure, Denny. What are you really going to do about Ms. Lincoln and Mr. Kincade, Denny?"

"I'm certainly going to protect my interests and my constitutional rights, that's all. Don't worry, and don't ask questions. The less you know, the better."

Chapter 58

Christine Milltown Lincoln got up shortly after her husband left for the office the next morning. She pulled on a robe, looked with foreboding into a mirror over her dresser and groaned, wondering if all women her age looked so bad in the morning.

Christine shook her head, then walked into the kitchen to prepare a pot of coffee. After measuring the correct amount from a can of ground coffee she kept in the freezer, she filled the water reservoir. Christine lifted up the plug, which she kept out from the socket for safety reasons, and reached out to plug it into the wall socket. For a moment, she hesitated, thinking the wire looked a little twisted. On closer inspection, she didn't see loose wires, and decided it was probably safe to use. She made a mental note to remind her husband to check it out later. Then, she picked up the plug and reached for the wall socket.

Before heading to her bedroom, Christine switched on the percolator. The familiar gurgling sound began almost immediately, followed by the warm scent of freshly brewing coffee.

Satisfied that essential task was underway, Christine went into the bathroom and turned on the shower to get it warm. Steam began to fill the bathroom almost immediately. She paused for a moment when she thought she heard a sound from the kitchen, opened the door and called out for her husband in case he had returned from work. There was no reply. Certain she couldn't have heard anything above the shower water and the background grinding sound of the heat lamp timer, she returned to getting ready for work.

Just then, the door bell rang. Not expecting anyone else, Christine assumed it would be her husband, forgetting something as usual. She put her robe back on, turned off the water, and went back into the living room. The doorbell rang again, and she opened the door.

"Christine Lincoln?" After the woman nodded to indicate that was who she was, Marina introduced herself, and said, "I'm a nurse at Haven General Hospital. Ms. Lincoln, I know this is unexpected, but would you be able to speak with me for a few minutes."

Christine was surprised and wary, and very rushed to get ready for work. "Maybe; what is it you want of me?" She pulled her robe closed more tightly, and kept the door open only a little.

"I think we knew each other from Haven High," Marina smiled, hoping to break the ice.

When Christine smiled some recognition, Marina said, "I'm friends with Mr. Charlie Kincade, an attorney who witnessed the altercation you had in Dr. Baatard's office yesterday."

Christine's face clouded over. "Oh, I see. But it was my understanding that Dr. Baatard was not going to press . . . I mean, make a complaint," she blushed.

"Oh, I don't know anything about that. I'm not affiliated with Dr. Baatard at all. You see, Mr. Kincade is a personal friend of mine. He called me and told me what he had witnessed; he was quite upset."

"Yes, but what exactly is it you want with me?" Christine asked. She knew her movement and her tactics were popular with some, but rubbed a lot of other people the wrong way.

"After hearing what had occurred, I naturally wanted to understand more. I want to know what Dr. Baatard did to make you react so strongly." Looking around, and feeling a little strange standing on the doorway, Marina asked, "Do you mind if I come in and speak to you?"

Christine thought it over, looked carefully at Marina, then took the latch off the door and motioned Marina inside. "Where did you say you work?"

"I'm a nurse at Haven General Hospital and I'm involved in the Quality Assurance program. Whenever something major happens, like a bad surgical outcome, I investigate. The hospital wants to be certain that if there is a way to improve its part of the delivery of health care, that the necessary improvements are identified." Christine seemed to Marina to be interested and intelligent, and not at all a violent woman.

"What exactly is it you want to know, Mrs. Bonnaserra?"

"I understand you said Dr. Baatard was a murderer. What did you mean by that?"

"He murders little children every time he performs abortions." Her face screwed up into a disgusted, painful little ball, as if she realized she had accidentally stepped in a pile of animal feces.

Marina winced at the way Christine described abortions. She had not gotten over the pain and suffering and guilt from her own abortion years ago. "But what made you physically attack Dr. Baatard?" Reflecting on the idea, it didn't seem all that unreasonable. There was something about Baatard she had detected lately, something sinister that made her cautious. Particularly after Dr. Ryder Vernor, who apparently may have had some very unusual contractual adoption relationships with Baatard, died in his presence.

"Tell me, Ms. Bonnaserra, what do you know about abortions?"

"Quite a lot. As I said, I'm a nurse." In fact, she knew very little technically about abortions, and had never witnessed one nor participated in one, other than her own, that is.

"But I mean, what do you really know about abortions? You know some of the technicalities, the physiology, but what do you really know about the pain, the terrible, haunting feelings, the guilt, the emptiness?" Lincoln's voice broke, and her eyes flooded with tears.

Marina tried to speak, but stopped short. Memories of her own abortion flooded her consciousness. She wanted to tell Lincoln just how much she really did understand, but could not form the words.

Lincoln looked into Marina's eyes and instantly she

knew. She reached out and held Marina's hands in hers. Her voice now only a choked squeak, she slowly nodded her head as she said, "So you've had one too."

Marina nodded imperceptibly, then looked away out of shame, but did not try to free her hands. The human touch felt particularly good just now. "It was almost eighteen years ago. Here, right here in Haven."

Lincoln gasped as she realized the coincidence. "Where, in Haven?"

"I really don't remember. It was some shabby little clinic over on the other side of town, that's all I remember. God, I feel so guilty whenever I think of what happened, what I allowed to happen. It still hurts so."

"We all hurt; Dr. Baatard hurts babies, and I hurt when he does that."

"But your feelings, . . ." Marina began.

"It's not just my feelings. Can't you understand?" she began to cry. "Sure my heart aches for those babies, and my body hurts too." Suddenly, Christine pulled the robe off her shoulder and over her right chest, exposing her right breast.

Shocked and surprised at the unexpected disrobing, Marina stared for several painful seconds at Christine's disfigured chest, the jagged scars, and most of all, the missing nipple. Helpless, she felt sharp pains ripping anew through her own chest, the parallels to her own breast undeniable. "How?" Marina began, but quickly ran out of words to say. She knew what she was seeing, exactly how it happened, and now knew completely why Christine was so angry. She knew, she understood, she empathized.

"I was raped, last year." She motioned to her breast, then said, her voice cracking, "That animal, he did that." It took several moments for her to regain enough composure to say, her voice reduced to a painful squeak, "And I got pregnant, again, and the baby was deformed, or so I was told."

"Only last year? Oh, I'm so sorry," Marina said. She wanted to get up and hug Christine, hold her, share her anger and sorrow, but she found it hard to move.

"And," she continued, her voice a choked-up sob, "I had to have an abortion, another abortion. I killed that little baby, Marina, just as much as Dr. Baatard did, and I just know that I'm going to rot in hell for it." She looked away, her jaw a trembling mass of wet tears.

They sat in complete silence for minutes - it seemed like hours, not looking at each other, unable to move. For Marina, the pain was more intense then she had felt in years. She knew that the bizarre cause of Christine's deformity had to have been the same as hers, even without seeing the teeth marks. The fact it happened last year could only mean one thing - the rapist was still alive, and here in Haven. The frightening feelings she had experienced were not alarmist paranoia, but a true sensing of his evil presence.

"Look. Mrs. Bonnaserra, I don't want to be rude, or anything, but I have to get ready for work," Christine finally said, her composure returning. "And as you can

The Surrogate

see, I haven't even started to dress yet. So, if you'll excuse me, I need to start getting ready."

"Of course," Marina said as she got up to leave. "Don't let me hold you up." She knew that Christine, so upset at having her violent confrontation yesterday brought up again, and the painful memory of her recent, disfiguring rape and subsequent abortion, wasn't interested in talking any more. Marina realized that nothing could come from pressing the point, she had already seen enough. Marina knew that she had suffered exactly the same disfigurement as Christine, and that could only mean the bastard who raped her, tore her flesh from her own body in that same way so long ago, was still alive, and still in this very city with her. She may even have seen him, and he may have seen her, certainly a creepy concept to consider. Did he remember her, recognize her, know where she worked, or lived? She was in danger, no doubt, just as she had been so many years ago, and she would never be able to sleep again until he was finally caught.

Moments after Marina left, the door rang again, and Christine opened it, expecting Marina had left something behind by accident. She was shocked to see someone standing there with a black ski cap over his head. Instantaneously, Christine was shot directly in her face with a spray of Mace, paralyzing her in blinding pain.

A hooded and enraged Denny Cruite shoved Christine back into her apartment, and too confused to cry out for help, Christine's dead weight fell onto the floor. Grabbing at her blinded eyes, Christine tried to roll away, but Denny followed Christine in, closed the door behind, then stood glowering over her as she writhed about in pain.

"I want," Denny kicked Christine in the side, "to give you," Denny kicked Christine in the back, "something to remember," Denny pulled Christine's hair and slapped her face, knocking a tooth loose and drawing blood, "next time you think about disrupting an abortion clinic." Denny violently kicked Christine in the head several times, causing her to cry out in pain, viciously stomped on her abdomen, and then left a crying and stunned Christine bleeding on the floor of her apartment.

Once outside Christine's apartment, Denny quickly removed the ski cap, calmly stuffed it in her purse, walked out to the elevator and left the building. Within minutes, she was back in the comfort of her home, where she showered, and threw her clothes in the washer, before returning to work.

The next morning, Baatard was shocked to note on the front page of the newspaper that a prominent anti-abortion protester, Mrs. Christine Milltown Lincoln had been attacked while at home yesterday morning.

A sick feeling came over Baatard as the unfortunate 'incident' which had taken place in his office in his office immediately came to mind, how Kincade witnessed the altercation, and how he had hit Christine Lincoln, even though it was in self-defense.

Certain that the police would be visiting him any minute, Baatard hurriedly placed a call to his attorney, Ellen Yee. Baatard thought about the conversation he had with Denny Cruite and wondered about her own role in this. He thought about Ramirez and the demands she was making. Baatard wondered if he was being set up to take the blame, and he needed to do something about it right now, to protect his own life.

Back at home, Marina's thoughts were occupied with visions of Dr. Ryder Vernor, of his wife Lissa, and now of the horror of Christine Lincoln. One was dead, and one was in a coma. Convinced she was in mortal danger, she took out the handgun she had impulsively purchased after Dr. Vernor's death. Marina knew that, untrained in the gun's safe use, she was more a danger to herself than to others with it. She had no experience shooting it, and no real understanding of how it even worked. She didn't even know how to load it.

After finding a suitable practice range and instructor from the gun shop, she made an appointment for lessons her next day off from work.

Chapter 59

Haven County Government Building
Office of the District Attorney

The Prosecutor's office for Haven County was cramped into the second and third floors of the Haven County Government Building. The entire office complex, which consisted of the courts, city offices and library, was housed in a fortress style brick building set apart on ten acres of prime land in the heart of Haven County. The buildings had aged red brick for an outer shell and an old but well-maintained inner appearance. The municipal complex had a friendly, hometown atmosphere to it, and the intrusion of weapons scanners had yet to make their ugly presence felt.

The County Prosecutor, Jane Omizawa-Shapiro, leaned forward in her chair as she looked quizzically at Charlie Kincade. She had been in the county prosecutor's office for almost twenty years now, ever since leaving law school and being appointed a trial case investigator. She was generally regarded as tough but fair, and was currently suffering under a horrendous case load. Her

husband, Dr. Sonny Omizawa, a local optometrist, rarely
saw Jane and often joked about how good that was for
their marriage. Jane didn't think him very humorous.

Lights for all four of her phone lines were lit: all four
lines were also placed on hold because she hadn't a
secretary to answer them at the moment. In addition, for
the last hour Jane had patiently been listening to the
arguments of Charlie Kincade, who was accompanied by
Marina Bonnaserra to bolster his position.

"Look, Charlie, I understand your emotional
involvement, but . . . " Jane said.

"Excuse me, but this isn't emotional involvement.
The facts here speak for themselves," Kincade politely
tried to correct her. He had disagreements with Omizawa-
Shapiro before: she always won. The prosecutor by
definition held all the winning cards. This time, though,
he somehow needed to make her see his point of view.

"First," Jane patiently explained, "there is no case, at
least not now. Second, the hospital and a group of
disinterested specialists have all cleared Dr. Baatard of
any negligence in the Lissa Vernor case. So, Charlie, I
just don't understand the problem," she sighed. Looking at
Kincade, she wondered if he were really cruel enough to
place one more burden on her already overburdened
shoulders.

"The problem, prosecutor, is in the big picture,"
Charlie persisted. "The case has a bad odor to it." He sat
rigid in his seat, the tension of making a losing argument
in front of Marina evident.

"Okay, if you won't consider the facts on the Lissa
Vernor case, how about what happened to Dr. Vernor,

then?" Marina added.

"As for her husband, Dr. Ryder Vernor, the coroner ruled the death was due to natural causes." Jane threw her hands up in the air, and picked up another pile of papers from her desktop, occasionally glancing at them.

"Oh, for God's sake, Jane." Charlie Kincade said. "Aren't we being blind to a conspiracy? The wife has a stroke under Baatard's care. Then, suddenly, while in a coma, she gets pregnant. She delivers, and while still in a goddamn coma, for Christ's sake. As soon as she delivers, bamm, what happens? Her husband, a doctor, dies while working with Baatard. Then Baatard claims the kid. What's it look like to you?" Not able to imagine how she could miss the obvious connections, Kincade wondered what motives other than overwork could make her not want to pursue Baatard more aggressively. "Oh, and I forgot, an abortion protester makes a scene in Baatard's office, and before you can say Right To Life, she gets viciously attacked in her own home."

"I agree with Charlie, your honor," Marina spoke up. "Taken individually, at least some of this might seem explainable, but taken as a whole, they just don't add up."

"Yes, taken together it does sound suspicious," Jane agreed. "But neither one of you would have to prosecute any case that would develop. As for the surrogate adoption mess, well that's gone to a custody hearing. There's nothing I can do about it. I can't interfere in an ongoing proceeding. So, what do you want me to do now?"

"For starts, how about just looking at the hospital QA hearing records? I could provide you with a summary," Marina offered. She had not cleared her presence here with Lemar Jackson, the hospital attorney, but was certain he would go along with her offer to the judge.

"I can't do that," Omizawa-Shapiro said, waving a handful of freedom-of-information subpoenas just given her by Kincade. "I want to remind you I'm a lawyer, not a doctor, Charlie. To adequately review these documents, even if I want to, I'll need to get in some additional specialists, and that would mean a big budget expenditure. It's money I don't have to spend. And for what?"

"I think there was a cover-up of Baatard's care of Lissa Vernor," Charlie said. Marina nodded her strong agreement.

"Well, that may be," Jane nervously laughed, "but I'm sure you don't need me to remind you that Medical malpractice can be tried in court. And medical misconduct is handled by BMQA."

"I tell you there's a cover-up," Charlie Kincade nearly yelled. He could see Baatard laughing at him behind his back, and it made him angry and frustrated. But he still could not begin to imagine what Baatard's involvement really was, or why. Overall, it just didn't make sense.

"There's absolutely no evidence for a cover-up, Charlie," Jane told him, shaking her head in disbelief. "It's all circumstantial. At best, you'll have dueling specialists in front of a hung jury. There's Beyond Reasonable Doubt here, Charlie. You're experienced in these things, Ms.

Bonnaserra, Nurse Bonnaserra. Don't you see what I'm trying to explain to you? You need to be practical, not emotional."

"Unfortunately, I have to agree with you," Marina conceded.

"Jane, the guy's already been investigated in Wisconsin, and God knows where else that didn't make it to the documentation stage. Look at these records," Kincade said as he handed Baatard's Wisconsin BMQA records to Jane over her desk. "Baatard was into problems with infertility evaluations, fraudulent practices with a sperm bank, phony billing, . . . "

"I see no convictions here. In fact," she said as she continued to examine the documents, "I find total exoneration on all counts. Baatard was accused but never taken to trial. In our system of justice," she made a distasteful grimace, "he's innocent until proven guilty."

"Exactly, that's my point," Kincade said.

"No, Charlie, that can't be a point of fact leading to further investigation. He wasn't charged because there wasn't reason to. We are presumed innocent in this country, all of us, including doctors you happen to loath. Hey," she chuckled, "can you find me one doctor anywhere in New Jersey who hasn't had a bad outcome, a dissatisfied patient, a family member disgruntled about their bill?"

"But these problems . . . "

"You mean these alleged problems which involved infertility evaluations, a questionable sperm bank, and billing practices? Are you saying that Dr. Baatard may have similar difficulties in the Vernor cases?"

"Not exactly, but . . . " Seeing he was arguing against cold prosecutorial logic, Charlie changed tactic. "Then there's the death of Dr. Vernor."

"As I already told you, the coroner has examined the case and ruled the death was accidental," Jane added. "Are you asking me to have the coroner reopen the case?"

"Why not?" Kincade asked her.

"No, the question is WHY? Do you have any evidence not available to the coroner that would have changed the determination of cause of death?"

"No." Kincade looked away briefly, then said, "And what about the custody battle over the Vernor child? Come on, Jane. You're a woman. Do you honestly believe a doctor's wife would try so very hard to get pregnant, go through all that trouble and expense for assisted fertilization or whatever the hell that hocus pocus crap Baatard does is called, and then agree to give up the child for adoption? And after acting as a surrogate? I don't think so," Kincade said, laughing nervously and shaking his head, "and neither do you. It just doesn't make sense, does it Marina?"

Marina indicated her agreement with Charlie.

"Okay, maybe it doesn't seem reasonable, but Baatard hasn't established his surrogate parentage yet. There's a custody hearing scheduled for next week, right?"

Kincade nodded yes. He would be there, representing what was left of the Vernor family and its interests. He wondered if he was sole determiner of what those interests were, at this point. He wondered if, as in a fairy tale, Lissa would wake up after a kiss, just in time for him to kill the dragon. He laughed to himself.

"I'm not saying I won't look into this," Jane said, seeming to bring the meeting to an end.

"Good," Kincade said. Finally, he felt that he was getting through to her.

"But, before I get involved in this case, I want to know the outcome of the custody hearing. Then, we can talk more," Jane said as she abruptly ended the conversation, turning her attention to a large collection of documents on her desk wrapped loosely in a folder. Several phones continued ringing unattended in the background.

Chapter 60

Baatard waited uncomfortably in Rubin's office the day after the QA hearing, shifting around in the chair, when Rubin finally walked in. Rubin had called him in unexpectedly, and Rubin's secretary had made the appointment through Sharlene without offering a reason for the meeting. Baatard angrily noted it was characteristic of Sharlene to not be attentive enough to ask for a reason.

"Thanks for coming, Damon," Rubin said, smiling and slightly out of breath. "I expected to be here sooner, but you know how that goes." Rubin shrugged his shoulders, and then feigned a smile. He reached over to the intercom and asked his secretary to hold all calls and visitors, except emergencies. Turning back to Baatard, Rubin said, "Well, I guess you're wondering why I asked you to come here."

"Yes. I assume it has something to do with a Vernor, which one I don't know," Baatard replied, shaking his head. He was feeling more like a criminal each day, although he never did anything to cause the Vernor's medical problems, at least those of Lissa Vernor. That he was the prime person under suspicion was a given, although the evidence was solely circumstantial. That kind of link smelled the worst, and the worse the smell, the longer it lingered.

"Damon, I'm not your enemy. I support you, and I

agree with the conclusions of the expert QA review of the Lissa Vernor case. So, I'm not here to hurt you."

"Good, I'm glad to hear that. Then I can go now," Baatard said, getting up from his chair.

"Damon, please don't make this so difficult for me."

"Really, what can I do for you?"

"I just want to ask you something about the Lissa Vernor case that has me puzzled. I assure you it's in utmost confidence," Rubin smiled. "Look, I'm taking no notes." Rubin held his hands up, opened the palms and waved them in the air.

"Okay, shoot," Baatard said as he shifted in his chair, somehow unable to get comfortable.

"It's about the infertility workup of Lissa. You said your evaluation of her was normal, so you decided to try ovarian stimulation."

"That's right. It often works in idiopathic infertility."

"Well, you're certainly the expert there. Tell me this, what was her husband's sperm count?"

"The what?" Baatard exclaimed. As soon as he heard that question, he knew that he had never really found the answer out. At the time it seemed insignificant, now it appeared negligent. He didn't know one of the most fundamental of facts in an infertility workup, and he should have known it right from the beginning.

"What was Ryder Vernor's sperm count?" Dr. Rubin repeated. "Surely you did one in your infertility workup of Lissa. I assume you established that Ryder's sperm count and morphology were normal and that Lissa was the problem since you decided to manipulate Lissa's endocrine system. Was the sperm count and morphology normal or not?"

"Was it normal? Was it normal?" Baatard repeated the question in a low voice, trying to stall. He was certain Rubin knew the answer, an answer he did not, and was baiting him. "That was a long time ago, Meyer. Give me a second to try and recall," Baatard said, scratching his head and looking up at the ceiling. "Well, I don't have the patient chart in front of me at the moment. Actually, as I remember it, I think I assumed Dr. Vernor's sperm count was normal."

"You assumed it was normal?" Rubin said, incredulous, almost laughing.

"Well, yes. As I remember it, Lissa told me Ryder recently had his sperm count evaluated. She wanted children, they had several years of unprotected intercourse, and she knew that was one of the things you check. So, she asked him to get it done."

"And Ryder did this sperm analysis before they saw you?"

"Yes, maybe, I think so. I, ah, well I had the impression Ryder was trying to keep the cost down so he took the initial steps in an infertility workup on his own. A sperm count would be one of the first things to do, and since he was a physician he could have easily requested an analysis on his own specimen. And, yes, it supposedly was done before his wife Lissa saw me professionally. "

"I see," Rubin said, holding his chin in his hand.

"Ryder, as I understand it, didn't want any children at the point in time when Lissa sought out my professional services. That was probably why Lissa wanted her additional efforts to become pregnant kept from her husband. I honored her request, of course, and therefore couldn't actually bring Ryder in for another sperm count." Baatard wondered what else Lissa was keeping from her husband, and from him. There were plenty of rumors.

"Did Lissa bring you in any documentation about her husband's sperm count? Perhaps there was a lab slip with a sperm count on it?" Rubin asked.

"No, I don't think so, but I could check if you wish. I assumed Lissa knew what she was talking about. As I remember it, she said Ryder told her his sperm count was normal."

"How about a name of a requesting physician or even the name of a lab performing the sperm count?"

"No, I don't think I have any records of that. But, I could check if you really need me to. Why?" He could see the freight train coming from miles away, aimed straight at his forehead. Like a deer paralyzed by oncoming headlights, there was no way for him to get off the tracks.

"Damon, you do know my surgical specialty, don't you?"

"Yes, of course I know that, Meyer. You're a urologic surgeon. Why?"

Chapter 61

Vena, having had several rather unpleasant legal experiences in her past, tried every way she knew to get Deanna to go with her to the custody hearing. Despite all the pleading and all the inducements on Vena's part, Deanna told Vena in the most clear and characteristic language, "No way." Not willing to accept the embarrassment and the isolation of going alone, Vena persisted and ended up asking Marina, out of desperation. She was relieved and somewhat surprised when Marina finally agreed to go with her.

Marina, interested in getting a good understanding of Baatard's involvement in the adoption, took the day off. She left Austin with a baby sitter she had started using, an older neighbor of hers. As she drove to the courthouse with Vena and Ephrim, Marina had a most unusual and uncomfortable feeling. Marina somehow attributed this strange ill-defined sensation to Ephrim, but couldn't understand why. Several times, Marina tried to tell Vena that things just seemed not completely right, but each time she held back. She didn't want to upset Vena more than she already had.

Vena brought Ephrim in a back holder, purse in one hand and baby bag in the other. When they got to the courtroom door, the guard asked Marina, a non-participant, to wait outside. Vena protested, wanting Marina in the courtroom with her for moral support, not outside. The guard would not be dissuaded. Since the jury waiting room was only a few feet from the courtroom and was not in use, Marina was allowed to go in there. Vena and Ephrim were searched, and then allowed to enter the courtroom.

Once inside, Vena anxiously looked around the courtroom for Kincade. Her anxiety level was raised to new heights when she found Kincade hadn't appeared yet. Vena wondered if something had happened to Kincade, if he had forgotten, had an accident, got lost, and whether she would now have to handle her legal representation alone. None of these possibilities seemed real, and she could feel herself moving rapidly to a panic state.

The courtroom was smaller than Vena had imagined it would be. The judge's bench was in front, with a clerk's desk to one side and the recorder to the other. A long wooden table stood about twenty feet in front of the judge, its top piled with documents, two water pitchers and glasses.

Baatard was already in the court room, as was his attorney Ellen Yee, and about twenty other people, none of whom Vena recognized. Nervous, Vena took Ephrim and left the courtroom to look outside for Kincade. She found Marina in the juror room, quietly reading some papers from work.

"I wouldn't be too worried about Charlie Kincade not showing up, Vena," Marina reassured her. Her past experiences in courtrooms, as an observer, with Lemar Jackson or with Charlie Kincade, all gave her something to compare to. She knew Vena had no such past experiences, or at least she thought so.

"Lawyers like a dramatic entrance accentuated by their absence," Marina continued. "They feed on the anxiety they cause. So, don't feed the bears," Marina knowingly smiled. It occurred to her she should take some of her own advice concerning Charlie Kincade. "How's Ephrim doing?"

"Ephrim is fine, Marina. Actually, he's sleeping right now," she said, looking at the blue bundle in the blanket lying over her shoulder. "I'm the one with the problem."

Just then, Kincade rounded the corner, curtly nodded recognition to Marina and Vena, and motioned for Vena to hurry up and go into the courtroom with him. "Come on, come on. They haven't started yet, have they?" Kincade said to her as he rushed into the courtroom.

Nearly a half hour later, an exasperated Vena came out of the courtroom with a crying Ephrim, and hastily handed him to Marina like he was radioactive. "God, Ephrim's being a real pain today. He just won't stay still and be quiet. Could you hold him for just a while, please?" Vena pleaded. "I think that he knows something is wrong that involves him."

"No problem," Marina said. "What's been going on in there, anyway?" She had been in many courtrooms over the years, searching for her rapist, a purpose which was totally dissimilar to this.

"Oh, God, it's so boring. First there was an opening

statement from the hearing officer. Then there was Kincade's opening statement, and then another opening statement by Yee. So far, the only person called to testify has been Baatard."

"What did Baatard say?" Lately, when Marina said his name, an uncomfortable feeling came over her. At this point, she wished she had used another doctor for infertility services, although she freely admitted the results had turned out exceedingly well.

"Baatard told the judge about Lissa's fertility problem and what he was doing about it. He said initially Lissa wanted a child to strengthen her marriage."

"But, I'm surprised in a way Lissa wanted a child. Somehow it doesn't seem like something she would do - it would be too inconvenient for her to go shopping," Marina quipped.

"I know what you mean," Vena said, an angry, jealous look clouding her face "Lissa told Baatard that she had brought up the idea to Ryder several times. Ryder told Lissa he wanted her but definitely did not want a child. Ryder also told Lissa that he didn't want her with a child. Unfortunately, she had her stroke before she could have known she was pregnant."

"Ironic, isn't it?"

"It's sad, Marina, that's what it is. Ryder found out about Lissa being pregnant about a month after her surgical accident. Then - and this is all according to

Baatard -" Vena cautioned, "Baatard told the court that Ryder approached him about Lissa getting an abortion. Baatard asked Ryder to wait a few days and think it over first."

"Baatard told Ryder about the pregnancy, and then Ryder asked him about an abortion? Are you sure?" Marina asked.

"Baatard told the court he had a client who wanted a child and was willing to pay for a private adoption," Vena said. "At first, Ryder wanted to go for an abortion," Vena continued. "According to Baatard, the money was a big temptation for Ryder. Ryder said he was under a tremendous amount of pressure, claiming Lissa had tried to ruin their marriage, and that her illness was now ruining his medical practice. Ryder did say that to me, too, Marina," Vena nodded. "Eventually, Baatard claimed Ryder caved in to the pressure and signed the surrogate adoption contract. Wild, huh?" Vena said, shaking her head.

"I see," Marina said, thinking about her own experiences with an abortion. Having been there, in the pits of hell, she could empathize with what Lissa might have felt if she had not had the surgical accident. As it was, Lissa now felt nothing, understood nothing.

Vena looked up at the ceiling, then over to a group of lawyers talking in a corner, each holding a paper coffee cup and eyeing young women as they walked by. "Lissa Vernor had a stroke before anyone else knew she was pregnant."

"What was Baatard's role in the planned adoption?" Marina asked.

Vena looked at her, shook her head and said, "Apparently Baatard's services as an infertility expert extend to these things too."

"It sure is amazing. It's almost like a TV movie. Did anything else happen in there?"

"One other thing," Vena said. "Baatard's attorney Yee started to discuss surrogate contracts. It was really boring and lost me in a few places. Then, Ephrim started fussing and I had to come out here."

Marina reached over and took hold of Ephrim. "I can take him for a while. You can go back in." She felt she could easily take care of Ephrim, and could well understand why Vena needed quiet and no distraction.

"Don't let anyone take my Ephrim while I'm away, okay Marina?" Vena said as she backed away toward the courtroom door.

"There's no need to worry," Marina said, bouncing Ephrim on her knee. She saw Vena look back nervously several times before waving one last time and finally reentering the courtroom.

Kincade came in and out of the courtroom, going over to a pay phone against the wall, then to the men's room, then back in to the courtroom. He also tried several times to speak with Marina. Each time, his conversations on how the case was going were interrupted by calls from the bailiff summoning him back to the courtroom.

Marina noticed several clerks in inexpensive and ill-fitting clothes and some uniformed police move in and out of the courtroom frequently, like bees buzzing around a hive. Only a few went into the courtroom Vena was in.

Vena came back out of the courtroom in another thirty minutes, and asked Marina, "How's Ephrim doing?"

"He's just fine, Vena," Marina reassured her. "If there's a problem, I'll call you. Just go back in and relax." As Vena turned and started back, Marina called out, "What's going on now?"

"It got really hot a few minutes ago. Attorney Kincade was great, he challenged everything. He said the surrogate contract was invalid, and he objected that the main participants were not here to speak."

"How could he expect Dr. Vernor or Lissa to be here?" Marina asked.

"I don't know," Vena said, shaking her head. "And the judge didn't understand this either. Kincade promised to explain this all a little later. Then Yee called me up to speak."

Marina looked up at Vena, and then said, "Oh. What did Yee ask?"

"She asked me a lot of questions whose answers were obvious, that's all. Like, she asked if I was the mother of Ephrim, which of course I'm not. Then she asked me if I was Ryder's wife, which of course I'm not, either."

"I think she was trying to both embarrass you, and to enter facts into the court record," Marina explained to Vena.

"Well, I guess. Then Yee asked how, if I wasn't Ephrim's mother, and I wasn't the wife of Ephrim's father, why was I living with him? That's a real slap in the face.

Can you believe cheap shit like that?"

Marina nodded sympathetically, but could very well understand.

"Anyway, I said I was his receptionist, and since his wife was ill, I was helping out with the child's care, that's all. Yee, she smiled kind of sly-like and said, "Oh, I'll bet you were, Miss Vena.""

"Now THAT was pretty low," Marina commented. True, but low.

"That's the truth. I told that little bitch that's all the relationship was. Yee didn't believe me, and I don't think the judge did either, if I can know by the look on a woman's face what she's thinking, and I believe I can. Then Yee said if I wasn't the mother or the wife of the father, what possible right did I have to the child? Can you believe the nerve of that bitch?"

Marina shook her head 'no' but understood Yee's logic. Yet, telling Vena this would have been unfair and not supportive. She knew Vena needed support right now more than anything else.

"Anyway, I didn't need to reply because Mr. Kincade stood right up and objected," Vena smiled proudly. "He said Ryder had provided in his new will for my having custody of Ephrim if anything happened to him. And that was supposed to be more important than any old surrogate contract." Vena looked at her watch nervously, then said, "Look, I've got to get back in there, okay?"

Marina paced back and forth with Ephrim for a little while, trying to calm him down. She was amazed at how comfortable she felt with Ephrim, and how easy it was to take care of him, almost like it was for Austin. But she still felt something to be wrong, terribly wrong, if only she could understand what it was. As Marina walked past the doors to the courtroom, she got an inspiration and calmly walked right in and took a seat in the back of the courtroom in the visitor's section. No one paid her attention.

The family court judge, Helen Newton, was addressing Kincade. "It is my understanding, counselor, that you are in possession of documents giving custody of the child Ephrim Vernor to you should anything make his parents or Vena Kleinman incapable of caring for him."

"That is correct, your honor," Kincade said. "Dr. Ryder Vernor, the father of the child Ephrim and the legal guardian of his wife Lissa, updated his will to say this just a few weeks before his death."

"I object to these supposed documents, your honor," Yee said. "The surrogate agreement documents supersede these supposed power of attorney papers in importance and by date."

Yee presented a long and detailed argument addressing these issues, including the calling of several expert witnesses. The judge, however, allowed the new will to be entered into evidence.

Judge Newton, chosen for her special interest in surrogate parentage contracts, appeared totally absorbed in the proceedings, at times almost enjoying herself. The

judge frequently asked questions, and when both
attorneys had completed their cases, Judge Newton was
ready to ask the attorneys to present their closing
arguments.

Charlie Kincade got up first, holding a large stack of
typed and hand written papers in one hand, and began to
speak. After only a few minutes, the judge interrupted
Kincade, and gently told him, "All right, Mr. Kincade, I
think that's all that I need to hear from you." Judge
Newton smiled reassuringly at Kincade, motioned for him
to sit, then turned to Yee and asked for her summation.

Kincade nervously smiled over at Marina, who
flashed him a confident thumbs up.

Yee noted the judge's negative demeanor and made
her presentation brief and to the point. The expression on
her face showed her concern at strongly suspecting she
lost. She reviewed her opening arguments on surrogate
parentage case law, the supposedly well-documented
contractual agreement between the parties, and the
extraordinary facts in this case. Yee then asked for
immediate honoring of the surrogate contract, and for
Ephrim to be awarded to Dr. Baatard's care. She argued
that further delay would only hurt Ephrim's emotional
development more.

Judge Newton folded her hands and gently laid them
on the bench top and smiled. Instead of asking for an
adjournment of several days for her to consider the case,

she surprised everyone. Looking at the packed court, Judge Newton announced she was prepared now to render her decision.

A silence fell on the room as everyone waited. Yee appeared as glum as Kincade seemed overjoyed. The judge leaned over the bench's side to confer with a clerk and one of the police. Then she straightened up and began to read her decision.

Marina was startled when, suddenly, one of the spectators rose from the back. "YOUR HONOR, YOUR HONOR," a young man with an intense scowl on his face yelled out. "I have something VERY important to say about this case before you announce your decision. Please hear me out. You must listen to me, your honor."

The courtroom was abuzz with discussion as a courtroom guard rushed toward the spectator. Judge Newton leaned over and spoke with another guard.

"What is your name?" the bailiff demanded. Both of the courtroom guards now moved toward the person making the unexpected interruption.

"Dr. Rudy Salvatore," the man said. He wore a neat, conservative two piece gray suit, glasses, and had his hair held back with a tight bow. A gold earring pierced his left ear lobe.

"And what is your relationship to the case, Dr. Salvatore?" Judge Newton asked, her hand grasping a pen, poised to take notes.

"I object, your honor" Yee angrily shouted out. "The testimony of this person has not been requested by the attorney for either party."

"Over-ruled. Continue, Dr. Salvatore," the judge said.

"I'm an obstetrics and gynecology resident at Haven General Hospital. I assisted in Lissa Vernor's care at the hospital, and I know something very crucial about this child, your honor. Please hear me out," Salvatore pleaded.

Judge Newton motioned with her hands for Yee to sit. She had Salvatore brought up to the front of the courtroom, all the while eyed carefully by wary guards.

A courtroom guard searched Salvatore and passed his driver's license to Judge Newton. The bailiff then administered the oath of testimony, following which Salvatore restated his name for the record.

"What is your relationship to the case, Dr. Salvatore?" the judge asked.

"I participated in the surgery on Lissa Vernor, the mother of Ephrim Vernor," Salvatore told the court. "And I also assisted in her post-operative care."

"I object," Yee yelled out. "The court had no opportunity to verify the veracity of these statements, and should they be prejudicial to my client, then . . . "

"I understand all that, counselor," the judge said. "Of course we'll need to verify everything that the witness says. Of course. But, let's hear him out, shall we? This is family court, not a criminal trial. Not yet, anyway. So, what is it you have to tell us, Dr. Salvatore?"

"I object," Yee shouted out again. "The questioning of this person is inappropriate. We have not had an adequate opportunity to prepare a cross-examination of any testimony to be presented." Yee was nearly screaming as she pounded her fist on the table, her face flushed with rage. Baatard had never seen Yee excited like this before, and was totally taken aback by all the sudden and unexpected happenings.

Marina watched Yee in action, and although she admired Yee's aggressiveness, she found her rather annoying. She noticed that Kincade generally ignored Yee, up to now.

"Overruled," the judge repeated, frowning her impatience at Yee. "Counselor will please contain herself."

"Mr. Kincade, I believe his name is, asked me to speak here," Salvatore said as he looked quickly at Kincade, then back to the judge.

"Mr. Kincade?" the judge eyed the defense table.

Kincade cleared his throat, and stared in amazement at Salvatore. "I'm not aware of doing that, your honor," Kincade said. He had heard of Dr. Salvatore, but never had met him.

"Mr. Kincade demanded Ephrim Vernor's father be brought into the courtroom for questioning, your honor," Salvatore said. "Isn't that correct?"

"I'm not under questioning here, nor is Mr. Kincade." Looking at some papers the court recorder handed her, Judge Newton said, "Mr. Kincade said he wanted the parents of the child to speak. But of course they can't. The husband of the mother, the legal father of this child is dead," the judge told Salvatore. "It's impossible for him to be here. It was only a rhetorical statement." Judge Newton looked over at the defense attorney's chair for support from Charlie Kincade.

"I really don't think the biological father is so hard to find," Salvatore said, looking at Baatard and Yee, sitting at opposite ends of a long wooden table.

Baatard looked in back of him at the closed and guarded courtroom doors, then leaned over and whispered something into Yee's ear.

"What are you getting at?" the judge asked Salvatore.

"First, the court needs to know Dr. Rubin performed a surgical procedure on Dr. Ryder Vernor: it was a vasectomy. Dr. Vernor was aspermic - by that, I mean that he was incapable of supplying sperm, and so he couldn't have been the natural father of Ephrim Vernor."

Baatard, caught completely by surprise at this information, medical information he should have known, dropped the cell phone he was playing with. The loud thud called attention to him, and to the trapped look on his blushed, guilty face.

Now, many things began to become clear to Marina. She wondered if this had something to do with the rumors of Lissa's continued running around. She had heard about it before Salvatore's confession, of course, from Vena, and before her, from others.

"I object," Yee yelled out, as did Baatard, followed by Kincade. All three sprang to their feet and faced the judge. Surprised at the concurrence of all their objections - a first of its kind - Yee and Kincade stared at each other for a few seconds.

"Over-ruled," the judge said. "Now, tell the court in your own words, and in a way that non-medical folks can comprehend, Dr. Salvatore, how you come to possess this information."

"I assisted on the vasectomy procedure on Dr. Ryder Vernor. You can check the medical record at Dr. Rubin's office if you don't believe me."

"And who is Dr. Rubin?" the judge asked Salvatore.

A great deal of discussion broke out in the courtroom, leading the judge to bang her gavel and demand quiet.

"Dr. Rubin is the Chief of Surgery at Haven General Hospital," Salvatore explained. "His specialty is urologic surgery. What I'm trying to explain to you, judge, is Dr. Ryder Vernor was not the father of this child. He couldn't have been, not after having a vasectomy."

"I object," Yee yelled out. "Your honor, we have not had an adequate opportunity to examine the credentials of this person. We have no way of knowing if he is a doctor, or to verify any of the statements he is making. Where is the documentation?"

"Over-ruled. Continue," the judge instructed Salvatore. "You'll supply documentation, I presume?" the judge asked Salvatore.

"Of course, your honor. But, I'll need the court's help in subpoenaing documents."

"It will be done," the judge replied, nodding to the bailiff. "Proceed."

"This is preposterous," Yee said.

"I beg your pardon, counselor," the judge said to Yee.

"That statement is in contempt of this court."

"I was referring to that man's statements, not your ruling, your honor. I apologize."

The judge uncomfortably nodded acceptance of the weak excuse and accompanying apology in Yee's direction. "Proceed, Dr. Salvatore."

"So you see, your honor, that's why Lissa Vernor couldn't get pregnant. Her husband had a vasectomy. Only, I don't think she knew that."

Marina doubted that. The Lissa she knew would have known everything about her men - even this.

"Why do you think that, Dr. Salvatore?" the judge asked.

Salvatore was quiet for a very long time before answering, "Because she was trying to get pregnant, and she assumed all along that she was the problem. And, and . . . because she didn't tell me anything about it."

"But, why would she discuss these matters with you?" the judge asked, her voice now almost a hush barely discernible in the dumbfounded and stunned courtroom.

"Well, you see, Lissa, Lissa and her husband and I, we were friends. We talked about a lot of different things. And, think about it, your honor. Lissa couldn't have known, otherwise I don't think she would have gotten hormone treatments. She really didn't need them since her husband was the problem all along. He had no sperm."

"Dr. Baatard?" the judge said, looking at the desk where Baatard and Yee were sitting. "I may call you back to the stand on this one."

"For a while, I wondered how I was going to get the courage to tell this," Salvatore continued, then broke down crying. After several minutes, he recovered his composure.

"Thank you for giving us this information. I guess what you're telling the court is that Lissa Vernor is the biological mother, but Dr. Ryder Vernor isn't the biological father. Is that correct?"

"That is correct, your honor."

"And how can this be verified?" the judge asked.

"Ask Dr. Rubin. He has the records of this outpatient surgery, Dr. Vernor's vasectomy. He will verify this. Genetic testing could have helped, if Dr. Vernor had been alive to supply tissue samples."

"I have those," Vena blurted out. Vena took several minutes to explain the existence of the genetic analysis she had found on Ryder, Lissa and Ephrim.

The judge was bewildered and well over her head in technology she could only begin to fathom. Judge Newton leaned over the bench and gave some orders to a bailiff, who then got up and left the court room. "Couldn't Dr. Vernor have donated sperm to a, a, a sperm bank?" the judge said, waving her hands in the air to help extract the difficult words. "That would still allow Dr. Vernor to be the biological father."

"Yes, I guess so. But that's not what happened here," Salvatore said, looking dejectedly at the floor.

"I object, your honor. This is pure conjecture on Dr.

Salvatore's part," Yee said.

"Over-ruled," the judge said. "Continue, Dr. Salvatore. Who do you think is the biological father?"

"Dr. Vernor is the biological father," Baatard yelled out.

The judge loudly banged her gavel several times and ordered Baatard to sit. "One more outburst like that, Dr. Baatard, and I'll hold you in contempt of court and have you fined and removed from this courtroom. IS THAT CLEAR?"

"Yes, your honor." Baatard looked around him for support, but found none and meekly sat back down.

"Good. Counselor, control your client please," Judge Newton firmly instructed Ms. Yee.

"Yes, your honor," Yee said, angrily looking at Baatard.

"Mr., I mean Dr. Salvatore, you may proceed," the judge said. "I believe you were about to tell the court who you think is the biological father of Ephrim Vernor."

"Yes, your honor. I'm the biological father, your honor," Salvatore whispered to the absolutely silent courtroom.

Marina had guessed this was coming, but still had a difficult time believing what she just heard.

"Do you mean you donated to a sperm bank, and somehow your sperm was used on Lissa Vernor, by accident?"

"No, not exactly," Salvatore said.

"I object," Yee called out.

"Over-ruled," Judge Newton repeated. "You may proceed," the judge told Salvatore. The judge was intently absorbed herself, and rested her chin in her hand as she focused her gaze and thoughts on Salvatore.

"Although I did donate once to a sperm bank, I don't think that's what happened here. You see, when I was taking care of Lissa Vernor in the Intensive Care Unit after her surgery, she developed a fever. I ordered a number of cultures of her blood, her urine and a vaginal culture. This was done to evaluate the cause of the fever and to adequately treat it."

"My client ordered Dr. Salvatore to do this as part of his flawless handling of the complicated Lissa Vernor case, your honor," Yee interjected. Yee looked over and smiled approvingly and admiringly at Dr. Baatard.

"I left the case before all the lab slips came back to Lissa's chart," Salvatore said, looking down at the floor. "Then, last week I had a meeting with Dr. Rubin."

Judge Newton whispered to the clerk, who shrugged her shoulders. After this, the judge turned back to Salvatore and said, "Excuse me. Continue."

"Yes, anyway, Dr. Rubin and I were reviewing a number of different things," Salvatore waved his hands vaguely in the air, "when we came to the fever that Ms. Vernor developed. Well, on the lab slip for vaginal culture there was a mention of some sperm seen on the microscopic exam. Dr. Rubin performed Dr. Vernor's vasectomy and therefore knew that Dr. Vernor was aspermic."

"Aspermic? Isn't that the word you used a few minutes ago?"

"Yes. It simply means, as a result of having a vasectomy, his semen didn't contain sperm. "

"I see," said the judge, leaning over on the bench and stroking her chin. "And just whose sperm do you think that might be, seeing as you have eliminated Dr. Vernor from the picture?"

"Mine," Salvatore replied faintly, his voice cracking, looking into his lap.

"I didn't quite catch that, Dr. Salvatore. Can you repeat what you just said?"

"I think the sperm was mine, your honor."

Near pandemonium broke out in the court room as everyone expressed surprise and disbelief and shock at what they had just heard. Judge Newton didn't even try to restore order, preferring to confer with the bailiff, then with the court guards, then called the attorneys to the bench. The discussion was heated and lasted for some time before the judge finally turned back to Salvatore.

"Dr. Salvatore," Judge Newton said, "The court would like you to amplify on your last statement. However, I must warn you that you are under oath and that some of the statements you make may involve your admission of commission of a crime. If so, these incriminating statements may be used against you. You may wish to avail yourself of the services of an attorney before answering. Do you understand this?"

"Yes, your honor. I've considered all this for months, and I am willing to clear my conscience right now, completely. This is very difficult to say," Salvatore nearly sobbed. "I loved Lissa, I loved her for years. I even dated her before she found Ryder. I don't even think Lissa really loved Ryder, just his money."

"I object," Kincade yelled out. "Witness is speculating on the private thoughts and feelings of a woman in a coma."

"Over-ruled, continue," the judge directed Salvatore.

"Lissa and I had the opportunity to meet often. Her husband was one of my attending physicians during my residency. Lissa came by the hospital occasionally to have lunch or dinner with him. We would meet when we knew Ryder was tied up somewhere else."

"And just what did you meet for? What did you do during these meetings?"

"What do you think?" Salvatore said. He tried unsuccessfully to smile.

"Oh. And where, ah, did you, ah consummate . . . " the judge waved her hand in the air, a puzzled and embarrassed look on her face.

"In the surgery resident's on-call rooms, in back of the surgery suites. There were no problems with having to rent a room, the privacy was good, there was easy access, and best of all no cost. The on-call rooms had many advantages. A lot of people 'did it' there, you know."

"No, I must admit I wasn't aware of that, Dr. Salvatore," the judge admitted, coughing into her cupped hand.

"We also met at her house, at the motel on first street, in my car, in her car, . . ."

"I get the point," the blushing judge interrupted. "And when was the last time you had intercourse with Mrs. Lissa Vernor?"

"A few hours before she was brought into the emergency room, I think," Salvatore said.

After several minutes of discussion, the judge announced, "Because of the unusual circumstances which have arisen out of the testimony of Dr. Salvatore today, I'm postponing my decision. Court will reconvene after genetic identity testing has been performed on Dr. Salvatore and the Vernor child."

Baatard leaned over and conferred with Yee briefly, Yee nodded and then said, "Your honor."

"Yes, attorney Yee. Do you have another objection?"

"No, Your Honor. But, my client wanted to bring to the court's attention that The Conceptions Foundation has the most advanced genetics laboratory in the entire state. He suggested that the court contact them to hasten the specimen's analysis."

"Thank you for the suggestion, counsel, but under the circumstances, I'm sure you will see why that's inappropriate. Bailiff will have the genetic testing papers on Dr. and Mrs. Vernor and the Vernor child, supplied by Ms. Kleinman, verified and entered into evidence. Bailiff will contact the medical examiner's office to explore who the state can use to accurately, impartially, and rapidly analyze the specimens. The delay for verification of these genetic tests will also give the attorneys enough time to prepare additional questions for the witnesses, including a chance to cross-examine Dr. Salvatore. Dr. Salvatore, this is already agreeable to attorneys Yee and Kincade. Are you willing to supply a blood sample to the court?"

"Yes, your honor, I am."

"Fine. In addition, I plan to examine the dates and authenticity of the custody and surrogate agreements presented to this court. When all determinations have been completed, we'll reconvene. The bailiff will make the appropriate arrangements. Dr. Salvatore, you may want to retain legal counsel yourself."

"Yes, your honor," Salvatore said, his voice now penitent.

"Good," Judge Newton said, banging her gavel. "We'll contact all the parties when the testing is complete and arrange a second hearing. This is to take no longer than thirty days. Until that time, the child will remain with Ms. Vena Kleinman."

"Your honor.," Yee called out.

"Yes, Ms. Yee? I suppose you object."

"Yes, I most certainly do, your honor. The surrogate papers clearly supersede here. The child will be harmed by being allowed to form an emotional bond with Ms. Kleinman, a bond which later will have to be broken."

"Over-ruled. I think that emotional bond already exists. Now, I want these genetic determinations to be made as quickly as possible. Attorneys Kincade and Yee, court will grant you access to copies of said genetic analysis documents for your own use, if you so request."

"Your honor. I strenuously object to the way these proceedings are turning out," Yee called out again. "Dr. Baatard is concerned that Vena Kleinman, now unemployed and emotionally unstable, will attempt to flee with the child."

"Over-ruled. The court has seen no evidence which would indicate that Vena Kleinman would act in that manner." Turning to Vena, the judge said, "Ms. Kleinman, the court instructs you to care for and return with Ephrim Vernor at such time as we'll notify you. Is that clear, Ms. Kleinman?"

"Yes, your honor," Vena said.

"Until such time as the testing is complete," the judge said, loudly banging her gavel, "the court is adjourned. The child will remain in the care and custody of Vena Kleinman until that time." The courtroom rose as the judge stood and left, then broke up into several groups anxiously discussing what had just transpired.

Chapter 62

It took Ramirez less than two hours to hear the disappointing and inconclusive results of the first court custody hearing and to also obtain copies of the genetic analysis papers that Vena had submitted. She examined the papers briefly and quickly surmised she didn't know what the hell she was looking at. Fortunately, she collected people who could tell her what she wanted to know, and called Denny Cruite again at her office.

When Denny picked up on her private line and heard Ramirez, she almost died. She immediately wondered if Ramirez was going to invite her out again somewhere else, but this time to ruin her career and all that she had built up.

"Yes, Mrs. Ramirez. I didn't expect to be hearing from you again so soon."

"Look, Denny, the reason I called is that some doctor named Salvatore is claiming to be the father of my son-to-be Ephrim. How can this be?"

"Well, that's just not so. That Dr. Salvatore must be lying or crazy or both. Mrs. Ramirez, you understand that the way the IVF was done, we definitely used a sperm sample donated from your husband."

"Yeah. But now Salvatore claims otherwise. That would make me very angry. I paid for that kid, but now, under these uncomfortable circumstances, well . . ."

"But I tell you that Dr. Salvatore is clearly wrong," Denny insisted.

"Maybe so," Ramirez countered, "But the child's caretaker, a woman named Vena Kleinman showed up in court with genetic evidence to that effect."

"Yes, I have a copy already. We have the finest lab in the states and are trying at this minute to prove her wrong."

"I got a copy too, so don't try to bullshit me with phony results, okay? Anyway, I'm glad you can prove this Salvatore wrong, and hope it turns out good, for your sake. I like you, Denny, so don't fuck with me." She laughed a course, wet laugh which ended in a cough. "Realistically, the child is unsuitable now. I'm afraid that the adoption's off."

"Unsuitable?" Denny nearly screamed, envisioning eight hundred dollars being flushed down the toilet. "Unsuitable in what way?"

"Simple. How can I adopt any child under these circumstances, Denny? I'm running for public office. A scandal like this would just kill my candidacy, rather than enhance my image, as I had hoped to accomplish."

"We plan to do everything possible to satisfy you, and you'll be hearing from me, Mr. Ramirez." Denny anxiously tried to reassure herself there was no possibility of an error here. Salvatore had not donated sperm, at least to the Conceptions sperm bank, so there was none lying around frozen away that could have been mistakenly used to fertilize Lissa Vernor's ova. Frank did the actual IVF, and although she had her doubts about his overall competence, a mistake in such a simple procedure was beyond even him. Besides, he didn't report any problems. Still, if Salvatore had slept with Lissa as he claimed he did, then it was conceivable that Ephrim had been born from that union, and not the IVF. After all, only about a quarter of IVF's actually took hold and resulted in a viable pregnancy.

"You can bet your sweet ass you'll be hearing from me too. I want some goddamn answers to this, and I want them soon. Or someone's going to be out some big bucks. And Denny, don't call me, unless I call you."

If there turned out to have been an error somewhere, Ramirez would find out - Denny realized that all too well. She also was quite aware that everything Baatard, Frank, and certainly she had worked so hard for would be ruined. Where, how could she run and hide from a woman like that? No, she would have to come up with a worst case plan that would allow her to live, no matter what happened.

Chapter 63

Home of Marina Bonnaserra

The phone rang shortly after nine in the evening, startling
Marina in the midst of her totally quiet home. Marina was
awake, unable to sleep, unable to read or paint or really
do anything after the startling revelations she had heard in
court, and she had spent a long time trying to sort out
their meaning in her mind. She looked at the phone while
it rang several more times before answering it. It was rare
when she got a call this late at night, unless it was an
emergency. Even cranks didn't bother with her.

The voice on the other end of the line was
mechanical, tinny, as if it were being electronically
altered, artificial. It was also totally devoid of emotion,
cold, threatening, and without a doubt masculine.

"Quit running after me, Marina," the disembodied
voice hissed. "Give it up. Let it go."

"Who is this?" Marina screamed. She had never in
her life heard a voice as disembodied like this, and she
had absolutely no idea who was really speaking behind
the disguise, nor what he was talking about. She was

angry at having her privacy invaded and her life's peace disturbed by so unwarranted an action, and wanted to slam the phone down hard.

"You know me," the weird voice said. "I'm your death love."

A terrible thousand thoughts rushed through Marina's frantic mind, all leading to sexual violence long past but not forgotten or forgiven. "What do you want?" she screamed.

"You can't get to me, but I can reach you any time I want to. What's more, I can hurt you infinitely more than you can hurt me."

Marina heard a click as the caller hung up. Just then, she heard a loud crashing sound coming from Austin's room, followed by Austin's shrill crying.

Terrified, Marina ran into Austin's room. Broken glass from a shattered window was strewn all over the carpet, crunching under her sneakers. A large gaping hole in the center of the window pane filled the curtains with the dark night air, forcing them to flap wildly like angry ghosts. A large rock rested in the corner.

Marina grabbed Austin and held him tight. He was crying and startled but at least seemed to be uninjured. Staring at the broken window, she couldn't believe this was happening to her. Her first thought was to look out of the window for the maniac who threw the rock, but she quickly decided against that. She had no way to be sure another rock wasn't already on its way up. Instead, she got down on the floor with Austin, grabbed the phone and called 911. Then she crawled into her bedroom and took out her own handgun. She had never used it, except to practice, but was certainly prepared to now.

The police arrived within minutes and cordoned off the area. Unfortunately, Marina had no neighbors within eyesight, leaving no witnesses. After searching the probable location the rock came from, and looking closely at a few tire tracks, they interviewed Marina.

An hour later, the police sergeant turned to Marina and said, "I'm sorry, but we don't really have a lot to go on here. I wish we had the Star 69 system, or at least Caller ID.

What's that? Marina asked.

"The Star 69 system is something that allows you to call back the last number that called you without telling you what it was, and Caller ID actually gives you the phone number of the guy who was terrorizing you. Unfortunately, Haven doesn't get either service yet. Anyway, my best guess is that it was just a prank.

"Your best guess." Marina yelled. "You think an attempt to kill my son was a prank? By whom?"

"Look, Mrs. Bonnaserra, . . . "

"That's Ms., if you don't mind," Marina corrected him. She could feel the blood rushing around in her head, and just wanted to do something, anything to kill that bastard who was torturing her so. She remembered the scar on Christine Lincoln's chest, warning her that her attacker was still alive and definitely nearby. The very thought gave her the chills and made her feel vulnerable. The forensic evidence she had recently obtained brought her one step closer to identifying him, but was she now getting too close? Apparently he knew she was closing in, and the rock was in direct response, a way to warn her off?

Her goal now was clearly to get out of her house. She didn't know where she would go, but she knew that she couldn't stay here, lest Austin become an innocent victim in a deadly chess game. That much was understood.

After the police left, Marina cleaned up some broken glass and taped up the gaping hole in the window pane. She pulled the shade down, moved some clothes and bedding from Austin's room, and locked his door. Then, she called Charlie.

It was late at night, and when Charlie answered the phone Marina could tell he had been sleeping. She apologized, her voice cracking under the strain.

"Marina, what's the problem?" Charlie groggily asked.

Marina told him what had happened, fighting as she spoke to remain in control. Now was no time to crack. Charlie was shocked at what had just happened, and offered to help in any way he could.

"Could Austin and I stay for the night? Just until we can make some other arrangements. Please," she pleaded. Although she could always stay at one of the nicer hotels near the hospital, she knew she would feel safer being with someone she knew and trusted.

Marina hid with Austin at Charlie's house overnight,

but in the morning she could see that Charlie was uncomfortable about their being there. The signs of Charlie's discomfort were subtle but everywhere. Although Marina would have thought otherwise, she really could appreciate where Charlie was coming from, and she couldn't really blame him, either.

Yet, her relationship with Charlie had changed again, and he was trying to do something significant, something meaningful by defending Vena and Ephrim. Marina admired the way Charlie handled himself in court at Ephrim Vernor's custody hearing, his forceful objections, his legal maneuvering. He seemed more masculine, and more appealing to her when he acted that way, and even more sexy.

After leaving Charlie's house, Marina took Austin to town, and bought a newspaper. She checked the want ads for some temporary housing, then stopped back at her house for some clothes.

She watched her house from a distance for a long time before going in. There were no cars nearby, and no evidence anyone was inside. After waiting a few more minutes, she quickly entered.

Going into her own house now had an entirely different flavor to it, one of fear, apprehension, stress. Once it had been violated by the rock, she could no longer think of it as her home. She entered quietly, and left the door open behind her, in case she needed to get out fast.

After rushing through to gather up some essentials, Marina started for the door. Just as she reached the doorway, the phone rang. Visions of the very same phone ringing last night filled her with fear. She stared at the phone for several rings before picking it up, afraid it would be 'him.'

"Marina?" the voice asked.

"Yes," Marina hesitantly replied.

"Oh, hi. This is Denny Cruite."

What the hell is she calling about now, Marina wondered. She was relieved at least it wasn't the crank caller. Marina felt more and more uncomfortable around Denny with each contact she had. There was just something very strange about her. Marina couldn't define the exact source of the feeling, but knew it's nature to be clearly caution and danger.

Denny explained that she had called to ask how she and Austin were doing.

Marina, on edge, needed to talk to someone, someone else besides Charlie. Another woman seemed most welcome, and she quickly explained all that had just happened. Denny was horrified, and invited Marina to stay at her house. She assured Marina she had more than enough room, and mentioned that her housekeeper was very good with children. Under the circumstances, Marina had few immediately available options other than returning to Charlie Kincade's, and that night took Denny up on the offer.

Chapter 64

Denny sat in her office, staring admirably at the highly favorable accounts receivable balance sheets for The Conceptions Foundation when her personal phone line rang. One thing for certain, she thought, the IVF clientele influx never ceased, despite occasional threats and problems with kooks the likes of Christine Lincoln. Picking up the phone, Denny was surprised and more than a little unnerved to hear Lydia Ramirez's bitingly cold voice on the other end. Hearing from Ramirez was never good, and Denny wondered what was upsetting Lydia now, and what Lydia would want from her. Forcing herself to be polite, she began by asking Lydia how she was doing, but was very reluctant to inquire into the purpose of her call. She was certain it would develop on its own.

"I think it would be a good idea if we met for lunch, Denny, and besides, I enjoy your company so much."

The voice was dry, flat, and threatening. Denny's skin began to crawl. The woman was a goddamn lizard, and Denny was afraid of actually becoming her lunch. She preferred the safer silence to coming out and saying No.

"How about Napoliatonio's Grill? It's just down the

street from you," Ramirez more stated than suggested.

Denny said she knew the restaurant, a dingy, old-style diner in the old town section near the rail yard, and only a few blocks from the central court complex. Its name was much superior to its cuisine. When Denny tried asking Ramirez if she was unhappy with someone or something, or more to the point, with her, Ramirez said only that there were a few things she need to discuss with Denny. With seemingly little choice, she agreed to meet Ramirez at Napoliatonio's Grill in thirty minutes.

An hour later, Denny found herself squished between the wall and Ramirez in a narrow booth in the back of Napoliatonio's Grill. All the waiters and the maitre d' seemed to know Ramirez, and gave her a wide berth and a great deal of privacy. Denny would have preferred less privacy, for her own sake. Ramirez ordered an appetizer plate and a glass of rose wine for herself, and a diet cola for Denny, and dismissed the waiter.

Never one herself to shy from confrontation, Denny could nevertheless sense the danger, and asked, "So, why did you want to meet? If it's about the child, then . . ."

Ramirez interrupted Denny with a dramatic sweep of her fork. "Look, Denny, my sources tell me there might still be a problem getting the other child. Is it so?"

"If you mean Ephrim Vernor, I'm confident it will work out," Denny desperately lied. "We have an excellent lawyer handling the case - Ms. Yee."

The waiter arrived with the appetizer tray, and the drinks. Denny took a sip of her cola, and Ramirez downed another glass of wine, and signaled for yet another.

"Yeah, I know about Yee. Real good legal, a real

bitch, but smart. But Denny, although I'd really like to adopt the child, I just can't get involved in embarrassing litigation. This particular adoption may just not work out. Unexpected things like this can happen."

"But . . . " Denny started to say.

"Oh cut all the bullshit." Ramirez interrupted angrily. "No child no money, no money no child. Got it?"

"But what about our fixed expenses, out lab fees, our doctor charges?" Denny protested. "The Foundation provides much more to its clientele than simply an infertility evaluation and assistance, its . . ."

"Tough. No child no money, period. What part of that don't you understand? And if I were you, there would be several other things I'd be more worried about than reimbursement for all your uninteresting little expenses, not to mention eight hundred thousand dollars."

"Such as?" Denny asked, fighting to remain in control of the situation, yet realizing all along she wasn't.

"Oh, try an extensive state investigation of The Foundation's services. Think you can withstand the scrutiny?" with a wink that threw daggers.

"I think so," Denny blustered, but it rang out unconvincingly to both.

"Bullshit." Ramirez said. "And there's another thing, Denny. I know a lot about you, more than you think I know," she laughed again, then stopped.

"Oh, what exactly do you mean?" Denny asked,

nervously. Her pale face began to flush as her mind raced over what Ramirez might actually know.

"If you don't deliver, well, then I'm just going to have to destroy that little clinic or foundation or whatever it is of yours that we both love so much, and most likely you too in the process." Ramirez patted Denny's knee again, this time more roughly, then stroked her cheek lightly. Ramirez's touch seemed to burn Denny's skin, and Denny recoiled from her seemingly threatening gesture, her face unable to disguise the fear she was experiencing. Ramirez gestured for Denny to take some food from the appetizer tray, but she indicated she would pass.

Ramirez waved her stylishly manicured hands as if to dismiss Denny's questions, and told her, "Enough with this stuff, Denny. That's for another time. Like I said, though, don't call me." She laughed heartily, patted Denny's knee lightly, then moved away, smiled another time, then got up and walked out, never turning back, leaving Denny seated alone in the booth. Denny's mind raced forward, trying to understand what had just occurred and how she could turn the situation around for her. She sensed a personal survival issue here of the utmost gravity.

Chapter 65

Several days passed since her home had been vandalized and she and Austin terrorized, and Marina found that staying at Denny's house proved much easier than she would have ever suspected. Denny and her housekeeper were excellent around Austin, and as a result Marina soon had little concern for leaving Austin there with them while she went to work.

Denny had generously provided Marina and Austin with a small but comfortable room in the back of Denny's house. It was attached, but with its own entrance, a kitchenette, and allowed Marina to come and go as she pleased without needing to interact with her host.

Marina had just arrived home from work, and, seated in Denny's living room with Austin, her mind began to wander. She thought about the time she spent with Ephrim Vernor at the courthouse. The unusual, conflicting emotions she experienced while holding Ephrim still troubled her. Her feelings were confused and unexplainable, and quite real. Denny's arriving home interrupted her thoughts.

"Marina, I was wondering if I could have your help?" Denny asked.

"Of course. I'll be glad to help you in any way that I

can. What do you have in mind?" Denny had asked so little of her, and yet seemed to be willing to give her so much.

"Do you remember when you went to the Conceptions Foundation seminar?" Denny asked.

Marina responded that she did.

"After the formal presentation was complete, one of our success stories came up to tell of her experiences. It's of great encouragement to other women when they see personally how successful pregnancies can result from our IVF services."

"Yes, I agree that the personal experience presented that day was very helpful." She thought it added a certain 'woman's touch.'

"We try to give such a testimonial at each presentation. The other day I was looking at Austin and thinking how beautiful he is, how healthy, and how smart. Now we really want you to tell your inspiring experiences at one of our Conceptions Foundation presentations," she smiled, bubbling with enthusiasm.

Marina was totally taken aback by this suggestion. "Oh, no, really, I don't think I'm your best choice. I'm not good at speaking in public, and really, I, no, I don't think that I'm the one you want." Marina looked up at the ceiling, eyes wide open, then shook her head. She had never been comfortable speaking in front of the public, in great part due to her unpredictable and embarrassing stutter, but how, after all Denny had done for her, could she refuse?

"Well, I strongly disagree, and, I hope you'll reconsider. You trust my judgment, don't you?"

Marina could only muster an uncomfortable smile. "Well, I think you'll be great. Please, let's talk about this again over lunch later this week."

Marina was silent for a few seconds, then said, "Well, okay, but this isn't a commitment; I'm only agreeing to consider it."

"Good," Denny said. "All I'm asking is for you to just talk about your experiences, that's all."

Marina went out with Denny for lunch the next day, meeting at a small coffee shop a block from the hospital. Although Denny still made Marina feel somewhat uncomfortable, Marina found she enjoyed speaking with Denny; Denny seemed so focused, so aggressive, so much in control. Marina admired those qualities in a woman. With Denny's unbridled enthusiasm, Marina sometimes had difficulty getting an edge in the conversation.

After the dessert and coffee were gone, Denny returned to business. "Marina, I understand that your mind is still not made up about being a guest speaker. I think that a tour of Conceptions Foundation might be helpful to you. I'm sure you'll find what you see there most interesting."

"Why not," Marina replied. She had never been inside the Conceptions Foundation building, and had a modest curiosity about what went on over there in "managed care-ville." Yet, she had to wonder why she had been chosen over the hundreds of other potential success stories that surely were available to Denny. She also wondered if her single status was a plus or a minus.

Conceptions Foundation was located on the high-rise strip running through central Haven, only a few blocks by foot from Haven General Hospital. The company's red logo was prominently displayed by a thirty foot high electric sign artfully hung at an angle near the building's top. Denny and Marina walked over from Haven General, along the car-less mall filled with planters and green strips. As soon as the guard at the lobby door recognized Denny, he released the magnetic lock, allowing them both in.

Anticipating Marina's concern about the locks, Denny explained, "We have occasional trouble with demonstrators. This keeps the building and its employees and guests safe and quiet," Denny gestured at the secure door.

Marina remembered Charlie Kincade's description of the disruption he had witnessed at Dr. Baatard's office. Then she remembered the horrible assault that had so recently occurred at Christine Lincoln's house.

Denny waited for Marina to sign in the log book and obtain a visitor's pass. "This way to the clinics, Marina," Denny said, taking the lead.

They passed through the very sleek lobby and entered Denny's office for a few minutes. Denny had a stack of messages, and needed to make several business calls. As Marina waited, she immediately noticed a large framed Mona Lisa print mounted on the wall behind Denny's desk. It seemed to her a little out of decor with the room and particularly with Denny's personality. Marina shrugged, having long ago given up trying to predict people's artistic preferences.

As she spoke on the phone, Denny appeared a little more nervous than usual, and began stroking her chin, but when she noticed Marina watching her, she uncomfortably smiled and stopped. "I've just got to catch up on a few calls. Please, make yourself at home," Denny said, gesturing around her.

After her phone calls were completed, Denny smiled and apologized for the delay. She had noticed Marina's interest in the Mona Lisa and commented, "I've often wanted to be a Mona Lisa myself."

The reply struck Marina as odd, prompting her to ask, "In what way?"

"Just to be special enough to have someone paint me."

"That's not so very difficult, Denny," Marina said. "I could do it, if you'd like." Many people around the hospital knew of her artistic hobby, and a few had seen her works. Although Marina occasionally did get requests for portrait work, she almost uniformly declined. This request was, under the circumstances, somewhat different.

Denny smiled, thanked Marina profusely for her offer, and agreed. Marina asked Denny for a recent photograph and Denny agreed to provide a nice eight-by-ten she had at home. They then made some vague arrangements for a sitting date in the near future.

Denny then escorted Marina back out from her office and into the hallway. As they made their way down the corridors, Marina looked into the open rooms they passed, noticing a private medical laboratory, rooms full of diagnostic ultrasound and x-ray equipment, examining rooms, and a medical chart room.

"It looks like there's a major medical group right here," Marina observed. "The Conceptions Foundation is not at all what I expected."

"Most people never get to see this part of The Conceptions Foundation, at least not yet," Denny smiled. "Actually, just about every Conceptions Foundation client at this time is seen by her own private physician. It's just like you were seen by Dr. Baatard. Diagnostic testing occurs in their offices, too, at least for now."

"But, why then do you have all this equipment?"

"Because the current way may not be the most efficient way," Denny smiled. "But, well that's for the business people to decide. I'm here strictly to help bring the joy of childbirth to as many women as I can who want it," Denny said, smiling saint-like. She gestured with pride at the facilities arrayed like armor around her. "Well, what do you think?" she asked, gesturing with her open hands, slowly turning around full circle.

"I'm certainly impressed," Marina said. She thought a minute, sighed, then said, "Okay, I'll do it. I'll talk about my own experiences with Conceptions Foundation, but for just one time. I want you to understand this is only to help other women learn how The Conceptions Foundation can help them. This isn't to increase your income."

Dimitri Markov

"Of course," Denny replied. "Anyway, Conceptions is a nonprofit foundation." Denny straightened her dress and nervously tossed her head to one side in a highly exaggerated way, almost a jerk. She took a pack of cigarettes from her purse, then quickly stuffed them back in when she remembered Marina's presence. "I'm so glad you've reconsidered. Good, then I'll be contacting you soon about the preparations we must make." Just then, an administrative person came up to Denny and whispered something into her ear, causing her face to frown. "Marina, dear, I must go right away to take care of a small problem. I'm so sorry to cut our visit short."

"It's no problem at all, Denny. I can find my way out. See you soon," Marina said as she waved good-bye and turned toward the front exit. As Denny walked away, Marina noticed how Denny's clothes seemed to fit her a little more loosely than usual. Remembering how ill Denny seemed to look lately, she wondered if Denny were losing weight.

Marina had gone only a few feet around a corner when someone put a hand on her shoulder, holding her back. Startled, Marina almost screamed as she stopped and whirled around. She was relieved but more than a little annoyed to find Frank Lieu lurking within inches of her.

"Hi, Marina. I thought I saw you walking around here today. How are you and your child?" Frank was wearing a

695

white laboratory smock, and clutched several laboratory notebooks in his hands. He had cuts on his face from razor nicks, and some food spots on his shirt. In addition, Frank was frowning and looked very stressed out.

"Oh, Frank, I didn't see you," Marina said. She could feel the rush of adrenaline jolting her body from being unexpectedly grabbed from behind, and tried to regain her composure. "You gave me such a start. You really ought not to surprise people like that, you know. Anyway, Austin and I are doing just fine, thank you."

"Good, good. Look, I'm sorry if I scared you," Frank said.

"Oh, it's all right. Forget it. Say, are you well?"

"All right, I guess," he replied unconvincingly. "Well actually, I've really got a lot on my mind." He seemed to fumble a few moments for the right words, then asked, "Would you like a cold drink before leaving? I could even show you the lab area where Austin began his life. That is, if you're interested," Frank said, looking shyly at his feet.

"I do have to get back to the hospital, but, I guess I have a little time free now. Sure, I can go with you." She had wondered about the IVF process more than once, and had actually meant to ask Denny if she could visit the embryology lab while on her tour here today.

A rushed and annoyed Denny, hurried back to her office from a particularly complicated set of malpractice suit reviews and new economic opportunities, and walked into the hallway just as Marina and Frank were headed away. Instantly recognizing them from behind, Denny was startled and couldn't believe her eyes. All she could think about was the tremendous amount of damage Frank could cause her if Frank ever divulged even one key fact of Marina's IVF to her. Her career in the IVF industry would be finished, and she could even go to prison. Frank knew, to some degree - and it was probably a very damaging degree, exactly what Baatard had done with Marina's ova. Frank knew, that Baatard, without Marina's permission, had directed that her ova be fertilized with Salvatore's foul sperm. Again without Marina's permission, several of the ultimately fertilized ova of high biological and commercial potential were expropriated. As if that were not enough, Marina had been intimately involved in the disruptive QA hearing over the poor outcome of the Lissa Vernor surgery, and perhaps she still was in a position to really hurt Baatard, the Foundation's principle physician.

Denny knew more clearly than she had ever known anything before that Frank had to be stopped, and stopped immediately before any damage was done. Denny had actually carefully planned how this might best be accomplished in her own mind, made the necessary preparations long before, back when Frank destroyed some other critical ova and the sensitive information somehow got out to Ramirez. Back then, Denny had been weak, too generous, and had never been able to make herself carry out the necessary actions, but now, circumstances were dangerously different. Always, she hoped, Frank would keep quiet, Frank could be trusted, Frank would not hurt The Foundation. Certainly, Denny could see now that she had been wrong, dead wrong. Fortunately, it was not too late. Frank was probably escorting Marina to the front door, as it was inconceivable that anyone would even consider taking her elsewhere inside The Foundation. Marina would be gone in minutes, and, she hoped, Frank would return to his lab.

Frank escorted Marina to the company lounge and bought them both a soda from a machine. He handed one can to Marina, opened his, then brought her over to the embryology lab area. "This is where I work," Frank said proudly, as he opened the door to his personal kingdom and let them in.

"Are you sure we can drink in here?" Marina asked, holding her can of soda up in the air for emphasis.

Frank looked at their cans of soda, then at the biohazard label on the door and then back at Marina. "Sure, he smiled. But, let's finish before we touch anything, just in case." Frank downed his can's contents in several large gulps; Marina took a few sips from hers before putting the can down.

The main embryology lab reminded Marina of several biotech companies she has seen recently on the evening news. There were bench top work stations with black marble surfaces, various gas and electric outlets, and equipment, lots of scientific equipment everywhere. "Frank, I'm impressed. You must be so smart. What is all this stuff?" she oozed, hoping to completely drop his guard, and extract as much information from him as possible.

"Well, we have the tissue culture incubators, microscopes, deep freeze units, . . . " Frank tried to explain to Marina what all the pieces of equipment were and what each was used for, with pride evident in his voice.

"I can tell you really like what you do," Marina told him. She could also sense something was definitely troubling him, something he was having a hard time disguising, and his uneasiness today only served to confirm that.

"Yes, it's very interesting, and I get to meet a lot of nice people. Like you," he tried to smile at Marina. "You know, I can still remember when I first saw you, the day of your ova harvesting procedure."

"You were there? I only vaguely remember anything about it," Marina said, suddenly embarrassed at the thought of how much of her body may have been opened for exposition to this geek.

"You bet I was. I brought all three of the embryo transfer tubes up for Dr. Baatard to use when you had your implantation."

"I don't remember any of this, Frank. Can you tell me more about the implantation procedure?" She had not heard of how many embryos were utilized in her IVF implantation procedure, but knew that commonly, more than two ova were implanted at a time. This was because the overall odds of success for each individual ova were only 25 or 30 percent, and by using several at once, the odds went higher.

"You weren't really looking down in that direction," Frank smiled boyishly, pointing to Marina's pelvic area. "Anyway, the ova recipient never is, you know," he smiled meekly at her, his teeth showing excessively. Some red gooey material stuck between the front crevice of his upper canine teeth, giving them an unwholesome appearance. "Anyway, Dr. Baatard inserted a speculum into your vagina, then he put an ova transfer catheter into your cervix."

Marina definitely remembered that part, the embarrassment and the discomfort.

"Baatard injected the fertilized ova into your uterus, and that was that," Frank said, rubbing his palms together. "It's pretty much as you saw on the video at the Conceptions Foundation seminar you attended a while ago. Remember?"

"Yes, vaguely. Then, what did Dr. Baatard do after he injected all the fertilized eggs?" Marina noticed Frank suddenly look embarrassed and turned away from her. "What's the matter Frank? Did I say something wrong?"

"Marina, I think you should know something. Dr. Baatard only injected one fertilized ova," Frank replied, looking away from her eyes.

"I'm afraid I don't understand." She was certain Frank was hiding something from her, and she suddenly had an urgent desire to know any and all important facts concerning her IVF. Frank, like all men she had known, was easy to read, and she hoped he would be just as easy to manipulate and extract information from.

"Well, it's very complicated. Let me put it this way," Frank nervously ran on. "We got eleven eggs from you in the initial harvesting, and I took them back to the lab here with me." Frank pointed casually to some equipment around him, then continued. "I put your ova in the tissue culture unit over there," Frank gestured to a refrigerator-like unit in the corner. "The next day, I found ten of the eggs were viable. I put them into ten separate growth dishes, like the ones over there," Frank pointed over to some equipment on the desk top.

Marina nodded and tried to keep track as best she could. She decided that now was not a good time to ask about the source of the sperm used to fertilize her ova. She wasn't sure she really wanted to know, or even if Frank did.

"Of those ten ova of yours, seven could be successfully fertilized. I grew those seven ova to the sixty-four-cell stage. Now, of those seven ova, five were males, which is the sex you specified, am I correct?" He looked in her direction, as if seeking approval.

"Yes, I wanted a son. Please go on." Her curiosity about the sperm source was almost unbearable, and she fought against asking Frank the details.

"Okay, of those five male fertilized ova, four had the intelligence genetic complex which Dr. B thinks might be associated with intelligence. That's an unusually high percentage, you know. We were impressed."

Marina nodded modestly. She had never heard the aloof Dr. Baatard referred to before as Dr. B, and found it amusing.

"Dr. B told me to freeze the two females, the one male without the intelligence genetic complex and also one other male with it. I let the other three males continue to develop in the tissue culture apparatus. Okay?"

"Yes, I think I'm following you. There's so much information that I need to know about this, and I'm amazed at what you have to tell me. You seem so bright. Conceptions Foundation is fortunate to have someone of your caliber," she smiled. Marina almost chided herself for manipulating Frank so brazenly, but could see no other way to accomplish per purpose. She had to find out what had happened, and certainly asking Baatard was not going to yield any useful information.

Frank, embarrassed, smiled at Marina and continued like a giddy child to tell her anything she wanted to know.

"So" Marina continued, "let me get this straight. There were four fertilized eggs, four males with the intelligence genetic complex plus three others. That means there were seven fertilized eggs. Correct?"

Frank nodded.

"There were seven potential children, my children. Right?" Marina asked, her voice displaying rising anxiety. "And I got three of them, right?"

"Don't get angry with me, Marina. I don't know. Dr. B asked me to bring him three of the male ova, and I did. I know he used the one, the one which I guess resulted in your child."

"But I thought you said you brought three fertilized

ova for implantation in me? Am I missing something?"

"I asked Dr. Baatard about the other ova, but he said he didn't want to risk multiple pregnancies in you, so he didn't use all the ova."

Marina nodded her head, then asked again what happened to the other two ova that Frank had prepared for use that day.

"I asked Dr. B about them, but he said only that he would dispose of them. Hey, that's all I know. Really, he's the boss," Frank told Marina, shrugging his shoulders and beginning to look even more worried and uncomfortable. He saw Marina wince in pain as he described 'disposing' of her fertilized ova, each of which could potentially develop into her children. Frank thought he understood her pain. "Hey, Marina, please, don't tell Dr. B I told you these things. He would be really angry. I hate it when he gets angry. He makes me afraid with his temper and throwing things and yelling. You know?"

"Why can't I just ask Dr. Baatard? They're my ova, aren't they?"

"I don't know. I guess so. Please just don't, and don't ever tell him how you found out, okay?"

"Sure, Frank, sure, if it really worries you so. Thanks for being so honest to me, though. I really appreciate that in a man, especially one so intelligent and caring as you." She was certain Baatard was perceptive enough to pick up the source of her information once she were to ask the question, but somehow she didn't care anymore.

Frank smiled, boyishly. "And never, never tell him I called him Dr. B. Okay?"

"Sure, Frank. I won't tell," Marina said, perhaps believing Frank, but distrusting Baatard. "But, there's one thing I don't know, that I'm sure that you can help me with." The question came out without her thinking about it, as if some force inside her brain made her mouth move.

"Shoot."

Marina frowned at Frank's choice of words, then continued. "I would like to know who the father of Austin is." Once she asked, she felt so ridiculous and stupid that she just wanted to walk out of the room and never look back.

"Oh, Marina. That's strictly confidential. Even I don't have the codes."

"Codes? What codes?"

"The codes to the frozen sperm samples. I can look up which coded specimen vial was used, but there's just no way I can figure out who donated," Frank told Marina, shaking his head.

Marina could sense that Frank was lying, or at least not completely telling her the truth. She would have bet anything he really knew the codes, even if he wasn't supposed to know. But, perhaps for Austin he really didn't know the codes. In that case, she reasoned, maybe Frank was hiding an error. Something in his mannerisms convinced her Frank wasn't telling her something important.

"No, there's definitely no way to know," Frank nervously shook his head. "There's definitely no way to know," he repeated. "But I can tell you this much. The sperm donor code was HR-39."

"Well then, who does know the codes?" Marina demanded, making a point of remembering 'HR-39.'

"I don't know," Frank admitted, shrugging his shoulders. "There are worse things to know about here than that."

"What do you mean by that?" She was right; there was something very wrong here at the Conceptions Foundation, and it concerned her ova. "Frank, you look very nervous. Is there a problem for you answering these questions?"

"No, I guess not. I'm not nervous either. It's just that, . . . " Frank stared out the lab window, looking back and forth down the hallway.

"Who are you looking for, Frank?"

"No one. Well, Mrs. Denny."

"You mean Denny Cruite? Are you worried about her?"

"You bet. She's one mean woman. If she ever finds out I had you in here or that I talked to you so much, she could make bad things happen."

"I don't see how."

"You just don't understand, Marina. Look, a while ago I made a mistake on a special fertilization request," Frank blurted out. He looked afraid, as if he expected someone to kill him. "The man involved doesn't tolerate mistakes. He fries people who cross him. Somehow they found out about what I did, by accident, and now they have me doing worse things."

"What worse things? What man is making you do these things? How is Dr. Baatard involved? Frank, tell me," Marina pleaded, walking to and holding his thin shoulders tightly in her hands.

Frank began to cry, and turned away. "I don't want to talk about it anymore." He began slowly walking back toward the lab door. "That's about all I have to show you right now anyway. Maybe sometime we could talk about this some more," he said, regaining his composure. His eyes nervously darted around the embryology lab, then fixed upon on a large piece of equipment which appeared to have been moved ever so slightly, as if someone had bumped into it.

Marina could almost taste Frank's fear. "Yes, maybe we could talk more again, sometime," Marina said.

"I think I should walk you out now. Please, just wait; I have to turn on a growth medium warmer bath. It will only take a minute." Frank walked over to a small electric water bath unit on a laboratory desk top and reached to a metal switch on the front control panel, then stopped as he heard the door open.

Denny poked her head inside, and started to say, "Frank, we need to talk," when she saw Marina. "Well, well, what a surprise," Denny exclaimed. The irritation in her voice was unmistakable. "Getting a tour of the lab, are you?"

"Yes, Frank was kind enough to show me a little of what my IVF entailed. It was very interesting."

"I'm sure it was," Denny glared at the helpless and uncomfortable Frank, then asked pointedly, "If you're not too busy giving guided tours and inviting the world in to the lab to contaminate our ova, could you see clear to spending a little time helping out on an unscheduled ova harvesting procedure?"

"Now?"

Marina looked at her watch, excused herself, and left quickly. She had learned many more disturbing facts than she could have imagined, whose significance she would need time to consider. In the meantime, she did need to rush back to her office - her afternoon schedule was packed.

Denny nodded annoyingly, and Frank told her that he needed to get his ova harvesting setup ready, and could then follow her in a few minutes. "I'm afraid that Dr. Baatard wants you now, Frank, and if I was you I'd get your scrawny ass in gear and come with me now," she said impatiently, tapping her foot and crossing her arms.

Frank grabbed a few essentials, put them on a small tray, and dutifully followed Denny down the hall, trailing like a wounded dog. When they got to the elevator, Denny told Frank that the procedure was only one floor down and they would take the stairs to save time. She reached over and opened the stairwell door for Frank, and let him carry the equipment tray in.

Glaring at his back as the door closed behind them,

The Surrogate

Denny angrily told him, "Frank, a little knowledge can be a dangerous thing, and in your case, I'm afraid it is," and with that said, she waited until Frank stood precariously at the top of the stairs before firmly planting her boot on his bottom and forcefully shoving him forward. Caught off balance, his shrieks echoed inside the empty stairwell as he fell forward, hit the side rail, and then tumbled down the stairs, before his limp and broken body came to rest, motionless, several floors below.

"Frank, you really ought to be more careful," Denny said, as she left the stairwell unseen and returned to her office.

Chapter 66

Emergency Paramedics arrived from Haven General ER within minutes of Frank's motionless body being discovered, but by then, Frank was obviously dead, and no effort was even expended for resuscitation. Dr. Damon Baatard, having been in the building, came down and witnessed the remaining moments of the attempt at rescue, and then pronounced Frank dead.

Detective Bruce Mitchell of the Haven Police drove in to examine Frank Lieu's body almost as soon as it was broadcast over the police radio. After speaking briefly with the only witness to have seen him recently, Marina Bonnaserra, Bruce ordered the Embryology Laboratory closed off and its contents impounded.

"You can't do that," Baatard protested. "We've got at least ten different sets of fertilized human ova in there, and they're due for implantation in the next few days. If no one goes in there to monitor them and change the fluid, they could die."

"Someone already has died, Dr. Baatard. I'm sure you agree that a person has more value than some eggs." After seeing that Baatard wasn't going to argue the point, Bruce asked Baatard, "I understand that Mr. Lieu worked for you. Is that correct?"

Baatard had never heard Frank given the dignity while alive of being called Mr. Lieu, and it sounded strange. "No, not really. Frank was an employee of The Conceptions Foundation. I don't know his supervisor's name, but you can get that from the Foundation's Director, Ms. Denny Cruite."

"I already plan to talk to her later," Bruce said. "For now, I want a word with you, Dr. Baatard."

Looking at all the people gathered around him, Baatard suggested meeting in his office, instead, and Bruce agreed. Moments later, Baatard shut the door to his office, and, looking as sincerely and calmly at Bruce as he could, he said, "That was truly awful, wasn't it? I mean, we've never had any accident like that happen around here before. Safety is a big issue with The Foundation."

"Death's never a pretty thing," Bruce stated matter-of-factly. "What was your relationship to the deceased, Dr. Baatard?"

"I am a participating physician at The Conceptions Foundation, and I refer a client's ovas to the embryology laboratory for preparation before implantation. Because of this, I see Frank quite frequently, often at ova harvesting procedures. In addition, I do a small amount of research in the laboratory, and Frank occasionally assists me in a small way. Nothing formal."

"Ms. Bonnaserra told me that Frank was speaking with Denny Cruite when she left."

"Mrs. Cruite is the Foundation's administrator, and probably stops in on people with critical positions, like Frank, frequently."

Bruce made some notes, then asked, "How well did

you know Mr. Lieu?"

"Our relationship was superficial, and restricted to work-related occasions. Of his personal life, I know little, except ..."

"Except what?"

"Oh, nothing. It's trivial, I'm sure."

"Try me," Bruce said.

"Frank is an immigrant, from Taiwan, I believe. Lately, he's made quite a number of trips back home."

"Maybe he's homesick?" Bruce suggested, skeptically.

"I guess, but his family immigrated here with him, and I believe they all live together near here somewhere. I wouldn't even mention this, but I've been to Japan, once, for a medical meeting, and I know how expensive it can be."

"Maybe he saves a lot."

"I guess, but I don't think that The Foundation really pays him a lot," Baatard said, leaving, by the tone of voice, the impression that there was more he could have said, but didn't.

"Did Mr. Lieu have any enemies?"

Baatard shrugged. "Who knows? None that I know of."

"Thank you, Dr. Baatard. You've been most helpful, and I'll probably need to speak with you again, okay?"

"Sure, detective, sure. Have a nice day."

"Where can I find Mrs. Cruite's office?"

"First floor, lobby." Baatard watched Bruce leave his office with certain determination in his step, and waited until he had taken the elevator down. After another minute, Baatard took the elevator down to the cafeteria in the basement, grabbed a cup of coffee, then headed for the Medical Records department to catch up on some work. There was little that he could do now for poor Frank.

Chapter 67

Hours later, Marina still had not recovered from learning of Frank's violent death. Just as she was horrified at Frank's death, she was equally furious, and offended with Baatard for not telling her about so significant a detail as destroying several of her fertilized eggs, her offspring. It was almost as if she were reliving her teenage abortion all over again. Perhaps it was the confusion surrounding Frank's death which animated her into action, but Marina went directly over to Baatard's office and marched up to the reception desk.

Marina demanded to speak with Baatard immediately, and a wary Sharlene could well recognize an ugly incident in the making. Attempting to diffuse the situation, Sharlene took Marina out of the waiting room and away from the other patients, and moved her back into Baatard's consultation suite.

Within minutes, Baatard came by the door to the room, and stared at Marina, unsure of the situation and of what had prompted her into coming here unannounced like this. He hoped it was not because of something damaging Frank may have told her before his death.

"Hello Marina," Baatard uttered almost mechanically, and with little effort at hiding his insincerity. "What a terrible day." He frowned as he walked into his office and over to the window, looking out. Then, he sat down and started leafing through a stack of mail while talking to her.

Marina simply stared at him, almost too angry to talk, until Baatard accidentally knocked over his coffee cup. "GODDAMNIT." he yelled out.

For the moment, Marina chose to ignore his profanity and tried to remain composed as she watched him quickly wipe up the mess he had just created. She had made him anxious, and this was good, she thought. "I appreciate your being able to see me on such a short notice, because I'm not doing well at all, Dr. Baatard, not well at all. I just came from a visit with Denny Cruite at the Conceptions Foundation building." Even the thought of her recent experiences there made her sick.

"I guess you heard about Frank Lieu?" Baatard asked, his voice unable to cover the insincerity it conveyed.

"Yes, I most certainly did."

"Terrible," Baatard echoed. "But, why were you there today?"

"Denny asked me to speak at a Conceptions Foundation seminar as a person who had a successful pregnancy, and she gave me a tour of the facilities as an inducement to my saying that I would. And shortly after that, the accident happened." She paused again, fighting to not seem a stereotypically frightened weak female. Visions of Frank's horrible death arose to her consciousness. She could almost hear Frank's desperately muted cry as his twisted body fell to its death, and it all sickened her. Her stutter began to reappear. Shit, she thought, not now.

"How horrible." Baatard uttered, his demeanor more one of arrogant confidence than empathy.

Marina watched Baatard squirm around in his chair, saw the actual fear on his face, and realized that Frank's death definitely meant something to him, and that it also contained a totally different meaning than for her.

"Yes, it was hell the way that man died. I was with him in his embryology lab at the Foundation building just before it happened. How horrible. The police said it must have been an accident, but, what a terrible way to die." she repeated.

Observing Baatard's strongly evasive and insincere reaction, Marina now wondered if Frank was actually killed for seeing her, or for what he knew, or did, or for something entirely different. She also wondered if Baatard felt himself in some danger, and why that might be? For now, she wanted to deal with her own pressing problems, and so she said to him, "The reason I'm here, Dr. Baatard, is not about Frank Lieu, surprising as it may seem."

"And just what might that be?" Baatard asked, anticipating what she was about to ask.

"It concerns my IVF. Somehow, it appears all is not as I thought it had been. As a matter of fact, I have a few important questions I need answers to right away," she continued.

"No problem, no problem at all," Baatard muttered. "Now, what's on your mind?" Baatard picked up some charts and shook off the spilled coffee onto the carpeted floor.

"There are a few details about my fertilization procedure I want to know, ah, know a little better." Marina purposely smiled sourly, like a tax auditor listening to an obviously fraudulent penitent. She crossed her legs and leaned back a little in the soft leather chair. Baatard was a liar, and realizing that, disappointing as it was, actually made her task in a way a little easier.

Baatard put down the mail, looked at Marina, and asked, "Why? Was there a problem?" He deftly moved his hand down to the side of his desk.

"I prefer you not record this, Dr. Baatard," Marina said. Marina had been warned about the recorder by Vena, although she didn't understand how Vena had known what resided under his desk. Finding this out only made her more suspicious of Baatard then ever.

Baatard, a puzzled look on his face, moved his hand away, then smiled, "Of course."

"Thank goodness there was no problem with my fertilization procedure, none at all. At least as far as I know. And what I want to find out from you is really very simple." Marina paused, then said, "How many eggs did you, as you say, 'harvest' from me?"

Baatard pushed a button on the intercom and said, "Sharlene, could you please bring me the Bonnaserra chart? And bring with a handful of paper towels too."

Within a minute there was a knock at the office door. Sharlene entered and handed Baatard a folder with colored tabs on the sides. Then she threw some paper towels on the puddle of coffee on his desk top, shook her head in amazement, and asked, "Do you need anything else?"

"No, thanks," Baatard told her.

Sharlene gave Marina an annoyed glance, then quietly left, shutting the door behind her on her way out.

Baatard opened Marina's chart, looked around, then matter-of-factly told Marina, "The records show that there were about eleven ova."

"There were about eleven," Marina repeated. "I see. And, what happened to all the ova? I mean, one obviously became Austin. But, what about the rest?"

"Why all the sudden interest, Marina?" Baatard asked. "It sounds almost like you've been talking to someone."

Marina could feel herself blushing, and knew Baatard was now certain she had spoken about this with Frank. "No, not at all," she lied. "As I said, It's just that I unfortunately saw a lot more than I bargained for today, with Frank having that deadly accident in your facilities. "Even the thought made her nauseous.

"I see, "Baatard said.

"While I was there, Frank Lieu took me for an impromptu tour of his laboratory. That was shortly before the accident happened. When I was in the embryology lab with Frank, of course, I began to think more about the details of my procedure. There's so much I just don't know about it." She stared directly at his face, but he avoided her eyes.

"Well, anyway, about your fertilization," Baatard said, still hoping to change from an uncomfortable subject. He leafed through her office chart, then said," I don't have the fertilization records in front of me just now. You see, they're separate papers and are stored in your file at Conceptions Foundation. That's where the actual fertilization was done."

Marina could feel her voice tighten up as her stutter grew, and she struggled to control it. "I'd appreciate it if you could follow up on this. It's important to me."

"Hum, I see," Baatard began. "Well, as best as I can remember, some eggs didn't fertilize, so they really weren't too much good for you, were they? Some were females, and you didn't want females, now, did you? And some didn't have the intelligence marker, so as you instructed me, those were discarded too."

"Discarded?"

"Well, perhaps I might better put it: those ova were not used. We don't destroy ova unless specifically instructed to do so by the client."

"How many of my fertilized eggs did you have available that were suitable?"

"There were about four, as best as I can remember." Baatard squirmed around in his chair, searching for a comfortable spot. "I know you may find it difficult to understand why I can't remember all the details about your particular *in vitro* fertilization procedure. But, really, I do perhaps five to ten a week on the average, and since

yours was over a year ago, well . . . " he chuckled
nervously.

"Certainly, I can understand that. Good, there were
about four fertilized ova then," Marina said, trying to keep
this meeting on track and businesslike. "And, of those
four, what happened to them?"

"They were used to fertilize you, that's what. There's
a twenty percent success rate nationwide for IVF, so one
successful pregnancy out of four ova is about average, I
would say."

"Are you saying you transferred all four ova into my
vagina during the implantation procedure?"

"Yes, but actually, they were inserted through your
vagina and into your uterus."

"Yes, of course that's what I meant." She didn't care
about the details of implantation right now. If her worst
suspicions were true, she might turn out to be the mother
of other children, somewhere else.

"Excuse me, Ms. Bonnaserra. I'm a busy person, a
very busy person. You appear to be looking for a specific
piece of information. If I knew what it was, perhaps I
could help you better. At this point, you sound more like a
police investigator," Baatard angrily told her.

"Yeah?" Marina smiled coyly. "Do you want a
lawyer present?"

"Of course not; don't be silly. Now, are there any
other questions you have for me today?" Baatard asked

Marina.

"Yes, I have just a few more. Please try to be patient. I'll be glad to pay you for your time if you like."

"No, of course not. Okay, ask away," Baatard said, looking at his watch.

"I had one child, Austin. So, what happened to the other three eggs?"

"Pay attention. I just got through telling you they were all used to fertilize you."

"I am paying attention, Dr. Baatard," Marina said sternly. He was treating her like a child again, and she resented it. "I remember in the Conceptions Foundation seminar that usually several eggs are implanted because less than half typically take root. Was that what happened in my case?"

Baatard looked like he was going to say 'yes,' but seemed to reconsider, then said, "No, now that I think of it, that's not exactly what happened." Baatard looked again at his watch, picked up her medical chart, then smiled and said, "Oh, I remember now. Of course. I decided to only implant one ova instead of all four. I didn't want you to run the risk of multiple pregnancies."

"But I thought you were expecting only a twenty percent take, and were planning to use all of the ova?" She knew there really were, at least according to Frank, three ova present, not four. Frank had already told her the other male ova with the intelligence genetic complex was frozen.

"Yes, well I changed my mind. I guess."

"You guess? And the other eggs? What happened to them?"

"They were too old to re-freeze, so I had to destroy them," Baatard said in a hushed voice, looking away from Marina.

"Oh," Marina said, then sat silent for some time. Visions of her teenage past were returning to haunt her. She began once again the uncomfortable process of reliving memories that she had long ago learned to carefully suppress.

"So, do you have any more questions?" Baatard asked, obviously annoyed and angry.

"Yes, just one. Who was the father?"

"I'm sorry," Baatard said. "Who was what father?"

"Maybe what I really mean to ask is, who donated the sperm?" She could see she was pushing Baatard, and was beginning to feel more than a little threatened, physically by him. Now she was no longer certain he wouldn't just jump out of his seat and grab her around the neck and start choking her. It was an unnerving sensation.

"As you may have guessed, on this subject there's absolute and complete privacy. The donors don't want to be identified. All sperm vials are coded, and I have NO idea at all who has the codes or where they're kept. I thought I explained all that to you before we began, and you accepted it. You acknowledged the conditions beforehand, in writing, I might add," Baatard said, holding up her chart. He got up, walked to the door and said, "Well, I hope that helps you. Now, I really have got

to get back to seeing patients. So, if you'll excuse me, . . .
"

Chapter 68

Marina left Baatard's office, totally unsatisfied with his shallow answers. Knowing full well when a man wasn't leveling with her - a matter she was experienced in - she called up Vena and asked if they could meet. Vena too had contacts with Baatard, and seemed to know his ways. Vena suggested it might help to have Kincade there, and said she would call Marina right back. A few minutes later, Marina picked up the phone on the first ring. It was Vena, as expected.

"Kincade said fine, he said ten minutes, and wanted to talk at a diner. He said he was hungry. Is that okay with you?" Vena asked.

"Sure," said Marina. "Did you ever notice how he always wants to meet at a diner? That's why he has such a problem with weight."

"Oh, I didn't notice. He looks pretty good to me," Vena replied.

Marina, somewhat taken aback at Vena's complimentary reply, wondered if Vena, with Ryder only so recently out of the picture, now had her sights on Charlie. She didn't know exactly how she felt about that, except it didn't sit right with her. Although Marina realized she certainly had no exclusive claim to Charlie, and didn't even know if he was dating other women - and he probably was, knowing him - Marina did care for him.

In some subconscious, ill-defined way she still wished for their relationship to develop into something more than it was, and was sorry that it had deteriorated so in the recent past.

They all met as planned at the Haven diner a short time later, took a booth in the back, and ordered some coffee. Marina strategically positioned herself next to Charlie, leaving Vena to sit across from them.

As she tried to hold onto to her coffee cup, Marina's hands still visibly trembled from having only hours ago learned of Frank's gruesome death. Marina started speaking first, and told Vena and Charlie what she had heard.

"Why did you go over there?" Charlie asked.

"I went over to Conceptions Foundation today, at Denny Cruite's invitation," Marina repeated, much as she had just done for Baatard. She observed Charlie frown, as he typically did, whenever she mentioned the name of Denny Cruite, and again wondered why he apparently disliked her so. "Denny wanted me to perform a public service testimonial at one of her informational presentations. On my way out, I met Frank Lieu, and he told me . . . "

"Frank Lieu?" Kincade smirked.

"He's the embryology technician for Conceptions Foundation," Marina explained. "At least, he was."

"Oh," Kincade nodded his head and took some notes. "That's an awfully funny name. It sounds kind of like . . . "

"I know," Marina said, cutting Kincade off and trying to ignore his childish humor. "Frank implied to me there was something unusual about the sperm used to fertilize my ova, which he identified as HR-39. Frank also said that usually, for a three ova implantation, he would load all the ova up into only one or two catheters. In my case, Baatard at first requested only one catheter, then changed his mind and ordered three separate catheters. Frank thought all three of my fertilized ova were to be used to impregnate me, but Baatard unexpectedly changed his mind, and used only one catheter, one ova. Baatard then left the procedure room with two unused catheters, and when Frank tried to ask what was going on, Baatard told Frank he didn't want to risk multiple pregnancies. He claimed he was going to destroy the unused ova."

"Did Frank tell you what he thought Baatard may have been up to?"

"No, but he was very fearful of both Baatard and Denny Cruite. Frank said he made a mistake on a 'special' fertilization, and they both were angry with him. Frank also told me that Denny could make bad things happen, but didn't elaborate on what or why."

"Denny is someone you really have to be careful of, that's for sure," Charlie said.

"Why's that, Charlie?" Marina asked.

"I'd like to tell you more, believe me, but I can't. Attorney-Client. But I think Frank's sense about her is right on."

"Talking about this made Frank very nervous, and he told me he had to get me away from him and from the lab. As Frank was getting ready to walk me to the Conceptions exit, Denny came by, and I took my leave, so as to not cause trouble for Frank. Shortly after that, he died." Marina said, struggling to keep her composure.

"It must have been terrible," Charlie agreed, shaking his head. He stroked his chin, looked quietly up at the ceiling, then asked, "Do you think it was an accident, Marina?"

"I heard that the paramedics think it was."

"But what do you think?" Charlie asked Marina.

"I think he did something or knew something that was a problem for someone. And I think he was killed because of that," Marina said.

Charlie Kincade thought about it for a moment, then asked, "Assuming Frank was correct, and that Baatard was not telling the truth, I wonder where exactly Baatard did go with the other fertilized ova after he implanted one in your uterus? Do you take Baatard at his word that the ova were destroyed?"

"He said he destroyed them," Marina shrugged. She no longer believed Baatard, and judging from Charlie Kincade's face, neither did he.

"Yes, but do you think there was a record of this?" Kincade asked.

"Frank didn't say," Marina replied.

Kincade said, "Well, if you can't find out what Baatard did with the ova, and you're thinking he may not be telling you exactly what he did do, then maybe knowing what else he did that day might help."

Vena nodded her head, and said, "I don't think Baatard would tell me, but maybe I can approach it another way. Deanna Baptiste said she knows some office staff in Baatard's office, and maybe she can help. Give me a day and let me see what I can come up with."

"It might be better if I call Deanna. I've already called her once before, and this is, after all, about my ova," Marina said.

Vena admitted that this approach made sense. She flashed Marina a confident look, but let her smile linger in Charlie's direction before getting up and leaving.

Marina paid the bill, something she had become used to around Charlie. He seemed perpetually short of cash. On their way out of the diner, Marina smiled at Charlie and said, "Hey, I'm seeing more of you these last few weeks than I ever did. And, have you noticed something?"

"What's that?" he smiled back at her.

"We're getting along better. I like that." She looked over at Vena's car as it pulled out of the parking lot, then held out for Charlie's hand. He took her hand in his and gave it a warm squeeze.

"Me too. But, I don't trust this Baatard. There's something about him, you know?"

"Yeah," Marina agreed. She was beginning to suspect what it was, too, and it frightened her. All the doubts she had about Baatard during the QA hearing over Lissa Vernor were raised anew and now given additional credibility.

Chapter 69

Deanna's Apartment

Marina knew that, to find out where Baatard had gone immediately after implanting her ova, she couldn't count on directly asking him. If he told her anything at all, it would probably be a lie. Other than Baatard himself, the most likely person to know that information would, she suspected, be his secretary/receptionist Sharlene. It didn't take too much imagination to guess what Sharlene's response to a request for that information would be.

Marina decided to try Vena's suggestion, one that wouldn't tip Baatard off to her inquiring, and called Haven General to speak with Deanna Baptiste. From what she knew of Deanna's personal life, mostly from what Charlie had told her, she thought Deanna could help her find about where Baatard had gone after Marina's implantation. Vena certainly thought Deanna might be able to help. After a few tries to different wards, the hospital operator transferred Marina over to the nursing office.

An annoyed scheduling nurse said that Deanna was scheduled to work the morning shift but had failed to show. She told Marina that no one answered the phone at Deanna's apartment and speculated that something had happened to her car. Marina, being a hospital employee, managed to get Deanna's address before hanging up.

Marina tried calling Deanna herself from a nearby pay phone, but unfortunately, the line was continuously busy. Relieved that at least she had located Deanna, Marina waited a little while and tried the phone again; it was still busy. Marina tried Deanna's phone one more time that afternoon to see if she could get through, then gave up.

Impatient and a little concerned, Marina drove over to Deanna's apartment building. It was an older brick and stucco converted condo complex next to a warehouse and a heavy equipment yard. A large black Doberman was tied up with a long clothesline leash in the front yard. It lunged viciously at her as she approached the front door, frightening her. The grass was uncut and trash littered the walkway. Although not enough to call the Health Department over, the lack of attention and caring was telling.

The lobby entrance was a clutter of gaudy, peeling paint and trashy photo reproductions of nameless Italian cities. No one answered when Marina rang Deanna's apartment from the massive button array at the main lobby. Marina tried the manager's apartment button next.

After the manager let her into the complex, Marina walked over to Deanna's apartment. The front door was closed but unlocked. Marina knocked on the door and rang the door bell for several minutes before going in.

Inside Deanna's dingy little apartment, the living room was dark and the shades were drawn. A mixture of stale food, cigarette and liquor odors lingered from the carpet. Marina could make out some magazines and two half-empty coffee cups on a small table in front of the couch. The furniture was old and had several cigarette burns on top. There were assorted stains and rips in the fabric of the couch and the curtains. A loose pile of old cigarette butts choked several ash trays. Clothes were strewn over the floor and on several pieces of furniture, and draped over an ironing board which stood against the wall in one corner of the room.

Marina called out for Deanna, and thought she heard a muffled sound from the back. She slowly walked down the darkened corridor, tripping over some clothes and a glass on the floor. A cat hissed and ran by her, startled more than Marina was. The bedroom door was ajar; Marina slowly pushed it open.

Marina found Deanna sprawled out on the bed, draped loosely in a pink baby doll night gown. Deanna's hair was a mess, her makeup was smudged and her eye shadow was runny, making Marina think that Deanna had fallen asleep without washing her face, perhaps while crying. Deanna was partially covered with a mixture of sheets, clothes and cigarette butts.

Deanna slowly turned her head in little jerks and tried to speak through a heavy slur. "Oh, Vena," she laughed. "I'll just bet I know who you're looking for."

"I'm not Vena. I'm Marina Bonnaserra, and I came looking for you, Deanna." Deanna looked like she had

Dimitri Markov

gone through hell, but at least she was alive.
Ignoring what Marina told her, Deanna cried out in a
slur, "Well, Ryder's not here tonight." Deanna put her face
in her hands, rolled over on her belly, and yelled, "Ain't
life a bitch?" Deanna gave several dry heaves, then
emitted a long wet cough.
"Why would Ryder be here, Deanna?" Marina
couldn't understand where Deanna was coming from.
Surely Deanna remembered that Ryder was dead. Marina
looked at the metal clip in an ashtray on the floor, and
saw some white powder and a razor blade on the night
stand. Almost exploding with anger, Marina said, "What
the hell does all this mean? What's been going on here,
Deanna?"
"Party time. I've had company."
"Who's been here with you?" Marina yelled out,
barely able to control her anger. She could hardly imagine
the scum who would spend their time like this.
"Oh, you'll never guess," Deanna teased.
"Try me." Pointing to the coke, Marina told Deanna,
"Where did you get all these drugs? It must have cost a
fortune."
"I've got expensive tastes," Deanna said. "Ryder
comes here all the time and sometimes he brings me a
gift. That is, he used to come here all the time. Now he
don't do that shit anymore." Deanna buried her face in a
pillow and cried out, "Because I killed him. Oh God, now

731

I just want to die. Leave me alone, please leave me alone and go away."

"Deanna, don't you remember? Ryder had a heart attack. You didn't kill him." At least, she didn't think so.

"He was electrocuted, Vena. And I did it to him," Deanna sobbed incoherently.

Marina could see that Deanna was delirious and hallucinating and still saw her as Vena, although there was absolutely no resemblance between herself and the lanky, buxom Vena at all, and was rather insulted at the comparison.

"That's impossible," Marina told her. "How could you possibly have killed Ryder?" At times she had wondered if Baatard somehow managed to kill Ryder, and whether his death was related to Lissa's surgical mishap. Even Charlie Kincade thought that might have been the case. Although it did seem to make sense, it also made too much sense, and somehow didn't seem consistent. Now apparently Marina was again wrong about Baatard.

"I put a shorted electro-coagulation probe in the OR, Ryder used it, and it zapped his heart."

"Why the hell did you do that?" Marina demanded, grabbing Deanna by the shoulders and shaking her. She was furious at Deanna for killing Ryder, an innocent man, a good man, and a good physician.

"I did it to get more drugs," Deanna said, looking around at all the drug paraphernalia in her room. "If I didn't, well, someone was going to tell the police that I was stealing drugs from the hospital. Then I'd go to jail again, and I'd rather die than go back there." Deanna tried to cry but in her stupor managed to only slobber.

"But why would you want Ryder dead?"

"Because Ryder promised to give his child up for adoption. Then, Ryder backed out. You don't back out of that kind of agreement just like that; there was too much money in it. That much I can say for sure," she said, gesturing broadly around her.

Marina knew as Deanna said this that, strange as it was, it did make a perversely distorted sense. It explained the surrogate agreement Baatard claimed to have for Ephrim Vernor. But why would Baatard now want to arrange for the adoption of a child? And why go through the trouble to use a surrogate when other means were more readily available - for the right price. Even more puzzling, who did Baatard want the child for? The questions kept on coming, but reasonable explanations lagged far behind.

Marina had to tell someone about this as soon as possible, and wondered if Charlie Kincade was her best bet. Certainly, it really depended on what she wanted done with the information. She also needed to get some help in here in a hurry, so that Deanna could be taken care of.

Suddenly, Deanna moaned loudly, "Oh God, help me," as she slumped off the side of the bed, hitting the wood floor with a heavy thud. Marina grabbed Deanna and shook her violently but couldn't get her awake again. Her mind raced as she grabbed the phone and dialed 911 to call for an ambulance. Marina knew it could mean jail for Deanna after she got out of the hospital. That is, if she lived long enough to make it to a hospital in the first place. Marina checked Deanna as carefully as she could, noting a reassuring steady breathing and a strong pulse.

Deanna might never live to tell her story again, and even if she did, probably she would never again admit to killing Ryder. Marina also realized that no one would believe what she claimed Deanna said.

Marina next called the housekeeper at Denny's house that was watching Austin, and was glad to hear Austin was well. As she put down the phone, Marina noticed a group of business cards held together by a red rubber band, stuffed under a doily by the night lamp. She took the cards and looked through, finding, among others, Ryder's and Baatard's office cards, and one from The Conceptions Foundation. The name on the card was Denny Cruite. Marina pocketed all the business cards.

Several anxious minutes passed for Marina, waiting for the paramedics to arrive. Deanna never woke up again, and although she was still breathing, what breaths she did take became more shallow and labored as time slowly passed on. A few minutes later, Deanna suddenly vomited all over herself and on the bed clothes. Despite that, she didn't awake, and ended up choking in her own vomit, leaving Marina disgusted and more frightened than ever. It was then that Deanna stopped breathing.

Her hands shaking, Marina frantically initiated CPR. All the times she had trained, the calm she was supposed to retain, all this went out the wayside in the reality of an imminent death. CPR was a task she had never actually learned well, other than a few courses in nursing school and refreshers at the hospital. Now, smelling the putrid vomit which pulsated out of Deanna's mouth, hearing the choking and gurgling with each ineffectual chest compression revolted Marina. She pressed on Deanna's chest with less force each time, now regretting not having called an ambulance as soon as she had found Deanna delirious.

Although Marina was certain Deanna would be dead by the time paramedics made it to Deanna's apartment, the emergency response team, a local volunteer unit, did finally arrive a long fifteen, anxious minutes later. It seemed to Marina like an eternity. The ambulance crew spent another fifteen minutes attempting to revive Deanna in her apartment before transporting her to Haven General.

The police who responded to the ambulance call stayed at Deanna's apartment after the ambulance crew took her away. It didn't take them long to find all the drugs, and comment that the 'strong shit' Deanna had used, as they crudely put it, probably O.D.'d her.

Marina, as the last person to see Deanna, was kept in the apartment for questioning. She couldn't be a great deal of help to the police, except to show them the business cards she found there. Her presence in the apartment placed her under suspicion of drug use also, and she was required to give a urine sample.

Marina already knew the police investigator, Bruce Mitchell, from her faltered rape investigation and Frank's accident. She told Bruce everything Deanna had told her, including Deanna's pointing to someone at Haven General as her drug supplier. Marina already had heard through the grapevine that Deanna was under suspicion of stealing drugs from Haven General, and it would have been only a matter of time before she would have been arrested at work.

Shortly into his questioning of Marina, Bruce was interrupted by a phone call. He grunted a few comments, then hung up. "That was a doctor at the emergency room at Haven General. They're pumping the stomach of your friend Deanna, and they think she's probably gonna live," he told Marina matter-of-factly.

Marina collapsed onto a chair, relieved. Why had Deanna taken drugs, she sobbed? Marina imagined that if only she had known, maybe she could have talked to Deanna, and stopped her self-destructive habit.

Bruce tried to comfort Marina as best he could, seeming to believe the story Marina had told him. When Marina asked Bruce what he was going to do, he told her, "Do? There's not a hell of a lot I can do, other than to book Deanna, at least right now."

"I don't understand?" Marina said, still crying and barely in composure.

"I need more evidence than the word of a strung-out drug addict that someone at your hospital supplied the drugs, or that it was as payment for assisting in murder, or arranging for an adoption. For now, I'm only willing to call this a simple drug overdose."

"A simple drug overdose? You've got to be kidding." Marina gasped. "Didn't you hear what Deanna told me?" Somehow Marina got a bad feeling that Bruce wasn't interested in or capable of pursuing any accusations against Baatard. The whole shocking affair was taking on the same sordid flavor of the seemingly half-hearted investigation of her own rape years ago, during the limited time it had been not at all aggressively pursued, and then unceremoniously dropped.

"I'll have to look around more first. And Marina, please, keep this conversation to yourself, okay?" Bruce asked her, then winked.

Marina didn't know exactly what Bruce meant, but the guilt she now felt profoundly shook her. Marina just couldn't accept that a nurse, even one as messed up as Deanna, would have made such a stupid mistake. She felt certain that someone at Haven General had intentionally given Deanna enough drugs to cause an overdose, that they probably wanted Deanna dead, and that someone would have to pay.

Chapter 70

Offices of Cornwall, Kincade and Santos, P.C.

Charlie Kincade had a bad feeling about the way the custody hearing would turn out. The courtroom gossip had the judgment circulating long before the scheduled reconvening later that day, at 4:00 in the afternoon, and the rumor Kincade heard was against him and his client.

Allowing Baatard to assume custody of Ephrim Vernor just didn't make sense; Kincade could only assume extraordinary outside pressure had been brought to bear on the court. He suspected the administrator of Haven General or Denny Cruite had government ties and had used every one of them. Baatard obviously had displayed just too good a track record at avoiding trouble and getting his way. First, Haven General absolving him of error in the Lissa Vernor case. Then, the coroner ruled Ryder Vernor's death accidental - a death Kincade now knew, based upon Marina's conversation with Deanna shortly before her I.D., to be intentional.

Kincade had to wonder, though, if all of what Deanna had told Marina was true. After all, Kincade knew the cause of Dr. Vernor's death was a bad heart rhythm, and most plausibly of natural causes. Unfortunately, Deanna was the only solid tie linking Denny or anyone to the murder, the evidence was only hearsay, and she was conveniently unable to talk about it now. Kincade had to wonder if Deanna's overdose itself was accidental, or if she simply knew too much.

But why, Kincade kept asking himself, would Ryder agree to give up his child? Did what Deanna suggest make sense? Much of it didn't, he had to admit. Some of it uncomfortably did.

Needing more ammunition for his case, Kincade called his legal clerk Andrea into his office. "Run a newspaper search on Dr. Damon Baatard," he asked her. "I just bet the crooked SOB is in some article somewhere. I just don't trust him. We've got to find something somewhere that will help us."

Looking up momentarily from the stack of surrogate documents he had been reviewing for hours, Kincade tapped a red lead pencil on his glass desktop. Acting on an inspiration based on what he had witnessed in Baatard's waiting room, he called after Andrea as she was leaving his office. "And Andrea, contact the local antiabortion league and ask them what they know about Baatard. Also, run a search on The Conceptions Foundation. Look for articles on complaints that may have surfaced about their billing practices, their sperm bank, the quality of care, complaints from local doctors of unfair competition. You know, the whole thing. Okay?"

Andrea came back in under four hours, surprising even Kincade, but could only tell Kincade she had found almost nothing of significance.

The Surrogate

Marina called over to Baatard's office later that day. Finding that Baatard was there, she left her office and walked over. She didn't ask Kincade about doing this before going, certain that he wouldn't approve, particularly with the custody case still undecided. Yet, Marina had a good professional relationship with Baatard before all these problems had begun, and felt that she at least could talk to him, reason with him. She kept reliving her last hours with Deanna, and wondered about Baatard's relationship to Deanna.

As soon as Marina walked into the office lobby, a scowl came over the face of Sharlene, Baatard's receptionist. Without saying a word to Marina, Sharlene got up from her swivel chair by the phones and rushed back into the exam area. It didn't take too acute a hearing level for Marina to hear Baatard shouting, "What the hell is SHE doing here? Get her out of here, you stupid bitch."

"Don't you talk to me that way, asshole. What do you think I am, some kind of fool?"

Marina heard a door slam, then saw Sharlene come back. She looked like she was going to kill someone.

"We don't show you listed as having an appointment today," Sharlene told Marina. Visibly upset, she forced herself to appear business-like and ask, "How may we help you?"

Marina could tell her visit had caused a problem for both Baatard and for Sharlene. She wished she could tell if it was for the same reason for each of them. Marina smiled coyly and explained to Sharlene that she wanted to discuss some 'personal matters' with Baatard.

"Oh," Sharlene blushed, anger uncontrollably sweeping over her face. "Dr. is occupied at the moment. Why not call back at some other time, and perhaps we can schedule you for an appointment?"

"I'd rather not do that. You see, it's very important and I do need to speak with him today, and I'm willing to wait." Marina could see her request didn't sit well with Sharlene, which was another reason she knew waiting would get her access - Baatard might think it the only way to get rid of her. She decided that it might be prudent to make Charlie Kincade at least aware of her presence here, and asked to use the phone.

Sharlene escorted Marina into the clerk's area where she could used the phone. Charlie was at the courthouse, so she left a message instead. When Marina was finished, Sharlene left her in the clerk's area instead of moving her back to the reception area, presumably to avoid the possibility of having Marina discuss unfavorable things with patients.

Marina passed the time waiting by looking at a Conceptions Foundation brochure she had brought with her from the waiting room. As she leafed through it, she came to an area describing services offered. Although she had not noticed it before, abortions and surrogate adoptions were indeed listed.

The office phone rang constantly, and Sharlene had to switch back and forth from the hold button. "Why not let me help you while I'm waiting?" Marina offered. "I think I can handle it. After all, I am a nurse, you know."

Sharlene seemed uncertain at first, but appeared rather harried and more than a little perturbed, and soon said, "Well, okay, I guess it will be all right." Sharlene quickly explained the button sequences to Marina, then just as quickly disappeared in the back room, not returning for several minutes.

Marina picked up a few calls, most of which were either requests for appointments or requests for Baatard to call this person or that lab. Marina asked Sharlene where the appointment books were kept, and was directed to another desk area by the window. Going over there, Marina found the current year's books, and got back to work answering calls while she waited for Baatard to see her.

Sharlene frequently got up from her desk, dashing back and forth to the exam areas. One of the times Sharlene was out of the reception area, Marina quickly searched the desk drawers by the appointment book and soon located a set of the past year's books. She opened the appointment book from last year and quickly looked up the date of her implantation. Immediately after the line where her procedure was noted, was written "Haven Convalescent rounds." Just then, Marina heard Sharlene's footsteps and shoved the old appointment book back into the drawer.

"Dr. is still very busy, and wants you to understand it may be hours before he can even speak with you. Sorry," Sharlene said insincerely, trying her best to smile. She sat down and wearily answered another phone call, but

appeared distracted and quite angry.
"Is there something that's bothering you that we could talk about?" Marina asked her. Something obviously was.
"I doubt it," Sharlene said, dejected.
"Maybe so, but I think we both have Baatard trouble." Marina knew that to be so, but could only speculate what Sharlene's problems with Baatard in particular were about.
"Yeah, maybe so," Sharlene sighed, not looking up from her work. Still, she seemed not willing or interested in amplifying her remarks.
The next time Sharlene left the room, Marina took the opportunity to leave. She had gotten more than she planned for.

Chapter 71

Home of Denny Cruite
Central Haven, New Jersey

Marina was again torn from a fitful sleep, her body
soaked in sweat, for the third time this night, and she
could feel the strain of sleep lost. Each time she was
awakened, she thought the reason to be the same - a
nightmare about four children crying, a burning
orphanage, and each time she was helpless to do anything
to save them. Her inability to help the children was
frustrating, unreasonable and probably the worst aspect of
her nightmare.

Marina checked on Austin in his crib next to her bed
and found him to be sleeping comfortably. That only
relieved her anxiety partially. Something was still
bothering her, something vague and subtle and very
terrifying, its identity too far removed from any reality
she knew of to give it real form. She wondered if it was
simply the unfamiliarity of living in another, strange
house, Denny's house. Frank's remarks about Denny,
made just before he died, kept recurring to her, adding to
the doubt.

Giving up on sleeping, Marina walked into the
kitchen and brewed a pot of tea. She put an English

muffin into the toaster, and waited at the kitchen table for it to pop up.

Sitting alone, she began to think about the time, so recent but so far, when Austin had been born. Although really only months ago, it now seemed like years. Her most fond memories were of his being brought to her for feedings. Perhaps it was the physical closeness, the bond, the act of giving life, nutrition to another human being. It was unfortunate that the damage to her one nipple made breast feeding often a painful affair for her. How ironic that her rapist could still hurt her so after all these years, even intruding into the intimacy she shared with her newborn. But even back at Austin's birth, Marina remembered having experienced vague and free-floating fears, nightmares which woke her from sleep, panic the nurses had tried to reassure Marina were not uncommon for new mothers.

Marina's thoughts moved to when she first read about the "miracle birth" of the woman in the coma - Dr. Vernor's wife Lissa. Austin's and that poor child's birth were so close. Why, she thought, they could almost have been brothers. Marina tried to laugh out loud at this thought, then began to feel very uncomfortable. A thought, a possibility too ridiculous to consider, too uncomfortable to believe, an evil, dangerous alternative reality floated poorly hidden just beneath her carefully constructed consciousness.

The Surrogate

Marina again heard Austin cry and got up to see what was the matter. She found Austin right where she left him, asleep in his bed. Yet, it seemed impossible to her that Austin could have cried out from the position he lay in; he seemed to have not even moved. The fresh, warm aroma of the tea and muffin followed her into their bedroom, and drew her back to the kitchen.

Suddenly, she heard the cry again and rushed back to Austin's crib. Still, Austin lay there, quiet. But this time the crying out of a child persisted, distinctly, pleadingly, even now, and she wondered if she were going insane. And, even more strange, she could swear that particular cry she heard, although like Austin's, may not have been his. She knew his own particular cry exceedingly well, and could pick it out of a crowd of other children, just like any mother could. But, this child's cry was slightly different, though, being almost like that of a wounded animal.

It was then she considered that she was hearing an altogether different child crying. She stared out of the empty window into the black city night, as if the angry darkness could provide her with answers to who that other child was.

Marina was unable to sleep for the rest of the night. The thought that she was hearing another child frightened her, and she kept wondering who it could be. Perhaps she was experiencing auditory hallucinations, perhaps she was going mad. She knew, though, she was sane, but faced with an almost insane explanation. The answer was all too obvious, but not one she was ready to face or to accept. Operating on a hunch, Marina called up Vena not long after sunrise and asked how Ephrim was doing.

Vena was crying and in a near state of panic. She said very little, and the two decided that it would be best to talk in person. When she arrived at Denny's house almost an hour later, Vena nervously looked Marina in the eyes and then glanced at Ephrim. "He must have known, Marina, Ephrim somehow must have known this would happen. The last night we were together he kept waking up and crying."

Marina was reminded of the children's voices she kept hearing in her dreams, and the trouble she had sleeping last night also. "Austin felt something was wrong too, Vena. Perhaps they both were concerned about the same thing?" Marina resisted the temptation to tell Vena of her suspicions about the two boys. She was sure they would sound too crazy, too unbelievable.

Vena, in tears, said that a second custody hearing had suddenly been called, late yesterday. The court-appointed forensic pathologist had reviewed the tissue samples from Dr. Rudy Salvatore, and Lissa and Ephrim Vernor. The conclusion was that Ephrim was not related to Salvatore.

"Well, I'm not surprised," Marina said. "I figured Salvatore must have been wrong. Ephrim doesn't have any of Salvatore's heavy Italian characteristics." Neither did Ephrim resemble Lissa Vernor, though, she thought. Nor, for that matter, did Ephrim resemble Vena Kleinman, she also considered, but decided against mentioning her observations to Vena, at least for now. "Then I assume they confirmed that Ephrim belonged to Ryder and Lissa."

"They didn't say, Marina. All the judge was interested in was verifying or disproving Dr. Salvatore's claim. The lawyers kept returning to that damn surrogate contract. Yee asked the judge to immediately honor the surrogate contract. Once it was determined Salvatore was definitely not the father, the surrogate contract was upheld and Ephrim was awarded to Baatard. I had to hand him over right then," Vena said, crying again.

"Oh, Vena, I'm so sorry. That must have been terrible." She could just picture the heart-rendering scene in her mind and was glad she hadn't been there. Marina was surprised that the judge gave that decision, after Charlie Kincade's rational analysis and presentation of the facts.

"Yeah, it was. I could have died, Marina. Ephrim knew something was wrong. He cried and cried. And that bastard Baatard didn't even know how to hold him. Some doctor he is. What a mess. I just don't see how the judge can allow something like that to happen."

"Don't worry, I'm sure all this madness will work out," Marina tried to reassure Vena, although from the worried look on her face, she could only have believed the opposite.

Marina left Austin with Denny's housekeeper for a few hours, then drove over to her own house. Marina had been home infrequently since being forced out after the rock throwing incident had disrupted her life. Since she had no further telephone threats, she had been considering moving back home, and probably would be doing so this week. Marina had to admit that, even with the lack of privacy, she liked the convenience of having Denny's housekeeper available to watch Austin, and also liked the additional sense of security she felt having others around her at home in the evening.

When Marina arrived at her own home, everything was just as she had left it, save for the fact that the broken window had been repaired, and an integrated security and fire alarm was now installed, as arranged for by none other than Charlie Kincade. New external light posts were mounted along all four sides of the house, and a motion sensor-controlled light was mounted over the driveway. She had wanted to have all these security measures in place before she moved back in, and now that they were complete, planned to do just that.

Chapter 72

Kincade had called for Marina at Denny's, and was directed to Marina's house. When he arrived, he put his arm around her shoulder, pulled Marina close and gave her a hug.

Marina was pleasantly surprised at his show of affection, put her arms around Kincade, and held him close. "Vena came by. She told me what had happened to Ephrim."

"I'm afraid there's little I can do about the court's custody decision at this point," Kincade said.

"Yes, I heard, but I can't accept that. Maybe there is something we can do," Marina said. "You better sit for this one, though. I don't know if you'll be able to believe what I'm going to say."

"It's going to take a very good idea to help this time, Marina," Kincade told her.

"Just don't think I'm totally crazy." Marina paused a moment to gain her composure, then continued. "I think Ephrim also is my biological child, and I'm his biological mother." She remembered when, just before the implantation of her fertilized ova, Denny had sent flowers to her hospital room. Then, Denny had asked if she could donate some ova to another woman. Marina had refused, but what if Denny had not respected her decision?

"I don't understand," Charlie said, startled. He laughed nervously, as if trying to dismiss the idea, then said, "I mean, this isn't a joke, is it? After all, we just got through with the courts dealing with Dr. Salvatore's parental claim. He did, at least, have sex with Lissa Vernor," Charlie said, sardonically.

Marina smiled warily, ignored Charlie's implied digs, then tried to explain what she knew and what she suspected. When she was finished, Charlie turned to her and said, "Hey, it's wild. But, I follow you. This is really preposterous, and I have no idea how the hell we could prove it, but it just might work. Now, at least, there's something I can go on." Kincade immediately made plans to contact the county prosecutor and allege medical fraud on Baatard's part.

"I think I can get at least a temporary stay on the custody award," Charlie told Marina. "Even if what Deanna told you is only hearsay, the county prosecutor might reconsider Ephrim's custody award. I think I can also get the social services people riled up enough to find out who is the ultimate adopting parent. They might reverse things, at least until Ryder's death is reinvestigated."

After a long and turbulent conversation with the county prosecutor, Kincade finally put down the phone. Marina could see his hand shaking as he turned back to her. "The prosecutor thinks we're all crazy, and she thinks that I especially am a pain in the ass, which is usual between us." Marina frowned. "I also think she believes me. At least she's willing to consider the possibility. Omizawa-Shapiro is sending out some people to bring Baatard in for questioning right now."

"Great." Marina exclaimed. If the county prosecutor gave her story even the benefit of a doubt, that was encouraging.

"The prosecutor wanted to know if we knew where Baatard might be. I said we would try to find out and get back to her."

"What about Ephrim?" Marina asked.

"There have been no papers filed to transfer custody to anyone besides Baatard. Not yet, at least," Kincade told her. "I presume now no court would ever honor such an additional custody petition. Ephrim must still be with Baatard."

"I'll call Baatard's office," Marina volunteered. After a few minutes on the phone, she reported that Baatard was not at his office today. Apparently this was a hospital day, at least according to Baatard's answering service. Marina tried the hospital, but Baatard wasn't logged in at the central switchboard or in the staff office either. After several anxious minutes of waiting, Baatard also didn't respond to an overhead voice page at the hospital.

Kincade tried calling Yee's office next, but Yee didn't know Baatard's whereabouts or at least wasn't going to say so. Somehow, Charlie just wasn't too surprised. Exasperated, Charlie threw his hands up in the air. "Any suggestions?" he asked Marina.

"Yeah, I got one," Marina said. She picked up the phone, had a quick conversation, then said, "I know Baatard's not at Haven General, but I think I'll go over there anyway. I'll call you later."

Half an hour later, Marina stood outside the hospital library, having just arranged to meet Sharlene there. As a woman, she sensed the animosity Sharlene had toward Baatard, and planned to play on their common loathing of him. Rather than remain standing there, Marina asked Sharlene to follow her out into the garden walkway to the hospital's rear. As soon as they were outside, Sharlene lit up a cigarette and took a long drag, holding the smoke in a long time before slowly exhaling through her nose.

Walking thoughtfully down the path, Sharlene said, "I've seen you around our office a lot lately. Now that your IVF was successful, and the QA hearings are over, just what are your continuing interests with Dr. Baatard?"

Surprised and frankly taken aback by Sharlene's intimations, Marina said, "If you mean, do I have or am I interested in a 'relationship' with him, the answer is most definitely NO. My only interest is in getting Ephrim back."

"Ephrim? Who's Ephrim?" Sharlene asked.

Marina was surprised that Sharlene didn't seem to know about such important matters which involved Baatard. Nevertheless, she explained the custody battle over Ephrim to Sharlene, then said, "When Baatard took custody of Ephrim, he took Ephrim away from Vena, and Vena was the only mother he ever knew."

The Surrogate

"My God, I'm so sorry," Sharlene said, almost at a loss for words. She dropped her cigarette on to ground, and covered her mouth with her hands, and appeared almost on the verge of fainting. "I knew that Dr. Baatard was involved with another adoption, but I never knew the child's name. How terrible for both Ephrim and for Vena."

"Yes, at this point Ephrim has no one else left, except his comatose mother, that is. He's basically an orphan, and now, for whatever perverted purpose, Baatard claims to own him."

"You know, I can believe almost anything about that son-of-a-bitch Baatard," Sharlene said. She opened her cigarette case and light another one. Sharlene took a deep drag, held it in for a long time while she thought, then slowly let the smoke escape through her nose. "But I'm sure he doesn't want the kid for himself. It must be for an adoption, as you said."

"He evidently had been planning this surrogate adoption for some time too. He claimed to have worked out a surrogate contract with the Vernors before Lissa Vernor got sick," Marina told her.

"A surrogate contract? You mean this wasn't a straight adoption?"

"Nope. Why do you look so strange, Sharlene?"

"Because I think I heard Baatard talking a few weeks ago to judge Lydia Ramirez about a surrogate contract. I guess this must have been the one."

"That's what I'm afraid of. Look, Sharlene, the police would like to speak to Baatard right now. I think he plans to turn Ephrim over to some other adopting couple, and I hope to find him before he does."

"But why do you care so much about Ephrim?" Sharlene asked. As Marina explained her possible relationship to Ephrim, Sharlene was astonished, yet seemed to believe Marina. "Maybe I can help," Sharlene told her.

"Thanks very much, Sharlene. You'll never know how much I appreciate this." She didn't know what additional perverted purpose Baatard still had for Ephrim Vernor, and could only hope that he wouldn't hurt him.

"Consider it my pleasure. That son-of-a-bitch Baatard has screwed me for the last time. Look, he's staff here at the hospital, and on the on-call schedule. I just bet his answering service could locate him for an emergency surgery," Sharlene smiled, using an old but effective technique of hers. Sharlene put in the call to Baatard's answering service, requesting him to contact the O.R. scheduling desk immediately. Then, she went to the O.R. to wait. She was pleasantly surprised when she got a call back in only twenty minutes.

"This is Dr. Baatard," he said, his gruff voice revealing his usual arrogance, and his annoyance at being paged.

"Hi, there, Damon. This is Sharlene," she said, a little too cheerily.

"I know who the hell you are, for Christ sake. Now what do you want, goddamnit? And why are you at the O.R. scheduling desk?"

"Oh, I'm just watching the phones for a friend, that's all."

"But I'm not scheduled today for anything, am I?"

"You weren't scheduled, Damon, but they may have an add-on. What's your availability?"

"Look, Sharlene, I asked you not to call me Damon when others could hear you, okay?"

"I'm alone here, lova bubba, so don't you worry your little head at all. Besides, you're not ashamed to be associated with me, are you? Or maybe you are embarrassed. What is it with you, anyway, Damon?"

"Maybe I act this way toward you because you're such a loser," Baatard sarcastically replied. "Anyway, my availability just now isn't too good. I'm on my way to Haven Convalescent Hospital. You got me on my car phone."

"Why are you going there?"

"I have to see one of my patients." He waited for a long several seconds before continuing. "I can't get back for at least four to six hours," Baatard said.

"Okey dokey, Damon." Sharlene paused to let him smoke about being called Damon again, then asked him, "What are you going to do down there, to visit a friend?"

"Oh, for god's sake, Sharlene. Let's not get into that jealous shit again, okay? It's nothing like that. You're the only one I have a 'special' relationship with right now, you know that. Anyway, when would I get the time," Baatard laughed nervously, then burped loudly into the car phone.

"Excuse you," Sharlene said, reprimanding him for being so gross. "It's just that sometimes I'm not so sure about your loyalty."

"You damn well know where I'm going, Sharlene."

"Yeah, I figured as much."

"When are you coming back?"

"Like I just said, later today," Baatard repeated, irritated as he forked over several dollars to the toll collector. "Is that soon enough for you?"

"I guess it will have to be. See you when you come back." Sharlene thought she heard a child's sounds in the background coming from the car phone. After she hung up, she immediately relayed what she had learned to Marina.

Marina thanked Sharlene, then picked up the phone again and called Charlie Kincade. "I think I know where Baatard has gone." Marina related what Sharlene said, and that Sharlene thought she heard a child's voice in the background. Charlie said he would relay this to the police, and hoped they could find Baatard. Mentally exhausted, she drove to Denny's home to pick up Austin. She planned to gather up her clothes, Austin's crib, and move back into her own place immediately.

Chapter 73

When no one answered the doorbell at Denny's house, Marina used her key and went inside. Denny's house was totally and uncharacteristically quiet. There were no responses to Marina's calling for the housekeeper, and also no child's sounds. Instantly alarmed, Marina walked nervously from room to room, then began to frantically run. Austin was nowhere to be found. She could feel little beads of sweat forming on her forehead, and a frightful sense of foreboding overcame her.

Minutes later, Marina finally located the housekeeper, terrified and tied up and gagged in a bedroom closet. A handwritten note was pinned to the front of her dress. Marina quickly untied the sash from around the elderly Philippine housekeeper's head, who then told Marina that a strange man whom she never actually saw broke in and tied her up, then took Austin and left.

The note simply said that if Marina stopped looking for her rapist and didn't go to the police, Austin would be returned. Marina was to paint the word 'accept' or 'reject' on a small canvas and display it in her window as she drove through Center Street, Haven at precisely 1 p.m. Panic-stricken, Marina instinctively reached for the phone to call the police, then held back, afraid of harming Austin. Instead, she called Charlie.

Charlie Kincade's advice to her was simple: he would

go to the police and let them handle this. They were, he explained, experienced and set up to dealing with kidnappings. In the meantime, Charlie wanted Marina to stay there and wait for the police.

Within minutes, several cars arrived at Denny's. A policewoman, whom Marina later learned was one of their hostage negotiators, interrogated her for almost a half hour. In the background, Marina could hear radio traffic between police indicating they were already out actively looking for Austin, and also for Dr. Baatard and Ephrim Vernor. Marina was relieved when the woman cop instructed her to officially accept the offer and do exactly as the kidnapper directed her to do, so Austin, at least, wouldn't get hurt.

Marina's mind was flooded by emotions and she felt totally incapable of thinking rationally. Under the circumstances, she felt she had no choice. She quickly painted the word 'accept' on a canvas she had in the back of her van, taped it to a window, and drove as instructed through Haven. As she painted the canvas, she wondered if this request to use a canvas rather than a piece of paper was simply coincidental, or if somehow the kidnapper knew she used canvasses, knew she was an artist. Not too many people knew that about her, making her wonder if the kidnapper was also her rapist, the evil she had pursued all these years, and just how much he knew about her. Then, shocked, she wondered if he knew her now, if he even had the nerve to deal with her from time to time, and if, impossible as the thought was, she knew him?

Depressed and fearful for her son's life, she had no desire to go anywhere after driving through Haven but back to her own home. Once there, the house echoed in the emptiness of Austin. Reminders of her Austin were everywhere, and for the first few moments, Marina could only cry, overcome by a devastating sense of hopelessness.

Marina unlocked Austin's room and went in. Small pieces of glass from the broken window were still on the floor and crunched under her shoe. She found a spot in the corner against the wall, slumped down and just sat there, motionless, staring out the window, wondering what she would do, uncertain if she would ever see her infant son again.

The rage Marina was feeling surged within her and she reached the point where she actually wanted to kill whoever had done this to Austin and to her. She wondered if it really could be the man who attacked her, after all these years. And why had he so suddenly reappeared out of nowhere? What was she doing, what had she been looking at these last few weeks that had taken her so close, so dangerously close to him, provoking him?

Inexplicably, her mind wandered to her last visit to Denny's office and the conversation there. Then, for some strange reason, her mind formed a clear image of the Da Vinci painting of Mona Lisa hanging so inappropriately behind Denny's desk. It seemed so out of character for Denny - too serene, too classical. This prompted Marina to wonder whether the painting was not just a random art choice but was instead in some bizarre way symbolic. Then something clicked in Marina's sub consciousness and she remembered the article she had read about the Mona Lisa. Suddenly, as an unbelievable connection was made inside her mind, it all became horribly, disturbingly clear.

Marina ran from Austin's room to her art studio and uncovered the portrait of Denny Cruite she had nearly finished. Frantically, she squeezed fresh oils from small colored tubes unto her palate, and quickly began to work. Denny's hair style was changed from long and blonde to something much shorter and dark brown, and masculine. Then, Marina changed the facial coloring a little, removing all evidence of makeup. A terrifying image began to appear right in front of her eyes, and she couldn't believe she, of all people, had been so blind. Marina worked feverishly, first removing almost twenty years of aging, then adding a few pounds of flesh as her brushes anxiously splashed and dabbed new colors in just the right places. Interesting, no changes were needed to Denny's evil eyes.

When it was complete, Marina stared at the altered painting for several minutes in disbelief. Then, she picked up the phone and called Charlie Kincade. When he answered, she simply said, "I've found the bastard, Charlie. After all these years, I've finally found him. And now, he's got Austin." After speaking with Charlie for a few minutes, she walked into her bedroom, opened the chest of drawers, and took out the handgun she had purchased long ago. Her hand shook visibly as she contemplated what she needed to do. This time, she said to herself, I'll be prepared. She checked to be certain her clip was full - it held ten bullets - firmly pushed it into the gun's metallic handle, then put on the safety latch and walked down the hall to her art studio.

Dimitri Markov

Chapter 74

Marina stood directly in front of the hated portrait of the beast, her rapist, her portrait, staring directly into the very eyes she had just finished painting. They were so cold, unmoving, dispassionate, and exactly as she had remembered those hateful portals of vision all these years. What degrading sights they had witnessed, including the defiling of her own body and that of Christine Lincoln. The thought made her sick, and in her heart she cried out for revenge. Now she finally knew exactly whose eyes they were, and revenge was within her grasp.

"Unbelievable," she said to herself, "unbelievable." The way he had fooled her, played with her, talked to her, and used her only made her more angry.

She slowly lifted up the gun and pointed it to the area between his eyes, flipped off the safety latch, and started to squeeze the trigger, slowly, in exactly the manner she had been instructed at the target range, but absolutely certain she could do the exact same thing when finally facing him in the flesh. But she was unable to wait, and had to release her tension now. Just one bullet into his hateful head, she thought, just one avenging bullet round deep into where the memory of all those filthy acts he did to her so long ago resided still. Just one bullet would end his memory forever, but it would not end hers. Her tortured memory could only end the same way - with her own death.

Just as she was about to fire off her first round, the door bell rang, startling her. She quickly placed the safety latch back on, put the gun in her skirt belt under her bulky sweater, picked up a small canvas to cover the bulge in front of her clothes, and went to answer the door. She was painfully aware just how flushed and nervous she must have looked. Hopefully, whoever it was would attribute her appearance to the terrible stress she was under.

To her horror, she saw the police through the peephole. She made the supreme effort to get a grip on her composure, prayed that they weren't here to give her bad news, quickly slipped the gun out of her belt, placed it on the closet shelf, and then opened the front door.

Marina was more than relieved to learn that the police were here simply to interview her. She wasn't surprised to learn that kidnappings in her quiet little Haven were extremely rare, and the police reassured her they were giving this their highest priority.

Charlie arrived after only a few minutes, and he and Marina then told the police about Denny Cruite. They tried to explain why they thought Denny had taken Austin. Now, both the police and Marina were looking for Denny, both for kidnapping and for another, long-unsolved crime. After a few more minutes of questions, and several calls from her phone, the police left. Marina was impressed with their attention to detail and their sincerity, but she had seen it all before, and had learned her lesson. She placed her trust only in herself, and could not make the mistake of depending on the police to rescue Austin.

As Charlie went into the kitchen to use the phone, Marina quickly took the gun from the closet and moved it into her purse. She managed to finish making the transfer just as Charlie walked back into the room.

Charlie stared at Marina and slowly shook his head, as if wondering what monkey business she had been up to while he was out of the room. Then, dropping whatever speculation had occurred to him, he said, "I think if we find Baatard, we'll be able to find Ephrim."

"Look Charlie, I know that finding Ephrim is a priority for us all, but my highest priority now is locating Austin."

"That's not going to be so easy, Marina. Assuming that Denny has Austin, she could be real trouble to find. Worse, she knows a lot about you - where you live, what car you drive, who you associate with."

"Then what do you recommend we do? I can't just sit here waiting for the police to rescue him. They have their priorities too. For now, they say finding Austin is the most important thing they're doing. It is for me too. But what if there is a bank robbery in the next hour? Their priorities will change, but not mine. No, I intend to go out and find my Austin."

"Marina, leave police work to the professionals. Believe me, that's not only the best way, it's the only way you're going to see Austin alive again." He gave Marina a look which indicated he meant everything he said, held her and gave her a hug of encouragement and then a furtive kiss, then left to his office, where he said he could do more good.

Marina remembered all too well the totally inadequate job the 'police professionals' did finding her rapist. She knew she just couldn't afford to trust Austin's welfare to their hands alone.

Unable to stand staying home alone and simply doing nothing, helpless while she presumed others were out looking for her kidnapped son, Marina drove over to Charlie Kincade's office. He had just gotten off the phone with the police; regrettably, they had no news on Denny Cruite, Ephrim Vernor, or her precious little Austin.

"That's it," Marina nearly yelled. "I can't wait any longer. I've got to do something, anything. Denny could be killing Austin right now, while we're sitting here just talking."

"Marina, listen to me," Charlie said, taking hold of her upper arm. "She would have no reason to kill your son."

"No, damnit, you listen to me." Marina yelled back, forcefully removing his grip on her. "I know that Baatard left almost an hour ago. Denny is nowhere to be found. There's no sign of any kids. Don't you see, he and Denny probably took both boys with them. They're probably going to hand Ephrim over to someone. God knows what they plan to do with Austin, but I've got to go there too. You can stay here if you want, but not me." She could see the indecisiveness in Charlie's eyes, and wondered if she would ever be able to count on him again?

Minutes later, a resolute Charlie and a determined Marina took Charlie's BMW and drove together. There was a chance they could find Baatard, knowing that he intended to visit the convalescent hospital. "Now Marina," Charlie sternly told her, "If by some miracle we do find Baatard, or better yet all of them, please stand clear while I notify the police. Let them handle this or it'll get all screwed up. I know, I've seen civilians mess up a perfectly good arrest. This is your son here, and you'd better leave his rescue to the professionals, okay?"

Charlie looked over at Marina and waited for a confirmation, but she didn't seem to comprehend what he was saying. Instead, she was contemplating and running over and over in her mind exactly what she would do to Baatard and Cruite when she caught up to them.

Kincade immediately called Haven Convalescent Hospital and learned Baatard wasn't there yet. Excited, he quickly made the drive with Marina, hoping to still catch Baatard and Ephrim.

A few minutes later, they parked in the near empty visitors lot of Haven Convalescent and got out. A black

Cadillac with New Jersey license plates was parked next to the side entrance of the one story extended ranch structure. Next to it stood a BMW with the letters "MD" in the license plate. "This could be Baatard's," Kincade said, pointing to the BMW.

"Maybe he's still got Ephrim with him." Marina said, hopefully. Still, first on her mind was locating her own son and getting him to safety. For now, Baatard was her best bet on locating Denny, who's car didn't seem to be here.

"I hope so," Kincade said as he reached for his car phone to call the police.

Marina was already out of the car and running toward the entrance, and hopefully to Austin, her purse clutched tightly in her hands. Charlie called after her to wait for the police, but just the thought of Ephrim possibly being inside the convalescent hospital along with Baatard overpowered any considerations of her own safety. Austin could be there too.

"Be careful," Kincade called after her. "Baatard's a crazy man. He might try to hurt you if he's in there."

Marina was more concerned with what else she might find inside. She patted her heavy purse before entering.

Chapter 75

Haven Convalescent Hospital
Haven, NJ

When Marina entered the side door of Haven Convalescent Hospital she was greeted by the icy stares of three obese nurses seated at the front nursing desk, perched like ancient guardians at the entrance to an Egyptian temple. Each wore a white pant suit with white doily caps, the appearance of which under less threatening circumstances might have given them the comical appearance of the Pillsbury doughboy. Like a gathering of ducks, their heads turned in mechanical unison in Marina's direction as she approached. The youngest one of the three, Nurse Ivory Peoples, finally uttered an insincere, "Can we help you?"

Trying to think quickly, Marina blurted out, "Yes, I'm here to meet Dr. Baatard." She desperately wanted to ask if Baatard had a child, her son, with him, but held back out of fear of warning Baatard.

Marina immediately was taken aback by the absolute stillness of the building, the emptiness of the corridors, the depressing dimness of the lights. In some ways it seemed like the mausoleum she had just been in - in this case a mausoleum for the living dead. The stench of urine and feces was overwhelming, and she had trouble imagining just how these nurses survived in this environment. Had they no sensibilities, she wondered? I guess you can get accustomed to almost anything, she thought, once again glad she had gone into administrative nursing.

"Dr. Baatard is over there," Nurse Peoples gestured with her pencil, her voice a monotone of indifference. "He's in Room 17." Then she looked away, picked up an uneaten sandwich off a patient's service tray and resumed watching the overhead TV with the other nurses. A soap opera completely absorbed their attention, one which odd enough took place in a hospital. Marina remembered the room number just given her as the one she had visited Lissa Vernor in, several months ago. Why was Baatard in there, she wondered?

Marina stared at the sandwich Peoples was eating and found that the visual image of eating in these surroundings made her stomach feel ill. As she started down the hall, the revolting odor of human waste made the convalescent home seem more like a filthy public bathroom at a bus station, and she felt confined and dirty. Marina covered her mouth with some paper tissue from her purse and continued walking. As she thoughts returned to Austin again, she wanted to run to that room, and struggled to maintain control.

An elderly man startled Marina when he darted out of a room, propelled forward in his wheelchair by the pulling of his crippled little feet against the floor. His contorted face half-smiled in Marina's direction, and his vacant head bobbed up and down to some hidden music. Saliva drooled in rivulets down one side of his crooked mouth as he muttered unintelligible things in several running conversations with no one. A horrendous body odor accompanied him that grabbed at Marina's throat and made her gag uncontrollably. Marina nodded politely to the man, carefully dodged what seemed to be a yellow puddle of urine forming next to his chair, then moved past several heaps of soiled linen lying on the floor in the hall. She made a personal vow never to allow herself to be put in so hopelessly degrading a place if she ever became too old to live independently.

The gray metal door to Room 17 was closed. Marina noticed four nameplate holders carelessly stuck at an angle on the door, three of which were blank. One nameplate had "L VERNOR" embossed on a black plastic strip, which did not surprise her. She stood next to the door and listened carefully for several seconds but heard no conversation from within. Ever so slowly, Marina nudged the door open, praying as she did so it wouldn't squeak, and hopeful her son would be safe and inside.

Two metal hospital beds were immediately visible through the wedge of light revealed by the door - both were empty. Metal pull blinds lay in front of the windows, a cheap tile covered the floor, and fluorescent lights hung from the ceiling. Several bulbs were out, but this seemed of no consequence. Scattered paintings of various styles hung on the walls, and a small room, probably a bathroom, was off to the back.

Marina moved the door open a little more, eliciting an annoying and revealing squeak; the sound she had inadvertently generated made her cringe. The three nurses watched her actions from the nursing station, their eyes glaring suspiciously down on her back as she still stood partway in the hallway. At this point, Marina felt pressured to finally go into the room before someone yelled down the hallway at her, or worse yet, used the overhead speaker.

Lissa Vernor lay exactly as Marina had left her months ago when she had first visited, in the bed nearest the window. She appeared to be asleep, or unconscious. A nursing clipboard with some loose papers on it hung from the foot of each bed. Baatard was seated by the bed, his chair facing away from the door and toward the wall, reading from papers scattered on top of the bed.

Marina held her breath as she entered the room, praying not to cause a disturbance. She was enormously relieved when Baatard didn't look up, probably only expecting one of the nurses. What she would do next, she had no idea, yet she was also certain Baatard would either have her son here or know where her son was. Although she couldn't understand why Austin was taken from her, she wanted him back, immediately and unharmed. At this point, she would gladly trade revenge for his safety alone.

A ray of light shown through a tear in the drawn curtain and reflected against millions of dust particles suspended in the air, imparting upon the room an eerie illusion of the abeyance of time. The room was uncharacteristically clean, considering what Marina had already seen of the rest of the facility, and remarkably free of odor. She noticed even her nose beginning to become accustomed to the pervasive foul background smell.

Lissa had lost a lot of weight since Marina had last visited her, and was now only a shell of her former self. Marina was struck by the extremely pale and paper thin appearance of Lissa's skin, as if it were not skin at all but instead crepe paper wrapping her tiny bones, and draping her empty eyes. A blanket was neatly drawn up to her chin and her arms rested peacefully on top of the covers. As Marina walked nearer to the bed, Baatard suddenly whirled around, startling her.

His eyes wide in surprise, Baatard screamed, "What the hell are YOU doing here?" He quickly stood up, hands clenched threateningly, and faced Marina.

"I'm looking for my son Austin, and I'm also looking for Ephrim Vernor," Marina said. She fully expected Baatard to hit her, and moved back from. "Someone stole them both, and I thought you would have them with you." Marina anxiously looked around the room for signs of children - baby bags, clothes, toys - but was disappointed to find there were none. She gripped her purse tighter, and opened the clasp in case she needed to reach inside in a hurry.

"I don't know where your precious little child is," Baatard snapped. "And as for Ephrim Vernor, he's certainly none of your goddamn business; he isn't your child at all. What the hell are you involved with Ephrim for, anyway?"

"Vena Kleinman was a friend of mine, and she asked for my help."

"Ah, Vena, that little slut. Ephrim wasn't her child either, and she never had any legal right to him. Besides, I understand Vena's out of the picture now, so Ephrim really isn't her concern any longer, is he?" Baatard smiled grimly.

Marina recalled Vena's gruesome accident, and that of Frank. She hoped that, if Baatard somehow was the cause of their deaths, then he, too, should suffer and die just as they did.

"Ephrim's none of your business now, either," Baatard said. "That child was conceived as part of a surrogate pregnancy and was legally adopted out."

"But, I thought the court awarded him to you?"

"I was the legal intermediate in the adoption proceedings, if that's what you're referring to" Baatard scoffed. "It's customary for the obstetrician to act as the legal intermediate for a private adoption. The actual adoptive parents assumed control of the child in a separate, private legal proceeding. By now, Vena would be out of the picture anyway."

"You're wrong about that, Dr. Baatard. Vena WAS Ephrim's legal guardian, and Charlie Kincade IS now."

"No, he is not," Baatard insisted. "That child was legally adopted out."

"Charlie and I don't think so, and we're having Child Protective Services reopen the custody hearing."

When Baatard angrily tried to object, Marina interrupted him. "Falsifying adoption papers is a crime, Dr. Baatard. Now, I want to know where Austin and Ephrim are, and I want you to tell me." Marina persisted, anxiously looking around.

"They're not here, as you can see. Ephrim is right where he belongs, with his new father and mother. As for Austin, I can't help you there either."

"I think that you have Ephrim with you," Marina persisted.

"I told you, Ephrim's with his adoptive father and mother, you nosy bitch. I gave him up only a few minutes ago. Fortunately, you just missed them, and if I were you, I definitely wouldn't interfere with these particular people. They have even less tolerance for annoying little people like you than I do. As for Austin, I know nothing. Whoever told you I had him was obviously mistaken."

"You're lying, Baatard. I know that now; you always have been a liar. Who has Ephrim and Austin, and where are they? Tell me." she screamed, as she stepped forward and pushed him on his chest.

Startled at being pushed by Marina, Baatard moved back. "That is very confidential, and definitely none of your business. Now, get the hell out of here, or I'll have the nursing staff call the police for trespassing."

"Don't you ever listen, Baatard? The police are coming, we've already called them. Now, tell me, was Lydia Ramirez the person who tried to adopt Ephrim?" Marina persisted. Her mention of Ramirez's name caused quite a look of surprise from Baatard. "Did Ramirez take Ephrim? Tell me." she screamed.

"I already told you that's none of your goddamn business," Baatard shouted, his face flushed red with rage.

"I think the medical licensing board would be more than a little upset to learn you tried to arrange an illegal adoption for the likes of Lydia Ramirez."

Obviously fighting to remain calm, Baatard said, "I should have never taken you as a patient, again. You're nothing but trouble."

"Again? What do you mean by that?" A strange feeling was developing in her subconscious, and a knowledge she long suspected was now fighting to reach her conscious level.

"Yes, again. Well, I guess you simply don't remember, do you?"

"Remember what? I don't know what you're talking about."

"You do remember your abortion when you were sixteen, don't you?" he sneered.

Marina could only nod that she did, afraid of what he was going to say next.

"Do you remember the doctor's name?" he asked in a mocking, rhetorical tone.

"He never said," Marina told Baatard. She vaguely remembered the doctor, and he didn't look at all like Baatard. Still, she knew she was young and frightened at the time, and tried to blot the entire event from her memory almost as soon as it had occurred. As she stared at Baatard's face for several painful moments, she began to realize the awful truth. Finally, she managed to say, "Oh, for God's sake. Don't tell me it was you?" But she knew it was so, and the idea that this hateful man had been involved in so painful an event of her teenage years bothered her terribly. "You're going to regret all of this, Baatard, I swear it. You'll pay for all the suffering you've caused me."

Baatard's face clouded over as he listened to Marina's threats, and considered the problems she could cause him.

Marina couldn't help but stare at Lissa' rather enlarged midsection. "What's wrong with her stomach? Does she have a cancer or something?" Somehow, Marina was afraid Baatard might answer her otherwise.

"No, it's not a cancer, fortunately. You see, Lissa is pregnant again," Baatard announced, leaning down and holding Lissa's hand. His words, considering the circumstances, were understandably devoid of any joy.

Marina stared into Baatard's eyes, hoping that she didn't correctly comprehend what he was implying.

"You could say you're going to be a mom, all over again."

"A mom? What the hell are you telling me?" Marina asked, her voice rising in anxiety. Suddenly she was overcome with a sickening realization. "The other ova, you don't mean . . . "

Baatard nodded, then slowly pulled back Lissa's sheet, displaying her pregnant, protuberant abdomen.

Marina gasped and almost fainted as she stared at Lissa, still in a coma and apparently carrying another of Marina's children. It was almost too much for her to comprehend. "What the hell are you doing here, you maniac?" Marina jumped back and headed toward the door. "You're crazy." Marina let out a scream for help. She only hoped Charlie could hear her and that the police had arrived by now.

A disturbed and detached look came over Baatard's face, making Marina feel strangely uncomfortable. "She's pregnant? I don't understand," Marina said, her voice now quavering.

"Well, I didn't have sex with her while she was in a coma, if that's what you're implying."

"Then how . . . "

"You see, there are many desperate people out there in search of intelligent, healthy male children, as you're used to putting it. Why, I never would have thought of this," he nervously chuckled, "but a while ago you actually helped me develop a wonderful idea. Yes, I think you should get all the credit. You wanted a child so badly you were even willing to use artificial insemination. When we were done with your implantation, there were some fertilized ova left over. Then, along comes Mr. And Mrs. Ramirez who offer Denny eight hundred thousand dollars for a child.

"All they wanted was to use some of your ova, that's all. Things sort of got self-perpetuating after that. Now,

Lissa is going to help one more family find happiness."

"You're crazy, Baatard."

"Well, actually, you two are sort of going to do this together," Baatard told her, his voice chillingly devoid of emotion. Running after Marina, he grabbing her hair from behind. Marina desperately reached into her purse and pulled out the handgun, now her only protection, her only way out now. She wanted to kill Baatard for all the terrible things he was doing to her and her child, her children, and was more than ready to do so. Marina struggled to turn and point the handgun at Baatard, but somehow he managed to grab it and pull it from her hand instead. Falling back hard against the wall in shock, Marina staring at the gun Baatard now held, wondering if he was going to kill her.

"I think you better come back here and sit," Baatard said, motioning to a chair with the barrel of the gun.

Marina slowly turned around and walked toward Baatard. "What are you going to do to me?" she pleaded. She desperately looked for a way to get the gun back and kill him first.

"Well, for one thing, you seem to have such choice ova, I want to have more of them. After the stroke I'm going to induce in you, why you can have this bed right here," he said as he lifted the gun and pointed toward the empty bed by the door.

Marina's heart rose as she heard the door behind her

open, expecting it to be Charlie. Instead, Joan Grizell, one of the staff nurses, came in, holding a medication tray with a syringe on it. Marina was relieved that at least one of the nurses had heard her cry for help and had responded. She could only wonder what had happened to Charlie. Then she saw the bizarre, serious look on Grizell's face as she turned around and locked the door behind her. Grizell picked up the syringe off the tray and started walking toward Marina.

Marina looked in terror at Baatard, holding a gun in his hand, pointed directly at her chest. She turned around and saw Grizell also walking toward her, the raised syringe pointed menacingly at her. Baatard motioned with his gun for Marina to sit on the bed.

Lissa Vernor, in and out of various stages of sleep for almost a year, was drawn into a subdued state of consciousness by all the noise and the acrid smell of gun oil emanating from the handgun. She had reached a state of semi-consciousness several times before, responding to a nurse who had spent long periods patiently working with her and reading to her. Now, she reacted instinctively to Baatard's grating voice, instinctively feeling that Baatard posed a threat to her. Reaching out from another level, Lissa moved her hand from under the sheet and through her clouded thoughts managed to grab Baatard's wrist.

Startled, Baatard turned to Lissa and was astonished to see her staring at him for the first time in almost a year. "Oh, my GOD." he yelled out.

"No, don't hurt me. Help." Lissa cried.

Grizell, trying to calm Lissa, moved closer and held

Dimitri Markov

her down in the bed. "There, there, Mrs. Vernor, everything is all right."

Taking advantage of Baatard's shock and momentary confusion, Marina lunged at him, trying to wrestle the gun away. Baatard screamed out and fought as they fell over Lissa's bed. Grizell jumped out of the way and tried to keep Lissa from falling out of bed. Marina grabbed for the only weapon she could find - a bed pan - and swung it hard at Baatard, grazing his head and then striking Grizell squarely on the forehead. Grizell whirled around, and fell on the floor, unconscious, dropping her syringe.

Baatard, only momentarily slowed, moved back and forcefully thrust his fist up, hitting Marina in the chin and slamming her head against the wall. Stars came out, the room swirled, and Marina almost lost consciousness as her legs gave way and she slumped to the floor.

Baatard angrily looked down at Marina's crumpled form, then kicked her side with his shoe. She made no movement. "You stupid bitch," Baatard sneered. "I'd love to just kill you and get it over with, but I need your body to carry your precious fertilized ova."

Despite feeling on the verge of passing out, Marina somehow managed to grab Grizell's syringe, which had rolled onto the floor by her side. Knowing this was probably her last chance to live, and her only opportunity to get free and save Austin, Marina wrapped her hand firmly around the syringe shaft. Just then, Charlie knocked on the door, and when he didn't get an answer, knocked again and called out for her. She heard the door unlock and Charlie stepped inside.

As Charlie looked at Baatard, he quickly realized he had made a big mistake. Baatard motioned with the barrel of the gun for Charlie to move away from the door and over to the bed. As Charlie moved slowly away, Baatard came up behind and hit Charlie hard on the head with the gun, knocking him out.

The moment Baatard struck Charlie, Marina quickly thrust the syringe deep into Baatard's leg, repeatedly stabbing him. The syringe needle penetrated deep through the muscle and she could feel it crunching into his bone. Marina desperately twisted and turned the syringe and repeatedly tore as much of his hated leg muscle and bone as possible.

Baatard screamed in pain and jumped back as he tried to pull the needle from his leg. Blood poured from the stab wounds, but rather than run from Marina, Baatard became even more enraged. He stared at the blood pouring down his leg in utter disbelief, as if it wasn't really his, then ran forward and kicked Marina in the head. Her head spun around and her body twisted from the blow, further deadening any precious consciousness she had remaining. Now, she was unable to think, to see, to feel, and had she had lost almost any will to fight back and resist this monster. Now, only the memory of her son kept her alive.

Baatard fell upon Marina and started insanely beating her head with the gun butt. Fighting against the clouds in her mind, fighting just to stay alive, Marina thought only of rescuing Austin. With all the remaining strength she was able to raise, she grabbed Baatard's other hand, which was smothering her mouth, and sunk her teeth deeply into his flesh, making him scream out anew in pain. Baatard relaxed his grip on the gun for only a second, and Marina desperately seized that chance. She forced herself to turn and grab Baatard around his neck, then tried to roll away from under him. As soon as she was free from underneath his weight, Marina rammed her knee into Baatard's groin. Baatard groaned and rolled in agony, and Marina quickly grabbed for the pistol. Baatard still had a good grip on it and wasn't going to let go of the pistol easily. It was then Marina heard the muffled burst of the gun between them go off and felt the force of the blast leaving the barrel. Moments later, she and Baatard slumped together in a tangled heap on the floor. She was totally numb, could feel absolutely nothing and was certain she was going to die.

The door to the hospital room opened, and Denny Cruite came running in, having heard the gunshot. Baatard had directed her to meet him here for the exchange of Ephrim, but she was characteristically late. Denny rushed over to the two bodies lying on the floor, and rolled Baatard's dead weight off Marina. As soon as Denny saw the pool of blood, she instinctively grabbed the gun, her eyes nervously darting around the room for anyone else.

Charlie Kincade groaned as he began to awake. He struggled to get up, but immediately froze in position when confronted with the barrel of Denny's pistol. "Hold it right there," Denny told Kincade. A cold chill ran down Kincade's spine as he realized his own gun was perhaps a hundred feet away, hidden uselessly in the glove compartment of his car.

"Get over there," Denny commanded Kincade. She indicated with her pistol barrel for Kincade to stand next to Marina. Kneeling down next to Baatard, she rolled him over. Miraculously, Baatard coughed up some blood, slowly sat up, and used his hand to cover a wound in his chest.

Kincade helped Marina to sit up. "Are you all right?"

"No, but I'll live," Marina croaked. The sound of her own words reverberated inside her skull, her head was pounding, her vision blurry. Terribly weak, she almost fell over again, and had to grab onto Charlie for support. Marina forced herself to think, to reply. Looking in Baatard's direction, she told Charlie, "I think Baatard shot himself when I tried to get the gun away from him." She felt more pain than she had ever felt in her entire life, and could barely stand or focus her eyes. As soon as Marina saw Denny standing there, a hatred such as she had never felt before seethed through her body, for she knew she was now looking at her rapist. They stared at each other, face to face, before Marina yelled, "Where's my son?"

Ignoring Marina, Denny told Baatard, "We've got to get you to a hospital."

Baatard nodded weakly, but was growing increasingly pale and appeared on the verge of losing consciousness.

Charlie Kincade knew he had to think fast. Turning to Denny Cruite, he asked, "Dennis, is that really you?"

"I'm sorry, who were you talking to?" Denny choked. Her facial expression rapidly changed from anger to surprise to embarrassment before settling on fear. That Kincade's remark meant something special to her was undeniable.

Baatard looked strangely at Kincade. "Hey, what are you talking about?"

"Don't you know?" Charlie asked Baatard. "That's Dennis, I mean Denny Cruite. We've known each other for quite a few years, professionally, that is."

Denny vigorously shook her head, denying all that Kincade was telling. But the sense of panic sweeping through her body was evident. She tried to move closer to Baatard, but he inched the other way.

"I defended Dennis on sexual battery charges years ago," Charlie explained to Baatard. "Of course, that was before he was called Denny. But hey, I can see you've changed quite a bit, Dennis."

Denny straightened up, and with every effort left to her, to him, tried to maintain her/his composure. "Yes, things are very different now. I got engaged a very short while ago, Charlie," Denny said. Her voice cracked as it seemed to drop to a slightly deeper, and much less flattering pitch as she lost control. From the look on her face, she must have realized she wasn't sounding in the least bit convincing to anyone. "It was shortly after the death of my former husband, Nevin."

Charlie Kincade stared at Baatard with a wry smile on his face, and flashed a devilish wink. "So, Baatard, don't tell me this is your new heart throb? Aren't you the man."

"That's right. What's it to you?"

"Well, not too much, I guess. Except, I think you've got weird tastes Baatard, that's for sure." he chuckled.

"What are you getting at, anyway?" Baatard angrily demanded. He coughed up a small amount of blood, then slumped back, drained, against the bed.

"Getting at? Oh, I think you know what. I mean, I think that you have more bizarre sexual preferences than I gave you credit for, Baatard, that's what I mean. One thing for sure, you kind of need a little truth in labeling here, if you know what I mean," Charlie gave Baatard a large wink and smiled coyly.

"Honey, we don't have to listen to this trash." Denny urged Baatard. "We've got to get you to a hospital. Let's kill them both and get out of here,"

"Shut up, goddamnit. I want to listen to him," Baatard snapped at Denny. "So, wise guy, what are you trying to tell me?"

"Only that, as I said, I used to know Denny when she was Dennis." Seeing that Baatard still wasn't getting it, or was refusing to, Kincade persisted, "Let me put it to you this way. What has thin hips, thin lips, a receding hair line and no ovaries? Want a little goddamn hint?" Charlie winked again.

Dimitri Markov

Baatard looked both agitated and confused as he glanced over to Denny, carefully examining her from head to toes. "No way," he insisted. "She's got a goddamn vagina. She's got breasts. No way could this be. You got to be crazy. C'mon, Denny, tell me it's not true." He looked pleadingly into Denny's eyes, searching for some explanation. Tellingly, there was none.

"She may have all those things, Baatard, but when I knew her she had a penis too," Charlie Kincade said. "Hey, she's fooled better judges of a woman's body than you."

"I'm afraid I don't know what you're talking about" Denny innocently told Charlie, trying her best but fooling no one. Her voice cracked as she tried to hold the façade of her life together.

"She dated Rudy Salvatore, and he was a physician, and one specializing in obstetrics and gynecology at that," Charlie told Baatard. "Denny fooled more than one doctor. Can you believe it?" Charlie laughed out loud.

"Hey, I fooled a lot more than Baatard and that fool Rudy," Denny bragged. "I fooled your stupid little girlfriend there for a long time. I know you and her been having sexual problems, and your relationship's been going nowhere. Not as though any of her relationships have gone anywhere. But ask yourself this, counselor, would you still want her if you knew she and I made it once?" Denny winked at Marina, crossed her arms and

787

gave a knowing glance at Charlie Kincade.

Marina, totally perplexed, yelled back at Denny, "This is ridiculous. I've only known Denny Cruite professionally, and there's certainly never been anything else between us, believe me, Charlie."

"Oh, come on now, don't tell me you've forgotten our little tryst about seventeen years ago. I thought it was much more memorable than that for you. For a while there, I'd thought you'd never be able to forget."

Marina and Charlie instantly knew what Denny was getting at. Denny, by her own words, confirmed that she was the man of Marina's nightmares, the monster Marina had compulsively painted so many times. Denny was the rapist, and Marina wanted to kill her right now, immediately, in front of everyone else. She knew she had to kill Denny, in order to be finally free of the nightmares and the tormenting guilt.

Denny saw Marina's intent, and taunted her, saying, "Go ahead, try to hurt me. You'll end up just like your fucking father did. He got too close, and you see what happened to him." Denny looked over to Baatard for support, but was disappointed to see that he was nearly unconscious from the continued bleeding. "Look, you love me, don't you?" Denny pleaded with Baatard. "Oh baby, what difference do a few minor physical appearances make anyway? I'm your woman, now. It's you I love."

"By the way, Baatard, you do remember Dennis' former husband Nevin? You know, the one who was so sickly and died about a year ago?" Charlie asked ironically. "I'm certain you'd be interested to know that

Nevin died from his pneumonia. But it was a very special pneumonia - pneumocystis. He had a complication of AIDS. That certainly puts anyone who had recent close contact with Dennis at risk too, I'd say."

Baatard in total disbelief let out one final painful groan as Denny pointed the gun at his head. For some strange reason, she paused and slowly turned it back around toward her. Denny paused again and appeared confused and lost as she moved the gun back at Baatard. "No, Denny, No No No," he pleaded. A loud crack shook the room as the gun went off. The recoil made Denny miss, leaving Baatard shot in the arm and slamming the gun hard against her chest with a thud.

Marina looked at Denny at that fraction of an instant and in horror clearly recognized the traces of the man who attacked her so long ago, haunted her dreams, ruined any attempt with normalcy she ever tried to have. And she acted to finally realize her obsession, impulsively seizing her opportunity. Marina ran at Denny and grabbed for her hand and for the gun, and they fell back together. The last thing Marina recalled was hearing a loud shot, and felt the blast impact her like a hammer blow and felt the gush of hot air, and she and Denny fell together onto the ground in a heap of tangled flesh.

It seemed to Marina like an eternity before she regained awareness, but she was at that moment thankful to be alive. Looking around her she could see Baatard, shot in the arm and lying on the floor bleeding and moaning. Next to her lay Denny, shot in the foot, and also crying and delirious.

Bruce ran into the room moments after the second shot was fired, followed by nurse Peoples. The morbid smells of gunpowder and blood mixed in the stale air. Two bodies lay in the center of the room connected by two pools of blood slowly running together - those of Dr. Damon Baatard and Denny, or Dennis, Cruite. Bruce could see Joan Grizell who lay unconscious by a nearby bedside.

Peoples quickly checked Baatard and Cruite, then looked at Marina and Charlie. "Fortunately, those two look all right," she told Bruce, motioning at Marina and Charlie.

"I got here as fast as I could, but I heard the shot before I could find you," Bruce told Charlie. "When I saw the bodies on the ground I thought that Baatard had killed someone. Apparently, I'm not that far off."

"When Denny realized how much she had deceived her last love and completely ruined her career, she shot Baatard." Marina told Bruce. "She was going to shoot herself too, but I managed to grab her gun, and it went off and I guess she shot herself."

"What about her?" Bruce asked, gesturing to Joan Grizell.

"Baatard told that nurse to attack me with a syringe, and she almost did," Marina said. "Fortunately, I managed to knock her out first."

Bruce nodded impressively at Marina, then went

over to Grizell and cuffed her to the bed, as she was just beginning to wake up. Police and ambulance crews started to arrive, and busily triaged the two gunshots and Grizell.

"Where are the children?" Marina started to ask Bruce.

"Good news. We think we found them," Bruce announced. "Apparently, Denny left them both with a sitter at the children's play area at The Conceptions Foundation. The Haven police are checking it out now."

"That's wonderful, I'm so relieved," Marina smiled as she held onto Charlie's arm.

Looking at the silent woman lying in the bed, Kincade asked, "Who is she."

"That's Lissa Vernor," Peoples said.

Kincade looked at Lissa strangely, and then said, "I think she looks pregnant."

"She is," Marina exclaimed. "And she may be a surrogate carrying my child, or at least another of my children."

"That's impossible," Kincade exclaimed. He looked carefully at Marina, and then asked, "It is impossible, isn't it?"

"No, I'm afraid not," Marina said. "I don't know for sure, but that's what Baatard claimed." She remembered that Lissa had managed to grab Baatard's arm a moment ago. She was happy to see a sign that Lissa might be recovering from her coma. It was a good thing for her and for the baby she was carrying.

"You got a lot of kids for a single babe, you know," Kincade joked, as he nervously glanced at Lissa Vernor.

"Yeah," Marina blushed. "And single parenting is hard work."

"I'm sure it is," Kincade agreed.

A thought of Christine Lincoln flashed by Marina's consciousness. Marina wondered if there was a way she might be able to involve Christine with these innocent babies. It certainly might be therapeutic for Christine, and worth reaching out to her.

"I think we all better all go down to the police station and sort this out," Bruce told them, shaking his head.

"Oh, by the way, I found out who the father is," Charlie told Marina as they were leaving the convalescent hospital together.

"Oh really. How did you do that?" Marina asked him.

"Let's just say I used a little creative file searching," Charlie joked.

Marina looked surprised as she said, "I don't know if I'm ready for this." She had a strange feeling she knew what Charlie was going to say. How ironic that Mr. Ramirez Salvatore, or even Baatard, anyone other than Charlie could be the father of her child, and maybe of all her children, and what a curse for those children too.

"Actually, it's really not too bad," Charlie said, reacting to the apprehension he read on Marina's face. "It seems the sperm donor code came out definite for some handsome devil named Charlie Kincade." Charlie looked carefully at Marina as he spoke, carefully gauging her reaction.

Marina's mouth hung open in total surprise, as she stared at Charlie. "You're kidding. You donated the sperm, Charlie? How did that happen?" Marina couldn't believe that Charlie had finally fathered her children after all these years of studiously avoiding doing exactly that. How inexplicable, and how ironic. Unable to conceive how Charlie could have planned this, she wondered if it was instead some colossal goof-up, or perhaps the fateful hand of God. Frank's bungling image flashed in her mind for an instant.

"After you gave me the genetic analysis on the Vernors, I petitioned the courts to open the sperm bank records. I was curious, and a little worried too. You see, I donated sperm once when I was in college."

"You donated?"

"Yes. I needed the money. Apparently, as luck would have it, my sperm was used on your ova, Marina." Charlie's face left little room to tell if he was pleased or perplexed.

Marina was speechless, uncertain how to cope with her new relationship to Charlie. It was like traveling for years, all the time avoiding one place, and still ending up there.

"Genetic analysis gave Baatard's mistake away," Charlie said. "And now, well, it seems I'm the father of all these kids. Well, at least I'm the genetic parent, as they say." His face grew silent.

"Well, what do you think about that?" Marina laughed out loud. "And here I thought you hated kids."

"I used to think so too," Charlie said. "Anyway, I don't think I'm ready to be the father of three rug rats. At least not alone I'm not." He smiled a little uncomfortably at Marina, then cautiously kissed her on the forehead and held her close. "Especially with my reassignment coming up."

"What reassignment?" Marina asked. It was just like Charlie to not directly tell her something important and then spring it on her as part of another conversation. She thought it was a peculiar avoidance mechanism of his, and one that made his accompanying boyish smile seemingly innocent and hard to be angry with. Sometimes she thought she knew him so well, but at other times she realized how very little she really did.

"Well, I passed my Colorado legal boards and I just accepted a position with a much bigger firm in Boulder. It was a real growth opportunity," he explained proudly.

"You've got to be kidding." Marina said, shaking her head. "Boulder?"

"In a way I do wish I were kidding," he murmured, looking down at his shoes. "I'm sure you wouldn't find living in Boulder interesting or appealing at all. Mountains, fresh air, open space. And I know how you hate the cold." He wrapped his hands warmly around their bodies and pretended to shiver.

"Oh, I wouldn't be so sure about that," Marina smiled.

Ethics Essays
of Donald H. Marks

Jonas Salk, Polio Vaccine and Vaccinating Against Hate. Thoughts on treating hate as an infectious disease. https://dhmarks.blogspot.com/2018/10/jonas-salk-polio-vaccine-and.html

Einstein, Relativity and Relative Ethics. Considerations on whether ethical decisions can be situational. https://dhmarks.blogspot.com/2018/10/einstein-relativity-and-relative-ethics.html

What I Have Not Told My Family About The Meaning of Time. Personal reflections on mortality. https://dhmarks.blogspot.com/2018/10/what-i-have-not-told-my-family-about.html

Available on search engines and on the author's blog https://dhmarks.blogspot.com

Made in the USA
Middletown, DE
27 October 2023

41248975R10440